Anonyr

Report of the Geological Survey of the State of Missouri

Anonymous

Report of the Geological Survey of the State of Missouri

Reprint of the original, first published in 1874.

1st Edition 2024 | ISBN: 978-3-36885-104-0

Verlag (Publisher): Outlook Verlag GmbH, Zeilweg 44, 60439 Frankfurt, Deutschland
Vertretungsberechtigt (Authorized to represent): E. Roepke, Zeilweg 44, 60439 Frankfurt, Deutschland
Druck (Print): Books on Demand GmbH, In de Tarpen 42, 22848 Norderstedt, Deutschland

REPORT

OF THE

GEOLOGICAL SURVEY

OF THE

STATE OF MISSOURI,

INCLUDING

FIELD WORK OF 1873--1874,

WITH 91 ILLUSTRATIONS AND AN ATLAS.

GARLAND C. BROADHEAD, STATE GEOLOGIST.

PRINTED BY THE AUTHORITY AND UNDER THE DIRECTION OF THE

BUREAU OF GEOLOGY AND MINES.

JEFFERSON CITY:
REGAN & CARTER, STATE PRINTERS AND BINDERS.
1874.

OFFICE OF THE GEOLOGICAL SURVEY,

ST. LOUIS, *August 31, 1874.*

To the President and Members of the State Board of Geology and Mines:

GENTLEMEN: I have the honor herewith to submit to you the Reports of the work of the Missouri Geological Survey for the years 1873 and 1874.

With this, Gentlemen, I have the honor to be

Your obedient servant,

G. C. BROADHEAD,

State Geologist.

PREFACE.

During the years 1873 and 1874, the Board of Managers of the Survey consisted of

Gov. SILAS WOODSON, ex-officio President.
Mr. EDWIN HARRISON.
Prof. FOREST SHEPPARD.
Hon. A. W. MYERS.
Hon. L. A. BROWN.
With A. A. BLAIR, of St. Louis, Secretary of the Board.

My predecessor in office, Prof. Pumpelly, sent in his resignation to take effect July 1, 1873.

At that time, the following persons were employed as assistants on the Survey :

G. C. BROADHEAD, Assistant Geologist.
Dr. ADOLF SCHMIDT, Assistant Geologist.
REGIS CHAUVENET, Chemist.
CHAS. J. NORWOOD, Assistant.
ALEX. LEONHÁRD, Assistant.
J. R. GAGE, Assistant.
P. N. MOORE, Assistant.
H. H. WEST, Assistant.
With Mr. T. J. CALDWELL, in the office, and
C. HENRICH, Topographer.

At a meeting of the Board on the 18th of June, 1873, I was unanimously appointed State Geologist to succeed Prof. Pumpelly.

On account of the depletion of the fund during the first part of the year 1873, I found it necessary on entering upon my duties as State Geologist to reduce the force engaged in the field. During the latter half of the year 1873, Dr. Schmidt, Mr. C. J. Norwood and Mr.

Chauvenet were employed, with Mr. Caldwell as draughtsman in the office and, part of the time, Mr. West assisted in the field.

During the early summer of 1873, Mr. P. N. Moore examined the Limonite deposits of the South-east, in the progress of which he examined ore beds in Madison, Bollinger, Wayne and Butler.

Mr. J. R. Gage examined certain lead deposits of Jefferson, Washington, Madison and St. Francois.

Dr. Schmidt, assisted by Mr. Alex. Leonhard, made a careful examination of the various lead and zinc deposits of Newton and Jasper counties.

Mr. Leonhard and Mr. Henrich made a topographical survey of the Granby lead mines.

Myself, with the assistance of C. J. Norwood and H. H. West, made detailed examinations of the coal formation and underlying rocks of Bates, Vernon, Barton and Cedar, and a survey of Jasper county. During the months of September, October and part of November, we made surveys of Howard, Linn, Adair and Sullivan counties.

During the spring and part of the present year, Dr. Schmidt made examinations of the lead deposits of Cole, Miller, Morgan, Moniteau and Cooper.

C. J. Norwood and H. H. West made surveys of the counties of Putnam and Schuyler and part of Chariton.

During the present summer, I have made detailed examinations in Madison and Cole, and have visited certain mines in Callaway and Moniteau.

During the past winter and part of the present summer, we were engaged in writing out our reports. We have been assisted in the office by Mr. T. J. Caldwell and Mr. T. A. Minor.

Mr. R. Chauvenet, our chemist, has been almost constantly engaged in making analyses of various ores.

I would state, in addition, that Dr. J. G. Norwood has kindly placed at my disposal copies of notes taken by him in Madison county several years ago.

I would state that our plan of working for the past year has been to look after those items of the greatest interest and economic value, and I have impressed upon the various assistants the importance of presenting the facts in the simplest form, so that they can easily be understood by the general reader. Of course, sometimes we have to use terms only pertaining to Geology, but this is found necessary in all professions. The lawyer, the merchant, the physician, the architect, the farmer, all use terms peculiar to their calling, and find it necessary to do so. Scientific men may be in search of certain facts; for their criticism and correct understanding, we often have to use terms only familiar to science, otherwise, our descriptions would seem awkward if not unintelligible.

The Board, by its action of last November, resolved to publish the next volume from the fund of the annual appropriation. This has necessarily very much limited our field work during the present season.

The number of men employed on the Survey during the first half of 1873 was such that the fund was very much reduced at the time I assumed the duties of State Geologist, and although I reduced the number of employes, still there remained less than $14,000 for the present year.

With this sum we have managed to do some field work and leave enough to publish the results of our last year's examinations.

An arrangement was effected with Gast & Co., of St. Louis, to engrave the maps and plates, and with Messrs. Regan & Carter, the public printers, to do the printing and binding. Mr. Gast has already exhibited proof sheets of plates, and they are well done, and compare favorably with similar work contained in other Geological Reports. Messrs. Regan & Carter, we know from previous experience, will do their work well, and we can safely say that our present volume, in style and execution, will favorably compare with other Geological Reports, and be highly creditable and a good recommendation for our publishers.

In our collection we have representative specimens of rocks, fossils, clays, and ores from each county or district examined.

Rocks supposed to contain hydraulic properties as well as fire clays have been collected. These we propose to have tested as to their useful qualities.

In our collection are numerous fossils from different formations. Many of these can not yet be distributed to the different State Institutions which under the law are entitled to collections, until they are carefully studied by the Palæontologist.

It is recommended, that a Palæontologist be appointed at an early day. Other States have published valuable contributions to Palæonthology, our valuable collections present an interesting field for study, and by the assistance of an able Palæontologist a handsome addition could be offered to science.

I take pleasure in acknowledging kindnesses shown by various citizens of the State during the progress of my work. Among these I might mention Mr. J. H. Nash of Cass, Messrs. W. W. Prewitt and J. M. Lowe of Vernon, Mr. Tucker of Barton, Mr. W. S. Tower of Jasper, Hon. L. A. Brown and J. C. Heberling of Howard, Hon. D. S. Hooper of Adair, and many others. I am also under particular obligations to Messrs. T. McKissock, Supt. St. Louis, Iron Mountain and Southern Railway, Mr. W. C. Van Horn, Supt. of St. Louis, Kansas City and Northern Railways and Mr. A. A. Talmage, Supt. of A. & P. Railroad, for free transportation over their several Roads.

GARLAND C. BROADHEAD,

State Geologist.

CONTENTS.

LEAD REGION OF CENTRAL MISSOURI.

APPENDIX A.

APPENDIX B.

APPENDIX C.

APPENDIX D.

APPENDIX E.

CHAPTER I.

HISTORICAL NOTES ON EARLY MINING IN MISSOURI.

BY G. C BROADHEAD.

The object of the early explorers through the province of Upper Louisiana, was the same that had actuated the early Spanish settlers of Mexico and other American provinces—the search after the precious metals.

In vain hope of discovering precious metals, the Governor of Louisiana prepared an expedition which, in 1705, ascended as far as the mouth of the Kansas River.

1715—1742.

In 1719 the Sieur de Lochon being sent by the West India Company, commenced mining on the Meramec.* He dug out a large quantity of ore, was occupied four days in smelting a pound of it, which they say produced two drachms of silver; but some suspected him of putting this in himself.

A few months after, he returned, and from two or three thousand pounds of ore extracted fourteen pounds of lead. Charlevoix, who passed here October 17, 1721, says they were then engaged in searching for a silver mine. The company being impressed with his accounts, sent a Spaniard named Antonio, who had been taken prisoner at the siege of Pensacola, was afterward a galley slave, and boasted of having wrought in a mine of Mexico. But he succeeded no better than De Lochon.

---

*Schoolcraft—Extracts from Charlevoix's journal.

About this time a company of the King's miners, under the direction of La Renaudiere, did some mining; but as he neither understood mining nor smelting, he failed in accomplishing anything.

A private company next undertook the Meramec mines. Sieur Renault, one of the directors, superintended the operations, and in June, 1721, he discovered a bed of Lead ore said to be two feet in thickness. Austin, in his communications, (1804,) speaks very favorably of Renault's mines.

These mines were worked by Renault until 1742. After that, they were not worked again until the present century.

La Motte, working under the direction of Renault, discovered the Mines a la Motte in 1720.

In 1763, Francis Burton discovered the rich mines known ever since by his name, and now called Potosi Mines; and in this neighborhood the lead mining was chiefly concentrated.

1798—1823.

Moses Austin was born in 1784, in Durham, Connecticut. In early life he moved to Virginia, at length settling in Wythe county, where he conducted an extensive Lead mine and founded the town of Austinville. In 1797 he journeyed on horseback from Austinville to St. Louis. At this time the only settlements between the falls of the Ohio (Louisville) and St. Louis, were at Vincennes.

Austin, very soon after his arrival in Missouri, obtained a grant of one league of land from the Spanish government, which he took possession of and sunk the first regular shaft in 1798, and erected a reverbatory furnace for smelting Lead.

Austin's mining operations included the Mine a Burton tract (Potosi). This was discovered by Francis Burton in 1763.

Austin's report in 1804, names ten principal mines, viz:

1. Mine a Burton.
2. Mine a Robina.
3. Old Mines.
4. Mine Renault.
5. Mine a Maneto.
6. Mine a la Plate.
7. Mine a Joe.
8. Mine a Lanye.
9. Mine a la Motte.
10. Mine a Gerbore.

Schoolcraft's list, made out in 1818, includes forty-six mines, mostly in Washington county (39); three in Ste. Genevieve; one in Madison, and two in Jefferson.

Schoolcraft, about this time,* speaking of the Potosi Mines, says:

The chief are Austin's, Bibbs', Jones', Mine a Robina, Old Mines, Bell Fontaine, Shibboleth and Mine a Joe, (Bogy Mine,) and were at that time reserved to the Government, and are leased to individuals by application at the War Department, under authority derived from the President, and the lessee paying one-tenth in Lead.

The price of Lead, at that time, was four dollars per hundred at the mines, with four dollars and fifty cents on the Mississippi at Ste. Genevieve or Herculaneum; the cost of transportation, seventy-five cents per hundred. The same mineral was then worth seven dollars per hundred at Philadelphia.

The quantity of lead annually smelted from the crude ore, was 3,000,000 pounds; and number of hands employed, 1,100.

Other mines worked about this time, were those near Prairie du Chien, worked by Sacs and Foxes; on the Des Moines, formerly worked by the French; on the Osage, Gasconade and Mine River of Missouri; on the White River and its tributaries; on the St. Francois; on the Arkansas, where silver is in combination; at Cave in Rock, Illinois; at Drennon Springs and Millersburgh, Kentucky; on New River, at Austinville, Wythe county, Virginia. At the latter place it had been worked for fifty years, and the mines were being still worked.

About 1820, Lead was found in the Southern part of Cole county, and about 1827, the first furnace was erected by Chouteau, of St. Louis.

From 1823 to 1850, Lead-mining was continually on the increase in Missouri.

The mines of Galena, Ills., were discovered in 1822, and actual work begun in 1827, and were very extensively worked for some seven years after.

In the Missouri Geological Report of Prof. Swallow, published in 1855, Dr. Litton furnished the fullest Report on Missouri Lead Mines that had yet been published. He describes a number of Mines in Washington county, and says that its area may be considered as one extensive "Lead Digging."

Since then no Report has been published of these Mines, but their yield continues good. Dr. L's Report also included certain Mines of Jefferson and Franklin, most of which are still worked with profit.

Mr. Meek, in his Report published at the same time as Dr. Lit-

* Schoolcraft, 1823.

ton's, says that Lead has been found in all parts of Moniteau where
the Magnesian Limestones exist. He enumerates 10 mines in Moniteau county. The most valuable he considers to be the High Point
mine. This was discovered in 1841. About 1846, a lead furnace was
erected in Camden county, probably the first built in Western Missouri.

Mr. Meek examined Miller county in 1855, and wrote his Report
in 1859. He speaks of Lead being found at several places North of
the Osage, and at one locality South of that River. His statements
would indicate that very little mining had been done in that part of
Missouri at that time.

Mr. Meek also says that Lead was found in nearly every township
in Morgan, but not over a dozen mines worked.

There really was not much mining done in Miller county until
1869, nor in Morgan until 1873. At this time there is a great deal of
mining being done in both Miller, Morgan and Cole.

At present the Lead Mines of Morgan, are by some persons
thought to be as valuable as those of Granby or Joplin.

Until recent years mining in South-east Missouri was confined to
surface mining. Now, deep shafts have been sunk in many places,
and rich yields of mineral obtained.

We may say that the mining in Central Missouri is yet near the
surface. When these have been chiefly exhausted, deep shafts will
be sunk, and reasoning on the experience of South-east Mines, we may
here expect to find rich Lead still lower down.

Dr. Shumard, in his various Reports from 1855 to 1859, speaks of
the existence of Lead in Ozark, Wright, Laclede, Pulaski and Phelps.
He considers the Eastern part of Crawford as constituting part of the
vast Lead District of South-east Missouri, and enumerates many valuable mines. He also speaks of the mines of Perry, Ste. Genevieve
and Jefferson.

Previous to 1857, Lead had only been found at three places in
Maries county. Within the past few years very valuable mines have
been developed in the Northern part of the county.

Although some Lead has been found in Osage, Texas, Wright,
Benton and St. Clair, no extensive mining has yet been prosecuted
in these counties.

Prof. Swallow, in his Geological Report of 1855, speaks of the
chief mines worked in the South-west at that time as those on the
Gravois and near Linn Creek, other mines near Cole Camp, in Benton
county and in Jasper and Newton. The Granby mines were discovered after his first visit to the South-west; a little mining had been

done two miles South of Carthage, near Minersville, on Turkey Creek, Shoal Creek, below Neosho, Sturgeon's prairie, Oliver's prairie, and a few other points. At present most of the Jasper and Newton mines have developed into exceeding rich mines.

Prof. Swallow's Report to the Pacific Railroad Company in 1859, enumerates 216 mines and 34 Lead furnaces in Missouri.

The Report of the Ninth Census for 1870, states that the product of Lead-mining in Missouri at that time, was $201,885, making it the second Lead-producing State in the Union. Wisconsin being the first, its yield amounting to $369,067.

The yield in other States was small. The returns include Lead mines in Illinois, Iowa, Kentucky, Missouri, Nevada, New Hampshire, New York, Virginia and Wisconsin.

The same Report gives returns by counties of Missouri, as follows :

Cooper	300
Franklin	27,630
Jasper	37,500
Miller	6,115
Moniteau	1,100
Newton	72,500
St. Francois	37,760
Washington	17,000
Webster	1,980

If this report be correct for 1870 it falls far short of the amount three years after, for Joplin alone, in 1873, produced over $500,000 worth of lead. Again, during the first six months of 1874 there were brought into St. Louis over the Atlantic and Pacific Railroad 5,050 tons of pig lead, worth in St. Louis $707,000.

HEAVY SPAR—SULPHATE OF BARYTA.

As long ago as 1822 Schoolcraft informs us that Sulphate of Baryta was crushed, powdered and mixed with white lead and used in painting, and that as much as 80 per cent. could be used. He speaks favorably of its use.

We can not find that it was much used in adulterating white lead until within the last fifteen years. At present vast quantities are used.

IRON.

In 1816 James Tong erected a small furnace for smelting iron near what is now called the " Shut In," on Stout's Creek, Iron county, three miles east of where Ironton now stands. He only smelted a small

quantity of ore, being forced to stop in consequence of the fall in all
kinds of produce and manufactures. This was the earliest attempt
to smelt Iron in any of the States west of the Ohio. The next furnace
was erected in 1823 or 1824. About that time a blast furnace was
erected in Washington county by Eversol, Perry and Ruggles, afterwards known as " Perry's Old Furnace." The ore was first obtained
from Clear Creek.*

The first bar of Iron, made out of pig metal in Missouri, was in
May, 1825, and the first blooms in 1832.

The next blast furnace erected was by Massey and James, in
Phelps county, which was completed in 1829, and has been in operation, at intervals, up to the present time. Their property, now known
as the Meramec Mines, was, for many years, known as Massey's Iron
Works and Mines. Their mine was opened in 1826. For many years
their iron had either to be hauled on wagons to the Missouri River or
else taken in flatboats down the Meramec.

About the year 1840 a furnace was erected on Sac River, in the
southern part of Cedar county. But little work was done. The owner
being financially embarrassed his creditors tore down the buildings and
destroyed the machinery. Since then no furnace has been erected in
that portion of Missouri.

In 1836 the Pilot Knob land was entered by Van Doren, Pease &
Co., who proceeded to form a company for speculation. They also purchased the Iron Mountain and laid off a city.†

In 1843 a charter was granted by the Legislature of Missouri to
C. C. Zeigler for himself and others, and in June, 1845, the "Iron Moun-
tain Company" was formed, a company composed of Jas. Harrison
and P. Chouteau of St. Louis; F. Valle, C. C. Zeigler and John P.
Scott of St. Genevieve; Aug. Belmont, Samuel Ward and Chas. F.
Mersch of New York, and E. F. Pratt of Fredericktown.

The Pilot Knob works were begun November, 1847, under the
management of C. C. Zeigler and E. F. Pratt. No mining had been previously done at these places.

In 1848 E. Mead of St. Louis, shipped metal from Iron Mountain
to England and the following spring he received it back manufactured
into razors and pocket and table cutlery by Jos. Rodgers and Sons,
Sheffield. These experiments proved the ore to be well adapted for
the manufacture of fine steel cutlery. In 1853 Child, Pratt & Co. had

---

*Mo. Geol. Rep., 1855, Pt. 2, p. 73.
†Western Journal and Civilian, vol. 8, p. 136.

large quantities manufactured into lock cases, and they were found to be superior to those made from other iron.*

The Report of the Ninth Census, 1870, gives the value of Iron produced in Missouri for that year as $491,496, which is but a small return when compared to Pennsylvania of $3,944,146.

ZINC.

The profitable mining and working of Zinc in Missouri belongs within the past decade; of Zinc blende within two years.

The first Zinc metal in Missouri was made at Potosi in 1867, by Geo. Hasselmeyer, and the next works started at Carondelet produced the metal in May, 1869.

*Western Journal, vol. 11, p. 371.

CHAPTER II.

BY G. C. BROADHEAD.

GENERAL GEOLOGY.

GEOLOGICAL RELATIONS.

As the names of the several formations, which occur in Missouri, require frequently to be named in a Geological Report, and as this Report may fall into the hands of many citizens of our State who are not familiar with such terms, it seems but proper to give a brief description of the various groups and their order of succession.

Until within a few years past, the Granites, Porphyries and other rocks of similar origin and constituency, were termed Azoic. Recent investigations, developing certain facts, have caused Geologists to discard this term and use that of Eozoic instead. Professor Dana* in his manual of Geology to such rock has applied the term ARCHÆAN, which may include rocks in which there is no evidence of any pre-existing animal life, or in which we find evidence of the first dawn of organic life.

About the origin of these rocks there certainly is but little known; we only recognize them as including the apparently oldest.

The Archæan time includes—

1. Azoic age.
2. Eozoic age.†

They are also subdivided into two periods :

1. The Laurentian, or oldest of the two, and,
2. The Huronian.

---

*Dana—Man. Geol., p. 146, etc., Ed. 1874.
†See Dana's Man. Geol. Ed. of 1874, p. 146 et Seq.

BY G. C. BROADHEAD.

Iowa.	Ohio.	Tennessee.	Canada.
		Alluvial........	
		Bluff.............. { Loam......	
		{ Gravel..........	
		{ Ripley...	
		Cretaceous........ { Green Sand....	
		{ Coffee Sand....	
	Upper...		Upper Coal ...
	Lower....	Coal Measures........	{ Middle......
	Carb. Conglom....		{ Coal...
		Mountain Limestone...	Millstone Grit.......
		{ Upper Silicious...	Gypsiferous Series........
		{ Lower Silicious.	(Lower Coal Measure)....
	Waverly....	Silicious Group. {	
			Catskill....
	Erie Shale....	Black Shale...	
	Huron Shale... {		
	Hamilton...	.●.	
	Corniferous...		
			Onondaga...
	Oriskany.		Oriskany Sandstone....
....one...		Lower Helderburg....	Lower Helderburg....
		{ Meniscus Limestone.....	
		{ Dyestone Group..........	Niagara....
		Niagara. { Wh. O. Mt. Sandstone.......	
		{ Clinch Mountain Sandstone.....	
	Cincinnati Group...	Nashville Group....	Hudson River....
			Utica...
		{ Lebanon Limestone......	Trenton...
		{ With Marble.....	Black River....
			Birds-eye....
			Chazy....
			Taconic....
...ne...			{ Calciferous....
			{ Sandrock....
		Knox Group. { Dolomite Shale....	
		{ Dolomite Sandstone....	{ Potsdam...
		Chilhowee Sandstone....	{ Sandstone....
		Ocoee Conglomerate and Slates...	
			Huronian....
			Laurentian....

1. LAURENTIAN.

This includes the chief Granite ranges of the Continent, extending from Labrador to the Arctic Sea, the ranges parallel to and north of the Laurentian chain of lakes, reaching from the St. Lawrence River to Lake Superior, the Adirondack Mountains of New York, Black Hills of Nebraska, and Granite and Porphery mountains of South-east Missouri.

The Laurentian rocks are either metamorphic or crystalline. They include Granite, Gneiss, Syenite, Crystalline Limestone (or Marble), Hypersthenyte. Iron ore and iron bearing minerals abound.

The rocks belonging to this system in Missouri include Granite, Porphyry, Specular and Magnetic Iron and some Slates.

The subdivisions of Geological time are—

I. ARCHÆAN TIME, including
    1. Azoic age.
    2. Eozoic age.

II. PALEOZOIC TIME:
    1. Age of Invertetrates, or Silurian.
    2. Age of Fishes, or Devonian.
    3. Age of Coal Plants, or Carboniferous.

III. MESOZOIC TIME:
    The age of Reptiles.

IV. CENOZOIC TIME:
    1. Tertiary, or age of Mammals.
    2. The Quaternary, or age of Man.

The following chart of Geological History shows the formation of Missouri opposite to equivalent formations in other localities:

GEOLOGICAL STRUCTURE OF MISSOURI.

In the order of succession the formations may be represented thus:

QUATERNARY.

Alluvium.
Bottom Prairie.
Bluff or Loess.

DRIFT:

Altered Drift, Sand and Pebbles, Clay and Boulders.
Tertiary?
Cretaceous?

CARBONIFEROUS SYSTEM.

UPPER CARBONIFEROUS OR COAL MEASURES:

Upper Coal.
Middle Coal.
Lower Coal.
Clear Creek Sandstone and Lower Coal.

LOWER CARBONIFEROUS:

Sandstone.

St. Louis Group:
St. Louis Limestone and Warsaw Limestone.

Keokuk Group:
Encrinital or Burlington.

Chouteau Group:
Chouteau Limestone.
Vermicular Sandstone and Shale.
Lithographic Limestone.

DEVONIAN SYSTEM.

Hamilton.
Onondaga.

UPPER SILURIAN:

Oriskany.
Lower Helderburg (Delthyris Shale).
Niagara.
Cape Girardeau Limestone.

LOWER SILURIAN SYSTEM.

TRENTON PERIOD:

Cincinnati Group—Hudson River Shale.
Receptaculite Limestone.
Trenton Limestone.
Black River and Bird's-eye.

MAGNESIAN LIMESTONE SERIES:
   1. Magnesian Limestone.
     Saccharoidal Sandstone.
   2. Magnesian Limestone.
     Sandstone.
   3. Magnesian Limestone.
     Potsdam Limestone.
     Potsdam Sandstone and Conglomerate.

ARCHÆAN:
     Greenstone.
     Porphyry.
     Granite.

QUATERNARY SYSTEM.

The Quatenary System is represented by one or all of its integral members throughout the State. Our soil is *alluvial* and generally reposes on one or the other members of the system.

The *Bottom Prairie* is generally a dark, tenaceous Clay, forming more often a flat prairie. Correct types of this formation are represented by the Mississippi bottom prairie from the Missouri River to Clarksville; the bottoms above Hannibal; the Waconda prairie in Carroll county; the Missouri bottoms in Holt and Atchison counties; Marais des Cygne bottoms in Bates county; Marmaton bottoms in Vernon county; Sac River bottoms in Cedar county; Grand River bottoms in Henry county; Big Creek bottoms in Cass county; Petit Osage plains in Saline county, etc. These Clays are black, stiff and pointed, with sometimes, but rarely, beds of sand, and often contains small concretions of Bog Iron.

BLUFF OR LOESS.

This is fully described in the County Reports. It occurs in the Missouri bluffs, forming a belt of several miles in width, extending from the mouth of the Missouri to the north-west corner of the State, where it is found just beneath the soil. It is generally a finely comminuted silicious marl, of a light brown color, and often weathers into perpendicular escarpments. Concretions of Limestone are often found, and to the marly character of these Clays may be ascribed the richness of the overlying soil. The Missouri hills are generally covered with heavy timber as far up as Holt county; further up they are often bare. The growth of timber is generally valuable, including such varieties as Walnut, Sugar tree, Hickory, Elm, Linden, Ash, Rock Chestnut, Oak, together with Redbud, Pawpaw, Grapevines, etc.

The "Bluff" is well represented in the hills of Glasgow, Kansas City and St. Joseph.

Receding from the river for ten miles the character of the Bluff changes to a stiff, tenaceous Clay, which may properly belong to the

DRIFT.

This formation exists throughout North Missouri. The upper members consist of stiff, tenaceous, brown, drab and blue Clays, often mottled and sometimes containing rounded pebbles, chiefly of granitic rocks. The lower division includes beds of dark, blue Clay, often hardening on exposure, frequently overlaid and sometimes interstratified with beds and pockets of sand, sometimes inclosing leaves and remains of trees. Good springs originate in these sand beds, and when they are ferruginous the springs are chalybeate.

The Lower Drift includes large boulders of various kinds of rock, chiefly granitic or metamorphosed rocks, of which Granite, Red Quartzite and Greenstone are the varieties more often found. These rocks are drifted from the far north; the Quartzite from Minnesota and North-west Iowa. The force of gravity generally causes the boulders to settle down near the streams; still they are sometimes found on high ground. They increase in quantity and size as we go north. In Sullivan county a Granite boulder was observed 20x24 feet. Boulders three feet in diameter are found as far south as Monroe county. They occur in North Missouri from low in the valley to an elevation of about 1,050 feet above the Gulf of Mexico.

The Missouri River seems to limit their southern extension, for along its southern bank, and in the bluffs above all known high water, it is only occasionally that drift boulders are found, and they are only represented by a few small boulders of Granite, Quartzite or Greenstone, and they are found no further south. But at a few localities rounded silicious pebbles are found. In St. Louis county, three miles north of Glencoe, there is a large deposit of these pebbles, among which I only recognized Quartzite, Greenstone and chert. These beds occur on a ridge, which is probably over 800 feet above the Meramec valley. Along the streams lower down are heavy deposits of river gravel, evidently originated on the ground—but we find nothing similar to that found on the high land. If convenient to St. Louis it would be exceedingly valuable. No better material could be procured for street paving. There appears in sight about 7,000,000 cubic feet. West of this the next deposit was observed near Big Salt Spring, in Saline county, but the quantity was limited.

On the top of the high ridges encircling the head of Panther Creek, Bates county, and at an elevation of about 1,000 feet above the sea, we find occasional small rounded pebbles of Chert. Similar pebbles were also observed on the high land, South-west of Carthage, Jasper county.*

The washings on the banks of the Maries des Cygnes, and a few other streams, disclose beds of rounded cherty gravel, occupying a position above the present ordinary high water mark.

In the beds of sand, with clay and vegetable remains, are also sometimes found the teeth, tusks and other bones belonging to the mastodon, horse, ox and other extinct animals.

It is very probable that anterior to the deposit of the last named rounded drift, etc., but subsequent to the age of deposit on the highest land that an immense lake covered a larger part of our state, including all of North Missouri. St. Louis county, the counties on the Missouri River above Moniteau county, and a portion of the border counties, while all Central and Southern Missouri formed an extensive area of dry land. As the waters of the lake subsided, currents originated, wearing away the surface of the lower lands, and moving with great force, sweeping in its path the horse, mammoth, etc., bore down the drift from the higher lands and deposited it along the valleys.

We have evidence also in North Missouri—of great erosion previous to the existence of this immense lake.

In Sullivan and Adair, solid Limestones and Sandstones occur to within a horizon of 50 to 60 feet of the higher hills.

In Adair, towards the East line, wells have been dug over a 100 feet without reaching solid rock, and at Edina, Knox county, a well has penetrated over 200 feet in these Clays. This area is now covered with Clays of the drift formation including remains of trees, etc., towards the bottom.

The extensive deposits of rounded gravel found in the Northern counties of Missouri, if convenient to cities, would be of exceeding great value in paving streets.

COAL.

We dwell but briefly on the Coal formations—this being elsewhere more fully treated in the county Reports.

The map of 1872 does not include all the Coal fields, but only an area of a little over 19,000 square miles. This includes over 8,000 square miles of upper Coal Measures. The upper Measures are mostly barren of Coal, or only contain an occasional seam too thin to pay for working.

The investigations of 1873 show a greater downward thickness of

---

* Neosho is 1,018 feet above the Gulf of Mexico. This locality is probably 150 feet higher, or about 1,160 feet above the sea.

the Coal formation in South-west Missouri, including beds whose position is probably below the beds of North Missouri.

Our examination of the South-western counties have enabled us to estimate the Coal area with a pretty near degree of accuracy. The total area of the Missouri Coal field we thus find to be 23,100 square miles.

COAL POCKETS.

Near the margin of the Coal, but disconnected from the regular Measures, are often found small pockets of chiefly cannel, but sometimes bituminous Coal. Although they are generally quite limited in extent, sometimes they contain enough Coal to occupy a good force of men for many years before they are exhausted.

LOWER CARBONIFEROUS OR MOUNTAIN LIMESTONE.

CHESTER GROUP.

In Southern Illinois, and Southwardly to Alabama, are beds of Limestone with some Sandstone and shales, reaching to as much as 1000 feet thickness.

This Group is almost entirely absent in Missouri, being only represented in South-west Missouri, by a Sandstone heretofore known in Missouri Geology, as the

FERRUGINOUS SANDSTONE.

This is generally found along the Eastern and Southern limit of the Coal field, passing beneath the Coal formation on the West. It varies from a few feet to 100 feet in thickness.

In Callaway it occurs both as a pure white Sandstone, a ferruginous Sandstone and a conglomerate. In Pettis and Howard we find it a coarse, whitish Sandstone. In Cedar, Dade and Lawrence a very ferruginous Sandstone, often containing valuable deposits of Iron ore. In Newton it occurs in useful flag-like layers,

Limestones of the Chester Group were recognized by Dr. Shumard in Perry county, 200 to 300 feet in thickness.

ST. LOUIS LIMESTONE.

This Group, next in descending order, forms the entire Group of Limestone at St. Louis, where it is well marked and of greater thickness than seen elsewhere in this State. It is more often fine-grained, compact or subcrystalline, sometimes inclosing numerous Chert concretions, and the beds are often separated by thin, green Shale-beds.

The chief fossils of this Group are Melonites, Bryozoons, *Litho-strotian* and *Producti*. It greatest thickness is not over 250 feet.

In this Group are now included beds which have been called Warsaw Limestone. It is subordinate and lies at the base of the St. Louis Group. It more often consists of alternations of calcerous shales and thin, irregular, coarse, Blue Limestone beds. *Archimedes* and *Pentremites* are the chief fossils.

The St. Louis Group includes the even-bedded Limestone of St. Louis, St. Charles and Alton, the equivalent beds at Spergin Hill, Indiana, the calcareo-argillaceous Shales and Magnesian Limestone of Warsaw.

Where the upper part of this Group forms the surface rock, we find numerous sink holes as at St. Louis and St. Charles.

KEOKUK GROUP.

The upper part includes beds of shale containing geodes of Quartz, etc., some of which are very beautiful. The lower beds are gray and bluish-gray, with lenticular and concretionary Chert beds, together with some massive Chert beds. *Archimedes, Hemipronites Crenistria* and Crinoid stems are numerous, and some fish teeth are found. This constitutes the Limestone at Keokuk, Iowa, the upper Limestone at Quincy and Hannibal, the Limestone in central parts of St. Charles county; it is also found in St. Louis, Boone, Howard and Cooper, is well developed in South-west Missouri, being found in Cedar, Barton, Vernon, Jasper, Newton and McDonald. It is the Lead-bearing rock of these South-western counties, and corresponds to the silicious Group of Tennessee. It is 200 or more feet in thickness.

ENCRINITAL OR BURLINGTON LIMESTONE.[*]

The upper beds are gray and cherty. The top beds in St. Charles county, include seventeen feet of thin Chert beds with alternate layers of red Clay. The middle beds are generally gray and coarse ; the lower ones gray and brown, with some buff beds.

Crinoid stems are common in nearly all the beds, hence it has been appropriately termed Encrinital Limestone.

The lower beds often abound in well preserved *crinoidæ*.

This rock occurs at Burlington, Iowa, Quincy, Illinois, Hannibal and Louisiana, Missouri, and is well exposed in most of the counties

---

[*] The objection to the term " Encrinital," is the fact that there are limestones belonging to other formations which abound in crinoid stems, and lithologically resemble this.

Being well developed at Burlington, Iowa, Prof. Hall first termed it " Burlington Limestone."

on the Mississippi River north of St. Louis; and from the western part of St. Charles to Howard county. South of the Missouri River, and along its south-west outcrop, it is not generally well developed.

In Green county it is quite cavernous.

It has not been recognized east of Illinois, and is not separated from other Carboniferous Limestones of Tennessee.

CHOUTEAU GROUP.

This Group, originally called " Chemung," in the Missouri Report of 1853, by Prof. Swallow, and also by Prof. Hall in his Iowa Report, since called the Kinderhook Group by Worthen in his Illinois Report, and also by White in his Iowa Report, is probably better developed in Missouri than in either Illinois or Iowa. Being first described by Missouri geologists, the term then applied, if correct, should remain. Palæontological investigations make it a matter of doubt about its being equivalent to the Chemung Group of New York, but of this I have not studied sufficiently to be entirely satisfied.

As there is much greater thickness and better development in Missouri, I shall choose to use the name of the chief member of the Group for the Group itself, and call it the Chouteau Group. Missourians who have read Swallow's Report, will at once understand what it means. It includes three principal divisions:

1. Chouteau Limestone, 100 feet.
2. Vermicular Sandstones and Shales, 75 feet.
3. Lithographic Limestone, 55 feet.

The Chouteau Limestone, in the upper part, is a coarse, gray Limestone, resembling the lower beds of the Encrinital Limestone. In fact, it is a bed of passage, as it often contains fossils common to both.

Next below is a thick bedded Magnesian Limestone, sometimes containing geodes of Quartz and Calcite of a peculiar form, with occasional Chert beds.

Lower down are thinner beds of dove or gray, fine-grained Limestone. This was observed of one hundred feet in thickness, near Sedalia in Pettis county.

VERMICULAR SANDSTONE AND SHALES.

The Sandstones of this division are generally soft and calcareous. They are easily recognized by being ramified by irregular windings throughout, resembling the borings of worms. This formation attains a thickness of seventy-five feet near Louisiana, in Pike county.

LITHOGRAPHIC LIMESTONE.

This, where normally developed, is a fine-grained, compact Llime-stone, breaking with a free, conchoidal fracture—closely resembling the well known Lithographic Limestone, but when exposed breaks into numerous perpendicular joints.

It might be that if quarries were well opened, good layers for lithographic purposes could be displayed.

The lithographic character is only seen in North-east Missouri, and as far as my observation has extended, only in Pike and Ralls, it being best developed at Louisiana, where it is fifty-five feet thick.

Where elsewhere seen, it somewhat resembles the upper beds of the Chouteau Group. At Taborville, St. Clair county, it is of a salmon drab color, occurring in thick beds having an open texture, and contains a well known characteristic fossil—*Pentremites Rœmeri*. Sh.

The Vermicular Sandstone and Shales preserve a uniformity of structure from Ralls to Greene county. It is seen in Ralls, Pike, Lincoln, Cedar and Greene. The Lithographic Limestone is found in Pike, Ralls, St. Clair, Cedar and Greene. The Chouteau in Knox, Marion, Ralls, Pike, Lincoln, St. Charles, St. Louis, Warren, Montgomery, Callaway, Boone, Cooper, Pettis, St. Clair, Cedar, Greene and Christian.

Fragmentary outliers of this group are occasionally found capping the higher ridges near the Arkansas line.

At base of this group, in North-east Missouri, a few feet of black Slate is occasionally seen.

DEVONIAN SYSTEM.

The *Hamilton* Group is found in Ralls, Pike, Lincoln, Warren Montgomery, Callaway, Boone, Cole and probably Moniteau; also in Perry and Ste. Genevieve.

Onondaga Limestone probably found in Cole, Boone, Callaway, Montgomery, Lincoln and Pike.

Total thickness of Devonian, about 100 feet.

UPPER SILURIAN.

Oriskany Sandstone is found in Ste. Genevieve and Ralls. On Salt River, above Cincinnati, it contains well known fossils of the Group.

In Cape Girardeau county, Dr. Shumard recognized the Upper Silurian, represented by—

Delthyris Shale (Lower Helderburg)... 350 feet
Niagara Group... 225 feet
Cape Girardeau Limestone.. 50 feet

He recognized the same beds in Perry and Ste. Genevieve counties.

In Montgomery and Callaway counties are about 20 feet of coarse gray crinoidal beds, which are probably Upper Silurian.

In Pike county, near Sugar Creek, are heavy beds of buff Limestone, affording a good building material, and equivalent in age to the well known Grafton quarry rock of Illinois, used extensively in St. Louis.

Dr. Shumard makes the Lower Helderburg 100 feet, and the Niagara 150 feet thick in Ste. Genevieve county.

LOWER SILURIAN.

This very important system reaches to a great thickness in Missouri, and covers over one-half the area of the State.

At the top we find the

CINCINNATI GROUP.

This, the equivalent of the blue Limestone and Shales of Cincinnati and of Madison, Ind., is represented in Missouri only by the upper shale beds, with an occasional flag-like Limestone layer. It is found in Ralls, Pike and Lincoln, and probably reaches to 100 feet in thickness—Prof. Swallow thinks 120 feet.

The mineral springs of Ralls and Pike seem to originate in these beds.

The Eastern equivalent of this formation is the Hudson River and Utica shales.

GALENA GROUP—RECEPTACULITE LIMESTONE.

This consists, in Missouri, mostly of beds of coarse gray or white Limestone—the Galena Limestone proper being wanting, and, as far as observed in Missouri, none of the beds are Lead-bearing. It occurs in Cape Girardeau, Perry, Ste. Genevieve, Jefferson, St. Louis, St. Charles, Warren, Lincoln, Pike and Ralls. Its greatest thickness (130 feet) is in Cape Girardeau. In St. Charles it is not over 40 feet, in Warren 30, and thins out in eastern part of Montgomery county.

TRENTON GROUP.

With this Group we include—

Trenton Limestone.. 150 feet

Black River Limestone..⎫
Birdseye Limestone...⎭ 70 feet

The Trenton Limestone is generally thin-bedded, dark ash, drab or gray, and sometimes magnesian. The Black River and Birdseye are often in even layers; the lower beds have sometimes mottled drab and reddish shades, often affording a pretty Marble. The Trenton is found from Cape Girardeau to Ralls county, and from St. Charles to Callaway, entirely thinning out in eastern portion of Callaway. The Black River and Birdseye are found from Cape Girardeau to Lincoln, and in St. Charles, Warren and Montgomery, thinning out in the latter county.

The entire thickness of this group is probably over 400 feet.

MAGNESIAN LIMESTONE SERIES.

This, as low in the series as the Second Sandstone, is probably the equivalent of the Calciferous Sandrock of the New York Geologists. The rocks below are the equivalents of the Potsdam formation. The Potsdam and Calciferous have been sometimes called " Primordial."

FIRST MAGNESIAN LIMESTONE.

This is generally a buff, open-textured, thick and even-bedded Limestone, breaking free under the hammer, and affording a useful building rock. A species of *Cythere* is often found; other fossils are rare. Dr. Shumard estimated its thickness in Ste. Genevieve county to be about 150 feet. In North Missouri, I observed it 70 feet thick in Warren county. It is found in Ralls, Pike, Lincoln, St. Charles, Warren, Callaway and Boone. South-westwardly, it is not well marked— in fact, I doubt its presence in some counties where, in regular sequence, it should be found. It occurs in Franklin, St. Louis and southwardly to Cape Girardeau county.

FIRST OR SACCHAROIDAL SANDSTONE.

This formation is well developed in Lincoln, St. Charles, Warren, Montgomery, Gasconade, Franklin, St. Louis, Jefferson, Ste. Genevieve, Perry and Cape Girardeau. Besides the above, it is also developed in a more attenuated form, in Callaway, Osage, Cole, Moniteau and Boone. It is the rock called in the Illinois, Iowa and Wisconsin Reports the St. Peter's Sandstone.

This Sandstone is probably destined to be one of the most usefu rocks found in Missouri. It is of a very white color and the purest Sandstone found in the State, and very suitable for making the finest glassware. Its great thickness makes it inexhaustible. I have observed it 133 feet thick in St. Charles and Warren, and in South-east Missouri it has been observed over a hundred feet in thickness. In Jefferson county, a large plate glass factory has recently been established, where they contemplate making glass equal to the finest French plate.

SECOND MAGNESIAN LIMESTONE.

This formation occurs in all the River counties south of Pike as far as the swamps of South-east Missouri, and is more often the surface rock in all the counties south of the Missouri and Osage Rivers to within 50 miles of the Western line of the State. It is generally composed of beds of earthy Magnesian Limestone interstratified with Shale beds and layers of white Chert, with occasionally thin beds of white Sandstone, and, near the lower part, thick cellular silico-mag nesian Limestone beds. The beds are more often of irregular thickness and not very useful for building purposes.

It is often a Lead-bearing rock, and most of the Lead of Cole county occurs in it. It is from 175 to 200 feet thick. Its fossils indicate it to belong to the calciferous Sand rock of New York geologists.

SECOND SANDSTONE.

This is much coarser than the first Sandstone, and occurs in much firmer beds—at the upper part are beds of intercalated Chert, often abounding in fossils. This rock is common in most of the counties of South-east and Southern Missouri. Thickness 50 to 150 feet.

THIRD MAGNESIAN LIMESTONE.

This, also, an important member, occurring in nearly all the counties of Southern Missouri, is generally a thick bedded coarsely cryslatine bluish gray or flesh colored magnesian Limestone, with occasional thick Chert beds. It is the chief Lead-bearing rock of South-east and Southern Missouri. In some counties it is as much as 300 feet thick, and Dr. Shumard supposes it to be over 600 feet in thickness in Pulaski.

THIRD SANDSTONE.

This was recognized in Camden and Dallas counties by Professor Swallow. Excepting in the borings of St. Louis County Insane Asylum well, I have not been able to recognize it. Thickness 82 feet.

FOURTH MAGNESIAN LIMESTONE.

Prof. Swallow recognized this rock on Niangua and Osage Rivers. It closely resembles the third magnesian Limestone, and may be included with it in Southern Missouri. Thickness 300 to 400 feet.

OTHER PRIMORDIAL ROCKS.

At the base of the unaltered fossiliferous rocks in Madison, St. Francois and Iron counties we find in the order of succession from the top the following strata :

6. Second Sandstone on hill tops.
5. Chert beds—fossiliferous.
4. Third magnesian Limestone.
3. Silicious or grit-stone beds with intercalated magnesian Limestone.
2. Marble beds.
1. Sandstone, conglomerate and Shales.

No. 3 is the Lead-bearing rock of Mine LaMotte and vicinity. Fossils have been obtained from Mine LaMotte and near Fredericktown which prove to be well known types of the Potsdam Group ; an intercalated shale bed at Mine LaMotte abounds in (*Lingula*) *Lingul ella Lamborni* Mk.

The Marble beds are not always present ; they seem to be confined to the South-west quarter of Madison and the Central and Northern parts of Iron and extend into Reynolds county. Their greatest thickness is not over 30 feet. ,

No. 1 is confined chiefly to the Northern part of Iron and Madison, extending to St. Francois. The entire thickness of this as well as the regular order of its various beds is rather difficult to arrive at. But we find both in Iron and Madison counties coarse conglomerates resting on Granite and Porphery. We also find Sandstones, which are sometimes very coarse, and at other times fine grained, resting on conglomerates. We also find Shale or Slate beds reposing on Granite and underlying Sandstone. Similar Shale beds are also intercalated with the Sandstone. In the neighborhood of Mine LaMotte this sandstone reaches to over 100 feet in thickness, and is also found to be the lowest rock directly resting on the Granite. Borings with diamond drill on the Mine LaMotte property indicate magnesian Limestone with some silicious beds 80 feet ; Sandstone 63 feet ; Granite.

On St. Francois River, in Madison county, these lower Sandstones rest directly on the Granite and are unaltered ; on Twelve Mile Creek, Madison county, the Marble beds and Sandstones rest unaltered on the Porphyry, and on Big Creek, Iron county, heavy beds of unaltered Magnesian Limestone rest directly on the Porphyry. We therefore know that the Granites and Porphyries of South-east Missouri are of much older age than the Magnesian series or the Potsdam.

BORINGS AT INSANE ASYLUM.

The borings in the well at the St. Louis County Insane Asylum serve to show the aggregate thickness of the various rock formations. An inspection of data show that some strata found in other portions of the State are here wanting, while other strata are much thicker.

Vertical section of borings at the St. Louis county Insane Asylum.

1. 40 feet Clays of the Bluff formation.
2. 80 feet of Coal Measures.
3. 670 feet of Lower Carboniferous rocks.
4. 93 feet of Chouteau Limestone.
5. 421 feet of Trenton, Black River and Birdseye Limestone.
6. 148 feet of First Magnesian Limestone.
7. 133 feet of Saccharoidal Limestone.
8. 517 feet of Second Magnesian Limestone.
9. 82 feet of Second Sandstone.
10. 83 feet of Third Magnesian Limestone.
11. 98 feet of Third Sandstone.
12. 384 feet of Fourth Magnesian Limestone.
13. 54 feet of Potsdam Sandstone.
14. 245.5 feet, mostly Granite, although a portion of the upper part may be Sandstone.
15. 40 feet of Granite.

The well terminated in Granite at 3,843.5 feet from the surface.

The above section was constructed after having made a critical examination of the specimens from the boring.

The following is a tabular view of the formations similar to those found in the well, and will serve to show the comparative thickness in other sections :

TABLE OF FORMATIONS.

Authorities: G. C. Broadhead (with W. B. Potter), B. F. Shumard, Meek.

Formations	Well at Insane Asylum	Professor Swallow's Report	Lincoln county (W. B. Potter)	St. Charles county	Maries county	Osage county	Warren county	Franklin county	Jefferson county	Ozark county	Wright county	Phelps county	Laclede county	Pulaski county	Crawford county	Miller county	Morgan county
Lower Carboniferous	670	1,145	370	266			132		60							20	10
Chouteau Group	93	205	100	40			37		51	50	70						25
Lower Devonian		125	36	14			40										
Upper Silurian		220					15		80								
Cincinnati Group		120	65	168			114								120		
Trenton	421	360	230				55		100								
Black River and Birdseye			30														
First Magnesian	148	190	50	94	85	25	84	175		80	250	30					20
Saccharoidal Sandstone	133	125	65	185			130		130			150					40
Second Magnesian	517	230	35	60	240	240	210	300	90	275	130	150	140	100		80	175
Second Sandstone	82	70			55	30		140				180	70			70	40
Third Magnesian	838	350			200	180		300		184			300	600	300		300
Third Sandstone	98	50														6	30
Fourth Magnesian	384	300													300	27	153
Potsdam Sandstone	54																
Potsdam Sandstone with Granite	245.5																
Granite	40																

The borings began at the bottom of a well 120 feet deep, with water standing at forty feet below the surface. At 134 feet, an eight or ten inch opening was struck, and the water sank to a depth of 128 feet. Salt water was obtained at 1,220 feet. At 1,225 and 1,262 feet from the surface a strong petroleum smell was recognized. Sulphur water was obtained at 2,140 feet. At 2,256 feet the water in the sand pump indicated three per cent. of salt; at 2,957 feet, four-and-a-half per cent.; at 3,293 feet, two per cent.; and at 3,367 feet, less than two per cent.; at 3,384 feet, three per cent.; and below 3,545 feet, seven to eight per cent.

Experiments with a Fahrenheit registering thermometer, indicated the following :

At depth of 3,127 feet.............................Thermometer, 106 degrees.
    "   3,129 "   ....   "   107   "
    "   3,264 "   ....   "   106   "
    "   3,376 "   ....   "   106   "
    "   3,473 "   ....   "   105   "
    "   3,604 "   ....   "   105   "
    "   3,641 "   ....   " $104\frac{1}{2}$ "
    "   3,728 "   ....   " $105\frac{1}{2}$ "
    "   3,800 "   ....   "   105   "
    "   3,887 "   ....   "   105   "

No tests of temperature were made above these depths.

In boring to the depth of 833 feet, the drill was often observed to be highly magnetized, but after passing that depth no further influence was observed.

Two wooden plugs, with iron screws at the end, were driven in, one at the 1,022 offset, the other at the 953 feet offset, in order to separate the fresh from the salt water. If withdrawn, the well would be clear from top to bottom. The five-inch tube, reaching to 1,022 feet, has been withdrawn, and a pump put down to 400 feet. This pump was worked a few days, the water found to be a little salty, and the supply limited.

The surface of the ground at the well is about 583 feet above the Gulf of Mexico.

The borings were made under the direction of Mr. C. W. Atkinson, who collected numerous specimens and carefully labelled them, and also filed a descriptive section, from which I obtained the necessary data, as above written.

CHAPTER III.

CAVES.

BY G. C. BROADHEAD.

Certain geological formations abound in caves, in others they are rare or are not found.

Caves occur in the Third Magnesian Limestone, Saccharoidal Sandstone, Trenton, Lithographic, Encrinital and St. Louis Limestones.'

That the St. Louis Limestone is cavernous is proven by the great number of sinkholes where this formation prevails, as at St. Louis and in St. Charles county. Small caves have been entered in St. Louis and found to connect with'sink-holes ; both here and near St. Charles good springs often issue forth.

In Eastern and North-east Missouri there have not been found many large caves in the Encrinital Limestone, but the lower beds of this formation in South-west Missouri often enclose very extensive caverns; among the latter may be included the caves of Greene county with some in Christian and McDonald. Those in McDonald I have not seen, but they are reported to be very extensive and probably are situated in the Encrinital Limestone.

SPECIAL DESCRIPTIONS.

On Sac River, in the North part of Greene county, we find a cave with two entrances, one at the foot of a hill, opening toward Sac River, 45 feet high and 80 feet wide. The other entrance is from the hill top 150 feet back from the face of the bluff. These two passages unite. The exact dimensions of the cave is not known, but there are several beautiful and large rooms lined with stalactites and stalagmites which often assume both beautiful and grotesque life-like forms. The cave has been explored for several hundred yards, showing the formations to be thick silicious beds of the Lower Carboniferous formations.

Knox cave, in Greene county, is said to be of large dimensions. I have not seen it but some of its stalactites are quite handsome.

Wilson's Creek sinks beneath Limestone and appears again below.

There are several caves near Ozark, Christian county, which issue from the same formations as those in Greene county. On a branch of Finly Creek a stream disappears in a sink, appearing again three quarters of a mile south-east through an opening 60 feet high by 98 feet wide. Up stream the cave continues this size for a hundred yards and then decreases in size, and for the next quarter of a mile further it is generally 10 by 14 feet wide. A very clear, cool stream passes out in which by careful search crawfish without eyes can be found.

There is another cave a few miles south of Ozark, and another ten miles South-east occurs in the Magnesian Limestone.

Two miles below Hannibal and a half mile from the Mississippi river, is McDowell's cave. This occurs in Lithographic Limestone, and is noted for being the place where Dr. McDowell deposited a relative's corpse to see if it would petrify. It faces the north, the entrance passing straight in is occasionally intersected by other narrow avenues crossing at right angles.

In Boone county there are several caves in Encrinital Limestone. Conner's, the largest, is said to have been explored for a distance of eight miles.

In Pike and Lincoln there are several small caves occurring in the upper beds of the Trenton Limestone, which are often very cavernous. On Sulphur Fork of Cuivre, there is a cave and Natural Bridge, to which parties for pleasure often resort. The bridge is tubular with 20 feet between the walls, and is 100 feet long.

At J. P. Fisher's on Spencer Creek, Ralls county, there is a cave having an entrance of 90 feet wide by 20 high. The Lower Trenton beds occupy the floor, with the upper cavernous beds above. On the bluff, at a distance of 150 yards back, there is a sink-hole which communicates with the cave. Within the cave is a cool, clear spring of water, and Mr. F. said he could keep meat fresh there for six weeks during midsummer.

In Pike county, near Matson's Mills, there are many sink-holes in these Trenton beds. In one of them I collected some pretty specimens of Arragonite. They often terminate in caverns.

The Third Magnesian Limestone which occupies such a large portion of South-west Missouri, often contain very large caves. One of them, known as Friedes' cave, is 6 or 8 miles North-west of Rolla, on Cave Spring Creek. It is said to have been explored for several miles, but I only passed in a few hundred yards. The stalactites here are very beautiful, assuming the structure of satin spar. A very clear stream of water issues out. West of the Gasconade, on Clifty Creek, is a remarkable Natural Bridge, which I have elsewhere described in Geological Survey of Missouri, 1855–71, page 16. ·

Mr. Meek and Dr. Shumard speak of the Third Magnesian Limestone as often cavernous. Mr. Meek speaks of a large and interesting cave on Tavern Creek, in Miller county. Dr. Shumard estimates a cave on Bryant's Fork, in Ozark county, to be a mile and a half long, and speaks of its containing many interesting stalactites.

There are many small caves in Third Magnesian Limestone in Pulaski county, along the Gasconade River. Some of them contain salpetre.

SUPPLIES OF WATER.

Springs are generally more abundant where cavernous rocks prevail. Streams will flow to the surface when underlying clay-beds prevent their downward passage. In certain Geological formations springs are more apt to abound, and in certain formations the water is better than in others. The purest water flows from Chert beds, or percolates through pure Sand, and is called soft or free-stone water. Water flowing through ferruginous Sands will become Chalybeate; that flowing through hale beds, containing iron pyrites, has often a strong copperas taste; that through Limestone, or from Limestone caverns, will taste of Lime, or is called " hard-water." The water flowing through pyritiferous Shales containing magnesia, will issue in what are ordinarily called Sulphur Springs; that flowing through shaly Magnesian Limestone sometimes originates Epsom Salt Springs.

Where certain Geological formations prevail, we may expect abundant supplies of water, while districts underlaid by other formations are comparatively arid.

Wherever Limestone No. 78, of the Upper Coal Measures prevail, we may expect good streams of water just beneath. Springs of any kind are not common in either the Middle or Lower Coal Measures, but are more commonly found where the Upper Coal Measures prevail.

The Drift in its beds of Sand interstratified with Clay, contains good reservoirs of water. These Sands being sometimes ferruginous, the water in such instances is Chalybeate.

The St. Louis Limestone being cavernous sometimes incloses large springs. The springs near St. Charles issue from this Limestone.

The fine springs of Jasper and Newton, flow from the Lower beds of Keokuk Limestone.

The clear, cool springs, often very large, of Greene, Christian and Lawrence, flow from the Lower beds of the Encrinital Limestone.

The Chouteau Group does not contain many springs, but Sulphur Springs sometimes flow from it.

At Louisiana, a very bold spring of good water flows from the face of a bluff of Lithographic Limestone.

We know of no springs of consequence flowing from Devonian Limestone.

The Upper Silurian system is too limited to generalize.

The Cincinnati Group affords the supply for most of the mineral springs of North-east Missouri.

The Trenton Limestone contains many sinks and caves in which are generally clear, cool pools of water.

Weak springs often flow from beneath the Saccharoidal Limestone.

In the Second Magnesian Limestone there are not often many springs.

The Third Magnesian Limestone is often cavernous, and affords beautiful, clear and cool springs of water. Some of the largest springs yet observed in Missouri, flow from these rocks. The largest known are on the Gravois, in Morgan county, in Camden, Dallas, and the spring at Meramec Iron-works, Phelps county.

The streams flowing through the Third Magnesian Limestones, are very clear, full, bold and rapid, and afford good water-power throughout the year.

Among them I would name Castor River, St. Francois, Black, Current, White, Niangua and the Gasconade, and their tributaries. They afford as fine water-power as any streams in the United States.

The streams flowing only through the Second Magnesian Limestone beds often become low, sink or dry up during the Summer season.

Those flowing through the Lower Carboniferous rocks of the South-west are clear, full and rapid, and afford a mighty water-power. Among them are Spring River, Center Creek, Shoal Creek, James' Fork of White River, Wilson's Creek, Finley Creek and the head streams flowing into Sac River.

The Streams originating and flowing through the Coal Measures are generally sluggish, and the smaller streams do not afford water-power sufficient for milling purposes.

The streams of North-west Missouri do not flow rapidly, but are constant running streams. Their main water-supply is derived chiefly from reservoirs in the Drift, but a portion of their supply is also derived from springs in the Upper Coal rocks.

[For Mineral Springs see Appendix.]

CHAPTER IV.

SOILS.

BY G. C. BROADHEAD.

The character and quality of all soils is mainly dependent on the underlying geological formations. Where Sandstones exclusively prevail, the soils will not withstand severe drouths, but with frequent refreshing rains are rendered productive. A soil composed in part of Sand, but also largely of Lime and humus or vegetable mould, is always productive. In wet seasons, the Sand affords proper digestion of refuse, decomposing vegetable matter, while the other useful promotives of vegetable growth push forward the crops to vigor and productiveness. Such soil we find on the Missouri bottom.

When the underlying material is clayey, with some lime but no sand and but little humus, we have a soil that will retain too much water on the surface to yield good crops, and in dry seasons the Clays are too hard for moisture to penetrate and reach the delicate roots and fibers of the growing crops. Such soil is common on the prairies of North-east Missouri.

When the subsoil approaches near the surface, our soils are not very rich; but when there is no underlying rock in sight, or it lies at a great depth, and the alluvial soil is a foot or more in thickness lying on the subsoil, and although it may not contain much Sand, we have a soil that will be abundantly productive in both wet and dry seasons. Such soil we have in North-west Missouri.

We do not here propose to go into a detailed description of our soils; such an article would be too elaborate for this volume; we only propose to discuss the geological relations of our soils.

Where Limestones prevail, our soils are black and productive, and give large yields of corn. Soils resulting from decomposition of Magnesian Limestone are black, warm and rich, suitable for corn, wheat, fruit and the vine. Where the Limestones contain Iron, the inter-mingling of the Iron with the soil produces a rich red or brown soil, yielding large crops, and capable of long endurance. Around mines of Iron, a luxuriant growth of vines and blackberry bushes will often spring up from the thrown out ferruginous debris.

At the Lead mines of Madison, the ground for many years has been dug over, and we find a luxuriant growth thereon.

Around Coal mines, where much Clay has been thrown out, the vegetation is slow to grow. Where calcareous Clays abound, as in the Bluff and Drift of North Missouri, we have several times had occasion to observe, along railroad lines, that these clays, when thrown out, mingle with the soil and impart additional fertility.

The bottom lands are all rich. The soil of those of South Missouri is sandy and gravelly, yielding abundant crops every year, and can generally be plowed soon after rains.

The soil of Missouri bottoms is composed of finely comminuted Sand and Clay, with some humus. In 1844, these bottom lands were covered with a greater depth of water than has been since known or had been known for a generation past. At the time of this flood, large deposits of Sand were formed in many places, and for several years after, no crops could be produced—corn was planted but would yield no ears. Since then these sandy lands have gradually improved, until at present heavy crops of corn are annually produced. This illustrates forcibly the imperishable nature of these alluvial soils. They have been subject to no overflows since 1844, and the only source of fertility has been from falling leaves, weeds and moisture.

Other bottom lands in North and West Missouri are, for the most part, based on the deep, black Clays of the age of the bottom prairie, and are always productive when properly ditched and drained, other-wise they often hold water too late in the season, and crops are some-times drowned out.

Other extensive tracts, similar in quality and richness to those just named, may include the swamp regions of South-east Missouri, embracing the counties of Pemiscot, Dunklin, New Madrid, Mississippi, Scott, Stoddard, and parts of Butler and Cape Girardeau. These lands are surpassingly rich, and large areas are still covered with swamps, but the time may be when many of them will be drained, and these reclaimed lands will then compete in productiveness with the richest lands in the world. Fine crops of cotton are annually raised in this part of Missouri, and these lands will yield from 75 to 90 bushels of corn per acre.

Exclusive of the swamp counties, the area of the State of Mis-souri may be divided into about four parts or districts.

FIRST CLASS.

The richest, including North-west Missouri, consists mostly of prairie, and is underlaid by the Upper Coal Measures, with the Middle Measures beneath and appearing along its south-east and eastern margin. A line entering the State in the north-west part of Vernon, passing north and east through the western part of Bates, thence eastwardly through the southern part of Cass, thence north-eastwardly to central part of Johnson county, on the line of Lafayette, thence eastwardly through southern portions of Lafayette and Saline, thence northwardly to Chariton in the direction of Salisbury, thence a little west of north to the northern boundary of the State in Mercer county, will include, on the west, the richest farming land in Missouri.

There are, of course, occasional tracts of inferior land included within these limits, but the soil is generally of uncommon fertility. This soil is generally based on a deep bluff deposit or on Limestone, and is for the most part calcareous. It is generally at least a foot thick and quite black, yielding good crops of corn, grass, pumpkins, squashes, potatoes, turnips, etc. The yield of corn will average fifty to seventy-five bushels per acre with ordinary cultivation, and lands that have been in cultivation thirty years yield as abundantly as when first cultivated. Blue grass grows well when the prairies have been grazed down. This is probably no better for wheat than the lands in Eastern Missouri; in fact, during similar seasons, the yield is not always as large per acre, but fine crops of wheat are often raised—frequently twenty-five bushels per acre—the general yield being from fifteen to twenty-five. Apples, and some small fruits, succeed very well, and occasionally there is a good crop of peaches. There seems to be no better soil for the gooseberry, and the cultivated grape grows to a large size, but the vines grow too luxuriantly.

As an evidence of the desirableness of this part of the State for farming purposes, although it is the most recently settled part of Missouri, it is now the most populous. The counties south of the Missouri River had become almost entirely depopulated at the close of the war in 1865, but now are as thickly settled as any counties in the State.

SECOND CLASS.

This lies just east and south of the first named. Its southern and eastern boundary passes through Barton into the western part of Cedar, thence through St. Clair, Benton, north-west part of Morgan, through Cooper, the southern part of Boone and Callaway, and eastwardly parallel to and within ten miles of the Missouri River to a point opposite the central part of St. Louis county. This district may also include extensive areas of the other counties lying southward along the Mississippi River, but not being familiar with them I am at present unable to classify their soils.

There are several well marked varieties among the soils of this district. That in the west and northern portion consists chiefly of prairie, often spreading out, in North Missouri, into flat prairies. That in the south-west is rolling country, with generally a sandy soil. The yield is generally from thirty to fifty bushels of corn per acre. The timbered lands in Eastern Missouri and in the counties along the Missouri River produce very fine crops of wheat, sometimes even yielding over twenty-five bushels per acre. A fine variety of tobacco is also produced on the thinner timbered lands. The hills near the Missouri River yield good crops of fruit nearly every year—the peach rarely failing, the grape always fine.

This division of the State we mark as Second Class, although it really does include some extensive tracts of first class land. Such may be found in Howard, Boone, Callaway, Marion, Ralls, Pike, Lincoln, St. Charles and St. Louis.

We have reports of as much as forty bushels of wheat per acre from Ralls, St. Charles, St. Louis and Perry.

In the counties of North Missouri and St. Louis county blue grass grows as fine as in the famous Kentucky blue grass region.

The underlying geological formations of this district are chiefly Lower Coal Measures and Lower Carboniferous Limestone. The richer lands are based on either Lower Carboniferous or Lower Silurian with rarely Devonian.

Near the Missouri and Mississippi rivers the soil is based on loose beds of Bluff formation, originating a rich mellow soil. In the interior of North Missouri it is mostly on stiffer Clays of Drift or Bluff and the soil is not so rich.

THIRD CLASS.

This occurs chiefly in South-west Missouri, becoming a narrow belt to the North-east, barely dividing the second from the fourth. It may include part of McDonald, Barry, Lawrence, Christian, Greene, Polk, Dade, Jasper, Barton, Cedar, Hickory, St. Clair, Benton, Morgan, Cole, Moniteau, Osage, Gasconade, Franklin, St. Louis and Jefferson, and a band passing southwardly. Some of the lands in Jasper, Lawrence and Greene are as good as those of the Second Class. The soil is generally somewhat gravelly and often mingled with red Clay. Good crops of wheat and corn and fine crops of fruit are produced,

especially in those counties along the Missouri River, whose hills
yield fine peach and grape crops every year.

In the South-west the soil is based on Lower Carboniferous and
Lower Coal measures; in counties along the Missouri River on Lower
Silurian, spread over with a pretty good deposit of Bluff Clays.

FOURTH CLASS.

This includes the main body of Southern Missouri, excepting the
swamp counties of the South-east and the other counties above
named. It constitutes an extensive tract, elevated higher than other
parts of the State, it being from 1,200 to 1,500 feet above the sea. It
is underlaid by the primordial Sandstones and Magnesian Limestones,
with an occasional elevation or peak of Porphyry or Granite in the
Eastern part. The country is broken by stream channels, cutting
down two hundred to three hundred feet below the tops of the bluffs,
with valleys often as much as four hundred feet below the main distant ridges.

Near the streams it is generally very rugged, with either abrupt
or long, steep ascent to the hills. When the main streams are wide
apart the country spreads back into a flat land with light colored soil,
supporting chiefly a growth of Post Oak; when a little more hilly
Black Oak and Black Hickory are common. With more soil there is
often a fine growth of White Oak, mingled with Sassafras, Dogwood,
etc. South of the main Ozark ridge, where the hills are either covered with Sandstones or Chert fragments, we find but little soil and
often a heavy growth of Pine. On the slopes from the Magnesian
Limestones are often seen fine Cedar groves.

There are extensive tracts within this District where the soil is
either too thin or too rocky to admit of present cultivation. But all
these lands will grow the Grape.

When those parts of Missouri that contain richer soil are entirely
settled up and the land costs too much for men of moderate means to
purchase, their attention will then be turned to this extensive District, where, by proper economy and thrift, good crops can be produced. At present twenty to thirty-five bushels of corn can be produced, or fifteen to twenty of wheat.

Of course, we occasionally also find very rich valleys, which
yield equal to any of the richer lands of the State. The valleys along
the streams near the South line produce fine crops of corn and cotton.

Other particulars regarding the soils and products will be found
in the various county reports.

TIMBER.

Most of Northern Missouri and the Western counties consists of prairie. The prairies, during the spring and summer seasons, are covered with a natural growth of many different species of plants, many of them having beautiful flowers.

These counties have generally belts of timber extending along the streams, affording a sufficient supply for fuel and other neighborhood uses.

The Missouri bottoms are generally heavy timbered with Cottonwood, Hickory, Walnut, Hackberry, Burr and Red Oak.

The counties along the Missouri River, from Platte eastward, often have heavy bodies of fine timber, but, until they reach Howard, are interspersed with occasional extensive prairies. Howard and those counties east have belts of ten to twenty miles wide, extending parallel to the Missouri River, and including the finest varieties of hard wood timber, such as Ash, Oak, Walnut, Sugar-tree, Hackberry, Hickory, Elm, etc.

A similar belt from fifteen to twenty miles wide, lies parallel to the Mississippi.

Along the Osage are heavy bodies of excellent timber. All the counties to the South contain heavy tracts of good timber, chiefly Oak. In South Missouri there yet remain large tracts of fine Pine lands not yet culled out, and that can be bought cheaply.

Yellow Poplar and Sweet Gum are common in the South-east counties south of Madison. The swamps abound in Cypress, Oak, Catalpa, Tupelo, Gum and Walnut.

In Southern Missouri open prairies are rare, but in their stead are occasional large tracts of barrens, or hilly districts covered with tall grass, on which are scattering, stunted Oaks, including Black Jack, Post Oak and Black Hickory. With this exception, the whole of South-east Missouri is one heavily timbered district, containing vast quantities of the finest kinds of timber suitable for making furniture and agricultural implements.

At present an immense number of these articles are imported into our State, thus taking the money out, when we ought to be more self-sustaining and manufacture our own farming implements and have a surplus to export. When our citizens devote more attention to manufacturing they will assuredly find prosperity attend them.

CHAPTER V.

MINERALS.

BY G. C. BROADHEAD.

IRON.

This, the most generally diffused of all our minerals, in some form or other, may be found in every county.

BOG ORE.

This is said to be found in the swamps of South-east Missouri. The surface deposits in other parts of the State often contain concretionary and amorphous forms of black, sandy material, containing as much as 14 per cent. of Oxide of Manganese, with about 18 to 20 per cent. of Oxide of Iron. Similar small concretions occur in the prairie Clays.

LIMONITE,

Or brown *Hematite*, is a very common ore, occurring in most of the counties of South Missouri. Drusy cavities in the Second Magnesian Limestone often contain pretty crystaline forms. In the same formation it is also found in a Stalactitic form.

GOETHITE,

A variety of brown Hematite, occurs in beautiful acicular crystals in Septaria of the Coal Measures of Adair county,

RED HEMATITE

Occurs in the Coal Measures of Linn, Adair, Sullivan, Henry, Vernon and Barton, and in other Carboniferous rocks of Callaway, Boone, Montgomery and St. Charles.

Beds of both Red and Yellow Ochre occur in many counties of Missouri, and afford an inexhaustible supply of good material for making paint stuffs.

CARBONATES.

The Spathic ores are chiefly found in the Coal Measures. The best and thickest layers are in Carroll, Johnson, Henry, Vernon, Barton and Cedar.

ANKERITE,

(A Spathic ore,) has been found in ores of Phelps county. Mr. R. Chauvenet's Analysis of it, gives Lime, 52.75; Magnesia, 20.45; Prot. Iron, 26.90.

SPECULAR

Oxide is found in larger masses than the other Iron ores; of such is the Iron Mountain in St. Francois county, Shephard Mountain and Pilot Knob in Iron county, Simmon Mountain in Dent county, Meramec mines in Phelps and numerous other deposits in Madison, St. Francois, Iron, Reynolds, Dent, Phelps, Crawford, Maries and Osage.

SULPHURETS.

Iron Pyrites is generally diffused, occurring in most of the Coal, and in the Shales and Slates, and scarcely any Limestone is free from it. The ash-blue Limestones, of the Coal Measures, contain it.

COPPERAS.

Sulphate of Iron is often abundant in the Coal Measures. In abandoned passages, at Coal Mines, it often occurs in long-wooly, thread-like crystals.

GOLD

Has been found in small quantities in the "Drift" Sands of North Missouri.

SILVER

Only has been found in small per cent. associated with Lead.

ZINC.

Zinc blende abounds at Granby and Joplin, and is found at many other Mines of the South-west. It is also found at the Lead Mines of

Franklin and Washington, and some other points in South-east Missouri.

The "pockets" of Coal, in Central Missouri, nearly all contain Zinc blende. The Lead Mines of Central Missouri also somtimes carry it.

It is, next to Iron, the most generally diffused metallic ore, although often found in only small quantities. It is found in nearly all the Geological formations. The St. Louis Limestone contains it in many places, although in very small quantities. It is occasionally found in small quantities in Coal Measure Limestone ; Ironstone concretions often inclose a nucleus of Zinc blende. Fragments of plant remain, often have minute cracks filled with Zinc blende, and it occurs in the interior of fossil shells.

SILICATE OF ZINC

Abounds at Granby and Joplin, and is found at most of the Lead Mines of the South-west, it is also occasionally found in Central Missouri and South-east Missouri.

CARBONATE OF ZINC

Occurs at Granby, Joplin, Minersville and Valle's Mines.

ZINC BLOOM

Is rarely found in Central and South-west Missouri.

GREENOCKITE,

(Cadmium Sulphide,) is found associated with Zinc blende in South-west Missouri.

COPPER.

No exclusive mining for Copper is now being done in Missouri. Mining has formerly been done in Shannon, Crawford, Jefferson, Franklin and Madison. Besides these counties, Copper is also found in small quantities in Miller, Cole, Cooper, Dade, Greene, Ozark, Wright, Phelps, Ste. Genevieve, Christian, Warren and Washington.

The ores of Copper are the blue and green Carbonates (Green Malactite,) and Sulphuret.

In Madison, it is intimately associated with Lead, Cobalt and Nickel.

NICKEL AND COBALT.

These ores abound at Mine LaMotte, and old Copper Mines in Madison county, and are also found at the St. Joseph Mines.

(Sulphuret of Nickel,) beautiful, hair-like crystals, are found in the St. Louis Limestone, St. Louis, occupying Drusy cavities resting on Calcite or Fluor Spar.

LEAD.

It is impossible to do anything like justice to this mineral in such a notice as this. Fuller information can be obtained from the county and special reports.

In South-east Missouri Lead is found both in Porphyry and in Magnesian Limestone. In Madison it occurs in small veins in Porphyry. It is found in paying quantities in the Lower Magnesian Limestones of Perry, Ste. Genevieve, Jefferson, Washington, Franklin, Gasconade, Osage, Maries, Crawford, Phelps, Pulaski, Morgan, Miller, Moniteau, Cooper, Cole and Camden. In South-west Missouri in the Lower Carboniferous rocks of Jasper and Newton, and in the Magnesian Limestones of Webster, Taney, Christian and Barry. It is also found in lesser quantities in many other counties.

Galena or Sulphuret of Lead is the chief ore obtained. Carbonate of Lead (*cerussite*) is also often met with. Phosphate of Lead (*Pyromorphite*) is sometimes, though rarely, found.

WOLFRAM.

This ore has been found in Madison county.

MANGANESE.

Manganese and Manganiferous Iron occurs in Iron county. Manganese occurs in other counties.

OTHER MINERALS, NOT ORES.

Carbonate of *Lime* (Calcite) seems generally diffused. It enters into the chief composition of all Limestones, and in many it occurs in natural crystals. The clear or transparent variety is common. At the Lead mines it is more often of a brownish tinge and generally modified in form, the more common of which is the Dogtooth Spar. Very handsome crystals can be obtained at the Lead mines of Cole county, and also at Joplin, Minersville, near Sarcoxie, and also in Christian county.

Arragonite is found in Mine LaMotte, and also in Jasper, Jackson and Lafayette counties. *Pearl* Spar is found in Second Magne-

G.S—4.

sian Limestone at Hermann. Violet colored Calcite is found on
Spring River, Jasper county.

Fluate of *Lime* (*Fluor Spar*). I only know of its being found
at St. Louis.

QUARTZ.

This, next to Calcite, is the most generally diffused mineral. Most
rocks contain it. Sandstone is nearly pure Silicia. The "mineral
blossom" of the Washington county mines is Quartz. It here occurs
in drusy cavities and in mammillary and botryoidal forms. When
viewed with a magnifier distinct crystals of Quartz appear, well defined. Lead is often associated with it. This form occurs in Washington, Jefferson, Madison and other counties. Large quantities are
brought to St. Louis and used for adorning parks and lawns. Veins of
Quartz, containing well defined, transparent and rose-colored crystals
occur, traversing the Granite of Madison county.

HEAVY SPAR—SULPHATE OF BARYTA.

The "Tiff" of the miners abounds at the Lead mines of Morgan,
Miller, Cole, Franklin and Washington. The finest crystals are found
in Cole, Miller and Morgan. They occur of both a clear and azure
blue, and amber color. The compact is generally white, but is sometimes tinged with Iron.

Large quantities of this is annually ground and mixed with the
commercial White Lead.

GYPSUM—SULPHATE OF LIME.

This mineral I have only found in the Coal Measures. It is sometimes found in joints of coal, but more commonly in the beds of Shale
or fire Clay. In all the counties where the Lower Coal Measures are,
we find Gypsum. It occurs crystallized, in the form of clear, transparent crystals, known as selenite. These crystals are often thickly
diffused through the beds of fire Clay. It abounds near Salisbury,
Chariton county, Knob Noster, Johnson county, and six miles north.

PICKERINGITE—HYDROUS SULPHATE OF ALUMINA AND MAGNESIA.

This was only obtained in Barton county, occuring as an efflorescence on Sandstone.

FELDSPAR.

Is only found in the Granites and Porphyries of Missouri.

MICA.

This mineral occurs abundantly in minute scales in nearly all the Coal Measure Sandstones—is sometimes also diffused through the Clay beds. It is one of the constituents of Granite, but in the Missouri Granites it is sometimes almost or entirely wanting.

HORNBLENDE.

This occurs in the Greenstones of Iron and Madison counties.

ASBESTOS.

This has only been found, associated with Greenstone, in Madison county.

BITUMEN.

Mineral Tar or Bitumen is found in many of the western counties, including Ray, Lafayette, Jackson, Johnson, Cass, Bates, Vernon, Barton and Jasper, and also westwardly in adjoining counties of Kansas. The particular localities, where found, and a description thereof, will be found in the several county reports. It seems to increase in quantity in the southern counties which contain it.

North of the Missouri River it occurs in the western and central parts of Ray county. Crossing the river it is said to be found near Blue Mills, in Jackson county, and detected in the boring of wells at Kansas City. Twelve miles south-east of Lexington, on the McCausland farm, it is found at many places oozing from between the Lower Sandstones of the Coal Measures. In the southern part of Cass are several Tar springs issuing from Sandstones of the Middle Coal Measures. Other localities further south are described in the several County Reports.

It has a vertical range through the various geological strata of over 600 feet. Its northward occurrence in Jackson and Ray, is in the upper part of the Upper Sandstones of the Middle Coal Measures; in Lafayette and Johnson, in Sandstone of the Lower Coal Measures; in Cass, in Sandstone of Middle Measures; at Parkersville, Bates county, in Sandstone of the Middle Measures, similar to that of Ray county; further south in Bates, in Limestones of the Middle Measures and in Lower Coal Measure Sandstones; in Vernon and Barton, in both Sandstone and Limestones of the Lower Coal Measures, and in the southern part of Vernon and in Barton counties most of the Sandstones are thoroughly saturated with it. In Barton and Jasper, we find it diffused through Lower Carboniferous Limestones, and is also generally dispersed in drops and massive forms in close juxtaposition with the Lead and Zinc of the mines, and sometimes coating nice calcite crystals.

Many of the rocks of South-west Missouri, especially the darker colored, when freshly broken, yield a strong bituminous odor, and the Sandstones are sometimes so highly bituminous as to be rendered quite black. Sometimes the rocks do not seem apparently to be bituminous, but upon striking them with a hammer the odor is readily distinguishable. When the tar is thrown in water and stirred, a beautiful display of irridescent colors appears on the surface.

I drank of the water of a spring on Shiloh Creek, in Vernon county, which did not apparently seem to be bituminous, but the taste of bitumen was very marked.

The so called Fort Scott Marble, common in the western part of Vernon, is a bituminous Limestone.

Most of the coals of South-west Missouri are very bituminous, which can often be detected by their smell. Black concretions in Clay Shale, in the western part of Vernon, often contain a good deal of free Bitumen. Its presence seems to have the effect of indurating the rocks—for the bituminous Limestone seems generally to be very hard. The Sandstones sometimes contain it in the form of small pockets of Asphaltum, but generally as a black, viscid tar.

The occurrence of Bitumen at so many places has given rise to much expenditure in search of oil, but all attempts have failed to reach any more abundant supply. From the evidences, I think it extremely doubtful whether there is sufficient quantity at any one place in Missouri to pay to work it. It seems too generally diffused, and does not appear to flow from any great reservoir. Probably the chief source of these bituminous deposits is in the Coal Measure Sandstones, from whence it has flowed out and entered other rocks.

An analysis of free Bitumen, from Minersville, Jasper county, by Mr. R. Chauvenet, gives:

Bitumen .... 95.75 per cent.
Ash (pale yellow)... 4.25 per cent.

Bitumen mixed with sand, from West Drywood, Barton county, gave:

Bitumen.. 44.74 per cent.
Ash... 55.26 per cent.

ROCKS.

CLAYS.

Fire Clays, possessing refractory qualities suitable for making fire brick, occur beneath most of the thicker Coal seams.

Good Potters' Clay may also be obtained, especially among the Coal Measure Clays. It is also sometimes found associated with Lower Carboniferous Rocks.

Kaolin is only found in South-east Missouri, where Porphyries or Granites prevail.

SAND FOR GLASS.

The Saccharoidal Sandstone, being clean and free from impurities, forms a very superior article for glass-making. It is generally very soft, making it easy to quarry. Its great thickness in this State also enhances its importance, and certainly no other portion of the Union is better supplied with pure Sand than Missouri.

It is 100 feet thick in Cape Girardeau, 80 in Perry, Ste. Genevieve and Jefferson and the western part of St. Louis county ; over 100 feet in Franklin, quite thick in Gasconade, 133 feet in St. Charles and Warren, becoming thinner in Callaway and Lincoln. With such thickness over such an area, there is room for many glass works.

LIME.

Most of the Limestone will burn into Lime, but the Lime is not all alike. The Limestones of the Coal Measures will burn into a good, strong Lime, but not a white Lime. The Lower Carboniferous Limestones generally will burn into a white Lime. Among the best we may include those of St. Louis, St. Charles, Boone, Louisiana, Hannibal, etc.

The Limestones of the Magnesian Series will not all readily burn into Lime, but such as do, afford a very strong Lime. Some of them would doubtless make a good Hydraulic Lime.

HYDRAULIC CEMENT.

The Limestones of the Coal Measures often afford a good Cement Stone. The Limestones near the hill top at Amazonia, Andrew county, have been proven to possess good Hydraulic properties. The Hydraulic Limestones have an uneven fracture, and generally a dull ashy appearance.

Some of the St. Louis Limestones also seem to be suitable for hydraulic purposes.

The Devonian Limestone of Callaway is said to resemble the Louisville Cement Stone, but no tests of its hydraulic properties have been made.

We feel confident in stating that we have abundance of good Hydraulic Limestone in our State, and that it abounds in many counties.

POLISHING STONE.

In Newton county, near Seneca, are extensive quarries of a porous rock, the composition of which is nearly pure Silica. This affords a very good Polishing Stone. Bricks of it are cut out, and the fragments ground up and made into blocks, and sold throughout the country as " Bath Brick." This rock may also be found in Jasper and McDonald counties.

NITRE—SALTPETRE.

Dr. Shumard mentions the occurrence of this useful earth as efflorescence on Sandstone in Ozark, and disseminated through Clays in caves of Pulaski county. I have also found it in caves of Maries county, and Saltpetre was formerly made in a cave at Portland, Callaway county. Its geological occurrence is in Second and Third Magnesian Limestones.

BUILDING STONE.

Our State is well supplied with the various kinds of stone needed in building. The extensive Gray Granite quarries near Knob Lick, St. Francois county, and Brown's quarry of Red Granite, in Iron county, near Iron Mountain, are beginning to supply St. Louis with a beautiful and durable stone. Similar quarries can be opened at other places in the same county; also in Madison and Ste. Genevieve. The Porphyries of these counties would be useful if they could be economically quarried. They all afford a valuable material for street paving.

The Third Magnesian Limestone, occurring in most of the counties of Southern Missouri, generally occurs in thick, strong and durable beds, but it being more difficult to open good quarries of it, it will remain unused for some time.

The Second Sandstone, when found, is generally in good, firm layers for building purposes.

The First Magnesian Limestone generally occurs in thick beds, is easily quarried and worked, and would afford a handsome and durable building stone. Such quarries might be opened in St. Louis, St. Charles and Warren counties.

The Niagara Limestone of Sugar Creek and Paynesville, Pike county, closely resembles its correlative beds in Grafton, Illinois, and will afford just as useful and handsome a building stone.

The Lower Carboniferous Limestones are generally durable, and, when used, afford a strong building stone.

Among the Lower Carboniferous Limestones the Burlington beds (Encrinital) will afford very thick and strong layers. The columns of the court-house and University at Columbia are constructed of it, and over twenty-five years' use have not impaired their beauty and durability.

The St. Louis Limestones have also proven to be durable, and are everywhere used in St. Louis.

The Sandstones of the Coal Measures being easily worked, occurring in even layers and afterward hardening, have become very desirable in building houses. The Lower Measures afford the best; those in the Upper Measures often contain some Clay in their composition, and disintegrate on exposure. Good quarries can be opened in Barton, Vernon, Cedar, Henry, Bates, Johnson, Lafayette, Carroll and Linn. Already have large quantities been shipped from Warrensburg, in Johnson county, to numerous distant points. The rock from these quarries is much valued, and can be quarried in any dimension desired. Similar dimension stone has been procured from the quarries near Miami, in Carroll county.

GRINDSTONES.

Many of the Coal Measure Sandstones possess a good grit, and from them excellent grindstones have been made. The best quality has been procured from the eastern part of Vernon and from Barton counties. Most of the other counties of South-west Missouri that contain Coal Measures also do afford good Grindstones.

MILLSTONES.

The Granites of the South-east have formerly been used for this purpose; other stones have been procured from Drift boulders of North Missouri. Some of the Chert beds have also been used, from rock obtained from interstratified beds of the Second and Third Magnesian Limestone. The Chert occurring among the Lower Carboniferous rocks of South-west Missouri, in outward appearance closely resembles the French Buhr. Beds of this Chert are well exposed in Newton, Jasper and Cedar counties. Some specimens from the last named county, under a strong magnifier, disclose minute crinoid stems. There would be danger of their breaking and becoming disseminated into flour, rendering it not very palateable.

SLATES.

In Iron county I have observed beds of Metamorphic Slates, in composition and general appearance closely resembling Roofing lates, but thus far have perceived no extensive quarries.

MARBLE.

Beds of buff, gray, flesh-colored, red and variegated Marble occur in the eastern part of Reynolds county ; Big Creek, Marble Creek and Stout's Creek, in Iron county ; Marble Creek, Leatherwood and Cedar Creeks, in Madison county.

These beds often possess great beauty and would be desirable for table-tops and mantles.

CHAPTER VI.

TOPOGRAPHICAL FEATURES OF THE SOUTH-WEST COAL FIELD.

BY G. C. BROADHEAD.

The general features of the Coal Measures of Bates, Vernon and Barton are similar. The lowest Measures are found in Barton, the highest in Bates. In Barton the base of the formation is seen, while in the North-west part of Bates the mounds are capped with Upper Coal Measures.

The evidences go to show that the agency by which the mounds were left as they now are passed in a Southerly direction, for near the State line is a range of mounds which is sometimes continuous for many miles, and can be traced from the Cass county line to Jasper. East of this, the mounds are more or less isolated but sometimes form chains for several miles. Their elevation above the plains below, is generally from 80 to 150 feet, more often capped by Limestone which has preserved them from entire destruction. The country of the plains slopes gently, so that it forms a beautiful farming country and lies well for the construction of public highways. A line of road could be easily and cheaply constructed near the State line passing at the base of the mounds and occasionally through gaps between them. Such a road would be convenient to some of the best Coal Mines in Missouri for a distance of 60 miles North and South. The central part of these counties also presents a favorable surface for the construction of railroads, and in some districts would pass near valuable Coal Mines.

At present there are large tracts of prairie overspread with a luxuriant growth of grass forming very fine grazing for stock.

SYNCHRONOUS BEDS.

In a certain county or adjacent district, the connected Section can generally be made and parallelism be drawn between remote outcrops in the same district. But when formations are separated by sev-

eral hundred miles, it is extremely difficult to do so. The Upper Coal
Measures are easily recognized, indeed the beds near the base of the
Upper Measures scarcely change in the distance of 150 miles.

With the Lower Measures it is different. In four or five counties
in North Missouri are found beds closely resembling each other.

The Rhomboidal Limestone of Howard, Randolph, Linn, Macon
and Adair, I regard as the same, and in these counties its associated
rocks, lying above, can be recognized occupying about the same distance apart at widely separated points, but the character of the rock
20 feet above this as found in Howard and Randolph seems very different from the same rock of Adair.

Now for other changes: Our observations tend to show that the
Chœtetes Limestone 20 feet above the Rhombidal may be the rock just
beneath the Lexington Coal. If so the Coal is wanting. Further investigations in other counties of North Missouri tend to show that this
Coal is probably not found north or north-east of Ray and Carroll. It
may be thinly represented in Livingston, and although seen in nearly
all the Missouri Bluffs in Lafayette county, we find that in going south it
becomes attenuated. While it is often 2 feet thick at Lexington, 20
miles south-west we find it only 1 foot thick. In Bates it may be the
8-inch seam near Butler (No. 57 of the South-west Coal Section) but
the other correlated rocks are different from those of Lafayette. The
Limestones and other rocks, with two seams of Coal well developed
at Fort Scott, and frequently met with in the western part of Vernon,
disappear northward. The Mulberry Coal of Bates county often 2½ to
to 3 feet thick, we find represented in the eastern part of Cass and
the western part of Johnson by a 1 foot seam, and at Lexington by a
thin band of shaly Coal. Further north it may be recognized in the
Coal at Graham's Mills, Livingston county.

MARAIS DES CYGNES COAL.

This Coal presenting a thickness of from 2½ to 5 feet appearing
near Moundville and in the south part of Vernon, next seen along the
line of Bates and Vernon, thence of good thickness near Richhill,
again on the waters of Panther Creek at several places, may be traced
by its thickness farther north and north-east through St. Clair into
Henry. Passing north-eastward we find it on Grand River near Clin-
ton and near Windsor. We are further inclined to draw a parallel
with this and the thick Coal in the eastern part of Johnson, west part
of Saline and a thick Coal in Chariton, Howard, Randolph, Adair and
Putnam counties.

The beds included below No. 16 of our South-west Coal Section
can all be found in Barton and Jasper, but probably do not all exist

in Vernon. The Coals below No. 16 although found south of Vernon were not all recognized in Vernon. In fact although the formations underlying Nevada are thick enough to enclose them we have no evidence as to their containing over two thin seams, and eastwardly toward Clear Creek, except in certain localities, there is only one to be seen. The Lower Coal Measures in the south-eastern part of Bates, although they give evidence of occupying the base of the Measures, do not indicate that the series below the Clear Creek Sandstone is present.

The Clear Creek Sandstone is probably the same as that found in the prairie two miles west of Rockville. Its equivalent may also be at the base of the Coal Measures in Henry county, and I consider it the Sandstone affording a good quarry rock at Brownsville, Saline county, where it occurs near the base of the Coal Measures. But the whole group below it as represented in Vernon, Barton and Cedar has not been recognized, and I think does not exist in North Missouri.

Some other beds can not be traced beyond a restricted limit. This difficulty is sometimes caused by interrupted masses of Shales preventing their being traced for any distance, and the absence of a well grouped collection of fossils. Some Coal beds of different horizons also seem to be formed under similar conditions. We are then apt to commit an error in correlation. An exactly correct grouping would therefore seem to be impossible.

Our grouped sections are approximately correct; entirely correct for a limited area of one or two, and even sometimes three or four counties, but for remote points of 75 or 100 miles or more we do not often have more than one stratum clearly defined. Other sections below or above may be entirely correct at one place but not entirely so at another.

Conclusion: That the Coal seams do thin out in a long distance is proved. That the Limestones do also is apparent. That entire groups may be wanting at remote places. *Per contra*, that Coal beds represented by a mere trace may form a thick and valuable seam at remote points.

Furthermore, that although good thick Coal seams are found of regular thickness along the line of outcrop, they may be absent beneath the surface west and north-west, where their correllators have dipped say 100 feet below the horizon. If reports of the borings in such districts are reliable, this fact seems partly proved. Examinations by shafts or with the Diamond drill would alone settle the matter.

The annexed General Section is compiled from notes taken in Bates, Vernon and Barton:

GENERAL SECTION of the South-west Coal Field in Bates, Vernon and Barton counties.

Number.	Thickness.	Description.	Total depth.
75	....	Blue and gray Limestone..	....
74	20 feet...........	Shaly slope..	478½ feet
73	8 feet............	Sandstone..	458½ feet
72	5½ feet..........	Brown shales with calcareous nodules and *Brachiopoda* large *Crinoid* stems.......................................	450½ feet
71	2 feet...........	Blue sandy shales containing fossils..............................	445 feet
70	20 to 34 inches	Coal (Mulberry)..	443 feet
69	2+ feet..........	Fire-clay	441 feet
68	11 feet...........	Slope..	439 feet
67	8 feet...........	Gray Limestone containing *Acheocidaris, Chaetetes, Fusulina* and *Syringapora*..	428½ feet
66	9 feet..........	Shales, some thin Limestone beds and fossils....................	420 feet
65	5 feet..........	Shaly slope...	411 feet
64	4 feet..........	Dark, ash-colored Limestone; brittle; breaks evenly and has but few fossils ; Bituminous...............................	406 feet
63	2 inches.........	Dark snuff-brown shales..	....
62	16 inches........	Hard Bituminous and slaty shales, with small round concre- tions..	402½ feet
61	8 inches.........	Hard, black, shiny band..	401 feet
60	1½ feet..........	Soft bituminous shales..	400½ feet
59	4 inches.........	Hard band..	399 feet
58	22 inches.......	Soft black bituminous shale......................................	399 feet
57	9 inches.........	Coal (Butler)...	398 feet
56	25 feet..........	Fucoidal Sandstone (lowest rock at Butler).....................	397 feet
55	2 to 4 feet.....	Limestone (upper Fort Scott Limestone).........................	372 feet
54	1 foot	Buff calcareous shales..	368 feet
53	4 feet...........	Bituminous shales	367 feet
52	8 inches........	Bituminous Coal (92 feet below Mulberry Coal).................	363 feet
51	3 feet...........	Shales and Fire-clay..	362½ feet
50	3 feet...	Fusulina Limestone (hydraulic)...................................	359½ feet
49	1 foot...........	Nodular Limestone shales and *Crinoids*.....................	356½ feet
48	3 feet...........	Blue and bituminous shales......	355½ feet
47	1 foot 6 inches	Bituminous Coal..	352½ feet
46	4 feet...........	Fire-clay...	351 feet
45	43 feet..........	Shales and Sandstone	347 feet
44	33 feet..........	Slope, shales and Sandstone concealed..........................	304 feet
43	1½ feet.........	Jointed bituminous Limestone....................................	271 feet
42	1½ feet..........	Calcareo-bituminous shales with fossils........................	269½ feet
41	6 inches........	Hard black slate..	268 feet
40	1 foot...........	Blue Limestone with fossils, *Pr. muricatus*...................	267½ feet
39	5 inches........	Shelly concretionary Limestone in one bed (Fort Scott Mar- ble)..	266½ feet
38	10 inches.......	Shelly bituminous shales with fossils............................	266 feet
37	8 inches........	Dark concretionary Limestone..........	265 feet
36	3 feet...........	Bituminous shales with large and some small Limestome concretions (Fort Scott Marble)................................	264 feet
35	2½ feet..........	Drab ochrey shale...	261 feet
34	2½ feet..........	Bituminous shales ; brown ochrey at the bottom...............	258 feet
33	1 foot...........	Coal (Cooks).........	256 feet
32	34 feet..........	Slope including a few thin Coal seams............................	255 feet
31	1 foot 6 inches	Coal...	221½ feet
30	15 feet..........	Slope..	220 feet
29	1 foot...........	Red Limestone...	205 feet
28	6 feet...........	Slope including beds of Carbonate of Iron.......................	204 feet
27	8 feet...........	Bituminous shales *Septaria*.....................................	198 feet
26	6 inches........	Hard slaty Coal..	190 feet
25	16 to 18 inches	Coal...	189½ feet
24	8 feet...........	Shales semi-bituminous at lower part.............................	188 feet

GENERAL SECTION—Continued.

Number.	Thickness.	Description.	Total depth.
23	2 to 3 feet.......	Coal..	180 feet
22	5½ feet............	Clay nodules and Selenite..	177 feet
21	4 feet..............	Sandstone and sandy shales..	172 feet
20	6 feet.............	Blue shales...	168 feet
19	2 feet 3 inches	Blue and bituminous shales calcareous and fossiliferous at the bottom...	162 feet
18	18 to 20 inches	Coal..	160 feet
17	9 feet.............	Gypsiferous Clay and thin Coal seams..	158 feet
16	50..................	Clear Creek Sandstone...	149 feet
		Base of Coal Measures—Bates and eastern and northern part of Vernon.	
15	1...................	Conglomerate and Iron ore..	99 feet

The lower continuation of this Section may be found in the report on Barton county.

CHAPTER VII.

CEDAR COUNTY.

BY G. C. BROADHEAD.

This county occupies rather a secluded position in the family of counties. Away from any railroad, navigable stream or great public highway, it is generally but slightly noticed.

Its area is 492 square miles. Most of the county east of the Sac River consists of timbered land.

The western half is chiefly prairie. Its surface is generally hilly, in fact, some portions especially that adjacent to the Sac in the southern part of the county, and a portion in the north-east is quite broken. The measurements of the highest bluffs in the county show those of Sac River to be from 130 to 165 feet high; the hills of the northern part 135 feet, and those on Childer Branch, in the north-east to be 200 feet.

The elevation of the highest ridges above the valleys of Sac River, is about 250 feet. Most of the western half of the county includes a somewhat hilly and rolling region, rising by long and gentle slopes from the lower valleys.

The district occupied by Coal Measures often contains Sandstone capped mounds with Keokuk Limestone at their base. A number of such mounds appear in T. 35, R. 27, between Alder and Horse Creeks, and are generally from 60 to 75 feet high. On the county line, near Clear Creek, we find long slopes extending to a high elevation.

Between the East Fork of Sac River and Bear Creek, the county is of an agreeable, undulating surface. The bottoms of Sac River are often a half of a mile wide, and from their margins the country often ascends very gradually.

TIMBER AND PRAIRIE.

The western half of the county is about equally divided into timber and prairie. Prairie occupying most of the higher ridges with a few stunted Back Jack Oaks on top of the sandy mounds, with the heavy bodies of timber mostly confined to the valleys and hills, for from 1 to 3 miles from the main streams. The portion east of Sac River consists mostly of timber with an occasional small prairie. Townships 33 and 34, R. 25, include fine bodies of large timber of the various kinds indigenous to this part of Missouri. In the northern part of the county the timber is stunted, and the county partakes of the character of "barrens." In this county several trees were observed which are peculiar to that portion of the State, lying east, but which are not found west, and among these I might name Alder, Sassafras, Spice Bush, Dog-wood, (*Cornus florida*) and *Bumelia lanuginosa*. White Oak is rare in the counties west, but abounds in Cedar county. For useful and durable timber, Cedar county includes an abundance of the best varieties. The timber on the Sac, especially between the Forks, is very large, tall and straight, and very abundant. Among the best varieties of timber in this county, we may include White Oak, Post Oak, Black Oak, Red Oak, Burr Oak, Hickory, Elm, Black Walnut, Birch, Sycamore, Coffee Tree, Honey Locust and Hackberry.

STREAMS.

Sac River, a swift, flowing stream with good power for regular water mills, flows through the county from south to north, cutting off one third of the county on the east. Bear and Spring Creeks are also regular flowing streams. Cedar Creek, West Bear Creek and their tributaries, become low, and even locally dry in extremely dry seasons.

Good springs are sometimes found and are often seen flowing from the lower beds of the Chouteau Limestone Group. The fine spring at Stockton flows from this formation. Other fine springs exist near East Bear and Spring Creeks. In some wells, in the southeast, the water has a remarkably pleasant taste. The water in the western portion of the county is not so agreeable, having occasionally a copperas taste. This is generally the result of flowing through the aluminous and pyritiferous Shales near the base of the Coal Measures.

In Sec. 9, T. 33, R. 28, from a very ferruginous Sandstone of the Lower Coal Measures, there flows a strong but pleasant tasting spring. The flow of water is sufficient for many to use from.

Another spring, of an equally strong taste but of weaker flow, was observed in Sec. 22, T. 34, R. 28.

GEOLOGY.

SURFACE DEPOSITS.

I saw no evidence of the existence of anything of older age than the *Alluvium* and *Local Drift*. The *Alluvium* includes the soils and all the recent deposits along the streams, and appears in their banks.

The *Local Drift*, which is only a subordinate member of the *Alluvium*, refers to the broken masses of rock, clay, etc., seen in gorges, ravines, or strewn along the flat margin of streams.

ROCK FORMATIONS.

Among these are included:

Lower Coal Measures	130	Feet
Ferruginous Sandstone	50	"
Keokuk Limestone	140	"
Encrinital or Burlington	20	"
Chouteau Limestone	40	"
Vermicular Sandstone and Shales	44	"
Lithographic Limestone	18	"
Magnesian Limestone	50	"

MAGNESIAN LIMESTONE SERIES.

At several places, low in the hills of Sac River, are outcrops of coarse, fine-grained and compact Magnesian Limestone, Cotton rock and Chert, which, from their position just beneath the Lithographic Limestone beds, we might at first glance think belonged to the First Magnesian Limestone.

But in the general absence of fossils, we have no data by which to determine. The lithological characters of some of these beds would indicate that they belonged to the Second Magnesian Limestone, and if so, the Saccharoidal Sandstone is wanting. In Sec. 34, T. 35, R. 26, on Sac River, Mr. Norwood observed an outcrop of beds of Cotton Rock and Chert. The upper bed was cherty, then followed 8 feet of drab, fine-grained and compact Magnesian Limestone (Cotton rock), with a dull, rough fracture, containing fucoids in relief. Underneath this was 4 feet of coarse and fine silicious Oolite. Some of the coarse pieces, with Oolites standing in relief and scarcely cemented at all. The fine-grained Oolites can only be clearly seen with a high magnifying power. The rock is very firmly cemented together, generally with silicious material, but sometimes a little Magnesian Carbonate of lime is insinuated.

In this case, the Oolites are very small and beautiful, having a central cavity. A fossil resembling *Straparollus reticulata (Sh.)* was obtained from these beds. This would indicate the formation to be the Second Magnesian Limestone.

Another small outcrop of similar beds was observed near the mouth of Bear Creek.

In the north-eastern part of the county, on the waters of Childer and Turkey Creeks, the Magnesian Limestone appears better developed, and some beds closely resemble those of the First Magnesian Limestone. They appear here as fine-grained, porous and light buff; fine-grained, drab, and silicious, dull, cherty, drab Limestones. We also found coarsely granular and crystalline Dolomites, of a gray, yellow and gray, bluish drab, and flesh color. A dark sub-crystalline, ash-colored bed, mottled with spots of white, decomposing, cherty nodules, was also observed.

Pleurotomaria and *Straparollus* were the fossils found.

About 50 feet was the greatest observed thickness of these beds in this part of the county.

At Dunagan's Mill, on Sac River, there occurs 18 feet of fine-grained, drab Limestone, with shaly partings, having 1 to 2 feet of olive Shales immediately above, containing Limestone concretions, and bands and concretions of Hornstone, with clouded bands of pink, purple and smoke colors. These beds, for the present, I refer to the First Magnesian Limestone. No fossils were observed.

CHOUTEAU GROUP.

The Group to which I apply this name includes those beds called by Prof. Swallow, in Missouri Report for 1855, the Chemung, also called Chemung by Prof. Hall in his Iowa Report, and by Worthen in his Illinois Report and White in the Iowa Reports, the Kinderhook Group.

The divisions seen in this county belonging to this Group include the Chouteau Limestone, Vermicular Sandstone and Shales, Lithographic Limestone.

G.S—5

Lithographic Limestone.

This, the lowest of the Group, is seen on Sac River at several points, being best developed at and near Dunagan's Mill, but not recognized in other portions of the county, excepting on Bear Creek. About 16 feet of this formation was observed at Dunagan's Mill, appearing thus :

No. 1. 5 feet mottled, fine-grained Limestone, with calcite specks disseminated, in tolerably even beds. Contains small fragments of *Crinoids*.

No. 2. 5 feet hard, thin-bedded, very fine-grained, light drab and somewhat silicious Limestone. No fossils seen.

No. 3. 1 to 2 feet olive shales with Limestone concretions.

No. 4. 18 feet Limestone.

No. 1 of this section is undoubtedly of the age of the Lithographic Limestone. I recognized it as of the same age as the beds at Taborville, St. Clair county, where it contains *Pentremites Roemeri*. Nos. 3 and 4 belong, I think, to the First Magnesian Limestone.

The entire section here would include :

No. 1. 39 feet cherty slope, with fragments of Chouteau Limestone near the lower part.

No. 2. 7 feet Vermicular Sandstone.

No. 3. 37 feet slope (Sandstone and shales.)

No. 4. 16 feet Lithographic Limestone.

No. 5. 18 feet First Magnesian Limestone.

The Lithographic Limestone, as it appears in this part of Missouri, is entirely different from that of North-east Missouri. It occurs here generally as a thick-bedded, buff brown Limestone with numerous minute cavities, which are generally cells vacated by fossils. Minute fragments of *Crinoid* stems and cells formed by their removal are commonly seen. *Pentremites Roemeri* being found, indicates the geological position of these beds. The rock here has a rough fracture, and would work easily and afford an excellent building material.

Vermicular Sandstone and Shales.

This formation is found next above the Lithographic Limestone. At Dunagan's Mill, it occupies a higher position in the hills, and is 44 feet in thickness, which is probably about its entire thickness in the county. It is found all along the bluffs of Sac River and Bear Creek, and of the upper portions of Turkey Creek.

Its characteristic features are a buff, brown, very fine-grained and sometimes calcareous Sandstone, generally traversed by windings of about an eighth of an inch in diameter, of a worm-like appearance.

The chief fossils observed were *Allorisma* ———, *Arca Missouriensis*, *Philipsia* ———, *Bellerophon* (like *B. carbonarius*), *Hempronites* ———, and *Aviculapecten Cooperensis*.

CHOUTEAU LIMESTONE.

This is somewhat limited in its outcrops.

Grayish, shaly Limestone was observed in the road east of Stockton. The upper buff and drab beds were seen on Bear Creek and Spring Creek.

Mr. Norwood observed on Bear Creek, near the east county line, fifteen to twenty feet thickness of these beds, the upper four feet being more fine-grained and harder than the lower; having a very rough surface; weathering with numerous small holes, and being flesh-colored and brown. The lower—ten to fifteen feet was of a light buff color, full of small drusy cavities set with mamillary crystals of Calcite.

On Sac River, below the mouth of Bear Creek, a high bluff is crowned with an escarpment of the upper, dark brown beds of this group. From the foot of the bluff, a thick bed of Argillo-Magnesian Limestone crops out, containing many small geodes of Quartz, and abounding in a coral resembling *Zaphrentis gigantea, and Spirifer Marionensis*. The interior of the fossils is sometimes of Calcite, and sometimes of Quartz, and both are often found in the same fossil.

The fossils observed in this Group were—in the Chouteau Limestone: *Orthis Mitchellini, Spirifer Marionensis, Zaphrentis* ———, *Terebratula fusiformis,* (?) *Spirifer lineatus, Orthis Vanuxemi, Athyris lamellosa, Cardiamorpha sulcata, Rhynchonella Cooperensis, Productus Shumardana, P. Pyxidatus, Euomphalus, Pleurotomaria* ———, *Fucoides Cauda-galli, Pentremites Burlingtonensis, Scaphiocrinus simplex.*

In Vermicular Sandstone—*Hemipronites, Arca Missouriensis, Allorisma* ———, *Aviculopecten Cooperensis*, and *Bellerophon* ———.

At Cedar Gap, one mile east of Stockton, the hills have Chouteau Limestone and Vermicular Sandstone above, with shales below, and on top are many loose fossils.

ENCRINITAL LIMESTONE.

This is not well developed, the lower beds appearing in the southern part of the county, near Sac River, and outcrops of gray, shelly

Limestone, referable to this formation, are seen along Bear Creek, near the east county line.

The fossils observed were *Actinocrinus sculptus, Euomphalus la tus* and *Spirifer striatus.*

In Sec. 36, T. 34, R. 25, Mr. Norwood observed twelve feet of gray shelly Limestone, with cavities lined with small crystals of Calcite, abounding in remains of Crinoid stems, but containing few other fossils.

It is probable that some of the gray Limestone beds near Stockton belong to this formation.

Hemipronites ———, *Spirirer* ———, *S.* ———, *Productus punctatus*, and *Bryozoa* were observed.

KEOKUK GROUP.

This formation occupies the greater portion of the western half of the county, forming the Bluffs of Cedar Creek, and appearing low down in the Bluffs of Alder, Horse and Bear Creeks.

Its greatest observed thickness could not be seen at any one place. In Sec. 12, T. 35, R. 28, 100 feet thickness was observed. Its greatest thickness is probably not over 35 or 40 feet more.

The beds are sometimes thick, but are more often thin and shelly, and nearly always of a uniform, light gray color. Intercalations of concretionary Chert occur mostly in the upper part.

The chief fossils observed were *Orthis dubia, Hemipronites crenistria, Productus mesialis, Pr. semireticulatis, Pr. cora, Spirifer* ———, *Zaphrentis Cliffordana, Philipsia* ———, *Chonetes* ———, *Terebratula parva, Rhynchonella subcuneata, Athyris* ———,

A solid Chert bed appears just above the highest Limestones closely resembling the French Buhr Stone. It contains very minute cells, resulting from the displacement of fossils, chiefly Crinoid stems·

FERRUGINOUS SANDSTONE.

This formation is scarcely recognized west of Stockton, only a few detached outliers being occasionally seen; but east of Sac River it forms the principal top rocks from the south to the north line of the county. Its general character is that of a coarse Ferruginous Sandstone, composed of rounded grains of pure Quartz, cemented generally with oxide of Iron, which is sometimes red, sometimes brown, and often ochrey. The rock is sometimes quite hard, and resembles Quartzite. No fossils were observed.

The greatest observed thickness was on Turkey Creek, where it often forms bold, steep and picturesque bluffs, which are sometimes weathered into a columnar front with partially formed caves. Weathered holes are often found, indicating that the Sandstone is alternately soft and hard.

The Iron ore of the eastern part of the county, has its origin in this Sandstone.

COAL MEASURES.

That division of the Coal Measures to which these rocks in this county belong, is the lower part of the Lower Coal Measures and lies below all known Coal formations of North Missouri, and includes beds of Sandstones, Shales, Ochre, Soft Hematite and Bituminous Coal.

The Sandstones are generally coarse-grained, micaceous and often ferruginous, being deep and bright brown and red in color. The lower beds are very coarse, even partaking sometimes of the character of a conglomerate, and are particularly ferruginous.

The equivalent of the Clear Creek Sandstone of Vernon county often occupies the highest ridges, and is generally even-bedded, forming a good building stone and a pretty good material for grindstones.

Mud-cracks, Fucoids and *Ripple-marks* are often characteristic of this Formation.

The following genera of plants were observed: *Sigillaria, Calamites, Lepidodendron, Syringodendron, Trigonocarpon* and *Cordaites.*

No Limestone beds were observed in the Coal Measures of this county, and only a fragment of a fossil shell was observed at one place in a thin bed of calcareous Ironstone. The greatest observed thickness was 130 feet.

ECONOMICAL GEOLOGY.

In a mineralogical point of view the Coal of this county may be considered about the most valuable product, although at present not so valuable because wood is abundant and cheap everywhere.

In sections 19 and 20, township 35, range 28, Coal has been mined at several places. First, on Wm. Taylor's land, from one to two feet is said to have been reached in his well at a depth of fourteen feet from the surface. It is immediately overlaid by one foot of Ochre and calcareous Ironstone. Three hundred yards south, on the land of Mr. Mulky, near the county line, a Coal, probably of a lower horizon, was observed sixty feet below the hill top. It did not present a very favorable appearance, the upper fourteen inches being soft and abounding in *Cordaites.* Then came six inches of blue Shale with three inches of shaly Coal below. The cap-rock was a shaly Sandstone. Firm beds of Sandstone occur two feet above the Coal, also near the hill-top, resembling the " Clear Creek Sandstone."

Miller's Coal Bank, one-quarter of a mile east of Taylor's, was so concealed, that I could not see its correct thickness. It was reported to be in two seams, each one foot six inches thick, separated by blue Clay. Five feet of blue Clay overlies the Coal. The Coal itself is deep black and shining, seems very bituminous, appearing, in fact, almost like an Asphalt. It has a little Iron Pyrites irregularly dispersed in small quantities in it, and contains faint plant streaks replaced by Pyrites. If as thick as reported this Coal may be of commercial importance at some future day.

Mr. H. West visited the Coal Bank of Ann Connor in north-west of Sec. 16 of same township, and found an 8-inch seam capped by 8 feet of thinly laminated Micaceous Sandstone, containing plants with other Sandstone beds above.

This is undoubtedly equivalent to Mulky's Coal, as is also probably a 6-inch seam found cropping out in Sec. 22 of the township, north.

There were no other Coal outcrops observed between Cedar and Bear Creeks, but Coal may be easily obtained at many places where it is now concealed.

Wm. Barden's Coal, in south half of Sec. 3, T. 34, R. 28, is 10 inches, capped with 3 feet of light blue Shales, with Sandstone in the Bluffs above. Lower Carboniferous Limestone occurs about 30 feet below the Coal. This is also probably the same bed as the last named bank.

A 4-inch seam appears lower down the valley, having Red Ochre bands in the underlying Shales.

Other principal outcrops appear in T. 36, Rs. 7 and 8. North of Cedar Creek, in the western part of T. 36, R. 26, about 2 inches of Coal crops out in a branch, and this may be the lowest Coal in the county. A section here is about as follows :

No. 1. 125 feet slope, with occasional outcrops of Sandstone.
No. 2. 2 feet Shales.
No. 3. 2 feet Sandstone.
No. 4. 2 inches Coal.
No. 5. 2 feet Blue Clay.
No. 6. Coarse-grained Sandstone.

At B. Marcus', in north-west Sec. 15, Coal crops out very favorably on the edge of a low bluff. Red and Brown Sandstone appear above, with ferruginous sandy Shales resting immediately on the Coal. The Coal is 16 inches thick, and weathers reddish-brown, the middle portion showing remains of plants and Mineral Charcoal, and occasional thin streaks of Iron Pyrites. The bottom part is deep-black, with an occasional layer of jet-looking Coal of one-third to three-sixteenths of an inch in thickness.

The same Coal as the last appears 18 inches thick at Lebec, capped by shaly Sandstone. Sandstone appears 30 to 40 feet higher, and is very ferruginous. The water flowing through it contains much Oxide of Iron. The general appearance of the Lebec Coal is like the middle portion of Marcus'. It also occurs in thin layers, and resembles Block Coal.

Mr. Norwood examined Joseph Miller's bank in Sec. 22, T. 36, R. 28. His section here was—

No. 1. 55 feet Sandstone at top; tumbled masses are seen lower down.
No. 2. 7 feet shaly Sandstone.
No. 3. 3 feet sandy shales in thin laminæ, containing *Ferns*.
No. 4. 1 foot hard, black, shiny Coal, in thin layers, containing a little Sulphur.
No. 5. 10 feet slope to Walnut Creek.

This Coal is probably the equivalent of the Lebec Coal, and underlies the county on the same horizon between these places. It has also been worked about a mile south of Lebec, near the waters of Clear Creek.

COAL EAST OF SAC RIVER.

These localities were examined by Mr. Norwood.

M. L. Parishe's Coal bank in the S. E. S. W. Sec. 13, T. 35, R. 26, formerly worked, but not recently. At present the driftings are in a bad condition.

An approximate section was obtained mainly from other persons, of which the following is nearly correct :

No. 1. Sandstone (Clear Creek).
No. 2. 10 feet Shales.
No. 3. 16 inches tolerably good Coal, containing a good deal of Pyrites and somewhat slaty at the top.
No. 4. 2 to 3 feet Shales and Clay, passing into a Sandstone below, containing *Stigmaria* and *Cordaites*.
No. 5. 18 inches Coal, more compact than the top seam; said to be also better, but still contains Pyrites.

The dip is south-west at one place and south-east at another.

Hosey's Coal bank, in N. E. S. W. Sec. 13, T. 35, R. 26, (worked when examined,) resembles Parish's but is not divided by seams. Its section is:

No. 1. 20 feet slope with Sandstone.
No. 2. 3 feet Coal with a few bands of Iron Pyrites.

The top layer is a heavy, dull black pyritiferous Coal, which weathers with a white material (Copperas) in joints. The layers are generally separated by Charcoal. Between this and the lower part is the " Smith's "Coal, which appears very different from the upper, the fracture showing a bluish [appearance, weathering yellowish brown. The bottom resembles the top.

Beuler and Chandler, in N. W. S. W. Sec. 13 and Trent, in N. E. Sec. 24, T. 35, R. 26, have the same Coal. The thickness at Beuler and Chandler's varies from 20 inches to 3 feet. The area of this small field is about 6 square miles.

The total area underlaid by Coal Measures in this county is about 124 square miles.

The exact aggregate thickness beneath the surface could not be obtained, owing to doubt regarding the number of coal seams.

But Cedar county is well supplied with Coal.

OTHER MINERALS OF CEDAR COUNTY.

IRON ORE.

This is found associated with Ferruginous Sandstone and also with the Coal Measures.

In Sec. 2, T. 33, R. 26, occasional masses of Limonite, generally a foot in diameter, were seen strewn along the hill-top. A few small excavations have been made here but no great amount of ore discovered.

Similar masses of Limonite were observed in Sec. 10, T. 33, R. 25, evidently associated with " Ferruginous Sandstone."

An analysis of Mr. Chauvenet gives:

Insoluble Silicious... 9.70
Peroxide of Iron.. 75.09
Water.. 11.61

Other ore beds of the same geological age were observed by Mr. Norwood, as follows:

On G. Callahan's land, in the E. half N. E. quarter Sec. 20, T. 34, R. 25, scattered fragments of sandy Limonite are seen strewn on the surface. Similar ore is also found on Jack Simmons' land, in the N.W.

Sec. 4, T. 34, R. 25, and at other places in this vicinity, wherever the Ferruginous Sandstone is exposed.

In Sec. 15, T. 34, R. 27, there is quite a deposit of Silicious Limonite. The ore occurs in large detached masses over the surface of a hill; many of the masses being 400 or 500 pounds in weight.

One old excavation, made about 30 years ago, exhibits 2 feet of ore, occurring irregularly, as if piled up. Some of the ore is soft and porous, other portions are hard and compact. It probably is of the age of Ferruginous Sandstone, although no rocks of this formation are seen in the vicinity. The Keokuk Limestone is found a little below. Mr. Chauvenet's analysis of this ore is as follows:

Insoluble Silicious matter	43.94
Water	8.91
Peroxide of Iron (Fe. 2, O 3)	47.02
Metallic Iron	32.91

In Sec. 30, T. 36, R. 28, I examined a deposit of Iron ore of similar character to that last described by Mr. Norwood. The bed is about 300 feet east and west by 50 north and south, and apparently very silicious. The ore is full of small cells and portions are somewhat ochrey. It reposes directly on *Lower Carboniferous Chert.*

It is probable that this description of ore is merely a replacement of Ferruginous Sandstone.

A partial analysis of this ore gives:

Insoluble Silicious	43.63
Peroxide of Iron	49.28
Water	7.08

IRON ORE OF COAL MEASURES.

This is generally softer and lighter, occurring as a red, yellow and brown Ochre and as a soft porous Limonite.

The chief place where this ore was observed was in Sec. 22, T. 34, R. 28. As this locality is interesting from the variety and peculiarity of its different rocks I insert it here:

No. 1. Slope from hill-top.

No. 2. 28 feet Clear Creek Sandstone, of a buff color, rather fine-grained, and occurring in flag-like masses.

No. 3. 5 feet outcrops of porous, brown Hematite—a portion a little ochrey.

No. 4. 1 foot 6 inches red and brown sandy textured Ochre.

No. 5. 7 inches Ochre, somewhat concretionary.

No. 6. 4 inches red, sandy shales.

No. 7. 1 foot blue, shaly Sandstone.

No. 8. 6 inches shaly Coal.

No. 3 occurs in large sized masses, a quarter of a mile west, strewn over about an acre of ground, so it is very probable that it underlies the intervening space.

An analysis, made by Mr. Chauvenet, of No. 3 of this section gives:

Insoluble, silicious matter... 4.71
Water.. 13.27
Peroxide of Iron (Fe2 O3)... 81.90

99.88
Metallic Iron Fe.. 57.33

An analysis of No. 4 gives:

Insoluble, silicious matter... 8.69
Water.. 12.59
Peroxide of Iron (Fe2 O3)... 78.30

99.58
Metallic Iron (Fe.).. 54.81

Nos. 4 and 5 would form a pretty and durable paint. These, together with No. 3, will serve to show that this is an important mineral locality.

We may also expect to find these beds at many other places in the neighborhood.

The above analyses of Nos. 3 and 4 show them to be good ores. No. 3, a particularly fine quality of Limonite, was also observed a quarter of a mile south-west.

We think we are correct when we say that there is about 16,300 tons per acre of ore—enough to supply a furnace for one year, smelting 45 tons per day, and on 40 square acres there would be amply sufficient to supply the same furnace for at least 30 years.

Our calculation is based on these beds extending over 40 acres, but the probability is that they really do extend over at least a mile square but driftings or shafts sunk to the same horizon could only determine this. In driving in these drifts, the miner would have a good roof of the overlying Sandstone, and the Sandstone itself is often a good gritstone.

But in this calculation, we have only taken note of the upper Limonite; if to this we add No. 4, our quantity is increased one-third to one-half. Just below No. 4 there is a 7-inch good bed of red and brown compact Ochre, which may yield from 30 to 40 per cent. of pure Iron. This, besides being a superior Ochre for painting, could also be smelted. The underlying Coal could also be utilized. The wood for burning into charcoal could be obtained at from one to three miles of this place. The nearest water power would be Bear Creek, one mile off.

Many years ago, parties began the erection of an Iron furnace on Sac River, in the southern part of the county, but the projector being involved in debt, was forced to abandon his work before completion.

LEAD.

There are reports of the existence of Lead in this county at several places, but they have proved, thus far, unworthy of notice. One locality on the old Cheshire place, now occupied by Mr. Prewitt, was examined by Mr. Norwood, who only found Calc Spar in Chouteau Limestone—no Lead at all.

At Mr. Kennedy's, on Sac River, four miles north of Stockton, a pit has been excavated to a depth of 40 feet in search of "mineral" of some kind. In the thrown out debris, I observed fragments of a bluish slaty rock and Iron Pyrites. This is the locality formerly reported by some wandering mineralogist to contain Antimony ; but if there ever was any Antimony here, he brought it in his pockets and it vanished with him. No useful ores or minerals, besides those above named. have been found in the county.

BUILDING STONE.

Near Dunagan's Mill, fine quarries could be opened of the Lower Chouteau or Lithographic Limestone. Also, good quarries of Cotton rock, of age of the First Magnesian Limestone. Other good quarries may be opened at various points on Sac River and Spring Creek. On Turkey and Childer's Creek, good quarries of Magnesian Limestone may be opened.

The "Clear Creek Sandstone," of the Lower Coal Measures, affords a superior building stone, and is sometimes of excellent quality for grindstones.

Good quarries may be opened in Secs. 12 and 24, T. 35, R. 26; also, near the hill-tops near Cedar and Horse Creek, and at other places northward near Clintonville, and along the north county line.

The Limestones on Cedar, Alder and Horse Creeks afford large quantities of excellent material for Lime, and may do also for all ordinary building purposes.

In the southern part of Sec. 6, T. 34, R. 27, I observed about two feet outcrop of silicious rock, lying just at the top of the Keokuk Limestone. This rock is very close-grained, and contains numerous minute cells, not many of them larger than a pin's head, and most of them, under magnifying power, proving to be cells vacated by Crinoid stems. This rock has the texture and general appearance of the French Buhrstone, and may be used for the same purpose. I would recommend that it be tried, it may prove valuable. It can be found at many places west of Cedar Creek, by carefully examining the horizon just at the top of the Keokuk Group.

AGRICULTURE.

We may divide the soils of this county into about four classes. The first or richest includes the bottom lands of the larger streams— a rich alluvium. The second class includes the soil between the forks of Sac River, and most of that between Sac River and Bear and Spring Creeks, also, a portion of the county near Stockton. The soil of the south-eastern part of the county is generally sandy. When much Iron and Lime are disseminated, it is rich, but when mostly sandy, is quite poor. The third class includes the soil on the hills and slopes in the western part of the county, capable of producing tolerably fair crops. The north-eastern part of the county embraces the poorest land—that on the ridges being very sandy and poor.

The staple crops are corn, wheat and tobacco. Some cotton is also raised, and when frost does not appear too soon, this is very successfully produced. Fruit will generally succeed very well.

CHAPTER VIII.

JASPER COUNTY.

BY G. C. BROADHEAD.

This county contains 643 square miles. Its surface is generally rolling, sometimes hilly near the larger streams, but is often gently undulating.

The principal streams are Spring River, Centre Creek, and North Fork of Spring River. The principal tributaries of North Fork are Little North Fork, Dry Fork, Buck Creek and Cow Creek.

The country, from between Spring River and the north county line, in Ranges 29 and 30, generally slopes very gently from near the streams to the far off hill tops. The contiguous bluffs, along the streams, are not often over 15 feet high.

Range 29 is poorly supplied with springs, and the streams do not generally run all the year. Dry Fork is indeed generally dry, except in pools, until it receives the water from Mr. Schooler's spring in Sec. 8, T. 29, R. 30. Below this the creek has a full supply of water, and runs rapidly all the year. Further west the country is a little more hilly, and that part of R. 32 of T. 30, underlaid by Coal Measures, has occasional mounds rising above the general surface. On Little North Fork, near the county line, the bluffs are sometimes as much as 70 feet high.

Spring River, a very rapid flowing stream, traverses the county from east to west, a little south of the middle. It has always an abundance of clear running water from many fine springs, but what is remarkable is that the surface drained by this river, forms a very narrow strip, rarely over two miles wide on either side the stream ; and for a long distance its tributaries are mere spring branches, or a water-shed from the neighboring hills. White Oak Fork enters it five miles west of the east line of the county. From this to the mouth of North Fork, we might almost say it has no tributaries for a distance, in a westerly straight line, for over 20 miles. Two miles below, it receives Pond Creek, but on the south side it has no tributaries in the county of greater length than two miles. The country on the south side is generally of gentle slope, from the top of the prairie to the stream.

Centre Creek, a rapid and constantly running stream, traverses the county, irregularly meandering from the east to the west line, about parallel to Spring River, and at an even distance of from four to five miles from that stream. It, together with its tributaries, governs the topography of all that portion of the county lying south of Spring River. Another remarkable fact connected with this stream, is that it has scarcely any tributaries coming from the north, but many on the south. Incidental to this, we perceive that its steep bluffs lie chiefly on the north bank, and the bottoms on the south side —like those of Spring River—are often wider, and their slopes from the neighboring hills are long and gentle. Its hills are generally of the same height as those of Spring River. Its tributaries, which as I said, lie on the south side, start from an easy, flat depression, near their sources; then a channel is formed, and we begin to see low bluffs, becoming higher as we descend.

The principal tributaries are Jenkins', Jones', Grove and Turkey Creeks. These smaller streams are well supplied from the purest springs, passing out of beds of clean gravel.

WATER POWER.

In Jasper there are no navigable streams, but its water power is equal to that of any other county in the State.

Spring River, Dry Fork, Centre Creek, Turkey Creek, Grove Creek and Jenkins' Creek, all afford a wonderful power for milling purposes. Some of the small streams, at their sources, have water enough for extensive manufacturing purposes. I might name the springs at Fidelity, those on Jenkins' and Jones' creeks, the spring at Scotland, that at Carthage, and that at Mr. Schooler's. These springs always afford an abundance of water, and do not freeze during the coldest of weather. The spring branch at Mr. Schooler's, never freezes for 200 yards from its source, and ice only begins to form a quarter of a mile from the spring.

The shafts at Leadville and Joplin generally reach strong streams of good fresh water. This the miners always turn to advantage, and use in washing their mineral.

AGRICULTURE.

Jasper may be considered one of the best agricultural counties of South-west Missouri.

The vallies along the large streams are generally broad, often a quarter to a half mile in width, and are very fertile.

That portion of the county north of Spring River, and east of North Fork, embraces the next best farming land. Good crops of wheat, and good average crops of corn are produced.

South of Spring River, rock often approaches near to the surface. Nevertheless, there are occasional tracts of very desirable land. The best land will yield 40 bushels of corn, or 15 to 18 of wheat.

In entering the county from the north, we are struck with the change of the soil and appearance of the crops. Having just left a sandy soil, we step upon a black and richer one. The Chert and Limestone soils are generally of a dark color, except when the red Clay comes near the surface.

Most of the crops peculiar to counties north of this, are raised here. Beside, good crops of cotton can be raised, and peanuts grow very well. The fruits have not as yet been much planted, but the soil and climate are such as to invite the planting of large orchards and vineyards.

SURFACE DEPOSITS.

The material overlying the solid rocks may be referred to "local agencies."

Solid beds of rock often appear on high ground, and can always be reached within a few feet of the surface. The soil and subsoil, both combined, are not often over two feet deep, with downward successions of red Clay and Gravel for from 4 to 8 feet, to solid Rock. The Gravel is even sometimes at the surface, and often within a foot depth. A similar succession of loose material, is also commonly found at the Lead mines. The banks of the streams, also, are similar, of which Centre Creek exhibits:

No. 1.   1½ feet dark soil.
No. 2.   2   feet red Clay.
No. 3.   3   feet Gravel bed to the water in creek.

On the prairie, two miles to the south-west of Carthage, excavations show water-worn Chert pebbles at the surface. At the old mines in Sec. 33, four miles south-east of Carthage, similar pebbles were observed. These were found at 60 to 70 feet above Spring River or Centre Creek; so it is quite evident that no recent agency could have deposited them there. They must therefore belong to the Drift, about its southern limit, but borne by currents from some place near by.

LOWER CARBONIFEROUS ROCKS.

In this county are found a part of the Lower Carboniferous Formations and the Lower Coal Measures. These divisions of the Lower Carboniferous appear to be mostly of the type of the Keokuk Group with overlying loose masses of Chert inclosing fossils representing a higher horizon. Some of them are fossils of the Keokuk, some of the St. Louis and others again of the Chester Group.

The Limestone with occasional Chert is found along all the streams in the county excepting the north-western part where we find the Coal Measures.

With regard to the thickness of the Keokuk Group in this county we find it impossible to determine owing to the various beds so closely resembling each other; the same fossils also occur in low strata and again are found higher up. So we found it impossible to trace out any bed by its fossils.

We find Limestones at the water's edge in the creeks which we also see within a few feet of the surface on higher ridges. These ridges being from 100 to 150 feet above the streams, probably not much more than 150, we therefore think we are safe in saying that there is 150 feet of this Group, but can not say how much more.

The Limestones are generally of a uniform bluish-gray excepting when they contain Bitumen, they are then of a darker color. They are also frequently a light or whitish-gray or drab; occur also in both thick beds and in thin shelly layers.

On Grove Creek, north of Scotland, an exposure of 57 feet of Limestone is represented by light gray shelly Limestone, at the top containing *Orthis Keokuk, O. dubia Productus cora, and Phillipsia.*

At 6 feet from top the Limestone is coarse ash-grey, and at 14 feet fine and coarse beds are seen containing *Orthis dubia.* At 22 feet it is coarse and Cherty; at 27, firm, hard Limestone; at 30 feet there is 2 feet of coarse Limestone. At 15 feet from the bottom the Limestone is hard and close-grained.

The remainder is coarse, thick-bedded Limestone to the bottom of the hill. These Limestones often have intercalations and lenticular beds of oolitic Chert both in their upper and lower parts. In the lower parts of the bluffs at Carthage are seen 2 feet of mingled Chert and Limestone. Similar beds were also observed on Center Creek. We also found Cherty beds with disseminated particles and fragments of Calcite. The Limestone beds are also often separated by Chert layers.

The fossils recognized in this group were *Achimedes* (rare) and other *Bryozoa, Zaphrentis centralis* (?) *Z.* ——, *Amplexus* ——, *Productus Wortheni, P. cora, P. Altonensis, P. magnus, P. mesialis, P. like P. alternatus, P. Flemingii*, (?) *P. setigerus* (?) *Spirifer pseudolineatus, Sp. subcuspidatus, S. Keokuk, S. lateralis, S. suborbicularis*(?) *S. incrassatus, S. Logani, S. increbescens* (?) *S. tenuicostatus, S. tenuimarginatus* (?) *Althyris Roissyi* (?) *Althyris planosulcata, Terebratula parva, T. trinuclea, Rhynchonella mutata, R. subcuneata, Camaraphoria subtrigona, Chonetes planumbona* (?), *Orthis dubia, Hemipronites crenistria, Aviculopecten* (2 *sp.*), *Myalina San Ludovici, Phillipsia* ——, & *Platyceras* ——, *Crinoid* stems are often abundant.

This rock with the upper broken members forms the main Lead-bearing rock.

In the eastern part of Jasper, on Spring River, at Tarter and Dudley's Mill, and on White Oak Fork outcrops were seen of a flesh-colored closely crystalline and very fine-grained Magnesian Limestone in very thick beds. On White Oak Creek a single 18 foot bed was measured. The rock is evidently altered from a pure Limestone to a Magnesian Limestone, for no well defined fossils are found. The process of alteration seems to have destroyed nearly all vestige of organic remains; a few small but vague and ill defined cells are left which were probably formerly occupied by fossils. I saw an obscure form of a *Spirifer* which may be *Sp. rostellatus* and a *Capulus*. Well defined Keokuk Limestone is found at a higher horizon, still I do not know that this may prove to be the lowest rock of the group.

On Turkey Creek there is an extensive exposure of heavy Chert beds, containing but few fossils but whose place is below the Limestone beds above named.

Near the mouth of Lone Elm Creek a Chert Knob 42 feet high is capped with 12 feet of solid Chert, with 30 feet lower slope over which are strewn large tumbled masses. Lower down on Turkey Creek, this Chert is seen extending quite across the creek and rising in the valley beyond not less than 20 feet thick. These Chert beds must be equivalent to those of Shoal Creek at and near Grand Falls described by Prof. Swallow in the Missouri Geological Report, 1855, page 95, of which he reports over a hundred feet thickness. Observing no strong

G.S—6.

dip that would throw this high in the bluffs, and from its being represented low on Shoal Creek and also on Turkey Creek, the evidence
would go to show that this underlies the county northward, but a gentle
dip has thrown it beneath the horizon for it is not again seen. It also
thins out northward for older rocks do not bring it to the surface reposing on them. It is rare in fossils and we have only reports of its
containing Lead.

UPPER CHERT BEDS.

Above the solid Limestone of the Keokuk Group masses of Chert
are found strewn over the surface in many places, and also interstratified with red Clay until we reach the bed-rock of Limestone. These
masses of Chert are often sharp and flinty, breaking into keen angular
fragments, but we also find a white porous Chert apparently partially
decomposed and sometimes very easily broken into the proper dimensions for making fences or foundations.

The thickness of this deposit is not often over a few feet, but excavations sometimes show it to be as much as 20 feet and formed of
broken layers interstratified with much red Clay. The red Clay would
probably make an excellent stone-ware for it is generally either nearly
pure Silica or Silicate of Alumina. This Clay was evidently at one
time Chert. I have found it under conditions that are incontrovertible.
In Keith's mine, Joplin, a red mass of Clay was noticed 9 inches by 5
inches thick of a flattened spheroidal shape, being broken it shows the
concentric rings always seen in such shaped Chert masses, but it was
quite soft and surrounded by decomposed Dolomite. Yellow and buff
and pure white Clay are also found. The white has the appearance of
common tallow. The fossils common in the Chert are *Bryozoa (several
sp.) Amplexus, Pentremites conoideus* ——, *Actinocrinus (?)* ——, *Zaphrentis* ——, a coral like *Rhombopora, Spirifer pseudolineatus, S.
subcuspidatus, S. spinosus, S. Keokuk, S. increbescens, Althyris pla
nosulcata, Rhynchonella subcuneata, Camaraphoria subtrigona,
Rhynchonella mutata, Terebratula fusiformis, Productus cora, Pr.
magnus, Hemipronites crenistria, Capulus* ——, *Aviculopecten* ——,
Avic. Indianensis, Myalina San Ludovici.

Dr. Owen, in his Report on the Geological Survey of Arkansas,
pages 105, 107 and 108, speaks of the Lead-bearing rocks of South-west
Missouri, and recognizing their equivalents in the northern counties
of Arkansas, pronounces them to belong to his "Barren Limestone
Divison of the Subcarboniferous Group, not to the Archimedes," and
further says that in Searcy county, Arkansas, there are over 200 feet
thickness, and that it is underlaid by 38 feet of Black Slate.

Upon examination of Tennessee Geological Report, pages 341 and 342, I find that the description of the Siliceous Group answers very well to that of the Subcarboniferous Lead-bearing rocks of South-west Missouri.

SPECIAL DESCRIPTION.

As Dr. Schmidt has in his Reports carefully given detailed descriptions of most of the mineral localities, I will only describe those not visited by him, and but briefly touch on others.

A well dug by Mr. John B. Travis, six miles north of Carthage, shows :

No. 1. 1 foot Soil.
No. 2. 2½ feet Gravel.
No. 3. 5 feet coarse bluish-gray Limestone.
No. 4. 2 feet Red Clay.
No. 5. 5 feet blackish-gray, bituminous Limestone, of coarse texture, containing a few small particles of Zinc blende.

I give this because it is the only place in Jasper county north of Spring River where the rocks show that they contain any Zinc. Excavations, in search of mineral, have been made in most neighborhoods north of the latitude of Carthage, but we have no information of profitable results. Between White Oak Fork and Spring River, are a number of barren excavations. Messrs. Marquis and Mulligan have sunk shafts at several places in Sec. 7, T. 28, R. 29, but found neither Lead nor Zinc. They have certainly shown an industrious perseverance, notwithstanding their ill-fortune.

One pit, near the bluffs of Spring River, is over 40 feet deep, with 1st, 6 feet of red Clay; 2d, 10 to 15 feet Clay and Gravel, then white Chert and red Clay to the bottom.

Another shaft close by, on the edge of the bluff, passed over 40 feet on the face of the Limestone, throwing out quantities of red Clay, Chert, and Calcite breccia.

Some beautiful specimens of Calcite, some of a violet-shade, were obtained here. Brown Calcite, with curved faces having a trace of Iron and of Magnesia, was observed in crevices in the Limestone. A half-mile, north-east, is a remarkably shaped cove 200 by 100 feet wide, sloping up gently to the surrounding hill and terminating at one end in a shallow sink-hole. A pit 44 feet deep was sunk here by Mr. Marquis, passing through Chert into Keokuk Limestone, but revealing no mineral.

At Tarter and Dudley's mill, on Spring River, in Sec. 15, T. 28, R. 29, I was informed that at one time about 2 wagon loads of Lead ore

had been dug out of the stream, and that Lead had been found associated with Chert in the hill about 100 feet above the stream.

Another locality in S. E. S. W. Sec. 2, T. 29, R. 28, was visited by
Mr. Norwood, who reports a shaft 34 feet deep passing through Clay
and Chert to Limestone. Small pieces of Galena, but in great quantity, were found in the Chert near the upper part.

PERRY'S MINES.

These are in N. E. Sec. 12, T. 27, R. 30, on land belonging to Wm.
Carnahan. The mining has mostly been done by Mr. Perry and persons
in his employ. They are situated on a gently sloping hillside, over
which are seen many shafts. The first pit is 25 feet deep, with all
Chert and red Clay for 19 feet, then blue Limestone with Zinc blende.
Fifty feet south-east, a shaft 40 feet deep reveals Limestone at 33 feet
from the surface. Another pit, near the last, is 33 feet deep, and from
it about 2,000 pounds of mineral have been taken out, some from the
Clay and some was found in detached cubes in the Limestone. One
hundred feet east is a shaft from which a quantity of Zinc ore was obtained. The ore occurred in a pocket-shaped longitudinal mass, entirely
giving out at one place but soon thickening. The Zinc blende found
here is desseminated through the Limestone. Silicate of Zinc also to
the amount of several hundred pounds has also been obtained both
from the Limestone and Chert. Two hundred yards east a shaft was
sunk in the valley 54 feet deep, but no Lead obtained, but many fine
Calcite crystals were brought up, some of them beautifully modified.

CARTHAGE MINES.

Some mining was formerly done at several places near Carthage,
mostly on land belonging to Messrs Tower and Regan. In N. E. Sec.
8, T. 28, R. 31, I observed a pit about 4 feet deep, showing chiefly a
reddish-brown heavy Spar with Limonite. This place is remarkable
as being the only locality where heavy Spar has been found in this
county. Masses of Chert are strewn on the hillside below. A high
mound in S. E. Sec. 8, is capped with Sandstone evidently of the age
of the Lower Coal Measures. On its southern end, a pit has been
excavated 55 feet deep. In the thrown out debris I observed Shales
and Sandstone with *Stigmaria* and Ferns, and masses of dark ash-colored argillaceous Limestone, showing obscure lines of fossils replaced
by Calcite, and also intersected by minute Calcite veins. The forms
of fossils were most too vague to determine their character, but
Bryozoa and a fossil which may be a *Rhombopora* were observed.

This rock has the appearance on one side of having been subjected to pressure, and of having slipped a little while in a plastic condition. It incloses Zinc blende, Calcite and Dolomite, with fragments of Coal and Bitumen and Iron Pyrites, generally associated as if in a vein. I could see no evidence of a large quantity of any useful mineral.

On Mr. Tower's land in S W. N. W. Sec. 17, situated on a flat depression of the prairie, are a number of old shafts bounded on the west by a shallow ravine running south. The deepest pits were about 30 feet deep, and occupied a space in the prairie of about 250x100 feet. No mining had been done for some time, consequently none of the pits were in a condition to be examined; we, therefore, are unable to treat of the occurrence of the ores. Lead ore, Zinc blende and Silicate of Zinc are found.

On other lands, of this same company, lying in Sec. 33, T. 28, R. 31, are evidences of extensive mining, but none of recent date.

Several pits were dug 50 feet deep, nearly all showing alternations of Chert and red Clay from the surface down. In some of them a fine-grained Limestone was reached at 10 feet. On the south-east slope were observed fragments of fine grained Sandstone of a good quality for whetstones, a portion containing remains of *Stigmaria ficoides*. This was from a shaft 50 feet deep. I was informed that 10 inches of Coal was found at the bottom. This must be in the form of a pocket, for in shallow pits, adjacent on the west, are Lower Carboniferous rocks. Some of the Limestones here are dolomitic, and some are bituminous. Some Lead has been found, but I could obtain no data as to quantity.

DAVIS' MINES,

Examined by C. J. Norwood. These mines, worked by Morgan Davis, on land belonging to Wm. McGowan, are located in N. W. N. E. Sec. 29, T. 28, R. 30. Only 60 pounds in all have been taken out here—in small pieces—the largest weighing only one and a quarter pound. This was found associated with red Clay and Chert, occupying a fissure in the Limestone. Mr. Davis has blasted considerably in the Limestone, and minute specks of Lead are found in the suture (*Stylolite*) joints of the rock. Keokuk fossils occur in the Limestone.

RICKER'S DIGGINGS,

Examined by C. J. Norwood. Several shafts have been sunk in Sec. 17, T. 28, R. 30, on the dividing ridge between Spring River and Centre Creek, one passing through 18 feet of Red Clay and Chert into Limestone. Another was sunk 25 feet through Sand and Clay Shales to Limestone. The Shale contains only nodules of Iron Pyrites, on which repose Zinc Blende in small quantities.

BROCK'S MINES,

Examined by C. J. Norwood. These are in S. W. S. E. Sec. 7, T. 27, R. 31. Two shafts have been sunk, one of them 21 feet deep through Red Clay and Chert, but no mineral obtained. The other shaft, 120 feet south-east, is 46 feet deep, but was in no condition for examination. The miners furnished the following section :

No. 1. 28 feet Red Clay and Chert.
No. 2. 1 foot soft, white, porous Chert, sometimes called Cotton Rock.
No. 3. 2 feet Red Clay.
No. 4. 15 feet gray, coarse Dolomitic Limestone, containing much Calcite and some flesh-colored Dolomite.

About 200 pounds of Galena have been taken out of No. 3. At the bottom the Galena seemed to enter a crevice in No. 4, but no heavier deposits were found. The bottom is a cherty breccia cemented by Dolomite. A small piece of heavy Red Limestone was picked up from among the thrown out debris, which may probably contain Oxide of Lead.

W. S. FLEMING'S DIGGINGS,

In N. W. N. E. Sec. 6, T. 27, R. 31. Several shafts have been sunk, passing through first 9 feet of Clay, with some Chert and entering Limestone. The shafts here have been dug 27 feet, obtaining only 150 pounds of mineral from one of them, but none in the others.

GROVE CREEK MINES.

A particular description of these mines will be found in Dr. Schmidt's Report.

CALVERT'S SHAFT,

Is 33 feet deep, and gives the following section :

No. 1. 1 foot Soil and Gravel.
No. 2. 2 feet Red Clay and a little Gravel.
No. 3. Mostly Chert and Clay, with Red and Yellow Clay below, extending to coarse, hard, Gray Limestone at 28 feet.

Lead was obtained at 26 feet, and thence to the bottom generally associated with Chert, but at the bottom it occurs in a hard, close-grained Limestone, the latter also containing angular pieces of Chert. Some Silicate of Zinc is also found. In another shaft, 40 feet distant, Lead was found at 15 feet depth, mixed with Gravel. Another shaft, 50 feet in depth, near Calvert's, has been worked for many years. Before the war 50,000 pounds of mineral were raised, and during the war some mining was done, and the mineral smelted on a logheap, covered with Clay. Sixty feet west of Calvert's, a shaft was sunk 60 feet deep, but no mineral found. Another pit, 75 feet south-east of Calvert's, 50 feet deep, in mostly Red Clay, with but little Chert, and some Galena, at 35 feet depth.

MOSES JEWITT'S SHAFT.

Some Chert and Limestone on one side; on the other crystals of Galena occur disseminated through Tallow Clay, and 10 feet above the bottom large cubes occur in the Clay. In cherty Limestone at the bottom are also large cubes of Galena. The Chert sometimes forms a brecciated mass, with Calcite, Clay, Galena and Silicate of Zinc.

SMITH'S SHAFT,

Thirty feet south of Jewitt's, is 50 feet deep. A good deal of Lead was obtained at about 15 feet depth. Red Clay occurs nearly to the bottom. During the winters of 1872 and 1873 300,000 pounds of mineral were obtained from this shaft alone. The bottom rock is close-grained Dolomite, containing angular pieces of Chert and disseminated cubes of Galena.

SMITH & ——.

Lead has been obtained here from the top down, mingled with Flint and Clay. Near the bottom occurs a hard and soft Silicious Limestone, containing Galena. A side drift was extended for 20 feet and another shaft sunk, and mineral obtained throughout, and in paying quantities. Another shaft, 75 feet east, and 50 feet deep, extends 10 feet below the Chert beds. At the bottom there is a red Limestone, containing Calcite. A little Zinc Blende has been obtained. In drifting northward to another shaft for 16 feet, 8,000 pounds of mineral were obtained. In a pit 20 feet south of Smith's, at 15 feet depth, Silicate of Zinc was obtained.

JOHN BROWN'S SHAFT,

In a pit in a valley a half mile south, Galena was obtained at 18 feet depth, from a gray porous Limestone. A little Zinc Blende was also found.

CLOW'S SHAFT.

This shaft is situated on the edge of a valley, and is 30 feet deep, passing through a loose local drift of Limestone, Coal Shale, etc., to Limestone. I was informed that 30,000 pounds of mineral had been taken out in one week. The Limestone is a coarse-grained Dolomite, containing innumerable disseminated particles of Asphaltum, which give it a dark gray appearance.

OLD DUFF'S AND OTHER DIGGINGS.

These mines are on the prairie, about half way from Scotland to Joplin, and are mostly abandoned. Occasionally some mining has been done. On H. Taylor's land, in Sec. 25, T. 27, R. 32, are about 18 shafts, indicating a superficial formation of red Clay, overlying coarse bituminous Limestone. Some mineral has been obtained here. On Moffit's and Sargent's land, in the same neighborhood, in Sec. 31, S. E., T. 28, R. 32, there are a good many pits and a few recent diggings. Silicate of Zinc and Galena have been found.

BIRCH'S MINES.

Location, S. W. N. W., Sec, 11, T. 27, R. 32. These mines, we may say, are tributary to the Grove Creek, being in sight. They occupy the highest part of the prairie and the shafts are sunk on level ground, showing:

No. 1. 1 foot dark Soil.
No. 2. 1½ feet yellow Clay, with but little Gravel.
No. 3. 2 to 10 feet red Clay and cherty Gravel.

Galena, Carbonate of Lead and Silicate of Zinc are the minerals found here. The shafts are from 30 to 40 feet deep, and from many of them there has been no mineral obtained. In Leverton, Davis & Co's shaft Lead was obtained from 12 feet depth to the bottom, 40 feet. The mineral was found diffused in buff and brown soft rock and Chert.

From March 1, 1873, to August 1st, these mines yielded 40,000 pounds of mineral. Recent information is that although at one time they did not yield well that they are now yielding profitably.

The Birch and Grove Creek Mines are leased by Davis & Murphy, and from March 15, to August 1, they have shipped 12 car loads of Lead from these mines, each car containing 270 pigs of 75 pounds each.

MINERSVILLE.

This is one of the oldest mining districts of Jasper, and is located on the Memphis, Carthage and North-western Railroad, being the main shipping point for all the Jasper county mines. The rock in the shafts, whether Limestone, Chert or Sandstone, is hard. The minerals obtained are Galena, Zinc blende and Carbonate of Zinc; some of the latter apparently recently formed in minute globules on brecciated Chert, containing Zinc blende—the formation having taken place since the Chert was quarried out of the shafts.

Bitumen is found in massive semiviscid form in the Limestone, and associated with beautiful crystals of Dogtooth Spar.

STEPHENS' MINES.

These are owned by Davis & Murphy, and are located in W. half N. W. Sec. 31, T. 27, R. 33, on slopes of a hillside, making into a narrow valley, tributary to Turkey Creek. The formations include Clay and loose Chert for 10 feet, then Chert and masses of Limestone, containing Zinc Blende and Lead. None of the shafts were deep when I visited the place. In Neeley's shaft, 21 feet deep, there was some Chert associated with a good deal of decomposed Dolomite at the bottom. In the latter quantities of Galena were being taken out. Mr. Neely reported that five men took out a little less than 6,000 pounds of Lead mineral in one week.

The Zinc Blende assumes the form and color of beautiful crystals, much of it of a Garnet color.

LEADVILLE.

These mines are two miles north-west of Joplin and extend a little over a quarter of a mile along a small valley, reaching north to Turkey Creek. Geo. Cavanaugh, Duff and Reanden worked here in 1851. Taylor bought them in 1851 and Orchard mined here in 1852. These old shafts still continue productive. One of them is 70 feet deep, in which mineral was obtained at 50 feet and below. At the bottom is solid Limestone with lenticular Chert beds, in which Galena and Zinc Blende occur in horizontal sheets, arranged as shown in Fig. 2.

In the *Horseshoe Diggings* mineral was obtained in large quantities from shafts not over 20 feet deep. A little higher in the hill a shaft 96 feet deep yielded very little mineral. Loose Chert was taken from the upper part. The lower 26 feet includes Limestone, brecciated and whitish Calcite.

In Phillips' shaft, at Leadville, gray Limestone was struck at 18 feet depth, which continued for 20 feet. He then passed a 20-inch band of Galena and Zinc Blende in Chert to a soft opening, with hard rock below. Beautiful crystals of Zinc Blende and Calcite were obtained at these mines, the Calcite being often in large, Amber colored "Dogtooth" forms.

JOPLIN.

Limestone crops out below the town in bluffs on the west side of Joplin Creek, for about 50 feet from the bottom of the hill, and on the east side of Lone Elm Creek, not far from Turkey Creek, for 25 or 30 feet up the bluff. In Byer's shaft, at the south-west corner of Joplin, occurs a solid Dolomite. So, although these Limestones extend at intervals high in the hills, excavations show the solid beds to be wanting in many places and their place occupied by loose Chert or large broken masses of Dolomite or decomposed Dolomite or red Clay. The Lead is to be found in these broken masses, mostly irregularly distributed. Excavations show this broken mass to be sometimes as much as 40 feet thick, resting against a solid wall of Limestone, a good example of which may be seen in Keith's shaft, on Porter's land. The driftings here extend about north and south and show that there is a north and south concealed line of bluff. The solid rock contains some Galena but it is mostly distributed in the soft mass. (See Fig. 3.)

Excavations in Joplin Valley frequently penetrate a blue, shaly Sandstone, which may probably belong to the age of the Coal Measures, but it is evidently a drifted deposit. We also hear of a little Coal being sometimes found, but these deposits are also mere pockets. Just west of Joplin, I examined one of these, showing the Coal to be of irregular form of deposit, thinning out entirely at one end. The other I could not see, but it also has proven to thin out in that direction. The quality is poor and quantity insufficient for profitable mining.

To show the progress of mining here, I give a few statistics, furnished by Thos. B. Dorsey, of mineral taken out on the Porter land— 120 acres:

Date.	Pounds.	Remarks.
1871. December...	4,150	....
1872. January...	8,245	....
February...	10,350	....
March...	63,402	....
April...	104,400	....
May...	98,000	....
June...	48,000	Water interfered...
July...	148,000	....
August...	101,000	}
September...	72,000	} Very dry. The mineral had to be hauled two miles to be washed.
October...	113,000	}
November...	104,000	....
December...	89,5(0	....
1873. January...	221,000	....
February...	255,000	....
March...	400,000	....
April...	355,000	....
May...	272,000	....
June...	176,000	....
July...	164,000	....

IRON ORE.

Small pieces of brown Hematite are occasionally met with, but none was observed in quantity sufficient for investment. At Mc-Daniel's, two miles east of Carthage, a piece measuring one foot by six inches was picked up. It was found with Chert, and may have originated from the upper Chert beds of the Lower Carboniferous Formation. In Sec. 34, T. 29, R. 30, and at several places in the neighborhood, small pieces of ore are occasionally found, but there is no evidence of any large deposit.

At Mr. Isaac Schooler's, in N. half S. E. Sec. 28, T. 29, R. 30, Mr. Norwood observed loose fragments of similar ore in a space of about

30 yards in circumference.   Its geological position is probably the
same as that of the other places just mentioned.

On Mr. Tower's land, in N. W. Sec. 8, T. 28, R. 31, a pit dug disclosed four feet of heavy Spar, with large streaks and pockets of
brown Hematite.

COPPERAS WELL.

At. J. S. McConnell's, Sec. 32, T. 30, R. 32, is a well of strong
mineral water.   Mrs. McConnell informed Mr. Norwood that if the
water were sweetened a little it would make excellent pickles.   This
proves it to contain sulphuric acid.   The well was 13 feet deep, of
which the upper 8½ feet of sandy Shale is divided from the lower 4
feet of sandy Shale by 6 inches of Coal.   The water was said to be
good when the well was first dug, but after using it a year and a half,
it became suddenly so strongly impregnated with sulphuric acid that
it was rendered entirely unfit to drink, and impossible to use for
washing.

BUILDING STONE.

The Limestones found on most of the streams are strong enough
and sufficiently durable for all building purposes, but are too often too
irregular in their beds.   They also contain too much Chert to recommend them very highly, but they will burn into excellent lime.

The Sandstones are more sought after for building purposes. They
may be found in good dimensions and in large quantity.   Good quarries can be opened in the northwestern part of the county, in T. 30,
Rs. 32 and 33.

COAL MEASURES.

BY CHARLES J. NORWOOD.

The Coal Measures are, with the exception of three or four small
basins, confined to the north-west portion of the county.   That part
embraced in T. 30, R. 33, and T. 30, R. 32, with about three sections of
T. 30, R. 31, bordering on the north county line.   They then spread
west into Kansas and north into Barton county, with the rocks dipping
a little north of west.   There are at least four and perhaps five distinct beds of Coal in this region, all of which have been worked at

one time or another. It must not be supposed, however, that Coal underlays the whole area laid down as "Coal Measures." For there is considerable undulation of the surface, the prairie spreading out in long, gentle rolls or slopes, with sometimes the Lower Carboniferous rocks approaching near the surface, covered by only a few feet of the Coal formation, and again rising in high mounds and ridges, some of them attaining a hight of 100 feet above the general plain. About one-half of the Coal beds occur only in mounds or ridges, and the presence of the others in the low land is governed altogether by the regularity or irregularity of the surface. Without a topographical survey having been made it is therefore impossible to designate in this report at just what points Coal may or may not be reached. It is believed, however, that at least one bed of Coal is co-extensive with that region included in the area marked as Coal Measures on the map. And this, although it may not be considered of commercial import-ance is still valuable as a fuel—taking the place of timber.

The thickest Coal is 18 inches, while the thinnest ranges from 11 to 14 inches. When capable of being stripped even these Coals are profitable in some parts of the Coal region.

The lowest bed is that seen near Medoc, on Little North Fork, at Mr. T. C. Arnot's Coal bank, and is probably equivalent to the lowest bed found at Cline's mound, in Barton county. It is 14 inches thick and covered by five and a half feet of blue, sandy, semi-bituminous Shale, with Sandstone still above. The Coal is made up of alternations of dull and shiny black layers. At the top there is considerable Pyrites, but towards the bottom the Coal is of good quality. A short distance down the creek Lower Carboniferous Limestone is found, occupying a *topographical* position above the Coal, the latter seem-ing to have been brought down by a fault. This is the more probable as the Coal lies pretty horizontally in the creek bed, while at Medoc, where the Limestone was observed, we find some 26½ feet of Lower Carboniferous rocks rising above the creek.

Near Mr. Arnots, another Coal was found occupying a position about ten feet above that Coal seen at his bank. The bed is fifteen inches thick. At the outcrop it is rotten, and of course we can not judge of its quality. This we believe to be a new discovery. It is capped by one foot of conglomerate, while above that four feet of hard gray Sandstone is seen.

At Mr. McConnel's, in S. half N. W. Sec. 32, T. 30, R. 32, a Coal bed is found occupying a position above Arnot's, and is probably equivalent to the Third Coal from the top at Cline's mound. Mr. McC's Coal is 11 to 12 inches thick, at one place covered by a foot of light blue sandy Shale, and at another by two feet of local Drift and soil, the Drift being composed of small fragments of Carbonate of Iron and Sandstone. Below the Coal is seen an ochreous blue Clay Shale. The same bed is worked by Mr. Thos. Smith just south of Mr. McConnell's, in S. E. S. W. Sec. 32, T. 30, R. 32, and is said to be 18 inches thick. North and north-west of Mr. McConnel's, Sandstone is found on a mound, being about 40 feet above Smith's Coal.

On Duval Creek, 7 to 14 feet of semi-bituminous Shale was observed occupying a position below the Coal. This Shale is above the Medoc Coal, and the Shale overlying the Medoc Coal may be a part of this. Of this, however, we have no proof, and it is doubtful; it (the Medoc Shale) may be considerably lower.

The following is a general section of rocks in sections 28, 29 and 32, T. 30, R. 32 :

SECTION A.

No. 1. 2 feet buff and grey micaceous Sandstone.
No. 2. 29 feet slope; mostly Sandstone.
No. 3. 5 feet sandy Shale.
No. 4. 12 to 18 inches Coal.
No. 5. 7 to 14 feet semi-bituminous Shale to bed of Duval Creek.

In Sec. 24 (?), T. 30, R. 32, Coal which may be referred to the top bed at Cline's mound, in Barton county, is found. At this place we find five feet of buff to brown micaceous, generally soft, coarse Sandstone overlying the Coal with ten inches of conglomerate, composed mostly of intercalated fragments of Ironstone. This is seen on a mound, rising 72 feet above the prairie level.

At Round Mound, in N. E. quarter Sec. 17, T. 30, R. 31, the same Sandstone is found, capping the mound, while 67 feet below, two feet of "Keokuk Limestone" (Lower Carboniferous) is found exposed in the prairie. The mound is 45 feet high.

Just west of Round Mound, there is a ridge upon which are two beds of Coal worked by Mr. Huntley. These beds may be referred to the two upper ones on Cline's Mound, in Barton county.

The following section exhibits the relative position of the strata:

No. 1. 17 feet slope covered by fragments of Sandstone.
No. 2. 10 inches coarse, gritty, reddish and gray Sandstone.
No. 3. 2½ feet drab and reddish Sandstone and Shale, with a few Carbonaceous streaks.
No. 4. 16 inches good Coal.
No. 5. 5 feet slope.
No. 6. 18 inches white potter's Clay.
No. 7. 1 foot red and ochreous Clay.

No. 8. 12 inches blue and semi-bituminous Shale.
No. 9. 11 inches Coal.
No. 10. 50 feet slope to prairie level.

From the foregoing observations, and with data obtained at Cline's Mound, we are enabled to construct the following approximate vertical section of the Coals:

No. 1. 55 feet slope, lower part covered with fragments of curiously ripple-marked Sandstone. This is from a high mound.
No. 2. 3½ feet Sandstone.
No. 3. 10 inches Conglomerate, not always present.
No. 4. 16 inches good Coal. Found on Mounds. (Equal to Upper Lamar Coal.
No. 5. 4 feet potter's Clay.
No. 6. 15 to 20 feet, Rocks covered.
No. 7. 5 feet sandy Shale.
No. 8. 12 to 18 inches Coal. Found on mounds and ridges. (Equal to Middle Lamar Coal.)
No. 9. 2 feet blue Shale.
No. 10. 14 feet semi-bituminous Shale.
No. 11. 5 feet Sandstone.
No. 12. 4 feet, Rocks covered.
No. 13. 2½ feet Sandstone.
No. 14. 5½ feet sandy, semi-bituminous Shale.
No. 15. 14 inches Coal. (Equal to Cline's Coal.)
No. 16. 25 feet slope (about this distance).
No. 17. Sub-Carboniferous Limestone.

The foregoing is not given as being an *exactly* correct section, for it was impossible to get a view of all the Rocks. The prairie is continually changing its level, with long, gentle slopes; and as there were no means to get the topography of the country, we could not use that as a basis for referring heights. However, we believe the section to be very near, if not quite correct.

In W. half lot 2, Sec. 2, T. 29, R. 31, Mr. James Goff has opened a Coal bank.

The Coal occurs in a basin formed in Archimedes (Keokuk) Limestone. The bed averages about 18 inches in thickness, and its greatest extent is N. N. E. The course of the exposed face of the bed is S. E. and S. W. At the S. E. end of the bank, Lower Carboniferous Chert is found covering the surface, fifteen feet above the topographical position of the Coal, which dips 20 deg. N., 20 deg. W.

At the north-west end Archimedes Limestone is exposed, occupying a position five feet above the Coal, which it cuts off. The Coal at this end dips 10 deg. S., 55 deg. E. The surface toward the north-east is pretty level, and is from 7 to 10 feet above the Coal. Toward the north-west, south-west and south-east, the Coal extends for a short distance only, being cut off by Lower Carboniferous Limestone, which is, we may say, the surface Rock. Toward the north-east, however, the Coal may hold out for several years. From the nature of the country, its exact limit in that direction can only be told by sinking shafts. It was supposed by many that the Coal would be found under the Limestone at the north-west end of the bank, and that it would be thicker and of better quality. This, however, is a mistake, as it is known that no Coal occurs under that series of Limestones, (in the United States,) of which the one in question is a member. Even if this Limestone belonged to the Coal Measures, the strong dip of the Coal would show that it will not be found under this particular one.

CHAPTER IX.

BARTON COUNTY.

BY G. C. BROADHEAD.

This county embraces an area of 580 square miles, including about 125 of timber, which is mostly confined to the immediate vicinity of the streams.

Timber is very scarce in the western portions of the county.

The general surface of the county is gently undulating or rolling, or occasionally relieved, at intervals of from three to ten miles, by a mound gently rising above the undulating plains to a hight of from 70 to 140 feet, but not often more than 100 feet, and often much less.

The bluffs along the streams are not often over 50 feet high. The most broken part of the county is that lying east of Horse Creek, in the north-east part of the county.

STREAMS.

None of the streams are rapid, nor are all of them constantly running; but, from the fact of their flowing through and over Sandstone, the water is not muddy, and is even at times very clear. The principal streams are: North Fork of Spring River, sometimes called Muddy; Little North Fork; Dry Wood and Little Dry Wood, and Horse Creek. The central portion of the county appears to occupy the position of a main water shed. From this the Dry Woods flow north and north-west, and the branches of Spring River southward. The streams flowing north toward the Osage, those on the south to Spring River and thence to the Arkansas. The North Fork, entering the county in the South-east, is arrested by a barrier of Lower Carboniferous rocks, and flows away to the North-west, skirting the line of the Coal Measures and the Lower Carboniferous rocks until it almost reaches the center of the county, where, no longer impeded, it curves around south-west and southwardly, still keeping the Lower Carboniferous formations on its left bank, and leaves the county with a slight dash across a low exposure of these rocks.

Where the Lower Carboniferous rocks appear, we find good springs; for instance, near Dublin and in Secs. 25 and 30 of T. 32 Rs. 29 and 30. There are some wells of good water in the county, but many of them, when they extend into the lower Shales of the Coal Measures, are of a disagreeable taste, either impregnated with Alum or Sulphate of Iron. In Lamar are several lasting springs of good water. Mr. Ward, in Sec. 33, T. 31, R. 30, has a well of excellent quality. The well is 52 feet deep, and has a general supply of about 30 feet of water, which mainly flows from a source 30 feet below the surface. The formation, passed through in boring this well, was mostly Sandstone, and two days were occupied in boring the well, at a cost of $1.00 per foot. Mr. Burr, three miles west of Lamar, bored a well 75 feet deep through Sandstone and Sandy Shales, at a cost of $1.50 per foot.

The streams, near their origin in the prairies, occupy a gently depressed valley for some distance, with occasional deep and wide pools with steep margins and full of water-plants, which look very beautiful in the flowering season. Among these I might name *Nymphœa odorata*, *Brasenia peltata*, *Nuphar advena*.

When the streams enter the timber their margins are fringed by Birch, Sycamore, Elm, Oak and Willow.

The first signs of a growth of timber on the prairies is the appearance of small persimmon bushes. They are very common nearly everywhere. On the high mounds occasionally are found a few small Cherry trees. Cherry Mound is so called on account of the presence of five small Cherry trees, the largest eight inches in diameter. There are no other trees of any kind within three miles. The seeds have been probably brought there by birds. Another low mound, three miles south, has two or three small Cherry bushes just growing up.

GEOLOGICAL FORMATIONS.

The superficial deposits of this county include Soils with sometimes a substratum of Local Drift of only a few feet thickness, and the *Alluvium* along the streams.

The rock formations include *Lower Carboniferous* and *Coal Measures*.

LOWER CARBONIFEROUS.

This system includes the Keokuk Limestone and overlying Chert beds, which present types of both the St. Louis and Chester Groups. These formations show an exposed surface of 77 square miles in the county.

KEOKUK GROUP.

This formation consists generally of a bluish gray or dark gray Limestone, generally Bituminous; the Bitumen being often found filling minute cavities in the rock. The Limestone is often in thick, even layers, is always coarse-grained and contains numerous fragments of Crinoid stems. The other fossils observed were : *Actinocrinus Gouldi (?)*, *Zaphrentis* ——, *Pr. punctatus*, *Pr. semireticulatus*, *Sp. pseudolineatus*, *Hemipronites crenistria*, *Platyceras* ——, *Philipsia* ——. The greatest observed thickness of these beds at one place was 25 feet. It is probable that they are about 75 or 80 feet thick in Golden Grove. I say so, because this Limestone was thrown out of a well on high ground near the southern edge of the grove, and one mile north Limestone of a similar age appears in the bed of a branch at about 75 feet lower down. They are also seen on Coon Creek and on North Fork, in the southern part of the county.

CHERT BEDS.

Above the Limestones are seen loose, irregular masses of Chert strewn over the surface, but in no place appearing in a solid cemented bed. The fossils most abundantly observed were : *Bryozoa*; but *Zaphrentis* —— ——, *Orthis dubia*, *Productus mesialis*, *P. semireticulatus*, *Hemipronites crenistria*, *Pentremites conoideus*, and *Granatocrinus granulosus* were also found.

The Chert on North Fork, near Dublin, abounds in *Retzia Verneuilana* and *Spirifer spinosus*, indicating a Chester type.

OLD DIGGINGS.

In Golden Grove, in Secs. 4, 8, 9 and 16, are 'many ruins of former shafts, most of them now nearly filled up. These old shafts are reported to have been here before the Government Surveys or first settlements were made. Some years ago a Mr. Little explored an old pit and it is said that he found an iron pan and part of an old pick handle. Others have made examinations and find the Chert beds including the overlying loose Chert to be 22 feet in thickness, reaching a Dolomitic Limestone. One shaft recently cleared, which I examined disclosed:

1. 6 Feet loose Chert and red Clay.
2. 16 feet regular but rough Chert layers.
3. Dark ash Magnesian Limestone.

An examination around and in these places did not show the presence of any kind of mineral.

A recent well at the hill-top on the edge of the prairie in S. E. S. E. Sec. 17, T. 31, R. 29, gives the following section:

1. 3 feet red Clay and Gravel.
2. 7 feet red Clay.
3. 7 feet masses of Limestone and Clay.
4. 10 feet Solid Limestone, coarse and fine dark grayish blue and bituminous, the Bitumen sometimes appearing in drops.

Zinc Blende and Iron Pyrites are also found in small quantities.

COAL MEASURES.

Barton county is underlaid by about 503 square miles of Coal Measures, including, with the mounds, a total aggregate thickness of about 300 feet. Without the mounds we have about 190 feet. These beds are referable to the Lower Coal Measures as heretofore interpreted in Missouri Geology, but nearly 150 feet belong to Measures which lie below the formations known as Lower Measures. These lower beds include Sandstones, Shaly beds and about 4 seams of Coal. The Sandstones differ in character from any of those of North Missouri. The farthest point north where similar Sandstones are seen is near Brownsville, Saline county. Being well developed on Clear Creek, Vernon county, we have in speaking of them applied the term Clear Creek Sandstone to the upper member. The other Sandstones below, are similar in character and texture. They occur in thick and thin, mostly even layers, sometimes ripple-marked, and sometimes with rugose irregular wave-like markings which seem to be the result of differently directed mud currents. Some markings also seem of Fucoids. The surface of lamination is also sometimes exceedingly smooth and even. These Sandstones are generally very firm and are even sometimes hard. They are mostly fine-grained and contain some Mica, and seem originally to have been very pure Sandstones, but are at present generally found completely saturated with Bitumen. Where pure they are of a bright drab or inclining to a buff color. When containing Bitumen they are dark gray to black and very hard, sometimes like a Quartzite.

Wherever the Coal Measures exist in this county, excepting on the higher mounds in the North-west, Sandstone occurs as the surface rock.

On North Fork, three miles North-east of Lamar, it occurs in 4 feet beds. Fragments of *Sigillaria*, *Lepidodenron* and *Calamites* were occasionally found.

At the base of the Coal Measures we find about 16 to 20 feet of blue sandy Shales which are often pyritiferous and sometimes aluminous.

Section of Strata below Fort Scott Series.

Number.	THICKNESS.	TOTAL THICKNESS.	DESCRIPTION OF MATERIAL.	
40	....	....	Rough mottled Limestone.	
39	63 feet...............	306 feet 4 inches	Includes Shales, a few Limestone beds and probably a few Sandstones.	
38	1 foot 6 inches	243 feet 4 inches	Even bedded jointed bituminous and very hard, deep blue Limestone.	⎫
37	1 foot 6 inches	241 feet 10 inches	Calcareous, bituminous and fossiliferous Shales.	⎪
36	6 inches	240 feet 4 inches	Hard black Slate.	
35	1 foot...............	239 feet 10 inches	Blue fossiliferous Shales containing *Productus semireticulatus*.	
34	5 inches	238 feet 5 inches	Bed of Shaly concretionary Limestone.	
33	10 inches	238 feet 5 inches	Shelly bituminous Shales.	Includes Prof. Swallow's Fort Scott Marble Series.
32	8 inches	237 feet 7 inches	Bed of dark concretionary Limestone.	
31	3 feet...............	236 feet 11 inches	Bituminous Shales with large bituminous Limestone concretions and round Shaly pyritiferous concretions.	
30	2 feet 6 inches	233 feet 11 inches	Drab ochrey Shales.	
29	2 feet 6 inches	231 feet 5 inches	Bituminous Shales with small concretions.	
28	6 inches	228 feet 11 inches	Brown ochrey Shales.	
27	1 foot...............	228 feet 5 inches	Coal.	⎭
26	34 feet...............	227 feet 5 inches	Slope with a thin layer of Coal.	
25	18 inches	193 feet 5 inches	Coal.	
24	15 feet...............	191 feet 11 inches	Slope.	
23	1 foot...............	176 feet 11 inches	Red Limestone.	
22	6 feet...............	175 feet 11 inches	Slope including beds of Carbonate of Iron.	
21	8 feet...............	169 feet 11 inches	Bituminous Shales with Septaria and a calcareous layer with fossils.	
20	6 inches	161 feet 11 inches	Hard slaty Coal.	
19	16 to 18 inches	171 feet 5 inches	Coal.	

Section of Strata Below Fort Scott Series—Continued.

Number.	Thickness.	Total Thickness.	Description.
18	8 feet..............	160 feet..............	Shales. Lower 2 feet deep blue and and semi-bituminous.
17	3 feet..............	152 feet..............	Coal.
16	50 feet..............	149 feet..............	Clear Creek Sandstone.
15	1 foot..............	99 feet..............	Conglomerate and Iron ore.
14	11 inches	98 feet..............	Coal (8 to 13 inches) (Upper Lamar.)
13	15 feet..............	96 feet..............	Sandstone.
12	6 feet..............	81 feet 11 inches	Clay—upper 4 feet is light drab, the lower is blue and semi-bituminous.
11			Thin layer of Limestone.
10	1 foot.....	75 feet 11 inches	Coal.
9	15 feet..............	74 feet 11 inches	Sandstone.
8	5 feet 6 inches	59 feet 11 inches	Semi-bituminous Shales not always present.
7	10 inches	54 feet 5 inches	Coal.
6	35 feet..............	53 feet 7 inches	Sandstone.
5	1 foot 6 inches	18 feet 7 inches	Shale.
4	1 foot 1 inch	17 feet 1 inch...	Coal, lowest at Clines'.
3	16 feet.,..............	16 feet..............	Blue Shales containing Alum and Sulphur.
2			Chert Beds.
1			Keokuk Limestone.

DESCRIPTIVE SECTIONS.

In order to show more particularly the order of succession of the various beds, I here insert a few sections obtained in various parts of the county.

In Sec. 15, T. 32, R. 29, we have:

No. 1.　30 feet mostly Sandstone in thick layers and ripple-marked.
No. 2.　Two feet outcrop of thin sandy layers.
No. 3.　1 foot rotten Coal.
No. 4.　16 feet sandy Shales with occasional ochrey bands and also a knife-edge of Coal.

The Lower Carboniferous Limestone occurs a short distance north, so we reasonably suppose that the above Section includes some of the lowest Coal Measure rocks.

The following Section includes some of the lowest Coal Measure rocks in the county:

Section of Cline's Mound—S. W. Sec. 34, T. 31, R. 31.

No. 1. 18 inches Shales and Sandstone.
No. 2. 8 to 10 inches Rotten Coal.
No. 3. 6 feet 6 inches Clay.
No. 4. 8 to 10 inches Crumbling Coal.
No. 5. 4 feet blue Fire-Clay.
No. 6. 8 feet Shaly Slope—Sandstone at the top.
No. 7. 1 foot blue Shales.
No. 8. Band of yellow Ochre.
No. 9. 2 feet 6 inches blue Shales.
No. 10. 2 inches concretionary band of Ironstone, breaking with smooth joints into blocks which are generally hollow.
No. 11. 1 foot 6 inches dark Semi-bituminous Slate.
No. 12. 7 to 10 inches Coal.
No. 13. 35 feet Slope, containing Sandstone.
No. 14. 12 to 18 inches light and dark-blue Shales.
No. 15. 12 to 13 inches Coal.

Section on Little North Fork at the South County Line..

This illustrates the Geological structure of the neighborhood as follows:

No. 1. 28 feet Slope, with outcrops of Sandstone.
No. 2. 5 feet Sandstone.
No. 3. 7 feet slope 30 deg., a thin Coal seam is probably concealed.
No. 4. 12 feet Shales.
No. 5. 6 inches blue Shaly Limestone.
No. 6. 7 inches Coal.
No. 7. 16 feet blue sandy Shales.
No. 8. 13 inches Coal in creek.

The neighboring hills are about 10 feet higher, and capped with tumbling Sandstone.

Section one mile west of Lamar.

This includes a portion of our Section at Cline's Mound, as follows:

No. 1. 10 feet Slope.
No. 2. 9 feet Sandstone in flag-like masses.
No. 3. 6 feet Sandstone, in 4 and 8 inch layers.
No. 4. 1 foot Conglomerate of Sandstone, Ochre and nodules of Carbonate of Iron.
No. 5. 10 inches Coal.

No. 6. 7 feet 6 inches Slope, with some Sandstone.

No. 7. 4 feet light colored Clay Shales.

No. 8. 1 foot 4 inches deep-blue Clay Shales.

No. 9. 13 inches Coal.

No. 10. 8 feet 6 inches Slope.

No. 11. 7 feet 6 inches thin and even layers, gray Sandstone, with some Shaly layers containing *Lepidodendron.*

No. 12. 13½ inches Coal.

Two miles west of this, on high ground in Sec. 28, Mr. Burr dug a well 75 feet deep, passing through 7 feet of soil and jointed Clay to Clay-Shale, which extended to 30 feet, at which depth 1 foot of hard rock was perforated, from which bituminous Sandstone extended to the bottom. No Coal was reported.

The highest rocks in the county appear in the north-west, capping the mounds and belong to the age of the lower part of the Middle Coal Measures and below the Fort Scott Group. As much as 50 feet of very bituminous Sandstone of the Lower Coal Measures crops out on Drywood and its various branches in the neighborhood, including 2 thin Coal seams. Just a little ways above the Sandstone we find 2 feet of good Coal capped by Shales and concretionary Ironstone bands. This Coal is 140 feet below the top of Blue Mound. On the mound, 10 feet below the top, there was a peculiar sandy textured Limestone (No. 37.) A little below the latter are many fragments and some stumps of *Coniferous* wood, measuring as much as 3 and 4½ feet across the surface. These stumps I regard as of the same Geological age as those found one mile east of Pleasant Gap, Bates county.

Section on Round Mound in Sec. 16, T. 33, R. 32—By C. J. Norwood.

This includes some beds of Limestone which may occupy a higher Geological position, as follows:

No. 1. 2 feet mottled, flesh and drab Limestone, containing *Spirifer lineatus.* I suppose this rock to be equal to the lowest rock at Butler, Bates county.

No. 2. 2 feet Slope.

No. 3. 6 inches Limestone, with much Calcite.

No. 4. 3 feet Slope.

No. 5. 1 foot drab Limestone, mottled with dark streaks.

No. 6. 3 feet Slope.

No. 7. 1 foot 6 inches drab Limestone, with nailhead Spar between the joints, contains fossils, including *Spirifer lineatns, Lophophyllum, Fusulina* and *Philipsia.*

No. 8. 11 feet Slope.

No. 9. 5 inches Sandstone.

No. 10. 16 feet Slope, with yellow Ochre at the lower part.

No. 11. 1 foot dark, ash shelly Limestone, containing *Productus muricatus*, *P. Prattenianus* and *Hemipronites crassus*, and abounding in *Chonetes mesoloba*.

No. 12. 10 feet Slope.

No. 13. 1 foot hard-blue, bituminous Limestone, breaking rhomboidally and containing *Spirifer plano-convexus*, and *Entolium aviculatum*, Crinoid stems and *Bryozoa*, (No. 38 of Gen. Sec.)

No. 14. 40 feet Slope to level prairie.

Coal 5 inches thick has been obtained in a neighboring well, which would place it about 50 feet below No. 13 of the above Section. On top of the mound a few masses of Limestone were seen containing *Chaetetes milleporaceus*, *Fusulina cylindrica* and *Zaphrentis*.

Section on West Fork of Big Drywood, in S. W. Sec. 21, T. 33, R. 33 —By C. J. Norwood.

No. 1. 12 feet Slope.

No. 2. 13 feet Sandstone.

No. 3. 3 feet 6 inches blue Clay Shales; bituminous Limestone at the bottom.

No. 4. 1 foot blue Shaly Limestone with fossils, including *Productus Prattenianus*, *Pr. muricatus*, *Hemipronites crassus* and *Chonetes mesoloba*.

No. 5. 10 feet 6 inches Sandstone and Shales.

No. 6. 5 feet Slope.

No. 7. 2 feet shaly micaceous Sandstone.

No. 8. 10 feet Slope.

No. 9. 13 feet 6 inches Sandstone and Shales.

No. 10. 18 feet Slope, to water in the creek.

On Mr. Boyd's land a well was penetrated in search of oil to a depth of 130 feet, passing through Sandstone and Shale beds. The upper bed, Mr. Norwood thinks, is the equivalent to No. 9 of his Section just quoted.

The top of the mound in Sec. 27, is about 50 feet above No. 1 of this Section, and is capped with 5 feet of Sandstone.

Coal, 18 inches thick, was obtained by Mr. Croghan in a well nearly at a vertical distance of 69 feet from the top of the mound.

The following includes the formation of Cherry Mound:

Section at Cherry Mound.

No. 1. 5 feet blue Shales.

No. 2. Yellow ochrey band.

No. 3. 1 foot 6 inches Limestone, weathers red and brown-ochrey.

No. 4. 3 feet blue Shales.

No. 5. 2 inches Coal.

No. 6. 1 foot blue Clay with *Stigmaria*.

No. 7. 2 inches Coal.

No. 8. 3 feet Fire-clay.

This mound presents an interesting appearance on the summit. A circular basin has been worn out by the action of the elements, leaving a 5 feet bank of Shales in the center, and just at the outer margin of the mound there is an elevated rim extending nearly around it, between which and the central small mound is the excavation of 5 feet depth. This peculiar appearance has given rise to curious speculations. Many persons thinking they see evidences of ancient mining, when a few minutes close observation and thought will at once show that these appearances can all be traced to natural causes. Cherry Mound is 70 feet above the neighboring plains, and about 80 feet above the Coal of Mr. Johnson, about 1 mile N. E.

ECONOMICAL GEOLOGY.

Of 503 square miles of Coal Measures in this county, there are about 480 underlaid by an aggregate of 4 feet of good Coal. With this is included a strip of 31 square miles in the western part of the county underlaid by 6½ to 7 feet of Coal. We will then have under 31 square miles the amount of 224,699,904 tons of Coal, and under 449 square miles the amount of 2,002,784,256 tons, or a total of 2,227,484,-160 tons. Allowing for a waste of one-third in mining, we still have 1,484,989,440 tons of available Coal in the county—sufficient for all county purposes during the life of the present generation, besides allowing for a large export.

As yet there has been but little mining of Coal in this county. The home market is very limited, and facilities for transportation are very poor. In the eastern portion of the county, fire-wood is generally easily obtained, but in the western part the inhabitants will have to use Coal. The county is at present but thinly settled, but when the population shall have increased, we may expect Coal mines to be opened in every neighborhood, and Coal to become a staple article of commercial value.

DESCRIPTION OF PRINCIPAL COAL BANKS.

Mr. Cline, at the foot of the mound, in Sec. 34, T. 31, R. 31, works a 13-inch seam. It lies in the bed of the branch, and is best worked in dry weather. The Coal is of good ordinary quality. An analysis by Mr. R. Chauvenet gave:

Water.. 1.54
Volatile.. 33.79
Fixed Carbon.. 50.21
Ash 14.46
Color of ash, gray; rather a large per cent.
Sulphur was rather high, being.. 5.588 per cent.

The seams at the upper part of the mound have also been worked at intervals, but are too thin for profitable working.

In Secs. 28 and 31 of the same township, an 8-inch seam is sometimes worked, which is probably referable to that just named. (No. 14 of County Section.)

In Secs. 6 and 7, T. 30, R. 31, a 15 to 18-inch seam is worked at the surface, on an open prairie, at several places. It here crops out in the edge of a ravine. On N. B. Wood's land, in Sec. 7, it is capped by thin layers of blue and bluish gray, fine-grained Sandstone. At Quillan's diggings, in the N. W. Sec. 5, the cap-rock consists of one foot of blue and semi-bituminous Shales. Three-quarters of a mile northwest of this, on Anderson's land, it is capped by light blue Shales, and 5 feet above there is a hard Sandstone. The Coal from these various places is mostly hauled to Lamar.

At Jno. Hubbard's, in N. W. Sec. 11, T. 30, R. 32, is an 8-inch Coal seam, probably equivalent to No. 14 of our County Section. Sandstone 21 feet thick lies 13 feet above it.

In S. E. Sec. 7, T. 30, R. 32, is an outcrop of Coal probably equivalent to the last, but only 5¾ inches thick. It has thin layers of Sandstone immediately resting on it, with an irregular, cellular Ochre bed sometimes as the cap-rock. This Coal I regard as the equivalent of Hubbard's, of one of the upper seams at Cline's and the top Coal at Lamar, or No. 14 of our General County Section. There has been considerable mining for it, but on account of its inferior thickness and close approximation to the overlying Sandstone, I imagine that the mining has been without profit. Its place is No. 3 of the Section on North Fork, at south county line.

On George W. Evans' land, in N. half N. W. Sec. 22, T. 31, R. 31, Coal No. 4 of our Section appears in the edge of a prairie branch. It is one foot thick, of good quality, but the water in the branch is a serious impediment to mining operations. The owners might do well to sink shafts a little way down on higher ground. The Coal would be reached at the same level, and there might be a little water sometimes in the way, but there would be no danger of being overflowed as there is at present. From this place the ground rises very gently back and the hills are low. Each of the three seams in the bluffs west of Lamar has been worked at various times. The Coal seems to be of a good quality and certainly underlies the country north and west. The lower beds may underlie Lamar.

Section at Tracy's, in N. W. N. E. Sec. 32, T. 32, R. 30.

No. 1. 50 feet Sandstone.

No. 2. 3 to 6 inches Coal. Seen as a rotten, smutty streak at "Trace's Bank," but up stream it forms a solid Coal seam, (No. 14 of General Section.)

No. 3. 3 inches ochrey Clay.

No. 4. 2 feet 3 inches dove-colored Fire Clay, with *Stigmaria*.

No. 5. 9 inches good bed of Ochre.

No. 6. 1 foot blue, olive and ochrey Clay.

No. 7. 3 feet blue Clay.

No. 8. 14 inches good Coal, (No. 10 of General Section.)

This Coal is worked at many places for $1\frac{1}{2}$ miles up the branch east, rising gently eastward.

Mr. Ward, on a neigboring hill, bored 52 feet, mostly through hard Sandstone, without any Coal. Near the foot of the hill, or 30 feet lower than the surface of the well, he struck the 14-inch Coal at 17 feet. This will seem to show that the boring in the well nearly reached the Coal, and also, between the points, there must be a dip of a little over 5 feet.

On Dr. VanPelt's land, in S. W. Sec. 16, T. 32, R. 30, a 1-foot seam is found in a well near the foot of a hill. This must be the equivalent of the lowest bed in the hill one mile west of Lamar. For 30 feet above, the formation appears to be mostly Sandstone. There are probably other Coals concealed.

On the north side of the Creek from the last named place, a Coal bed appears in the bed of the Creek, capped by 3 feet of buff Clay Shales—the latter overlaid by thick beds of Sandstone. Its entire thickness could not be seen, and only 1 foot was exposed, but I was told it was 2 feet thick. This Coal is probably the equivalent of the bed sometimes worked on North Fork in north part of Sec. 30, T. 32, R. 29. At the latter place it is reported to be 28 inches thick, but being in the bed of the stream, I could not verify the information. It is probably the lowest Coal in the county, and is probably also the same that crops out in Sec. 34, T. 32, R. 29. It was reported to be 18 inches thick, but was so covered with debris that I could not see it.

On land of Gaddy's, in N. W. N. W. Sec. 3, T. 32, R. 29, Sandstone rests directly on Coal which was reported to be 12 to 14 inches thick. It was concealed by rubbish when I was there, but I suppose it to be equivalent to No. 7 of our Section.

The Coal last named was also seen at the corner of Cedar and Dade counties, 13 inches thick, and capped by Sandstone containing intercalations of Ochre. The rocks here dip 5° W.

Another place where it was found was in S. E. Sec. 16, T. 33, R. 29, on land of David Bass. The Coal here is 16 inches thick and capped by 21 feet of Sandstone—the upper part in thick layers, the lower thin and even, and separated by partings of blue Shale.

In T. 33, R. 30, are several outcrops of thin Coal seams, but they have only been worked for neighborhood uses.

Cherry Mound has been already noticed.

One mile north-east, on Mr. Johnson's land, a third seam of Coal was observed, presenting the following section:

No. 1. 3 feet Soil and Clay.
No. 2. 3 inches concretionary red Ochre.
No. 3. 1 foot 3 inches blue and semi-bituminous Shales.
No. 4. 6 to 8 inches Coal.
No. 5. ½ inch yellow Ochre.
No. 6 Blue Clay.

As to the exact geological position of this Coal, I am not certain. It is probably equivalent to the seams seen by Mr. Norwood four or five miles north, and also reported to be in the well in Sec. 17, T. 32, R. 32, 14 feet from the surface.

North of this, on East Drywood, Coal has been mined at several places.

In Sec. 25, on W. H. Curless' land, a 13 to 18 inch seam was observed, 4 to 10 feet above the water. A little further up stream, a one foot seam was being mined in the bed of the creek, probably 10 to 15 feet below the other seam. These seams must underlie the surrounding country.

In the north part of Sec. 34, T. 31, R. 33, was observed a 16-inch Coal occurring thus:

No. 1. Sandstone.
No. 2. Few feet of slope.
No. 3. Band of red concretionary Shales.
No. 4. 2 feet dark ochrey Shales.
No. 5. 2 feet blue Shales.
No. 6. 16 inches Coal.
No. 7. Slope, with Sandstone below.

This is probably equivalent to the Coal of Johnson's, above named. If so, I think I am correct. It must underlie all of the intervening country.

Mr. Norwood records a Coal of the same thickness from the well of Mooney, in Sec. 23, T. 31, R. 33. He also makes it equivalent to an 8-inch seam cropping out in Sec's 3, 10, 11 and 13 of the same township. He has estimated this Coal to be 50 feet below the Coal (No. 17) of our section.

Passing over an exceedingly gently rising country for three miles north-west, and at an assumed elevation of 40 feet higher, we approach Martindale's bank. This is the furthest southern outcrop of the 3-feet Coal—No. 17 of General Section. The location is S. E. S. W. Sec. 30. T. 31, R. 33, near the top of a low mound. The Coal is about 3 feet thick, but of impure quality, containing a good deal of Iron Pyrites, sometimes in thin bands. It is overlaid by 4 to 5 feet of blue Clay Shales, with some sandy layers, capped by a rough Ochre band. The mound limits this bank to a few acres in extent. Dipping northward, we next see it at Beebe's, in Sec. 7 of the same township, just below the general level of the prairie. It crops out here in the edge of a gently flowing prairie draw, but its working is some what interfered with by water. The Coal contains a little Iron Pyrites.

An analysis of Beebe's Coal by Mr. R. Chauvenet, gave :

Water.. 1.12
Volatile.. 34.98
Fixed Carbon... 50.68
Ash (color of ash, pinkish gray)... 13.22
Sulphur.. 6.48

The per cent. of water is small; fixed Carbon very fair; but ash and Sulphur too much.

The next point north where observed, was on the land of Dr. Morerod, in the south part of Sec. 19, T. 32, R. 33, capped by blue and red Shales, and of a uniform thickness of three feet. Three-quarters of a mile south, Mr. Barker struck this Coal in a well, at a depth of 68 feet, passing through an 8-inch seam at 23 feet. This thick Coal seems generally to dip north and west, as indicated from the above, and a few outcrops further east. On Henry Flack's land, in the north part of Sec. 29, of the same township, it crops out on the south side of a gentle draw, eight feet above the valley near by, and three feet thick, the upper six inches crumbling; that below being hard, shining and bituminous.

I append an analysis of this Coal by Mr. Chauvenet, from which it appears more favorably than that of Beebe's—the Sulphur being 2.969 per cent. and other constituents as follows :

ANALYSIS.

CONSTITUENTS.	Top.	Middle.	Bottom.
Water	2.14	1.89	1.54
Volatile	33.56	34.09	37.51
Fixed Carbon	56.02	58.71	56.65
Ash	8.28	5.36	4.30
Color of ash	Faint purple gray.	Purple gray.	Drab.

In Sec. 22, on the land of Tucker, Ward & Co., it is 28 inches thick, and capped by six feet of blue Shales, the lower two feet of a deeper blue, and semi-bituminous.

The Coal is hard, black and shiny, with an efflorescence of Copperas on the surface. We find Sandstone 20 feet above. The Coal here is well situated for mining, being 12 feet above the valley.

A Coal that I refer to this bed, has been worked at several places south-west of Leroy. In Sec. 19, T. 33, R. 33, we find :

No. 1. Sandstone.
No. 2. Blue and drab Shales.
No. 3. Blue Shales with concretions of red Ochre.
No. 4. 4 inches blue Limestone, changing to a bright brown Ochre.
No. 5. 21 inches bituminous Shales.
No. 6. 2 feet Coal.

The following is an abstract of C. J. Norwood's notes not included in the above.

McKERROW'S COAL.

Locality, S. E. Sec. 30, T. 33, R. 32, on the East Branch of Big Drywood. The Coal is made up of alternating shiny black and dull black layers with Charcoal partings. Markings of *Stigmaria* were observed and masses of Iron Pyrites also occur. The Coal is 45 to 50 feet below the base of Round Mound.

NEIL & GILBERT'S COAL.

This has been worked up and down a dry prairie branch for 200 or 300 yards. The Coal is 2 to 3 feet thick, equal to No. 17 of general section and separated by a pyritiferous band. The top, of 5 inches, is of poor quality, becoming better as we approach the lower part.

The lower 18 inches is hard, compact, and shiny black. Excepting the dividing Pyrites band we find scarcely any other impurities, but near the middle of the seam a Sulphur efflorescence proceeds from the joints and the upper layers have plates of Carbonate of Lime inserted in the joints. Immediately over the Coal is 3 to 4 feet of shaly Sandstone with occasionally a conglomerate, formed of the overlying Sandstone, cemented by oxide of Iron. Twenty-five feet above this Coal are beds of Sandstone which were traced to the south part of Sec. 6, T. 32, R. 33. At this point a 6-inch seam of coal occurs a little above the Sandstone and capped by Bituminous Shales, enclosing pyritous concretions, containing *Productus muricatus*. When this Shale thins out we find it replaced by $\frac{1}{2}$ to $2\frac{1}{3}$ft of local drift, formed of Sandstone and a Bituminous Shale, cemented by Oxide of Iron into a conglomerate. David Nenger, in N. E. Sec. 30, T. 33, R. 33, has the same Coal as Neil and Gilbert's. In Sec. 17, T. 32, R. 33, a 10-inch seam, corresponding to the one of Sec. 6, is seen. Twenty-three to 36 inches of Coal (No. 17) is opened in the north part of Sec. 19, T. 32, R. 33. At one place it is covered by a conglomerate, at another by 18 inches of sandy Shales. Coal has been mined at several places in Secs. 10. 11, 13 and 14, T. 31, R. 33, of varying thick ness, from 8 to 18 inches. Mr. Kent's, in S. W. Sec. 17, T. 31, R. 32, is 12 inches; Mr. Stinnet's, Sec. 34, T. 32, R. 31, is 11 inches; O. Rising's, in the N. E. quarter Sec. 30, T. 35, R. 31, is 15 to 18 inches thick, covered by sandy Shales, excepting local drift at one place.

One and a-half miles south of Lamar, on a branch heading south, 14 inches of Coal, equivalent to the middle Lamar Coal, crops out. A 6-inch, dark streak appears 10 feet above with Sandstone 12 feet above it. Mr. Richards, near Lamar, struck 8 inches of Coal in his well. Mr. Norwood thinks this is 12 feet below the lowest Lamar Coal. The equivalent of the last is also found at Mr. Catlins', in the S. E. S. W. Sec. 27, T. 33, R. 31, and at Mr. Broadhurst's, in S. W. N. W. Sec. 16, T. 33, R. 29, being 18 to 20 inches thick at the latter place. Coal, equivalent to the middle Lamar Coal, is found on Isaac Van Nice's land, in S. E. S. W. Sec. 6, T. 32, R. 29; at Mr. Hazleton's, in N. W. Sec. 6, and at Mr. Crabtree's, in N. E. Sec. 22, T. 33, R. 30.

In S. E. Sec. 28, T. 32, R. 29, Mr. Sparks has 22 inches of Coal, which may be equivalent to the upper (?) Lamar Coal. Harrington's Coal, 12 inches thick, in Sec. 20, T. 31, T. 30, and Trace's, in N. W. N. E. Sec. 32, T. 32, R. 32, are each equivalent to the middle Lamar Coal.

IRON ORE.

There are found in this county red and brown Hematites, Carbonate and Sulphuret of Iron and Ochres. The Sulphuret is generally diffused, but in small quantities in some of the Coals.

No extensive deposits of good ore are observed, but the lower Coal often carry just above them beds of Ochre or soft Hematite or ferruginous conglomerate. The Upper Coal, one mile west of Lamar, is overlaid by an irregular bed of from 3 to 12 inches, which is sometimes a conglomerate of Carbonate of Iron, a little Sandstone and some Ochre. At other times it is a cellular, soft Limonite, with minute Limonite concretions alternating with a bright yellow Ochre. A specimen of this, analyzed by Mr. Chauvenet, gave—

Insoluble Silica.. 31.51
Water (H. 2, O.)............... .... 12.02
Peroxide of Iron (Fe. 2, O. 3)... 56.29
                                                                      ———
                                                                      99.82
Metallic Iron (Fe.).. 39.40

This contains too much Silica to be valuable.

The brown, cellular ores, abundant in many other places, would give about the same analysis.

They have been incidentally noticed in speaking of the Coal and can only be valuable as material for Ochre paints. In Secs. 18 or 19, T. 33, R. 33, the Shales over the Coal contain several concretionary bands and detached concretions, arranged at regular horizontal intervals through the Shales. The bands are from 1 to 2 inches thick, formed of an outer soft brown or red crust, then a soft, deep, bright red Ochre, with an interior of $\frac{1}{8}$ to $\frac{1}{4}$ of an inch shell of hard red Hematite. The interior is sometimes filled with soft yellow Ochre, at other times is hollow and supported by small vermicular stalactites of Hematite.

An analysis by Mr. Chauvenet gave—

Insoluble Silica.. 24.81
Water (H. 2, O.).. 11.90
Peroxide of Iron (Fe. 2, O. 3)... 63.20
                                                                      ———
                                                                      99.91
Metallic Iron... 44.24

A good quality of soft Limonite was seen on the prairie in N. E. Sec. 23, T. 33, R. 33. The bed is about 2 feet thick and is exposed as broken strata of 40 feet long by 20 wide, on the edge of a shallow ravine. Across, on the other side of the ravine, are a few masses of the same ore, showing it to be a regular bed. The quality is very similar to a deposit occurring in the Lower Coal Measures of the south-west part of Cedar county. Some of it is soft and shaly while other por_tions are hard. Further investigations may prove it to be of greater extent, if so it would be valuable. Eleven inches of crumbly Coal was seen in the ravine a little higher up.

CARBONATES.

In the S. E. S. W. Sec. 10, T. 33, R. 33, on land of a St. Louis banking company, there is exposed a 5-inch, band of rather poor Carbonate of Iron, in drab and Ochrey Shales. Below this and separated by blue Shales is a thin seam of good, black, shiny Coal.

An analysis of the Iron ore by Mr. Chauvenet gave—

Insoluble Silica... 21.10
Metallic Iron.. 33.12

This is probably the equivalent of the same bed found in the north-west part of Jasper county and reported to contain silver. (!)

BITUMEN.

This product is quite common, being found somewhere in every neighborhood. The Lower Keokuk Limestone, in Golden Grove, shows it very plain and some of the Limestones are nearly black. In a well, at the edge of the prairie, the Keokuk Limestone is quite bituminous, and occasional drops of Tar are seen.

On North Fork, in Sec. 25, T. 32, R. 30, borings were made in the bed of the stream for oil but were soon abandoned. In a well 30 feet deep, dug in Sec. 18, T. 33, R. 30, bituminous Sandstone was struck at 12 feet from the surface. At L. Z. Burr's, in Sec. 28, T. 32, R. 31, in a well 75 feet deep, bituminous Sandstone was entered near the bottom.

A well dug 19 feet deep in Sec. 2, N. W. quarter, T. 30, R. 33, exhibits—

No. 1. 6 feet Clay and local Drift.
No. 2. 11 feet hard, dark blue, black Sandstone, nearly as hard, and very much like Quartzite, highly saturated with Bitumen.
No. 3. Deep blue Clay Shales, with a good stream of pleasantly tasted water.

At Curless', in Sec. 25, T. 33, R. 33, a 50 foot outcrop of Sandstones shows most of the beds to be very bituminous. At Leroy they are similar, some beds being quite black and fetid. In fact nearly all the Sandstones in the north-west part of the county seem to be saturated with Bitumen. All of a chocolate color are bituminous, the darker colored containing a large per centage.

There is a Tar spring in the N. E. Sec. 29, T. 33, R. 33. At this place, the Bitumen regularly oozes from between the layers of the rocks and from the Sandstones, forming a thick indurated mass on the surface. On the land of Mr. Boyd, in N. E. N. E. Sec. 29, T. 33, R. 33, a bore was sunk to a depth of 130 feet in search of Petroleum. A gentleman living near gave Mr. Norwood a journal of these borings, as follows :

    No. 1.   30 to 40 feet Sandstone.
    No. 2.   2 to 3 feet Soapstone.
    No. 3.   50 feet Sandstone and some oil.
    No. 4.   4 feet Shales.
    No. 5.   Coarse, bituminous Sandstone, in which the boring was stopped.

This boring was made under the superintendence of Mr. Samuel Rose.

Some of the Sandstones are sufficiently saturated with Bitumen to burn for several minutes when ignited.

But although Bitumen seems to be nearly everywhere in Barton county, yet I do not think that it exists in quantity sufficient at any place to justify attempts at boring for it. It is too generally diffused, not in sufficient quantity, or not enough separated from the rock at any one place.

BUILDING STONES.

Excellent quality of Sandstones, in good even layers, exist nearly everywhere in the county.

GRITSTONES OR GRINDSTONES.

In nearly every neighborhood are found layers of Sandstone, possessing a good grit for grindstones or whetstones. I might particularly name a quarry in Sec. 31, T. 31, R. 31; also, in Sec. 17, T. 32, R. 33. At these places the rock is fine grained, nearly white, and of a very pure quality. Similar beds exist nearly everywhere in the western half of the county, and by careful examination may be often found.

LIME.

The Limestones on North Fork, near Dublin, in Golden Grove, and at Avery's, in Sec. 25, T. 32, R. 30, would no doubt burn into a good quality of Lime.

OTHER MINERALS.

ZINC BLENDE,

In small quantities, has been found in the Keokuk Limestone at Mr. J. H. Wolfington's, at the edge of Golden Grove.

I saw no *Lead*, although the inhabitants, for some reason, think they ought to have it. The old diggings in Golden Grove do not prove its existence there, still I do not say it does not exist there—it may be found. The Limestones are of the same geological age as the Lead bearing rocks of Jasper, but because they are it does not follow that they certainly bear Lead in Barton. The same Limestone at many places in Jasper contains no Lead.

A white, silky-looking mineral was obtained by Mr. Norwood from McKerrow's Coal bank, which, on analysis by Mr. Chauvenet, corresponds very well with *Pickeringite* (Dana), a rare substance. Its analysis is as follows:

Water (H2, O)	44.64
Sulphuric Acid (H2, O4)	35.77
Alumina (Al2, O3)	15.55
Magnesia (Mg. O)	2.92
	99.91

This occurred as an efflorescence on Sandy Shales, in bands of one-half to two and a half inches, of which there were observed four.

MINERAL SPRINGS.

At many places in this county the water in wells has a bitter, disagreeable taste, owing sometimes to the presence of Sulphate of Iron (Copperas), but oftentimes to Sulphuric Acid. That at Newport penetrates the lower blue Pyritiferous Shales, and is very unpleasant to the taste.

At Thos. Gaddy's, in N. W. N. W. Sec. 3, T. 32, R. 29, the water has a strong copperas taste. It is 27 feet deep, having penetrated through Sandstone into Sandy Shales, with Pyritiferous concretions.

At Wm. Rector's, in N. W. Sec. 35, T. 33, R. 29, the well is 34 feet deep, with 18½ feet of water in it most of the time, at which depth it gives a weak taste of Alum, but is really not very unpleasant to taste, and can be used for washing purposes. Mr. Rector has used the water constantly for 18 years, and his family have enjoyed good health. Horses and cattle will not drink it. When the water is dipped out, that flowing in has such a strong Alum taste that it can not be used for a week. In 15 days it will rise to its average depth. When very strong, it can not be used for washing or cooking, nor will it make coffee.

Mr. Rector informed me that the rock structure consisted mostly of Sandstone, with 14 inches Coal at 18 feet depth and a 3-inch streak of Iron ore.

There is said to be another Alum well in this neighborhood, but it did not come under my notice.

These Alum wells may be valuable in the future.

At Milford, Mr. T. B. Hendron has two wells, from one of which I collected water for analysis. This water has a disagreeable taste, will act on the bowels, but is said to be healthy and can not be used for washing.

The well is 21 feet deep, passing through—

No. 1. 15 feet Clay.
No. 2. 6 feet Blue Shales.

Sulphuric Acid is the main cause of the bad taste of this water.

The other well, 100 feet deep, is said to be much stronger, but there being no means of hoisting the water, I can not say how it tastes. Mr. Hendron says that if a chicken is stewed in the water it will be too bitter to eat.

At Mr. Comstock's, in Sec. 23, T. 33, R. 33, are two wells containing water of a disagreeably strong taste. This is probably owing to the presence of Sulphate of Lime.

The disagreeable taste of much of the water of the northern part of this county is owing to either the presence of Sulphuric Acid or Sulphate of Lime.

AGRICULTURE.

The soil of Barton is not so rich as that of many other counties, but there are some very good tracts of land in the county. The gently undulating and sloping surface lies very well for farming, but the Sandstone so often approaches the surface as to seriously impede cultivation. Quite a good body of land for agricultural purposes is that near the west line extending from Martindales to Leroy; but this is sometimes spotted with light and poor soil. Another body of good land lies in the northern part of the county, north-west of Doylesport; also in the south-east, near Golden City.

The best land, with careful cultivation, will yield 62 bushels of corn per acre, and 11 to 15 bushels of wheat. But some lands I should think might yield a greater quantity of wheat.

The county at present is but thinly settled, chiefly owing to the fact that large tracts of land were withheld from the market on account of uncertainty of titles, but at present the titles are adjusted, the land is in market, and offered very cheap and in quantities to suit the purchaser.

The grasses flourish, and the prairies afford fine grazing for stock.

But few fruit trees have yet been planted, but the soil and climate indicate that they would succeed well.

CHAPTER X.

VERNON COUNTY.

BY G. C. BROADHEAD.

This county contains an area of 848 square miles.

At a general glance it appears to consist principally of prairie, but excepting the southern portion, some of the country between East and West Drywood, and the flat ridge and slope lying between the waters of Marmaton and East Drywood, on one side, and Clear Creek on the other, timber is generally convenient. With proper care in its preservation, the quantity is amply sufficient for all the inhabitants for many years. Still those persons on the wide prairies, do not often have to haul fire-wood or other timber, more than four or five miles ; and most of them are also well supplied with good Coal seams underlying their farms, although but few of them are exposed to view. On Little Osage and Marmaton, the timber belts are often over a mile in width. On East Drywood they are over two miles, with still wider belts on Clear Creek.

All the streams are tributary to the Osage, to seek which they preserve a general north-east course.

The main ridges have also a north-east trend.

The Osage touches the border for ten miles along the east part of the north line of the county. Its two principal streams, the Marmaton and Little Osage, drain the entire western half of the county. Clear Creek drains the south-east quarter, and Horse Creek, a tributary of Sac River, just enters, and passes out of the south-east corner of the county. None of the streams flow rapidly; the smaller ones even, become quite low during dry seasons. The Osage, Little Osage and Marmaton, flow continually ; although the two latter, in dry sea-

sons, become in shoaly places almost dry. The difference of elevation of ordinary water in Marmaton, from high water, is 22 feet; the
height of banks above ordinary stage of water, on the low bottoms, is
16 feet; the higher banks, 25 to 28 feet. The banks of Muddy Creek
are 20 feet high.

The bottoms of the larger streams, are generally wide. Those of
Marmaton and Little Osage, in many places, measure a mile across.
The bottoms along the lesser streams, are correspondingly wide.

The Uplands may topographically be divided into three classes,
viz.: The flats or plains, stretching off from the foot of the mounds to
the low ground; the mounds, and the hill lands. The country adjacent to Clear Creek, and its various forks, is generally 60 to 70 feet
above the valleys, being a little broken near the streams. This district, extending quite to Nevada, including the south-east quarter of
the county, has for the most part a gently undulating surface, passing
to the higher lands near Nevada City, which are about 125 feet above
the valley of the Drywood. North-east of Nevada, reaching to the
Osage, we find the same gently sloping country, excepting part of T's
36 and 37, of R. 30, north of Walker Station. It is here diversified by
clusters of mounds, reaching more than 100 feet above the general
surface of the prairie. Blue Mound is 150 feet high, and can be seen
from a long distance. Timbered Hill, near the mouth of Marmaton and Little Osage, is a round, isolated mound, 170 feet above the
Marmaton, and over 100 feet above the surrounding plain. Being several miles from other marked elevations, it is seen for many miles off.
North of the Little Osage, a series of mounds extends east and west
along the county line, at an elevation of over 100 feet above the
gently stretching valley at their base. This undulating valley, from
30 to 50 feet above the river bottoms, extends westward and blends
into the higher lands further west.

Most of the country in R. 32, lying between Marmaton and Little
Osage, consists of a gently undulating plain, not more than 40 to 50
feet above the principal streams. Further west, in R. 32, we find the
mounds rising still higher. These mounds continue on southward
through the county, interrupted sometimes for several miles by the
streams.

From Moundville, a high ridge, or series of connected mounds,
trends off to the south line of the county, rising near the northern
and middle line to 140 feet above the lower valleys, or 80 to 100 feet
above Moundville valley. From this range the country slopes off
gently and gracefully to the Drywoods. The occasional occurrence
of these mounds gives a charming variety to the landscape. Many
of them can be seen at a long distance, and from their summits the

views are often very fine. Their line of junction with the lower plains is often easy, and with many farms in view, the whole combined is pleasing and interesting.

The easy and gently sloping country below the mounds, presents a surface well adapted for the construction of public highways. Railroads of easy grades and long tangents, could be cheaply constructed in several directions through the county. The counties north and south, being of similar topography, the construction of such highways would be comparatively easy.

SURFACE DEPOSITS.

Undoubtedly this county has been subjected to glacial agency at some former period of time.

Its results may be seen in the isolated mounds and deep valleys between. The amount of erosion must have been of great force and of long continuance, if we view the mounds and long stretches of distance from one to the other. When protected by the upper series of Limestones, the erosion was not complete; but if these Limestones were much broken, or entirely absent, leaving the Sandstones exposed, the waters would rush down with resistless force, and bear away all the softer material; leaving, for example, a long stretch of plains from the county line north of the Osage to Moundville, over 12 miles in length. From the direction of most of these mounds, I would suppose the force to have generally been from north to south.

No Drift pebbles were seen on high ground, but some wells expose rounded Gravel and Sand. Near Nevada, I heard of a Gravel bed containing logs, etc., in a well 16 feet below the surface.

The bank of the Marmaton, at Boswell's, is 25 feet high, and composed of a brownish Clay.

LOWER CARBONIFEROUS.

Limestones referable to the Keokuk Group appear from beneath Lower Coal Measures at several places in the county. On Horse Creek we find exposed about 25 feet thickness, the beds generally of a gray color, with a few feet of buff-brown Limestone about the middle portion. The next exposure north of this is in Secs. 5 and 6, T. 34, R. 29, on a branch of Clear Creek. Next north is a limited exposure in Section 16, T. 35, R. 29. A little north of Virgil City, we find occasional outcrops as far north as Sec. 13, T. 36, R. 29, and thence up Clear Creek to White Oak Mills. One mile south-west of Bellevoir, a 12-foot outcrop of cherty, bituminous Limestone occurs 40 feet above the water. This would make over 50 feet of this formation at this place. The only other place where observed was in Sec. 20, T. 36, R. 31. When seen, the beds are generally of a bluish gray color, often slightly bituminous and containing many *Crinoid* stems. The other principal fossils observed were *Spirifer Keokuk, Orthis dubia, Chonetes* ———, *Productus Wortheni, Productus semireticulatus, Terebratula* (ovate formed Sp.), *Rhynchonella mutata, Retzia Verneuiliana, Athyris planosulcata, Phillipsia* ———, *Zaphrentis* and *Archimedes.*

This Limestone is chiefly valuable for making Lime, and at Mr. Hatteen's, near Marmaton, north of Nevada, one layer making excellent hydraulic cement is found.

COAL MEASURES.

There are 90 to 125 feet of mostly Sandstone and Shales in this county, including from the base of the Coal Measures to No. 23. This embraces one good, workable Coal with other thin seams. Sandstone is the chief element of this Group and appears on the surface or crops out on the streams in all that portion of the county east of East Drywood and lying south of the Marmaton and Osage, excepting the Mounds near Walker's Station, where it is below the surface. We find these Sandstones occupying T. 35, R. 32. and extending up and along the Drywoods to the county line.

On the Marmaton, above the mouth of Muddy, are exposed 30 feet of bituminous Sandstone. On Newton's farm, two miles northwest, near the line of Bates and Vernon, it is quite black, with tar oozing out from between the strata. Near Nevada, and extending north to Marmaton, Sandstone, with occasional shaly beds, occurs, thus indicating a thickness of about 125 feet of the same Sandstone. (Its main or upper bed of 50 feet being well developed on Clear Creek, we have, for convenience, spoken of it as the *Clear Creek Sandstone.*)

On Marmaton, in Sec. 9, T. 36, R. 31, the rocks seen are:

No. 1. 40 feet Sandstone.

No. 2. 25 feet olive Shales.

No. 3. 10½ inches Coal.

No. 4. 1 foot calcareo-pyritiferous bed.

No. 5. 7 feet Shales and Fire Clay. In the lower beds are concretionary, plant-bearing beds of Carbonate of Iron, which turn red on exposure. A Coal seam was observed, 8 inches thick, at one place, but thinning out at 25 feet in either direction.

No. 6. 1 foot Coal.

No. 7. 6 feet silicious and ferruginous beds, with *Stigmaria ficoides.*

The Sandstones near Nevada are generally soft and often colored a reddish brown ferruginous, but there are some good, solid beds for building purposes.

On Big Drywood, in Sec. 25, T. 35, R. 33, large, tumbled beds of Sandstone are exposed, resting on about 25 feet of sandy, blue and drab Shales, the latter containing some peculiar, cup-shaped fossils, which may be *Fucoids*.

On McKill Creek, near the south line of the county, are exposed hard beds of dark, chocolate colored, bituminous Sandstone. At White Oak Mills, on Clear Creek, there is a good exposure of the lower beds.

Section at White Oak Mills.

No. 1. A few feet Slope from hill-top.

No. 2. 25 feet "Clear Creek Sandstone," tolerably fine-grained, with some micaceous beds. A few remains of plants are seen. It occurs generally in even flags which make good grindstones.

No. 3. 21 feet Slope. A thin Coal seam in the lower part.

No. 4. Outcrops of Shale and fragments of Coal.

No. 5. 33 feet Slope to water in Clear Creek. The lower 12 feet being Lower Carboniferous Limestone.

Three-quarters of a mile south, 12 inches of Coal were observed in place, about 15 feet below No. 2 of the above Section. The Coal was capped by light blue Shales.

One mile east of White Oak Mills, our Section includes both this Coal and the shaly seam at the Mill, and the rocks appear in the following succession:

No. 1. 5 feet Sandstone.

No. 2. 12 feet drab, sandy Shales.

No. 3. 5 feet thin layers of Sandstone.

No. 4. 2 inches rotten Coal.

No. 5. 32½ feet deep blue Shales, with bituminous layers. Ten feet from top is a seam of bituminous Coal.

No. 6. 1½ feet Shales, with concretions of pyritiferous Limestone from 6 inches to 1½ feet diameter, separated by *Cone in Cone.*

No. 7. 2½ feet black Shales.

No. 8. 6 inches rough, sandy, pyritiferous Limestone, containing a *Gasteropod.*

No. 9. 4½ inches Coal.

No. 10. 2 inches black Slate.

No. 11. 2 feet Fire Clay.

No. 9, of this Section, is probably the exposed Coal seam at White
Oak Mills, and the Coal in No. 5 the equivalent of that seen a half mile
south of the mills. The same Coal also appears in the creek bank a
mile above the mills. The Sandstones of this Group are often of remarkably firm texture and generally very durable. They are sometimes ripple-marked, and we also find numerous rugose, wavy markings, such as would be formed by loosely and gently flowing mud, but
can not be referred to such a cause, for there is no Clay in their composition. It may be *Fucoidal*.

In the neighborhood of White Oak Mills I observed some fine specimens of *Sigillaria* and *Lepidodendron ; Calamites, Stigmaria* and
Coniferous wood are also seen. The fossil forms called *Sternbergia*,
are also not infrequent. These Sandstones are sometimes ferruginous
and small quantities of good quality of brown Hematite are of frequent occurrence. Chalybeate waters are also rather common.

Near White Oak Mills the Sandstone did not seem to be bituminous, and in the Nevada Sandstones only minute traces of Asphaltum
were observed. Considerable Iron is seen near Nevada, but too intimately connected with the Sandstone to be valuable.

From our observations the position of the strata is nearly horizontal. From the east line of the county to the line of R's. 32 and 33,
and from the south line to the Marmaton the dip from this west and
north limit is west and north.

MARAIS DES CYGNES COAL.

The well-known Coal occurring as a 3 to 6 feet bed, sometimes
worked at many places between the Little Osage and Marias des
Cygnes, as far west as the line of R's. 31 and 32, I shall speak of as
the Marais des Cygnes Coal, and the group of rocks occurring with it
as the Marais des Cygnes Group. In the eastern half of the county it
may only be found in T's. 36 and 37 of R. 30. The lower part of Timbered Mound includes this and other Coals.

Section at the Base of Timbered Mound.

No. 1. Sandstone.
No. 2. 2½ feet seam of rotten Coal.
No. 3. 3 feet thin layers of drab and yellow Sandstone with *Stigmaria*,
       sometimes replacing Fire-clay.
No. 4. 2 feet yellow and blue banded Clay with Selenite.
No. 5. 1 foot red and yellow Clay.
No. 6. 2½ feet rough nodular silico-ferruginous rock, with Selenite.
No. 7. 4 feet blue shaly Sandstone, with sandy Ironstone.
No. 8. 6 feet blue Shales, with calcareous Ironstone—contains plants.

No. 9. "Cone in Cone."

No. 10. 2 feet semi-bituminous Shales.

No. 11. 2 feet 3 inches blue calcareous, bituminous and pyritiferous Shale, containing *Pr. muricatus*, etc.

No. 12. 18 to 20 inches Coal.

No. 13. 6 feet Fire-clay, upper half blue, the lower brown and gypsiferous.

No. 14. 2 inches Coal.

No. 15. 1½ feet Clay and blue concretions.

No. 16. 1½ feet dark-blue Clay.

This Section includes the Marais des Cygnes Coal, and the lower beds closely resemble those cropping out on the Little Osage, in Sec. 22, T. 37, R. 33. About 24 feet above the Marais des Cygnes Coal is often found a ferruginous Limestone, with its upper part shelly and weathering red, the lower a dark-ash, and often jointed. It is No. 29 of our General Section, and was seen on Timbered Hill and south of Moundville, at Todd's, in Sec. 9, T. 37, R. 33, and in Sec's. 11 and 15 of T. 37, R. 33. The presence of this rock would indicate that Coal is below it at no great depth. Its characteristic fossils are *Productus muricatus, P. Prattenanus, Chonetes mesoloba, Spirifer cameratus, Sp. lineatus, Sp. planoconvexus, Athyris subtilita*, a small *Discina* and *Bellerophon Montfortianus*. This Limestone is marked No. 29 of our Section.

At Todd's we find :

No. 1. 29 feet shaly Sandstone and sandy Shales.

No. 2. 3-inch band of fossiliferous Ochre.

No. 3. 10 inches drab Shales.

No. 4. 3½ feet Limestone, No. 29.

No. 5. 8 feet drab Shales.

No. 6. 10 to 11 inches Coal.

BITUMINOUS LIMESTONE GROUP.

This includes 60 to 70 feet of Shales, with 2 or 3 thin seams of Coal and some black calcareo-bituminous concretions, and a dark-blue bituminous Limestone in the upper part.

Section on the Little Osage, in Sec. 16, T. 37, R. 33.

No. 1. 31 feet bank of the stream.

No. 2. 21 feet Gravel bed.

No. 3. 16½ inches even layer of Limestone jointed perpendicularly, No. 43.

No. 4. 6 inches olive calcareo-bituminous Shales.

No. 5. 10 inches black semi-bituminous Shales, containing *Spirifer planoconvexus*.

No. 6. 6 inches bituminous Slate, with a few fossils.
No. 7. 1 foot roughly fractured blue Shales, abounding in *Productus muri-*
        catus.
No. 8. 4½ to 5 inches bed of shaly concretionary Limestone, contains *Pro-*
        ductus Prattenianus and *Productus muricatus.*
No. 9. 10 inches shelly blue calcareous Shales.
No. 10. 8 inches dark concretionary bed, like No. 8.
No. 11. 3 feet bituminous Shales.

The jointed Limestone of this Section occupies the bed of the
Little Osage, two miles east, where I obtained some good characteristic
fossils, including *Spirifer lineatus, Terebratula bovidens, Productus
Nebrascensis, P. Prattenianus, Chonetes mesoloba, Aviculopecten
occidentalis* and *Allorisma regularis.* This Limestone is generally
recognized by its even bed, and being jointed by vertical cracks into
rhomboidal masses, very hard and heavy, and giving out a bituminous odor. It is much used for building and looks well in a wall.

Going southward it is found on Marmaton at Alexander's Ford,
southward near Cox's, and half way up the mounds south of Moundville. In R. 33, near the line of T's 36 and 37, are seen the beds underlying this Limestone, with the Coal, which occurs 20 feet below.
On Cook's farm, three miles south-west of Moundville, the Limestone (No. 43) is found with the Coal 30 feet below. Five feet below
the Limestone, the Shales inclose large black bituminous concretions.
These concretions were seen at several places in this vicinity; also,
in the northern part of T. 36, R. 33, and at some other localities, but
never forming a continuous bed. They correspond to what is known
as the Fort Scott Marble, but cannot be considered of much value for
such purposes.

FORT SCOTT GROUP.

This includes the highest Rocks seen in the county. They occupy
all the higher lands in R. 33 and R. 32, north of the Little Osage.
This Group embraces several thick beds of Limestone, which are useful for making lime, and two beds of Coal. Our section on the
mounds below Moundville, was the only place where the beds were
found connected with other lower Rocks.

Moundville Section.

No. 1. 6 feet Slope from hill top.

No. 2. 12 inches gray Limestone, weathers in part brown.

No. 3. 8 inches buff and brown Limestone.

No. 4. 4 feet 2 inches bituminous Slates, inclosing small, flattened concretions. These Slates are jointed regularly—S. W. 45 deg., and N. W. (?) 45 deg., magnetic course.

No. 5. 17 inches Coal—No. 52 of General Section.

No. 6. 11 feet Slope.

No. 7. Outcrop of rough mottled Limestone.

No. 8. 63 feet Slope.

No. 9. Jointed bituminous Limestone.

No. 10. 15 feet Slope.

No. 11. 1 foot Coal—No. 47 of General Section.

No. 12. 50 feet Slope.

No. 13. Red Limestone.

No. 14. 22 feet Slope.

No. 15. Thick Coal—No. 23 of General Section.

(For the section at Fort Scott, Kansas, see our General Section, Nos. 44 to 55. No. 44 contains many concretions of yellow Ochre.)

The top Limestones below Moundville, contain *Campophyllum*, (?) *Lophophyllum proliferum*, and *Crinoid* stems. At other places were observed *Spirifer lineatus, Archæocidaris* ————, and *Productus splendens.*.

The next lower Limestone (No. 50) contains *Productus punctatus*, *P. muricatus, P. costatus, P. Prattenanus, Rhynchonella Osagensis, Hemipronites crassus, Crinoid* stems, *Fistulapora nodulifera,* and *Fusulina*.

ECONOMICAL GEOLOGY.

COAL.

Most of the Coals seem to contain an excess of Bitumen, and are generally of good quality. Good beds may be obtained in most sections of the county. In the central and eastern parts, the seams are thin, and not often well exposed, and but little mining has been done. The seams in the south-eastern part of the county lie below the other Coals in Cedar county, mentioned in the geological description of that county, and are all below Coal No. 23. They are generally thin, and apparently horizontal; and wherever found exposed, may reasonab.y be supposed to be continuous for several miles beneath the surface. Near White Oak Mills are two thin seams—one of a foot thickness, the other a little thinner. They underlie the country south, and may underlie that on the west as far as Nevada.

The upper of these Coals is probably the representative of No. 70 of the General Section.

In T. 34, R. 29, thin streaks of Coal are met with in digging wells, but further west, on McCarty's Branch, an 18 inch seam is exposed.

In T. 34, R. 30, are found thicker Coal beds, but it is very probable that one of the seams is the equivalent of that last above named.

On Dillon's land, in the north-west corner of Sec. 23, T. 34, R. 30, we find exposed:

No. 1. Hard, coarse, dark-gray Sandstone, in irregular layers.
No. 2. 6 inches Coal having a bituminous odor. Appearance, bright and shiny.
No. 3. 3 inches black Clay and bituminous Shales in thin laminæ.
No. 4. 12 inches hard black shiny Coal.
No. 5. Thick layer of Sandstone—appears a little below.

Section on McLaughlin's land in Section 21 of T. 34, R. 30.

No. 1. Clay and tumbled flags of Sandstone.
No. 2. Coal divided thus:

  a—10½ inches soft Coal.
  b—11 inches good Coal, jointed with Calcite in joints, lower layer irridescent.
  c—1 inch Clay and pyritiferous band, with *Cordaites*.
  d—8 inches impure Coal, with Iron Pyrites in joints.

A section a half mile west of this place, gave:

No. 1. Sandstone.
No. 2. 2 feet cellular silicious Kidney Iron Ore.
No. 3. 3 feet drab and blue sandy Shales.
No. 4. 2 feet Coal.
No. 5. 20 feet Slope to water in creek.

In the Creek are deep blue Shales, with concretions of Carbonate of Iron. This Coal, with thickness as above, may underlie most of this township and the next one west. There is a probability, but I express it with hesitation that it may be the equivalent of the Moundville Coal and the thick Coal of the northern part of the county, or No. 23 of our General Section. It is undoubtedly the equivalent of the Coal examined by Mr. Norwood in T. 34, R. 31, and of the thick Coal in R. 33 of Barton county.

On McKill's Creek, in T. 34, R 33, are indications of two thin Coal seams, but I only saw one of 7 inches thickness.

On Lander Branch, in the north-west part of Sec. 6, T. 34, R. 31, a 1 foot Coal seam has been occasionally worked. This may be the same Coal that is found four miles north-west, near Drywood. It is probably the equivalent of No. 10 of our Section.

Section at John Murray's, N. W. Sec. 30, T. 35, R. 31.

No. 1. 6 feet Sandstone.   In the lower part is an irregular mass of " Kidney Ore."

No. 2. 1 foot to a few inches of shaly, blue Limestone, sometimes thinning out.

No. 3. 1 foot blue Shales.

No. 4. 1 foot Coal, said to thicken to 18 inches.   No. 10 of General Section.

No. 5. 6 feet blue Shales.

No. 6. Said to be 8 inches of Coal in the water.

Horizontally north, we may expect this Coal to underlie Nevada.

MARAIS DES CYGNES COAL.

At Moundville, a shaft 34 feet deep has penetrated the thickest known bed of Coal in the county. Mr. Harvey Karnes, the proprietor, informed me that the material consisted of—

No. 1. 6 feet Soil and Clay.

No. 2. 10 inches fragments of Sandstone.

No. 3. 5 feet Soapstone and Clay Shales.

No. 4. 12 to 18 inches Limestone.

No. 5. 5 feet red Clay.

No. 6. 17 feet light colored, Clay Shales.

No. 7. Coal.

It was impossible, on account of the water in the sump and bad air in the chambers, for me to recognize the total thickness of the Coal. About 4 feet was exposed, but Mr. Karnes gave me the following order of succession, with the thickness of the various layers :

No. 1. 30 inches Coal.

No. 2. 11 inches Clay.

No. 3. 11 inches Coal.

No. 4. 7 inches Clay.

No. 5. 30 inches Coal.   Lower 10 to 12 inches of good blacksmith quality.

No. 6. 20 inches layer of compact, hard Coal, with splintery fracture—between a cannel and a bituminous Coal.

The Coal is limited just north and east, and extends southward for three miles within a belt a mile wide. It then passes under the mounds, terminating probably five miles south of Moundville, and includes here a district of about eight square miles. This Coal seam may underlie the mounds north of Walker's, but the evidences are that it is not so thick as the Moundville bed. Timbered Hill embraces it, but only 2½ feet in thickness. In Secs. 5 and 6 of T. 37, R. 31, and in T. 38, R. 31, are the best exposures of this Coal in the county. It is here mined at various places in open pits, and from the east line of T. 38, R. 31, for five miles west. The principal mines are owned by Dr. Bryan, Bougham, Cox, Denton, Ewell, Balder, Brand and Parker. The outcrops are in flat draws traversing the plains, sloping southward from the high mounds on the county line from 10 to 15 feet above the elevation of high water in the Marmaton, and generally are very favorably situated for mining. The Coal varies in thickness from 3 to 4½ feet, being intersected by a thin band of Pyrites about the middle. The upper 2 feet soon cracks and crumbles on exposure. The part below the Pyrites band is said to be the best smiths' Coal, and only that portion at the bottom cakes, the other part burning to a white ash.

Dr. Bryan's, in N. E. Sec. 36, T. 38, R. 31.

The Coal is 4 feet thick and crops out 4 feet above high water in the Marmaton. The lower 2 to 2½ feet is hard, black and shining, and apparently of good quality.

J. D. Cox's Bank, in S. E. Sec. 26, T. 38, R. 31.

This is 11 feet above high water. The total thickness is 53 inches, and is divided thus:

> No. 1. 5 inches crumbling Coal.
> No. 2. ¼ inch Mother of Coal.
> No. 3. 9½ inches black, shiny Coal.
> No. 4. 1½ inches Mother of Coal with Coal.
> No. 5. 14 inches hard, black, good Coal.
> No. 6. 3 inches band of Pyrites and Coal, with efflorescence of Sulphate of Iron on exposed surface.
> No. 7. 2 feet hard, black, good Coal.
> No. 8. Shaly Coal at bottom.

E. S. Ewell's, N. E. S. E. Sec. 27, T. 38, R. 31.

> No. 1. Gentle slope, terminated by a break showing 1½ feet of Clay, Sand and Gravel.
> No. 2. 8 inches soft, black band of decomposed Coal.

No. 3. 10 inches blue Fire Clay with a brown tinge.
No. 4. 3 inches band of brown and olive Clay.
No. 5. 4½ feet yellow-stained, blue Clay Shales.
No. 6. 6 inches soft, black, bituminous Shales.
No. 7. 4 feet Coal—the upper 1 foot soft, below it is hard, black and shiny. It
contains but little Iron Pyrites with some Mother of Coal, and on
exposure weathers brown along the joints.

A short distance off, it is shaly at a foot from the bottom, above
the middle it is irridescent, and near the top the layers have Charcoal
partings.

Benjamin Parker's, in N. W. Sec. 5, T. 37, R. 31.

No. 1. 1½ feet brown, sandy soil, with signs of brown Ochre at the bottom.
No. 2. 18 inches rotten Coal.
No. 3. 4 feet brown and blue Fire Clay.
No. 4. 4 feet 3 inches dark blue Clay.
No. 5. 39 inches Coal; a 2-inch pyritiferous band occurring at 18 inches from
the top. While the upper portion has plates of Pyrites insinuated
between the joints, the lower has Calcite plates.

This is said to be a good steam Coal. In the middle of No. 3 are
found pyritous concretions, containing *Pr. muricatus*, and *P. Prattenanus* occurs in the lower part. The Coal here is about 20 feet
above high water mark of the Little Osage. Our section shows certainly two distinct Coal beds, 8 feet apart. At Ewell's, the upper one
is five feet from the lower one.

These Coals are not seen further west, being concealed by higher
rocks. In T. 36, R. 33, at several places on land of Kountz, Todd and
others, are beds of Limestone, which I am disposed to refer to that
lying 20 to 30 feet above these Coals, and the Coal on the land of
Kountz is probably the upper seam just spoken of. This is worked at
several places in this neighborhood, but is only 1 foot thick.

On Mrs. Kauffman's land, at the corner of Secs. 28, 29, 32 and 33,
there is exposed 13 inches of good Coal, which may be one of the
seams, but the topography of the county would rather indicate it to
belong a little higher in the series.

At Jas. R. Strong's, on the Little Osage, in Sec. 22, T. 37, R. 33,
there are exposed several thin seams of Coal, whose occurrence nearly
resembles the beds at the base of Timbered Mound, thus:

No. 1. 5½ feet light blue, Ochrey Shales in thin laminae.
No. 2. 10 inches Coal.
No. 3. 2½ feet good Fire Clay.
No. 4. 3½ feet brown gypsiferous Shales.
No. 5. 6 inches Coal.

No. 6. 3½ feet blue Shales, in thin laminae, with incrustations of Selenite, and having brown partings and also enclosing brown Limestone nodules.

No. 7. Fossiliferous calcareous stratum.

No. 8. 2 feet bituminous Shales.

No. 9. 15 inches Coal.

No. 10. 3 feet Clay, containing Limestone nodules in the lower part.

The Coals of this section and others just previously discussed may be looked for beneath the surface in all the county west and north.

The next most important Coal in ascending series is No. 31. But few outcrops of it were observed. The furthest west and north is on the land of Hogan, near the mouth of Duncan Creek. It underlies the country north and about half of T. 37, R. 33.

South of the Little Osage, in Sec. 2 of T. 36, R. 33, it has been worked on a flat depression on the prairie. With its associated rocks it appears thus:

No. 1. 2 feet bituminous Shales with large, dark bituminous Limestone concretions and some small, round concretions. (No. 36. Gen. Sec.)

No. 2. 2½ feet drab and Ochrey Shales.

No. 3. 2½ feet bituminous Slates, with small, round concretions.

No. 4. 6 inches brown Ochrey Shales.

No. 5. 1 foot Coal. (No. 33. Gen. Sec.)

This Coal has also been worked two miles north-west. Its eastern limit in this neighborhood is probably the line of Rs. 32 and 33, extending south to Sec. 13, thence passing north-west around the heads of streams flowing south to Sec. 8, and thence south and south-east, first appearing on the creek in Sec. 21.

Mr. Willis Hughes has a Coal bed 13 inches thick in the bed of Cottonwood Creek, in Sec. 21, T. 26, R. 33. This I also refer to No. 33. A well dug just above and extending nearly to the Coal affords a plentiful supply of slightly chalybeate tasted water. In digging the well large, black bituminous concretions were taken out.

A mile below, on the land of J. Ditzler, in Sec. 28, the Coal is exposed in the bank of the creek, 10 feet above the water and 12½ inches thick, and of good quality. Just over it there is exposed:

No. 1. 3 feet hard, bituminous Slate, containing small concretions.

No. 2. 6 inches chocolate and ochreous Shales.

No. 3. 1 foot blue Clay Shales.

No. 4. Coal.

Thirteen to 15 feet above the Coal the bituminous Limestone (No. 43) lies in jointed flags, strewn along the surface of the prairie in very even layers of 16 inches.

Two to three miles south of the last place the above Coal is mined at several places on the land of Mr. Cox and others.

On the land of Mr. Cox, in Sec. 6, T. 34, R. 32, (No. 33) is 20 inches thick, cropping out in the edge of ravines sloping from mounds down to the plains below. No. 43 lies 30 feet above, and just over the Coal is a local band of shaly bituminous Limestone, such as is often found enclosed in bituminous Slate.

Coal, which may also be referred to the beds just named has been mined at several places in Secs. 28 and 32 of T. 34, R. 32.

Section at Wm. M. Shinn's, S. W. Sec. 28, T. 34, R. 32.

No. 1. 18 inches Soil.

No. 2. 1 foot ash-blue Limestone, weathering brown and full of fossils, including *Productus Muricatus* and *P. Prattenanus.*

No. 3. 17 inches olive calcareous and Clay Shales, containing *Chonetes mesoloba, Rhynchonella Osagensis,* and *Rhombopora lipidodendroides.*

No. 4. 3 inches bituminous Shales.

No. 5. 1 foot olive Shales.

No. 6. 2 feet bituminous Shales, full of small, round concretions.

No. 7. 9 feet mostly drab Shales, with many round, hollow concretions, the outer portion of which is formed of several concentric layers of ochreous Iron ore, the interior studded with Iron Pyrites, changing to Sulphate of Iron on exposure.

No. 8. 18 inches Coal.

No. 9. Fire Clay.

A quarter of a mile west the Coal is 1 foot thick at the outcrop.

FORT SCOTT COAL BEDS.

The equivalent of these Coals was first observed in Sec. 36, T. 38, R. 32. A section here shows—

No. 1. 2 feet Limestone.

No. 2. 9 inches olive Shales.

No. 3. 1 foot blue Shales.

No. 4. 1 foot blue, passing into bituminous Shales below.

No. 5. 1 foot Coal—No. 52 of General Section.

This seam passes under the mound north and west, and was not again seen in this part of the county. This is probably the same Coal as E. T. Welsh's, in Sec. 20, T. 39, R. 32. At this place I only observed a rotten outcrop.

CASSEL'S COAL, SEC. 7, T. 37, R. 33.

No. 1. 2 feet 2 inches broken mass of Limestone.

No. 2. 6 to 12 inches Calcareous Shales, with fossils, *Chonetes mesoloba, Lophophyllum and Fusulina.*

No. 3. 5 inches ash drab Limestone.

No. 4. 4 inches Clay Shales.

No. 5. 1½ inch dull drab Hydraulic Limestone.

No. 6. 2 feet blue and olive Shales, with small oblate Limestone concretions.

No. 7. 16 inches bituminous Slate. Concretions contain *Discina* and minute specks of Zinc Blende.

No. 8. 1 foot Coal, (No. 47) and equivalent to the Lower Fort Scott Coal, weathers mostly brown and contains very little Sulphur.

This Coal underlies the country north, and may be found in the western part of the next township south. I only observed it on the head of Shiloh Creek, near the State line, where it varies from 7 to 12 inches in thickness.

Its overlying beds are—

No. 1. 4 feet Limestone.

No. 2. 6 inches to 1 foot olive and drab Shales.

No. 3. 1 foot to 16 inches blue Shale.

No. 4. 9 to 10 inches bituminous Slate.

No. 5. 7 inches to 1 foot Coal.

Farther south these Coals are only seen in the high mounds south of the Marmaton.

In Secs. 6 and 7, T. 34, R. 32, and the Sections just west, they may be found under an area of about two miles square. The mines are mostly on the lands of Webster, Karnes and English. The Coal where I observed it was 17 inches thick, and lying very favorably for open working. I refer this bed to the Upper Fort Scott seam, or No. 55. The lower seam I did not find, but presume it exists in the neighborhood.

Vernon County Coalfields.

T.	R.	No. of Seams.	Thick.	Area in sqr. miles.	Am'nt in tons.
34	33	Two together amount to............	26 inches......	3	7,248,348
34	33	Two together amount tc............	2 feet..........	50	111,513,600
35	33	Two together amount to............	41 inches......	(?)	34,390,432
35	33	One.......................................	3 feet..........	36	120,434,688
36	33	One.......................................	1 foot.........	6	6,690,816
36	33	One.......................................	2½ feet......	36	100,362,240
37	33	One.......................................	3 feet..........	36	120,434,688
37	'33	One.......................................	1 foot.........	4	4,460,544
38	·33	One.......................................	4 feet..........	12	53,526,528
34	32	One.......................................	2½ feet......	3	8,363,520
34	32	One.......................................	1 foot.........	6	6,690,816
34	32	One.......................................	5 feet..........	10	55,756,800
34	32	One.......................................	1 foot.........	36	40,144,896
35	32	One.......................................	8 inches......	....	....
36	32	One.......................................	8 inches......	....	....
37	32	One.......................................	2 feet..........	20	44,605,440
38	32	One.......................................	3 feet..........	12	40,144,896
34	31	One.......................................	7 feet..........	36	281,014,272
35	31	One.......................................	1 foot.........	36	40,144,896
36	31	One.......................................	1 foot.........	32	35,684,252
37	31	Three together equal to............	6½ feet......	2	14,496,768
37	31	One.......................................	10 inches......	36	33,454,080
38	31	Two, 4½ feet and 1 foot..............	5½ feet......	9	55,109,232
34	30	One.......................................	2 feet..........	48	107,053,232
35	30	One.......................................	1 foot..........	36	40,144,896
36	30	One.......................................	6½ feet.........	2	14,496,768
36	30	One.......................................	1 foot..........	36	40,144,896
37	30	One.......................................	18 inches......	36	60,217,344
34	29	One.......................................	18 inches......	36	60,217,344

Vernon County Coalfields—Continued.

T.	R.	No. of Seams.	Thick.	Area in sqr. miles.	Am'nt in tons.
35	29	One....................................	2½ feet.........	18	40,181,120
36	29	One....................................	1 foot.........	30	33,454,080
37	29	One....................................	1 foot.........	36	40,144,896
		Total tons of Coal in county.....			2,650,816,252

OTHER MINERALS.

IRON ORE.

No thick or extensive deposits were observed. The lower Sandstones, especially those near the Coal, often enclosed deposits of Kidney Ore or Ochre, but the first often contained too much Sand. Beds of the other may be found extensive enough to form a good Ochre. We may also expect to find in the lower members good beds of Brown Hematite similar to that found in Cedar county.

The Shales near the base of Timber Hill enclose bands of Carbonate of Iron of several inches thickness. This would probably realize 40 to 50 per cent. of pure metallic Iron. The overlying debris was such that I could not determine the number or thickness of these layers.

GYPSUM.

This is found diffused in the Under Clays of the Coals. Its occurrence is mentioned above in the description of the various Coal beds. The principal observed localities were in the road just west of Moundville, near the base of Timbered Hill, and at Strong's, on the Little Osage. Its value in this country would only be to mingle with the soil when it is deficient in Lime.

FIRE CLAYS.

Most of the Coals are underlaid by beds of Clay suitable for making fire brick. On Marmaton, in Sec. 9, T. 36, R. 31, there is exposed 7 feet of Clay.

Near the base of Timbered Hill there is 3 feet and 3 feet at Strong's, on the Little Osage.

Nos. 46 and 51 of the General Section would probably make good fire brick.

HYDRAULIC LIME.

On Hatteen's land, three miles north of Nevada, is a Limestone that has been burned for hydraulic purposes. The bed occurs between layers of Lower Carboniferous Limestone, those above and below not being Hydraulic.

Limestone No. 50 of our Section is the rock used at Fort Scott for making Cement. I have not heard of its being used in Vernon, but it may be found in most of the mounds occurring a little above the lower Fort Scott Coal.

The Lower Carboniferous Limestones on Clear Creek and near Bellevoir and at Hatteen's, afford a useful material for burning into Lime.

BUILDING STONE.

The Sandstones afford the best building material. Good quarries are near Nevada, but the best may be opened on the waters of Clear Creek.

Even, firm and durable beds were observed at White Oak Mills, and formerly very good grindstones were made here as well as at several other places in the neighborhood, and were quite an article of export. The rock forms an excellent grit suitable for grindstones and coarse whetstones, and may in the future be a valuable source of revenue to the inhabitants. Besides the above, similar beds may be found in other parts of the county where the Sandstone is well developed.

SOILS AND PRODUCTS.

In Vernon we find about every variety of soil including rich, poor sandy, and of stiff Clay.

The bottoms on the principal streams are wide and very productive. The soil on the mounds and along their slopes may be considered the richest upland, and sometimes the mounds almost encircle extensive valleys of rich land. These valleys when nearly surrounded by mounds are not only of rich soil but are delightful spots on which to dwell.

One such is the Kauffman valley, located in Secs. 21, 28, 29, 32 and 33, of T. 37, R. 33. In the northern part of the next township south is an elevated plateau of rich land which slopes off and bears southwardly along Cottonwood Creek.

Near Pleasant Valley there is some good land. Another district of productive land is that in T. 38, Ranges 31 and 32.

The valley stretching off from Moundville southwardly lies beautifully for cultivation, and yields abundant crops of corn and wheat. Another rich valley lies along Upper Drywood and McKill's Creek. Around the mounds near Walker's Station, are also some bodies of good land.

The lands will generally with proper cultivation, yield 50 to 60 bushels of Corn per acre. When not properly cultivated 35 to 50.

When the slopes from the mounds blend off into the neighboring valleys and stretch off beyond into a wide plateau, the land is not so rich; of such is part of T. 36, Ranges 32 and 33, near the Marmaton. The prairie north of Boswell's, shows a portion of very good land, but it is often spotted with lighter or poorer soil. At the origin of some of the dry branches in this vicinity the banks break off suddenly, soon disclosing a light-ash soil. These places have also very much the appearance of Buffalo wallows. Most of the soils east of East Drywood and south of Marmaton are either quite sandy or else of a thin light-ash color. The latter we find around Nevada and on the prairies south. At the edge of the timber the soil is nearly always sandy, supporting a growth of Black Jack, Post Oak and Black Hickory. Sometimes a few Chincapin Oak bushes appear, but Black Jack is generally the leading tree, extending first and farthest out on the prairie.

The soil in R. 29 is generally very sandy.

These soils of course are not so rich as the first named, but during seasonable years good crops can be produced. During the year 1873, up to August 1, the corn gave promise of an abundant yield, but lack of after rains caused premature drying of the blade, and the bright hopes indulged in were disappointed. On the sandy Black Jack lands the wild grape grows very finely, and should there be a great demand for grapes and wine, we could point to no more suitable soil than these lands.

But few orchards were observed, and no vineyards.

This county is well adapted for growing wheat and oats, and good crops are raised. Castor beans are a successful crop, producing 50 bushels to the acre.

TIMBER.

The bottoms of the Marmaton, Little Osage, the Drywoods and Clear Creek furnish an abundant supply of good Timber. White Oak is probably not to be found in the western part of the county, but is abundant near Clear Creek. On the valleys of the Marmaton, Little Osage and Osage Rivers, we find numerous Pecan trees. Other useful trees observed were Shell-bark Hickory, Burr Oak, Ash, Elm, Black Walnut and Birch.

WATER.

There are not many springs in this county. They may be found on the waters of Clear Creek, in the South-east part of the county, and sometimes flowing from beneath Limestone in the western part.

The chief source of water supply is from wells or cisterns. Cisterns are more reliable for good water, as the well water is often impregnated with disagreeable salts. In some neighborhoods wells have to be bored very deep to reach water. In Southeast Sec. 20, T. 35, R. 32, a well 80 feet deep passed through chiefly Sandstone with some Shale. The water obtained is bituminous, and a black tar coating is formed on the well rope.

A small spring on Shiloh creek flowing from Shales indicates a slight bituminous taste.

On Clear Creek, in the eastern part of the county, are several very fine Sulphur Springs of very pleasant taste. The water seems to contain chiefly sulphuretted hydrogen. The flow being abundant and the water pleasant and healthy, give promise that at some future day they may be much resorted to.

Three miles North of Nevada is a pleasant Chalybeate Spring. In Nevada, at Dr. Hunter's, there is a strong Epsom Salt Well. In Southeast part of T. 37, R. 33, some of the water is of disagreeable taste, and is unfit for cooking. It seems strongly impregnated with Sulphuric acid, and this, chemically united with Lime, gives a very unpleasant taste to the water flowing through some of the Shale beds of the lower Coal Measures.

REPORT OF C. J. NORWOOD.

MINERAL SPRINGS.

In N. W. Sec. 28, ? T. 36, R. 31, there is a fine Chalybeate Spring. At present no care is taken of it. A "gum" holding 5 or 6 gallons, forms the reservoir, the water coming up at the bottom and issuing from under Sandstone near by. The water flows at a rate of about 2 gallons per minute, and is very pleasant to the taste. In the hottest days the water is as cool as if ice were in it. I am told that during the summer this spring is much visited by parties at and near Nevada City.

In S. E. qr. S. W. qr. Sec. 16, T. 35, R. 29, Mr. J. S. Grisham, also has 2 fine Sulphur Springs. The stream bubbles up from a dark-gray Sand, and is quite strong. A Shaly bed containing Iron pyrites occurs below the spring, but whether this has anything to do with the properties of the water, is doubtful. The water is pleasant to the taste, and the springs afford a great deal of the water.

On Capt. Houtzes' land, in N. W. S. E. Sec. 1, 36, R. 29, there are 2 Sulphur Springs. The water here, like at the former localities, is collected in "gums." In spring No. 1, which is on the south side of a small branch emptying into Clear Creek, the water flows at the rate of three-fourths of a gallon a minute. Spring No. 2, which is on the north side of the creek, has a much bolder stream, flowing at the rate of 3 gallons a minute. These form the head of a branch flowing into Clear Creek, and the water in each is very pleasant to the taste.

Samples were collected for analysis.

COAL MEASURES.

The following embraces an account of the various localities of Coal visited:

At "Blue Mound," in N. W. quarter N. E. quarter Sec. 10, T. 37, R. 30, bituminous Shale, which overlies Coal No. 14 of the General Section, is seen at the base of the mound, 145 feet from the top. The mound is capped with Limestone equivalent to the lowest seen at Butler, Bates county. The rocks seen on this mound, with the description of each, are included in Section A, on a succeeding page. The Coal was covered so that the thickness could not be determined.

The same (?) bed is found at Mr. Brown's, in N. E. quarter Sec. 2, T. 37, R. 30. The Coal itself was covered by water at the time of my visit, but the following were exposed above it:

No. 1. 5 feet light blue and ochreous argillaceous Shale, with concretions of yellow Ochre. The lower part has two thin streaks of Coal, and is marked by remains of plants.

No. 2. 1 foot + hard semi-bituminous Shale.

No. 3. ——? Coal.

A short distance from where the foregoing were seen, an outcrop of gray Sandstone, whose position is above No. 1, was observed. At "Timbered Hill," a high mound in N. W. qr. Sec. 14, T. 37, R. 31, higher rocks and Coal were found. The following is a Section of the strata exposed.*

---

* The fossils of each stratum, with a more careful description of the rocks, will be found in Sec. A, on a succeeding page.

No. 1. 10 feet gentle slope from hill top.
No. 2. 1 foot Limestone. Top rock at Fort Scott.?
No. 3. 11 feet Slope.
No. 4. 3 feet + Sandstone.
No. 5. 50 feet Slope, covered with fragments of Sandstone.
No. 6. 24 feet Slope, with outcroppings of argillaceous Shale at the top and bottom.
No. 7. 4 inches + Limestone.
No. 8. 5½ feet Slope.
No. 9. 2 to 4 feet mottled Limestone.
No. 10. 4 feet Slope.
No. 11. 2 feet + Limestone.
No. 12. 3 feet Slope.
No. 13. 14 inches ashy-blue Limestone.
No. 14. 3 feet bituminous Shale.
No. 15. 2½ feet Shale—calcareous.
No. 16. 6 inches blue sandy Ironstone.
No. 17. 16 feet Slope.
No. 18. 11 inches Coal.
No. 19. 36 feet Slope to water in Marmaton.

Timbered Hill was settled by two French gentlemen named La Timbre. In consequence it was called "La Timbre Hill," this was corrupted into "Timbered Hill," and now it is so called by some, ignorant of the source whence it receives its name. The latter, however, is a very appropriate name, as the mound is thickly timbered, with also a great deal of underbrush, and is sometimes called Brushy Mound.

About three-quarters of a mile south of the mound, at a ford of Marmaton, in S. W. qr. Sec. 14, T. 37, R 31, lower rocks are exposed, including two beds of Coal. The upper bed is from 2 to 3 feet thick, and is rotten at the outcrop. It is No. 23 of the General Section, and may be the "Marais des Cygnes Coal" of Bates county, and the northwest part of this. The second Coal is about 25 feet below the upper, and is 20 inches thick. This is No. 18 of the General Section.*

A full description of the strata here, will be found included in Sec. A.

At the group of mounds, in the vicinity of Walker, two Coal beds are found exposed, associated rocks equivalent, in part, to those seen on Timbered Hill and Blue Mound. These mounds are known, I believe, both as the "Howard" and the "Dodson Mounds.

The following is a General Section of the rocks, etc., exposed:

---

*It is also seen at Mr. Shaver's, (?) in Bates county, in S. W. N. E. Sec. 2, T. 38, R. 30.

No. 1. 2 feet coarse Sandstone.
No. 2. 8 feet Slope.
No. 3. 8 feet drab and blue Limestone.
No. 4. 6 feet Slope.
No. 5. 6 feet Limestone—mottled color.
No. 6. 11 feet Slope.
No. 7. 6 inches ashy-blue Limestone.
No. 8. 2 feet Slope.
No. 9. 6 inches + bituminous Shale, No. 14, Timbered Hill Sec.
No. 10. 11 feet Slope.
No. 11. 5 feet Clay.
No. 12. 18 inches Coal.
No. 13. 29 feet Slope.
No. 14. 3 to 4 feet calcareo–bituminous Shale.
No. 15. 2½ feet Coal. Lower Coal at Ford of Marmaton, south of Timbered Hill.
No. 16. 20 to 35 feet Slope, to prairie level.

Both of the Coal beds have been worked a little here, and are of fair quality. Upon the supposition that the three-foot Coal seen at Marmaton Ford, is *persistent* in this direction, it may be looked for as being present in No. 13 of the foregoing Section, its place being about 20 feet above No. 14. It, however, may not be present, and the space filled up by Shales, etc. In the former case there would be three beds of Coal on these mounds—one of 18 inches, one of 2½ feet, and one of 2½ to 3 feet in thickness—making a total thickness of from 6½ to 7 feet.

The following is a General Section of the Rocks, etc., on

Blue Mound, (A,) Timbered Hill, (B.) Marmiton Ford, (C) and the Walker Mounds (D).

SECTION A.

No.	Feet.	Inch's	DESCRIPTION OF STRATA.	Locality
1	10	....	Slope from top of Timbered Hill...............................	
2	1	....	Compact, drab Limestone, weathering, ash color, and containing *Spirifer lineatus*..................................	B.
3	11	....	Slope..	
4	3	....	Buff Sandstone...	B.
5	50	....	Slope covered with fragments of Sandstone...............	B.
6	10	....	Slope	

SECTION A—*Continued.*

No.	Feet.	Inch's	DESCRIPTION OF STRATA.	Locality
7	2	....	Very coarse-grained Sandstone, made up of large and small grains of Quartz. (Local ?)........................	D.
8	3	....	Drab and blue Limestone, weathering, buff and chocolate color. Abounds in *Chaetetes milleporaceus*, and *Fusulina cylindrica*, and contains *Athyris*, *Spr. lineatus*, *Lophophyllum proliferum*, etc.; equivalent to the lowest Limestone at Butler, Bates county........	
9	1	....	Slope.........................	
10	....	4+	Hard, dark blue Limestone, containing *Ch. mesoloba* and *Rhynconella Osagensis*. May be No. 43................	B.
11	3	6	Slope.........................	
12	4—6	....	Drab and gray mottled Limestone, Sometimes abounds in *Productus muricatus*.....................................	B and D.
13	4	....	Slope.........................	
14	3	....	Blue Limestone, with a thick chocolate colored crust. Abounds in *Ch. mesoloba*, and contains *Prod. muricatus* and *Fistulipora nodulifera*.......................	B.
15	3	....	Slope.........................	
16	1	2	Ashy blue, tolerably fine-grained Limestone, weathering buff. Fossils are *Chonetes mesoloba*, *Prod. costatus* and *Spr. cameratus*	B and D.
17	3	....	Bituminous Shale.........................	B and D.
18	2	6	Blue and ochreous calcareo-argillaceous Shale..............	B.
19	....	6	Sandy Ironstone, with *Crinoid* columns......................	B.
20	11	....	Slope.........................	
21	5	....	Clay.........................	D.
22	1	6	Good Coal, sometimes only 11 inches........................	B and D.
23	3	....	Fire-Clay.........................	B.
34	6	....	Sandstone.........................	C.
25	3	....	Coal—varies from 30 to 36 inches............	C.
26	7	....	Gypsiferous Shale.........................	C.
27	....	2	*Tutenmergel*.........................	C.
28	....	2	Coal	C.
29	....	6	Sandstone, with *Stigmaria ficoides*	C.
30	1	....	Fire-Clay	C.

No.	Feet.	Inch's	DESCRIPTION OF STRATA.	Locality
31	15	....	Dark semi-bituminous Shale, with layers of Carbonate of Iron, (Iron Stone,) and a thin Limestone bed, abounding in *Prod. muricatus*, and containing *Discina, Pr. Nebrascensis* and *Ch. mesoloba*...................	C.
32	2	. 6	Bituminous Slate, containing *Brachiopoda*.....................	C and D.
33	2	6	Coal, sometimes only 20 inches..............................	C and D.
34	2	....	Fire-Clay...	C.
35	45	....	Slope...	
36	2+	....	Sandstone..	A.
37	44	....	Slope...	
38	1+	....	Bituminous Shale..	A.
39	(?)	....	Coal...	A.

Four miles north-east of Walker, near the M. K. & T. R. R., Mr. Haines has opened a Coal bank. It is worked both by drifts and shafts, the manner owing altogether to the nature of the surface. The Coal, as seen where it had been worked by a drift, is 2½ feet thick, and not of very good quality, being crossed by seams of Iron Pyrites. A good opportunity for examining the Coal was not afforded, and no reliable opinion can be given as to its quality. It is covered by seven feet of Sandstone, which I regard as the equivalent of No. 24, Section A.

On the road to Nevada, Sandstone which underlies the lowest Coal at Walker's, and which is called the "Clear Creek Sandstone," in this report, is seen cropping out at intervals from Walker to Nevada. The prairie is undulating, sometimes making long, sweeping slopes, and the Sandstone is the surface Rock for long distances.

It is exposed around Nevada City, and on the Marmiton. In N. E. S. E., Sec. 18, T. 36, R. 31, on the Marmiton, there is 12 feet of it exposed 4 feet above the water.

Three-quarters of a mile down stream, it is seen reaching a thickness of 40 feet. One quarter of a mile still further down, it forms the face of the Bluffs, varying from 40 to 60 feet in thickness, and at one place on the creek even attaining a thickness of about 75 feet. The major part of it is excellent building Stone, and can be easily quarried. Springs issue from beneath this Sandstone, but they nearly all are of a slightly Chalybeate nature—some of them very much so.

On a small creek emptying into the Marmiton, one mile and a half west of Nevada, part of the strata below this Sandstone come to view in the following order:

No. 1. 12 feet gentle Slope from prairie.
No. 2. 16 feet slope at an angle of 35 deg., covered with fragments of Sandstone.
No. 3. 8 feet buff and gray Sandstone. " Clear Creek Sandstone."
No. 4. 6 feet Slope.
No. 5. 10 feet deep blue, arenaceous Clay.
No. 6. 12 to 18 inches Coal.
No. 7. 18 inches Fire Clay.

On Mrs. Wade's land, in S. half, S. E. qr. Sec. 30, T. 36, R. 31, Coal, which is probably equivalent to No. 14 of General Section, is exposed. Twenty feet of thick-bedded, gray Sandstone rests upon it. The "Clear Creek Sandstone " is exposed on Mr. Hatteen's farm, in N. E. qr. Sec. 20, T. 36, R. 31, with sub-carboniferous Limestone still below. The Section there is:

No. 1. Slope.
No. 2. 33 feet "Clear Creek Sandstone."
No. 3. 22 feet Slope.
No. 4. 8 feet sub-crystalline, gray and bluish gray Crinoidal Limestone. This is divided in three parts, thus:

> (a) 3½ feet crystalline, bluish gray Limestone.
> (b) 1 foot Limestone; is not so crystalline as a, harder, bluish drab in color, weathering chocolate brown, and contains Chert.
> (c) 3½ feet Limestome like a.

Division b is said to make excellent cement, and a and c make fine Lime. The rock is much quarried and used for the latter purpose. *Spirifer Keokuk* was the only fossil found. This may be equivalent to the Limestone seen on Osage River above Bellevoir, at Stratton's.

At Messrs. Foland & Leslie's Bank, in N. E. part S. E. S. E., Sec. 8, T. 36, R. 31, Coal is seen, the exact position of which, in regard to the other rocks of the county, could not be determined. It, however, evidently occupies a place in the " Clear Creek Sandstone Series," and is very likely towards the bottom.

A Section of the strata is:

No. 1. 6 feet Slope, covered with fragments of Sandstone.
No. 2. 6 feet + gray Sandstone.
No. 3. 3 feet Slope.

No. 4. 9 feet ochreous Shale.
No. 5. 9 feet light blue, arenaceous, slaty Shale.
No. 6. 15 to 18 inches good Coal.
No. 7. 8 inches calcareo-arenaceous band.
No. 8. 6 feet arenaceous Shale, sometimes passing into Sandstone.
No. 9. 2 to 11 inches Coal. Not persistent at this place; thins out in a distance of 50 feet down stream.
No. 10. 2 feet Fire Clay, with *Stigmaria ficoides.*
No. 11. 6 feet blue and drab argillaceous Shale, with thin layers of Ironstone.

Coal, equivalent to the upper bed at Fort Scott, (Kan.,) is found at Mr. Thaler's, at or near the head of Willow Creek. It is reported to be from 11 to 18 inches thick, but being covered when the locality was examined, but little can be said about it. It is said by blacksmiths to answer their purposes admirably.

At Mr. Samuel Parker's, in S. W. qr. N. E. qr. Sec. 34, T. 38, R. 32, on Reed's Creek, Coal is found which I am inclined to place as equivalent to John Schrum's, (Bates county.) It is overlaid by—

No. 1. 4 to 6 inches chocolate colored Limestone abounding in fossils, viz.:
         Rhynchonella Osagensis, Ch. mesoloba, Athyris, Prod. muricatus and
         Spr. lineatus—the latter very abundant.
No. 2. 2 inches green Clay.
No. 3. 2 to 3 inches layer of buff, sandy Limestone.
No. 4. 4 inches olive colored Shale.
No. 5. 11 inches dark blue Clay.
No. 6. 3 feet bituminous Shale.
No. 7. 4 feet blue and green Clay streaked with yellow.
No. 8. 18 to 20 inches Coal of good quality. Is hard, shiny, black, breaks in
         angular fragments, and is apparently free of Sulphur.

One hundred yards down stream, 3 feet of blue and ochreous Clay, containing *Stigmaria ficoides,* is exposed below No. 8. *Productus muricatus* and *Spr. lineatus* are the only fossils seen in the Limestone (No. 1) at this place.

Another Coal is seen on Mr. Parker's place, in N. W. part N. E. qr. N. E. qr. Sec. 34, T. 38, R. 32, with the following order in the overlying strata:

No. 1. Long, gentle Slope.
No. 2. 1 foot hard, dark blue, pyrito-calcareous bed abounding in fossils, viz.:
         Ch. mesoloba, Ch. Verneuiliana, Prod. muricatus, Athyris, Lophophyllum proliferum, and a small *Orthoceras(?).*
No. 3. 5 inches yellow Clay, with streaks of Coal.

No. 4.   15 inches Coal, rotten at the outcrop.

No. 5.   5 feet Slope.

No. 6.   ? Coal covered by water. No. 8 of preceding Section.

About three-quarters of a mile above the foregoing locality, near Mr. Yates', 3 feet of Limestone, light drab, mottled with bluish drab spots, and weathering buff, is found 31 feet above the creek. Five feet below it, 8 feet of Shale and Sandstone are seen. This resembles the lowest Limestone at Butler, Bates county, very much, and may be its equivalent. Its position is above the Coals seen at Parker's, but the exact distance could not be determined. In N. E. N. E. Sec. 22, T. 38, R. 32, 7 feet of Sandstone was found resting on the Limestone just mentioned.

At Mr. Bogan's Coal Bank, in S. E. N. W. Sec. 31, T. 38, R. 32, we find—

No. 1.   4 inches shelly, pyritiferous Limestone, with *Lophophyllum*, *Ch. meso-loba*, *Pr. muricatus* and *Hemipronites*.

No. 2.   3½ feet blue Clay.

No. 3.   13 inches Coal.

No. 4.   6 inches Fire Clay.

No. 5.   5 feet Slope.

No. 6.   2 feet blue Clay.

No. 7.   21 inches hard, dark blue, rhomboidally-jointed Limestone, (No. 43 of General Section.)

No. 1 is not constant; sometimes it is seen resting 6 inches over the Coal. A short distance down stream, the Coal rests on No. 7. Unfortunately, the rocks could not be traced, so as to determine whether the Coal rises again. No. 7 seems to be taken up with Clay and Marlite. There is a fault between this place and a point one-quarter of a mile down stream. At the latter place, Sandstone (which occurs above No. 1 of foregoing Section) is seen dipping 10° N. 50° W., while only a hundred or so feet up stream, it lies horizontally.

The "Fort Scott Marble," (No. 43,) with its associated Coal, is found at Mr. Geo. W. Harris', in S. E. S. W. Sec. 31, T. 37, R. 33, on Little Osage River. It is 14 inches thick, containing fossils; 3 feet below it there are 3 feet of bituminous Shale, with large spherical concretions, of dark-blue bituminous Limestone. Below this the Section is:

No. 6.   6 inches dark pyrito-calcareous Shale, with small concretions.

No. 7.   2½ feet blue Clay.

No. 8.   12 to 14 inches Coal—No. 33.

No. 9.   8 feet ochreous and blue Clay.

No. 10.   2½ feet (?) Coal—No. 31. ?

No. 11.   3 feet Slope to water.

The Sandstone overlying the Fort Scott Marble, is the formation farther down the Little Osage. This Limestone (Fort Scott Marble) is seen cropping out in Sec. 33, (?) T. 36, R. 32, exhibiting a thickness of 2½ feet, with Shaly Sandstone above.

At Mr. Henry Shackelford's, in N. E. S. E. Sec. 3, T. 35, R. 33, Coal No. 33, of General Section, is found. It is covered at one place by from 2 to 2½ feet of bituminous Shale, containing *Discinu Missouriensis* and a *fish tooth ;* at another it is overlaid by 2 feet ochreous and blue Clay, with large concretions.

At Mr. Alfred Cox's, in N. W. qr, of S. E., Sec. 3, T. 35, R. 33, it is again found. The same Coal is also worked at Mr. Hugh Cox's, in N. W. qr. N. W. qr. Sec. 3, T. 35, R. 33, and at Mr. Buck Cox's, in S. W. S. W. Sec. 34, T. 36, R. 33. Adjoining the latter place, in S. E. S. E., Sec. 33, T. 36, R. 33, the Coal comes to view once more.

At this place it is overlaid by—

No. 1. 1 foot Slope ; concretions of dark-blue bituminous Limestone, containing *Goniatites*, occurs at the top.
No. 2. 2 feet bituminous Shale.
No. 3. 2½ to 4 feet blue Shale and ochreous Clay.
No. 4. Coal—No. 33.

A higher Coal is exposed on an irregularly shaped mound, in N. W. qr. S. W., Sec. 4, T. 35, R. 33, on land belonging to Mr. Fairchild. It is about 85 feet above Cox's, and is equivalent to the Fort Scott Coal, No. 52 of General Section. The bed is 7 inches + thick, overlaid by 1 foot bituminous Shale, with large concretions disseminated. The Fort Scott Marble is found in the road one-quarter of a mile W. of N. of the mound, being about 80 feet below the Coal.

At Mr. Jaret Meddlin's, in S. W. qr. Sec. 5, T. 35, R. 33, there are three Coal seams, all close together, all of which are below the Fort Scott Marble. They occupy a place in No. 32 of the General Section, about the top. The upper bed may be No. 33, but this can not be said with certainty.

The following is a Section of the strata :

No. 1. 23 feet Slope, from Fort Scott Marble.
No. 2. 5 feet ochreous Shale.
No. 3. 10 to 12 inches Coal.
No. 4. 10 feet ochreous Clay.
No. 5. 1 foot good Coal.
No. 6. 9 inches to 3 feet pyritous Shale ; thins out to the west.
No. 7. 9 inches to 17 inches Coal, very good quality.
No. 8. ——? blue Clay.

It will be seen that there is a total thickness of from 2 feet 10 inches, to 3 feet 5 inches of Coal. This can be worked by stripping, for a considerable area.

The Fort Scott Coal is worked quite extensively about one mile and a half S. W. of Clayton, by the OSAGE COAL AND MINING COMPANY. The Coal is from 12 to 28 inches thick, and of good quality. It is compact, shiny-black when fractured, and is apparently pretty free from sulphur. I am told that it is, and it has every appearance of being, excellent smithing Coal. It has a rusty appearance between the perpendicular joints, and (as does the Fort Scott Coal, wherever I have seen it,) assumes a reddish brown exterior (due to Oxide of Iron) when taken from the bank and left exposed to the atmosphere. There are about twelve openings at this place, and the Coal is worked by stripping.

At the N. E. part of Clayton, the bituminous Shale (No. 36, Gen. Sec.) which is seen at B. Cox's, crops out in a little ravine near Mrs. Dunn's house, indicating the presence of Coal, No. 33, of General Section. Two miles and a half S. W. of Clayton, the Fort Scott Marble is exposed along a ravine in the prairie. This is the N.W.qr. Sec. 28, T. 35, R. 33, and Coal may be considered as being present from 10 to 15 feet below the surface. At the Iron bridge across Big Drywood, near the mouth, in N. E. qr. Sec. 7, T. 35, R. 32, the Clear Creek Sandstone is exposed for 46 feet. At the edge of the water, 8 inches of Coal, (No. 14) is found below the Sandstone. Some of the Sandstone beds are excellent for building purposes, and, as such, have been used in the construction of the bridge piers.

At J. S. Grisham's, in S. E. S. W., Sec. 16, T. 35, R. 29, Coal (No. 10) is seen near his Sulphur Springs. About 37 feet above it the Clear Creek Sandstone is exposed, exhibiting a thickness of 40 feet. There is said to be a Coal visible under this Sandstone further up the creek one-quarter of a mile below Grisham's; 5 feet of Keokuk Limestone was seen in the creek, forming the bed of the creek in part. The fossils found are *Rhynconella subcuneata, Spr. Keokuk, Hemipronites Keokuk*, a small *Productus*, an *Euomphalus* or *Straparollus, Chonetes* and *Zaphrentis*.

The Clear Creek Sandstone is the formation along Little Clear Creek. No Coal was seen or heard of as being exposed on this stream. This Sandstone also underlies that section of country included in Rs. 29, 30 and 31, T. 35.

In the eastern part, Sec. 25, T. 37, R. 29, the country is very hilly, sometimes rising in mounds 100 feet above Kitten Creek, near by. The tops of the mounds are capped with large fragments of Clear Creek Sandstone, which are very ferruginous. Some of the fragments have large cracks, which have been filled up with oxide of Iron. Farther north, in Sec. 24, of the same township, ferruginous Sandstone, with sandy Limonite is found on a ridge. The Iron ore is too silicious to be of practical value.

The country generally, bordering on St. Clair county, is hilly, consisting of mounds and high ridges, sloping gradually off to the prairie level, with the "Clear Creek Sandstone" as the cap rock. Sometimes this is quite ferruginous, so much so as to resemble Hematite, and some persons have supposed it to be valuable as an Iron ore, but it is not. A regular outcrop of the Sandstone is hardly ever seen, it merely coming to the surface. This Sandstone is seen occupying the prominent points from Sec. 24, T. 37, R. 29, along Clear Creek, passing through the western borders of St. Clair and Cedar counties as far up as T. 37, R. 29, and beyond.*

On McCarty's Branch, in S. E. quarter, Sec. 6, T. 34, R. 29, Keokuk Limestone is exposed, and at Mr. Reavis', in E. half lot 2, Sec. 6 of the same township, Coal (No. 4 of general section,) is found 35 feet above the Limestone, and is 10 inches or more thick. Mr. S. H. Avery has the same Coal on his place in S. W. quarter Sec. 7, T. 34, R. 29, where it is from 14 to 20 inches thick, and dipping 10° S. 47° W. It is also on Mr. Rodman's place, in S. E. quarter (?) Sec. 12, T. 34, R. 30.

The Marais des Cygnes Coal (No. 23 of general section) has been opened by the Messrs. Ferry, in S. E. quarter, Sec. 10, T. 34, R. 31. They report it as being "from 4½ to 5 feet thick, resting on hard, black slate" (calcareous Shale?). It is overlaid by 6 feet of Soil, Clay and Drift, the Drift coming immediately over the Coal. The Clear Creek Sandstone is exposed in the N. W. quarter, Sec. 15, about one-half mile south-west from Ferry's. In this region it is generally bituminous in part, the bitumen often oozing out and forming small pools of a tarlike substance. This mineral Tar is sometimes used by the farmers in the neighborhood of these "springs"—as they are called— on the axles of their wagons, and I am told it answers their purpose as well as pine Tar. In N. E. N. E. Sec. 16, T. 34, R. 31, Mr. Maxwell in digging a well, passed through the Clear Creek Sandstone, reaching Coal (No. 14 General Section). He reports it as being 2½ feet thick.

Coal (No. 33) is found on Mr. S. W. Harrison's land, in N. E. S. E. Sec. 1, T. 34, R. 33, from 14 to 20 inches thick. There is also a bed of good, red Clay Paint on his place, one foot or more in thickness. Mr. H. mixed some of the earth with water and painted his fire-place, the color produced being reddish brown. On a mound, at Mr. Drum-

*This resembles the "Ferruginous Sandstone" of Prof. Swallow, and might very easily be taken for it. It is, however, undoubtedly a member of the Coal Measures.

mond's, in Sec. 7, T. 34, R. 33, the top Coal seen at Fort Scott is found. The following is a section of the rocks:

No. 1. 2 feet drab and gray, and drab spotted with brown, brittle Limestone, in thin layers, *S pr.* (*Martinia*) *lineatus*, *Murchisonia* and *Lophophyllum proliferum*, were found.

No. 2. 5 feet Slope.

No. 3. 4 feet nodular, drab, fine grained Limestone, with a thick buff crust, containing *B. percarinatus*, *Spr. lineatus ?* *Pleurotomaria sphærulata*, etc.

No. 4. 3 feet bituminous Shale, with small concretions containing *Discina* and a *Fish tooth*.

No. 5. 1 foot Coal—No. 52 of Gen. Sec.

No. 6. Long gentle slope to prairie level.

SUB-CARBONIFEROUS—"HALLEY'S BLUFF," ETC.

OBSERVATIONS ALONG OSAGE RIVER.

The Clear Creek Sandstone is found cropping out in the hills at Belvoir, the lowest exposure being about 45 feet above the Osage. Below Belvoir it approaches nearer the water, and there is said to be Coal exposed beneath.

At Mr. John Stratton's Lime Kiln, about one mile above Belvoir, in S. E. quarter N. quarter Sec. 26, T. 38, R. 30, Sub-carboniferous Limestone comes to view. At this place we find 12 feet of crinoidal, bluish gray and gray crystalline Limestone, occupying a position 40 feet above the Osage. In the bottom 10 feet a concretionary bed of Chert occurs, containing *Bryozoans*, etc. The Limestone burns into excellent Lime, which is transported long distances for use.

One quarter of a mile above Stratton's, the Sandstone seen at Belvoir crops out 74 feet above the Limestone. It is very probable that this Limestone is brought up by a slight "uplift" in the rocks, as the overlying Sandstone seems to be thrown off to the east and west, being 45 feet above the Osage at Belvoir and from 25 to 30 feet above the river at Halley's Bluff. At the latter place the space between the Sandstone and the water is known to be filled by Coal Measure rocks.

HALLEY'S BLUFF,

Above Belvoir, on the Osage River. This place is quite celebrated in Vernon county on account of some "Old Diggings"—as they are termed—being there. They consist of a series of circular holes, 23 in number, dug down in the lower part of a thick Sandstone, which forms the face of the bluff, and is a member of the Coal Measures. The holes are 5 feet deep each on an average; they are larger at the bottom than the top, being three feet across at the top, and five and a half feet in diameter at the bottom. They are only from one to three feet apart, and follow the course of the outcrop of the Sandstone, which is north and south. They appear to have been made by some such instrument as a pick—faint marks as of such a tool being still visible. At one place there are six holes, side by side, forming a double row; the rest are single, following one after another. These are supposed by many to be the remains of excavations, made by French, Indians, Mexicans or Spaniards for mineral. In this I can not agree with them, as the only metal to be found in the rock is a little sandy Hematite and Ochre Concretions. From the regularity in the order, and the manner in which the holes were made, in the nicety with which they were formed, and regularity of size, I am led to believe them to be remains of old Caches made by former traders with Indians, or parties who were necessitated to conceal their goods. At one hole a peculiar mark (Fig. 4 a) was noticed cut in the Sandstone. Whether this was made by the maker of the hole, or at some later period, I will not undertake to say, though it is badly weather-worn. These holes are without doubt quite old. An Ash tree, two inches in diameter, was found growing out of one, and a Red Oak, four inches in diameter, out of another. Col. Boughan, who has lived near here for twenty-six years, and was one of the early settlers, says they were here when he came, and at that time no one knew for what purpose they were dug, nor how long ago. Figure 4 shows end-view of the parallel holes.

A section made here is as follows:

No. 1. Long Slope.
No. 2. 30 to 40 feet gray and buff Sandstone; the lower part containing concretions of very Silicious Hematite.
No. 3. 16½ feet Slope.
No. 4. 17 feet blue and buff Sandy Shale, with many lenticular concretions of Indurated Sandstone.
No. 5. 4 to 6 inches Coal.
No. 6. 4 feet Slope to Osage River.

It seems to be a prevailing, but mistaken opinion, that there is much mineral in this locality, such as Iron, Lead, etc. This is, no doubt, caused in a large degree by the supposition that the Caches are the remains of *old mines*. No Iron (except as noticed above) or Lead was found, nor is there any probability of there being any in *place*. It is *possible* for both Lead and Iron, as well as Gold and Silver or Copper, to have been brought here by *Drift;* but even if this were so, it would be a very unsafe venture to expend much capital in searching for it.

On Mr. Garrison's farm, in south part S. E. Sec. 36, T. 38, R. 30, there is said to have been an old furnace. Mr. Garrison informed me that formerly there was a chimney built of Sandstone and put together with mud, standing on the spot, but that he had taken it down. I could, therefore, form no opinion for what purpose it was built, nor was there anything else there to give me an idea. An outcrop of "Clear Creek Sandstone,"(?) 20 feet thick, with knife edges and thin seams of Coal intercalated, was observed. There is said to be, and probably is, a Coal seam a few feet below it.

There seems to be a disposition among some persons in this county to spend much money in searching for Lead, etc. It will be much better and more profitable, however, for them to invest their capital in opening up their great Coal region, for it is there their mineral wealth lies.

POTTERS' CLAY.

In the N. W. qr. Sec. 14, T. 35, R. 33, a good bed of Potters' Clay was found. Whether it belongs to the period of the Coal Measures or the Drift, we are unable to say—though we are inclined to place it in the latter formation. Exactly how thick the bed is could not be determined. Two feet and a half of it was exposed, and it extends over several acres. We understand that this is the Clay that is used in the Deerfield Pottery, and it is capable of making good earthenware—such as crocks, jugs, etc. The bed is overlaid by 2 feet of Local Drift, composed of Chert, Gravel, Ochre, etc.

MINERAL TAR.

On Mr. Markham's farm, in S. E. N. W. Sec. 24, T. 35, R. 30, there is a "Tar Spring" issuing from Sandstone. The Bitumen oozes out very freely, and bursts from the ground in several places. It comes up from a fissure in the Sandstone (Clear Creek?), and forms pools on the surface. Upon exposure it becomes quite hard—somewhat resembling Asphaltum. Mr. M. uses it on his wagon in the place of grease, pine tar, etc.

On Mr. Clay McCoy's land, (near Markham's,) there is also a quantity of Bitumen.

On Dr. Lipton's farm, formerly owned by Mrs. McCoy, in N. W. S. W. Sec. 27, T. 34, R. 30, there is both a Tar and Sulphur Spring. The water issues from beneath Sandstone and is slightly charged with Sulphur, while the Tar (Bitumen) issues from the rock itself, and flowing into the water gives both the taste of Tar and Sulphur. I am told that this water was formerly highly esteemed for its medicinal properties by persons living in the neighborhood.

SULPHUR.

On Mr. Batz's land, in Sec. 23, T. 34, R. 30, a good Sulphur Spring bursts from the ground, and is used by him.

CHAPTER XI.

BATES COUNTY.

BY G. C. BROADHEAD.

The area of this county is 873 square miles. Its surface is formed of agreeably undulating plains, terminating in the west part in a north and south range of mounds with other mounds in different parts of the county. These mounds, in the western part, are generally from 80 to 100 feet high. Six miles northeast of Butler, there are several of 80 to 100 feet in hight. From these, for 6 miles north-west, our route would pass low mounds to a continuous range extending 6 miles further. We then reach a broad valley, 100 feet lower than the mounds and over 6 miles wide. Crossing the Miami Fork, we are again in the region of the mounds, and these continue to the south line of the county, only occasionally interrupted for a few miles by the streams and valleys. South of the Marais des Cygnes, the county is for the most part hilly and rolling, occasionally broken by wide valleys along the streams. In R. 31, along the south county line, is a range of mounds extending east and west, passing south-westwardly and uniting with the high land in Vernon. Ts. 41 and 42, R. 29, are somewhat broken, the streams being separated by ridges often 200 feet high, rising by long slopes from the valleys. Passing southward over a rolling country to the waters of Panther Creek, we find a high, semi-circular ridge curving around the head of this creek, 240 feet in hight, and extending from Hudson south-west to Pleasant Gap and southeast for several miles. Within this high ridge or rim is the beautiful, undulating valley between Camp and Panther Creeks, elevated 30 to 40 feet above the stream. From there the country slopes off into a beautiful plain towards Prairie City and Papinsville.

A line passing north-west from the north-east part of T. 39, R. 29, to the north-west part of the county will touch along the principal dividing ridge and probably the highest ground in the county. It will also divide the waters of Grand River on the north from those of the Osage on the south. The principal tributaries of Grand River are Deep Water, Cove Creek, Peter Creek, Elk Fork, Mingo, the Deer Creeks and Mormon Fork. These generally start from broken depressions in the prairie, and pursue their course with increasing width of valley. Some of the valleys are sometimes a quarter to one-half mile and more in width, blending into a little more elevated plain. Grand River Bottoms are wide, with occasional ponds and marshes.

The chief tributaries of the Osage, making southward from the ridge above named, are Mulberry Creek, Miami Fork and Panther and Camp Creeks, with other lesser streams—as Shaw Branch, Willow Creek, Double Branches, Mound Branch, and Bone Creek and Knob Creek, forks of the Miami.

The banks of the Osage are generally about 25 feet high. Its channel being often full, it is rare that it can be forded, even at very few places. With some necessary improvements in the channel, it could easily be made navigable for light draft boats every year up to Papinsville. This place is 240 miles by boat from the mouth of the Osage, and light draft steamers have occasionally been up to this point. The bottoms of the Osage are generally 2 to 3 miles wide, but are often quite flat and marshy. Other streams have reasonably wide bottoms.

South of the Osage, we also find the streams originating from breaks in the high lands, thence passing off through widening flats to the Osage. These include Walnut Creek and its fork Gillen's Creek, Burnett's, Cottonwood and Muddy Creeks.

SURFACE GEOLOGY.

That this county has been at some former time subject to extreme denudation, is evident from the isolated mounds often seen. Their summits are probably of the same elevation as the higher ridges in the eastern part of the county. There has been a scouring from north to south, leaving isolated mounds protected from destruction by cappings of Limestone. In the eastern part of the county the Limestones on the summits are the same which may be found beneath the base of the western mounds. The force of the glacial action which has caused this has been such as to bear away all Drift pebbles from the surface excepting when on the higher grounds. On the mounds east of Pleasant Gap, are often seen quantities of rounded Gravel, mostly siliceous. The banks of Camp Creek have exposed at one place a bed of similar Gravel with Sand. Among these latter pebbles I obtained one of quartzitic conglomerate.

At Burnett's ferry the banks of the Osage show:

No. 1. Soil.
No. 2. 12 feet brown sandy Clay.
No. 3. 10 feet blue Clay.
No. 4. Bed of rounded siliceous Gravel.

These Gravel beds are occasionally met with at other places along the Osage. Wells dug at Papinsville show it to be 35 feet thick, of which 31 feet was yellow Clay resting on 4 inches of blue Clay and Gravel. Beneath this was found a thin sandy stratum enclosing a tooth of an extinct species of horse. Still beneath was a Gravel bed of 5 feet thickness, the pebbles mostly rounded and some adhering together. The pebbles are mostly siliceous, associated with fragments of Coal and Iron Ore.

From similar beds in the banks of the Marais des Cygnes, bones and tusks of Mastodon have been obtained.

COAL MEASURES.

Bates county is underlaid throughout by the Coal Measures. Including Upper, Middle and Lower Measures, there are in all about 500 feet of vertical thickness.

The Lower Measures, including the Marais des Cygnes Coal, crop out in T. 38, and part of T. 39, Ranges 29, 30 and 31, and the eastern part of R. 32. The lowest rocks to be seen in the county are on and near Panther Creek.

At the ford west of Rockville we find:

No. 1. Sandstone extending most of the way from the hill at Rockville probably, 30 to 40 feet.
No. 2. 5 feet drab sandy Shales.
No. 3. 6 feet blue Shales, enclosing three concretionary beds of Carbonate of Iron, each varying from 2 to 5 inches in thickness.
No. 4. 4 inch bed of carbonate of Iron in the creek.

These ores may in the future prove valuable.

The Lowest Coal Measure rocks in the county were penetrated in Mr. Seclinger's Well in E. hf. N. W. qr. Sec. 15, T. 38, R. 30. The well is 105 feet deep, and all Sandstone, (the upper 16 feet shaly) except the lower 4 feet of Slate. This Sandstone is seen in the Osage River at Papinsville.

Near the head of Panther Creek we find a gray Limestone supposed to be the equivalent of the lowest at Butler, 220 feet above the
valley of Camp Creek. This Limestone seems to crown the neighboring hills at many places. Below it there seems to be sandy Shales
nearly to the valley. Near the head of the eastern fork of Panther
the thick Coal is found. Judging from the topography of the surrounding country, this Coal must be about 220 feet below the gray
Limestone just above named.

In the south part of Sec. 28, T. 39, R. 29, is a remarkable exposure of 19 feet of dark bituminous Shale, mostly slaty, and enclosing
large dark bituminous Limestone concretions in the lower part. It is
very probable that this may be only a few feet above one of our thick
Coal seams.

The following section taken two miles north of Pleasant Gap,
shows the highest formations in this vicinity :

No. 1. Brown Sandstone.
No. 2. Rough coarse gray Limestone.
No. 3. 12 feet Slope.
No. 4. 10 inch brown Limestone contains *Fusulina*, *Chaetetes*, *Crinoid stems*
         Spirifer lineatus and *Spiriferina Kentuckensis*.
No. 5. 1 foot 6 inches Bituminous Shales.
No. 6. 9 inches hard black Slate, with many small round concretions.
No. 7. Sandy bituminous Shales.
No. 8. 6 feet soft sandy Shales.
No. 9. 26 feet Sandstone in flags.
No. 10. 1 foot calcareous Shale with fossils.
No. 11. 6 inches Shales with thin laminæ of Coal.
No. 12. 6 inches Coal.

This Group of rocks probably includes the equivalent of the Fort
Scott Group, but it is almost barren of Coal. The Limestones Nos. 2
and 4 of the above Section are found at the head of all the streams
north of this as far as the head-waters of Cove and Peters' Creeks.
They also crown the hills within 20 to 40 feet of their tops between
Pleasant Gap and Butler, and we suppose them to be the equivalents
of Nos. 50 and 55 of the General Section of the South-west Coal.

Sandstone No. 56 of our South-west Coal Section is the highest
rock seen just above the Limestones last spoken of. It is generally a
coarse deep brown Sandstone, sometimes affording a good building
material, but broken masses from it are often found in a pulverulent
condition, which mingling with the soil gives it a deep brown appearance.

The Iron set free also very much assists in promoting fertility.
This is found on all the higher ridges of R. 29 and T. 39. R. 30, and oc-

casionally on the north. Obscure remains of plants, with an occasional fragment of *Stigmaria ficoides* are sometimes found.

Near Johnstown are seen rocks whose position can be but little above the thick Coal of Panther Creek. At Shelton's, on Rockbottom Branch, are seen—

No. 1. 1 foot Ochrey Shales.
No. 2. 6 inches crumbling Coal.
No. 3. 13 feet Shale, with a few inches of nodular calcareous Ironstone near the middle.
No. 4. Sandy and Ochrey Shales.
No. 5. 1 foot blue and semi-bituminous Shales.
No. 6. 8 inches red Ferruginous Limestone, abounding in fossils, including *Pr. muricatus, Sp. planoconvexus, Sp. cameratus* and *Athyris* ——.
No. 7. 10 inches Slaty, Bituminous Coal.
No. 8. 18 inches (?) Coal.

This Section may be considered an exhibit of what we may find at many places on Deep Water for three or four miles north-west; also in the valley of Cove and Peter Creeks.

At Mrs. Hackler's the Coal has been mined in the bed of the creek, and on the hill over a hundred feet above is seen the brown Limestone, named above as occurring at the head of Panther Creek.

The following Section shows a partial connection of the Butler rocks with the Upper Coal Measures :

Section by C. J. Norwood, from the top of the Mound, in N. W. Sec. 28, T. 41, R. 30, southwest to a branch of Mound Creek.

No. 1. 15 feet Slope from the top of the mound.
No. 2. 3 feet Limestone (No. 72 Upper Coal Measures.)
No. 3. Outcrop of Sandstone.
No. 4. 100 feet Slope.
No. 5. 5 feet rough, gray Limestone, shelly at the top and containing *Chœtetes.*
No. 6. 27 feet Slope.
No. 7. 1 foot hard brecciated Conglomerate, made up of fragments of *Chœtetes,* Carbonate of Iron and Limestone ; contains *Sp. lineatus, Athyris* ——, *Ch. mesoloba, Fusulina* ——, *Archœocidaris* and *Lophophyllum*—Dip. 15 deg. S., 50 E.
No. 8. 4 inches Calcareous Shales, passing into a Conglomerate.
No. 9. 9 inches Conglomerate, like No. 7.
No. 10. 9 inches Shales, with streaks and knife edges of Coal, and inclosing a little Gravel.

No. 11. 1 foot Conglomerate—harder than No. 7; sometimes changing to a hard, coarse-grained, reddish Limestone.

No. 12. 13 feet sandy and Clay Shales, with many concretions, and contains beds of Carbonate of Iron, one of them 6 inches thick.

No. 13. 3 feet blue and drab coarse brittle Limestone, containing *Fusulina* and *Spirifer lineatus*.

No. 14. 6 inches green argillaceous Shales.

No. 15. 1 foot bituminous Shales, containing *Discina* and small flattened and round Concretions.

No. 16. 1 foot 6 inches dark-blue Shales, with a hard calcareo-sandy band near the bottom, containing *Chonetes* ——.

Butler Section.

No. 1. 2 feet 6 inches fine-grained and drab Limestone.

No. 2. 6 feet Limestone nodules, abounding in *Hemipronites* ——, *Spirifer cameratus*, *Productus costatus* and *P. Prattenianus*; also contains *Synocladia* ——, and *Sp. planoconvexus*. In some of the nodules *Fish-teeth* are found.

No. 3. 2 feet olive colored Clay Shales.

No. 4. 14 feet Slope.

No. 5. 1 foot 6 inches bluish-gray Limestone, containing *Sp. lineatus*, *Pr. costatus*, *Archæocidaris*, *Fusulina* and *Chætetes milleporaceus*.

AT BRAGGIN'S:

No. 6. 13 feet Slope.

No. 7. 3 feet outcrop of ash-blue Limestone.

No. 8. 4 inches dark, olive Calcareous Shales.

No. 9. 1 foot hard-jointed, bituminous Slate, with small Concretions.

No. 10. 2 feet sandy, bituminous Shales, with hard nodules of Limestone.

No. 11. 8 feet olive Shales.

No. 12. 8 inches Coal.

No. 13. 6 inches soft, thin Laminæ of bituminous Shales, with knife edges of Coal—seen at Braggin's.

No. 14. 25 feet Sandstone—at Butler.

No. 15. 4 feet ash-blue Limestone.

No. 16. 10 inches blue Shales.

No. 17. 10 inches bituminous Shales.

The upper part of this Section to No. 7 is seen at Butler; also Nos. 14 to 17. The intermediate beds are concealed at Butler, but exhibited at Braggin's, one mile north-east.

The beds seen next below this Butler Section are thick exposures of soft Sandstone, which, eastward on Mound Branch and four miles south between Possum Creek and the next Branch south, thicken up to 80 feet.

The upper beds of the Butler Section are just below the Mulberry Coal; in fact, I am inclined to think this Coal may yet be found in the highest hills at Butler. These are well developed on Miami Fork and Mulberry Creek. Their relation to the Coal can be obtained from our South-west Coal Section.

The beds from No. 67 to 72 and 73 are here generally found, and are well exposed at some of the Coal banks. Nos. 57 and 67 are connected by their intermediate beds at Jas. H. Becket's, in N. E. S. E. Sec. 10, T. 40, R. 32. The Limestones near No. 67 and above, appear at many places on Mulberry Creek, on the south side of Marais des Cygnes. These rocks appear nearly everywhere on the waters of Walnut Creek, and are also found at the head of Duncan's Creek.

Near New Home, and on the waters of Burnett's Creek, Prior's and Reed's Creeks, are beds which may be referred to the Fort Scott Coal. But the Fort Scott Coal itself was not certainly recognized. On the above named streams, further south in Vernon, are thin seams of Coal, which can certainly be referred to the Fort Scott Group. The evidence is that the Coal thins out north and north-east.

BEDS ABOVE THE MULBERRY COAL.

In Sec. 11, T. 40, R. 33, is a mound 85 feet above the general surface of the prairie. Its cap rock is a Limestone, apparently belonging to No. 74 of the General Section of the Upper Coal Measures of 1872. It abounds in *Lophophyllum* and also contains *Productus Nebrascensis*. On the prairie, 102 feet below, we find a Limestone which is probably No. 75 of the South-west Coal Section. The mounds in Secs. 27 and 28 of the next township north, 80 to 100 feet high, are also capped with Limestone of the Upper Coal Measures. The farthest limit south where we have recognized any Upper Coal Measures is on the top of a low mound in Sec. 5, T. 38, R. 33. On the mounds, 6 miles north-east of Butler, are also found Upper Coal Measure Limestones. The latter mounds are 120 to 140 feet high. Farther west and north-west the mounds develop into continuous ridges, for example at West Point and at Parkersville and north-west. They are all capped with Upper Coal Measure Limestones, including from No. 72 to No. 80 of our General Section of the Upper Coal Measures, 1872.

No. 72 contains some well preserved and fine specimens of fossils,

G.s—11.

including, near Holderman's, *Orthoceras*, (large species) *Nautilus*, (2 or 3 species, probably 4) *Cyrtoceras*, *Pleurotomaria* like *P. turbiniformis*, *Schizodus Wheeleri* and *Pinna peracuta*. In Sec. 11, T. 44, R. 33, *Productus Nebrascensis* and *Lophophyllum proliferum*.

ECONOMICAL GEOLOGY.

LOWER COAL BEDS.

The Lower Coal Series in Ts. 38 and 39 of Rs. 29 and 30, may include two or three seams. The lowest workable bed of 18 inches to 2½ feet has been worked on E. Shaver's land, near Willow Branch, 3 miles north-east of Papinsville; at Hamilton's, one mile north-east of Prairie City and 1½ miles north, near Shaw Branch; at J. M. Williams', on Camp Creek and on Panther Creek. The entire thickness of the bed at Williams' was not seen, only 1½ feet being exposed. Mr. Williams says it is 3 and 4 feet thick. If so it is the equivalent of Yates' Coal on the head of Panther Creek. From its topographical position I was inclined to refer it to a bed occupying a little lower horizon. A black, bituminous Limestone, with *Pr. muricatus* and a calcareous conglomerate, containing *Orthoceras Rushensis* occur just above it. This shows that the Coal here and that at Shavers may be the same, for a similar Limestone is also found at the latter place, containing, besides the above named fossils, *Productus Prattenianus*, *P. Nebrascensis*, *P. semireticulatus*, *Hempronites crassus* and a small *Lingula* and *Discina*. At Shavers the Coal is 22 to 26 inches thick.

Section on Hamilton's land in S. E. Sec. 7, T. 38. R. 29.

No. 1. Soil and Drift of rounded Pebbles.
No. 2. 1 foot 4 inches black Shales.
No. 3. 6 inches soft brown Shales.
No. 4. 2 feet 4 inches black bituminous Slate.
No. 5. 2 feet Coal with sulphurous incrustations on the surface.
No. 6. Fire Clay.

Hallam's Coal, examined by C. J. Norwood, in N. E. Sec. 11, T. 38, R. 30, is 1½ to 2 feet thick.

This coal underlies at least 5 sections in the north-east part of T. 39, R. 29, and dips beneath the surface of the townships west and north.

Section at Mrs. Annie Holt's, S. W. Sec. 14, T. 39, R. 29. (By J. C. Norwood.)

No. 1. 2 feet local Drift.

No. 2. 1 foot 6 inches argillo-calcareous Shales, with lenticular concretions of Ironstone.

No. 3. 6 inches semi-bituminous Shales.

No. 4. 27 inches bituminous Shales.

No. 5. 4 to 5 inches concretionary deep blue, hard pyritiferous Limestone, abounding in *Productus muricatus* and also containing *Spirifer cameratus, Athyris subtilita, Chonetes mesoloba, Polyphemopsis* and *Pleurotomaria spherulata.* A yellow Clay sometimes replaces the Limestone.

No. 6. 2 to 3 feet Coal, generally free from Sulphur.

No. 7. 5 feet blue argillaceous Shales.

No. 8. 2 feet blue argillaceous Shales containing Selenite.

No. 9. 2 to 4 inches good Coal.

No. 10. 3½ feet Fire Clay.

This Section closely resembles the Section taken at the foot of Timbered Mound on the Marmaton, in Vernon county. I regard the Coals as identical.

D. Wall's Coal is the same as Mrs. Holt's. It is found in a branch in S. E. N. W. Sec. 23, T. 39, R. 29, and is 3½ feet thick. A bed of concretionary Limestone, abounding in *Productus muricatus* and containing *Entolium-aviculatum, Hemipronites, Productus Nebrascensis, Naticopsis,* and *Chonetes mesoloba,** occurs immediately above. This is overlaid by bituminous Shale.

The coal also crops out 2½ feet thick at Dr. Taussy's, in N. E. S. E. Sec. 15; M. Baily's, S. W. N. W. Sec. 23; T. James, S. W. S. W. Sec. 13, and John's, in S. E. N. E. Sec. 14, all in T. 39, R. 29. In T. 38, R. 29, it it is also found on McDouglas' land in N. W. S. E. Sec. 11, and Mr. Campbell's, in S. W. S. E. Sec. 2. At Joseph Wilson's, in N. W. S. W. Sec. 14, T. 39, R. 29, the Coal is 3½ feet thick.

Near the head of Panther Creek Coal 3 to 4 feet thick is worked on the land of Gilbreath and of Yates in Lot 1, N. E. Sec. 4, T. 39, R. 29. A section of Yates' discloses:

No. 1. 4 feet thin layer of drab and brown Sandstone.

No. 2. 2 feet sandy, chocolate colored Shales.

No. 3. 2 feet sandy bituminous Shales.

No. 4. 6 inches calcareo-bituminous Shales with *Pr. semireticulatus.*

No. 5. 41 to 48 inches Coal.

---

*In these fossils we have an analogy to the Coal of Colonel Williamson, near Windsor, Henry county. We suppose it to be the same Coal.

Although thicker, the associated beds would indicate this to be the same Coal as that at Williams' and Shaver's. Further north and west this Coal has not been seen, but certainly could be reached by shafts sunk to the proper depth.

On low ground near Mormon Fork, in Sec. 35, T. 34, R. 32, I was informed that parties boring for oil, reported about the following section:

> No. 1. 30 feet Sandstone.
> No. 2. 270 feet Soapstone.
>> At 175 feet from the surface, 2 feet of Coal was reported, and 6 feet Coal at 225 feet.

The well was bored 525 feet, passing chiefly through Sandstone and Soapstone. There seemed to be a marked discrepancy in the statements of different persons as to the depth of the Coal. Mr. Holderman's account gives two seams at 300 to 320 feet, the upper 3 feet, the lower 9 feet, with a 3 feet bed at 80 to 100 feet. The latter is probably the Mulberry Coal ; the others are lower Coals—Nos. 18 and 23 of our Southwest Coal Section, and the same that are found at Yates'. In these two statements of the boring, although the reports show a discrepancy of from 80 to 100 feet, I still feel confident of the fact of the Coal existing at a depth of not over 350 feet from the surface.

On Panther Creek, a short distance below Yates', on the land of Jno. Atkinson, another thin seam crops out above the Coal of Yates'. The section here is:

> No. 1. Clay.
> No. 2. 8 feet Bituminous Shales, with a 1 foot layer of black septaria, 3 feet from top.
> No. 3. 6 inches hard, slaty Coal, passing from Cannel to Bituminous.
> No. 4. 16 to 18 inches Coal.
> No. 5. 3 feet gray Fire-Clay.
> No. 6. 5 feet blue Clay Shales.
> No. 7. Coal of Yates'.

The upper Coal—No. 4 of this Section—bears a close resemblance in its associated strata, to the lower Coal of Timbered Hill. If it is, we have three workable Coals within a short vertical distance of each other.

At Ewell's and Parker's are two seams near together, which seem to lie above the lower Timbered Hill Coal.

LOWER COAL SOUTH OF THE MARAIS DES CYGNES.

On Jno. Schrum's, in W. hf S. W. Sec. 30, T. 38, R. 31, is a 1 foot seam, with 2 feet Ochreous Clay beneath. A good seam of 18 inches is reported to be 2½ feet below this Coal, but was not exposed.

Hanley has the same Coal in N. E., Sec. 20, T. 38, R. 31.

In S. E. S. E., Sec. 31, T. 39, R. 31, on C. W. Bridgewater's land, we have:.

No. 1. Soil.

No. 2. 8 to 10 inches Clay.

No. 3. 6 inches Pyrito-calcareous bed abounding in fossils *Athyris, Sp. cameratus, Chonetes* —————, *Pr. costatus,* and *Pr. muricatus.*

No. 4. 18 inches to 2 feet good Coal.

At H. Bridgman's, in S. W. qr. of the same section, is the same Coal, but thicker, At the latter place it is 3½ feet thick, capped by 5 inches of Ochreous Shales, separating it from the Bituminous fossil bed.

Section at Benham's Coal Bank, N. E. S. E. Sec 36, T. 39, R. 32.

No. 1. Soil.

No. 2. 18 inches Limestone Nodules and Chert. (Local Drift.)

No. 3. 12 to 18 inches dark calcareo-Bituminous Shales in thick laminæ.

No. 4. 0 to 3 inches Ochreous Shales.

No. 5. 12 to 18 inches Coal in water. (No. 25 ?)

On Mr. Carr's land in S. W. Sec. 33, T. 39, R. 31, is the same Coal as that of Bridgman's. The section here is :

No. 1. 1 to 2 feet Calcareous Shale, somewhat Bituminous and rotten, abounding in fossils : *Pr. Prattenianus ;* also contains *Chonetes, Pr. costatus, Hemipronites, Orthoceras Rushensis,* and a small *Pleurotomaria speciosa.* (?)

No. 2. 4 inches Ochreous Shale—few fossils.

No. 3. 4 to 5 feet Coal ; upper 2 feet rotten at the outcrop ; the rest of good quality.

Aerhardt, near by, has the same Coal, but it is covered by 3 to 5 feet of hard, calcareous Shale, at the top passing into blue Limestone, with a thick buff crest. Most of the Coal is covered by water. 3 feet was seen at the opening of the drift by which it is worked.

On the land of Miss Nancy Morse in Sec. 35, T. 39, R. 32, I observed a good bank of this Coal. It was said to be 4 feet thick, but I

could only see 3 feet, the remainder being under water.   It is a good
hard Coal, containing very little Pyrites.

The above are the principal outcrops in this neighborhood.   It
will at once be apparent that these Coals underlie the county, from
its south line to Rich Hill, and westward.

COAL IN THE NORTH-EAST PART OF THE COUNTY.

On the branches of Deepwater, Cove and Peters' Creeks, are
seams of good Coal, but not of great thickness.   The Coal is jet black,
shiny, and has been opened at many places.   There are two seams occurring in the edge of the valleys.   Its Geological position is above
the last spoken of.

At John Young's, in N. W. Sec. 24, T. 40, R. 27, some open mining
has been done, exposing the following :

No. 1.   4 feet Clay Shales.
No. 2.   8 inches Slaty, Pyrito-calcareous band.
No. 3.   1½ feet dark blue Shales.
No. 4.   2 inches hard Calcareous Shaly band.
No. 5.   1½ feet Bituminous Shales, with a Pyrito-calcereous band.
No. 6.   1 foot Bituminous Shales.
No. 7.   Coal. Saw 13 inches. It is said to be much thicker, but on account
        of the water, I could not see it all.

On Mr. Newberry's land, at the fork of Mission Branch, a half
mile from South Deepwater, 10½ inches Coal crops out at several
places near the water's edge.   The Coal is of good quality, and capped
by drab sandy Shales.

At several places around Johnstown, on Peter McCool's land, are
outcrops of two thin Coal seams.   The upper one in his pasture, is 1
foot thick; the upper and lower part, a bright Coal of good quality;
the middle dull and crumbling.   A foot of blue Fire-Clay appears
underneath, which is ramified by black plant roots.

The lower Coal is seen just below the town near Deepwater, and
affords the following Section :

No. 1.   Sandy Shale.
No. 2.   1 foot blue Shale.
No. 3.   4 inches hard-brown ferruginous Limestone, containing *Pr. murica-
        tus* and other fossils.
No. 4.   2 inches blue Shales.
No. 5.   3 inches reddish-brown ochrey Shale.
No. 6.   2½ feet blue Clay Shales.
No. 7.   3 inches hard calcareo-pyritiferous band.
No. 8.   1 foot Coal.

These Coal seams are also sometimes worked at Shelton's and O'Neal's, one mile north-west, of which a Section may be found above in geological description.

Higher up Deepwater, on land of Pogue, in S. E., Sec. 15, T. 41, R. 29, the upper of these seams is 11 inches, with 15 feet of chocolate and blue sandy and ochrey Shales above, and 8 inches of Clay Shales in thin laminæ, inclosing knife-edges of Coal just over the Coal. Three-quarters of a mile south-west, and near Deepwater, on the land of Mr. Loggan's, the Coal has been 'occasionally dug out. Specimens shown me were of good quality, and the seam reported to be 12 to 13 inches thick, but was entirely covered with Shaly debris at the time of my visit. This Coal has also been mined on the land of Mrs. Johnson, three-quarters of a mile west. Further west it is not seen, being covered by upper strata. Northwardly, on Cove Creek, on Mrs. Hackler's land, about Sec. 34, the same Coal was formerly mined.

A Section from the hilltop gives:

No. 1. Coarse brown Sandstone in flags.
No. 2. Outcrop of gray and dove-colored Fusulina Limestone, containing *Spirifer lineatus*, (No. 55 of South-west Coal Sec.)
No. 3. 22 feet Slope.
No. 4. Fragments of bright brown shelly Limestone.
No. 5. 86 feet gentle Slope, with occasional outcrops of Sandstone.
No. 6. 15 feet ochrey and sandy Shales.
No. 7. 2 feet blue Shales.
No. 8. 6 inches outcrops of bituminous Shales *Pleurotomaria* were observed.
No. 9. 18 inches? Coal concealed.
No. 10. Yellow Fire-Clay.

On David Gilbert's land, in Sec. 26, T. 42, R. 29, one mile north-east, Coal 14 inches thick is well exposed in the edge of a branch capped with 1 foot of Shaly pyritiferous and bituminous Limestone bed, containing many fossils, chiefly *Productus semireticulatus*, with very long spines. It also contains *Pr. Prattenanus*.

On Peter Creek, in N. W., Sec. 21, T. 42, R. 29, I observed a 1 foot seam of Coal lying near the water's edge. Underlying it is 8 feet of Fire Clay, containing crystals of Selenite (Gypsum,) and numerous *Stigmaria* rootlets. Probably the same Coal we have just been speaking of, is found in Sec. 16, T. 39, R. 31, also near Stumptown on the waters of Double Branches.

FORT SCOTT COAL.

This Coal was not recognized in the north part of the county, although portions of its representative beds may exist in T. 42, R. 29. It may be also represented on the head of Burnett's Creek, Prior's and Reed's Creek. Its greatest development is further south.

No. 57.—This Coal is found on Braggin's land, near Butler, underlies Butler and is the Coal at Smith's 2 miles south-east. I also suppose it to be that Coal seen by Mr. Norwood on the land of Pearson, in N. W. N. W., Sec. 25, T. 42, R. 30. I also observed it on the land of H. Becket, in S. E., Sec. 10, T. 40, R. 32. It may also be found near Mulberry Creek, in Sec. 9, T. 40, R. 33, and southward. It may also be found in some of the mounds south of the Maries des Cygnes in R. 33. On account of its thickness, it is not often worked. It is from 8 to 9 inches thick.

NO. 70.—THE MULBERRY COAL.

This important Coal, mined at several places on Mulberry Creek, occurring from near its head to the Marias des Cygnes, and south of this stream to the county line, at many places in R. 33. It is also occasionally seen at many places near the Miami and its waters, from a few miles west of Butler to Sec. 24, T. 41, R. 33. It is also probable that the thicker seams on the waters of Deer Creek and the Coal of Bone Fork may be referred to the Mulberry Coal. We thus perceive its range to be quite extensive in Bates county, which is important considering its thickness. The general dip of the rocks in this county to the north-west carries it beneath the surface of the formations of T. 44, Rs. 32 and 33. Its greatest observed thickness was 3 feet, and general thickness 30 to 32 inches.

SPECIAL DESCRIPTION OF THE MULBERRY COAL BEDS.

The farthest southern extension of this Coal is in Secs. 18 and 19, T. 38, R. 33, at the south-west corner of the county, on land of the heirs of Leonard. On these lands it is 34 inches thick, appearing in shallow excavations on the almost flat prairie, the upper 10 inches crumbly, below it is a hard, firm, black Coal apparently free from Sulphur. It has a capping of 4 feet of sandy Shales, and dips gently southward. Limestone No. 67, of the S. W. Coal Section, appears 6 feet thick a short distance down the branch, with a Shaly fucoidal Sandstone 10 feet below it.

In Sec. 7, T. 38, R. 33, Coal has been occasionally taken out. Three feet above the Coal occurs a blue calcareous flag-stone, inclosing carbonaceous remains of fossils.

CONLEY'S MINES.

This is located in N. E., Sec. 18, T. 39, R. 33, on a high point of prairie about 30 feet below the higher prairie. It is 34 inches thick. A Limestone appears at 26 feet above Section at the bank, is :

No. 1. Soil and Local Drift.
No. 2. 4 inches band of yellow Ochre.
No. 3. 5 inches dove-colored Clay, with thin seams of Coal.
No. 4. 5 inches rotten Coal.
No. 5. 28 inches good Coal.
No. 6. Black Clay with Stigmaria scars and nodules of Pyrites.

A half mile south-west of Conley's, is Lewis' Bank, said to be about the same thickness, but it was not worked. Coal also is seen on a branch of Walnut Creek, in Sec. 15. One and a half feet were exposed, but it was said to be three and a half in all. A half mile west, on McGarrity's land, it is 27 inches thick, and of good quality and dipping west. It is here only covered by a few feet of the local Clays.

Mrs. Woodfin's Coal Bank, in N. E. Sec. 10, is 30 inches thick. Only occasionally worked.

At A. G. Wilson's, in Lot 2, S. W. Sec. 30, T. 29, R. 32, the same Coal has been mined. Drab and olive Shales are the immediate overlying rocks, with Limestone 8 or 10 feet above. The Coal was concealed at the time of my visit. Mr. Wilson says it is 3 feet 3 inches thick.

FOSTER'S COAL BANK, N. W. N. E. SEC. 21, T. 39, R. 33.

This was examined by Mr. Norwood, who reports the Coal 3 feet thick; the upper 15 inches soft and mostly free from Sulphur, is separated from the lower part by an ochrey Clay seam. The lower part has thin plates of Calcite between the joints, and when exposed appears rusty. Limestone, containing *Sp. lineatus*, is seen 5 feet below the Coal.

Mr. Beard, in N. E. N. W. Sec. 33, T. 39, R. 33, was reported to have 3 feet of Coal, but it was not exposed to view.

Manning, also, in N. W. Sec. 33, T. 39, R. 33, has the same Coal, said to be 32 inches thick. On a mound on the prairie, at 137 feet above Manning's Coal, the Upper Coal Measure Limestone is found, probably referable to No. 79 of the Upper Coal Measure Section of 1872.

Bender's Coal, in N. E. S. W. Sec. 32, T. 39, R. 33, is 30 inches thick.

The MULBERRY Coal, we thus see, underlies most of T. 39, R. 33, and nearly all of T. 38, R. 33, that is included in the limits of Bates county.

Passing to the north side of the Marais des Cygnes, the first are a series of banks examined by Mr. Norwood in Sec. 6, T. 39, R. 33.

At A. J. Dunlop's, in Lot 45, Sec. 6, T. 39, R. 33, is seen:

No. 1. Slope from above.
No. 2. 20 feet coarse, gray Limestone.
No. 3. 13 feet Slope.
No. 4. 3 feet dark blue Clay Shales, with seams of yellow Ochre. The lower part contains Pyrites. Within the mines the Clay becomes hard enough to form a good roof.
No. 5. 18 inches to 4 feet Coal; averages 3½ feet.
No. 6. 1 foot Fire Clay.
No. 7. 5 feet Slope.
No. 8. 5 feet drab, ferruginous Limestone.

Mr. Dunlop had drifted in about 25 feet, and each man would average 50 bushels per day.

WM. ARNOTT'S, ON LOT 44, SEC. 6, T. 39, R. 33.

This Coal is 2 feet to 2 feet 4 inches thick, being of better quality at the bottom and having Calcite between the joints. The top is somewhat rotten, and on the exposed surface has generally a rusty appearance. The Coal has an inclination of 5° towards the north. The Shales here do not form as good a roof as at Dunlop's, on account of transverse joints. The middle of the Coal is traversed by a pyritiferous band. Only a short distance off, another entry was made into the hill, at which place a 6-inch band of black Chert rested on the Coal.

Mr. Norwood reports other Coal banks in the same neighborhood, viz.:

John Reel's, in Lot 37, Sec. 6, T. 39, R. 33; J. P. McGraw's, in N. E. N. W. Sec. 21, T. 40, R. 33; Hiram Williams', in Sec. 21, T. 40, R. 33; and T. Williams', in S. E. Sec. 16, T. 40, R. 33.

JOHN NICHOL'S COAL, ON MULBERRY CREEK, IN SEC. 28, T. 41, R. 33. (Examined by C. J. Norwood.)

The seam is 3 feet thick—the upper 1 foot the best—with a roof of 5 feet of Shales abounding in concretions and concretionary Limestone beds, the lower beds being very fossiliferous. This bank is only worked in the winter.

COOPER'S COAL BANK, "OLD VERNON MINES," N. E. S. E. SEC. 5, T. 40, R. 33.

A good deal of mining has been done at this place, but it is only occasionally worked. At 10 feet from the outcrop, the Coal measures 34 inches, and is of apparently good quality with occasional shiny bands. It contains a little Sulphur and has Calcite plates between the joints. The upper 10 inches crumbles somewhat. The Coal is said to cake a little. The under-clay is 4 feet thick. Over the Coal are Shales with Limestone nodules abounding in fossils, including *Productus Prattenanus*, *Chonetes mesoloba*, *Athyris subtilita*, and large and small *Crinoid* stems.

In Sec. 9, T. 40, R. 33, I observed an outcrop of 2 feet 7 inches of crumbling Coal.

A little mining has been done at many places in this vicinity. Shafts on the prairie, between Mulberry Creek and Miami Fork, have also struck the Coal at several places.

On Miami, the farthest place north where this Coal was observed was on the land of L. N. Thornbrough, in Sec. 24, T. 41, R. 33. The Section here is:

No. 1. 8 feet Clay and Soil.
No. 2. 3 feet calcareous Shales, with shaly Limestone layers and concretions.
No. 3. 6 to 8 inches Coal and Shales.
No. 4. 12 to 14 inches Coal.
No. 5. 3 feet Fire Clay.

At Swink's Mill, near by, Limestone, whose position is known to be below the MULBERRY COAL, appears in the creek. In it were observed small *Crinoid* stems, *Fusulina* and *Spirifer lineatus*. Some mining has been done on the land of Jeremiah Reed, one mile south.

EMBERSON KEATON'S, SEC. 29, T. 41, R. 32.

The Coal here is said to be 2 feet thick, and crops out near the edge of the water. The Section is:

No. 1. 6 feet hard, chocolate-colored Sandstone in thin layers.
No. 2. 4 feet Shales and Limestone nodules, with large and small *Crinoid* stems and plates, *Pr. Prattenianus*, *P. splendens*, *Chonetes mesoloba*, *Athyris* ———, *Sp. cameratus*, *Sp. planoconvexus*, and *Lophophyllum*.

WM. T. GOODMAN'S BANK.

This is three-quarters of a mile south-east of the last, and about 100 yards from Miami Fork. The Section here is:

No. 1.   5 feet brown Sandstone in thin, cross-laminated layers.
No. 2.   3 feet olive Shales, with small Ironstone concretions and a few fossils—
          Athyris, *Productus* ———.   Sometimes thins out.
No. 3.   1½ feet smooth, yellow, ochreous Shales, with concretions of Carbon-
          ate of Iron.
No. 4.   1½ feet blue Shales.
No. 5.   3 feet good Coal.   Entire thickness not seen, but said to be 3 to 4 feet.
No. 6.   About 15 feet of Slope to Limestone in the creek.   The Limestone con-
          tains *Archaeocidaris megastylus* and *Syringapora multattenuata.*

Although mining has not recently been very regularly conducted here, the evidence is that there has been a good deal of work done, and considerable Coal taken out.   The upper 2 feet of "Peacock" Coal seems to be of fine quality, is more valued by the blacksmiths, and is quite hard, irridescent and shiny.   The lower part is only used for fuel and has a dull look.

Philip Hecadon's Bank, N. W. N. E. Sec. 16, T. 40, R. 32.

The Coal here is 31 to 34 inches thick.   The upper 15 inches a very good black and shining Coal.   This is divided from the lower portion by a 1½ to 2 inch Pyrites band.   The top Coal Mr. Hecadon says will sell in Butler at 25 cents per bushel, while the lower would only bring 14 cents.

This Coal is much esteemed by blacksmith's, is good charring Coal, and does not cake.   The overlying material here is similar to that at Goodman's.   The Sandstone occurs above, which is separated from the Coal by 7½ feet of sandy and calcareous Shale.   The Coal crops out along a branch for 100 yards above.   The working is done from an entry running back 80 yards.   On Page's land, a quarter of a mile south of Hecadon's, the Coal is 27 inches thick, and worked by surface stripping.   The Coal seems to be of about the same quality as that at Hecadon's.

WRIGHT'S COAL.

The MULBERRY COAL is worked on the lands of Wright and Wall, in Sec. 8, and of Dobbins, in Sec. 9, T. 40, Range 31.   The banks are all near each other, on a rolling prairie hill-side situated well for working.

The Coal is 2 to 2½ feet thick, of which 1½ feet is of good quality. It has a roof of 8 feet of Shales.

North-west, on Bone Fork, Mr. Norwood examined several Coal banks equivalent to the MULBERRY COAL.

The Coal is $2\frac{1}{2}$ feet thick, and overlaid by shaly Sandstone, and is worked by shaft and drift.

Conard's, S. E. S. E. Sec. 31, T. 41, R. 31, has the same Coal.

Mrs. Bowman, in S. W. Sec. 32, T. 41, R. 31, has Coal varying from 18 inches to $2\frac{1}{2}$ feet. Higher up the valley of Bone Fork in Sec. 28 or 29, is an 18 inch seam of Coal, which may be the one just spoken of.

THE COAL OF T. 42, R. 31.

At several places in this Township are outcrops of a thin seam of 8 inches of good Coal, but at only one place do excavations reveal a good, thick workable Coal. This is on the land of Moudy, in the west part of Sec. 26. The Coal was struck in digging a well several years ago. A shaft one hundred feet south of the well was sunk to the Coal, which gave the following succession of rocks:

No. 1. 10 feet Clay.
No. 2. 3 feet impure Limestone.
No. 3. 3 feet light dove Soapstone.
No. 4. 10 inches mottled light and dark colored brecciated Limestone.
No. 5. 7 feet soft bluish dove calcareous Shales.
No. 6. 4 feet (?) Coal thickens on one side.

It is probable that the Coal in Moudy's Shaft is the MULBERRY COAL. When the place was examined the shaft had not quite reached the Coal. Since that they report finding 4 feet of Coal.

The thin seams of this Township occupy a horizon but little removed from the Mulberry Seam.

Good workable Coals are said to exist very near Crescent Hill, but at present none are apparent.

On McCraw's land, near Mormon Fork, the Coal is said to be $2\frac{1}{2}$ feet thick, and on Ohler's land, $2\frac{1}{2}$ miles south-west, 18 inches of Coal is reported to be found in the banks of the creek.

The MULBERRY COAL we find is often of irregular thickness, varying from 20 inches to 3 feet, and sometimes 4 feet. It crops out over a larger extent of country than any of the other Coals of Bates county, and as above noted, may be found in R. 33, from the south line of the county to the middle of T. 41, is also seen at many places in T. 40 and 41, of R. 32, and 41 of R. 31, and portions of T. 40 and 42, of R. 31, and although not seen, it underlies the country north-west.

REVIEW OF PRECEDING PAGES.

One-half of T. 38, Rs. 29 and 30, are underlaid by at least 2 feet of good Coal.

Township 39, R. 29, is certainly underlaid by two seams of Coal, one of them 2½ to 4 feet, the other 18 inches, or a total average of say 2⅝ feet, and there may be another.

In T. 39, R. 30, only a 1 foot seam is exposed, but the Coals of the Township east may also underlie it. We would then have 4½ feet to underlie this Township.

In T. 40 and 41, R. 29, although only two thin seams are exposed, still, in portions, shafts sunk may reach the same Coals as those in the Townships south. The total thickness seen and concealed, is 4½ feet under 72 square miles, with another of 1 foot under at least one-half these two Townships, or a total average of 5 feet.

Township 42, R. 29, having about 26 square miles in Bates, may average the same number of feet as T. 41, (or 5 feet.)

Townships 40, 41 and 42, R. 30, are probably underlaid by 5 feet of Coal, although it all lies deep.

About 8 square miles of W. part of T. 38, R. 31, are probably underlaid by about 4 or 5 feet of Coal.

Of T. 39, R. 31, twenty miles are underlaid by 5 feet.

Township 40, R. 31, must be underlaid by the thick Coal found south and east, averaging 3½ to 4 feet, with another seam of 1½ feet. Twenty-four miles are underlaid by another seam of 9 inches, and 8 miles by 2½ feet. To reach thick seams at Butler, shafts would have to be sunk from 140 to 240 feet.

Most of T. 41, R. 31, is underlaid by about 8 feet of Coal.

T. 42, R. 31, has under it about 6 feet of Coal, mostly lying deep.

T. 38, R. 32, twenty-four square miles are underlaid by about 5½ feet of Coal,

One-half of T. 39, R. 32, or 20 miles, by 6 feet.

T. 40, R. 32, twenty-seven square miles are underlaid by from 8 to 9 feet, and 12 miles by 6 feet.

Ts. 41 and 42, R. 32, 69 square miles are underlaid by 8 feet, all lying deep.

In R. 33 about 164 square miles are underlaid by 8 feet of Coal. Of this 2 to 3 feet are easily obtainable, except in 1½ townships.

From these data we calculate the amount of Coal in this county to be 5,397,748,857 tons.

The following tables show the analysis made by R. Chauvenet of some of the principal Coals:

NAME OF COAL OR OWNER.	WATER	VOLA-TILE.	FIXED CARB.	ASH.	COLOR OF ASH.
Wm. Arnot, lot 44 of Sec. 6, T. 39, R. 33..............	4.55	33.45	48.74	13.26	Reddish brown.
Wright's, 3 miles north-west of Butler. (1)......	2.37	36.01	57.79	3.83	Light brown.
Do. ....(2)......	2.62	37.79	55.74	3.85	Light brown.
Do. ....(3)	2.42	35.99	55.77	5.82	Light brown.
W. F. Goodman's, 18 inches from top.....................	4.57	45.30	48.08	2.05	Light brown.
Cooper's, No. 1..................	5.58	36.04	48.29	10.09	Rusty brown.
" No. 2..................	5.07	38.13	47.99	8.81	Pinkish brown.
Hecadon's, top......	2.57	44.93	49.71	2.78	Pink.
" 1 foot from top..	4.89	42.39	50.18	2.54	Light brown.
" near bottom.....	5.09	35.36	47.51	12.04	Light brown.
B. Yates, on Panther Creek—top.	1.96	36.29	48.19	13.56	Light gray.
" " bottom.	1.87	30.95	47.89	19.29	

(Left side bracket label: MULBERRY COAL.)

Wright's, average per cent. of Sulphur 3.55.
Hecadon's, average per cent. of Sulphur from the 3 Coals mixed 1.86.
B. Yates, average per cent. of Sulphur from Coals mixed 4.10

BUILDING ROCK.

Stone, for all ordinary purposes, can be obtained in most neighborhoods, but superior building rock is not of general occurrence.

A good Sandstone quarry was noted on the prairie three miles west of Rockville, and the Sandstone immediately around Rockville affords a tolerably good building material. Good quarries of Sandstone may be opened just south of Possum Creek. The best exposure of this Sandstone is on Mound Branch, east of Butler. The rock of this quarry will favorably compare with the Warrensburg Sandstone, of which it is probably the equivalent. Thirty-five feet total thickness was here observed. On Possum Creek it is about 80 feet thick.

Limestones, suitable for making ordinary Lime, can be obtained in easy distance of most neighborhoods.

FIRE CLAY.

Good beds of Fire Clay can be found beneath most of the Coal seams.

Gypsum or *Selenite* seems generally to abound in the under Clays of the lower Coal beds.

IRON ORE.

At several places in Ts. 38 and 39, R. 31, are large masses of cellular brown Hematite of light specific gravity. Excavations may prove these beds to be thick and valuable enough to work, provided they are not too silicious.

On the slopes of Sand Mound, at the county line, and also north of Rockville are similar exposures of ore, but it is often too silicious.

West of Rockville, in bank of Panther Creek, are broken and lenticular strata of Carbonate of Iron of sufficient thickness to claim attention.

MINERAL WATERS.

In Bates, as in Vernon, are found wells of disagreeably tasted water. Mr. Newberry, in Sec. 22, T. 40, R. 29, has a well 18 feet deep, of very cool water, but alas, to the parched man it brings poor relief. It has a strong Epsom Salts taste. It acts somewhat on the bowels, does not cook well and will not wash. The lower 8 feet of this well is said to be in black Shales. Two miles east, John Young has a well with water having a pleasant Sulphur taste.

At Wilcox's, west of Crescent Hill, is a well over 80 feet deep, which was reported to be saline, but I could not discover it, which fact might have been owing to the abundant rains just previously fallen. About 57 feet of water generally stands in it. The water is said to wash well, but gives the clothing a yellow color unless rinsed in other water.

At Parkersville some Mineral Tar colors the Sandstone and small quantities drip from the crevices. Near Mr. Holderman's, a well was bored over 500 feet for oil but obtained none. Another small Tar spring, flowing from Sandstone, is in Sec. 23, T. 40, R. 33. The flow is weak, and on stirring the water a beautiful irridescence is seen on the surface, formed of plays of green and red, beautifully arranged. On Mulberry Creek, west and north-west of this, the Limestones indicate the presence of Bitumen by their odor.

Four miles south of Butler, small drops of Tar are seen upon fracturing the Limestone. In this instance the Tar occupies cavities formerly tenanted by fossils.

At Braggin's, east of Butler, is a soft Sandstone, impregnated with oil. A Chalybeate spring also issues from the same Sandstone.

At H. B. Francis', in the S. E. Sec. 4, T. 40, R. 33, is a weak flowing but strongly impregnated Alum spring. It issues from Shales just below Limestone No. 67.

On the land of Moses Martin, in S. E. Sec. 18, T. 40, R. 32, is a Salt and Sulphur well. The well is 117 feet deep from the surface of the high prairie. Epsom Salt water occurs near the upper part. That towards the bottom tastes of Sulphuretted Hydrogen. Mr. Martin says that the formations passed through were chiefly Sandstone with a 4 foot Limestone bed at 22 feet and at 32 feet Coal and Slate. Then below were Soapstone and Sandstone, containing Bitumen in the lower part. When first bored the well was left dry. Returning several days after there was found to be 60 feet of water in the well. At 60 feet depth a cavity containing gas was entered and an explosive report was heard 50 yards off. Even now if the water drops below 60 feet reports are sometimes heard. The water is said to be soft and better for washing than rain water.

FRESH WATER.

Some parts of the county are well watered, in others the supplies of water are weak.

There is a good spring of water at Butler, and water of good quality is easily obtained in wells.

On a ridge, in T. 38, R. 32, good water is obtained at easy depth.

At New Home there is a large spring of excellent water which never fails. There are other good and never failing springs in south part of T. 39, R. 32. One very pretty spring was observed on Mr. Ward's land, in Sec 35, flowing from Limestone high up in the hills.

In a deep shaded glen, on Richard Bleven's land, in S. Sec. 21, T. 39, R. 30, a very pretty and full flowing spring was noted.

Around the base of the hill, at the head of Peter's Creek, are wet places, indicating the existence of concealed springs. Springs may generally be found on the sides of the high mounds. One very excellent one is on the mound in Sec. 9, T. 41, R. 33.

AGRICULTURE.

In portions of Bates county are large bodies of excellent land, and there is also some thin soil in the county. About the thinnest soil is that north of Butler, including the north part of T. 40, part of

G. S—12

T. 41, and part of T. 42, R. 31.   The soil on the plains around the head of Miami Fork in T. 41, R. 32, is quite thin.

Where wood-land occurs on the hill-tops the soil is more often poor; for example, the country south of Possum Creek, slopes to Mound Branch and head of Panther Creek.   Most other portions of the county include tracts of rich soil.

The best lands will produce yearly 60 bushels of corn per acre, other lands 35 to 45 bushels.   Good wheat crops are also generally raised.   The natural prairie grazing is good and there are still large tracts of immense prairie land open for common grazing.   Blue grass has begun to take well.

There are but few bearing orchards in the county but we see no reason why fruit may not be successfully produced.

TIMBER SUPPLY.

Although Bates is a prairie country we find extensive bodies of good timber along the larger streams, especially on Grand River, Mormon Fork, the Marais des Cygnes and Miami and Mulberry Creeks, with good bodies near head of Panther Creek, a good deal of timber along Mound Branch and Walnut Creek.   Among the best varieties are Hickory, Oak, Elm, Honey Locust, Ash, Linden and Sycamore.   I saw no White Oak trees.   A few may probably be found near the head of Panther Creek.   Pecan occurs on the Marias des Cygnes.

CHAPTER XII·

HOWARD COUNTY.

BY G. C. BROADHEAD.

This county is one of the original "Old Counties" of Missouri, and was probably first settled a little prior to 1807. Although the first settlers had to contend with the cunning of the savage, the country settled up very rapidly prior to the admission of Missouri as a State, and that many of the early settlers were men of energy and means, seems proven by the age of the improvements in the county. Many of the farms are well improved, and the buildings first-class, large, substantial and convenient.

The area of this county is about 463 square miles, with a frontage on the Missouri River on the west and south, of 34 miles.

It originally consisted nearly altogether of timber, with two small upland and two bottom prairies, which are now under cultivation.

The bluffs, near Glasgow, rise to a hight of 260 feet above average water mark in the Missouri ; and this is probably about the general elevation of the high lands throughout the county. The river bluffs, at the western border of the county, are steep and sometimes perpendicular, but on the southern border are more gentle.

The streams more often pursue their way 150 feet below the tops of the ridges, and the valleys are connected with the ridges by long and very often easy slopes.

The south-eastern portion of the county is not as hilly as some other districts, We here have, near the Missouri, some steep bluffs with White Oak growth. Near the Bonne Femme, and south of Fayette for several miles extending to the Missouri Bluffs, is a tract of rich, rolling, heavily timbered land, including many varieties of excellent timber, such as White, Red and Rock Chestnut Oak, Black Walnut, Elm, Hickory, White Walnut, Ash and Linden. South-eastwardly from Fayette, is a similar country, and also westwardly, to Glasgow, but here it is more hilly.

Towards Boonsboro, and west, an occasional sharp and crooked ridge occurs, covered with a heavy growth of chiefly White Oak.

The north-western part of the county sustains a growth of timber similar to that lying south, but the country is not so hilly, and in fact, the slopes are quite gentle.

The north-eastern part of the county is broken and hilly, and sustains chiefly a growth of White and Post Oak.

In speaking of the trees of this county, I would say that Black and White Walnut are very abundant, being very common over most of the county. Blue Ash and Sassafras abound; this county being almost the western limit of the former in North Missouri. The Spice Bush (*Laurus benzoin,*) is common on the Missouri Bottoms, but Dogwood (*Cornus florida,*) is rare, and is not probably found further west. Many of the trees on the ridges, including Walnut, White Oak, Red Oak and Rock Chestnut Oak attain a great size. One of the latter, which I measured, was 13 feet 3 inches in circumference, 3 feet above the ground. This tree was on the Missouri Bluffs; in the bottoms, Cottonwood, Elm and Sycamore grow to a very large size.

The principal streams in the eastern part of the county, are Moniteau Creek (Manitou,) with its tributaries, and Bonne Femme. This last rises about the middle of T. 52, R. 15 W., and flowing in a southerly direction, empties into the Missouri about three miles below Boonville, Cooper county. The principal tributary of Manitou Creek in this county, is Hunger's Mother,* which heads in the north-west part of T. 51, R. 14 W.; and the principal one of Bonne Femme is Salt Fork, rising in the south-eastern part of T. 52, R. 15, and flowing south-west empties into the Bonne Femme in the north-west quarter of Sec. 30, T. 51, R. 15.

Other streams flowing southward, are Salt Creek and Sulphur Creek, and those running westward, are Richland, Hurricane, Gregg's and Bear Creeks and Doxy's Fork. They all run into the Missouri, and some of the smaller ones on entering the bottom, waste their waters on the flats and are lost.

---

*This stream, it is said, received its name from a party of hunters, early settlers, who were hunting bears, and meeting with no success, got out of meat on this creek. Bad weather came upon them, and they were prevented from hunting and threatened with starvation. They therefore christened the creek "Hunger's Mother."

The inhabitants of the county depend chiefly on cisterns and wells for drinking water, but some fresh water springs are occasionally found.

SURFACE DEPOSITS.

The *Alluvium* does not materially differ from that found in other counties, and which has been so often described. It includes the soils, washings and recent deposits along the streams.

The *Bluff* or *Loess* formation is well developed in this county, consisting in the main of finely comminuted Sands and Clays, with occasional small Gravel beds. The Clays are generally of a dull, brown appearance, and at one place, near Boonsboro, I observed a bed having a purplish tint.

Near Sulphur Lick, blue sandy Clay underlies brownish Clay, from which it is separated by a ferruginous sandy band. A similar appearance was observed at Glasgow. The lower bluish beds, more probably belong to the Drift formation.

Drift boulders, of Granite, Greenstone, Quartzite, etc., are found strewn along all the valleys and occasionally the blue Clay is seen.

On Salt Creek, near the bottoms, alternations of variously colored Sand appear in the following order:

No. 1. 20 feet Bluff Clay.
No. 2. 1 foot 2 inches black Sand.
No. 3. 6 inches brown Sandstone.
No. 4 6 inches brownish and green drab banded Sandstone.
No. 5. 10 feet layers brown, yellowish or greenish comminuted Sand.

This may be called "Altered Drift;" that is, it has been removed from its first place of deposit, and arranged again in regular layers.

No well marked beds of Drift were seen in the county, but it is probable that most of the valleys are underlaid by these deposits, and large boulders of Granite, Quartzite, etc., were occasionally found, clearly referable to this era of deposit.

PALEOZOIC ROCKS.

We find the following Groups in this county, referable to the Carboniferous system:

COAL MEASURES.

Ferruginous Sandstone.. 50 feet.
Archimedes Limestone, (St. Louis Group, Warsaw Limestone)........... 40 "
    "   "   (Keokuk Group)..................................... 35 "
Encrinital or Burlington Limestone.. 60 "
Chouteau Limestone.. 75 "

IRREGULARITIES OF STRATA.

Starting from Glasgow with the beds of the lower Coal Measures in sight, we find at Bluffport that these beds have receded in the hills, and the Keokuk Group, 35 feet in thickness, appears at the water's edge. Going southward, we find that the rocks continue to rise, and more rapidly, to about three miles north of Lisbon. Two miles north of this place, the lowest rock at Bluffport has risen over a hundred feet.

We are now opposite an anticlinal axis, spoken of by Mr. Meek in his report on Saline county.

From this point the Rocks dip rapidly in a southern direction, and at Lisbon the Keokuk Group is again at the bottom of the hill. From this, eastwardly, we observe a gradual depression of strata, until we approach New Franklin. East of this point, the strata again gently rises, and at Rocheport the upper portion of the Burlington Group is seen 60 feet up in the Bluffs.

Along this line are also occasional undulations, or irregular depressions and elevations. One and a half miles west of Mr. L. A. Brown's, the Ferruginous Sandstone appears in the Bluffs, 38 feet in thickness, resting on 24 feet of Limestone. A hundred yards east it is at the base of the hill. A half of a mile east, it was observed lying in a nearly horizontal position, and a little further east it dips 26° with a magnetic course of S. 43° E. It soon rises, however, to a hight of over 40 feet, and a few miles further east, almost thins out near the lower part of the hill.

CHOUTEAU LIMESTONE.

This formation is only brought to view in the western part of the county, near the mouth of Richland Creek, and extending southward along the Bluffs for about 2 miles. The upper 15 feet appears to be somewhat Argillaceous and Magnesian, close-grained and in thick, substantial beds, useful for building purposes. The lower portion is probably Hydraulic, the upper 4 feet being a pure drab, while the other beds are of a buff-drab color. Below these are thin, shelly and semi-crystalline dove-colored Limestones, containing occasional geodes filled with Calcite.

The fossils observed were *Pr. Murchisonianus, Rhynchonella Cooperensis, Sp. Marionensis,* and *Sp. cuspidatus.* The lower part of the Magnesian division, shows many small cells formed by the decomposition of the fossils, chiefly *Crinoid* stems.

Only about twenty feet thickness of the upper beds of this Group, was seen, but these rose over 50 feet in the Bluffs opposite the uplift above Lisbon. We have reason to suppose that this 50 feet is occupied by lower beds of the same Group.

BURLINGTON LIMESTONE.

This is the next overlying formation found in this county, and is the equivalent of the " Encrinital."

The beds belonging to this Group are, in this county, generally of a very coarse structure, the coarse layers being of a very loose texture, and abound in many *Crinoid* stems throughout.

At the base of the formation, is 10 feet of a buff color, with white *Crinoid* stems, which makes an excellent building stone. The upper 5 feet is fine grained, while the lower is a much coarser Rock. The next beds above this 10 feet are generally of a light or whitish gray color.

At Burkhart's Salt Spring, there is a Bluff of 30 feet of irregularly bedded brown and gray coarse Limestone, containing lenticular forms of Chert.

Just above Rocheport, Mr. Norwood measured about 60 feet of gray and crystalline Limestone, the two upper beds, of 20 to 30 feet being arranged in alternate layers of Limestone and Chert, many of them coarse, friable and light gray; others dark gray and fine-grained, with but little Chert in the lower part. These beds belong to the middle division of Prof. Swallow's Encrinital Limestone, including No. 3 and probably No. 5, those above and below these divisions not being recognized.

The structure known as " Stylolite," is often seen, and seems very characteristic of this formation.

Fossils are often abundant, but cannot always be separated from the Rock and their organic matter is generally replaced by white Calcite.

Those observed were *Spirifer striatus, Sp. suborbicularis* (?), *Orthis Swallovi, Or. Mitchellini var. Burlingtonensis, Chonetes Shumardana, Athyris incrassatus, Zaphrentis centralis, Actinocrinus concinnus* (?), *Actinocrinus* (2 or 3 undet. species) and *Platycrinus*

——.

This formation is seen in the Missouri Bluffs near the mouth of Richland Creek, and for several miles north and south; it being brought to view on the anticlinal, passing east and west. In going east, it is not seen again until we approach New Franklin.

It is found on the Bonne Femme as far north as the northern part of T. 49. From New Franklin eastward, it occupies a strip of the Missouri Bluffs, three miles in width, extending to the Boone county line. Its greatest thickness is, near Rocheport, about sixty feet, and on the anticlinal, in the western part of the county, it is not much more.

The Limestones of this Group can, most of them, be burned into good Lime.

KEOKUK GROUP.

In the western portion of the county we find, overlying the last named Group, beds of mostly coarse-grained, gray Limestone, with sometimes a slight bluish tint, and also occasional reniform masses and lenticular beds of white Chert. Some of the Limestone layers are shaley, others are thick-bedded and afford a good building material.

These beds crop out along the Missouri Bluffs, from Bluffport, for about nine miles, dipping beneath the overlying beds of the Warsaw Limestone (St. Louis Group) about one and a half miles south of Lisbon. Specimens of fossils can not often be obtained, but the rocks at Bluffport abound in the most characteristic. Those observed at the various outcrops were: Of Brachiopods, *Camaraphoria subtrigona Productus setigerus, Pr. punctatus, Spirifer Keokuk, Sp. neglectus, Sp. Logani, Sp. pseudo-lineatus, Sp. striatus, Sp. tenuimarginatus, Sp. rostellatus, Sp. subcuspidatus* and *Terebratula parva;* of Gasteropods, a *Platyceras ;* of Trilobites, a *Phillipsia,* and of Radiates, *Zaphrentis centralis, Z. Cliffordana, Trochophyllum Verneuiliana.* Crinoid stems often abound, but of fish remains I only obtained the tooth of *Cladodus laminoides* from the lower beds, two miles north of Lisbon. One specimen of *Sphenopterium depressum* was also obtained.

ST. LOUIS GROUP.

The beds occurring in this county, which I have assigned a place in this Group, are alternations of brown and gray Limestone, mostly in thin layers, separated from each other by Shales which are sometimes a few inches thick and often more than a foot. These beds were formerly called, by Mr. Hall in his Iowa Geological Report for 1858, the "Warsaw Limestone." Worthen, in Vol I of the Illinois Geological Report, and White, in the Iowa Geological Report, 1870, assign them a place in the St. Louis Group.

After inspection of the fossils, I choose to place these beds subordinate to the St. Louis Group.

I was unable to determine the exact thickness of this formation in the county; but three-quarters of a mile west of Mr. L. A. Brown's they were seen forty feet in thickness from the base of the hill up, the lower fifteen feet of coarse gray Limestone, containing *Archimedes Wortheni* and *Oligoporus Danæ.* Near this place the rock is somewhat fractured, and contains a good deal of *Arragonite. Archimedes* is very abundant, as are also *Pentremites conoideus* and several species of *Zaphrentis.* But the most abundant fossils are *Fenestella* and other species of *Bryozoa.* The following is a list of the fossils obtained in this county from this formation. Crinoids, *Dithocorinus ficus, Pentremites conoideus, Platycrinus planus, Pterocrinus crassus* and stems and plates of undertermined species; Echinoids, *Oligoporus Danæ;* Polyps, *Zaphrentis centralis, Z. Cliffordana*(?), *Z. spinulifera, Z.——, Z. Syringopora——,* and *Pyrgia Mitchellini* (?); Bryozoa, *Archimedes Wortheni, Ar. reversa. Fenestella St. Ludovici, Fen. hemitrypa, Coscinium saganella, Cos. escharensis, Polypora Varsoviensis* and *P. Halliana* ; Brachiopods, *Athyris——, Hemipronites——, Productus Cora, Pr.——, Rhynchonella mutata, R. subcuneata, Spirifer Keokuk, Sp. Leidyi, Sp. tenui-costata, Sp. spinosus, Terebratula Roissyi, T. trinuclea;* Pteropods, *Conularia Missouriensis;* Gasteropods, *Dentalium venustum,* and Conchifers, *Myalina St. Ludovici.*

Strata belonging to this Group are found at Boonslick, near Lisbon, and occasionally in the Missouri Bluffs as far east as Sulphur Creek and for several miles up the latter stream. It is wanting further east.

FERRUGINOUS SANDSTONE.

This rock is next in ascending series, and its geological position in the county is at the top of the Lower Carboniferous System.

In Callaway, Cedar and Lawrence we find a very Ferruginous Sandstone above all other Lower Carboniferous rocks, and under the Coal Measures. We, therefore, conclude that these rocks are of the same Geological age.

Wherever observed in this county it is almost a pure white within the quarries, becoming of a light buff or drab shade near the surface. Its percentage of Oxide of Iron seems small, and only an occasional brown spot can be observed in it.

No fossils were seen in it, and only from its position in reference to underlying and overlying rocks are we justified in assigning it this position.

Two miles below Lisbon it is 50 feet, and one mile above Mr. L. A. Brown's, it is 38 feet thick. It was not seen north of Lisbon, and thins out in an eastern direction, not being found east of Bartlett Branch.

UPPER CARBONIFEROUS OR COAL MEASURES.

The greater portion of this county is underlaid by the formations which include the Middle and Lower Coal Measures. The lowest beds of this Group found in the county may be seen near the Missouri Bluffs.

A section on a branch of Salt Creek, in the S. W. qr. Sec. 5, T. 49, R. 17, shows the following:

No. 1. Clay containing Ochre on which are tumbled masses of soft brown Limestone.

No. 2. 2 feet outcrop of Coal smut, showing a blue Clay band in the middle; (this is probably the equivalent of C. J. Norwood's Coal " E."

No. 3. 2 inches brown Shales.

No. 4. 9 feet 6 inches Shales and Fire Clay, mostly Clay, with some yellow Ochre.

No. 5. 2 inches rotten Coal.

No. 6. 4 feet blue Fire Clay.

No. 7. 10 feet Shaly Sandstone.

No. 8. 3 inches Coal.

No. 9. 4 feet mostly sandy Shales.

No. 10. Outcrop of Shaly Coal,

No. 11. 4 feet 6 inches Fire Clay.

No. 12. White Sandstone, (Lower Carboniferous,) 10 feet of this was found in the bluff below.

One hundred yards east of this place is 4 feet Limestone resembling that found overlying the Coal near Boonsboro, and lying irregularly.

No. 2, of the above section, is probably the equivalent of the Coal of H. L. Brown, which crops out a quarter of a mile lower down the branch. This Section will give an idea of the lowest Coal formation seen in this county.

The micaceous Sandstone which, according to Prof. Swallow, occupies the top of the Lower Coal Measure, is well exposed at the mouth of Hurricane Creek to a hight of 61 feet. At the top we find 14 feet of Shaly Sandstone, then 7 feet 9 inches of pretty good building rock, generally in even layers but with occasional Shaly pockets containing thin Coal seams. Below this is 5 feet of an irregular and sometimes Shaly layer of brown and gray Sandstone and black Shale beds, with *Calamites*, *Lepidodendron*, etc. The lower 34 feet is somewhat Shaly, the upper portions concretionary. Up Hurricane

Creek, at Turner's, Mr. Norwood's measurements show about 50 feet of this Sandstone resting on a Limestone, which we are disposed to regard as the equivalent of the Limestone lying 10 to 16 feet above the Glasgow Coal, and the apparent dip of the Glasgow rocks to the south is sufficient to reconcile their observed position.

Opposite the lower ferry landing, at Glasgow, the Limestone is 26 feet above the river, and one-half to three-quarters of a mile west it is 53 feet. If we allow a dip of 27 feet for three-quarters of a mile, or 36 feet per mile, which is not too much, our Limestone would be 46 feet below the bed of the water at the mouth of Hurricane Creek. But the formations being concealed between Gregg's and Hurricane Creeks, we can not truly say that they are so much depressed. In fact, we believe, they are not, for we have a measured thickness of over 60 feet Sandstone at the mouth of Hurricane Creek, and at Turner's only 50 feet, and if we base our calculations, for thickness, on the dip, our thickness would undoubtedly be too great.

Our Glasgow Section shows the micaceous Sandstone high up in the hills with another Sandstone near the water.

This Section is as follows:

No. 1. 16 feet sandy Shales, with beds of Sandstone in the upper part.

No. 2. 8 feet blue Clay and Shales, in thin laminæ.

No. 3. 1½ inches Carbonate of Iron.

No. 4. 8 inches blue Clay Shales.

No. 5. 4 inches shelly Ferruginous Limestone; weathers red, and contains *Ch. mesoloba* and *Pr. muricatus.*

No. 6. 4 feet Shales.

No. 7. 20 inches mottled deep-blue and drab Limestone, inclosing *Stigmaria ficoides*, which show on the weathered surface. *Brachiopods* are rare, but *Sp. lineatus* was found. A fragment of a plant was found with crystallized centre of red heavy-spar and Calcite.

No. 8. 2 feet 6 inches Shales.

No. 9. 10 inches Clay with Limestone nodules.

No. 10. 2 feet 3 inches deep-blue, fine-grained Limestone, brown-specked, and containing Calcite specks. Fossils observed, were *Fusulina cylindrica* and *Sp. lineatus.* This rock weathers brown.

No. 11. 16 feet 9 inches blue and drab Shales (jointed,) with Ochre between the joints.

No. 12. 1 foot outcrop of Coal, decomposed near surface.

No. 13. 4 inches band of rotten Coal and yellow Ochre.

No. 14. 3 feet blue Clay and streaks of yellow Ochre.

No. 15. 12 feet blue and drab Shales in thick laminæ, with sandy ochreous bands containing ferns.

No. 16. 20 feet blue sandy Shales and Shaly Sandstone, some very finely rippled marked.

Opposite the ferry landing, in town, three-quarters of a mile below, we find :

No. 1.   3 inches Limestone.
No. 2.   3 feet 6 inches dark-blue Shales.
No. 3.   6 inches blue Fire Clay, with Coal streaks.
No. 4.   6 to 9 inches brown Fire Clay.
No. 5.   3 feet 9 inches Limestone—No. 7, of Section just described, and only
       10 inches separates this from the Limestone No. 10 of last Section.
       Instead of 16 feet 9 inches to the Coal, we have just 10 feet, showing
       that some beds have been thickened and others are thinned.

The Limestone (7) of the Glasgow Section is seen on the Salisbury road, in the bluffs of Doxy Fork, we therefore suppose that the Glasgow Coal may be obtained here.

A general section of rocks near Fayette, would embrace over a 100 feet of Coal Measures from No. 12 of General Section, (O. J. N.) downwards, including Coal "D" (?) and also Coal "B" with many intervening Strata wanting.

Our general Section here is about the following :

No. 1.   25 feet Slope from hill-top.
No. 2.   2 to 7 feet bluish-drab Limestone, very nodular on top, and abound-
       ing in *Chœtetes milleporaceus ;* also containing *Fusulina cylindrica,*
       Athyris subtilita, Sp. lineatus and a *Nautilus.*
No. 3.   2 feet Fire Clay.
No. 4.   11 feet brown Shaly Sandstone.
No. 5.   14 feet blue sandy Shales, has an occasional ochrey band, the lower
       4 feet being calcareous, with Limestone nodules.
No. 6.   14 inches Limestone of a deep ash-blue color, which breaks rhomboid-
       ally—No. 15 of the General Section.
No. 7.   10 inches Bituminous Shales. Upper 2 inches are dark blue with gray
       fucoidal markings.
No. 8.   1 foot 5 inches black Slate.
No. 9.   9 inches Coal.
No. 10.   1 foot Fire Clay.
No. 11.   10 inches nodular Limestone belt.
No. 12.   7 feet Shales.
No. 13.   10 feet Limestone.
No. 14.   10 feet Shales.
No. 15.   1 foot 4 inches Limestone containing *Pr. costatus P. punctatus Ath. subt-*
       lita and *Sp. cameratus.* This Limestone is probably Hydraulic.
No. 16.   6 inches Shales.
No. 17.   1 foot Magnesian (Hydraulic) Limestone.
No. 18.   70 feet probably all Sandstone and Shales.
No. 19.   8 feet 1 inch blue Limestone.

No. 20.   2 feet 4 inches Shales.

No. 21.   9 inches blue shelly Limestone.

No. 22.   8 inches black smut—not persistent.

No. 23.   6 inches ash-blue Limestone.

No. 24.   4 inches Clay.

No. 25.   2 feet 8 inches bituminous Shales, containing septaria and also very small, round concretions.

No. 26.   1 foot blue carbonaceous Shales.

No. 27.   1 foot blue Shales, abounding in *Pr. muricatus*, and also contains a good deal of Iron Pyrites.

No. 28.   Coal said to be 1½ feet thick. Has been worked at many places around Fayette.

No. 29.   2 feet 6 inches blue Fire Clay, yellow streaked, and contains Stigmaria at the top.

No. 30.   1 foot bright brown and gray Clay, containing Selenite.

No. 31.   3 feet gray sandy clay, containing minute specks of Iron Pyrites, and also of Mica.

ECONOMICAL GEOLOGY.

Probably the lowest workable Coal seen in the county is that of H. L. Brown, which crops out in the edge of a branch of Salt Creek, in the S. E. qr. Sec. 6, T. 49, R. 17. The rocks here are dipping at 7 deg. N., 40 deg. W. Up the creek a short dirtance eastward, the Lower Carboniferous Limestones are seen underlaying the Ferruginous Sandstone. Still higher up stream bituminous Shales are seen dipping W. at an angle of 24 °., and about 16 feet above the lower Carboniferous Limestones. This bituminous Slate is probably equivalent to a similar bed found overlying the Coal. According to measurement made a quarter of a mile up stream, the Coal is 30 feet above the Ferruginous Sandstone. (See Fig. 5.)

The section at Brown's Coal bank is as follows:

No. 1.   1 foot 6 inches drab argillo-calcareous slaty rock.

No. 2.   1 foot 6 inches bituminous Shales.

No. 3.   2 feet 6 inches bituminous Slate containing a small Discina.

No. 4.   9 inches slaty Coal.

No. 5.   12½ inches good Coal.

No. 6.   1 inch dark dove colored Clay.

No. 7.   2 inches impure Coal.

No. 8.   10 inches dark dove colored Clay.

No. 9.   3-3½ feet Coal of good quality.

This Coal probably underlies one-half of Ts. 49 and 50, R. 17, but owing to its extreme dip and the difference of the angle of dip or repose at other places, it is impossible to say to what extent or to what depth it may be found.

About three miles west of this, and on the land of Mr. R. C. Johnson, in Sec. 3, T. 49, R. 18, a little Coal in detached masses has been
obtained from a small eroded space in the lower Carboniferous Limestone and Sandstone. It is probable that this was not originally
formed but drifted into this pocket. This locality was examined by
Mr. C. J. Norwood. Mining for Coal here would be time and money
lost.

Mr. Norwood examined Tatum's Coal in Sec. 16, T. 50, R. 17, the
oldest worked bank in the county. It is 24 to 33 inches thick, and
there is a probability that it may be the equivalent of Brown's Coal,
and it may underlie all of the east half of the Township, and extend
under the county east.

THE FAYETTE COAL.

Coal has been mined at various times near Fayette, on Adams
Creek, but recently there has been but little mining done.

Coal "B" has formerly been mined one mile north of Fayette,
where it crops out about 30 feet below the hill-top. It underlies the
county to the west and south-west for five or six miles.

On the land of Todd and Hughes, three miles South-west of Fayette, on the Boonsboro road, it is seen about the same distance below
the hill-top. At these several places it is 9 inches thick.

A rotten streak of this Coal appears on the Fayette and New
Franklin road, two miles south of Fayette, and 50 feet below the hill-
top. In the valley below are seen the bituminous Shales overlying
the lower Fayette Coal. Its thickness could not be seen near Fayette,
as no mining had recently been done, but going southward 4 miles, we
find this Coal high in the hills and worked at many places near the
Franklin road.

On Dr. J. P. Beck's land, in Sec. 29, T. 50, R. 16, it is 22 inches
thick and capped by 22 inches of Clay Shales, with 2 feet of bituminous Slate still above, extending to the overlying Limestone. The blue
Clay Shales vary in thickness from 2 to 4 feet, the under-clay being 4
feet. Beneath the latter is a bed of Sandstone.

The under-clay at Fayette is 6 feet 6 inches in thickness.

The overlying Clay Shales at Beck's abound in many fossils transformed into Iron Pyrites.

On A. L. McCullough's land, in Sec. 4, T. 49, R. 16, the Coal is 50
feet below the hill-top and 60 feet above the Encrinital Limestone, or
47 feet above the Lower Carboniferous Chert.

This Coal has been mined at various other places in the center of the county, and from observations, we are inclined to say that it certainly underlies the whole of the township in which Fayette is situated, as well as that immediately west, north-east and east, with the greater portion of the townships south and west.

Near Boonsboro, both on the head waters of Salt Creek and Bartlett Branch, it is found, but it is only mined at a few localities.

It is well exposed on the land of John S. Snoddy, in W. half S. W. Sec. 15, T. 49, R. 17.

West of Snoddy's, on Adam Gilmore's land, the Coal is 16 inches thick, with 16 inches of Slate resting immediately on it, separating the Coal from 1 foot of thick layers of bituminous Slate, which seems to be almost a Cannel Coal.

Less than a quarter of a mile from the last place, and on John Callaway's land, we found the Limestone closely resembling that on the branch just west of Boonsboro, at an elevation of 6 feet above the Coal just named. The Coal is 18 inches thick and has 2 feet of blue Shales separating it from the overlying bituminous Slate. Below the Coal is 4 feet of Fire Clay, invariably resting on Limestone; the upper and lower portions of the Clay are blue, the remainder is yellowish.

From inspection of these Sections, we find slight discrepancies in them, but there is a general semblance of parallelism throughout. The same bed in a short distance presents variations in its overlying beds. Sometimes bituminous Slate rests immediately on the Coal, then a little distance along, we find it separated by Clay Shales. There are certain common features in each, although often widely separated by distance. *Pr. muricatus* is the prevailing fossil, and the fossils are all replaced by Iron Pyrites. At Dr. Scroggins' Coal Bank, they oxidize soon after exposure. At this place are two fossil bands, one a little above the Coal and the other 3 or 4 feet still above. The other principal fossils observed were *Sp. cameratus*, *Ch. mesoloba*, *Hemipronites crassus* and *Ch. Verneuiliana*. At Beck's were observed *Nuculana bellistriata*, *Myalina Swallovi* and *Edmondia reflexa*—all beautifully replaced by Pyrites. At Scroggins', besides these, we found *Pleu. carbonaria* and *Solenomya radiata*, and also a thin upper band containing *Sp. planoconvexus*.

The Coal at these outcrops is generally conveniently situated for mining.

At many places, the Coal seams are concealed by deep Drift deposits, but when found near the railroad they will always be profitably worked.

The seam cropping out in the bluffs just above Glasgow, appears to poor advantage at its outcrop. It is said to be 20 inches thick, this is very probable, and it may sometimes be thicker.

Coal " B " is found on the head-waters of Hurricane, Gregg's and Fristoe's Creeks, 9 inches to 1 foot. At Turner's it is about 45 feet below the hill-top, and if the strata are nearly horizontal, it may be found at about the same elevation throughout this vicinity.

The Glasgow Coal is low in the adjacent valleys.

In the western part of T. 52, R. 16, Coal " B " is about 30 feet below the hill-top, and 9 inches thick.

Howard county contains about 380 square miles of Coal Measures, including in a large portion three and sometimes four Coal beds, of which one is from 2 to 3 feet thick, another $1\frac{1}{2}$ to $2\frac{1}{2}$ feet, another 6 inches, and a fourth one from 9 to 30 inches in thickness.

We find them distributed, in aggregate thickness, over the various townships of the county about as follows :

RANGE	TOWNSHIP	THICKNESS OF BEDS.	TOTAL THICKNESS.		AREA IN SQUARE MILES.	AMOUNT IN CUBIC FEET.
			Feet.	Inches.		
14	49	One bed..	1	5	$2\frac{1}{2}$	98,736,000
14	50	*Three beds—17 inches, 18 inches to 28 inches, 2 feet...........................	3	11	$15\frac{1}{2}$	2,306,164,400
14	51	Three seams—9 inches to 1 foot, and 22 inches to 30 inches.................	4	9	30	3,972,672,000
14	52	Same...	4	9	5	662,112,000
15	49	One seam—10 inches to 18 inches....	1	2	18	585,446,400
15	50	Two seams—1 foot to 15 inches, 18 inches to 30 inches......................	3	2	36	3,178,137,600
15	51	Three seams—9 inches, 1 foot, 22 inches to 30 inches......................	4	9	36	4,767,206,400
15	52	Two seams—1 foot, and 2 feet to 3 feet 9 inches..............................	3	8	17	1,737,753,600
16	49	One seam—1 foot 6 inches..............	1	6	18	753,716,800
16	50	Three seams, two in north half—7 inches, and 1 foot 6 inches, 17 inches to 22 inches....................	1	10	18	2,676,326,400
16	51	Two seams—1 foot, and 2 feet.........	3	...	36	3,010,876,200
16	52	Two seams—9 inches, and 2 feet......	2	9	28	2,146,636,800

*Average total thickness.

Coal Beds of Howard County—Continued.

RANGE	TOWNSHIP	THICKNESS OF BEDS.	TOTAL THICKNESS.		AREA IN SQUARE MILES.	AMOUNT IN CUBIC FEET.
			Feet.	Inches.		
17	49	*Two seams—15 inches, and 3 feet....	2	2	19	1,147,660,800
17	50	Two seams—1 foot, and 2 feet 9 inches..	3	9	36	3,763,584,000
17	51	*Two seams—9 inches to 15 inches, and 2 feet 6 inches..	3	6	26	2,936,524,800
17	52	Two seams—1 foot 6 inches, and 2 feet	3	6	15	1,533,312,000
		Total				35,276,836,200

This gives an aggregate of 35,276,836,200 cubic feet, and taking 80 pounds as the weight of a cubic foot of Coal, (25 cubic feet per ton of 2,000 pounds,) we get 1,411,073,448 tons for the amount of Coal in this county, most of which can be easily mined.

If we deduct from this the amount which the 9-inch seam will afford, which equals 317,813,600 tons, we still have 1,093,259,688 tons of Coal in this county.

BUILDING MATERIALS.

Generally speaking the Coal Measures do not afford a superior article for building purposes. The Rhomboidal Limestone has been used in the construction of culverts on the Louisiana road, for which purpose it seems to do very well, as it occurs in layers of uniform thickness and of a smooth surface. But it contains, as do many of the Coal Measure Limestones, too much Iron Pyrites, and on open air exposure is apt to crack and fall to pieces.

The Sandstones of the Coal Measures are also too apt to disintegrate, because they contain so much argillaceous matter. The Sandstone quarry at the mouth of Hurricane Creek contains some very good and thick layers, but I do not consider the rock by any means to be of superior quality.

* Average total thickness.

Better quarries may be found in the Lower Carboniferous rocks, which occur at intervals from Bluffport to Rocheport. In the Rocheport Bluffs are fine exposures of the Burlington (Encrinital) Limestone, which is both durable and one of the best rocks for making Lime. The lower beds of this formation appear in the Missouri Bluffs near where Richland Creek enters the bottom, and are there from two to four feet in thickness, forming a superior building stone. These latter rest immediately on the

Upper Chouteau Limestone Beds,

Which also afford an equally good building rock. Unfortunately these outcrops are generally overlaid by thick formations of other Limestones, rendering them in most cases difficult to obtain.

Ferruginous Sandstone.

The Ferruginous Sandstone is well exposed in the Missouri Bluffs, near the line of Rs. 17 and 18. Its beds are even, the color a pretty delicate, grayish drab or almost white, appearing of a somewhat buff tint on exposure. It is easy to work, and I regard it as a superior and very durable building stone. Good quarries can be opened in this vicinity.

Keokuk Limestone.

The Keokuk Limestones are often sufficiently durable for building purposes, but are too irregular in thickness to be much sought after, excepting for ordinary uses, but some of the beds would burn into good Lime.

Coal Measure Limestones.

Some of the Coal Measure Limestones would burn into Lime, but the article would not be so white, nor so good in other respects as that burned from the Lower Carboniferous Limestones.

The *Chaetetes* Limestone would probably make the best Lime of any of the Coal Measure rocks.

HYDRAULIC CEMENT.

Mr. Norwood makes mention of a Limestone found at Wiseley's Mill, Burton and Roanoke, which he thinks would burn into good Lime. He regards it as No. 11 of his Section.

I think it probable that a Limestone, occurring about 15 or 20 feet below Coal " B," may be a good Cement stone. The only place where I observed it was about a mile north of Fayette, but Mr. Norwood observed it in Sec. 22, T. 52, R. 16.

The Limestone overlying the Coal in some respects resembles a Hydraulic Limestone, and that in the bluffs above Glasgow may be somewhat Hydraulic.

The proper tests will determine if we are correct in calling these Hydraulic Limestones.

IRON ORE.

Thin layers of Clay Ironstone are occasionally found in the Shale beds, but were not observed in sufficient quantity or richness at any place to pay for mining.

Mr. Norwood observed 1 foot of argillaceous red Hematite resting on Lower Carboniferous Chert between Fayette and Rocheport, about Sec. 34, T. 49, R. 15.

FIRE CLAY.

Good beds of Fire Clay may be obtained from beneath most of the Coal beds. That beneath the Fayette Coal appears to be of good quality, and sufficient thickness to work. This Clay as seen appears thus:

No. 1. 2 feet 6 inches blue Fire Clay, with occasional yellow streaks.
No. 2. 1 foot bright brown and grey Clay, containing Selenite (Gypsum) in minute forms.
No. 3. 3 feet gray sandy Clay, containing a little Iron Pyrites and minute scales of Mica.

At Dr. Beck's the Fire Clay is 4 feet thick. The under-Clay of the Glasgow Coal is 3 feet in thickness, and that at Switzer's Mill is about the same.

GYPSUM.

This mineral in the form of Selenite, is often found intercalated with the beds of Fire Clay, but the crystals are too small and too much dispersed through the Coal to be useful for making plaster of Paris. It could be used as a fertilizer, but the Howard county lands are generally rich enough without having to use it.

HEAVY SPAR.

Crystals of Barytes of a pink color occur in the Limestones at Glasgow.

MINERAL SPRINGS.

The mineral springs of this county from their number and reputation are entitled to notice.

They occur in nearly every portion of the county, and nearly all of them are briny, and from some of them Salt was made as much as 65 years ago. Formerly it would pay to make Salt, but facilities of transportation and the low price of the imported article has superceded its home manufacture.

In importance we may regard Boonslick as of the first, Burkhart's as of the second, and that of Fayette as of the third class.

Boonslick is in Sec. 4, T. 49, R. 17.

The surrounding hills are of gentle slope, overlaid by a deposit of the Bluff formation, supporting a growth of chiefly White Oak. The valley of Salt Creek is 300 to 400 feet wide, and covered with a deep Clay formation, the lowest Clays belonging, probably, to the Drift period.

Limestone of the age of the Archimedes Limestone of the Lower Carboniferous, crops out in the head of a valley N. W. of the main springs.

No other outcrops of solid Rocks were observed in the vicinity, but the Coal Measures are supposed to underlie the neighboring hills, as they indeed crop out in a valley half a mile to the south.

There are four Salt Springs and one well at Boonslick, each one affording a free supply of water, all quite strong of brine. A white deposit is found on the surface of the ground at some of the springs, and a black at others. (Fig. 7 is on a map of spring.)

I am indebted to Dr. J. C. Heberling, of Boonsboro, for much valuable information in regard to the history of these springs. The first Salt was made here in 1807; Nathan Boone manufacturing it in 1810. His old works, on a mound in the valley N. W. of the main spring, and just east of a small branch coming into Salt Creek from the west. Other old Salt works were on the east side of another small branch. Large beds of charcoal and ashes are almost the only remains of the former works, but Salt was made here at various times, and almost constantly until about the year 1855 or 1856. The Salt made here was sold in 1837, at 1 cent per bushel, and rating a bushel at 50 pounds, this paid very well. As an evidence of former work here we would state that for 4 square miles around Boonslick, the timber has been entirely cut off at various times, for fuel for the Salt works. At the present time these grounds are entirely covered over with a thrifty growth of young White Oak, with some Walnut, Black Oak and Hickory. These trees are mostly 6—8 inches in diameter, but many are as much as 1 foot.

Dr. J. C. Heberling, W. N. Marshall and others, are the present owners of the property. In 1869 they began to bore for Salt water, and continued their work until the fall of 1872, when the boring had reached a depth of 1,001 feet. They then stopped work. At 37 feet water was obtained; at 68 feet, weak Salt water; and at 163 feet 9 inches, the size of the stream had increased a fourth, with per centage of Salt about the same as the outside stream, or 4.5 per cent.

At a depth of 481 feet they report a vein of Salt water, with an increased strength of one-third. At 707 feet 9 inches, a small addition of water was reached. Also a strong offensive gas, with a corresponding increase of strength of the brine from 4.5—9 per cent (double).

A 10 inch square wooden conductor was put in to the bottom of the quicksand—22 feet. Below this a 1½ inch pipe was inserted, from which the flow is about 30 gallons per minute. The volume of water is sufficient for a 2½ inch pipe.

The record of the borings was kept by Mr. Marshall, who furnished me a copy. I find that there must be an error in classifying the rocks, doubtless arising from an imperfect knowledge of Geology, and not having the necessary means of determining the constituents.

The quicksand extended to 22 feet. From this to 37 feet is evidently a drifted mass of Gravel, Limestone and Flint. Two feet of Coal were reported at 40 feet, and a 7-inch seam of it at 82 feet. The record further shows Limestone and Flint to 150 feet depth. From this down, is mostly Sand and Flint, with some Limestone. At 1,001 feet the boring terminated in a crevice.

BURKHART'S SPRING.

This spring is 2 miles west of New Franklin, at the edge of a small valley coming into the Bonne Femme from the west side. The water issues forth very freely from the valley Clays, not very far from a Bluff of Burlington Limestone. A white deposit is formed in the bed of the branch. In former times, considerable Salt was made here.

LEWIS SPRING.

The Lewis Spring, near Glasgow, is on the land of Jno. F. Lewis, 1½ miles from Glasgow, on the west branch of Gregg's Creek. The Salt water here flows from Clay at several places within a space of 12 feet square. In some places a white, and in others a black deposit is found in the bed of the rivulet.

There is another small Salt spring on Bear Creek, just outside of the limits of Glasgow.

A weak-flowing Salt spring appears on the west side of Sulphur Creek, near where it enters the Missouri bottoms.

On the flat below the railroad depot at Fayette, is a Salt and Sulphur Spring, of about the strength of the Lewis Spring. The cattle have formed, by licking and tramping, an extensive lick 50 by 100 feet. This was originally known as Buffalo Lick, and 2,800 acres of the neighboring lands were originally reserved as Saline lands, for the use of the State.

Simpson's Lick, or Simpson's Branch, one mile from the Missouri bottom, is a weak Salt spring. No Salt was ever made here, although the land was entered for " Saline Lands."

SALT WATER SPRINGS.

BY C. J. NORWOOD.

There are a number of Salt water springs in the eastern part of the county, at all of which Salt has been made at one time or another.

On Mrs. Wilhite's land, in N. W. quarter Sec. 2, T. 49, R. 15, there is a weak Salt spring. This was formerly known as the Moniteau Lick. Four thousand acres of the adjoining lands were originally selected for the use of the State. On the Messrs. Morriss' land, in Sec. 34, T. 50, R. 15, there is another which affords a great deal of water, but which is also weak. Judge Wade Jackson says that he made Salt from the water of each of these springs, but that it required from 500 to 600 gallons of water to make a bushel of Salt. He then dug a well on his place, in Sec. 35, T. 50, R. 15, to the depth of 50 feet, to Limestone, and then bored 250 feet. After boring 200 feet he struck Salt water, but it being no stronger than the water in the springs he bored 50 feet more, and, obtaining no water at that depth, abandoned the enterprise. It is his opinion that the water obtained by boring contained less Sulphur and Magnesia than that in the springs. It all probably came from the same source.

On Judge McCafferty's land, in E. half S. W. quarter Sec. 16, T. 51, R. 15, there is an old lick which is known as " Cooley's Lick." Mr. McCafferty states that Salt was first made here fifty or sixty years ago, and that John Cooley made Salt at the lick in 1841. He says he first saw the spring in that year, and at that time there were

trees growing up from old stumps that he judged to be thirty years
old. According to Mr. McCafferty's calculations Salt must have been
made here as far back as 1811. Mr. McCafferty has owned the lick for
twenty-five years, and made Salt in 1862, using the few remaining
kettles that were first used fifty or sixty years ago. He was unable to
state how much water was required to make a bushel of Salt, but
says that in making a bushel he burned four cords of wood. At one
time he would obtain more Salt from a certain amount of water than
at another. The water has a Sulphurous smell, and leaves and pieces
of wood left in the spring are soon covered with a yellowish white
coating.

At Mr. Adams', in the N. W. quarter, Sec. 33, T. 49, R. 15, there
are several Salt and Sulphur springs combined. In some the Salt predominates and in others the Sulphur. They are all close together and
the water is weak, about 700 gallons of it being required to make one
bushel of Salt. Salt was made here forty years ago.

AGRICULTURE.

The principal crops raised in this county are Corn, Wheat and
Tobacco; the next succeeding are Oats, Rye and Barley.

The average yield of Corn in the eastern part of the county is 35
bushels per acre. The hills in the western and south-western portions of the county will yield much more. The richest lands are said
to produce as much as 85 bushels to the acre, and the Missouri bottoms from 40 to 70. Mr. L. A. Brown raised over 70 bushels of Barley
per acre by subsoiling and harrowing well. Mr. Brown also informed
me that he raised 89 barrels of Corn on 4½ acres of Missouri bottom.
I should think 50 to 60 bushels of Corn per acre a fair average for the
best uplands in the western and south-western portion of the county.

The crop of Wheat will vary with the season. In the north-eastern
part of the county 10 to 15 bushels is the average yield, while in other
parts it is 20 to 30 with an average of 17 bushels. Most of the land
will produce 1,000 pounds of Tobacco and 40 bushels of Corn to the
acre.

The poorest lands are in the north-eastern part of the county.
The central, southern and western portions include lands that will favorably compare with the richest lands of Missouri.

The grasses seem to grow well and the surface of all the pastures
is generally covered with a luxuriant growth of blue grass (*Poa
compressa*) which is considered the best grass for grazing purposes.

This county is well supplied with bearing orchards and produces annually large quantities of fine apples. Other fruits do as well as in most of the counties along the Missouri River.

TIMBER.

Probably no county is better supplied with good varieties of hard timber than this. Among the best we may include White, Red and Burr Oak, Rock Chesnut and Pin Oak, Laurel Oak, Black and White Walnut, Elm, Sugar Tree, Ash, Linden, Birch, Sycamore, Cottonwood, Honey Locust and Wild Cherry.

COAL MEASURES.

BY C. J. NORWOOD.

Coal, the most abundant and important mineral in the county, is found in every township, and in some of them in nearly every section. It and its accompanying rocks occur very irregularly, sometimes thinning out and again thickening up. This is especially the case in the eastern part of the county. Near Sebree we find a Coal bed (Coal D) overlaid by Limestone and Shales, the whole forming an aggregate thickness of 35 to 40 feet. As we go north this Coal, with the accompanying rocks, entirely disappears. A more perplexing case occurs north-east of Sebree. At Digg's Coal bank the Coal (No. 56) is overlaid by 38 feet of Sandstone and Shales, while three-fourths of a mile west " Coal D " was also found, and which by measurement was *apparently* only *four* feet above the former (Coal E.) This apparent close proximity is explained, however, by the fact that the Coal (E.) seen at Diggs' was found to be dipping 10° S. 65° W., while Coal D. was dipping strongly east of north.

From the foregoing it will be seen that the construction of a correct vertical section of the rocks in the county was attended with much difficulty.

The following section, it is believed, will be found to be correct:

COAL MEASURES OF HOWARD COUNTY.

Number	Feet. Inches.	General Section.	Total feet.	Localities.
		30 to 50 feet Bluff and Loess.		
1	30 feet............	Buff, brown, gray, buff-spotted, with red or brown, buff-striped with red, and red micaceous Sandstone, which is generally soft, though sometimes found in hard, compact beds; mediumly fine-grained; at about the middle it is very ferruginous, and has many round cavites, which give to that portion of the rock a very rough appearance, contains *Sigillaria, Calmites*, etc..................................	30	Q. F. Beach's near Roanoke. Mr. Snell's in Sec. 28, T. 49, R. 15, and generally along the Fayette and Rocheport roads, to within 7 miles of the former.
2	——(?)............	COAL A.		Beach's.
3	17 feet............	Sandy Shale; red near the middle, olive above and below.......	47	
4	2 feet.............	Rough-bedded, light-drab or gray fine-grained Limestone, abounding in *Fusulina; Athyris subtilita*, and *Spr. lineatus*, are also abundant, and large *Crinoid* columns found....................	49	Squire Phelps', at Roanoke.
5	3 feet.............	Olive and dark calcareous Shale, containing *Prod. splendens, Athyris subtilita, Hemipronites crassus, Retzia punctulifera, Chonetes*, and abounding in *Spr. (Martinia) planoconvexus*.......	52	" " " "
6	½ inch...	Coal smut......................................	....	
7	1 foot	Very nodular, ash-drab or gray argillaceous Limestone abounding in *Fusulina cylindrica*...............................	53	" " " "
8	7 feet.............	Shale and nodules of decomposing argillaceous Limestone........................	60	
9	2 feet.............	Fine-grained, drab, sometimes silicious Limestone, with a brown crust; fossils are *Arcæocidaris megastilus*, large *Spr. lineatus*, etc...............................	62	" " " "
10	1 foot 6 inches..	Thin beds of Limestone and marlite, abounding in organic remains. *Spr. lineatus, Spr. planoconvexus*, (especially abundant,) *Athyris, Hemipronites crassus, Prod. costatus, Pr. punctatus*, (?) *Chonetes mesoloba, chonetes* ——, (?) *Synocladea biserialis, Archæocidaris megastylus, Fusulina cylindrica*, and *Crinoidal* columns being found	63	" " " "

Coal Measures—Continued.

Number	Feet. Inches.	GENERAL SECTION.	Total feet.	LOCALITIES.
11	7 feet........	Irregularly bedded Hydraulic Limestone. The top is very light-drab and generally shelly, the bottom being more compact, fine-grained and bluish-drab; sometimes this rock is divided into several beds, the upper part abounding in *Chonetes mesoloba*, containing large *Spr. lineatus*, *Athyris*, *Spr. cameratus*, *Hemipronites crassus*, *Prod. costatus.* and *Pr. semireticulatus*, while in the lower part *Spr. lineatus*, *Spr. cameratus*, *Prod. splendens*, *Spr. planoconvexus*, *Spr. Kentuckensis*, *Retzia punctulifera*, *Lophophyllum*, arms of *Archaeocidaris megustylus*, *Fusulina (robusta?)* and *Phillipsa major*, are found......................	70	Roanoke, Burton and Wiseley's mill, north of Fayette.
12	7 feet..............	Rough, somewhat nodular, irregularly bedded, mottled, dove and light-drab, or blue and drab, fine-grained Limestone; generally occurs in large, ill-shapen blocks projecting from the sides of the hills; abounds in *Chætetes milleporaceus*, which occurs in large mamilliary masses, and from this peculiarity it has been called ...... CHÆTETES LIMESTONE. This is division A.	77	Highest rock on the hills, south-east of Fayette. Near Mr. Garner's, in Sec. 20, T. 52, R. 16. Near Burton, Roanoke, and in the hills on the Fayette and Rocheport roads, in Sec. 5, T. 49, R. 15.
13	2 feet 6 inches..	Hard silicious, light-blue Limestone weathering ferruginous brown; full of large masses of *Chætetes*, and is division B, of the "Chætetes Limestone;" *Fusulina cylindrica* (abundant,) *Athyris*, *Spr. lineatus*,*Spr. planoconvexus*, *Prod. costatus*,*Lophophyllum proliferum*, and *Acrhaeocidaris*, were found.........	80	Roanoke. Wiseley's mill N. of Fayette, not often exposed.
14	25 feet..............	Sandy Shale, sometimes passing into Sandstone....................	105	McCrary's on Hackley's Branch.
15	3 feet..............	Hard, fine-grained dove to dark-blue "*Rhomboidal Limestone*," so-called because it occurs in rhomboidal bl'ks.	108	Roanoke on Doxy's Fork. Sebree. Burton, Boonsboro.
16	6 inches	Drab Shale...........	....	
17	1 to 2 feet...	Bituminous Slate..................................	110	
18	9 inches	COAL B.—This is sometimes, though very seldom, 30 inches, and is often only 6 inches..	111	Very often exposed.

The column between "Total feet." and "LOCALITIES" for rows 12–13 is labeled vertically: "Chætetes Limestone."

Coal Measures—Continued.

Number	Feet. inches.	GENERAL SECTION.	Total feet.	LOCALITIES.
19	5 to 13 feet.......	This includes Shales and Nodules of Limestone, or beds of Limestone, separated by Shale. Excepting the north-east part of the county, we generally find Shales with Limestone Nodules occupying the whole thickness. The Limestone beds are always arenaceous and of a light drab or gray color, mottled with dove or blue spots. *Prod. Prattenianus* var. *æquicostatus* is the characteristic fossil ; *Prod. semireticulatus, Pr. costatus, Athyris* and a *Phillipsia* are also found..	124	Burton. Railroad cut near Russell. Mont. Reynolds in Sec. 35, T. 52, R. 15, and Mr. Garners, in Sec. 20, T. 52, R. 16.
20	1 foot 8 inches..	Hard, fine-grained, compact Limestone in from 1 to 3 beds ; color deep ashblue, with chocolate to buff exterior.	126	Sec. 22, T. 52, R. 16
21	8 inches	Clay ; color green.............................		
22	1 foot 3 inches..	Dark argillo-bituminous Shale, with many small, round concretions of dark colored Limestone....................	128	
	6 inches	COAL C.—This is often not thicker than 2 inches, and only a smut................		Sec. 35, T. 52, R. 15, Burton.
24	2 feet.............	Fire Clay....................................	130	
25	3 feet.............	Blue and buff argillaceous Shale.........	133	
26	10 feet...........	Sandy Shale and thin beds of Sandstone....................................	143	R. R. cut, east of Sebree.
27	4 feet.............	Red sandy Shale..........................	147	Hurricane Cr., SE of Glasgow.
28	6 inches	Reddish and greenish-gray, impure arenaceous Limestone ; not persistent......................................	148	R. R. cut, east of Sebree.
29	2 feet 6 inches..	Blue, sandy Shale, with concretious of Ochre	150	
30	6 feet.............	Thin-bedded Sandstone....................	156	
31	3 inches	Yellow Ochre..............................		
32	8 feet.............	Sandy Shale..............................	164	
33	16 to 25 feet.. ..	Sandstone :—The upper 8 feet is shaley, but the lower is compact ; is micaceous, and brown to buff, or even gray ; generally soft. Some parts contain many remains of plants. "Micaceous Sandstone" of Prof. Swallow (?)......	189	Hurricane Creek, near Mr. Turners.

Coal Measures—Continued.

Number	Feet. Inches.	GENERAL SECTION.	Total feet.	LOCALITIES.
34	2 feet..............	Very rough, irregularly bedded Limestone, weathering light drab tinged, with brown, and with a sandy appearance on the surface ; fracture shows dove to blue, sometimes mottled with gray ; is fine-grained and breaks with an imperfect conchoidal fracture. The fossils are *Spr. lineatus*, *Spr. planoconvexus*, *Pleurotomaria* (small sp.) and *Loxonema* (?)......................	191	Sebree.
35	1 foot..............	Nodular Limestone...........................	192	
36	2 feet..............	Greenish drab calcareous Shale, with occasional small calcareous Nodules..	194	
37	5 inches	Somewhat concretionary mottled blue and gray Limestone	195	
38	8 inches	Variegated greenish drab and dark, calcareous Shale, full of remains of fossils. The following are all that could be recognized : *Chonetes mesoloba* (abundant), *Sp. planoconvexus*, and *Crinoid* columns............		
39	2 feet 3 inches..	Hard, fine-grained, compact, light drab (or gray) mottled, with dove (or blue) Limestone. Rough on surface, and weathers a light ferruginous tinge ; it is rich in fossils, which are mostly found on the surface, and are : *Spirifer lineatus*, *Spr. plano-convexus*, *Spr. cameratus*, *Spiriferina Kentuckensis*, a large *Spirifer* resembling and possibly is a large variety of *Spirifer cameratus*, *Athyris*, *Prod. Costatus*, *Productus* ——(?), *Hemipronites crassus*, *Chonetes Verneuiliana*, *Ch. mesoloba*, *Aviculopecten interlineatus*, *Pleurotomaria* (small sp.) *Bellerophon* (small sp.), *Rhombopora Lepidodendroides*, *Fusulina cylindrica* and *Crinoid* colums. It contains a little Chert in vein like forms, and which often decomposes upon exposure to the weather................	198	Sebree, in Railroad cut west of town.
40	5 feet..............	Olive sandy Shale...........................	203	
31	3 feet 6 inches..	Dark bitumino-argillaceous Shale........	206	
42	6 inches	Clay Ironstone (Carb. Iron). This often looks like an ordinary blue, impure Limestone, and is no heavier, and again it is very heavy and dark-blue. *Crinoid* columns were found in it......	207	Sebree.
43	6 inches	Shale..................................		

! *Coal Measures—*Continued.

Number	Feet. Inches.	General Section.	Total feet.	Localities.
44	2 feet...............	Bituminous Slate................................	209	
45	1 foot 6 inches..	Coal D.—This sometimes thicken to 2½ feet................................	211	Sebree.
46	5 feet...............	Fire (?) Clay	216	
47	1 foot...............	Bed of concretionary Limestone. This is local...........................	217	Sebree.
48	7 feet...............	Sandy Clay and Shale, with minute selenite crystals at the top................	224	
49	6 feet...............	Sandstone—gray banded with brown, and full of pyritiferous concretions, which weather out on exposure, leaving the rock full of small round holes	230	
50	4 feet...............	Dark-blue Clay...........	234	
51	4 feet...............	Green and light-blue Clay................	238	
52	10 feet............	Thin bedded Sandstone..	248	
53	16 feet.............	Sandy Shale................................	264	
54	10 feet.............	Argillaceous or (locally) arenaceous Shale, with ochreous concretions and thin layers of Clay Ironstone (Carb. Iron)................................	274	
55	1 to 2 feet........	Very dark-blue Pyrito-calcareous Shale which is often quite hard at Digg's Coal bank, and abounds in *Prod. muricatus, Pr. punctatus* (?), *Astartella vera* (?), *Hemipronites crassus, Myalina Swallovi, Aviculopecten recta-laterarea, Aviculopecten* —— (?) *Orthoceras Cribrosnm* (?) are also found, and are coated with Iron Pyrites.......	276	Near Sebree. Skinner's Coal b'k on Bonne Femme, near Burton, and Dr. Beck's (?), in Sec. 32, T. 50, R. 16.
56	2 to 3 feet........	Coal E.—This is divided about the middle by a Clay seam, and reaches a thickness of 39 inches................	279	Diggs. near Sebree. Skinner's on Bonne Femme north of Fayette, etc.
57	1 foot 3 inches..	Dark Clay................................	280	
58	6 inches	Clay, with Selenite. This is sometimes indurated................................	281	
59	2 to 10 feet......	Blue, argillaceous Shale and Marlite....	291	
60	2 feet...............	Hard, blue and dove colored, fine-grained Limestone; rough on the surface................................	293	Diggs and Skinners.

Coal Measures—Continued.

Number	Feet. Inches.	GENERAL SECTION.		Total feet.	LOCALITIES.
61	2 feet +............	Green, sandy Shale, with calcareous concretions at the top, and abounding in Spr. plano-convexus ; Pr. muricatus, Chonetes mesoloba and Crinoid columns were also found.................		295	
62	54 feet (?)........	Slope..			
63	50 feet.............	Ferruginous Sandstone...............	LOWER FERROUS. CARBONI-		Mo. River Bluffs.
64	40 to 50 feet.. ...	Keokuk (Archimedes) Limestone			½ mile below Lisbon.
65	50 to 60 feet......	Burlington Limestone			Opposite Rocheport, Boone county.
66	75 feet...............	Chouteau Limestone..................			Near the mouth of Richland Creek.

REMARKS ON THE GENERAL SECTION.*

No. 2—This is said to be from 3 to 4 feet thick, but I can not vouch for it, as I was unable to see it at the locality where it is said to reach that thickness.

Nos. 10 to 11—Archaeocidaris megastylus seems to be characteristic of these rocks, and was not found below No. 11.

No. 12—This is the easiest recognized rock in the county, always abounding in huge masses of Chætetes milleporaceus, and the only rock in the county containing that Coral in abundance. It is probably the equivalent of No. 36 of Prof. Swallow's Section of the Missouri Coal Measures.† It is equivalent to No. VI of the Randolph County Section.

No. 15 varies greatly in its lithological characters. At one locality it may be seen very dark blue with a great deal of Iron Pyrites (Iron Sulphid) and inclined to be shelly, while at another point it is fine-grained, compact and an excellent building stone. It always occurs in rhomboidal blocks, the joints being sometimes filled by Calc Spar or Carbonate of Lime. There is one marked peculiarity about it—in the northern part of the county it is nearly always seen full of small round cavities, caused by the weathering out of small masses of Iron Pyrites, while in the southern part it was nowhere found exhibiting this character. It generally occurs in from two to four beds and three feet thick. It is the equivalent of No. IX of the Randolph County Section, of No. 5 of the Muscle Fork Section, in Macon county, and possibly (?) of No. 44 of Prof. Swallow's Section of the Coal Measures.‡ It is usually silicious.

No. 18—This is occasionally worked, but only for domestic use. The discovery of thicker Coals has rendered the mining of it for any other purpose unprofitable. It was found showing a thickness of 30 inches at only one locality.

* No. 1—I think this must be the upper Sandstone of the Middle Coal Measures, equivalent to the Sandstone at Kirksville, Adair county, and to the Sandstone near Milan, Sullivan county.—G. C. B.

† See First and Second Annual Reports of the Geological Survey of Missouri, 1855, page 83.

‡ It is more probable that it is lower, and equivalent to No. 41 of General Section Middle Coal Measures, 1872, by Mr. G. C. Broadhead, (published in Geological Report for 1872.)—B.

No. 23—This is hardly ever more than a smut, and is sometimes merely a black streak in Clay. At one locality it was said to be 18 inches thick and of good quality, having been used by smiths. It is the equivalent of No. XVI of the Randolph County Section, and of No. 58 of Prof. Swallow's (?).

No. 27—This often thins out.

No. 28—This is not persistent for long distances.

Nos. 29 to 32, inclusive, are often wanting.

Nos. 33 to 51, inclusive, seem to be wanting as we go north from Sebree.

No. 45 (included in the above)—This is probably No. 68 of Prof. Swallow. It is the first really workable bed in descending order.

Nos. 34 to 39 are probably the equivalents of the Hydraulic Limestone of Prof. Swallow, (No. 66 of his Coal Measure Section.)

No. 49 is the equivalent of No. XX of Randolph county.

No. 54 is the equivalent of No. XXII of Randolph county.

No. 56—This is the best Coal in the county, and has but little Iron Pyrites in it, and is equivalent to No. 24 of Randolph county. It is probably the equivalent of No. 74 of Prof. Swallow's Section of the Missouri Coal Measures.[†]

No. 60—This, as seen at Digg's Coal Bank, near Seebree, is very rough and nodular at the bottom; it is gray or drab, mottled with deep blue or dove, weathering with a mottled appearance. The fossils found are *Athyris*, *Hemipronites crassus*, *Spr. lineatus* and *Fusulina cylindrica*. It *lithologically* resembles No. 30.

No. 33 may be the Micaceous Sandstone of Prof. Swallow, which is regarded as the dividing line between the Middle and Lower Coal Measures of Missouri. Should this be true, we find that there are in this county 164 feet of the Middle and 131 feet of the Lower Coal Measures—this latter including the Sandstone No. 33.

The "Chætetes Limestone" is the best and most reliable guide to one in search of Coal in this county, and may be denominated the *Key* to the Coal Measures in Howard county. This is true because it is the easiest recognized and more universally exposed throughout the county than any other rock.

Twenty-five feet below it we find the highest Coal, which is coextensive with the country. It is true there is a Coal above it said to be 4 feet (?) thick, but I think its area is necessarily quite limited from the position it occupies in the hills. I refer to Coal A.[†] Taking the "Chætetes Limestone" as a starting point, one may judge (by referring to the General Section) at about what depth Coal may be reached in different localities, always bearing in mind that the strata are liable to thicken or thin. For instance, in sinking for Coal at Burton or Roanoke, we must not expect to find "Coal D," for it thins out towards the north. That this is the case will be shown farther on.

---

* Vide First and Second Annual Reports of the Geological Survey of Missouri, by G. C. Swallow, 1855, page 87.

† I was unable to see this Coal, and can not vouch for its thickness being "four feet."

" Coal A" is the highest in the county, and has been worked at Mr. Q. F. Beach's in S. E. Sec. 25, T. 52, R. 16. A shaft was sunk on the side of a ridge here, reaching the Coal at 21 feet. At the time of our visit, the shaft was closed up, the mine having fallen in. A gentleman in Roanoke informed me that he understood the Coal had given out, and that this was the cause of the mine being abandoned. Not being able to enter the mine, I can only give this report for what it is worth—expressing no opinion as to the truthfulness of it.

The next Coal below that just spoken of, was first seen at Mr. Steven Garner's, in S. hf. N. W. qr. Sec. 20, T. 52, R. 16, and is " Coal B."

It is the most extensive Coal in the county, being found in every township north of T. 49, and in some of them in nearly every section. Unfortunately, it is not thick enough to be of *commercial* importance, but still it would furnish the farmer, if necessary, with all the Coal he would need.

At Mr. Garner's the Chætetes Limestone is found twenty feet above this Coal, and rocks as low as No. 33 exposed below.

The following section was made at and near Mr. Garner's, and will serve to show the relative position of the rocks in regard to this Coal.

No. 1. 20 to 40 feet Slope.
No. 2. 5 feet rough bedded, fine-grained dove and gray hard Limestone, abounding in masses of *Chætetes milleporaceus*. (Chætetes Limestone—Division A).
No. 3. 3 feet light blue and ochreous Clay Shale.
No. 4. 3 feet Clay.
No. 5. 12 feet Slope.
No. 6. 6 inches to 2 feet "Rhomboidal Limestone."
No. 7. 9 inches drab Shale.
No. 8. 2 feet Bituminous Slate.
No. 9. 9 inches "Coal B."
No. 10. 8 feet Slope.
No. 11. 5 feet greenish arenaceous Shale, with thin beds and nodules of bluish drab Limestone, thickly distributed through the Clay or Shale.* (No. 19, General Section.)
No. 12. 20 inches hard, compact, fine-grained, chocolate and grayish colored Limestone in three layers.

---

* This explains the mottled appearance of No. 19, when seen as a compact Limestone. The bluish drab spots, are purer Limestone and harder than any other part of the rock. From these data we would conclude that the Shale (No. 11 of the above Section) which incloses the nodules, has simply received an excess of Lime, and become harder and compact, the nodules being so firmly cemented and so completely surrounded by Lime as to escape detection in the compact rock, and as they retain their original color when the rock is fractured, they are only seen as bluish drab spots on an ash gray or light drab ground.

No. 13. 2½ feet olive, slightly calcareous Shale.
No. 14. 1 foot dark blue Shale, with knife edges of Coal. (Coal C.)
No. 15. 15 feet Slope.
No. 16. 6 inches indurated gray Sandstone.
No. 17. 10½ feet Sandstone.
No. 18. 5 feet + Sandy shale.

Coal B is also found at Mr. Turner's in Sec. 22, T. 51, R. 17, on a ridge the course of which is east and west along Hurricane Creek.

The Coal at this point is about 9 inches thick, with the Chætetes Limestone exposed only 12 feet above. As there are still lower rocks exposed here than at Mr. Garner's, the following section is given:

No. 1. 25 feet Slope.
No. 2. 4 feet + Chætetes Limestone.
No. 3. 10 feet Slope.
No. 4. 1½ feet blue and dove fine-grained Limestone. ("Rhomboidal Limestone.")
No. 6. Coal B.
No. 7. 18 feet Slope.
No. 8. 1 foot + fine-grained chocolate colored Limestone.
No. 9. 1 foot green Clay.
No. 10. 25 feet Slope.
No. 11. 23 feet Sandstone. (No. 33 of General Section.)
No. 12. 30 inches very rough, bedded, drab Limestone, breaking with a rough fracture; weathers ash gray, with a sandy appearance. Fossils are *Spirifer (martinia) lineatus, Prod. semi-reticulatus Zaphrentis* ————,(?) and a fragment of *Chætetes.*
No. 13. 5 feet Limestone in from 4 to 8 beds, which may be classed thus, beginning with the top:
  (*a*) 14 inches blue and sometimes dove, fine-grained, hard Limestone; irregularly bedded, weathers brown, and has a rough fracture. Calcite is disseminated in specks and thread-like veins; a little rose colored Baryta (?) was also observed.
  (*b*) 34 inches hard, fine-grained, light drab splintery Limestone, with minute specks of Calcite disseminated. Weathers drab and occurs in large, irregularly shaped blocks, caused by water wearing large fissures in the rock.
  (*c*) 14 inches hard, compact, fine grained, dove colored Limestone, breaking with a sub conchoidal fracture. At the center the rock is blue.
  (*d*) 9 inches + hard, deep blue, compact fine grained silicious Limestone, with a thick chocolate colored crest. Has many specks of Calcite distributed throughout.

Some of the foregoing beds appear to possess "Hydraulic Limestone properties."

G.S.—13.

The " Chætetes Limestone " is also found high up in the hills in
the southern sections of T. 51, R. 17, and in the north part of T. 50, R.
17. In Sec. 14 of the latter Township, it is seen near the top of the
hills, with from 15 to 20 feet [of greenish drab sandy Shale immediately below it.

The following is a General Section of Ts. 50, 51 and 52, R. 17:

Section.

No.	Feet.	Inch's	GENERAL SECTION A.	LOCALITY.
1	60	....	Slope...	
2	1	6	Buff to brown argillaceous Limestone Slope..........	
3	4	0	Slope...	
4	....	6	Very even bedded chocolate and drab, fine grained Limestone..	B. M. Crary's
5	5	0	Clay...	
6	1	6	Irregularly bedded, blue, drab and dove colored fine grained Limestone, abounding in *Fusulina cyl-indrica.* No. 11 Gen. Sec................................	" "
7	5	0	Clay...	
8	6	0	" Chætetes Limestone "...........................	On nearly all the high p'nts.
9	15—25	0	Sandy shale in thick laminae.......................	
10	2	0	" Rhomboidal Limestone...........................	S 26, T 50, R 17
11	....	9	Drab Shale...	
12	1	0	Bituminous Slate	S. 22, T. 1, R. 17
13	....	15	COAL B...	
14	....	14	Fire Clay with *Stigmaria ficoides*	
15	8	0	Slope.:..	
16	5	0	Greenish colored clay with beds of Limestone and Limestone Nodules. No. 19 Gen. Sec.................	
17	....	20	Hard fine grained Limestone.......................	
18	2	6	Yellowish slightly calcareous Clay.................	
19	1	0	Dark blue Clay, with a black streak and a few par-ticles of Coal. The streak is " Coal C "...........	
20	3	0	Slope	
21	6	0	Greenish and olive sandy Shale in thin laminæ.....	
22	4	0	Red arenaceous Shale.............................	S 15, T 59, R 17
23	3	0	Green sandy Shale.................................	

Section--Continued.

No.	Feet.	Inch's	GENERAL SECTION A.	LOCALITY.
24	8	0	Slope......	
25	23	0	Sandstone, soft and micaceous. No. 38 of Gen. Sec	S 22, T 51, R 17
26	6	6	Blue, dove and drab Limestone...............................	Glasgow.
27	16	9	Blue and drab Shale..	
28	(?)	....	Bituminous Shale...................................	S 16, T 50, R 1 7
29	2	9	" COAL D."...	J. Tatum's &
30	....	4	Rotten Coal and yellow Ochre............................	Glasgow.
31	3	0	Blue Clay with streaks of yellow Ochre................	
32	12	0	Blue and drab sandy Shale with bands of yellow ochre, in which ferns are abundant................	Glasgow.
33	20	0	Deep blue sandy Shale and finely ripple marked Sandstone	Glasgow.
34	(?)	0	Slope..	

In T. 50, R. 15, the strata from No. 12 of the General Section to No. 19, inclusive, are seen. These rocks are well exposed on the Mt. Gilead Road, two miles east of Fayette, in Sec. 7, T. 50, R. 15. The " Chætetes Limestone " is only two feet thick at this point the "Rhomboidal Limestone " 9 inches, and " Coal B" 15 inches thick, and seen only as a smut. On Mr. Pierce's land, a short distance south-east of the road, the strata thickens up and the Coal assumes a thickness of 30 inches. This, however, is maintained for only a short distance, and thins rapidly to the south.

In Sec. 14, T. 50, R. 15, lower rocks are found, but they dip so rapidly and disappear so suddenly that they can be traced for only a short distance. A Section made here is as follows.

SECTION 15.
No. 1. 35 feet Slope.
No. 2. 10 inches hard, light drab to grey mottled, with fine-grained, dove-colored Limestone. No. 39 of Gen. Sec.
No. 3. 3 feet Clay.
No. 4. 6 feet blue and green areno-argillaceous Shale, with ochreous bands.
No. 5. 6 feet argillo-bituminous Shale.
No. 6. 8 inches dark blue Clay-ironstone, containing small Crinoid columns, the organic matter of which has been replaced by brown carbonate of Iron.

No. 7.   3 feet 6 inches bituminous Slate.

No. 8.   5 feet dark blue Shale with lenticular concretions of blue Limestone.

No. 9.   6 inches bitumenous Slate; this is quite hard and calcarous, with pyritous bands. Contains *Cordaites?* and an imperfect form of a curious fucoid remotely resembling *Caulerpites* (*Chondrites colletti?*)

No. 10.   6 inches bitumino-argillaceous Shale, full of charred remains of plants.

No. 11.   4 feet Clay—mostly Fire Clay.

The rocks dip 1 foot in 16 feet, course N. 15° W. Considering No. 2 as No. 39 of Gen. Section, " Coal D " should be found here.

I suspect that the Shale (No. 10) has taken its place. This is very possible as the Shale is a mixture of Clay and charred remains of plants, and it is known that Coal D thins out toward the north.

In T. 50, R. 14, the rocks from No. 12 to No. 61 are found exposed, and all within an area of a mile and a half. In the S. W. quarter Sec. 7, in a cut of the Louisiana Railroad, the following section was made :

No. 1.   12 feet gentle Slope.

No. 2.   2 feet very rough, irregularly bedded Limestone, weathering light, drab tinged with brown, and with a sandy appearance. The prevailing color is blue or dove, but this is occasionally mottled with light drab spots; is fine grained and breaks with a sub-conchoidal fracture. The organic remains are *Spr.* (*Martinia*) *plano-convexus*, *Spr. lineatus*, a small *Pleurotomaria* and *Crinoid* columns.

No. 3.   12 to 18 inches very loosely cemented nodular Limestone—marlite ?

No. 4.   2 feet greenish drab Calcareous Shale.

No. 5.   5 inches Concretionary Limestone.

No. 6.   4 to 8 inches variegated, greenish drab and dark Calcareous Shale. Fossiliferous.

No. 7.   27 inches hard, fine grained, compact Limestone, rough on the surface and weathering with a light ferruginous tinge. The color is light drab to gray, mottled with blue or dove. It is traversed by thin vein-like masses of Chert, which decompose upon exposure and assume either a buff or ashy white color. It abounds in fossils, for which see No. 39 of General Section. This corresponds to No. 7 of the Glasgow Section.

No. 8.   5 feet sandy Shale.

No. 9.   3½ feet dark argillo-bituminous Shale.

No. 10.   2 to 6 inches Clay Ironstone (?) containing *Crinoideæ*.

No. 11.   6 inches bituminous Shale.

No. 12.   2 feet bituminous Slate.

No. 13.   18 to 20 inches Coal D.

No. 14.   12 feet Clay and Shale, with a concretionary bed of argillaceous Limestone. The lower 7 feet of the Shale is sandy, with small crystals of Gypsum.

No. 15. 6 feet of gray, banded with brown, very fine grained Sandstone. It is
full of pyritiferous concretions, which weather out, leaving small
round cavities. Upon long exposure it disintegrates and then remains a loose bed of sand.

No. 16. 4 feet dark blue and purple Fire Clay.

No. 17. 4 feet green Clay to water in Manitou Creek. Going eastward from
here the rocks rise and a lower series come to view, as is exhibited
in the following section :

Sec. 18, at R. Diggs' Coal Bank, located in N. E. quarter Sec. 8, T. 50, R. 14, one mile N.
E. of Sebree.

No. 1. 110 feet Slope from hill top.

No. 2. 10 feet thin beds of Sandstone interstratified with Shale.

No. 3. 16 feet sandy Shale.

No. 4. 10 feet argillaceous Shale with thin layers of Carbonate of Iron. Shale
is semi-bituminous at the top.

No. 5. 2 feet hard dark blue calcareo-pyritiferous Shale, abounding in *Produc-*
tus muricatus, and other fossils, for which see No. 55, General Section.

No. 6. 2 feet 6 inches good, shiny black Coal. Has a pyritiferous Clay parting
(often indurated) at 21 inches from the top. But little pyrites was
seen, and to all appearances it is an excellent smithing Coal. The
Coal is said to occasionally attain a thickness of 3 feet. It dips 10
deg. S., 65 deg. W. mage. course. This is "Coal E."

No. 7. 2 feet Clay.

No. 8. 2½ feet very rough mottled deep blue and gray or light drab Limestone.
Bottom quite nodular. This is No. 60 of General Section and lithologically closely resembles No. 39. A close examination, however,
shows it to be different.

No. 9. 2 feet green sandy Shale, with small calcareous concretions.

No. 5 does not appear to be constant. At one opening it was not
seen at all, while only 50 yards away it was found exhibiting its full
thickness and containing its characteristic fossils. From its presence
here I am disposed to regard this Coal as equivalent to that seen at
Dr. Beck's, but the question arises, where is the Limestone and bituminous Slate seen over Dr. Beck's Coal? This Limestone, however,
may have thinned out, (which I think probable,) which would be no
uncommon occurrence in this county. Dr. Beck's Coal may be a
higher one, but still it is hardly probable that two different beds of
Shale would be found, both abounding in *Productus muricatus* and
each containing other fossils of the *same species*.

Unless an 18 inch bed, seen in the north-west part of T. 49, R. 15, is lower, this is the lowest Coal in the county, and I suspect that the 18 inch bed referred to is " Coal D."

On the ridge, a little east of north of Mr. Diggs', in S. E. Sec. 5, T. 50, R. 14, on Mr. Wm. Davis' land, " Coal D " is found, with the rocks from No. 39 to 49 exposed. The Coal is only 6 inches thick. By long measurement it was found to be 25 feet above the Coal (E) at Mr. Diggs'. This measurement, however, was made with a pocket level; and as benching had to be often resorted to, we can not reasonably expect this to be exactly correct. South-west and west of Mr. Diggs' bank still higher Coals are found, and also most of the strata from No. 15 to No. 45 are exposed. The top of the ridge upon which the rocks crop out is 160 feet above the Manitou bottoms, and is perhaps as high if not higher than any other point in the township.

The top rock, which is the Rhomboidal Limestone (No. 15 of General Section,) is 83 feet below the top of the ridge, and about 40 feet above the site on which Sebree stands.

The highest Coal (Coal B) is found 2 feet below the " Rhomboidal Limestone," and 79 feet below this. Coal D crops out, and is on a level with the Manitou bottoms. South of this place, in a cut of the Louisiana Railroad, about one quarter of a mile east of Sebree, the rocks from No. 20 to No. 32, (General Section,) inclusive, are exposed, with a local (?) bed of arenaceous Limestone interpolated in the Sandstone and Shale. The Shales here contain some yellow Ochre ; not enough, however, to be worked with profit. " Coal C," is represented at 'this place by merely a black streak, coming 2 feet below the upper Limestone, which is 2 feet thick.

From the foregoing data it will be seen that in this township (T. 50, R. 14) there are four distinct beds of Coal, two of which at least, (Coals D and E) are workable beds.

These are all in the neighborhood of Sebree, and will be of commercial value should the Louisiana Railroad be completed.

In the next township north-west (T. 51, R. 15) there is a great thinning out of the strata. This is illustrated by two sections made on Mr. T. B. Harris' land near Burton.

The first section was made in the N. E. qr. Sec. 20, and is as follows :

No. 1. 22 feet Slope from the " Rhomboidal Limestone."
No. 2. 5 feet thin bedded Sandstone.
No. 3. 5½ feet Sandstone in one thick bed. Good for building.
No. 4. 25 feet Sandstone and sandy Shale.
No. 5. 5½ feet blue argillaceous Shale, with thin bands of Clay Ironstone.
        No. 54.

No. 6. 18 inches + black Shale filled with *Productus muricatus*, etc. No. 55.

No. 7. Coal E—The thickness could not be determined. It has been worked by smiths, and it is said to have answered their purpose well.

Rocks whose Geological position is 213 feet above the Coal, (No. 7 of the foregoing Section,) are found on the hill just south, on the south side of Salt Fork, occupying a topographical position only 86 feet above it; a discrepancy of 127 feet !

This is shown in the following section:

No. 1. Shaly Slope.

No. 2. 3 to 5 inches greenish, gray, coarse-grained, argillaceous Limestone, very fossiliferous.

No. 3. 15 inches olive and blue calcareous Shales ; fossiliferous.

No. 4. 2½ feet hard, fine-grained, dove-colored Limestone, occurring in thick, irregularly shaped blocks. Organic remains are abundant, including *Productus splendens*, (*P. Longispinus ?*) *Spr. cameratus*, *Spiriferina Kentuckensis*, *Spr.* (*Martinia*) *plano-convexus*, *Athyris*, a small *Chonetes*, and *Archæocidaris megastylus*. This a fine building stone, and has the appearance of a Hydraulic Limestone. No. 11 of General Section.

No. 5. 3 feet " Chætetes Limestone."

No. 6. 25 feet Slope.

No. 7. 1 foot + " Rhomboidal Limestone.

No. 8. 60 feet Slope.

No. 9. Coal E.

It will be seen that it would be useless to bore or sink for Coal D in this locality.

The same may be said of the adjacent country around. On Bonne Femme Creek, in S. E. N. E., Sec. 18, T. 51, R. 18, Coal E is found occupying a position only 93 feet below the "Chætetes Limestone," Coal D being entirely absent. This is seen at Mr. Skinner's Coal bank. The Coal is of very good quality, and as usual divided a little above the middle by a Clay parting. Eleven feet below the Coal, No. 60 is seen exposed in the bed of the Creek, the space between the Coal and Limestone being taken up by argillaceous Shale and Marlite.

This same arrangement of the rocks was observed at several places, and we may therefore reasonably conclude that Coal D and its associate rocks thin out toward the north ; and from observations made north of Sebree, we may regard the north line of township 50 as *about* the northern limit of it—at least in this county.

On Judge McCafferty's land, in Sec. 20, T. 51, R. 15, Coals B and C are found with the Rhomboidal Limestone exposed above Coal B.

No. 19 of the General Section, is at this place a compact bed of Limestone abounding in *Productus prattenianus*, and containing *Pr. semireticulatus*, *Athyris subtilita*, and a *Phillipsia*. (*P. major Sh*)

Coal B is only 8 inches thick, and Coal C varies from 1 to 9 inches. The rocks dip 9° S., 62° W., Magnetic. .One quarter of a mile southeast of Burton, No. 19 is again found exposed, and 27 feet below it, 13 feet of the Sandstone and Shales which overlie Coal E, are seen cropping out in the bank of a small branch which empties into Salt Fork. We may therefore conclude that Coal E will be reached by sinking a shaft here, commencing at the lowest point, within 25 or 30 feet. Just north of Burton the lowest rock exposed is No. 19, the Rhomboidal Limestone being found above it.

The Sandstone, No. 1, of the General Section, was first observed on the Renick road, in Sec. 35, T. 51, R. 15, where it is 12 feet + thick, very soft and ferruginous at the bottom, and 15 feet above division A of the Chætetes Limestone.

At Mr. Robt. Reynolds', in N. E. S. W. Sec. 10, T. 51, R. 15, No. 19, is found presenting a thickness of 4 feet. Thirty-eight (38) feet below it the Shales which overly Coal E were seen, and, we therefore conclude that this bed would be reached within a few feet[*]

At Mr. Montivell Reynolds, in N. E. qr. Sec. 2, T. 51, R. 15, the Limestone No. 19 was seen, with the Rhomboidal Limestone occupying a position 9 feet above it. The Coal (B,) which occurs under the latter Limestone, is at this place only 2 inches thick—and merely a smut. According to Mr. Reynolds' Coal C, occurs in the bed of the creek, and is 18 inches thick. This being correct, the Coal is thicker here than at any other locality. It was supposed that the Coal would reach a thickness of 4 feet, farther in the hill. This supposition is probably based upon the idea that this bed is the same as that seen at Mr. P. M. Pitney's, which is a mistake, as the latter is a lower and thicker bed. We may safely say that Mr. Pitney's Coal will be reached at a depth of perhaps less then 50 feet. This estimate is based upon the opinion that Coal D, and its accompanying strata are here, as elsewhere in this Township, wanting. Should it be present, however, the depth will be greater, as will be seen by referring to the General Section. From this place on to Mr. Nath. Pitney's, in N. E. qr. Sec. 36, T. 52, R. 15, the rocks from No. 15 to No. 19, are the ones found exposed. At Mr. Pitney's, a lower series come to view, being those rocks from No. 15 to No. 60, inclusive. The lowest rock, (No. 60,) is 22 feet above low water in Salt Fork. Coal E is seen here, presenting a thickness of 31 inches.

---

[*] I was afterwards informed that Coal has been taken out here—the thickness however was not known.

At Mr. Nath. Robb's, in the S. E. qr. N. W. qr. Sec. 36, T. 52, R 15, a bed of Coal 2 feet thick was found, which is probably the same bed as that spoken of above; but as there were no rocks exposed either above or below it by which to identify it, this can not be said with certainty. It is first-class Coal, but little pyrites or Carbonate of Lime being present. It has a Clay parting at the middle, as does Coal E.

On Mr. T. M. Pitney's land, in the E hf. Sec. 25, T. 52, R. 15, a Coal bed, which may be referable to Coal E, is being mined by the "UNION COAL AND MINING COMPANY." It is worked by a "slope," the mouth of which is on a level with the bottoms, and ten feet above the level of Salt Fork. The Coal, according to measurement, is on a level with the bed of the creek.

This Coal is not positively referred to Coal E, for no rocks by which to arrive at any positive conclusion were found. But as it is undoubtedly one of the low Coals, and as we are confident no lower Coal will be found in this county as thick, there is not much proba-bility of there being a mistake as to its equivalency.

The following is a Section of the strata exposed :

No. 1. Long Slope.
No. 2. 3½ feet gray Sandstone.
No. 3. 11 feet blue Clay.
No. 4. 5 feet hard, blue pyritiferous Shale, containing many small pyritous concretions and bands.
No. 5. 39 inches Coal; the upper 3 inches is worthless, being merely layers of Coal and pyritous bands ; this leaves 3 feet of pretty good Coal.

At the time this mine was examined, (Nov. 4th,) although it had been opened but a short time, a large quantity of Coal has been taken out. It has been opened well, and reflects credit upon the manager. Col. Elliott,* who is connected with this Company, informed me that it is the intention to work their Coal at this locality extensively.

From this place, on to Roanoke, higher rocks come to view at intervals. Near Roanoke, the rocks from No. 3 to No. 15, inclusive, are exposed on Mr. Phelps' land, in N. E. Sec. 15, T. 52, R. 16, and fol-lowing Doxy's Fork, into Sec. 16, there is a very good exposure of these rocks.

The following condensed Section is given :

---

* I am under obligations to this gentlemen, both for his hospitality and kindness, in giving me localities. He also located the M., K. and T. R. R. on the map, from Fayette northward into Randolph county.

No. 1. Shaly Sandstone and Shale. (No. 3 of General Section.)

No. 2. 2 feet rough, light drab to gray, fine-grained Limestone, with specks
       of Calcite disseminated. For fossils, see No. 4 of General Section.

No. 3. 3 feet olive and dark calcareous Shale, abounding in *Spr. planocon-
       vexus*, and containing other fossils.

No. 4. ½ inch Coal Smut; not persistent.

No. 5. 6 inches very nodular, ash, drab and gray argillaceous Limestone,
       abounding in *Fusulina*.

No. 6. 7 feet Shale and masses of buff cellular Limestone.

No. 7. 2 feet fine-grained, drab Limestone, with a chocolate crust. (No. 9 of
       General Section.)

No. 8. 1 foot Shale and thin beds of Limestone.

No. 9. 6 feet irregularly bedded Limestone; the top is very light drab and
       shelly, whilst the lower part is compact, fine-grained and bluish
       drab, with Calcite disseminated in small specks. (No. 11 of Gene-
       ral Section.)

No. 10. 15 inches blue and dove-colored Limestone.

No. 11. 10 inches bluish gray Limestone.

No. 12. 3 feet "Chætetes Limestone," division A.

No. 13. 2 to 2½ feet Chætetes Limestone, division B.

No. 14. 17 feet Slope; argillaceous Shale is seen at the top.

No. 15. 2 feet Rhomboidal Limestone.

No. 16. 2 feet argillo-bituminous Shale.

No. 17. 9 inches (?) Coal B.

On Mr. Q. F. Beach's land, in Sec. 25, T. 52, R. 16, the rocks from
No. 1 to No. 12, inclusive, are found. The Sandstone, No. 1, is 23 feet
thick, and overlies the Coal formerly worked by Mr. Beach.

This, in conjunction with the Sections made at Roanoke and Mr.
Garner's, will include all the rocks in this township, (T. 52, R. 16.)

At Wisely's Mill, in S. W. qr. Sec. 22, T. 51, R. 16, the strata from
No. 3 to No. 17, inclusive, are exposed. The rocks here are very
irregularly bedded, and dipping in all directions.

At Page's Coal Bank, in S. E. qr. Sec. 18, T. 49, R. 15, the following
Section was made:

No. 1. Slope.

No. 2. 25 to 30 feet Sandstone. (No. 1 of General Section.)

No. 3. 5 feet blue and ochreous Shale.

No. 4. 1 foot hard, compact, blue to dove-colored Limestone.

No. 5. 3 inches dark Clay.

No. 6. 3 to 4 inches somewhat pyritiferous Limestone.

No. 7. 2 feet bituminous Shale, with dark blue calcareous concretions.

No. 8. ——? Coal, said to be 18 inches thick.

The position that the rocks from No. 3 down should occupy in regard to the General Section, we were unable to determine, but suspect they are near the base of the Coal Measures. The same rocks are seen at Mr. Snell's, in N. W. Sec. 28, T. 49, R. 15, overlying an 18-inch bed of Coal. The Section is :

No. 2. 2 feet fine-grained Limestone. (No. 4 of Section at Page's.)
No. 3. 18 inches bituminous Slate and Shale.
No. 4. 18 inches Coal.
No. 5. 15 feet Slope.
No. 6. 5 feet Clay and Lower Carboniferous Chert.
No. 7. 5 feet Slope.
No. 8. Burlington Limestone.

It is, I believe, a generally supposed thing in this neighborhood' where the Burlington Limestone is exposed, that by sinking a shaft from 15 to 40 feet below the Limestone, a bed of Coal 30 *feet* thick will be reached. This was caused by a Pennsylvania gentleman saying that he had 30 feet of Coal under just such a looking Limestone as this is here. As it has been proved that no Coal occurs under this formation in the United States, it will be useless to dig for it at this point.

LIST OF COAL BANKS.

In the following list there are many localities given at which the Coal is too thin to work, but it must be remembered that the Coal beds mentioned are only those that are exposed or very near the surface at each locality. Except in the cases where the lowest Coal (E) is mentioned, there is every probability of finding a thicker bed by sinking shafts.

OWNER.	LOCALITY.			COAL.		REMARKS.
	Section.	Township.	Range	Thickness.	Number .:	Worked or not.
				Inches.		
Q. F. Beach	S. E. 25	52	16	?	A	Not worked at present—covered.
S. T. Garner	20	52	16	9	B	Not worked ....
?............................	22	51	17	9?	"	" " ....
?......	N. E. 15	50	17	12	"	" " ....
B. M. McCrary	N. E. 11	50	17	12	"	" " ....
?............................	4	49	17	15	"	Has been worked by local smiths.
S. Garvin	28	50	17	20	B?	Has been worked............

List of Coal Banks—Continued.

OWNER.	LOCALITY.			COAL.		REMARKS.
	Section.	Township.	Range	Thickness.	Number....	Worked or not.
—— Hatfield	?	50	17	....	B ?	Near Garvin's, and is worked.
Mrs. Hackley............	26	50	17	....	B ?	Covered; worked extensively at one time.
?	7	50	15	15	B	Not worked ....
—— Pierce...............	S. E. 7	50	15	18 to 30	"	" " " (has been).....
Mrs. Howard............	N. E. 10	50	15	?	"	" " " " .....
?	N. W. 27	51	15	22	"	" " " ....
?	N. pt. 17	49	14	17	"	" " " ....
Judge McCafferty...	S. E. 17	51	15	8	"	" " " ....
Judge McCafferty...	N. pt. 16	51	15	9	"	" " " ....
T. B. Harriss............	20	51	15	?	"	" " " ...:.............
M. Reynolds............	N. E. 2	51	15	2	"	" " " ....
James Ware	S. W. 35	52	15	12	"	" " " ....
—— Pattison............	16	52	16	9	"	" " " ....
Rice Pattison............	S. E. 9	52	16	?	"	" " " ....
James Sperry	N. W. 17	52	16	8	"	" " " ....
Richard Lee............	S. W.? 17	52	16	?	"	" " " ....
Dr. Walker...............	S. E. 5	52	16	....	"	Worked but little...........:.
?	S. W. 22	51	16	13	"	Worked for domestic use.
?	S. E. 5	49	15	10	"	Not worked ....
?	24?	50	16	?	"	This is at the Bonne Femme bridge, on the Fayette and Rocheport road. Worked but little.
?	N. W. 29	50	15	?	"	Covered; has been worked
James McDonalds ..	S. W. 5	49	15	?	"	Has been worked; Covered.
Barton*	S. E. 34	49	15	?	?	This was covered; has been worked.

* Mr. B.'s Coal was covered, and its position relative to the General Section could not be ascertained. Everything was in a confused state. Masses of Sandstone No. 1 and of the Rhomboidal Limestone were found, but they appear to have been transported by water. The Coal is found in a valley running north and south, with the Burlington Limestone on one side and the Coal on the other.

List of Coal Banks—Continued.

| OWNER. | LOCALITY. | | | COAL. | | REMARKS. |
	Section.	Township.	Range......	Thickness.	Number....	Worked or not.
McCafferty	S. E. 17	51	15	1 to 9	C	Not worked ....
M. Reynolds	N. E. 2	51	15	18?	''	Has been worked a little..
?	N. E. 10	51	15	12	''	Not worked ....
J. Tatums................	W. hf. N. E. 16	50	17	24 to 33	D	Worked...........................
?	S. W. 7	50	14	18 to 20	''	Worked occasionally ......
—— Powell	N. W. 18	50	14	18 to 28	''	Worked............................
—— Grigsbey........	19	50	14	....	''	'' ....
William Daviss........	S. E. 5	50	14	6	''	Not been worked. May thicken after going into the hill a distance.
?	W. hf. 8	50	14	24	''	Do not think this Coal is known.
N. Robb....................	S. E. N. W. 36	52	15	16 to 24	E?	Very good Coal; worked but little.
N. Pitney	N. E. 36	52	15	31	E	Not worked ....
T. M. Pitney	S. E. 25	52	15	39	''	Worked extensively ....
Dr. J. P. Becks........	32	50	16	22	E?	Worked...........................
Dr. J. P. Becks........	29	50	16	22	E	'' ....
T. C. Boggs............	4 and 5	49	16	....	......	....
R. Diggs.................	N. E. 8	50	14	30	E	Said to reach 36 inches, and is worked extensively; very good Coal.
—— Skinner	N. E. 18	51	15	30	''	Worked ....
T. B. Harriss...........	N. E. 20	51	15	?	''	Not opened ....
R. Reynolds............	S. W. 10	51	15	?	E?	'' '' ....

CHAPTER XIII.

LINN, SULLIVAN, ADAIR.

BY G. C. BROADHEAD.

These counties, having many features in common, their topography somewhat similar and their geological structure alike, are therefore grouped together. Our annexed Geological Section is also applicable to either county. It had to be constructed from materials from each county, for all of the beds of one county can not be connected without using Sections observed in the other counties. The shafts at Brookfield and St. Catherine have also aided us very much.

GENERAL VERTICAL SECTION.

Number	THICKN'SS		TOTAL.		DESCRIPTION.	LOCALITIES.
	Feet.	In.	Feet.	In.		
1	13	......	13	......	Soft Sandstone............................	
2	8	......	21	......	Limestone : Gray and ash-colored. *Prod. splendens* abounds, also contains *Aviculapecten inter lineatus, Sp. (Martinia) lineatus, Orthoceras.* Lower bed is jointed.	Alum Creek and Milan.
3	20	......	41	......	Sandstone and Shales..................	
4	2	6	43	6	Coal and Clay—(20 inches good Coal)— Alternate strata of Coal and Clay........	Milan and Spring Creek.
5	60	......	103	......	Sandstone.................................	Spring and Locust Creek and Wilhite Branch.

Up. Coal Measures

General Vertical Section—Continued.

Number....	Thickn'ss Feet.	In.	Total. Feet.	In.	Description.	Localities.
6	....	10	104	.....	Deep blue, shaly Limestone. Abounds in *Pr.Prattenianus,Pleurotomaria spherulata, Macrocheilus,* etc...............	Spring Creek, Blaylock bridge, near mouth of Montgomery Branch, and at Glidewell's.
7	2	......	106	......	Deep dull blue calcareous Shales. It abounds in fossils similar to the last, especially *Pleurotomaria*; also contains *Bellerophon* (2 species), *Astartella vera, Nucula ventricosa*.................................	"
8	....	4	106	4	Dull blue argillaceous Limestone...........	"
9	16	......	122	4	Shales, with rough calcareous nodules...	"
10	2	......	124	2	Bituminous Shales.............................	"
11	....	2	124	6	Shaly bituminous Coal.......................	"
12	18	......	142	6	Blue Shales, calcareous Ironstone in the middle....................................	"
13	2	6	145	......	Bituminous Shales.............................	"
14	....	6	145	6	Coal...	"
15	4	......	149	6	Green Shales..................................	West of Kirksville, near Linneus, on W. Locust Creek, and at T. Cassady's.
16	4	......	153	6	Red Shales....................................	
17	5	......	158	6	Sandstone.....................................	
18	11	......	169	6	Red Clay and sandy Shales, with Red Hematite nodules............................	"
19	3	6	173	......	Limestone: Greenish drab with shaly partings	Nos. 19 to 31 inclusive, found near Linneus, on Locust Cr'k, at Henry's mill, and on W. Locust Cr.
20	1	......	174	......	Mottled fine-grained Limestone, with many Calcite specks................	
21	....	10	175	......	Green Shale with *Chonetes mesoloba* and *Spirifer planoconvexus*........................	"
22	....	5	175	3	Green calcareous Shales—contain *Retzia punctilifera, Hemipronites crassus, Chonetes mesoloba, Prod. splendens, Spiriferina Kentuckensis*........................	"
23	2	......	177	3	Green Shales with fossils in upper part...	"
24	1	4	178	7	Blue Limestone: Abounds in *Athyris subtilita*...................................	"
25	4	......	182	7	Green Shales...................................	"
26	....	6	183	1	Rough nodular Limestone, full of *Chonetes granulifera*.............................	"

General Vertical Section—Continued.

Number	Thickness Feet.	Thickness In.	Total Feet.	Total In.	Description.	Localities.
27	7	.....	190	1	Shales, full of *Chonetes granulifera*, *Hemipronites*, *Pr. splendens*. Olive colored near upper part, blue below................	Nos. 19 to 31 inclusive, found near Linneus, on Locust Cr'k, at Henry's mill, and on W. Locust Creek.
28	....	6	190	7	Fine grained, dove colored Limestone—fracture splintery to sub-conchoidal. Contains minute calcite specks—(Flagstone)........................	"
29	....	4	190	11	Clay...........	"
30	....	7	191	4	Bituminous Shales........................	"
31	3	6	194	10	Clay and calcareous shales, abounding in fossils, mostly *Athyris subtilita*; also contains *Pr. costatus*, *Meekella*, *Spir. cameratus*, etc........................	"
32	....	10	195	8	Green Clay........................	At last named localities and on Big Creek, west of Kirksville.
33	2	.....	197	8	Yellow Clay........................	"
34	....	6	198	2	Brown Limestone........................	"
35	....	8	199	.....	Olive Clay........................	"
36	....	11	199	11	Limestone........	Near mouth of Big Creek, in Adair county, and at Coalson's mill, Linn county.
37	1	.....	200	11	Olive Shales with calcareous nodules......	
38	6	.....	206	11	Blue Shales: One foot from top is a nodular Limestone bed........................	"
39	1	.....	207	11	Nodular Limestone........................	"
40	4	.....	211	11	Limestone: Fracture shows a dove color; weathers brown—one bed................	"
41	23	.....	235	.....	Sandstone, mostly shaly........................	"
42	....	10	235	10	Limestone—shaly on upper surface; below, breaks vertically into rhomboid masses. Fucoids on worn surface......	Nos. 42 to 47 inclusive, are found on Muscle Fork, Linn Co.; Baker's mill, Coalson's mill, Bayles' mill, Dumy's mill, and at Withrow's mill
43	1	.....	236	10	Soft, bituminous Shales........................	
44	1	.....	237	10	Hard, black Shale—fucoidal. Contains small gray concretions........................	
45	1	.....	283	10	Deep blue black Shales........................	"
46	....	10	239	8	Black calcareous Shales, abounding in fossils, *Sp. cameratus*, *Pr. muricatus*, *Myalina subquadrata*, *Pr. Prattenianus*.	"
47	....	8	240	4	Soft blue Shales........................	....
48	....	8	241	.....	Dark gray concretionary Limestone with remains of plant leaves and *Stigmaria*	Sugar Creek, Adair county.

General Vertical Section—Continued.

Number	THICKNESS Feet.	In.	TOTAL Feet.	In.	DESCRIPTION.	LOCALITIES.
49	4	......	245	......	Fire-clay..	Sugar Cr., Adair co
50	7	......	252	......	Shales and thin Limestone layers..........	" "
51	10	......	262	......	Slope—probably all Shales....................	At Dumey's and at Hurburt's Mill—
52	1	6	263	6	Limestone...	now Miles' Mill.
53	....	6	264	......	Drab argillo-calcareous Shales..............	" "
54	2	......	266	......	Black Shales with a few flattened concretions..	In Linn county, at Miles' Mill.
55	....	¼	266	¼	Shaly bituminous Coal........................	" "
56	5	......	271	¼	Clay and shaly slope...........................	" "
57	3	......	274	¼	Thin bedded, hard chocolate colored Sandstone.......................................	" "
58	30	6	304	9	Shales—mostly argillaceous.................	" "
59	1	6	206	3	Coal—is the Coal at Nutter's and the upper Coal at St. Catharines', and also in Brookfield shaft....................................	Brookfield and St. Catharine's shafts
60	20	......	326	3	Shales and Clay concretions in the lower part...	Brookfield shaft.
61	1-1½	......	327	6	Hard Limestone.................................	" "
62	43	.....	370	6	Shales sandy at top............................	" "
64	4	......	374	6	Limestone and Shales. Bed near upper part often abounding in *allorisma*........	Spring Creek, Sullivan and Adair cos.; Shut-eye Cr.
65	1	.....	375	6	Shales..	Adair co.
66	....	6	376	......	Bituminous Shales.............................	" "
67	3	......	379	......	Coal separated by a 3 inch Clay seam.....	" "
68	1	......	380	......	Clay	" "
69	4	......	384	......	Brown friable Limestone — sometimes jointed......................	Abernathy's branch Adair co.
70	17	......	401	......	Sandstones and sandy Shales blue and drab.............................	" "
71	6	.....	407	....	Dark Clay and sandy Shales.................	" "
72	1	......	408	......	Shaly black carbonaceous Limestone.....	" "
73	2	6	410	6	Bituminous Shales..	" "

General Vertical Section—Continued.

Number...	THICKNESS		TOTAL.		DESCRIPTION.	LOCALITIES.
	Feet.	In.	Feet.	In.		
74	....	8	411	2	Black calcareous carbonaceous Shales, full of remains of fossils ; *Sp. cameratus*, *Pr. costatus*, *Chonetes mesoloba*, *Athyris*...	Abernathy's branch Adair county.
75	1	6	412	8	Black Shales..	" "
76	....	2	413	......	Ironstone with fossils; *Pr. Prattenanus*, *Hemipronites*, *Athyris subtilita*............	Joab's Cr., Adair county.
77	4	......	417	......	Clay..........	" "
78	4	......	421	......	Ash colored, weathers to drab, fine-grained. rough friable Limestone–only observed *Pr. Prattenanus*..................	" "
79	47	......	468	......	Clay and Shales...................................	Brookfield shaft.
80	3	6	471	6	Coal separated by thin Clay seam..........	Nineveh, on Rye & Hazel Crs., and in Brookfield shaft
81	3	......	474	6	Fire-clay seam...................................	
82	....	9	475	3	Hard and bluish drab and blue Limestone....................................	" "
83	....	9	476	......	Deep blue black Shale..........................	" "
84	2–5	.	480	......	Hard ash colored argillaceous Limestone	" "
85	15+	......	495	......	Sandy Shales....................................	" "

SULLIVAN COUNTY.

BY G. C. BROADHEAD.

This county is very regular in shape, being 24 miles N. and S., by 27 E. and W., and embraces an area of 648 square miles. Spring Creek, in T. 64, R. 18, runs south-eastwardly. All the other streams preserve a nearly southerly course, and the trend of all the main ridges is nearly in the same direction.

A portion of the county is quite broken. This may include that watered by Spring Creek, with the region between East and West Locust Creeks, in T. 61 and 62, and near Big Locust as far north as the northern part of T. 63, and near E. Locust, in T. 64. But the hills are not often over 150 feet in hight. It is also somewhat hilly near Medicine Creek and Muscle Fork.

The remaining portion of the county is rolling and undulating, and near Yellow Creek we find very gentle Slopes.

The prairie streams or " draws," near their sources, have generally steep banks, and at their origin we often find a flat, sloping valley, with no water channel; but tracing them down, we soon find a precipitous wash exposing three or four feet of dark, rich Soil.

TIMBER AND PRAIRIE.

Range 20, as far as the northern part of T. 63, mostly comprises good bodies of timbered land, with White Oak for the prevailing timber. Good Black Oak and Hickory abound near the southern county line; between Big and West Locust Creeks, Ash, Elm, Linden and Hickory are abundant. The remainder of the county mostly consists of prairie, with belts of timber a half mile in width, adjacent to the principal streams. In the northern part of the county we often find Burr Oak and White Oak on the ridges, with Swamp White Oak, Elm, Hickory, etc., on the bottoms. At the margin of the prairies are thickets of Pin Oak, Hazel, Cornus, Cherry, Plum, etc. The remaining trees and shrubs of this county are similar to those of Adair. White Walnut is abundant on Locust Creek, and this I find to be its extreme western limit in Missouri, nor is it found south until we reach the Missouri River.

STREAMS.

Spring Creek, East Locust, and Big Locust are pretty running streams; the other streams are rather dark and sluggish. The county affords but few springs, and persons have generally to depend on cisterns, and in newly settled places some have no other drinking water but that which they procure from standing pools in the "draws." Water may be obtained at reasonable depths by digging. On high grounds it may be reached at thirty (30) feet, and in the "draws," at the heads of hollows, at ten (10) to fifteen (15) feet.

SURFACE DEPOSITS.

Beneath the recent Alluvium we find beds of Sand, Clay and boulders belonging to the Drift formation.

In Sec. 5 of T. 61, R. 21, we find, next beneath the soil, five or six feet yellow, jointed Clay, resting on six to twelve feet of blue Clay, with yellow Clay, Sand and Gravel at the bottom. In the beds of Sand and Gravel are generally good reservoirs of water.

A well at Milan exhibits—

No. 1. 16 feet of yellow Clay.
No. 2. 4 feet of coarse Sand.
No. 3. 9 feet of dark-blue Clay (jointed) and boulders.

Igneous boulders of various kinds of rocks are often met with, and they mainly constitute the lower part of the Drift formation. We sometimes find the more comminuted material loosened, and borne away by abrasion of waters through long periods of time, leaving very large boulders exposed.

On Spring Creek I observed a Granite boulder eight by six feet, and on the prairie, near Beardstown, a still larger one, measuring 75 feet in its irregular circumference, 12 feet high, 25 feet long and 14 feet across the top; not less than 100 cubic yards were exposed. These boulders are red feldspathic Granite, and must have been borne a long distance, certainly not less than 500 miles.

Among other boulders I saw Amygdaloid, Quartz, and some small pieces of red and amber colored Agate.

CARBONIFEROUS SYSTEM.

In Sullivan and Adair counties we find beds clearly referable to the Upper Coal Measures, which do not exist in Linn. Around Milan, and westward to Locust Creek, beds of the Upper Coal Measures appear near the hill-top, and from 60 to 80 feet below, outcrops were seen by Mr. C. J. Norwood, of rocks which he refers to No. 85 of the General Section of the Upper Coal Measures. He also obtained the following General Section of the rocks in the vicinity of Milan, referable to the Upper Coal Measure strata:

No. 1. 1 foot Marly Shale.

No. 2. 5 feet finely oolitic Limestone. Upper part is a single 4-foot bed, stained with Oxide of Iron; contains *Pr. Nebrascensis, Pr. Prattenanus*, a large *Productus, Athyris subtilita*, and *Sp. cameratus*.

No. 3. 3 inches compact drab Limestone.

No. 4. 13 feet Slope.

No. 5. 1 foot fine-grained, thinly-bedded, semi-oolitic Limestone.

No. 6. 1 foot Slope.

No. 7. 5 feet rough and irregularly bedded Limestone. Upper beds are gray and drab, and fine-grained. Some portions in thin beds. Fossils *Athyris subtilita, Sp. cameratus* and *Crinoid* columns.

No. 8. 1 foot Calcareous Shale.

No. 9. 2 feet 6 inches hard, compact Limestone, both coarse and fine-grained buff and drab. Many obscure fossil forms appear on the surface. The bed includes *Athyris subtilita, Pr. costatus, Hemipronites crassus, Lophophyllum proliferum* and *Crinoid* columns.

No. 10. 6 inches olive Shale.

No. 11. 3 inches ash-gray, rough, argillaceous Limestone.

No. 12. 15 feet Slope; fragments of Sandstone appear.

No. 13. 1 foot † drab to dove colored, fine-grained, rhomboidally-jointed Limestone. 3 layers, fracture chonchoidal. Fossils are *Pr. splendens, Athyris subtilita* and *Ch. Verneuiliana*.

No. 14. 4 feet hard, coarse-grained, shaly Limestone, with *Athyris subtilita*, and *Pr. splendens*.

No. 15. 5 feet 6 inches Slope.

No. 16. 2 feet hard Limestone, containing much Calcite.

No. 17. 1 foot Slope.

No. 18. 3 feet rough, irregularly bedded Limestone; shelly at the top and more compact toward the lower part. Many small *Crinoid* columns are seen; contains, besides, *Pr. Americanus, Pr. splendens, Athyris subtilita*, and *Chonetes*.

No. 19. 1 foot buff and olive calcareous Shales.

No. 20. 2 feet 3 inches drab and dove-colored Limestone; jointed rhomboidally. Occurs in three layers; upper being coarse, and the lower layers fine-grained, with Calcite disseminated; breaks irregularly, and contains many fossils, including *Pr. costatus, Pr. splendens, Athyris subtilita, Sp. cameratus, Spr. plano-convexus* and *Crinoid* stems.

The lower beds, resembling No. 74 of the General Section of upper Coal Measures of 1872, appear on the hill at Milan They are also seen on the hills three miles to the north-west, cropping out 20 feet above the Coal (a 2-foot seam.)   At Milan this Limestone is seen 22 feet above the Coal, the latter appearing here only as a black, smutty, rotten streak. This Limestone may therefore be said to be a guide to the Coal, and as such should be carefully noted. We found it a mile east of Milan, of a drab inclining to a soft buff color, containing many specks and aggregations of Calcite throughout. It weathers with a brown ochrey crust, and is jointed; the joints generally lined with nail-head Spar, and sometimes with greenish blue Sulphate of Baryta. *Productus longispinus* and *Athyris subtilita* are the most common fossils, but *Rhombopora lipidodendroides*, *Spirifer Kentuckensis*, *Hemipronites crassus*, *Aviculopecten interlineatus*, and *Lophophyllum proliferum* are also found. It is found on Wilhite Branch, in Sec. 1, T. 26, R. 21, (with other related beds,) exposed and dipping eastward 1 foot in ten in the following order :

No. 1. 5 feet Blue Limestone, with *Pr. Nebrascensis*, *Pr. costatus*, *Pinna peracuta*.

No. 2. 22 feet Slope, exposing tumbled masses of brown Limestone.

No. 3. 3 feet 6 inches gray oolitic Limestone. (79 of General Section Upper Coal Measures.)

No. 4. 9 feet thin layer of gray and ash-blue Limestone.

No. 5. 2 feet Shales.

No. 6. 1 foot 6 inches even-bedded gray Limestone.

No. 7. 1 foot 6 inches olive Shales.

No. 8. 2 feet ———— ————.

No. 9. 1 foot 6 inches Bituminous Slate and Shales.

No. 10. 8 inches Limestone.

No. 11. 6 inches Clay and Limestone nodules.

No. 12. 3 feet sandy Shales.

Although there is here seen a stratum of black or Bituminous Slate, (No. 9,) we should not therefore suppose that we are near a bed of Coal. The simple fact of the existence of a Slate bed, is not certain proof of the existence of Coal. But in this case we may expect a thin bed of Coal about 25 feet below the Bituminous Slate.

Beds of Limestone, Shale and Coal, nearly related to the above, are found near Spring Creek, in the western part of R. 18. They appear there in the following order :

No. 4. 46 feet Slope from top of hill.

No. 2. Tumbled masses of blue and drab Limestone.

No. 3. Outcrop of shelly, gray Limestone, full of *Chonetes Verneuiliana*.

No. 4. 5 feet Slope, on which are found fragments of ash-blue Limestone full of *Pr. Nebrascensis.*

No. 5. 3 feet rough, Cherty Limestone, bluish-drab, contains *Pr. longispinus.* (No. 83. of Section, Upper Coal Measures.)

No. 6. 23 feet Slope, mostly Shales.

No. 7. 3 feet dark Shales.

No. 8. 6 inches Limestone bed full of fossils : *Pleurotomaria spherulata, Macrocheilus, Nautilus,* etc. It also contains minute veins of Zinc Blende.

No. 9. 3 feet 9 inches to 7 feet Bituminous Shales.

No. 10. 1 foot 6 inches Coal. (Mrs. Downing's.)

No. 11. 2 feet Shales with plants, including *Ferns, Annularia, Calamites, Sigilariœ,* etc.

With regard to the definite area of the upper Coal Measures, in this county, we cannot estimate exactly what it is, but they extend over several miles on the west side of Spring Creek—four or five miles near Milan, and at least a couple of miles near Wilhite Branch. It may be much more, but we do not know.

SANDSTONE AND OTHER LOWER BEDS.

No. 5 of our General Section, is the next most important member. It is generally a coarse, somewhat buff or brown Sandstone, more often soft, but sometimes hard enough to form a good building material. It is also frequently Shaly, the latter beds generally more or less argillaceous. It is also micaceous. Its fossils are *Calamites* (sometimes large species) and *Ferns.* About 50 feet thickness of these beds can be seen near Milan—nearly as much on Wilhite Branch, and 60 feet on Locust Creek, above Blaylock bridge ; and about the same thickness on Spring Creek.

It underlies the two eastern ranges of townships of the county.

We consider this Sandstone to be the upper member of the middle Coal Measures, and it closely resembles the same formation in Jackson, Cass and Livingston counties.

Nos. 6 and 15 inclusive, were found on Locust Creek Bluffs in several places. I first observed the upper beds in bluffs just below the mouth of Montgomery Branch. The lower were next observed at Mr. Glidewell's, in Sec. 30, T. 63, R. 20, and on Locust Creek west. At the first locality we find beneath the Sandstone ten feet of blue Clay Shales, with brown olive concretions resting on a deep-blue argillaceous and fossiliferous Limestone. Near Blaylock bridge we find similar beds with a second Coal seam of 6 inches 20 feet below the upper seam. The upper seam is only 2 inches thick, and slaty with one and a half feet of bituminous Slate overlying it. The lower 6-inch seam has been worked. These seams are too thin to be valuable.

Nos. 6, 7 and 8, the latter eighteen (18) feet above the upper thin Coal seam, are sure guides to its position. No. 8, as far as seen, is entirely non-fossiliferous, but Nos. 6 and 7 abound in fossils nearly alike in both members, and grouped so that the bed is easily recognized, some species being thus associated that are not found elsewhere in this district. The fossils are numerous and often well preserved, and comprise the following: *Polyphemopsis paracuta, Pleurotomaria spherulata, P. Grayvillensis, P. speciosa, Bellerophon carbonarius, B. percarinatus, B. Montfortianus, Macroheilus inhabilis, M. ventricosus, M. Newberryi, M. ———, Euomphalus rugosus, Soleniscus typicus,(?) Astartella vera, Nuculana bellistriata, Nucula ventricosa, Schizodus curtus, Allorisma, ———, Spirifer (Martinia) planoconvexus, Productus Prattenanus, Chonetes mesoloba, C. Verneuiliana, Hemipronites crassus, Orthoceras Rushensis, Nautilus, (2 Sp.) Phillipsia.*

Some of these fossils were found in abundance, others were wanting. *Pleurotomaria spherulata* is the most abundant—a large *Machrocheilus* comes next in order.

Nos. 9 to 14 were not observed on Spring Creek, and may have thinned out or been worn away previous to the deposition of the next succeeding members.

An outcrop of red Clay and sandy Shales was seen in Sec. 19, T. 64, R. 18, underlying the Sandstone, (No. 5,) and at one place we find beds of rough Limestone only 16 feet below the Sandstone. This Limestone resembles No. 19 of our Section, and Coal seams Nos. 11 and 14 seems wanting.

The Group of 38 feet of Limestone and marly Shales from Nos. 19 to 40, is well recognized wherever seen. The Limestones are generally rough-bedded and separated by Shaly layers, the latter more often of a dirty buff, the Limestones of a drab or greenish drab. Fossils are abundant, especially *Chonetes* and *Athyris subtilita* and *Pr. costatus*. No. 31 abounds in some places in *Pr. costatus* and *Ath. subtilita*.

At Field's mill, on Locust Creek, Mr. Norwood obtained three and a half feet of irregularly bedded drab and greenish drab Limestone divided into four beds, separated by greenish Shales, and abounding in *Chonetes, Productus costatus, Hemipronites* and *Spirifer planoconvexus*. Mr. Norwood thought that this Group very much resembled the rocks immediately over the Lexington Coal, Lithologically and Palæontologically, but if they are the equivalents of the Lex-

ington Group, we will be compelled to state that the Lexington Coa
is not found in Sullivan county.

On West Locust Creek, in the middle of Sec. 14, T. 62, R. 29, at the
foot of a bluff 100 feet high, we find an outcrop of red Shales containing nodules of red Hematite reposing on a rough bed of drab Limestone 2 feet in thickness. Below the latter are Clay and Limestone
nodules abounding in fossils, including *Ath. subtilita*, *Ch. mesoloba*,
Hemipronites crassus, *Pr. costatus*, *Retzia punctilifera*, *Rhynconella Osagensis*, *Spr. lineatus*. This Group of fossils belongs to Nos.
21 and 22 of our General Section.

On Locust Creek, S. W. Sec. 8, T. 62, R. 20, these beds are seen
occurring thus:

No. 1. 3 feet Limestone, (Nos. 19 and 22 of Gen. Sec.,) color greenish-gray
and full of small fossils, *Pr. splendens*, *Spr. planoconvexus*, *Hemipronites*, etc. On exposure this rock breaks into rough masses.

No. 2. 1 foot green fossiliferous Shales.

No. 3. 8 feet nodular Limestone, ash-gray, and full of *Pr. costatus*, containing also *Pr. Prattenanus*, and a very large *Athyris*.

At the mouth of a branch on Locust Creek, near Glidewell's, we
found:

No. 1. 5½ inches dove-colored Limestone, fine-grained, and traversed by
small Calcite specks and veins in every direction. This would be
pretty if polished. Spoken of as "flag-stone bed."

No. 2. 3 feet green and yellow Clay.

No. 3. 3 feet yellow Clay, with many fossils, *Sp. cameratus*, *Hemipronites
crassus*, *Lophohpyllum* ——, corresponds to No. 31, of our General
Section.

At Blaylock bridge, we find in the bed of the creek 3 feet of
rough nodular Limestone, containing *Pr. costatus*, *Ch. mesoloba*, *Ch.
Smithi*, (?) *Ath. subtilita*, *Allorisma* and *Hemipronites crassus*. At
this place this bed is but little below No. 14 of our General Section.

Our Section at Henry's mill presents some of the beds of our General Section, very favorably for observation, we therefore insert it at
this place:

No. 1. 8 inches bluish-drab Limestone.

No. 2. 4 feet green Shales.

No. 3. 6 inches rough nodular Limestone full of *Cho. mesoloba*.

No. 4. 7 feet olive Shales, full of *Ch. mesoloba*, *Pr. splendens*, and *Hemipronites crassus*.

No. 5. 6 inches flag-stone. No. 28, of General Section.

No. 6. 4 feet 6 inches blue Shales and Limestone nodules, full of *Ath. subtilita*, also containing *Pr. Nebrascensis, P. splendens, Meekella striatocostata, Ch. Smithi, Hemipronites crassus, Sp. Kentuckensis, Lophophyllum proliferum, Arehaeocidaris.*

No. 7. 4 feet light-blue or greenish Shales and Limestone nodules. The Shales are dark-red near the lower part.

No. 8. 1 foot 6 inches drab and light-blue Limestone, weathering to drab and brown, and containing *Pr. Prattenanus, P. costatus, Ath. subtilita, Phillipsia, Meekella, Chonetes mesoloba.*

No. 9. 1 foot blue calcareous Shales.

No. 10. 1 foot 6 inches Shaly dark-blue argillaceous Limestone, with but few fossils, contains a fish tooth.

No. 11. 2 feet blue Shales.

No. 12. 6 inches blue Shaly Limestone.

No. 13. 2 feet Shales, blue above and dark below.

From the northern part of T. 64 we find the rocks gradually rising to the north-east. At Crumpacker's Mill some of the members of the last sections are seen resting on a lower Sandstone, in the following order :

No. 1. Slope from the top of a low hill.

No. 2. 3 feet rough drab Limestone, containing *Bellerophon, Ath. subtilita, Fish teeth, Fusulina cylindrica, Rhombopora.*

No. 3. 1 foot green Shales with *Crinoid* stems and *Ch. granulifera?*

No. 4. 10 inches red Shales.

No. 5. 1 foot 6 inches green Shales.

No, 6. 3 feet nodular Limestone and Shales.

No. 7. 6 inches olive Shales.

No. 8. 1 to 3 inches Limestone resting on No. 9, and abounding in *Sp. planoconvexus,* also contains *fish-teeth.*

No. 9. 2 feet 6 inches Sandstone with *Chondites colleti?*

No. 10. 22 feet mostly sandy Shales.

The upper beds here are evidently equivalent to the lower strata at Henry's Mill. *Hemipronites crassus, Pr. longispinus, Sp. Kentuckensis, Sp. planoconvexus* and a *Chonetes,* were also found at this place.

Although beds of the series last described occur on Spring Creek, they are nowhere well exposed. We find beds occupying a higher position, also beds which lie below, but the intermediate ones are not seen. With the lower beds are found the Spring Creek Coal, to be spoken of in the following pages.

In the western part of Sullivan county we find no exposures of solid beds of rock. On West Locust Creek, north of T. 62, there are only a few out crops of soft Limestone.

ECONOMICAL GEOLOGY.

We will now discuss such Coals as are mined, or worthy of particular notice.

Mr. Norwood observed on and near Big Locust Creek, in the southern part of the county, the following Coal banks :

Maloney's, in S. W. N. E. Sec. 18, T 61. R. 20, appearing thus :

No. 1. Upper Slope.

No. 2. 5 feet dark drab Clay Shales.

No. 3. 3 to 6 inches dark blue-black Limestone (sepataria) containing *Cardium Lexingtonensis.*

No. 4. 2 to 5 inches brown, coarse-grained, tolerably soft, argillaceous Limestone.

No. 5. 5 to 7 feet bituminous Shales with large dark-blue hard and brittle Limestone concretions containing a small *Allorisma, Pleu. speciosa, Rhynconella*——, *Nucula*——, Bellerophon and *Cardiamorpha Missouriensis.*

No. 6. 1 foot 6 inches Coal.

From the fossils and associate rocks, I am disposed to believe this Coal to be the equivalent of the Coal worked three miles to the southwest of Laclede, Linn county, and on Black Water, Johnson county, as also that of the Mulky Coal, in Lafayette county. From the fossils in the overlying beds, Prof. Worthen, of Illinois, thinks there is a close resemblance to Coal No. 3, of the Illinois Geologists. But there are more than three Coals below this in the Missouri Coal Field.

At Mr. Kirby's place, in the N. E. S. W. Sec. 21, T. 61, R. 20, the same bed of Coal is worked. At this place it is covered by from 2 to 6 feet of bituminous Shale, containing large silico-bituminous concretions. The Coal is traversed by many joints, often slightly curved, which are generally filled with Calcite, and sometimes, but not often, with a little Iron pyrites. It seems to be of alternate layers of coarse rough fracture, and very fine, smooth, fracture, shiny or jet coal ; faint plant impressions are seen on the surface of the deposit.

Near Field's Mill, Sec. 8, T. 61, R. 20, this Coal has been found, but it is not worked. It is said to be eighteen inches thick, but it was only partially exposed. In Sec 14, T. 61, R. 20, it occurs in a very irregular bed. Slate and Limestone, with fossils, are found similar to the bed at Moloney's.

THE LOWER SPRING CREEK COAL.

Coal No. 67, of our Section, has been found at many places on Spring Creek. At present most of the mines are filled up. To show its position with the beds of our Section, I will here introduce a few descriptive sections. On the land of J. Bookout, near the line of Secs. 27 and 34, T. 64, R. 18, we have :

No. 1.　6 inches bluish drab Limestone, weathering drab, full of *Pr. costatus*
　　　　P. Prattenanus, *Ch. Verneuiliana*, *Meekella striato-costata Bryozoa*.

No. 2.　10 inches Limestone—finer grained than the last. Color, ash to drab
　　　　weathering brown. Contains *Allorisma regularis*, *Aviculopecten
　　　　occidentalis*.

No. 3.　2 feet tough and nodular ash-grey Limestone contains but few fossils.

No. 4.　1 foot 6 inches pea green friable and shaly Limestone, containing
　　　　large *Crinoid stems Sp. Cameratus Hemipronites*, *Ch. mesoloba*, *Pr.
　　　　longispinus*.

No. 5.　2 feet olive shales with streaks of Coal and nodules with a small
　　　　Discina.

The Coal is just beneath, and was concealed, but it is said to be 2¼ feet thick.

Coal has been worked at various times on the bluffs of Spring Creek below this. Mr. C. J. Norwood obtained the following Section at Avery Woods', in N. E. Sec. 27, T. 64, R. 18 :

No. 1.　Slope with red Shales containing nodules of red Hematite near the
　　　　lower part. (No. 16 of General Section).

No. 2.　3 feet rough nodular gray Limestone.

No. 3.　1 foot coarse grained Limestone containing *Ath. sublilita*, and abound-
　　　　ing in *Sp. planoconvexus*.

No. 4.　9 feet Slope.

No. 5.　8 feet green sandy shales with thin beds of sandy Limestone nodules
　　　　in the upper part, and a thin layer of hard Sandstone.

No. 6.　8 feet calcareous Sandstone.

No. 7.　3 feet olive Shale.

No. 8.　3 feet shaly slope, Limestone at bottom, with *Archæocidaris*.

No. 9.　1 foot light-blue and gray, even-bedded, sandy Limestone, containing
　　　　Sp. planoconvexus, *Pr. longispinus*, *P. costatus*, *Rhynconella*, *Chonetes
　　　　mesoloba*, *Hemipronites crassus*, *Lophophyllum proliferum*.

No. 10.　2 feet black Shale.

No. 11.　1 foot even layer of drab, earthy Limestone, containing *P. costatus*,
　　　　Hemipronites crassus, *Athyris subtilita*, *Crinoid* stems and *Bryozoa*.

No. 12.　1 foot blue Clay.

No. 13.　3 to 4 feet Coal (concealed).

No. 14.　Blue Clay.

No. 15. 8 feet Slope.

No. 16. 2 feet irregularly-bedded, fine-grained, hard Limestone.

No. 17. 15 feet Slope to creek, with out-crops of Sandstone.

On the north side of Spring Creek, on Beeler's land, we find :

No. 1. 1 foot 6 inches drab (Hydraulic?) Limestone, containing *Allorisma*, *Meekella striato-costata*, *Chonetes*, *Pr. costatus*, *Hemipronites crassus*, *Athyris subtilita*, with *Caulerpites marginatus* (?) on lower bed.

No. 2. 8 inches olive Shales.

No. 3. 1 foot 4 inches rough, ash drab Limestone.

No. 4. 6 inches Shales, with layer of nodular Limestone.

No. 5. 1 foot Shales.

No. 6. 6 inches bituminous Shales.

No. 7. 7 inches Coal—bright black, with Calcite in joints.

No. 8. 2 inches black, carbonaceous rock, approaching, in general appearance, "Mother of Coal," but can hardly be called the normal "Mother." It presents a dull, black appearance; has an irregular fracture, with occasional shiny Coal particles, and contains carbonaceous matter throughout, and some Iron Pyrites.

No. 9. Coal, (thickness not seen.)

Eleven feet lower down is a thick bed of brown Limestone. The total thickness of the Coal is said to be three feet.

At Jack Conklin's near the county line, the Coal is three feet in thickness, and capped by a six-inch layer of bituminous Shales and one foot of olive Shales (calcareous) above, with a roof above these, of four feet of Shales and Limestones, similiar to those at the above named places.

In Secs. 18 and 19 of T. 64, R. 18, Coal (No. 4 of General Section) was mined in several places; but for what reason I can not say, unless for want of a good market, they are all abandoned at present. I only (1873) could see it at Mrs. Downing's. It is here 18 inches thick, and reached by a horizontal Drift. Up a branch, westward about half a mile, one foot of poor slaty Coal crops out at the foot of the hill. On another tributary, one quarter of a mile south, the Coal was observed two feet in thickness, and 19 feet above the branch. It rests on about two feet of clayey Shales, containing plants, which is succeeded below by gray, shaly Sandstone. Thirteen feet below the Coal we find four feet of a shaly Sandstone, containing a seam of Coal of from one-half to three-quarters of an inch in thickness, with a lower seam of three inches. Three-quarters of a mile north of Downings, on the west side of Spring Creek, the Coal is seen 35 feet above the valley. The total thickness is not seen, but is probably two feet.

This Coal crops out in the ravines on the lands of David Sodder, in the S. W. quarter Sec. 27, T. 63, R. 20, and occurs thus:

No. 1.   16 feet Slope, with Limestone in loose masses, containg *Aviculopecten,*
        interlineatus, Rhombopora and *Pr. longispinus.*
No. 2.   18 feet Clay Shales, in thick laminæ.
No. 3.   26 to 30 inches Coal and Clay, arranged as follows:
        a.   6 inches olive Shales (clayey).
        b.   10 inches Coal.
        c.   2 inches ash-colored Clay, with Selenite.
        d.   1 foot 6 inches black Shales.
        e.   4 to 5 inches rusty Coal.
        f.   3 inches Clay.
        g.   1½ inch Coal.
        h.   1½ inch Clay.
        i.   3½ inches Coal.

This is succeeded by a bed of Fire Clay, and then Sandstone.

From examination near Milan we are induced to say that this Coal passes under the town, at about 100 feet below the hill-top, or 50 feet above the valley of Locust Creek, in which borings were being made for Coal. Examining our Section, we would then have for prospective beds to be found in the boring, and taking the surface for unity, at 227 feet, 18 inches of Coal; at 298 feet, 2½ to 3 feet of Coal, and at 387 feet, 3½ to 4 feet of Coal.

The Coal of David Sodder's may be found, by examinations, by digging about 80 or 100 feet below the top of the ridge, at or near Milan, for two or three miles N. W., and as many south. It may also be found under an area of several square miles, near Spring Creek. It is a soft and brittle Coal, with a middle, dull black seam of four inches, and an occasional thin, jet-black, shiny layer of one-sixteenth to one-eighteenth of an inch in thickness. This seam is jointed, the joints are filled with white and brown rust. Plant-like impressions occur between the seams. The bottom seam of three and one-half inches is soft and brittle, splitting into thick layers, and is also jointed with Calcite between the joints. An occasional thin seam of Pyrites and a little mineral Charcoal occur on the layers, and faint plant impressions are seen on the beds of deposit.

Mrs. Downing's Coal, already mentioned, occurs in Sec. 18, T. 64, R. 18, and is supposed to be the same bed as Sodder's. The bed is 18 inches thick and the Coal is hard and jointed. It splits into thick layers and breaks in large masses, but often in a sub-conchoidal form, being bright shiny and irridescent in color. Iron pyrites sometimes incrust the joints, and a white powder is found in them.

Besides the Coals above mentioned we find in Sec. 34, T. 62, R. 21, an outcrop of 7 inches of Coal, capped by 3½ feet of dark blue Shales which underlie 1½ feet of bituminous Shales. The Coal is underlaid by 1½ feet of Fire Clay. This Coal is probably No. 14 of the General Section.

We may safely expect to find this county underlaid by the same beds as Linn, under the entire surface of 648 square miles—say 6½ feet in thickness, to which add 2 feet of Coal, underlying an area of about 10 square miles, and we have 4,719,255,552 tons of Coal in this county.

CLAYS.

The under Clays of some of the Coal beds may afford good material for fire-brick.

One and a-half miles south of Milan, Mr. Norwood observed about 10 feet of good Potter's Clay, occurring in a valley between two hills. Good beds of this Clay may be found in other parts of the county, but are at present so deeply covered with recent deposits as to entirely conceal them.

Beds of good Red Ochre are not much exposed but may be looked for on the waters of Spring Creek, also on Locust Creek, west of Milan, in Secs. 10 and 11, T. 62, R. 21, Sec. 9, T. 63, R. 20, and Sec. 13, T. 63, R. 20. These red Shales sometimes contain nodules of red Hematite, but I saw but few of them in this county. At Thompson Cassady's the red Shales contain red calcareous Ironstone nodules, also thin calcareous Ironstone beds, and minute scales of bright Iron oxide sometimes occupy fractures in the shaly beds. The oxide seems to have infiltrated the cracks and the Shales seem soon after to have been pressed together, leaving a coating of a bright metallic appearance. Some of the nodules are Ochrey, as are also some of the Shales.

BUILDING STONE.

Good building material is not abundant in the county, although there are many quarries containing rock very suitable for walling wells or common rough stone-work. In Rs. 18 and 19 and as far north as T. 64, we only occasionally find beds of Soft Sandstone. On Yellow Creek, near the southern line of the county, is a Limestone bed which I suppose to be equivalent to No. 42 of General Section. In T. 64, R. 18, we find both Sandstone and Limestone.

The Sandstone near Clark's old place, is found in very thick beds, but I can not class it among first rate building material.

The Limestone overlying the Coal, near the eastern county line, is probably a Hydraulic one.

The best quarry to be seen in the county is that of James Webb, in Sec. 29, T. 64, R. 20. The succession of beds appear thus :

No. 1.   1 foot hard gray Sandstone.

No. 2.   4 feet 6 inches brown ferruginous, calcareous conglomerate.

No. 3.   1 foot 6 inches to 3 feet coarse Limestone, passing into a Clay, conglomerate.

No. 4.   15 feet soft, deep brown Limestone.

No. 5.   3 to 4 feet gray, fine-grained, freely working Sandstone—an excellent building material.

Nos. 1 and 5 are composed of minute grains of rounded Quartzose Sand, cemented by calcareous matter, effervescing freely. No 1 is much coarser than No. 5.

A Sandstone quarry on Wilhite Branch appears thus :

No. 1.   1 foot 6 inches fine-grained, drab colored Sandstone.

No. 2.   5 inches shaly Sandstone.

No. 3.   9 inches coarse, soft and brown specked Sandstone.

No. 4.   4 feet 6 inches fine-grained, brown specked Sandstone.

These beds are thick enough for most purposes, and the quarry will in time be valuable, but I consider the quality only second rate. There are in this neighborhood many outcrops of good Limestone suitable for the manufacture of Lime; also others near Milan.

Rock is scarcely ever seen in the south-eastern part of the county, for it is covered mostly with deep Drift.

A blue Limestone (probably No. 42) was only seen on Yellow Creek, Sec. 35, T. 61, R. 18.

The quality of the Sandstone is generally inferior, and not many beds will stand exposure.

CHALYBEATE SPRING.

In Sec. 34, T. 64, R. 21, a spring whose waters are considerably impregnated with Iron, issues from the Sandstone.

SOIL AND PRODUCTS.

The soil of Sullivan is generally good. The richer lands lie near Big and Little Yellow Creeks, East Locust Creek and parts of Ts. 63 and 64, R. 21 W., near Elmwood Branch. These lands produce fine crops of corn in most seasons, and with proper care 60 bushels of corn or 25 bushels of wheat in good seasons. Fifty bushels of corn per acre is considered a good crop. The soil on the hills between East and West Locust Creeks is very often thin, but can produce good crops of wheat in favorable seasons. Unless wheat is well put in the winter frost is apt to kill it out. Spring wheat is successfully raised.

Most vegetables of this climate are produced, and apples of fine quality are grown.

Grasses succeed well, the blue grass springing up everywhere, and I saw as good Timothy meadows as I have seen anywhere.

CHAPTER XIV.

ADAIR COUNTY.

BY G. C. BROADHEAD.

GEOGRAPHICAL DETAILS AND SURFACE CONFIGURATION.

Adair county embraces an area of 567 square miles lying in the northern part of the State, and is divided by a main north and south ridge into two portions. That east of this ridge is watered by streams flowing toward the Mississippi. West of the "Divide," the streams flow off to the Missouri. The topographical features of these two portions of the county are different. While the eastern portion is gently sloping and undulating, the western is more often hilly and broken. In the eastern part the "Drift" is deeply strewn over the whole surface, entirely concealing all solid rock formations. We also find a deep "Drift" deposit in the west, but the wearing of the stream channels has left exposed along their margins, and frequently on hill sides above, the Sandstones, Limestones, etc., of the Coal Measures.

TIMBER AND PRAIRIE.

Belts of timber are found in the eastern part of the county, near the streams, and sometimes on the adjacent hills. The "bottoms" consist mostly of prairie. West of the "Grand Divide," we find the Chariton hills covered with timber, often of large size and of good quality, consisting mostly of White Oak, and some Black Oak, with

occasionally Hickory. The bottoms are supplied with a heavy growth
of timber, and on the tributaries of Chariton and on Spring Creek,
are fine groves of Sugar trees. Adjacent and north of Spring Creek
are good bodies of timber, but in the south-western part of the county
the hills barely support a growth of Scrub Oak, (chiefly,) giving to
this region the appearance of " Barrens."

The Barrens include most of the county west of the Chariton
River and south of Spring Creek, and consist of irregular, winding
and sharp ridges of from 100 to 150 feet in hight, with but little soil,
being composed in the main of Drift—Clays, Sand, Pebbles and Boulders.

The following is a list of the trees, shrubs and vines found in this
county:

Crab Apple,	Black Jack Oak,	Red Bud,
Aspen,	Button Bush,	Rose,
Ash,	Coralberry,	Raspberry,
Red Birch.	Red Cherry,	Green Brier,
Bladdernut,	Choke Cherry,	Hackberry,
Buckeye,	Cottonwood,	Hazel,
Box Elder,	Dogwood, (2 species,)	Black Haw,
Bitter Sweet,	American or White Elm,	Gooseberry,
Pignut Hickory,	Red or Slippery Elm,	Shell-bark Hickory,
Honeysuckle,	Post Oak,	Thick Shell-bark Hick-ory.
Ironwood,	Swamp White Oak,	Sumach,
Honey Locust,	Chinquepin Oak,	Poison Oak,
Linden,	Pin Oak,	Thorn, (several species,)
White Maple,	Spanish Oak,	Black Walnut,
Sugar Maple,	Laurel Oak,	White Walnut,
Red Oak,	Burr Oak,	Waahoo,
White Oak,	American Plum,	Red Root.
Black Oak,		

Aspen (*Populus tremuloides*) was observed but rarely. I also
found it in Sullivan county, on Locust Creek. It may be found in
some of the counties to the north-west. It is a very pretty and well
formed little tree.

Burr Oak trees, with elongate acorns, often abound on the hills
in this county, and north, and west, but no further south.

STREAMS AND SPRINGS.

The streams flowing east of the " Divide " are sluggish, and during dry seasons contain but little water. Those west are clear, and mostly pretty streams, with beds of clean Sand. On the Chariton River are several good mill sites, and the stream affords sufficient power for milling purposes during the greater part of the year.

Springs are rare.

Water for drinking or domestic use is obtained from cisterns or wells. At Kirksville, and on the prairies east, good water in quantity sufficient for most purposes, is obtained at from 20 to 30 feet, and rises up through beds of Drift Sand. The water in the Chariton tributaries, is sweet and pleasant to the taste. In some of the streams flowing through beds of Sandstone, the waters partake very much of a Chalybeate character, and such is the character of the water in Hazel and Hog Creeks, and a few others, which have marked diruetic properties. There are several fine Chalybeate springs near Mr. Hendren's, on Hog Creek.

SURFACE GEOLOGY.

The surface deposits consist of Alluvium and Drift. The Alluvium includes local and recent deposits along the streams, and the soil.

BLUFF.

The upper 8 to 15 feet of the Clays resting just beneath the soil, such as we find in the eastern part of the county may be a representative of the Bluff.

Near Meek's mill, on Sugar Creek, we find exposed 8 feet of Clay, brown at top, becoming darker below, and containing white calcareous concretions. These Clays are generally marly, and good fertilizers, and when mingled with the surface soil impart additional fertility.

DRIFT.

Below the Clays last named, we find beds of Clay with smal rounded pebbles; and still lower is found sandy Clay with pebbles.

These latter beds are often reached at 4 and 6 feet below the surface, but are generally deeper. In digging wells, water is generally obtained in the Sand and Gravel beds. Still lower we reach beds of blue Clay, and masses of large rounded boulders. The abrasion pro-

duced by the agency of water, will sometimes present the lower beds
on the surface, and along the streams are often found large boulders
of igneous rocks.

A section on Sugar Creek presents the following:

No. 1. 15 feet Slope from hill-top.
No. 2. 8 feet Clay, brown at top and contains white, calcareous nodules,
     (concretions.)
No. 3. 15 feet beds of white Sand, brown Sand and pebbles.
No, 4. 10 feet mass of boulders, pebbles and Sand.

At Nineveh, we find exposed 20 feet of Clay, dark blue and brown
mottled in the upper portion, the lower part being brownish mottled.
This rests on a 6-inch bed of brown Sand, which again reposes on a
3-foot bed of blackish Clay, with pebbles. The Sand beds here thicken
up, and we again find a mass of black, soft Sandstone.

On the Barrens, in the southern part of the county, the beds of
"Drift," containing round pebbles, are often at the surface, and hence
the poor character of the soil.

The boulders consist of Granite, Syenite, Hornblende, Greenstone,
Quartzite, Jasper, Quartz, Agate and Limestone.

In the lower beds of the Drift there is sometimes found associated
with the blue Clay or with the Sand and Gravel beds, in juxtaposition,
masses of leaves, sticks and bark. These are found sometimes as much
as 100 feet below the surface.

From wells dug in the northern and eastern parts of the county,
we have proof that the "Drift" spreads over this district to a depth of
175 feet.

We suppose the ridge at Kirksville to be as high as any other part
of the county. Levelings show that it is 180 feet above the bottoms
of Chariton River. The Limestones on Big Creek extend as much as
40 feet above Chariton bottoms, with at least as much as 40 to 60 feet
of Sandstones and Shales above. This would leave not over 80 or 100
feet of Drift at and south-west of Kirksville. Borings at Mr. Eley's,
12 miles north-east of Kirksville, extended 175 feet through Drift,
reaching blue Clay at 55 feet. This shows that throughout the eastern
part of the county there exists a deep glacial trough, extending, probably through the Coal Measures and reaching nearly to Kirksville—
since filled with Clays and boulders.

LOWER CARBONIFEROUS ROCKS.

The eastern strip of 12 miles in width, extending from the north
to the south line of the county, exhibits no regular strata of rock, but

from the position and inclination of the strata appearing on the west,
we believe we can safely say that most, if not all, of this part of the
county is underlaid by Coal Measure rocks. These rocks, when seen,
are those of the Lower Coal Measures, and extend from the mouth of
Rye Creek northward along and near Chariton River. Beds a little
higher, geologically, appear on Spring Creek and on Shut-eye Creek.
In the western tier of townships, we find the upper Sandstone of the
Middle Coal Measures, or No. 5 of our General Section. This Sandstone appears near the hill-top near the head of most of the streams
near Kirksville—sometimes in very thick beds. On Alum, it occurs
in thick beds at one place, having the lower part eroded leaving
the upper beds overhanging. A white substance, either Alum or
Sulphate of Iron deposited on the surface in small quantities—hence
the name Alum Cave and Alum Creek. The Sandstone here is
traversed by a few minute Coal seams, and the lower part contains
a little red Ochre. Other beds just beneath are shaly for 10 feet,
then giving place to about 5 feet of rough conglomerate.

At Miller's Mill, on Alum Creek, there is 44 inches of dark, ash blue
Limestone—the upper 26 inches being shelly and variegated with
occasional dark specks, while the lower 18 inches is an even-bedded,
jointed Limestone, the angles forming rhomboidal blocks. Its fossils
are *Sp. lineatus, Avicpec, interlineatus* and *Orthoceras*. This rock I
supposed to be near the base of the Upper Coal Measures, and is
probably No. 74 of the General Section of 1872, or No. 2 of our General County Section. The beds and fossils are just like the rock over
David Sodder's Coal, near Milan. The fossils found here are *Pr.
longispinus, Avicpec, carboniferus* and *Orthoceras*.

Up a small branch coming from the north, we found the rocks
(Limestone) dipping 5° to the north. A little further up, there is 5
feet of bituminous Slate, but no Coal. Our section in this neighborhood would be:

No. 1. Sandstone.

No. 2. Bituminous Shale.

No. 3. A few feet Slope.

No. 4. 4 feet of Limestone.

No. 5. 2 feet dark blue Shales.

No. 6. 28 feet of Sandstone.

No. 7. 2 feet red and green Shales.

No. 8. 1 foot of red Shales, slightly sandy.

No. 9. Rough beds of fine-grained Limestone, corresponding to No. 19 of our
General Section.

These beds may be found on Alum Creek, at Dumy's, Sharr's Mills and on Big Creek hills at many places. The upper strata are well represented about one mile west of Kirksville, where they form benches across the stream. Mr. Norwood made the following section here:

No. 1. 3 feet drab and greenish drab, irregularly bedded, mostly compact, hard, fine-grained and sometimes mottled Limestone. Contains but few fossils and only found *Ath. subtilita* and *Crinoid* columns.

No. 2. 1 foot 6 inches rough, mottled bluish and light drab Limestone, nodular at the top and containing *Sp. planoconvexus*, *Ath. subtilita* and *Crinoid* stems.

No. 3. 10 inches olive and blue calcareous Shales, containing *Cho. mesoloba* and *Sp. planoconvexus*.

No. 4. 5 inches greenish-drab and gray argillaceous Limestone, contains *Retzia punctilifera*, *Sp. planoconvexus*, *Hemipronites crassus*, *Fusulina cylindrica* and *Rhombopora lepidodendroides*.

No. 5. 2 feet Shale, olive above and passing into argillo-bituminous below, with calcareous nodules throughout, containing *Pr. longispinus*, *Hemipronites crassus*, *Sp. Kentuckensis*, and *Chonetes*.

No. 6. 1 foot 4 inches ash drab, irregularly bedded, fine-grained Limestone, full of Calcite veins and specks, and abounding in *Athyris subtilita*, also containing *Pr. longispinus*, *Sp. perplexus*, *Fusulina cylindrica*, *Sp. planoconvexus*, *Bryozoa*, etc.

No. 7. 2 inches yellowish green Shales, abounding in *Pr. longispinus*, also containing *Hemipronites crassus*, *Sp. planoconvexus* and *Chonetes*.

No. 8. 1 inch black Shale.

No. 9. 2 feet dark green Shales.

No. 10. 1 foot to 6 inches nodular Limestone and Shales, containing *Bryozoa*, *Fistulapora* and *Hemipronites*.

The above section includes from Nos. 19 to 40 of our General Vertical County Section. This group is found on the head of all the little branches of Big Creek, and on the hills near the Chariton, also on Sugar and Alum Creeks, on Ely's Creek, high in the bluffs of Billy's Creek and of Spring Creek.

No. 27 of our General Section, was not observed in this county, but I think it may be found in some places after removing overlying debris. It is well exposed at Henry's Mill, Sullivan county.

No. 28 is very fine-grained, traversed by minute veins and specks of Calcite, and would look well if polished. It occurs in a very even bed, is of a uniform dove color. It is found on Big and Sugar Creeks and on Billy's Creek, near Campbell's, and lower down. Obscure remains of very minute (almost microscopic) fossils, are sometimes abundant. Below the last we have 3 to 4 feet of shelly Limestone, sometimes a greenish Shale and always full of fossils mostly *Ath.˙subtilita* and *Pr. costatus*; other fossils seen were *Ath. Missouriensis, Hemipronites crassus, Meekella, Sp. cameratus, Pr. Nebrascensis, Lophphyllum,* and a fish tooth.

These beds being almost entirely made of fossils, are easily recognized. They are found at most places where the last named Limestone beds are, and are also recognized in Sullivan, Linn, Macon and Randolph counties.

The strata next below No. 40 crops out near the mouth of Big Creek. No. 39 may be considered the upper part of No. 40, always occurring with it, but differs in being rough and sometimes nodular, whereas No. 40 is a single bed 4 feet thick of ash-blue Limestone, and may be Hydraulic. It crops out on the hill-side at Sharrs' Mill, and at Williams' or Dumy's Mill.

No. 42 is a well marked Limestone, although not so well marked in this county as it is farther south, yet we may always recognize it by its associate beds and fossils therein. Its upper and lower surfaces are generally slaty, its lower surface often traversed by a vermicular *Fucoid.* The solid interior breaks by vertical planes into rhomboidal blocks. It is generally at a nearly uniform vertical distance of 23 feet below the Limestone No. 40, of our General Section, from which it is separated by a Sandstone which is generally shaly, and the upper beds are somewhat nodular.

No. 46 is well recognized by its fossils, *Pr. muricatus* being most abundant. It also contains *Pr. Prattenanus* and *Sp. cameratus, Hemipronites crassus* and *Ath. subtilita.* On Sugar Creek *Myalina subquadrata* was obtained, and I would add that I have not observed this fossil at any lower horizon, with one exception, in Linn county, where it occurred about eighteen feet below. Heretofore I have considered its lowest horizon to be the base of the Upper Coal Measures. The rocks we have just been speaking of, together with other lower and associated beds, are well exposed on Sugar Creek, near its mouth, their thickness differing a little from that seen at other places, We here find :

No. 1. Shaly Sandstone and sandy Shales.
No. 2. 10 inches dark blue-black shaly Limestone.
No. 3. 10 inches black bituminous Shales.
No. 4. 20 inches hard black Slate, corresponds to No. 44 of our County Section.

No. 5. 5 inches soft bituminous Shale.

No. 6. calcareo-bituminous Shales (fossiliferous).

No. 8. 8 inches fine-grained, compact and dark concretionary Limestone, with some carbonate of Iron. Contains obscure remains of roots of plants, and is slightly mottled with a conchoidal fracture.

No. 9. Fire Clay.

No. 6 corresponds to No. 46 of our General Section. Besides the last mentioned fossils, we here find *C. Vernuiliana* and *Ath. subtilita.*

Near the waters' edge, at Williams' Mill, we find 18 inches of compact and drab or dull ash-blue Limestone (No. 52 of Gen. Sec,) containing *Pr. semireticulatus* and *Allorisma.* The rocks from Nos. 53 to 63 inclusive, are but poorly represented in Adair county. No. 59 is probably the equivalent of the Coal near McPhetridge's, and that at M. Gray's on Hog Creek.

Nos. 64 to 74 are found on Spring Creek and some of its tributaries, and on Shut-eye Creek. These beds do not materially differ from their corresponding equivalents in Sullivan county, and I shall not therefore dwell much upon their mode of occurrence. Mr. C. J. Norwood obtained the following Section in the edge of Putnam county, in S. W. Sec. 17, T. 64, R. 17 :

No. 1. 35 feet Slope of 25 deg.

No. 2. 1 foot 3 inches hard, finely cemented, calcareous conglomerate.

No. 3. 2 feet Slope.

No. 4. 1 foot 6 inches buff and brown, somewhat sandy, coarse, argillaceous, rough-bedded Limestone, with fossils, including *Sp. cameratus, Macrocheilus inhabilis,——Bellerophon ——, Pleurotomaria ——,* and abounding *Bell. percarinatus.*

No. 5. 14 feet alternations of sandy Shales and Shaly Sandstone.

No. 6. 5 feet Clay Slope.

No. 7. 1 foot 9 inches light-blue, hard and compact Limestone, containing a few fossils, including *Sp. planoconvexus, Ath. subtilita, Pr. longispinus, Sp. cameratus* and *Lophophyllum.*

No. 8. 6 inches olive Shales.

No. 9. 2 feet bituminous Shales and Slate.

No. 10. 2 feet 9 inches Coal, divided by a thin Clay seam.

No. 7 of this section is probably the equivalent of No. 64 of the General Section. As such it was seen at John Shibley's, being there 5 feet above the Coal, abounding in *Allorisma regularis* and also containing *Athyris, Meekella, Chonetes, Aviculopecten* and *Schizodus Wheeleri.*

On Abernathy's Branch we observed:

No. 1. Slope.
No. 2. out-crop of drab Limestone (No. 64 of Gen. Sec.) with *Pr. costatus*, and *Meekella striatocostatus*.
No. 3. 1 foot olive Shales, containing *Chonetes mesoloba*, *Hempronites crassus*, *Pr.*——, and *Athyris*.
No. 4. 1 foot 6 inches nodular Limestone and Shales.
No. 5. 8 inches light-blue Clay Shales.
No. 6. 8 inches bituminous Shales with gray bands.
No. 7. 5½ inches Coal.
No. 8. 3 inches blue Clay.
No. 9. 1 foot Coal.
No. 10. 1 foot Fire Clay, blue above, passing into brown below.
No. 11. 4 feet brown nodular Limestone (few fossils).
No. 12. 12 feet Sandstone, nodular at top, becoming Shaly below.
No. 13. 6 feet 6 inches blue Sandy and Clay Shales.

On Joab's Creek a half mile from Spring Creek, our Section includes some of the members of the last Section, with other lower beds, thus:

No. 1. 10 inches black Coal Smut (No. 67 of County Section).
No. 2. 1 foot 6 inches blue Clay.
No. 3. 6 inches bluish drab, weathering to drab, fine-grained Limestone.
No. 4. 6 inches drab, sandy Clay.
No. 5. 16 feet drab, shaly Limestone.
No. 6. 6 feet dark Shales, Clay and Sand.
No. 7. 1 foot black, shaly and carbonaceous Limestone.
No. 8. 2 feet 6 inches bituminous Shales.
No. 9. 8 inches black, calcareous and bituminous, shaly band, full of fossils *Pr. costatus*, *Athyris subtilita* and *Cho. mesoloba*.
No. 10. 2 inches blue-black Ironstone, containing *Pr. Prattenanus Hemipronites crassus* and *Athyris subtilita*.
No. 11. 4 feet ash-colored Fire Clay.
No. 12. 4 feet rough, ash drab, fine-grained and friable Limestone. Only observed *Pr. Prattenanus* (No. 78).

The lowest rocks of the county are those associated with the Nineveh Coal, and are seen at Beeman's bank.

COAL.

We find there are about three good workable seams of Coal in this county. The lowest is that worked on the Chariton and its immediate tributaries in the northern part of the county. It is from three to four feet thick, and is occasionally mined in R. 16, from Rye Creek northward.

The Section at Beeman's mine, S. E. Sec. 3, T. 63, R. 16, exhibits the following:

No. 1. 50 feet Slope.

No. 2. 1 foot 6 inches hard, bluish drab, coarse-grained Limestone; sometimes drab with ferruginous spots, showing remains of UNIVALVES in relief.

No. 3. 11 inches hard, tough and coarse-grained, gray and brown-specked Limestone, with much Calcite (disseminated). Numerous fossil remains are seen on surface (in relief).

No. 4. 3 feet drab Clay.

No. 5. 6 to 9 inches soft, brown Limestone; fracture shows a bluish drab color.

No. 6. 1 foot 3 inches Clay; buff and green above, passing into black at base.

No. 7. 2 feet bituminous Shale.

No. 8. 1 inch shaly Coal.

No. 9. 1 foot 6 inches Fire Clay.

No. 10. 2 feet green, shaly Sandstone.

No. 11. 1 foot greenish-gray, soft Sandstone.

No. 12. 3 feet sandy Shales.

No. 13. 10 feet blue Clay Shales.

No. 14. 35 feet Sandstone and Shales.

No. 15. 3 feet bituminous Shales.

No. 16. 2 feet 6 inches hard, shiny, black Coal.

No. 17. 1 foot 2 inches Clay.

No. 18. 1 foot poor Coal.

No. 19. 3 feet Fire Clay.

No. 20. 1 foot 6 inches hard, blue and drab mottled Limestone, contains *Athyris subtilita* and *Pr. Prattenanus*.

No. 21. 9 inches deep-blue, sandy Shales.

No. 22. 2 to 3 inches hard, ash-colored, argillaceous Limestone, abounding in *Crinoid* stems and black specks throughout.

No. 23. 15 feet blue, shaly Sandstone, with thin layers and nodules of yellow Ochre.

The Coal dips up the river five feet in three hundred feet, and varies from three feet and a half to four feet in thickness. The dark streak, fifty feet above the Coal, is probably the equivalent of the Spring Creek Coal. The Coal here is, as it is everywhere, separated by a thin Clay seam, and this in some cases nearly thins out. That above the upper stratum is the best. There are, as shown above, three feet and four inches of this Coal at Beeman's, near Nineveh. It resembles a little that of Kirby's in Sullivan county, and is black with a dull band. It is jointed somewhat irregularly, and sometimes has slightly curved surfaces, with Calcite plates in the joints and mineral Charcoal on the beds of deposit.

This Coal is well situated for drainage, twenty feet above water in the Chariton River, having a very good bed of Fire Clay for the floor.

It is also worked by Stout and Holmes, in S. W. N. E. Sec. 2, T. 63, R. 16 ; E. Besanco, N. W. N. E. Sec. 2 ; J. Porter, N. E. N. W. Sec. 2 ; J. Snyder, in N. E. N. E. Sec. 3, and Mr. Motter, in N. W. Sec. 2 ; all in T. 63, R. 16.

Most of these have shafts sunk to the Coal, which is generally at from fifteen to twenty-five feet below the bottoms of Hazel Creek. At some places it is reached by drifts. At the above places it is found to be generally from three to four feet thick, with a roof of from one to five feet of black Slate. In ravines, at Nineveh, the Coal is seen from three to four feet thick.

Watson's shaft was sunk in the bottoms of Rye Creek, one mile above Conner's mill, but was abandoned on account of the supposed poor quality of the Coal. The depth of the shaft was reported to be forty feet, and passed only through Sandstone to three feet of Coal. The Sandstone thrown out was whitish-gray and micaceous, containing carbonaceous remains of plants.

Near the mouth of Rye Creek, on W. Conner's land, the Coal has been mined at several places, but is rather low in the valley, and at the time of my visit the pits were all filled up with water and debris. The Coal is covered by about three feet of bituminous Shales, with thick beds of Sandstone above. The bituminous shales contain many small *Gasteropods*. The fossils found here were *Pr. muricatus, Pr. Prattenianus, Lingula, Solenomya,* and *Hemipronites crassus ;* also a minute *Macrocheilus, Pleurotomaria* (minute sp.) resembling *P. spaciosa, Petr. occidentalis, Actæonina minuta,* and *Streptacis Whitfieldii.*

If our General Section is correct for the central and southern part of the county for concealed formations, a shaft at Kirksville would have to be nearly 500 feet deep to reach this Coal, so strong is the dip of the rocks to the south.

SPRING CREEK COAL.

Our next and higher Coal in this county is from 50 to 80 feet above the first and lowest. I have called it Spring Creek Coal, because it is best developed, and only seen on Spring Creek and its tributaries, and streams close by. It may be found on McPhet-

ridge's Branch, on W. Shott's land, and also on that of Mr. McPhetridge. It is occasionally seen near Spring Creek to the north-west,
and, also, on Abernathy's Branch to its head, and on some of its tributaries. It has been mined at various places near Shut-eye Creek, and
certainly underlies all of R. 17, Ts. 63 and 64, and part of the Range
east, varying in thickness from 2 to 3 feet and is worth mining for, the
only drawback at present being lack of transportation to market. Mr.
Norwood .observed this Coal on E. Burns' land, (in the edge of Putnam county,) in N. W. qr. Sec. 17, T. 64, R. 17, 33 inches thick, and divided by a 2-inch Clay seam.

At John Shibley's, on Brush Creek, in Sec. 30, T. 64, R. 16, some
mining was formerly done, and the Coal reported to be 3 feet. The
upper layer of 1 foot in thickness, is of poor quality. That below is
hard, good Coal, but contains a good deal of Iron pyrites. This is
separated from the lower Coal by a 2-inch seam of Clay. The lower
bed is the best. The cap rock is Limestone, and is 6 feet above the
Coal, abounding in *Allorisma regularis*.

On the land of G. Sizemore, N. E. N. W. Sec. 9, T. 63, R. 17, the
Coal is only one and a half feet thick. The Limestone is separated
from the Coal by 2 feet of blue and black Shales. The Coal is the
same as that of Shibley.

Gardner's Coal bank is in N. W. Sec. 10, T. 63, R. 17, and Seaman's
north-west of it.

At Jno. M. Williams' Coal bank, in T. 63, R. 17, N. W. N. W. Sec.
15, the upper seam of 18 inches is separated by a 3-inch layer of light-
blue Clay, from the lower 13 inches of good Coal, the latter containing a very little Sulphur. A specimen taken from the top of the
seam closely resembles that of John Stanley's, being, however, a little more jetty, and having bright, brown rust in the joints. It is a
very good looking Coal. A specimen from the bottom seam was of a
dull-black color, with some bright bands and thin jetty layers. The
joints have a white lining and sometimes a dull irridesence. An occasional layer of Charcoal is sometimes found between the beds. The
total thickness of the seam is 31 inches.

At John Stanley's bank, a short distance north of M. Williams
and across the branches, we find the beds differing very little.
We here find :

No. 1. 6 inches Coal with Clay streaks.
No. 2. 1 foot Coal.
No. 3. 3 inches Clay.
No. 4. 1 foot 1-inch Coal.

The coal from the bottom seam is bright, shiny and hard, with long, smooth joints,containing some jet-black bands, which are jointed, but also break with a sub-chonchoidal fracture. It contains a little decomposed Calcite in the joints.

On P. Day's land, in S. W. N. W. Sec. 15, this Coal has been mined at several places, but all were abandoned at the time of my visit to this place. I was informed that it was three feet thick.

Other thin Coals, occupying a higher Geological position, were observed, and among which were the following:

On Billy's Creek, on the land of John Campbell, a one foot seam crops out just above the water's edge, with its associate rocks, appearing thus:

No. 1. 6 feet Local Drift.
No. 2. 3 feet thin layers of soft Sandstone.
No. 3. 6 inches black calcareo-carbonaceous Ironstone.
No. 4. 2 feet 6 inches bituminous Shales.
No. 5. 1 foot 2 inches Clay Shale.
No. 6. 1 foot Coal.

In the overlying bituminous Shales are occasional concretions of black Limestone, containing *Cardium Lexingtonensis*, and a *Gonitite*, also fish spines. No. 3 contains plant remains, probably *Lepidophyllum*. These fossils indicate that this Coal may be equivalent of the Coal at Moloney's, in Sullivan county, and the probable equivalent of the Mulky Coal, in Lafayette county. Campbell's Coal in S. E. S. W. Sec. 36, T. 63, R. 17, occurs, as is shown in the above Section in a seam one foot in thickness, and is of a dull-black color and jointed, with a very little Iron pyrites and a little Lime between the joints.

At Milton Grays, in S. W. S. W. Sec. 18, T. 62, R. 16, a seam of Coal 4 to 8 inches thick appears dipping 1 foot 6 inches in 5 feet N. 30° W. It is capped by 2 feet 6 inches of bituminous Shales, which is again overlaid by blue argillaceous Shales with blue Fire Clay beneath. Mr. Norwood regards this Coal as equivalent to that of Nutter's on Muscle Fork, Macon county, or No. 59 of our General Section. A Coal, probably equivalent to the last named, crops out on a small branch of Mc-Phetridges' Creek, one foot in thickness, and capped by 30 inches of bituminous Shales. A quarter of a mile below are found the beds of the Spring Creek Group. This Coal very much resembles that of Kirby's in Sullivan county. Its rough fracture and frequent irregular joints, filled with Calcite, give it a general gray appearance. It also has faint plant impressions and mineral Charcoal on the beds of deposit.

We may safely say that nearly three-fourths of Adair county or 380 square miles, are underlaid by the same Coal that we find in Linn, and if so we have 2,754,385,920 tons of Coal in this county. Shafts of sufficient depth will reach one, two or three of these beds in Rs. 15, 16 and 17.

CLAYS.

Nos. 16 and 18 of our General Section would make good PAINT. They appear at many places in the county and are well exposed in the bluffs of Big Creek, west of Kirksville, and at many places in the hills quite to Chariton River. They seem mostly free from Sand and entirely free from Lime. On William's land, in N. E. S. W. Sec. 12, T. 62, R. 16, the washings in an old road expose twelve feet of mostly deep brick-red Clay, free from Lime and Sand. This Clay is also well exposed in bluffs opposite Sharr's mill. At this place we find two distinct beds separated by three feet of Sandstone, the upper being 11 feet and the lower 4 feet thick. On the land of S. A. Lutze, west of the Chariton River, in Sec. 16, T. 62, R. 16, this Clay is used for making pottery. The Clays are dug out of the hill side on the place, exposing about 4 feet of red Clay. Fifteen feet above the red there is a mottled buff and drab, smooth Clay. Mr. Lutze mixes the red and light colored Clays together, and by this combination forms a good potter's Clay. Several feet of red Clay were seen on Alum Creek, but it was sandy and micaceous, with obscure fern impressions. These red Clays were also occasionally exposed on Sugar and Billy's Creeks.

IRON ORE.

On the Chariton River, two miles north of the south county line, numerous masses of Septaria are washed out of the Shales and strewn along the river bank. The joints of these are mostly filled with clear Calcite, and this is often studded with beautiful minute crystals of Limonite (hydrated sesquioxide of Iron). These often shoot out from between Calcite crystals, in which position we find them closely adhering at their base and thence diverging. There is an occasional clear crystal of Quartz entirely enclosing these beautiful black Limonite crystals. This variety of Iron ore is called Gœthite.

The Limonite is also sometimes collected in small globules on these crystals of Calcite. These globules vary in size from a pin-point to that of one-sixteenth of an inch. The largest seen was three-quarters of an inch in diameter. The Calcite is generally a regular rhomboid but is sometimes modified in form and has its surface sometimes covered with a pale, flesh red.

SELENITE.

The Fire Clay of the lower Coal sometimes contains a small quantity of Selenite crystals.

HYDRAULIC LIME.

No. 40 may prove to be a good Hydraulic Lime rock. It is four feet thick at the mouth of Big Creek, and may be found in most of its bluffs, and also on Sugar Creek.

No. 52 may also be Hydraulic. It was only observed at Dumy's mill.

The middle bed of No. 64 may also prove to be a good Hydraulic Limestone, being found everywhere that the Spring Creek Coal is. No experiments have yet been made on any of these rocks.

The upper beds on Big and Sugar Creek will make very good Lime for all ordinary purposes.

CHAPTER XV.

LINN COUNTY.

BY G. C. BROADHEAD.

This county embraces an area of 612 square miles and occupies a central position in North Missouri. It is traversed through the middle in an east and west direction by the Hannibal and St. Joseph Railroad.

The streams preserve a general course from the north to the south, those in the eastern portion being tributaries of the Chariton River, those in the west of Grand River. Muscle Fork, in the east, is the main western tributary of the Chariton, the other streams bearing their waters to Grand River.

Range 18, drained by Muscle Fork, has its peculiar topography quite distinct from that part of the county lying west. While the former is quite hilly and often broken, especially in Ts. 59 and 60, near their eastern line, we find the country lying west gently undulating and rolling.

The bottoms of Locust and of the Yellow Creeks vary from a half of a mile to a mile in width, and their outer margins blend by an easy slope with the higher lands. The lesser streams are also flanked by low hills of very easy ascent.

TIMBER AND PRAIRIE.

The bottom lands more often consist of prairie with timber growing along the margin of the streams and on the adjacent hills. We find, with a few exceptions, similar timber in this county to that of

G.S—17.

Adair and Sullivan.   White Walnut and Aspen are not found nor do we find Burr Oak growing on the hills.

This county may be considered as the southern limit of Choke Cherry in this part of Missouri.

The bottom lands of Locust Creek often afford a fine quality of Black Walnut timber.

The most extensive and best body of timber may be found north of Linneus near Locust Creek, and between Main Locust and West Locust to the north line of the county.

WATER SUPPLIES.

Good living water, except in wells, is scarce. There are but few springs, and in extremely dry seasons many of the wells become dry. In wells water is obtained at variable depths, and some have been dug as deep as eighty feet without obtaining water. A shaft at Brook-field struck a strong vein of water in Sand at a depth of eighty-three feet below the surface, while a well in the town reached a strong stream at fourteen feet. At the railroad tank a very bold stream was struck at a depth of forty feet, and anywhere in the neighborhood of Brookfield water may generally be obtained at from thirty to forty feet.

Mr. Huffaker, in Sec. 19, T. 59, R. 18, says that water may be ob-tained on the prairies in his neighborhood at a depth of from fifteen to twenty feet.

The variable depth at which water is obtained in this region is owing to the irregular character and thickness of the Drift Sands and Clays.

These deposits are formed of alternations of Clay, Sand and Gravel of irregular thickness, the beds of Sand being sometimes near the sur-face and again much deeper. It is in these Sand and Gravel beds, when they repose on tenaceous Clays, that we may look for water. The Clay prevents the water from sinking to a greater depth, and when there is a large pocket of Sand resting on the Clay we may find an extensive reservoir of water. In some wells the water is hard in others soft. The former may be caused by the water "seeping" or rising slowly up through overlying porous and calcareous Clays. If wells are walled with Limestone the waters may be impregnated sometimes with Lime.

Throughout the country cisterns are very much relied on for sup-plies of water, and the farmers often make ponds in the "draws" for he use of their stock.

QUATERNARY DEPOSITS.

The soil and recent deposits along the streams we recognize as alluvial. The wide bottom prairies, with a sub-stratum of black jointed, tough Clay, containing brown streaks, and occasionally small black, concretionary forms of Bog Iron ore, may be referred to the age of the bottom prairie of Professor Swallow.

It is possible that some of the beds of brown jointed Clays exposed in the railroad cuts may be representatives of the Bluff, but I am inclined to refer most of the latter Clays and also the underlying blue Clays, with rounded pebbles and boulders, to the Drift period.

On Locust Creek, near the north county line, we find exposed—

No. 1. 6 inches dark, laminated, sandy Clay.

No. 2. 3 feet dark soil and jointed Clay.

No. 3. 5 feet brownish black Clay near the top, shading into a yellow Sand near the bottom.

No. 4. 1 foot yellow Sand.

No. 5. 1 foot light brown Sand.

This section seems to be mostly of ancient Aluvium. A well in Sec. 9, T. 58, R. 20, revealed 33 feet of mostly yellow Sand and dark Clay, with fragments of Coal and pieces of wood near the bottom.

The washings in a road near by, disclose small Iron and Sand concretions, with a 4 to 5 inch dark ferruginous band. These formations may be referred to the Drift period. The Drift does not differ materially from what we find in neighboring counties, and is generally a brownish Clay with a little Sand, resting on beds of Sand, Gravel or boulders, with blue Clay or boulders below.

There is no doubt but there is as much as 80 feet thickness of Drift in the county, and we find in it similar boulders to those found in the adjoining counties.

GOLD IN THE DRIFT.

Near Yellow Creek, in the northern part of the county, we have reports of grains of Gold being found mingled with the Sand, but in small quantity. We do not think that any valuable deposits of the precious metals will ever be found in Missouri associated with these Sands. Mr. Norwood found a particle of Gold in a Quartz boulder in the southern part of the county.

DIP.

The rocks on Locust Creek, south-west of Laclede, I consider Geologically below those on the creek, northward. A little south of west from Laclede, on Locust Creek, there are exposed beds indicating a strong westward dip. These rocks are Sandstones and Shales, No. 5 of our General Section; and at the south end of the Bluff are seen the beds of No. 18.

At Perry's (formerly Withrow's) mill, in S. E. Sec. 27, T. 59, R. 21, the Rhomboidal Limestone (No. 42) is near the water's edge. Three miles north, at Miles' (formerly Hurlburt's) mill, No. 42 is 23 feet above water. This would indicate a rise northward of 23 feet, to be added to the descent of the stream, which would probably be as much more. This rise continues a little way into Sullivan county, where the beds probably slightly incline north to the northern part of T. 62, when they again rise, and continue to do so to the northern line of the county.

In the southern part of Linn county, the rocks preserve a constant westerly dip from the Macon county line to Laclede, of about 4⅔ of a foot per mile, or nearly 50 feet from Muscle Fork to Yellow Creek. Further west they indicate a rise. Along the eastern line of the county, the dip is northward, for we find that from the vicinity of the Hannibal and St. Joseph Railroad to New Boston, the corresponding rocks are depressed to the extent of 170 feet, as referred to the stream. The true dip north may be about 60 feet in that distance, or 5 feet per mile.

On Yellow Creek there is a general rise to the north, although the strata undulate somewhat. No. 42 is seen 25 feet above the stream at Yellow Creek, on the Hannibal and St. Joseph Railroad, and 1½ miles north, at Coalson's old mill, it is seen in the bed of the stream. At Baker's old mill, 2 miles further north, it is still in the bed of the stream. We find it occupying the same position at Bayles' old mill, in Sec. 6, T. 59, R, 18, and also in the edge of Sullivan county. This indicates a regular rise to the north, and as we saw it on Muscle Fork, 6 miles east, dipping north, there must therefore be an axis between which bears somewhat to the north-west.

In Adair county, the rocks gradually rise from the southern part of the county north, bringing to view rocks which are 200 feet beneath the surface near the southern county line.

COAL MEASURES.

The rock structure of this county includes beds of the middle Coal Measures.

Those seen, lie between the lower part of No. 5 and No. 62. Out-crops occur only in detached exposures, and hence it would be impossible to form a connected vertical section from material gathered within the bounds of this county.

GEOLOGICAL DESCRIPTION.

Near the line of Secs. 13 and 24, T. 57, R. 21, on the land of Turner's heirs, and of Edwards, we observed outcrops of rocks which we are disposed to regard as the lowest seen in the county. The Coal seam worked here we regard as No. 67 of our County Section, and the same as the working seam in the Brookfield and St. Catharine shafts; thus indicating a remarkable rise in the strata as we go west from Brookfield. We are probably right in this supposition, as the rocks on the Chariton, southward, are quite low in the series. From this place the formations dip westwardly.

Our section here is appended :

No. 1. 2 feet bluish gray, shelly and fine-grained Limestone.

No. 2. 5 feet sandy Shales.

No. 3. 2 feet Shales containing a 4-inch Clayey Ironstone bed, gradually merging into a 2-feet bed of Ferruginous Limestone.

No. 4. 4 feet blue Shales.

No. 5. 1 foot dark blue, concretionary Limestone, breaking with straight, even joints, and weathering brown. It contains *Sp. lineatus*, *Pr. muricatus*, *Pr. semireticulatus*, *Sp. cameratus*, and *Entolium aviculatum*.

No. 6. 2 feet bituminous Shales, with small gray concretions.

No. 7. 6 inches Shales, containing pyritiferous Limestone concretions, which are often decomposed on the surface, leaving a nucleus of blue Limestone within. These are sometimes entire, and are often reduced to a fine brown powder.

No. 8. 6 feet 6 inches blue or dove-colored Shales, with cleavage joints, in which Selenite is sometimes found.

No. 9. 7—8 inches Coal.

No. 10. 1½—2 inches Clay.

No. 11. 11 inches Coal—(11 to 11½ inches).

No. 12. 4 feet blue and drab pyritiferous Clay.

No. 13. Sandstone.

This Section very nearly resembles the Section at Switzer's mill, on Chariton, and, I think, we probably have the seam Coal.

East of Yellow Creek, in T. 57, Rs. 18 and 19, Messrs. Norwood and West observed beds of Limestone, which, upon inspection, I think, are included between Nos. 40 and 52.

On Rariton Branch, Sec. 36, I observed :

No. 1. Drift.

No. 2. 2 feet 2 inches blue jointed Limestone, (Rhomboidal,) with white *Crinoid* colums.

No. 3. 3 inches variegated dark pyritiferous and fucoidal Limestone.

No. 4. 6 inches fucoidal Shales.

No. 5. 1 foot bituminous Slate, containing small, flattened concretions.

No. 6. 3 feet 6 inches calcareous Shales, with many fossils chiefly in the upper part, including *Pr. costatus*, *Pr. muricatus*, *Ath. subtilita*, *Cho. granulifera*, *Ch. mesoloba* and *Hemipronites crassus*.

No. 7. 3 feet buff Clay.

No. 8. 1 foot 3 inches nodular Limestone and Clay, containing *Ch. mesoloba* and *Ch.* ——.

No. 9. 1 foot 6 inches compact, light dove-colored Limestone, of uneven fracture, weathering brown. (No. 52, Gen. Sec.)

This last is the lowest rock at Yellow Creek east of Brookfield. No. 42 is also found near-by in the bluff, and about 15 feet above.

On East Yellow Creek, near the railroad, these are also seen, and No. 42 is occasionally found cropping out near the water's edge as far as the Sullivan county line. It is very evenly-jointed by vertical planes into regular Rhomboidal blocks, with an angle varying from 109° to 120°, forming at various places beautiful paved beds, over which the stream flows. At Bayles' old mill it is 18 inches thick, and jointed, quite regularly, presenting the appearance of a paved floor.

At Colson's mill the joints point N. 41° W., S. 38° W. and N. 6° W.

It contains but few well-defined fossils, and we observed only *Sp. lineatus*, a *Pleurotomaria* and *Lophophyllum*. It effervescences freely with acid.

In Sec. 33, T. 57, R. 18, were found No. 40, and a more crystalline Limestone which occurs above it.

In S. W. N. E. Sec. 33, T. 57, R. 18, Mr. Norwood observed No. 31, and its correlated beds lying as follows :

No. 1. 15 feet upper Slope.

No. 2. 1 foot 7 inches greenish, drab Limestone; the upper portion breaks roughly, the lower part has a smooth even fracture; it occurs in two beds divided by a Clay seam containing *Crinoid columns*, *Lophophyllum proliferum;* The Limestone contains *Pr. splendens* and *Loph. proliferum.*

No. 3. 3 feet green Shales and Limestone nodules, abounding in *Sp. planoconvexus*, *Pr. splendens* and *Hemipronites crassus*.

No. 4. 1 to 2 feet hard, calcareous conglomerate, containing *P. Prattenanus*, *Hemipronites* and *Crinoid* stems.

These beds also appear in Secs. 9 and 24, T. 57, R. 18. Mr. Norwood's Section, at Hayney's mill, in Sec. 12, T. 57, R. 19, includes rocks
of No. 52, and related beds, to wit:

No. 1. Slope.

No. 2. 1 foot 6 inches Limestone, the upper 6 inches is soft, rough-bedded
and weathers buff; the lower part is fine-grained ash-blue and
rhomboidally jointed in even layers; the direction of the joints is
N. 40 deg. W., and S. 45 deg. E. The fossils seen were *Spr. lineatus* and *Sp. cameratus*.

No. 3. 1 foot coarse, brown, friable Limestone, almost entirely made up of
Crinoid columns; also abounds in *Ath. subtilita*, *Sp. cameratus*, *Sp.
Kentuckensis*, *Hemp. crassus*, *Pr. costatus*, *Pr. semireticulatus*, *Myalina Kansasensis*, *Lohophyllum proliferum*, *Archaeocidaris* spines, *Crinoid* plates and *Synocladia beserialis*. Many of the fossils are
weathered and stand out in relief.

No. 4. 6 feet sandy Shales.

Mr. Norwood's Section, in the edge of Macon county, two and a
half miles N. E. of Bucklin, at Mr. Nutter's, includes the beds of rock
occurring above the Rhomboidal Limestone, and the strata, to a considerable distance below, as follows:

No. 1. Long and undulating Slope.

No. 2. 1 foot hard, fine-grained and mottled-drab and chocolate colored
Limestone, (with fossils same as those of No. 40.)

No. 3. 25 feet Slope.

No. 4. 1 foot 6 inches Rhomboidal Limestone, (No. 42,) containing *Sp. lineatus*.

4. *a* bituminous Shale. ⎫
4. *b* 7 inches Coal. ⎭

No. 5. 10 feet Slope.

No. 6. 1 foot 6 inches dove-colored, fine-grained silicious Limestone (No.
52,) weathering brown, breaking with somewhat irregular fracture; contains *Pr. costatus*.

No. 7. 30 feet Shale, with small pyritiferous concretions in the upper part;
it also contains a few Sandstone layers.

No. 8. 8 feet shaly Slope.

No. 9. 18 to 26 inches Coal.

No. 10. 5 feet Slope to water in the creek.

Beds above the last described, appear a half of a mile above on
the State road, in the following order:

No. 1. 10 feet purple and green Clays.
No. 2. 5 feet Limestone and Shales, with fossils. (No. 31.)
No. 3. 4 feet calcareous Shales.
No. 4. 6 inches brown nodular Limestone.
No. 5. 8 feet dark, purple and green Shales.
No. 6. 5 feet Limestone. (No. 40.)

Similar beds to these, including the purple Shales, were absent on Muscle Fork, near New Boston. Mr. Norwood found these purple Shales in Sec. 6, T. 59, R. 18, on Little Yellow Creek. A quarter of a mile lower down stream is the old " Bayles' Mill Site," with the rhomboidal Limestone, (No. 42,) in the bed of the creek. He observed similar beds in S. E. Sec. 19, T. 60, R. 18.

The "Athyris bed " (No. 31) was seen on Wyatt's Branch, in Sec. 15, T. 58, R. 18, and on Winegan Creek, in the southern part of T. 59, R. 18, abounding in fossils, the most abundant being *Ath. subtilita*, and also containing *Pr. costatus, Pr. muricatus, Pr. Prattenanus, Pr. punctatus, Hem. crassus, Sp. cameratus, Sp. Kentuckensis, Meekella striatocostata, Chonetes* ————, *Allorisma* (small species), *Lophophyllum proliferum, Archæocidaris megastylus.*

On the Trenton road, a half mile from Linneus, our Section includes the following :

No. 1. Drift.
No. 2. 5 feet red Shales, with occasional green streaks.
No. 3. 1 foot olive sandy Shales.
No. 4. 3 inches Sandstone.
No. 5. 6 feet 6 inches drab Sandstone in thin layers.
No. 6. 3 feet red and green Shales.
No. 7. 6 feet red Shales, containing nodules of red Hematite, (No. 18 of our General Section.)
No. 8. 6 inches shaly nodular Limestone, abounds in *Ath. subtilita.*
No. 9. 6 inches green Shale.
No. 10. 1 foot 8 inches mottled drab and yellow Limestone in one bed.
No. 11. 6 inches soft yellow Limestone, containing *Pr. splendens, Cho. mesoloba, Ath. subtilita* and *Crinoid* stems.
No. 12. 1 foot Shales, abounding in *Sp. planoconvexus, Retzia punctilifera, Ch. mesoloba* and *Crinoid* plates. (No. 22 of General Section.)
No. 13. Nodular Limestone full of *Sp. planoconvexus.*

In Sec. 31, T. 59, R. 20, on W. H. Garret's land, are 15 feet of red Shales, with an occasional green streak. These Shales abound in nodules of red Hematite, containing *Discina nitida*(?) and *Myalina Swallovi.*

A greenish Limestone, abounding in *Athyris subtilita*, is found in the branch just below, and further up the branch we find about 15 feet of Sandstone, (No. 5.) This Sandstone also crops out on Locust Creek, a little south of west from Laclede, 25 feet thick, is micaceous, the upper beds being very soft and containing small concretions of Oxide of Iron. The lower part occurs in beds of 3 and 4 feet thickness. Just beneath is 8 inches of sandy ferruginous conglomerate, with thin seams of Coal and a 4 inch bed of Carbonate of Iron below. The Sandstone contains *Calamites*, and the Iron bed abounds in remains of a beautiful species of *Ferns*.

At Perry's, formerly Withrow's Mill, on Locust Creek, the rocks have a local dip of 5° and a course of S. 40° E., and include from No. 42 upwards, lying in the following order :

No. 1.   15 feet Slope, with tumbled masses of bluish drab Limestone on the lower part.

No. 2.   2 feet rough looking, nodular, bluish drab Limestone, corresponding to No. 40.

No. 3.   7 feet thin layers of Sandstone.

No. 4.   11 feet drab and micaceous sandy Shales.

No. 5.   1 foot 6 inches blue Limestone. The upper 4 inches is dark, shaly and fucoidal, and contains *Chonetes* ———, *Ch. mesoloba*, *Pr. muricatus*, *Sp. planoconvexus* and *Archæocidaris*. The lower part of the bed is firmly and evenly jointed, and corresponds to No. 42.

No. 6.   2 feet 6 inches bituminous Shales.

No. 7.   2 feet soft, black argillaceous and pyritiferous Shales abounding in fossils, mostly *Pr. muricatus* and *Hemipronites crassus*.

No. 8.   1 foot dark blue Clay.

Several miles further up stream, at Miles', formerly Hurlbert's' Mill, we find these rocks well exposed, and also some lower beds, as follows :

No.   1.   10 inches Limestone, (No. 42 of General Section.)

No.   2.   2 feet dark Shales.

No.   3.   10 inches drab Shales with fossils, (No. 46 of General Section.)

No.   4.   5 feet dark green Clay.

No.   5.   2 feet 6 inches ferruginous Shales with fossils in the upper part.

No.   6.   1 foot 4 inches ferruginous Limestone ; fracture shows a dove color.

No.   7.   6 inches argillaceous Shales.

No.   8.   2 feet black Shales, containing small flat concretions.

No.   9.   ¼ inch shaly Coal.

No. 10.   5 feet shaly Slope.

No. 11.   4 feet shaly Sandstone.

ECONOMICAL GEOLOGY.

There are but few outcrops of Coal in this county, and excepting the shafts at Brookfield and St. Catharine, there has been very little searching for Coal.

A thin Coal seam is sometimes seen just under No. 45. It varies from 2 to 4 inches in thickness and does not get any thicker in this county, and is wanting in the counties north. It underlies most of the eastern part of Linn county, but was not seen on Locust Creek, and may be looked for about 2½ feet below the Rhomboidal Limestone, (No. 42). It occurs as follows at Baker's Old Mill, on Yellow Creek:

No. 1. 1 foot 4 inches Rhomboidal Limestone, (No. 42 of General Section.)
No. 2. 2 feet bituminous Shales.
No. 3. 6 inches very thinly laminated bituminous Shales, containing Iron
        Pyrites concretions and fossils.
No. 4. 4 inches Coal.
No. 5. 2 feet Fire Clay.

Near Yellow Creek, in the west part of Sec. 4, we find:

No. 1. 6 inches blue Limestone; total thickness not seen. (No. 42.)
No. 2. 2 feet 6 inches bituminous Shales.
No. 3. 6 inches blue Shales.
No. 4. 2 inches impure Coal.
No. 5. 2 feet Fire Clay.

COAL (NO. 59 OF GENERAL SECTION.)

This Coal, formerly worked by Mr. Nutter in the edge of Macon county, a little above water in Muscle Fork, one and a half miles north of the Hannibal and St. Joseph Railroad, is, I think, the 15-inch seam found 70 feet below the surface, in the Brookfield shaft, and 20 feet below the surface in the shaft at St. Catharine.

A seam of 10 inches has been formerly worked at several places in T. 60, R. 20, but is now seldom mined. One of the chief of these is on the land of Jacob Vanbibber, in the southern part of Sec. 26, T. 60, R. 21. It is here overlaid by 1 foot 6 inches of bituminous Slate, which underlies 30 feet of bituminous Shales. Immediately over the Coal is a 2-inch pyritiferous bed, abounding in *Pleurotomaria carbonaria*. The seam varies from 10 to 16 inches, and the Coal occurs in very even layers, some of which are bright jetty, others dull or dark black. Calcite plates are found in the joints, and the beds show impressions of plants of very fine texture. The cross fracture shows black and shiny like tar.

This Coal was also formerly worked on Thos. Carter's land, in N. W. S. W. Sec. 23, and on Robt. McQuann's land. I could not obtain the necessary data for the Geological position of this Coal. It may be Nutter's, and may, probably, be a higher Coal. This Coal was also seen on Dr. W. R. Robinson's land, in S. W. Sec. 7, T. 60, R. 20, varying from 6 to 10 inches, with overlying beds, as follows:

    No. 1. Sandstone.
    No. 2. 1 foot 6 inches Limestone.
    No. 3. 6 feet drab Shales.
    No. 4. 2 feet bituminous Shales.
    No. 5. ½ inch Coal.
    No. 6. 2 inches Clay.
    No. 7. 5½ inches Coal.
    No. 8. Fire Clay.

The following is the Section of the Shaft at St. Catharine :

    No. 1. 14 feet Clay.
    No. 2. 6 feet rotten Slate.
    No. 3. Flinty Sandstone.
    No. 4. 1 foot 4 inches Coal.
    No. 5. 2 feet 5 inches Clay.
    No. 6. 22 feet Soapstone.
    No. 7. 1 foot hard Limestone.
    No. 8. 6 feet blue Sand.
    No. 9. 40 feet Soapstone.
    No. 10. 2 feet 2 inches Coal. Bottom of shaft. Below this a boring was
             made, and passed through the following :
    No. 11. 3 feet Fire Clay.
    No. 12. 8 feet hard, flinty Sandrock.
    No. 13. 60 feet Soapstone.
    No. 14. 4 feet 6 inches black Slate.
    No. 15. 2 feet 6 inches Coal.
    No. 16. 4 feet Fire Clay.
    No. 17. 35 feet Soapstone.
    No. 18. 3 feet Coal.

For the above section I am indebted to Mr. Wm. H. Elliott, the owner of the mine.

No. 10 is a seam which is worked; the Coal resembling somewhat that of Kirby's, in Sullivan county. It is black and shiny, with darker, fine-grained jet bands, with smooth joints, and occasional thin pyrites bands. Calcite occurs in the joints, and the beds of deposit show layers of mineral Charcoal and faint plant impressions.

The following is the section of the Brookfield shaft and bore

BROOKFIELD SHAFT AND BORE.

Number	Thickness.	Total Thickness.	Description.
1	30 feet.................	....	Surface deposits. The Rhomboidal Limestone should have come in here, 17 feet below the surface, but for some reason it was not found.
2	1 foot 10 inches..	31 feet 10 inches...	Hard rock, next below No. 42, and found in the bed of the creek near by.
3	16 feet.................	47 feet 10 inches...	Fire Clay and Shales.
4	25 feet.................	72 feet 10 inches...	Soapstone.
5	1 foot 3 inches...	74 feet 1 inch......	Coal (Nutter's).
6	14 feet.................	88 feet 1 inch......	Fire Clay and Shales.
7	6 feet.................	94 feet 1 inch......	Rock concretions.
8	1 foot 8 inches...	95 feet 9 inches...	Hard rock.
9	52 feet 8 inches...	148 feet 5 inches...	Soapstone.
10	2 feet 4 inches...	150 feet 9 inches...	Coal—working seam.
11	16 feet.................	166 feet 9 inches...	Brown Fire Clay and Shales.
12	8 feet.................	174 feet 9 inches...	Brown rock concretions.
13	6 feet.................	180 feet 9 inches...	Black rock concretions.
14	10 feet.................	190 feet 9 inches...	Fire Clay.
15	8 feet.................	198 feet 9 inches...	Sandrock (lowest rock at Joab's Creek)
16	3 feet.................	201 feet 9 inches...	Fire Clay.
17	4 feet.................	205 feet 9 inches...	Soapstone.
18	8 inches...	206 feet 5 inches...	Slate.
19	5 feet.................	211 feet 5 inches...	Fire Clay. Bottom of shaft. Below this the boring discovered the following ·
20	8 feet.................	219 feet 5 inches...	Soft Soapstone.
21	4 feet.................	223 feet 5 inches...	Fire Clay.
22	14 feet.................	237 feet 5 inches...	Soapstone.
23	4 feet.................	241 feet 5 inches...	Fire Clay.
24	2 feet.................	243 feet 5 inches...	Soapstone,
25	2 feet 1 inch......	245 feet 6 inches...	Coal.
26	5 inches...	245 feet 11 inches...	Fire Clay.
27	6 inches...	246 feet 5 inches...	Coal.

Brookfield Shaft and Bore—Continued.

Number	THICKNESS.	TOTAL THICKNESS.	DESCRIPTION.
28	15 feet...............	261 feet 5 inches...	Fire Clay and Shales.
29	8 feet...............	269 feet 5 inches...	Sandstone.
30	10 feet...............	279 feet 5 inches...	Soapstone.
31	8 inches...	280 feet 1 inch......	Hard rock (Pyrites).
32	10 feet...............	290 feet 1 inch... ..	Soapstone.
33	6 inches...	290 feet 7 inches...	Slate and Shales.
34	4 feet...............	294 feet 7 inches...	Rock concretions.
35	2 feet..	296 feet 7 inches...	Hard rock (not bored through).

The Coal of "Turner's heirs," already mentioned, is in the lower seam irridescent, smoothly jointed, with some pyrites plates on the joints and some rather beautiful and irridescent Charcoal, formed of finely striated plants on the beds of deposit. The upper seam differs from the lower in that the Coal is not irridescent.

Edward's Coal, near that of "Turner's heirs," is very similar to it, but the lower seam is not quite so irridescent.

From careful inspection of our Sections above noted, we find in Linn three Coals suitable for working that may be reached by shafts. The upper one is from 15 to 17 inches in thickness. The next below is from 2 to 2 feet 4 inches, and the lowest, which is deep below the surface, is from 3 to 4 feet. The upper seam crops out just beyond the eastern margin of the county and is 70 feet below the surface at Brookfield. The next is 73 feet below the first and the third and lowest is, as estimated by borings, 65 to 90 feet lower. These two lower beds are the most important, and, as I think, underlie most of the county. Their total aggregate thickness amounts to about 6½ feet, which, if found under 598 square miles, (probably a fair average,) gives us as the quantity of Coal under the surface in this county the amount of 4,557,560,832 tons.

CLAY AND RED OCHRE.

Beds of good potters' Clay may be found at many places in this county.

At Kelsey's pottery, on Dr. Fellow's land, two miles south-west of

Laclede, there is manufactured a good stoneware from Clays obtained on the edge of the neighboring creek.

The exposed beds appear there thus:

No. 1. Soil on top.
No. 2. 2 feet yellow Clay with Ochre.
No. 3. 4 feet blue Clay.
No. 4. 2 to 3 feet blue Clay with red streaks and a dark streak at top.
No. 5. Good, smooth potters' Clay.

A bluish drab calcareous Clay, obtained half of a mile west of Linneus, on the land of Wm. Harrison, is used to glaze the ware of this establishment.

These Clay beds are regular Shales of the Coal Measures and underlie a large portion of the county.

On W. H. Garrett's land, one mile north of Linneus, are seen about 15 feet of red Shales, which are occasionally streaked with green and contain nodules of red Oxide of Iron, which sometimes contain a little Carbonate of Lime. The Clay also contains some Lime where there are remains of fossils. These nodules, however, occur in regular layers and do not injure the main body of the Clay, which also becomes a valuable material for paint, and in taking it out for that purpose the Iron nodules can be reserved to be carried to a furnace. I do not know, however, that their quantity would be such as to warrant the erection of a furnace on the ground, but they could be profitably transferred to one. These red Shales are also exposed on the Locust Creek bluffs, southeast of Laclede.

BUILDING ROCK.

On the west side of Locust Creek, in Sec. 10, T. 57, R. 21, is a low mound, which seems mainly to be composed of Sandstone. On its eastern side a quarry has been opened disclosing about 15 feet of a superior quality. The upper portion is in thick beds of from two to five feet. Then comes two feet shaly rock, separating it from the lower portion, which is in layers one foot in thickness. It is mostly a light drab Sandstone, formed of minute rounded silicious grains, cemented in part by calcareous matter, and contains scales of Mica. It very much resembles the Stone from Whiterock quarry, Carroll county, to which it is in no way inferior. Sandstone of inferior quality is found in a good many parts of the county, but this one I regard as a good stone, and it will be of great value.

The blue Limestone, No. 42, has been used, but except when well exposed, it will not be quarried on account of the quantity of worthless material required to be stripped. It is generally in even layers and jointed into long regular blocks, with smooth and even faces. It was seen at the following places : Baker's mill, 17 inches thick; near the railroad, 1 foot thick; Bayles' old mill site, 18 inches ; Coalson's old mill site, 17 inches, divided into 2 beds, the upper being 11 inches; on Rariton Branch, 22 inches ; D. Becket's quarry, Sec. 17, T. 58, R. 20, 17 inches, in 2 beds of 5 and 12 inches; Withrow's old mill, 18 inches. At the latter places it was used in the abutments of the bridge near by and procured in blocks 4 to 8 feet long and 18 inches thick. A very good quality of this rock and one which does not require much stripping, is found on the east side of Yellow Creek, two miles east of Brookfield.

On Moore's land, near this place, is a quarry of rock differing prob - ably from that last named.

The beds of gray and drab Limestone, found near Linneus and along Locust Creek north, and in Ts. 57 and 58, R. 18, will make a tol- erably fair article of Lime but are not useful for other building pur- poses.

HYDRAULIC LIMESTONE.

It is probable that some of the Limestones in this county may be Hydraulic, but as yet no experiments have been made with a view to this purpose. They may include No. 52, occurring in Yellow Creek, east of Brookfield, and No. 40, at Coalson's old mill site, and those oc- curring southwardly on East Yellow Creek.

CHAPTER XVI.

Prof. G. C. Broadhead, *State Geologist*:

Dear Sir: The following reports on Putnam and Schuyler counties, embrace the major portion of my labors in the field during the months of May and June, of the present year. Much credit is due my assistant, Mr. H. H. West, for valuable aid rendered in the prosecution of the work. I take this opportunity to publicly return thanks to the following named gentlemen for the many favors shown me, and information furnished: Hon. M. Marshall and Mr. Hoskinson, of Unionville; the Messrs. Dickerson, of Dickerson's Mill, Putnam county; Mr. Henry Miller, editor of the *Excelsior*, Lancaster; Mr. Richard Caywood, Mr. Silas Breckenridge, of Schuyler county, and Mr. Henry Shaw, of Centerville, Iowa, who furnished me with valuable information concerning the heights of different points in Schuyler county, and to all those who aided me in different ways.

Respectfully,

CHARLES J. NORWOOD.

August 1, 1874.

PUTNAM COUNTY.

BY CHARLES J. NORWOOD.

———

Putnam county, one of the extreme northern counties of the State, bordering on Iowa, is bounded on the North by parts of Wayne and Appanoose counties, Iowa; on the west by Mercer; on the south by Sullivan and part of Adair, and East by Chariton River, which gives to that border a very irregular outline, and separates this from Schuyler county. The Burlington and South-western Railroad traverses the county in a west of South direction, passing through Unionville, the county seat. The county was first organized in 1845. Dodge county was added, and its area is now about 523 square miles. It is nearly three times as long as wide, being 36 miles long and 14 miles wide, exclusive of the 3 miles offset in the South-east. About two-thirds of its area is wooded, the timber in the west growing along most of the streams, sometimes extending to a distance of 4 miles on each side, while the eastern half is nearly all timber.

TOPOGRAPHY.

Taken as a whole, Putnam county is hilly and broken. There is of course also much level land, comprising the bottoms along the different streams, such as Blackbird, Medicine Creek, Chariton River, etc. There are also many localities in the western part, where the country is rolling, spreading out in beautiful and undulating prairie land. This part of the county is not so broken as the eastern portion, and there is greater uniformity in the surface configuration, which fact is very apparent to one passing over the prairies. In the west, the surface usually rises gradually from the streams, and spreads out in a series of long, irregular, wide, flat ridges, with gently sloping sides, which are from 150 to 200 feet above the streams. The valleys between the ridges are usually shallow, and often wide.

There is one general system in all of these ridges: they are nearly all parallel with each other, and have a general trend about N. 30° E. The country will then vary from the hilly, to the gently rolling prairie, the latter however being of comparatively small extent. In the eastern portion, as before stated, the country is more broken, and seemingly without any system; the ridges are irregularly winding, and have no special trend. The country is well drained by nature, long, narrow ravines transporting the water from the highlands to the streams.

In the west, in a few instances, only, do the hills rise immediately from the streams ; a wide bottom generally comes between, and even then the rise is gentle. In the east there is, as a rule, a bluff on one side and a' bottom on the other; the width of the bottoms varying greatly—in some instances they are quite wide, and again hardly an eighth of a mile in lateral extent. Along the Chariton they are occasionally a mile and a half, or even more, in width.

The site of Unionville is, perhaps, the highest point in the county, and a point on the railroad, about 5 miles north-east of the town, called "The Summit," may rank next.

HYDROGRAPHY.

SPRINGS AND WELLS.

Springs are rare in the county, and on the hills it is very seldom that water is reached in wells.

In the bottom land water is obtained by going to a depth level with or below the bed of the neighboring stream ; but even this gives out during very dry weather. In most cases the wells would have to be sunk to a depth of from 75 to 100 feet, or even more, on the ridges, to obtain a supply of water. This is rendered necessary by the thickness of the Quaternary deposits, which must be passed through. As well digging is attended with considerable expense and time, the farmer, after passing down from 20 to 30 feet in search of water without success, usually converts his unfinished well into a cistern.

STREAMS.

The principal streams are Medicine Creek, East and West Locust, in the western part; and North Black-bird, South Black-bird, and Shoal Creeks, in the eastern portion of the county.

There are two systems in the streams: Those in the west, head in the north and flow south, draining the country, from the east and west; while those in the eastern part start from a highly elevated ridge or plateau, the trend of which is north-east and south-west, and flows in a south-eastwardly direction to Chariton River, draining the country on the north and south. Thus it will be seen that the county is well provided with natural drainage. Some of the creek bottoms are exceptions, and must be drained by artificial means, such as ditching, etc.

GENERAL GEOLOGY.

The Geological formations found in the county include the Quaternary, and that division of the Carboniferous age known as the Coal Measures.

QUATERNARY.

This overlies the whole county, and in the western half attains great thickness, entirely concealing the Carboniferous rocks. There the high hills and ridges seem to be entirely composed of this formation. The deepest cuts made by streams exhibit only Quaternary deposits, and the deepest wells on the ridges are entirely in Clays, etc., of this age.

The following are the divisions of this formation, as found in Putnam :*

I.—ALLUVIUM.

This attains a thickness of from 25 to 35 feet, including the soil and Clays and Sand found along the various streams. On some of the streams, where the channel has been changed, small islands have been formed almost entirely of Sand belonging to this system. Some of these islands show a thickness of from 15 to 20 feet of Sand.

II.—BOTTOM PRAIRIE.

On the Chariton River, and at some localities along Shoal Creek, this reaches a thickness of from 10 to 15 feet.

III.—DRIFT.

This is especially thick, varying from 50 to at least 75 feet or more. This includes Sand, Gravel, Clays, etc. At one locality along Shoal Creek, from 20 to 35 feet of Drift Sand alone was observed. Large and small boulders of Syenite, Granite, Quartz, Quartzite, Greenstone, etc., and Quartz with Tourmaline, Hematite, Copper, and

* These divisions have been so often and minutely described in former Reports, it is deemed unnecessary to do so here.

small grains of Gold, were found in this formation. Some of the boulders are planed off one side, with parallel scratches extending across, exhibiting plainly the action of a glacial force.

CARBONIFEROUS.

COAL MEASURES.

The whole county is underlaid by this formation, but it is only in the eastern half that any of its strata are visible, the Quaternary deposits effectually concealing them in the west. The area of the Coal Measures—that portion of the county where the rocks approach near the surface, or are exposed—may therefore be laid down as about 246 square miles, not quite one-half the area of the whole county. The total thickness of the formation, as found exposed, is 205 feet. In this thickness there are three Coal seams, one of 3 to $3\frac{1}{2}$ feet, one of 2 feet to 28 inches, and one with 18 inches, with also many small streaks of from $\frac{1}{8}$ of an inch to 2 inches in thickness. The thickest Coal is also the highest, while the thinnest is the lowest. From the top Coal to the middle, or next one below, there is a space of 104 feet, filled up by Shales, Limestones and Sandstones; the lowest bed is found at from 15 to 20 feet below the middle one. The general dip of the Coal is a little south of west. There are, naturally, many local dips and disturbances, the result of *local* causes, such as undermining by water, etc.

The following is a Vertical Section of all the rocks and Coal beds in the county that are exposed to view. By carefully examining the rocks in the neighborhood and referring to the Section, one will be enabled to estimate at what depth Coal may be reached in different localities:

GENERAL SECTION.

Number	Thickness.		Total.		Description of Strata.	Locality.
	Feet.	Inches.	Feet.	Inches.		
1	20				Hard, gray, compact, micaceous Sandstone; some parts marked by Carbonaceous stains	Big Sandy.
2	7	27			Slope probably all Sandstone.......	
3	2	6	29	6	Limestone; top nodular, mottled, dove and drab, and fine-grained; this graduates into compact, hard, fine-grained, light, dove or bluish drab. Then the rock almost imperceptibly passes into an ashy-drab, fine-grained, somewhat earthy Limestone. Fossils are *Prod. splendens*, (*P. longispinus*, (?) *Chonetes* ——, (?) *Spr. lineatus*, and *Fusulina cylindrica*, the latter with *Spr.* (*M.*) *planoconvexus* is abundant.........	Railroad cut, three miles north Unionville. South of Blackbird and high points throughout N. E. and S. E. portion of the county.
4	1		30	6	Green argillaceous Shale.............	
5	2		32	6	Rough, irregularly-bedded, very hard and tough, both fine and coarse-grained Limestone; is often quite silicious; variable in color; where most silicious, it is cream-colored, and then varies from mottled-bluish or ash-drab, to speckled-brown and cream colored; the color is sometimes gray, and occasionally blue, or bluish gray. Generally, though not always, weathers with a thick, brown crust, which is soft and often decomposes and forms a brown powder; Calcite is disseminated in specks, small masses filling cavities, and thread-like veins, a nodular bed occurs at the top and bottom—this, however, is sometimes wanting. Fossils are numerous, especially *Spr.* (*M.*) *planoconvexus*, (which covers the surface,) and *Rhynchonella Algerii*, (?) *Athyris subtilita* and *Chonetes* ——,(?) are also found; fracture variable—often rough and sometimes sub-conchoidal.	Same localities as No. 3.
6	10		42	6	Green and reddish-colored argillaceous Shale......................	" "

General Section—Continued.

Number.....	THICKNESS.		TOTAL.		DESCRIPTION OF STRATA.	LOCALITY.
	Feet.....	Inches...	Feet.....	Inches...		
7	10	....	52	6	Sandstone and sandy Shale; Upper 6 feet generally buff and soft, also micaceous; lower part very soft, gray, micaceous and shaly..............................	
8	4	....	56	6	Red and green areno-agillaceous Shale...........................	
9	1	....	57	6	Hard, blue and gray Limestone, with a thick brown crust; color varies from blue to ash, *Chœtetes milleporaceus*, *Fusulina robusta*, (?) and *Crinoid columns*, are the fossils; sometimes only 6 inches thick........................	
10	....	6	58	....	Calcareous Shale; often absent...	
11	2	....	60	....	Greenish and ashy drab, compact, tolerably hard, close-textured, even-bedded Limestone; weathers with a thick, light ferruginous brown crust. Fossils are *Athyris subtilita*, large *Spr. cameratus*, *Spr.* (M.) *planoconvexus*, *Rhynchonella Algerii*(?), *Discina* ——(?) *Fish tooth* and *Crinoldal* columns..................	On railroad, north of Unionville.
12	5	....	65	....	Red and blue areno-argillaceous Shale	
13	....	9	65	9	Ash blue, generally jointed, argillaceous Limestone. Upon fracture the rock appears to be somewhat sandy, and upon exposure for a few minutes assumes a greenish tinge. Occurs in one bed. Fracture variable— where very argillaceous it is hackly, but at other places it is sub-conchoidal. Upper and lower surfaces shelly, and where they have not been exposed for a long period, covered with organic remains, viz.: *Hemipronites crassus*, *Athyris subtilita*, *Meekella striatocostata*, *Spr. cameratus*, *Spr. Kentuckensis*, *Prod. costatus*, *P. Prattenanus*, *Rhombopora lepidodendroides*, *Synocladia biserialis* and *Chondrites Colletti*..............	Wherever Coal A is found. Blackbird, Mrs. Markham's, etc.

General Section—Continued.

Number	Thickness.		Total.		Description of Strata.	Locality.
	Feet	Inches ...	Feet	Inches ...		
14	1	....	66	9	Dark blue argillaceous Shale.......	
15	1	6	68	3	Green calcareous Shale, with a nodular bed of Limestone at the middle. *Chonetes mesoloba* and *Hemipronites crassus* abound.....	
16	3	....	71	3	Irregularly bedded, ash drab and blue, earthy Limestone, some parts marked by dark windings as of fucoids. This rock is quite variable in its lithological characters. It is generally quite shaly and is often seen only as a calcareous Shale with occasional indurated spots. The bottom 12 inches is inclined to be nodular. Contains *Meekella striatacostata, Athyris subtilita, Spirifer cameratus,* very large *Spr.* (*M.*) *lineatus, Spr. lineatus,*var. *perplexus, Chonetes* ——, *Allorisma* (sometimes abundant), large *Crinoidal* columns, *Peripristis semicircularis,* etc. Equivalent to No. 64 of Sullivan county	North and South Blackbird, Big and Little Sandy and Shoal Creek.
17	1	6	72	9	Drab and green Shale with occasional Limestone nodules. Fossils are *Productus costatus, Pr. punctatus. Pr. muricatus, Hemipronites crassus, Chonetes mesoloba,* etc.............................	
18	1	....	73	9	Dark pyrito-calcareous Shale, full of *Spr.* (*M.*) *planoconvexus,* and containing *Chiton, Discina,* and a *Rhynchonella.* Seldom present.................................	Mrs. Markham's Coal Bank.
19	....	6	74	3	Bituminous Slate. This sometimes reaches 3 feet...........................	
20	....	3	74	6	Dark Shale.................	

General Section—Continued.

NUMBER	THICKNESS.		TOTAL.		DESCRIPTION OF STRATA.	LOCALITY.
	Feet	Inches ...	Feet	Inches ...		

21	3	6	78	9	COAL A. This varies from 3 to 3½ feet, and is sometimes found to reach a thickness of 4 feet. It generally has two clay partings, thus :
					  a. 2 feet Coal.
					  b. 2 to 4 inches Clay.
					  c. 1 foot Coal.
					  d. 1 inch Clay.
					  e. 4 inches Coal.
					This is the Coal commonly found cropping out throughout the eastern half of the county, and may be said to be the only "*sur-face Coal*" coextensive with the country. This is the bed worked (with but few exceptions) wherever Coal is opened in the county. Equivalent to No. 67 of Sullivan county....................
						Shoal Creek — on nearly all its branches. The Blackbirds, Big Sandy, and the Chariton River.

22	2	....	80	....	Fire Clay—impure....................	
23	1	....	81	....	Hard, mottled, ashy white, nodular Limestone ; occurs in large nodules	
24	1	....	82	....	Drab and ashy white, very friable Limestone, abounding in *Prod. muricatus*, and containing *Spr. Kentuckensis, Athyris subtilita, A. Maconensis, Hemipronites crassus, Chonetes mesoloba, Ch. Smithii*, etc....................	South Blackbird.
25	4	....	86	....	Ash to blue or drab, compact, close-textured, thick - bedded, hard Limestone with, generally, a thick, brown crust. Varies from 3 to 5 feet in thickness. Contains *Polyphemopsis* ——— *?*, *Athyris subtilita, Prod. costatus, Pr. muricatus, Pr. splendens* (= *P. longispinus ?*), *Hemipronites crassus, Chonetes mesoloba, Allorisma* (rare), *Lophophyllum proliferum*, and *Crinoidal* columns	Near Dickerson's Mill, Galt's Mill, near Hartford, etc.
26	3	....	89	....	Argillaceous Shale; white, striped with buff...........	
27	12	....	101	....	Sandy Shale with ochreous concretions. Sometimes passes into Sandstone.	
28	5	....	106	....	Argillaceous Shale...............	

General Section—Continued.

Number	Thickness.		Total.		Description of Strata.	Locality.
	Feet	Inches	Feet	Inches		
29	....	2	106	2	Very impure, sandy, dark pyritiferous, shaly Limestone, breaking with a hackly fracture. Has cavities filled with a brown powder. Fossils are *Spr. cameratus, Prod. costatus, Hemipronites crassus, Chonetes* and *Crinoid* columns. Equivalent to No. 72 of Sullivan County Section. This is remarkably constant	
30	2	6	108	8	Dark, semi-bituminous Shale, with large and small black *Septariæ*..	
31	3	....	111	8	Bituminous Slate; at the middle a hard, very fine-grained, black, slaty Limestone occurs, having the same joints as the Slate, the thickness of which is from 1 to 2 inches..................................	
32	....	6	112	2	Calcareous Shale full of fossils. Contains *Prod. costatus, Pr. muricatus, Spr. cameratus, Athyris Missouriensis, Chonetes mesoloba, Ch. Smithii (?)*	
33	....	2	112	4	Coal. Very seldom present	
34	1	6	113	10	Calcareo-bituminous Shale...	
35	5	....	118	10	Calcareo-argillaceous Shale	
36	1	2	120	....	Bituminous Slate—is sometimes Shale	
37	1	....	121	....	Argillaceous Shale	
38	1	3	122	3	Yellow Limestone. Often decomposes into a bright yellow powder Is also seen as a jointed, hard, compact, fine-grained Limestone—color ash, changing to drab.................................	
39	1	2	123	5	Black argillo-calcareous Shale. Has a banded appearance. Small concretions occur in it.............	Baugh Branch— No. 1.
40	....	$\frac{1}{8}$	123	$5\frac{1}{8}$	Coal streak...........................	"
41	1	....	124	$5\frac{1}{8}$	Drab Clay...........................	"
42	....	$\frac{1}{8}$	124	$5\frac{1}{4}$	Coal streak........................	
43	....	4	124	$9\frac{1}{4}$	Clay	

General Section—Continued.

Number......	Thickness.		Total.		Description of Strata.	Localities.
	Feet......	Inches...	Feet......	Inches...		
44	3	....	127	9¼	Greenish drab argillo-calcareous Shale, with small flattened concretions and thin, hard argillo-calcareous bands....'............	
45	2	6	130	3¼	Very light ash, fine-grained, rough friable Limestone—argillaceous. No fossils found....................	
46	2	....	132	3¼	Blue Clay..............................	
47	3	....	135	3¼	Hard, dark blue, thinly laminated, sometimes slaty Shale, with large spherical concretions of bituminous Limestone. Some of the concretions abound in *Cardium* (?) *Lexingtonensis*, and contain *Cardiamorpha Missouriensis*, *Discina nitida ?* *Goniatites planorbiformis*, *Aviculopecten*, large *Orihoceras?* and *Orthoceras Rushensis*	
48	....	½	135	3¾	Coal........................	
49	2	....	137	3¾	Fire Clay............................	
50	6	....	143	3¾	Shale...	
51	3	....	146	3¾	Buff and gray micaceous Sandstone	
52	13	....	159	3¾	Micaceous sandy Shale.............	
53	5	....	164	3¾	Bluish argillo-arenaceous Shale, with large septaria, some of which contain *Zinc blende* and *Stigmaria ficoides*...................	Baugh Branch—No. 1—near Dickerson's.
54	15	....	179	3¾	Dark blue Shale ; becomes hard and slabby and blue black at the bottom..................	Shoal Creek, at Dickerson's mill.
55	2	....	181	3¾	Soft bituminous Shale; often passes into slate, or imperceptibly into No. 54. Large, dark pyritous concretions occur immediately at the bottom..........	" "
56	2	4	183	7¾	Coal B : Divided by a Clay seam, thus......................... *a.* 18 to 24 inches in Coal. *b.* ½ inches in Clay. *c.* 4 inches Coal.	Wild Cat and Shoal Creek, near its mouth
57	2	....	185	7¾	Fire Clay.....	

General Section—Continued.

Number......	THICKNESS.		TOTAL.		DESCRIPTION OF STRATA.	LOCALITIES.
	Feet......	Inches......	Feet......	Inches......		
58	2	6	188	1¾	Sandstone, full of Stigmaria ficoides..	
59	15	....	203	1¾	Thinly laminated, sandy Shale, with carbonaceous markings and thin argillo-calcareous layers. Varies from 15 to 20 feet in thickness..........................	"
60	1	˙6	204	7¾	COAL C.................................	Wild Cat, at Mrs. Parton's.
61	1	†	205	†	Fire Clay...............................	

ECONOMICAL GEOLOGY.

COAL.

This mineral underlies the whole county but is easily accesible in the eastern half only, which may be denominated the "Coal region." This part of the county is peculiarly favored in this respect. Though there is but one thick bed, still this is, we may say, coextensive with the whole region, being easily reached, either by drifting or shafting, in nearly every part of the eastern half of the county. In the extreme south-eastern part of the county, however, it is high up in the hills, and is often entirely wanting, owing to the irregularity in the surface features of the country. But when the thick bed (Coal A) is absent, two thinner ones approach near the surface. One of these lower beds, (Coal B) is 28 inches thick, and is worked with profit in regions where Coal A is not present. This Coal (Coal B) appears to thicken as it goes south. It is equivalent to No. 80 of the Adair, Linn and Sullivan county section, which represents it as being from 3½ to 4 feet thick, and worked in Adair county, on the Chariton River, above Nineveh. Only a few exposures of it were seen in this county, but I hardly think it will be found with a thickness over two feet and a half.

The lowest Coal found (Coal C) occurs from 15 to 20 feet below Coal B, and was nowhere seen showing a thickness greater than 18 inches. It is only in the south-eastern part of the county, and near the Chariton River, that it is found near the surface. Not much mining has been done in the county heretofore, but at present it promises to become quite an industry. A great deal of land has already been leased for mining purposes, and her Coal region bids fair to become a source of great wealth to the county. For this to come to pass, however, the mining must be *systematic*, and considerable outlays be made for the proper machinery, etc. With a railroad running east and west through the county she will be enabled to supply Coal to the north-western counties of this State and beyond. A road running in this direction has, I understand, already been located. Unfortunately, the present road, the Burlington and South-western, passes through the western border only of the Coal field.

The Coal, as seen in the banks, is remarkably dry and soft, and is apparently free from sulphur. Average samples have been collected of Coals A and B for analysis, which will be found in Mr. Chauvenet's report.

COAL A.

This is variable in thickness, varying from 32 inches to 3½ feet. At one place I was told that it reached four feet, but was unable to see it, as loose dirt had slipped from above and concealed it.

The first locality examined where this Coal is exposed was at

MRS. MARKHAM'S COAL BANK,

in Sec. 29, T. 66, R. 18, on a branch emptying into Blackbird Creek. At this place the following Section was made:

Section 9.

No. 1. 49 feet Slope with fragments of Limestone No. 5, and with outcrops of red Clay.

No. 2. 3 feet + blue argillaceous Shale.

No. 3. 9 inches ash blue, jointed, argillaceous Limestone. No. 3. General Section.

No. 4. 1 foot dark blue argillaceous Shale.

No. 5. 18 inches to 2 feet green calcareous Shale, with Limestone nodules at the middle.

No. 6. 3 feet irregularly bedded ash, drab and blue, earthy Limestone— sometimes imperceptibly passing into calcareous Shale.

No. 7. 9 inches drab Shale with occasional Limestone nodules.

No. 8. 1 foot dark pyrito-calcareous Shale.

No. 9. 6 inches bituminous Slate.

No. 10. Coal A. Said to be 3 feet in thickness.

The same Coal is found at Mr. Davis Dickerson's, on Dickerson's Run, in N. E. qr. S. W. qr. Sec. 7, T. 65, R. 16.

The Section here is.

No. 1.　85 feet Slope from hill top.

No. 2.　6 inches ash blue, fine grained, compact Limestone.　No. 13, General Section.

No. 3.　5½ feet, nearly all bituminous Slate.

No. 4.　4 feet Coal.　This Coal was not visible, and thickness is given upon authority of Mr. Dickerson.　Coal A.

. No. 5.　4 feet Slope.

No. 6.　3½ feet argillaceous, ash-blue Limestone.　No. 25 General Section.

No. 7.　10 feet + sandy Shale and Sandstone.

This Coal is well exposed at many localities in this neighborhood, on Baugh Branch, Nos. 1 and 2, Parker's Branch, etc., and drainage is easily obtained.　At a few places it has already been opened, among which are Mr. Rose's and Mr. N. Livsey's banks.　At Dickerson's Mill, at 103 feet below the Coal No. 4 of the foregoing Section, Coal B is exposed, on the bank of Shoal Creek.　This will be mentioned further on.　At Galt's Mill, in S. E. qr. N. E. qr. S. W. qr. Sec. 35, T. 67, R. 18, on Shoal Creek, Coal A is found in the hills, seen only as a smut or rotten Coal.　By following the bed farther in the hill, however, it will no doubt become of good quality.　The Coal is found at a hight of 44 feet above the Creek, with a Slate No. 31, 32 feet below and 11 feet above the Creek.　A drift had been started in under this Slate, in search of Coal, but of course without success.　By referring to the General Section it will be seen that the next workable Coal below this Slate, is Coal B, 69 feet below.　It is a mistaken idea, that wherever there is black Slate there must also be Coal.

Coal A is also seen cropping out on the ridge, east of Hargrave's (Chariton) Mills, and is worked by Mr. H., one-quarter of a mile away. On the hills, around Woodard's Mill, in S. E. qr. Sec. 30, T. 67, R. 17, it is also exposed.　At Mr. Well's, in the S. W. qr. N. W. qr. Sec. 29, T. 67, R. 16, it is worked occasionally, and is said to reach a thickness of 3½ feet.　From Mr. Wells' it enters Iowa, and is worked quite extensively at Pleasant View (Hill Town), in that State.

COAL B.

This is not so extensive a "surface Coal" as Coal A, being found only in the south-east part of the county, on Chariton River, and on Shoal Creek, near its mouth.　At Mrs. Nancy Parton's, on Wild Cat Creek, in S. E. Sec. 6, (?) T. 64, R. 16, both Coal B and Coal C are exposed, with the following order of succession in the strata :

No. 1. Long Slope—perhaps 75 feet.
No. 2. 10 feet + deep blue, slabby Shale—argillaceous.
No. 3. 28 inches Coal, with a thin Clay parting 4 inches from the bottom.
No. 4. 15 to 20 feet thinly laminated blue and drab sandy Shale.
No. 5. 18 inches Coal C.
No. 6. Fire-Clay in the bed of the creek.

Mr. Preston Munlick has the same Coal on his place, two miles down the stream.

At Mr. Jno. A. Ledford's, in S. W. qr. N. E. qr. Sec. 31, T. 65, R. 17, Mr. West found Coal which I regard as Coal B. The following is a section made by him at this point:

No. 1. Slope.
No. 2. 24 feet argillaceous drab Shale. *Tutenmergel* occurs in the lower part.
No. 3. 2½ feet bituminous Slate, with large flattened concretions.
No. 4. 18 to 24 inches Coal. This is about 30 feet above South Blackbird Creek.

At Mr. Dickerson's mill, Coal B is again found exposed, exhibiting a thickness of 22 inches. It is overlaid by 5½ feet of dark blue Shale, passing into semi-bituminous Shale at the bottom, with large pyritous concretions just over the Coal. There is considerable Sulphur in the Coal at this point, present as an efflorescence on the surface. The rocks and Coal are very irregular here, there being several breaks in the beds.

This region seems to be specially favored by nature. In the hills Coal A is found; while in the lowland Coal B will be reached at a shallow depth.

From my observations in the county, I feel safe to state that there is hardly an acre in the eastern half without at least one of the three Coals on it, and within easy reach. Some of the creek bottoms are exceptions; for though the Coal may have been there at one time, it has subsequently been removed and replaced by later deposits.

The following is a list of most of the banks and outcrops of Coal in the county:

Coal List.

Number...	Section.	T.	R.	Owners.	Coal.	Remarks.
1	24	66	19	G. Corpron...............	A.	Reached in shaft at 45 feet below railroad.
2	29	66	18	Markham & Bentley..	"	Coal banks worked more than any others.
3	N. E. S. E. 20	66	18	J. F. Crabtree...........	"	Crops out; also a bank.
4	S. E. N. E. 34	66	18	Thos. Loyd...............	"	Crops out.
5	S. W. 35	66	18	Hugh Roberts...........	"	Crops out.
6	N. W. S. E. 14	66	18	Gus Wessel............	"	Old bank.
7	S½ S. W. 5	66	18	....	"	Reached in shaft at 40 feet below railroad.
8	N. E. N. W. 4	66	18	....	"	Crops out in railroad cut.
9	N. W. 34	67	18	———Bramhaul.....		
10	N. W. 27	67	18	....	"	Crops out.
11	N. E. S. W. 35	67	18	....	"	Crops out around Galt's mill.
12	S. W. 27	67	18	....	"	Crops out.
13	N. W. S. E. 32	66	17	——— Hockins......	"	Old bank—worked but little.
14	N. E. N. E. 30	66	17	J. W. R. Shelton.....	"	Partially opened bank.
15	N. W. N. E. 30	66	17	C. P. Torrey............	"	Crops out.
16	N. W. S. E. 19	66	17	Jas. Triplett............	"	Crops out and worked a little.
17	N. E. N. E. 27	66	17	....	"	Crops out at 50 feet above Shoal Creek.
18	30	67	17	....	"	Crops out S. and E. of Woodard's mill.
19	S. W. S. W. 29	67	16	——— Wells.........	"	Bank.
20	S. E. N. W. 4	66	16	M. A. Hargraves......	"	Crops out in hills, and is also worked.
21	N. E. S. W. 7	65	16	——— Dickerson...	"	Crops out.
22	S. W. N. W. 7	65	16	——— Rose..........	"	Bank.
23	N. E. 32	65	17	I. Featherly..............	"	Crops out.
24	N. E. S. E. 26	65	18	H. H. Green............	"	Worked.
25	S. E. S. W. 23	65	18	....	"	Crops out in the road.
26	1	65	18	....	"	Crops out near Cooley's mill.
27	S. E. 10	65	18	....	"	Old bank, worked but little.
28	S. W. 20 (?)	65	18	Wm. Bruce.............		
29	S. E. (?) 20	65	18	——— Holmes (?)......	"	Old bank.
30	S. E. 18	65	18	——— Jones (?)........	"	Banks.

Coal List—Continued.

Number.	SECTION.	T.	R.	OWNERS.	Coal.	REMARKS.
31	S. W. 18	65	18	—— Jones............	"	Old bank.
32	S. E. S. E. 12	67	17	....	"	Crops out—36 inches.
33	N. E. N. E. 11	67	17	—— Wages	"	Bank.
34	1	67	17	N. Livsey................	"	Bank.
35	N. W. 17	64	17	E. Burns................	"	Old bank—abandoned.
36	S. W. N. E. 6	65	16	—— Dickerson	B.	Crops out.
37	S. W. N. E. 31	65	17	J. A. Ledford..........	"	Crops out.
38	S. ½ N. E. 21	65	17	H. Houtz.............:.....	"	Worked a little.
39	S. E. 6 (?)	64	16	Nancy Parton	"	Worked a little.
40	S. W. 9 (?)	64	16	Pres. Munlick..........	"	Worked a little.
41	S. E. 6 (?)	64	16	Nancy Parton..........	C.	Crops out.

Beside the foregoing, there are many localities where Coal crops out; generally Coal A, and where a little work has been done, but which are unnecessary to mention.

LIMESTONES.

Nos. 3 and 5 of the General Section will burn into good Lime, and are found high up in the hills. The other Limestones are too argillaceous to make white Lime—or of the best quality.

HYDRAULIC CEMENT.

No. 25 appears to possess properties which render it suitable for this purpose.

BUILDING ROCK.

Numbers 3 and 5 are excellent building stones, being easily dressed, and capable of standing the weather. No. 1 will also do well for building when a Sandstone is desired, and Nos. 7 and 27 are sometimes (though seldom) suitable for that purpose.

SAND FOR MORTAR.

The Sand along Shoal and other Creeks may possibly answer for mixing mortar, though it is generally exceedingly fine and dirty.

ROAD MATERIAL.

The Gravel along Chariton River will answer for this purpose.

PAINT CLAYS.

Part of No. 6 will make paint, capable of being used for ordinary painting.

FIRE CLAYS.

This is found in connection with all the Coals, but it is of inferior quality.

IRON ORE.

Fragments of compact red Hematite were found in the Drift, but no ore of practical use occurs in the county.

COPPER.

Small masses of native Copper are said to have been found in the Drift in the eastern half of the county. Many suppose "a vein to run throughout the county, but to one acquainted with such matters this is evidently a mistake; neither will there be any of importance found, occurring in any other way in the county.

GOLD.

I was told by several persons that Gold has been found in minute grains in different parts of the county. This being the fact it is found in Drift. The impression prevails among many that Gold will be found in "paying quantities somewhere in the county." This, however, is a great mistake, and it is an utter waste, both of time and money, to search for it. The same may be said of

LEAD.

The occasional finding of small grains does not militate against this fact in the least.

TIMBER.

The greater part of the eastern half of the county is well timbered. There is also much good timber along the streams in the western part. In the bottoms the trees often grow to a great size,

G. s—19

and make good lumber. There are quite a number of saw mills in the county, most of which were in operation at the time of my visit, and they are fast turning the woods into lumber. Along Chariton River and Shoal Creek there are many Sugar trees, and much sugar is made from them.*

The principal trees of the county are Red, Black, White and Black-jack Oaks, Shellbark and common Hickory, Elm, Black Walnut (some trees of great size), Linn (scarce), Ash, Maple, Sugar Tree, Buckeye, Red Haw, Crab Apple, Wild Cherry, Willow, Cottonwood, Red Birch, etc.

AGRICULTURE.

SOIL.

There is a great diversity in the soil. It varies from a rick, black loam, as found in the bottoms, to a sandy, yellowish or reddish clayey mixture. In the bottoms, especially along the Chariton River and Shoal Creek, the soil is black, deep and rich, while on the high land it is of a clayey character, reddish or yellow in color, and often cold and poor. The red Soil is the best. On most of the ridge land the Soil is thin and poor, but there are spots of excellent ground on the wide ridges.

CROPS, Etc.

Some parts of the county are well adapted for wheat, others for tobacco, and others for oats; but taken as a whole, corn is the most reliable and profitable crop. Oats will rank next. Wheat has not had a fair trial, as it seems to be a settled thing that it will not do well here. The consequence is that most of the flour used in the county is brought from Iowa. The farmers should pay more attention to it; they have the land to raise it. They may not get such large crops as are raised in other parts of the State, but they at least will have enough to supply home consumption.

I was told that rye was formerly successfully cultivated; the average yield being between 35 and 40 bushels to the acre. There

---

* It may be of interest to some to know the following yield of the Messrs. Dickerson's (Dickerson's Mill) Sugar Camp this Season :

No. of pounds sugar made.. 2,135
No. of gallons of syrup made... 37
No. of trees tapped... 466
No. of gallons of water obtained...13,916
No. of days engaged.. 25

The above was furnished me by Mr. Dickerson.

are many fine meadows in the county, sown in timothy, the average yield of which is 1½ tons to the acre. In some localities it is heavier, a few meadows bringing as much as 2 tons to the acre; this is a rare case, however.

The following are carefully averaged yields to the acre, of the various products raised, being made up from the reported yields of many of the best farmers in the county:

CROP.	LOWEST YIELD.	HIGHEST YIELD.	AVERAGE.
Corn*..........................	15 bushels.............	60 bushels.............	37½ bushels..... ...
Oats.............................	20 bushels......	40 bushels.............	30 bushels...........
Wheat..........................	Can hardly average	—so little raised.......	....
Tobacco........................	But little raised......	....	800 pounds.........
Rye..............................	A little raised.......	....	27½ bushels.........
Timothy Hay.................	....	....	1½ tons...............

STOCK.

The farmers are beginning to pay some attention to raising cattle; "Short-horns" and "Devonshire" being the breeds in favor. But few fine horses or mules were seen raised for other than home use.

---

* Mr. Dickerson (Dickerson's Mill) informed me that he has averaged 65 bushels of corn to the acre on his bottom land every year he has raised it. This is in the Sugar Tree country.

CHAPTER XVII.

SCHUYLER COUNTY.

BY CHARLES J. NORWOOD.

HISTORICAL, Etc.

This county lies immediately east of Putnam county, with the Chariton River as the dividing line. On the north it is bounded by parts of Appanoose and Davis counties, Iowa; on the east by Scotland county, and on the south by Adair county. In form it is nearly square, though a little wider east and west than north and south. It is crossed by two railroads—the St. Louis, Kansas City and Northern, and the Missouri, Iowa and Nebraska—both of which are in operation.

The county was organized about the year 1846, and the county business transacted at a small place called Tippecanoe, which has long since passed away. Afterwards Lancaster was selected as the county seat and a court house built. This place is not situated exactly in the center of the county, but still is easily accessible from any part. The county is a small one, its territory being embraced in an area of about 342 square miles.

TOPOGRAPHY.

The county varies in its surface features from the broken to rolling and even flat. It is about evenly divided in these characters. The broken or hilly uplands gradually descend into level lowlands, which pass by gradual slopes into gently rolling or undulating prairie, and this, in turn, as it nears the streams, becomes hilly and often quite broken. In the northern part of the county, the rolling character seems to predominate; the surface usually rises gently from the bottoms, gradually merging into rolling land, which will again vary from flat to undulating prairie. This is especially the case in that part of the county east of the " Grand Divide." This Grand Divide is a highly elevated plateau, which appears to be a continuation of the Grand Divide between the Missouri and Mississippi Rivers, having an irregular north and south course, and at some points rising to a height of 180 feet above Chariton River. The country slopes off irregularly from this ridge or divide, becoming quite hilly on the west toward Chariton River, but more gentle on the east. The south-eastern corner of the county is extremely broken, rising into rough ridges and hills in the vicinity of streams, and extending a considerable distance on each side of them. Most of the broken land lies near the Chariton River. The bottoms along the streams vary in width from one-eighth of a mile or less to two miles. The latter is the width of the Chariton River bottoms at some places. Lancaster is, perhaps, the highest point in the county. Downing, which is about one mile and a half west of the east line of the county, is 100 feet lower, and is from 50 to 60 feet above the Chariton River bottoms. The country immediately east of Lancaster is made up of rolling prairie and low, flat ridges, with wide, shallow valleys between. It is very seldom that the streams are in immediate contact with the hills; usually a " bottom " is interposed between, extending on both sides of the stream. With but few exceptions, this is the case even on the Chariton River. It will be seen by the foregoing that but little of the county is so broken as to render it unfit for cultivation.

HYDROGRAPHY.

STREAMS.

The county is cut up by numerous small streams—mostly branches of Fabius River. The principal ones are Chariton River, Middle Fabius, South Fork of Middle Fabius, North Fork (of Fabius), South Fork of the North Fork of Fabius, Bushy Branch, Elm Creek, Lick Creek and West's Branch. The Grand Divide is naturally the great water-shed of the county, and those streams on the east flow south-east, while those on the west flow south-west. The banks of the streams are usually low, seldom more than 5 feet in height. The beds

of most of the streams are muddy, and as a consequence good fords
are rare in wet seasons, when the creeks are full.

WATER POWER.

Except on the Chariton River, there are no good localities for
water mills. On that stream a few have already been built and are in
operation. The other streams are, in ordinary seasons, too shallow
and sluggish to afford sufficient power for mill purposes. There are,
however, quite a number of steam saw mills (usually with a grinding
attachment) in the western part of the county.

WELLS AND SPRINGS.

Water is easily obtained anywhere by digging wells. On most of
the ridges it is reached at from 15 to 25 feet, while at Lancaster, I am
told, a good supply may be obtained within 40 feet, this being the
maximum depth of many of the wells. Many of them are much less,
perhaps owing to the irregularities of the surface.

GENERAL GEOLOGY.

There are but few exposures of rock in the county, and these are
confined to the western border, along Chariton River, and are only
found north of the dividing line between townships 65 and 66.

The Quaternary formation effectually conceals any rocks there
may be in the remainder of the county.

The formations found in the county include the Quaternary and
Coal Measures.

QUATERNARY.

This formation overlies the whole county, and is remarkably
thick, when it is taken into consideration that only three of its four
divisions are present.

These divisions are Alluvium, Bottom Prairie and Drift.

Alluvium and Bottom Prairie present their usual characteristics,
and are found along the various streams and in the valleys.

As is the case in Putnam county, and in fact in all the northern
counties of the State, the Drift is remarkably thick. Nearly all of
the material going to make up the hills (especially in the eastern part
of the county) may be referred to this formation. Also the Gravel,
some of the Sand beds, etc., along the creeks. Clays enter largely in

the formation, and I was inclined for awhile to believe some of the upper beds referable to the Bluff or Loess formation ; this, however, I now think, is not the case. Or if so, it is very sparingly developed. It was not deemed necessary to make an exact measurement of this formation, nor would it really have been possible to do so ; but it undoubtedly reaches a thickness of 100 feet or more.

Boulders of Syenite, Granite, Diorite, Rosy Quartzite, fragments of Hornblendic rock, Chloritic schist, etc., were observed in this formation. Some of the boulders are rounded on one side, while the other is planed off smooth, with occasionally parallel grooves or scratches. This is evidently due to glacial action.

COAL MEASURES.

Although the rocks are concealed by Quaternary deposits throughout nearly the entire county, still it is very probable that the whole county is underlaid by Coal Measures, and it is thus laid down on the map.* As there are but few rock exposures in this county, I visited Pleasant View, (Hilltown,) Iowa, where the same Coal is worked that is seen on Chariton River in this county. By examining the rocks associated with the Coal there, and following down Chariton River, carefully examining every point where any exposures of rocks, Coal, etc., were to be seen, I am enabled to construct the following vertical section :

---

* The extreme south-eastern part of the county may be an exception to this. Sub-carboniferous rocks of the age of the St. Louis Limestone, are known to occur in the south-west part of Scotland county, about 6 miles east of south of Memphis, and they may extend into this county. This will be determined when the examination of Scotland county is made.

General Section.

No.	Feet.	Inches.	DESCRIPTION OF STRATA.
1	3	6	Red and green Clay.
2	1	....	Hard blue and gray Limestone, with a thick brown crust. Color varies from blue to ash. Contains *Fusulina robusta*, minute *Crinoid* columns, and *Chaeletes milleporaceus* both in large and small masses.
3	....	6	Buff calcareous Shale.
4	4	....	Hard, thick-bedded Limestone, usual color blue, shading to dove, but is also yellowish drab in some localities; fine-grained and generally compact, though sometimes it is shelly on top; weathers with chocolate brown or buff crust; the upper surface is often covered with finely comminuted fragments of fossils, which stand out in relief. Fossils *Prod. Splendens, Athyris Missouriensis, A. subtilita, Rhynconella Algerii,* (?) *Discina Missouriensis, Spr.* (M.) *plano-convexus, Chonetes mesoloba, Ch. Verneuiliana, Lophophyllum proliferum,* etc.
5	1	....	Blue calcareous Shale; abounds in large *Crinoidal* columns, and contains *Meekella striato-costata, Prod. costatus, Athyris, Chonetes,* etc.
6	2	6	Blue Clay, banded with yellow.
7	3	....	Soft Limestone; color variable, changing from blue to bluish drab, mottled with chocolate. Weathers with a deep brown or buff crust. Sometimes is quite friable, and passes into calcareous Shale, with large nodules of Limestone.
8	1	....	Drab calcareous Shale.
9	2	....	Limestone. Occurs in several layers. The upper is somewhat concretionary or nodular, has a soft, brown crust, is 12 inches thick, and abounds in fossils on the surface, of which *Pr. Prattenanus* and *Ch. mesoloba* are the most conspicuous. The lower part occurs in two rhomboidally jointed beds which are tolerably regular and compact, and contain *Sp. cameratus, Ch. mesoloba, Crinoid* columns, etc.
10	1	....	Buff, calcareous Shale, passing into Limestone.
11	6	....	Drab argillaceous Shale.
12	1	....	Bituminous Shale.
13	3	....	Bituminous Coal. Ranges from 3 to 3½ feet. Equivalent to Coal " A" of Putnam.
14	2	....	Under Clay.
15	1	....	Hard, mottled, ashy-white Limestone—ashy white splotched with yellow. Varies from compact to friable.

*General Section—*Continued.

No.	Feet.	Inches.	DESCRIPTION OF STRATA.
16	4	6	Limestone, usually divided thus:
			a 2 feet soft buff Limestone, containing *Prod. costatus, Prod. Prattenanus, var. æquicostatus. Athyris, Schizodus, Ch. mesoloba* and *Crinoid* columns
			b 1 foot drab and ashy white, very friable, and nodular Limestone, abounding in organic remains, viz: *Prod. muricatus,* (especially abundant) *Spr. Kentuckensis, Athyris subtilita, A. Maconensis, Hemipronites crassus, Chonetes mesoloba,* etc,
			c 1 foot compact, ash-colored argillaceous Limestone.
			d 6 inches friable Limestone, with the same fossils as in *b.* *
17	2	....	Compact, ash-colored Hydraulic (?) Limestone. Varies from 2 to 4 feet.
18	2	6	Bluish white clay, with buff or yellow bands.
19	17	....	Dark-bluish, argillo-sandy Shale, with small concretions of Iron-stone.
20	5	....	Drab, sandy Shale.
21		2	Dark, earthy, Shaly pyritiferous Limestone, breaking with a hackly fracture. Contains *Spr. cameratus, Ch. mesoloba,* and *Crinoidal* stems.
22	3	.	Dark semi-bituminous Shale, with large concretions of bituminous Limestone,
23	3		Bituminous Slate.

* Sometimes all below *b* are compact and connected with No. 17.

By comparing the foregoing Section with that of Putnam county they will be found to correspond in many instances. The Limestones overlying and underlying the Coal however, are not so compact, and differ in a few other points. These Limestones appear to become more argillaceous as they enter Iowa, occurring in thinner individual layers, but with a total thickness greater than in Missouri. No. 23 of the Schuyler county Section is equivalent to No. 31 of Putnam county; by examining the Section of the rocks in the latter county, two Coal beds will be found to occur below the Slate (No. 31), one at a depth of 69 feet, and another at a depth of 91 feet. These same Coals may be looked for in this county. Carrying our General Section down, with the aid of that made in Putnam county, we will have as No. 24, a space of 69 feet, then as No. 25, 28 inches Coal, then a space of from 15 to 20 feet, and then 18 inches Coal. The Coal bed No. 13

of the Section, is the only one exposed in the county. Upon first entering the county, it was supposed that the Chariton River Coal (No.
13 of the General Section) extended, perhaps, entirely across the
county east and west, but this is now known not to be the case. From
the fact that all the Coal that has been discovered near, or east of
Lancaster, was found only in *isolated masses, broken, worn and mixed
heterogeneously with the Drift*, and with its *associate rocks* occurring
also in the Drift, *and from deep borings* which have been made in
search of the mineral, but without success, we are naturally led to
believe *it will not be found in place* in the *eastern* part of the county.
Several localities were visited at which Coal had been found, but at
no place was there the least resemblance to a regular bed. Sometimes large masses have been found, but it usually occurs in small
lumps or mere particles. That this Coal is the same that is worked
on Chariton River, is proved by the occurrence of fragments of well
recognized Limestone in the Drift with it. A line has therefore been
drawn on the map marking the supposed eastern limit in this county
of the Chariton Coal.

Much interest is exhibited as to the finding of Coal in the county,
especially in the eastern part, and this region was specially studied with
that in view. It was known that the only Coal that had been found was
discovered in detached masses only, and many theories have been advanced by gentlemen living in the county as to the cause of it. A
few are that "it has tumbled from above;" "that the Coal *rises* from
the west—comes up above the surface, and in consequence has no
regular bedding;" "that it is a system of faulting," and that it "occurs in pockets." I can agree with none of the foregoing. There
appears to have been at one time (prior to the deposition of the
Drift,) a wide valley in the east, with the Coal—now known as the
Hilltown or Chariton River Coal—near the surface, while the western
region was made up of high hills, with the Coal well protected, deep
beneath the surface. (This is represented by Figure A.) The waters
immediately preceding, and during the Quaternary period, then came,
tearing away a certain amount of material, taking part of the capping
off of the western hills but leaving the Coal on account of its thick
covering; while the Coal in the east, being in a valley and near the
surface, was, with its associate rocks, torn from its bedding. Figure
B is a rude representation of the face of the country after this denudation had taken place, preparatory to the disposition of the Quaternary. While this was taking place the waters in the eastern valley
were acting toward the western hills in the same manner that the rivers of our day, during a high stage of water, do toward their bluffs—
gradually cutting them away. But before this was entirely accom-

plished the waters receded, the deposition of the Drift was completed, and the Coal in the west left unharmed. Between the hills of this county and those of Putnam county, there also seems to have been a valley—shallow, though it may have been, and wide. Through this valley Chariton River cut its way, gradually becoming deeper and deeper, the channel narrowing the while, and alluvial deposits covering its former tracks, till at last it has reached its present depth and flows in its present channel. Figure C represents the structure of the country as it is at present.*

Although the Hilltown or Chariton River Coal does not extend across the county it is very probable that the two lower Coals of Putnam county do. I refer to Coals B and C of the Section made in that county. This, however, is not a *settled* fact, for sub-carboniferous rocks are known to occur in the south-west part of Scotland county, about six miles south-west of Memphis, and as no bores have been made in the eastern part of this county, nor any examinations in Scotland county, it is not known how far west these sub-carboniferous rocks extend as the "surface rocks."† The exact facts in the case can only be made out by a series of borings, or when Scotland county is examined, should it be desired to sink a bore or shaft either in the eastern or other part of the county, I would advise that it be commenced at as low a point as can be obtained. For the benefit of those who may propose to bore for the lower coals (B and C of Putnam county), the depth at which they should be reached at a few points is given. At Lancaster, at from 250 to 275 feet; at Downing, 150 to 175 feet ; at Griffin, 210 to 230 feet; at Glenwood, 235 to 260 feet.‡ It must be borne in mind that the foregoing calculations are based upon the belief that the two Coals which occur below the Slate, No. 23 of the General Section, are coextensive with the county. I have no doubt but that they extend at least to Lancaster and beyond, but in the southeast corner of the county they may possibly be cut off.

---

* It must be understood that these figures are not intended to represent the *exact* aspects of the country; they are merely rough sketches to illustrate the explanation that it may be more clearly understood.

† By " surface rock " is meant (in this case) the *first* rocks below the surface.

‡ The latter calculation is based upon the opinion that Glenwood is lower than Lancaster.

ECONOMICAL GEOLOGY.

COAL.

This mineral has been pretty fully discussed under the heading of "General Geology," and a few remarks added here will end the subject. There have been but few mines opened in the county, and these are in the north-west corner. The oldest mines are said to be those of Mr. Elijah Mock, worked near Hargrave's Mills. In this vicinity there are several openings. Mr. Al. Mock and Mr. Parsons also have mines near the mills. In the N. E. quarter Sec. 27, T. 67, R. 16, Mr. Samuel Scott has a shaft, situated on North Polecat Creek, Mr. Wm. James, in the N. E. S. E. qr. N. W. qr. Sec. 34, T. 67, R. 16, works the same Coal. His mines are operated by drifts, of which there are three. These gentlemen all work the same Coal (No. 13 of the General Section), the average thickness of which is $3\frac{1}{2}$ feet. The dip of the Coal is not quite 5 feet to the mile ; course about S. E., or, more correctly, east of south. It perhaps rises as it nears Adair county, as a much lower Coal is worked on Chariton River, near the mouth of Hazel Creek, in that county, and the fall of the river is hardly sufficient to overcome this dip, and allow the lower Coal to be exposed.

ROAD MATERIAL.

The Gravel found at some points along Chariton River will answer very well for this purpose.

BRICKS.

The Clay covering many of the ridges will make excellent bricks

OTHER MINERALS.

No useful minerals other than Coal were found in the county.

AGRICULTURE.

This county, though not rich in mineral deposits, is, as a whole, well adapted for farming. The Soil varies from black to reddish. On many of the ridges it is thin and poor, but in the valleys, (which are numerous), it is rich and deep. There are one or two objections to the valley land, which, however, can be overcome. The Soil is, as a general thing, wet, waxy and apt to be cold. This can be remedied by a system of drainage and fertilizing.

The subsoil is a stiff Clay, impervious to water, and, consequently, in wet seasons the water upon reaching this Clay is arrested and keeps the Soil not only moist, as it should be, but *wet*. This trouble can be remedied by digging holes to a depth of from 8 to 10 feet (or even less) in the Clay, at different points in the field to be cultivated. Then by a series of ditches, each ditch terminating in one of these holes, the land is easily drained. These ditches can be arranged at such convenient distances from each other as not to interfere with the cultivation in the least. I was told by a gentleman who has a farm of just such land as I speak of, that the best fertilizer he has tried is *Buckwheat*. He sowed the buckwheat one season, plowed it in, and the next season his crops were nearly doubled. Manuring the land will be a great benefit to it.

The following is a list of the various products raised in the county, with their average yields. Many farmers raise much more than the average crops, but the list will, I think, be found correct for the whole county:

Corn	30 bushels to the acre.
Oats	35 " "
Wheat	15 " "
Buckwheat	40* " "
Rye	40 " "
Timothy	1 to 1½ tons per acre.

Until within the last few years but little attention has been paid to raising wheat. The farmers have to contend with the chinch bugs in their spring wheat, and unless protected from the winds, the fall wheat is frozen out.

ORCHARDS.

Many fine looking young apple orchards were noticed in the county, and I understand considerable attention is now being paid this fruit. But few orchards are bearing at present, being too young. About 10,000 apple trees, some pear trees, plums, etc., have been set out in the county. Indeed, there is hardly a farmer in the county who has not an apple orchard of some size on his place. But few peach orchards have been set out, the reason being, so I am told, that they do not do well.

---

* It must be remembered that a great deal—sometimes nearly one-half of the buckwheat shatters off before it is harvested.

GRAPES.

Much attention is being paid to grape culture. Nearly every farmer is trying the experiment of raising them, and I am told successfully. The *Catawba* and *Isabella* varieties seem to have been the favorites, but they are not as thrifty as the *Concord*.

TIMBER.

The major part of the county is heavily timbered, consisting of Black, Red, Rock Chestnut, Pin, Laurel, some Post and White Oak Common and Scaly-bark Hickory, Elm, Black Walnut, some Ash, Red Haw, Crab-apple, a little Wild Cherry, Hazel, Sumach, etc.

CHAPTER XVIII.

ANDREW COUNTY.

BY G. C. BROADHEAD.

ITS GEOLOGY.

SURFACE CONFIGURATION.

This county contains about 455 square miles. Its surface presents quite a variety, including from the rugged and irregular broken, to the smooth and gently undulating plain.

That part, lying near the Missouri and Nodaway Rivers, is quite broken, the bluffs often reaching above 145 feet, and near the mouth of Nodaway River are as much as 330 feet high. Approaching the prairie, we find a gently rolling country. North and East of Savannah, the county is rolling and gently sloping. On Platte River. from Whitesville to Rochester, and on One Hundred and Two, from Ogle's Mill to Singleton's Mill, the bottoms are narrow, and bluffs often 90 feet high; south and north, along these streams, the bottoms are very wide, the hills low and slope very gentle.

TIMBER.

The wood-land occupies more than two thirds of the area of the county. The Missouri hills are well supplied with good timber, including White Oak, Red Oak, Black Oak, Burr Oak, Black Walnut, Cherry, Elm, Ash, Sugar Tree, Coffee Tree, Honey Locust, Hickory and Linden. The bottom lands also contain much fine timber.

STREAMS AND SPRINGS.

The Platte and River One Hundred and Two, flow through the county from north to south. The Nodaway, a much larger stream, flows along its Western border, and the Missouri bounds it on the South-west. On the Nodaway there are several Mills, and the supply of water is sufficient to keep them employed during the dryest seasons. Good springs abound. Just west of Savannah there is a very fine one, which affords ample daily supplies of water to many of the citizens.

GEOLOGICAL FORMATIONS.

In this county are found the Quaternary and a portion of the Upper Coal Measures.

QUATERNARY.

Under this head we find the Alluvium, Bottom prairie Clays, Bluff and Drift. The bottom prairie is best seen along bottoms of Platte River.

The Bluff or Loess overspreads the Missouri Bluffs to a considerable depth.

The " Drift " is not well exposed, but boulders of igneous rock, including Greenstone, Granite, red Quartzite and quartzose Conglomerate, are found nearly everywhere. Just below Amazonia the railroad excavations have exposed some 20 or 30 feet of Clay, Sand and rounded boulders of igneous rocks ; but none of very large dimensions. In S. E. part of county, a boulder of Granite was obtained which measured 12 feet by 10 feet by 7 feet.

On land of Monroe Foltz, near mouth of Nodaway River, the " Bluff " Clays contain irregular lumps of bog Iron ore. These pieces are not very hard, nor are they very heavy ; they are of a black color, and have a very dark brown or blackish streak.

UPPER CARBONIFEROUS STRATA.

The rock strata in this county belong to the Upper Coal Measures, and are included between Nos. 186 and 127 of General Section of Upper Coal Measures, * with a total vertical thickness of from 370 to 400 feet.

No. 186 is the highest well recognized rock, seen. It may be found near the hill tops from near the mouth of Nodaway River as far up as Ohio Mills. Its total thickness, anywhere seen, is about 15 feet. It is a grayish-drab, irregularly bedded, generally occurring in layers of about 6 inches thick, separated by buff, shaly partings. Its principal fossils are *Sintrilasma hemiplicata, Athyris subtilita, Spirifer*

---

* Missouri Geol. Surv. 1872--Part II--p.p. 91, 92 and 93.

Kentuckensis, and *Retzia punctilifera.* The Limestone is unsuitable for any purpose excepting to make rough walls or burn into lime.

Our Section at Ohio Mills include a part of this number, correllated with Lower beds, thus :

No. 1. Slope from hill top.

No. 2. 3 feet drab Limestone, containing much Calc Spar, and a few fossils, corresponds to No. 186 of Gen. Sec.

No. 3. 5½ feet Shales, buff, calcareous above—argillaceous below.

No. 4. 2 feet fine-grained, grayish drab Limestone, with many minute Calcite specks diffused, would look well if polished; weathers brownish. Corresponds to No. 184.

No. 5. 11 feet Slope.

No. 6. 2 feet buff porous and buff brown Limestone, No. 182.

No. 7. 35 feet Slope to bottoms.

No. 8. 10 feet of alluvial bank, concealing rocks.

No. 9. 9 by 2 feet—greenish drab Limestone, contains *Fusulina*, *Productus*, etc. A portion is Shaly. No. 171.

No. 10. 3 feet greenish, Shaly Limestone, containing *Chonetes*, *Sp.* *Kentuckensis*.

On Lincoln Creek, a half mile from Nodaway bottoms, our Section shows :

No. 1. 25 feet Slope, at an angle of 15 deg.

No. 2. 65 feet 35 deg. Slope ; at 20 feet from top are fragments of buff Limestone ; at top is found Limestone corresponding to No. 186.

No. 3. 10 feet sandy and argillaceous Shales.

No. 4. 1 + foot dark, coarse shaly Limestone, containing *Myalina* ; corresponds to No. 171.

No. 5. 10 feet 30 deg. Slope ; near the lower part are outcrops of green Clay Shales.

No. 6. 1½ feet greenish, drab and shaly Limestone ; resembles No. 171.

No. 7. 1½ feet of Shales and shaly Limestone.

No. 8. 2½ feet of argillaceous Shales ; blue at top, olive and bluish below.

No. 9. 12 feet buff, and a portion shaly and cellular, and mostly rough Limestone, corresponds to No. 161.

No. 10. 6 + inches Clay Shales.

No. 11. 3 feet Slope.

No. 12. 4 feet brown Limestone, containing large *Crinoid stems*, *Productus*, etc. No. 160.

Two miles up the creek the Limestone, No. 160, is found resting on 15 feet of green Shales. A quarter of a mile further, the hill is 161 feet high, with Limestone No. 186 near the top, and No. 160 at 107 feet lower down, resting on sandy and argillaceous Shales.

G. s—20

Near mouth of Nodaway, we find No. 186 near hill-top, and more than 200 feet below, No. 150 is seen above the waters' edge. Two and half miles west of Savannah, Nos. 160 and 161 crop out near the creek. In Shales underlying No. 160 observed a cylindrical form 5 inches in diameter with a central axis. The outside was somewhat rugose, all other markings rather obscure. I suppose it to be a fragment of a plant nearly related to *Stigmaria.* Lower down stream Limestone appears.

The brown Limestone, at Caldwell's quarry, one and a half miles south of Savannah, belongs to No. 160 of General Section. It is here found 4½ feet thick, and quite ferruginous, rather roughly-bedded in two layers of nearly equal thickness, and works rather freely.

Near this place, No. 160 presents some curious results of exposure. The entire stratum is a little over 4 feet thick, and intersected by vertical cracks, on either side of which the rock is of a different color, the mass presenting alternations of brown and gray colors.

In the railroad just north, the rocks, whose position is from 15 to 25 feet higher in the series, are well exposed, thus :

Section 45.

No. 1. 18 inches dark-ash, shelly Limestone, some of it brownish below, contains *Myalina subquadrata*, and abounds in *Fusulina cylindrica*. No. 169.   b

No. 2. 3 feet dark, olive Shales. No. 168.

No. 3. 1 foot nodular and shelly Limestone and Shales. No. 167.

No. 4. 22 inches even-bedded, drab Limestone. No. 167.

No. 5. 5 inches ash-gray fusulina Limestone. No. 166.

No. 6. 3 feet nodular and shelly fusulina Limestone, abounding in fossils, including *Hemipronites crassus, Athyris subtilita, Prod. Nebrascensis, Prod. costatus, Sp. cameratus, Spr. planoconvexus, Chenomya Minehaha, Allorisma* ——. *Syringapora multattenuata, Fusulina cylindrica, Fenestella* ——, and *Crinoid* stems. No. 166.

A General Section of rocks seen around Savannah, mostly on the branch two miles north-east, is about the following :

No. 1. Shales.

No. 2. 18 inches to 2½ feet of blue, shelly Limestone, containing *Fusulina* and *Myalina.*

No. 3. 1 foot dark, olive Shales. No. 168.

No. 4. 1 foot of nodular and shelly Limestone and Shales.

No. 5. 22 inches even-bedded, drab Limestone, containing *Syringapora multattenuata Fusulina cylindrica, Myalina subquadrata Terebratula bovidens, Spirifer cameratus, Sp. Kentuckensis.*

No. 6. 2 inches ash-gray fusulina Limestone. No. 166.

No. 7. 3 feet shelly and nodular Limestone, abounds in *Fusulina*, also contains *Syringapora multattenuata*, *Pr. Nebrascensis*, *Athyris subtilita*, and *Allorisma (Chenomya) Minehaha*.

No. 8. 3 feet dark Shales. No. 165.

No. 9. 1 foot bituminous Shales. No. 164.

No. 10. 4 inches dark-ash Shales with *Fusulina*. No. 163.

No. 11. 10 inches dark-ash colored shaly Limestone, abounds in *Fusulina* and contains *Athyris*.

No. 12. 9 feet yellow calcareo-argillaceous Shales, with thin Limestone bands. No. 161.

No. 13. 4½ feet, mostly buff or brown Limestone. No. 160.

No. 14. 23 feet of sandy and Clay Shales, near the upper part is 4 feet of light blue Clay Shales; then a half inch bituminous Shales; then 10 feet of Shales and thin Sandstone layers; then 2 to 5½ inches Coal. Nos. 155 to 159.

No. 15. 2 feet mottled, coarse, ash-blue and gray Limestone, abounds in *Fusulina*, and contains *Astartella vera*. No. 154.

No. 16. 9 feet Shales. No. 153.

No. 17. 8½ feet of coarse, bluish-gray Limestone, is oolitic, and abounds in *Fusulina*, also contains *Myalina Swallovi*, *Aviculapecten* and *Monoptera* ; is sometimes cross laminated, and affords a strong and useful building rock. No. 152.

No. 18. 1 to 2 feet Shales. No. 151.*

No. 19. 20 feet irregularly bedded blue and ash-colored Limestone. No. 150.

No. 17 is quarried in many places on creek N. E. of Savannah, and formerly was hauled to St. Joseph.

The upper members of this Section are rather better developed on creek one mile north of Savannah, where they appear in succession as follows :

Section 43.

No. 1. Outcrop of yellow Limestone on hill.

No. 2. About 20 feet Slope.

No. 3. 2½ feet dark, ash-blue Limestone, abounds in *Fusulina cylindrica*. No. 169.

No. 4. 6 feet dark, olive Shales. No. 168.

No. 5. 4 feet drab Limestone, weathering a little buff; contains *Bryozoa*, *Hemipronites*, *Chonetes*, *P. Nebrascensis*, *Sp. Kentuckensis*, *Syringapora multattenuata*, *Fistulapora nodulifera*, *Athyris subtilita*, *Terebratula bovidens*, *Meekella striatacostata* and fragments of *Nautilus*. (2 sp). No. 167.

No. 6. 3 feet dark Shales.

No. 7. 1 foot bituminous Shales.

*These numbers often and in general terms referred to in this county Report, are numbers in the Ceneral Section, Upper Coal Measures, 1872.

The lower members of this Section correspond to those of the previous Section. On another branch coming from south, observed the following succession :

No. 1. Outcrop of dark, ash-gray Limestone, which is sometimes a little brownish, abounds in *Fusulina*, and also contains *Athyris* and *Myalina*. No. 169 of Gen. Sec. Upper Coal Meas., 1872.

No. 2. 10 feet Slope, with debris from above.

No. 3. 4½ feet dull gray, shelly Limestone, abounds in *Fusulina* and *Athyris*.

No. 4. 3 feet shaly Slope.

No. 5. 5 feet yellow and olive Shales.

No. 6. 5 feet brown Limestone.

No. 7. 15 feet thin-bedded, shaly Sandstone, containing two thin bands of Coal ; a half-inch band occurs at 4 feet below the top, a 1-inch band near the lower part. This includes Nos. 155 to 159.

Limestone No. 150 is one of the most characteristic Limestones seen in the county. It occurs mostly in irregular layers, separated by blue or buff Shales, and seems generally to break into irregular angular fragments on exposure. *Fusulina cylindrica* is quite abundant, especially near the middle portion, in which are also handsome *Bryozoans*, *Fistulapora nodulifera*, *Rhombopora lepidodendroides* and *Chonetes* ———, which are abundant in middle beds. *Productus Nebrascensis*, with its interior replaced by crystallized Calcite, is common near the upper part. *Orthis carbonaria* is occasionally abundant near the lower part. This Limestone is generally over 20 feet thick. It caps the hill at Amazonia, and one mile up the bluffs there is a large quarry opened, which exhibits most of the beds. Some of the middle blue and drab argillaceous beds at this place have been burned and made into a pretty fair article of Hydraulic Cement. Several specimens of it were shown me which had stood different tests, and I could find no fault with them. This rock crops out on branch, two and a half miles north-east of Savannah. On Hundred and Two River, south-east of Savannah, and as far north as line of Ts. 60 and 61, it occupies the upper part of hills on Niagara Creek, near Rochester, at about 60 feet above the Coal, which is sometimes found at the foot. It is found as far north, on Platte River, as Whitesville; and occupies the uplands in south part of county, between Missouri Bluffs and One Hundred and Two River.

This Limestone often incloses many concretionary forms of Chert. At the bridge on One hundred and Two River, we find the upper beds containing a good deal of Chert, with one solid Limestone bed, 7 feet thick, at the lower part. Near Whitesville it is underlaid by five feet of blue and bituminous Shales, of which 2½ feet are bituminous. In the northern part of Sec. 15, T. 60, R. 34, we find, at 21 feet below No. 150, 2 feet of a thick-bedded drab Limestone, which is probably referable to No. 143. In the same neighborhood, on land of Wm. Huffaker, red and green Shales appear about 50 feet below No. 150, the lower green layers, containing Septaria. Beneath the last we find 3 inches brown, sandy Shales overlying a 1-inch band of bituminous Coal. Still below is an outcrop of 5 feet of ash-blue Limestone, shelly at top. This last named Limestone I refer to No. 137. At Jessup's Mill red Shales appear at 55 feet below No. 150, resting almost directly on No. 137, which, at this place, is 9 feet thick.

In bed of Platte River, at Rochester, we find 3 feet of Limestone; color, dark, ash-gray at top, bluish-gray below, containing *Productus Nebrascensis, Aviculopecten occidentalis* and *Athyris subtilita.* At low water this rock is well exposed. It is traversed by many vertical cracks, leaving the rock, as it were, divided into many very regular rhomboidal forms. The angle of fracture is 60°. This rock probably corresponds to No. 128. Farther down the river, observed about 20 feet of Shales underlying it.

ECONOMICAL GEOLOGY.

BUILDING STONE

Suitable for most purposes, may be found conveniently in all neighborhoods excepting in the northern part of the county. The strongest and most durable stone may be found in No. 152. There is a good quarry of this rock about a mile above Amazonia, on the railroad. Fourteen and a half feet are here exposed, more than I have seen at any other quarry. It is bluish gray oolitic, and with no Shale partings. At Lander's quarry, 2½ miles north-east of Savannah, we find 8 feet 9 inches of it, of relative thickness of 3½ feet, 14 inches, 6 inches, 14 inches, then shaly beds, with a 2 feet coarse gray bed at bottom. These beds are sometimes cross-laminated. One opening presents 6 feet thickness, which is cross laminated for over 50 feet—the angle of cleavage about 30°.

PAINT BEDS.

Red Shales are found at several places in this county, and they would undoubtedly make good paint. They are found at several places near Amazonia. On the hill above town, and on creek, one and a half miles up, there is exposed about 4 feet of good average quality of pure red Ochre. Appearances of these beds are also seen in Rochester road, 3 miles east of Savannah; also 2 miles south of Whitesville, and on land of Wm. Huffaker.

CARBONATE OF IRON,

In form of Septaria, concretionary and lenticular forms, and in thin bands, is occasionally found in Shale beds, but insufficiently for economic purposes.

COAL.

No valuable Coal beds exist in this county. A few miles northeast of Savannah we find thin bands but too thin for any economic purpose. One of these thickens to 5 inches on land of Wm. Barr, in S. W. quarter Sec. 16, T. 59, R. 36. The Coal crops out at the waters' edge for 50 feet along the stream, resting in the water near the middle line, where it is thickest, and rising each way to a height of two feet above the stream and 25 feet above and below, presenting the cross section of a basin. At the lower end of the outcrop the Coal is 6 inches thick, alternating with bituminous Shales and rests unconformably on Shales. At the upper point of outcrop the Coal is 3 inches thick and conformable with the Shale.

The Coal here can not be extensive as it is thicker near depression of the basin in the creek, thinning towards either end. Blacksmiths have used it in welding iron. On the bank, 200 feet off, a pit was dug by Mr. P. P. Chamberlain, some years ago, 29 feet deep to the Coal. Limestone, No. 160, crops out in the ravine east, about 15 feet above the Coal.

Coal has been worked at several places on Niagara Creek, but it is a thin seam, not over 10 inches thick. I regard it as equivalent to the Coal near Hall's Station, Buchanan county. In S. W. quarter, Sec. 13, T. 59, R. 34, when exposed, it presents the following appearance :

No. 1. 1 foot soft brown and rough Sandstone.
No. 2. 22 inches drab and brown banded sandy Shale.
No. 3. 5 inches bituminous Coal—poor quality.
No. 4. 9 inches blue shaly Clay ; contains ferns and other plants.
No. 5. 1¾ inches of bituminous Coal of good quality.
No. 6. 3½ inches blue shaly Clay.
No. 7. 2 inches bituminous Coal.
No. 8. 2 inches indurated blue Clay.

In some places we find above No. 1 a few feet of Shales, containing concretions of Kidney Iron ore.

The nearest workable Coal that can be reached by shaft in this county is the Lexington Coal; it lies about 800 feet below the lowest observed rocks on Platte River, or over 1,100 feet below the horizon of Savannah.

SOIL.

The soil of this county is generally rich but is susceptible of several divisions. We have the hills near the Missouri River, which are capable of producing fine crops of wheat. Adjacent, we find the richer lands supporting a growth of Elm, Linden, Paw-paw and Ironwood, which are equally wheat producing, and well adapted for corn and hemp. Then we have the Black Oak, Red Oak, Elm and Hazel lands near river One Hundred and Two, and near Fillmore. These lands produce fine corn crops and sometimes good wheat crops. The soil of the western and southern parts of the county is based on a deep bluff deposits. Lime, resulting from disintegration of the Limestone beds enters largely into the composition of the soil of most of the timbered land. Near Lincoln's Creek are rounded Limestone hills with rich valleys between. The prairies are rich and produce good crops of corn.

Most fruits of this latitude grow well in this county, especially may this be said of apples.

CHAPTER XIX.

DAVIESS COUNTY.

BY G. C. BROADHEAD.

GENERAL DESCRIPTION—TOPOGRAPHY.

This county is nearly equally divided by the main West Fork of Grand River entering the north-west part of the county and irregularly meandering to the south-east corner. Of the tributaries on the north side, their general course is south; of those on the south side, north-east. The chief tributaries entering from the north are Clear Creek, Muddy, Cypress, Big Creek and Sampson Creek; those on the south side are Grindstone, South Big Creek, Larry, Honey and Marrowbone. These streams sometimes become quite low and almost dry in extreme dry seasons, but Grand River affords sufficiency of water for milling purposes the greater part of the year.

The bluffs near the streams are generally from 30 to 50 feet high rarely reaching 100. But the summit of the ridges is often 60 to 100 feet above the valleys.

Near the tributaries coming from the south the country is often hilly and rugged, but the higher ridges rarely exceed 200 feet above the valleys. The hills are more elevated near Gallatin and South Big Creek, where they are sometimes abrupt. In other portions of the county the slopes are gentle. T. 61, R. 29, is somewhat hilly, but the hills are not very high.

The amount of prairie exceeds the timber, but Grand River bottoms afford an abundant supply, and the adjacent hills also, of first rate White Oak and Red Oak timber.

On Grand River bottoms the following trees and shrubs are found, viz.:

Crab Apple,	Gooseberry,	Red Oak,
Ash,	Shellbark Hickory,	Pin Oak,
Prickly Ash,	Pignut Hickory,	Laurel Oak,
Red Birch,	Ironwood,	Plum,
Box Elder,	Honey Locust,	Rose,
Waahoo,	Linden,	Raspberry,
Black Cherry,	Sugar Tree,	Redbud,
Choke Cherry,	White Maple,	Sycamore,
Cottonwood,	Mulberry,	Sumach,
White Elm,	Burr Oak,	Black Walnut,
Red Elm,	Swamp White Oak,	Willow, etc.
Hackberry,		

In Forks of Big Creek and Grand River are fine bodies of White Oak timber.

SPRINGS AND WELLS.

Good, lasting springs exist at the following places: In S. W. Sec. 27, T. 59, R. 27; a very fine spring in S. W. of S. E. Sec. 19, T. 59, R. 27; at Wm. Smoots, in N. E. Sec. 25, T. 59, R. 28; in N. W. Sec. 19 and S. W. Sec. 9, T. 61, R. 27; Sec. 21, T. 59, R. 26; at John Winn's, in N. W. Sec. 8, T. 61, R. 27, a good well of water.

Borings in yellow Clay, at Winston, reach water at 50 feet. At James McGuire's, on top of prairie near Larry Creek, Mr. Norwood obtained a Section, as follows:

No. 1. 12 feet yellow Clay.
No. 2. 12 feet blue Clay, with wood and charcoal.
No. 3. 2½ feet Sand.
No. 4. 20 feet blue Clay to Sand, in which water was obtained.

At Wm. Brennan's, near Honey Creek, 5 miles south-west of Gallatin, a well was dug 54 feet deep, revealing (according to Mr. Brennan) the following:

No. 1.   1 foot Soil.
No. 2.   3 feet yellow Clay—subsoil.
No. 3.   4 feet white Stratum.
No. 4.   12 feet joint Clay, with a few small pebbles and boulders.
No. 5.   20 feet blue Clay ; some water seeping in at top.
No. 6.   1½ feet red hard Sand, dipping a little as if water-worn.
No. 7.   7 feet coarse, yellow Sand.
No. 8.   3 feet blue Sand, with sticks and leaves at bottom.
No. 9.   3 feet dark colored Clay Shales.

In No. 5 there was found, at 35 feet from surface, an elm stick 5 inches in diameter, a grape vine 2 inches thick having the bark on, also Walnut and Elm chips.

Jas. McGaugh, in S. E. Sec. 27, T. 59, R. 28, found a Walnut log in his well at 40 feet below the surface.

Near corner of Secs. 28, 29 and 33, T. 59, R. 26, Mr. Snyder has a well 70 feet deep. In digging it he passed through Sand resembling river Sand, and blue Clay. At bottom, he encountered a pine log 6 feet in diameter ; he recognized the wood and bark. It is now covered with Quicksand. [The formations in these wells all belong to the " Drift."]

GEOLOGY.

QUATERNARY.

Besides the Alluvium and other recent deposits, we occasionally find boulders of Granite, Quartzite and Greenstone.

The brown Clays overlying the prairies may be referred to the " Bluff" formation. They are as much as 90 feet in depth, as indicated by wells near Winston. They are stiff and tenacious, with occasional Gravel and Sand beds, and soft, earthy Limestone concretions.

COAL MEASURES.

The solid rock formations belong to the Coal Measures, and include about 50 feet of the upper part of the Middle Coal Measures, and about 530 feet of Upper Measures, including in the uppermost rocks found near No. 125 of General Section Upper Coal Measures, (Missouri Report, 1872,) to No. 70.

It was impossible to obtain an entire, connected Section from rocks seen in the county, but seeing a well known bed here, but not its correlative beds, the latter can be supplied from examinations at points on the Missouri River.

The highest rocks were those observed near Winston. We there find beds identical with those seen at Weston, and included within the horizon of Nos. 121 and 125 of General Section Upper Coal Measures, 1872.

The Sandstones of the Middle Coal appear on Lick Fork, and occasionally on Grand River as far up as a little north of the center of the county.

A Section at top of Middle Coal Measures, on railroad, 4 miles below Gallatin, appears thus:

No. 1. 20 feet Slope; tumbled Limestone.

No. 2. 20 feet to railroad.

No. 3. 18 feet Shales; lower part concretionary.

No. 4. 1½ feet of blue Shales, containing *Eumphalus rugosus*, *Bellerophon*, etc.

No. 5. 6 inches blue, rough, nodular calcareous Sandstone.

No. 6. 18 feet Sandstone to river.

Other Sections on the Chillicothe and Omaha Railroad, above Gallatin, expose the lower part of the Upper Measures very well:

Section one and a half miles north of Gallatin, on R. R.

No. 1. 6 feet Limestone. No. 74.

No. 2. 4 feet drab sandy Shales. No. 78.

No. 3. 2 feet Sandstone.

Three-quarters of a mile further the upper Limestone just named, is 3 feet thick, forming a fine quarry of building stone, at level of railroad track. Limestone No. 78, appears 20 feet above.

A half mile further, we find in railroad cut:

No. 1. 3 feet drab, nodular Limestone.

No. 2. 4 feet thick bed of mottled, dark and light-colored, fine-grained, compact Limestone.

No. 3. 12 feet of Limestone. No. 78. *Fusulina* and *Prod. splendens* appear 4 or 5 feet from bottom.

At Groomer's mill, the last named Limestone occupies the bed of Grand River, as also that of Big Creek, at Pattonsburgh, and of Cypress Creek 2 miles east.

A half mile above Groomer's mill we find higher Limestone; those from 81 to 84 being well represented, thus:

Section 113.

No. 1. 12 feet Slope.

No. 2. 5 feet 8 inches irregularly bedded, bluish-gray Limestone, somewhat cherty, contains a few *Producti*. No. 84.

No. 3. 8 inches olive Clay Shales.
No. 4. 5 inches blue Clay Shales. No. 83.
No. 5. 14 inches bituminous Shales.
No. 6. 10 inches soft, black Shales.
No. 7. 19 inches dark Shales, with thin layers of pyritiferous Limestones.
No. 8. 5 feet dark-blue Clay. No. 80

Persons must not be deceived by the presence of these beds of bituminous Shales. They do not indicate the immediate vicinity of a bed of Coal, nor will they change to Coal. They will burn some, but not to ashes.

On Sampson's Creek, 4 or 5 miles north-west of Pattonsburgh, are beds of buff Limestone, probably very good for burning into Lime. The Geological position may be as high as No. 93. In creek 3 miles east of Pattonsburgh, No. 78 appears. Eighty-six feet above, we find a blue Limestone containing *Prod. Prattenanus, Pr. splendens, Pr. Nebrascensis, Lophophyllum.* Five feet higher, is found a coarse, ash-colored Limestone, containing large *Prod. costatus, Sp. cameratus, Nautilus,* etc. The latter I suppose equivalent to No. 91. Less than a mile north of the last named locality, we find a Limestone about 25 feet from hill-top, which I think must be the equivalent of No. 87, of General Section of Upper Coal Measures. It is irregularly bedded and cherty, containing some fine fossils, which are sometimes chalcedonic. The lower 10 inches abounds in *Fusulina cylindrica;* in beds above, observed *Prod. costatus, P. punctatus, Sp. cameratus, Prod. Prattenanus* and *Aviculopecten carboniferus.* Just beneath is 7 feet of irregularly bedded, ash-blue Limestone, weathering buff and with shaly partings. *Meekella striato-costata* abounds. Shaly beds at top abound in *Fusulina.* Other contained fossils, are *Prod. Prattenanus, Prod. splendens* and *Hemipronites crassus.* The presence of *Meekella* in this bed of Limestone, seems to identify it, wherever found in the county.

A brown dendritic Limestone crops out at 3 feet above the upper 9 feet of the above Limestone.

The Section at Gallatin, on the north side of the town, includes the Limestone last named, as well as others above and below, and is as follows:

Section 120.

No. 1. 35 feet from hill-top.
No. 2. 1 foot of coarse, ferruginous Limestone, contains *Athyris, Bryozoa, Crinoid* stems, etc.
No. 3. 2 feet Slope.
No. 4. 1½ feet of rough looking drab Limestone.

No. 5. 8½ feet of Shales.

No. 6. 2½ feet of ferruginous Limestone, containing *Corals, Fusulina* and *Crinoid* stems; upper part is very fine-grained, compact, drab and brown.

No. 7. 2½ feet Shales, with thin beds of fossiliferous Limestone; fossils, *P. Prattenanus, Hemipronites*.

No. 8. 23 feet shaly Slope.

No. 9. 4 feet outcrop of irregular bedded, bluish drab Limestone, with vein of Calcite, and abounding in *Meekella striato-costata*. No. 87.

No. 10. 16 feet Slope.

No. 11. 1 foot of coarse, hard, blue Limestone, containing arms of *Archæocidaris, Crinoid* stems, *Allorisma, Phillipsia*. 85 *d*.

No. 12. 2 feet Slope. 85 *c*.

No. 13. 8 feet of nodular and shelly, fine-grained, light-drab Limestone, full of small holes. No. 84.

No. 14. 1½ feet of drab, suboolitic Limestone, contains *Hemipronites, Prod. Prattenanus, Retzia punctulifera, Spr. Kentuckensis, Spr. cameratus, Athyris, Crinoid* stems and fucoids.

No. 15. 5½ feet of irregular bedded, bluish-drab Limestone, with Shale partings and Chert concretions, contains *Fusulina* and *Athyris*. No. 83.

No. 16. 2 feet shaly and irregular concretionary Limestone beds. No. 83.

No. 17. 2 feet 7 inches Limestone, in apparent thick beds, but separated by irregular lines of deposits; abounds in *Prod. splendens*, and also has *Prod. Costatus. Athyris*, and *Spr. lineatus*. No. 83.

No. 18. 2 feet Shales, with 2 thin concretionary Limestone beds. No. 83.

No. 19. 2½ feet deep-blue, shaly, fucoidal Limestone, abounds in *Hemipronites, Pr. Prattenanus, P. splendens, Sp. cameratus* and *Terebratula bovidens*. No. 83.

No. 20. 2 feet 2 inches gray Limestone, in 4 beds like No. 15.

No. 21. 10 inches olive Shales.

No. 22. 1 foot bituminous Shales.

No. 23. 4 feet blue and black Shales, passing to a blue Fire Clay beneath.

No. 24. A few feet Slope.

No. 25. 10 + feet of Bethany Falls Limestone. No. 78.

Just south-east of Gallatin, the lower members of the above Section appear connected with still lower beds, thus:

Section 130.

No. 1. 2 feet bituminous Shales.

No. 2. 11 feet Slope.

No. 3. 19 feet Bethany Falls Limestone. No. 78.

No. 4. 5 feet light blue Shales, contains *Lingula, Discina*, etc.

No. 5. 1½ foot of bituminous Shales. 77*a*.

No. 6. 10 inches jointed, bluish drab Limestone. 76 *c*.

No. 7. 10 feet 4 inches Slope. 75 and 76.

No. 8. 8 feet ferruginous Limestone. No. 74.

The above Section will serve to show the arrangement of strata near the base of the Upper Coal Measures. A quarter of a mile west of the C. R. I. and P. R. R. depot, at Gallatin, are outcrops of beds of Limestone not seen in Section 120, but connected with No. 11 of that Section, thus :

No. 1. 2 feet nodules of Limestone on Slope.

No. 2. 6 inches blue Limestone, full of *Crinoid* stems ; also contains *Fistulapora nodulifera, Sp. Kentuckensis, Chonetes Verneullana.* 85 *d.*

No. 3. 8 inches of alternate beds of blue Limestone and Shales. Fossils abound, including *Crinoid* stems, *Chonetes granulifera, Rhombopora* ——*;* in lower part are *Schizodus Wheeleri, Myalina subquadrata, Nautilus* ——*, Hempronites crassus.*

The beds last named, wherever found, abound in beautiful and often rare fossils, or at least only peculiar to this Geological horizon. Other places, where found, were on Larry Creek, Big Creek and on head-waters of Honey Creek, near Brennan's and near David Smith's. The Section near Brennan's appears thus :

Section 119.

No. 1. Slope.

No. 2. 6 feet of blue ("*Meekella*") Limestone ; abounds in *Meekella ;* and also contains *P. costatus, P. splendens, P. Nebrascensis, Sp. cameratus. Pinna peracuta, Prod. prattenanus* and *Fusulina.* No. 87.

No. 3. 2 feet buff Shales, with Limestone concretions.

No. 4. 4 feet blue Shales.

No. 5. 9 feet Slope.

No. 6. 2 feet Limestone and Shales, subdivided thus :

    a. 6 inches Limestone. Fossils are *Chonetes Verneuillana, Prod. costatus* and *Crinoid* stems.

    b. 5 inches blue Shales.

    c. 6 inches blue argillaceous Limestone.

    d. 1 foot of concretions of Limestone, full of fossils.

    e. 1 foot of blue Clay Shales, containing *Chonetes Verneuillana, Sp. planoconvexus.* Lower part has *Schizodus Wheeleri, Myalina subquadrata, Prod. Nebrascensis, Hemipronites.*

The blue crinoidal Limestone above these fossil beds is also found three-fourths of a mile south of Pilot Grove.

There are numerous outcrops of Limestone near Alta Vista and Victoria, which belong to a higher position in the section than those above named; but their exact horizon I was unable to locate.

Near Winston are beds much higher than those of the Gallatin Section, and probably above those at Alta Vista. A section three-fourths of a mile north-west of Winston, on the creek, presents the following arrangement of strata :

No. 1. Long Slope from top of hill, probably 80 feet.

No. 2. 1 foot olive Shales.

No. 3. 3 inches deep blue, hard, crystalline Limestone, contains *Aviculopecten occidentalis*.

No. 4. 1 foot 9 inches Shales, dark chocolate above, blue below.

No. 5. 9 inches dark ash, concretionary, argillaceous Limestone.

No. 6. Thickly laminated, lead and olive colored Shales, containing remains of plants.

No. 7. 2 to 4-inch bed of impure Carbonate of Iron.

No. 8. 2 inches thinly laminated gray Shales, with *Myalina Swallovi*. No. 123.

No. 9. 1 to 3 inches Coal—good. No. 123.

No. 10. 1 inch shaly bed of Sigillaria; corresponds to a bed found at Weston.

No. 11. 4 feet light-blue Shales.

No. 12. 2½ feet compact, buff Limestone—shaly.

No. 13. 1 foot light-gray, sandy textured Limestone.

No. 14. 1 foot 9 inches light-blue silicious Limestone.

No. 15. 10 inches variegated and banded brown and gray Limestone.

No. 16. 16 inches hard, heavy-blue, silicious Limestone, containing *Myalina subquadrata*.

No. 17. 3½ feet of olive Shales.

No. 18. 1 foot yellow, ochrey Limestone.

No. 19. 2½ feet hard Limestone; resembles No. 17.

Many other Sections of the strata were taken, but the above are the most complete, and will materially assist the local student in investigating the rock structure in this county, and comparing them with those in other localities; and by aid of the General Section, published in Vol. of 1873, he can see the exact connection of these beds with those above and below, and can also ascertain if there be any valuable Coal near by.

PALÆONTOLOGY.

Certain beds of dull blue Limestone, interstratified with blue Shales are found peculiarly rich in fossils. They are often of large size, and the same species seem here to be better developed than else-where seen. These beds occur just west of Gallatin; also on head-waters of Honey Creek, on South Big Creek, and on Larry Creek. The beds correspond to a portion of No. 85 of Section of Upper Coal Measures, and the fossils are *Productus prattenanus, P. Nebrascensis, P. costatus, P. splendens, P. punctatus, P. symetricus, P. Ameri-*

canus, Chonetes Verneuillana, Spirifer cameratus, Sp. Kentuckensis, Sp. lineatus, Terebratula bovidens, Hemipronites crassus, Meekella striotocostata, Aviculopecten providencis, Avic. occidentalis, Athyris subtilita, Aviculopinna Americana, Nuculana bellistriata, Nucula ventricosa, Leda oweni, Myalina Kansasensis, M. subquadrata, Allorisma ——, Pinna peracuta, Schizodus Wheeleri, Eumicrotis Hawni, Retzia punctulifera, Allorisma granosus, A. Topecaensis, Bellerophon ellipticus, Plurotomaria ——, Macrocheilus inhabilis, M. ——, Cyrtoceras ——, Archæocidaris ——, Scaphiocrinus hemisphericus, Synocladia biserialis, Rhombopora lepidodendroides, Fistulapora nodulifera, Fusulina cylindrica.

ECONOMICAL GEOLOGY.

The beds of Limestone in sight are the only valuable mineral product easily obtained. Beds of good building rock are convenient in most neighborhoods, and the Limestones will generally make good Lime.

At Elijah Whitt's, on the N. W. of S. W. qr. Sec. 6, T. 58, R, 27, is the quarry from which the rock was obtained and used for building the county jail. The quarry rock is 4 feet 9 inches thick, in two layers, the upper of one foot, the lower 3 feet 9 inches. It is a coarse bluish gray and brown specked Limestone.

At Mr. Daniel Smoot's the rock is 3 feet thick, and said to afford a good fire rock. The rock may be referred to No. 84.

The Limestone equivalent to No. 85 *d*, is generally from 8 to 12 inches thick, and affords a good building rock, and will also burn into good Lime. It occurs west of Gallatin at Daniel Smoot's, Wm. Brennan's, on Big Creek, near Harman's, near Pattonsburgh and near Pilot Grove.

Limestone No. 74 is in very thick beds; is durable and strong. It occurs east and north-east of Gallatin, and on the railroad at several places between Gallatin Station and Jameson.

CLAY FOR PAINTS.

Red Shales are found on the banks of Big Creek, near Harman's, and would probably afford a very suitable material for painting of most common buildings.

COAL.

No bed of Coal worth working appears in the county. The 3 inch seam near Winston can not be expected to thicken much. A shaft sunk there would reach a Coal seam at 625 feet that would vary from 1 to 3 feet in thickness. Seventy feet lower, another bed of about 2 feet would be reached. A few thinner seams, but none thick enough to be worked, would be passed through nearer the surface.

On Hurricane Creek three-fourths of an inch of Coal has been found. This is not expected to become thicker. It is at least 250 feet above any bed thick enough to work.

A thin Coal seam is reported to have been found on or near Lick Fork. This would also be over 200 feet above any workable seam of Coal.

A seam of Coal of a few inches thick may also be occasionally met with between Gallatin and Jameson. Its position would be about 20 feet below the thick bedded ferruginous Limestones which appear in several places. This also is over 200 feet above any workable Coal seam.

A shaft sunk at the depot of the Chicago and South-western Railway, Gallatin, would have to be extended downwards for 280 feet to reach a workable Coal seam. A seam would be struck at about that depth which would vary in thickness from one to two and a-half feet, with a two feet Coal bed 70 feet lower, and a 20-inch seam still lower,

SOIL.

The soil in this county is generally good, in fact a large proportion of the county contains rich soil which is very productive. In some districts where the rock approaches too near the surface the crops are too apt to fail in dry seasons. The land is mostly rolling and lies well for cultivation. T. 60, R. 27, has very rich soil—that near Alta Vista; also near Gallatin, and the S. E. part of T. 60, R. 29.

The above comprises the best portions of the county. Other portions are scarcely inferior. Much of the soil near the streams and especially that on the Grand River hills, is highly calcareous, resulting from disintegration and decomposition of the Limestones.

Corn is the staple crop produced.

Wheat requires to be put in with care.

CHAPTER XX.

COLE COUNTY.

BY G. C. BROADHEAD.

The area of this county is 391 square miles, exclusive of that part of the Missouri River which may be included within its bounds. It is generally hilly and some portions are much broken, the hills often rising above the valleys from 200 to 300 feet. In the western part, the hills do not extend to as great height as they do further east. Measurements on the Moreau show that the ridges are about 270 feet above the stream; also, that the high bottoms are 17 feet above the lower bottoms. We find along both the Moreau and the Osage, a second bottom or terrace, 10 to 17 feet above the recent alluvial bottoms. This older or higher terrace, has generally under-clays resembling the Bluff to which—or to a very little more recent age—it may be referred. The character of the growth partakes very much of that of the richer uplands, consisting of White Oak, Red Oak, Hickory, etc. The low, or alluvial bottoms, mainly support a growth of Sycamore, Maple, Hackberry, etc.

The surface of the county indicates that it originally was mostly covered with a heavy timber growth, with probably less than 20 square miles of prairie.

SURFACE GEOLOGY.

Excavations reveal, resting on the solid beds of Magnesian Limestone, from 2 to 6 feet of Gravel and Clay ; usually about 2 to 3 feet. These deposits are generally present, and separate the underlying rocks from the superincumbent Bluff. The Gravel seems mostly to be divided from the Chert beds of the neighboring rocks, and is sometimes found a little worn. Granite boulders of the Drift period, are not common; a few small ones, only, have been found near the Missouri River, but none much over a foot in diameter.

The Bluff formation is partially developed, being thicker near the Missouri, and attenuated south and west. Mr. Ott, in his well at Marion, penetrated through 43 feet. In other neighborhoods, it is not often over 5 feet in depth. The washings between South and North Moreau, prove it to be 5 feet.

The Alluvium includes the soil and more recent deposits along the streams.

ROCK STRUCTURE.

Among the solid formations of the county are recognized:

OUTLIERS OF COAL MEASURES,
ENCRINITAL LIMESTONE, (BURLINGTON.)
CHOUTEAU LIMESTONE,
DEVONIAN,
FIRST MAGNESIAN LIMESTONE,
SACCHAROIDAL SANDSTONE,
SECOND MAGNESIAN LIMESTONE,
SECOND SANDSTONE,
THIRD MAGNESIAN LIMESTONE.

COAL MEASURES.

We find no regular, connected or extensive Coal field in this county; but there are many small deposits or "pockets" of Coal, chiefly in the western part of the county. Some of these have been entirely exhausted; others appear of limited extent.

In S. W. Sec. 2, T. 44, R. 13, Mr. Elston sunk a shaft 50 or 60 feet in Coal. Extending an entry a few feet in one direction, he passed through the Coal and struck the wall rock of Magnesian Limestone. A few feet in the opposite direction, he sank another shaft, passing down the face of the solid rock. This deposit was found about 20 feet from the top, on a gentle slope, and near a depression between two hills.

Not far from this "pocket," Mr. Elston, in pursuing his investigations, revealed about 20 feet thickness of hard, black Slate. He used this Slate in burning lime, and found that it blazed up brightly, affording a strong heat and accomplishing the desired purpose; but like all Slate would not burn to ashes.

The excavations on the railroad disclose "pockets" which are sometimes filled with tumbled masses of rock from the surrounding

strata, and often with beds of Shales of the Coal Measures. The surface of the ground at these places, seems to have been level with that
adjacent, previous to the railroad excavations. I observed one such
place near Elston, where there was about 30 feet cutting, the formations being Second Magnesian Limestone. Suddenly the solid rock
ended, and was replaced by loose, large and small masses of rock and
Clay, extending longitudinally for about 50 feet, when the solid rock
again continued on without interruption. This did not seem to extend much if any over 50 feet transversely. The ground surface above
was nearly level. In such holes we believe Coal has frequently been
drifted.

BURLINGTON (ENCRINITAL) LIMESTONE.

This formation occupies a limited area in the northern part of T.
45, R. 13, and T. 46, Rs. 13 and 14 W.

Where observed it was of a coarse and often loose texture, in
thick beds and containing many *Crinoid* stems. Its color is generally
gray, with the lower beds inclining to brown. Fifty feet was the greatest thickness observed, just above Marion.

CHOUTEAU GROUP.

In the same district where the Burlington Limestone occurs, we
also saw the Chouteau Limestone underlying it. The upper beds are
thick and of an ash color; the lower beds are generally thin. Fossils
observed were *Fucoides cauda-galli, Spirifer Marionensis, Rhynchonella gregaria, Leptœna depressa.* The greatest observed thickness was 35 feet.

DEVONIAN SYSTEM.

At Marion, there is seen 35 feet of Calcareous Sandstone immediately underlying the Chouteau Limestone. *Atrypa reticularis* and
other Devonian fossils were observed. This may probably be the
Onondaga Limestone. Underneath it is 2 feet of heavy, crystalline
Limestone.

LOWER SILURIAN SYSTEM.

MAGNESIAN LIMESTONE SERIES.

The subdivisions of this Series recognized in this county include
the Saccharoidal Sandstone, 35 feet; Second Magnesian Limestone,

175 feet; Second Sandstone, 30 feet; and Third Magnesian Limestone, 170 feet.

The First Magnesian Limestone may be represented by certain beds on Rock Creek and near by on the Missouri River, but the evidence was not strong enough in its favor.

SACCHAROIDAL SANDSTONE.

Wherever observed, it was found to be a heavy-bedded, white, pure, friable Sandstone, always finer grained than the Second Sandstone. At the mouth of Rock Creek, 35 feet thickness was observed.

We often find it occupying valleys or depressions in older rocks. It occurs thus near Rock Creek; also, near Elston. A half mile east of Elston, 6 or 8 feet of it was observed in a massive form and purely white, occupying the bed of a small branch. A few hundred yards south-west, 5 or 6 feet occupies the point of a hill—the mass of the hill being of Second Magnesian Limestone.

SECOND MAGNESIAN LIMESTONE.

This formation includes the entire rocks in sight along the route of the Pacific Railroad from Osage to the west county line, and of the Missouri bluffs from the mouth of Osage River nearly to Rock Creek. It is the surface rock on all the county north of the Moreau, and of Ranges 10 and 11. The lower beds form the bluffs along the Missouri from Osage to Jefferson City and on Wear's Creek.

This Limestone, although geologically an important member of the group of rocks, is of but little value as a building stone. It contains, throughout, numerous Chert beds, generally occurring in a concretionary form, inclosed in greenish or drab Shales. Over 90 feet, at the upper part, consists of alternation and mingling of Chert, Shale and Magnesian Limestone—the latter, when in thin drab layers, is generally termed "Cotton Rock," and when of uniform thickness is much used for ordinary buildings; the beds are frequently argillaceous, from which circumstance they will not stand exposure. When not too argillaceous, it forms beautiful and excellent building material. The beds are often very irregular, sometimes undulating, then abruptly broken. They are also often exceedingly rough on the surface. But the Cotton rock layers are generally very uniform in thickness. The beds lower down are much thicker and are silicious. The lower 40 feet is fucoidal and contains many small cells which sometimes contain a white powder. Fossils are rare; fucoids occur throughout.

The following Section, taken at Moreau bridge of Pacific Railroad, exhibits very finely the structure of the lower beds :

No. 1. Sandstone.
No. 2. 8 feet Cotton rock and Magnesian Limestone.
No. 3. 11 feet Cotton rock; fucoidal cavities occur in the lower part, which are often occupied with Iron Pyrites.
No. 4. 6 feet gray, silicious Magnesian Limestone.
No. 5. 18 feet.
No. 6. 4 feet Sandstone and silicious rock.
No. 7. 8 feet thin beds of Cotton rock, Magnesian Limestone, Chert and Shale.
No. 8. 3 feet Sandstone; fucoidal on surface.
No. 9. 4 feet silicious Magnesian Limestone.
No. 10. 13 feet thin, shaly beds of Cotton rock and Magnesian Limestone.
No. 11. 20 feet heavy beds of cellular Magnesian Limestone.

The last member of the above Section is 40 feet thick on the Osage.

The beds of the lower members of the last Section often form glades, sometimes of several acres in extent, and almost bare of vegetation. These glades support a scrubby growth of bushes, the most common being the *Bumelia lanuginosa*, which, although common on the glades of South Missouri, is not found in the northern part of the State. Its general appearance is much similar to the Osage Orange, and it may be useful in making hedges. The bluffs on railroad above Jefferson City exhibit very well the strata above those just spoken of.

A Section in bluff just west, is as follows :

No. 1. 7 feet bluff formation.
No. 2. 2 feet Gravel and Clay.
No. 3. 4 feet green Shales.
No. 4. 12 feet silicious Magnesian Limestone, with thin beds of Chert.
No. 5. 2½ feet of drab Cotton Rock.
No. 6. 3 feet drab Magnesian Limestone, with numerous small cells, containing a white powder.
No. 7. 3 feet silicious Magnesian Limestone.
No. 8. 9 feet drab Cotton Rock.
No. 9. 12 feet hard, silicious Magnesian Limestone, interstratified with Chert.

The bed 8, of this Section, is easily recognized all along the bluffs above. On the fractured joints No. 8 frequently presents beautiful dendritic markings, some assuming characteristic arborescent forms. This stratum often contains nodules of Iron pyrites, which oxydize on exposure, giving the rock a brown, spotted appearance.

The Chert is often beautifully oolitic. The total thickness of the Second Magnesian Limestone formation in Cole county is a little over 170 feet.

The only fossil observed in this county, that could be directly
traced to this rock, was a *Lingula*, found in beds of Cotton Rock near
hill-top at Jefferson City, and in similar beds lower down; I also
found at Elston a *Straparolus*, *Loxonema*, and *Chemnitzia*. (?)

SECOND SANDSTONE.

This is generally a very coarse-grained rock, of a light-gray or
buff appearance. Its total thickness about 30 feet. It may generally
be recognized from the occurrence of the overlying Chert beds. These
beds are compact, cellular or oolitic; the cellular beds are full of minute, round cavities, from size of a pea to a hickory nut, which are
often studded with minute quartz crystals. This stratum has also
been denominated "Buhrstone," and is immediately recognized wherever found.

The following Section on South Moreau, shows relation of these
beds.

No. 1. 35 feet Second Magnesian Limestone.
No. 2. 6 feet silicious Magnesian Limestone, with strata of sandy Cotton
        Rock.
No. 3. 8 feet silicious rock, a portion brecciated and a portion cellular. Buhr-
        stone beds.
No. 4. 3 inches oolitic Chert.
No. 5. 6 inches coarse Sandstone.
No. 6. 5 feet silicious Magnesian Limestone, containing a few small angular
        Chert fragments.
No. 7. 4 feet Chert bed.

A half mile west of St. Thomas, are exposed:

No. 1. 10 feet amorphous and cellular Chert, with Iron ore.
No. 2. Second Sandstone.

The Second Sandstone is well exposed on the Vienna road south
of the Moreau. A few fossils are occasionally met with, generally
strewn over the surface below the Second Sandstone. Their Geological position is either in the lower part of the Second Magnesian
Limestone or the Chert beds of the Second Sandstone. Comparing
them with fossils labeled by Dr. Shumard, they may include the following species: *Murchisonia Ozarkensis*, *M. carinifera*, *Pleurotomaria turgida*, Hall. *Raphistoma subplana*, *Straparollus reticulata*,
S.——, and *Orthis antiqua*. The type of these fossils is that of the
Calciferous Sandrock of the New York Geologists.

THIRD MAGNESIAN LIMESTONE.

This, the lowest formation in the county, is principally developed along the Osage River in the southern part of the county. It is not found below Castle Rock, but develops high in the bluffs of Bois Brule and Little Tavern. The beds are generally thick, and are either coarse-grained Dolomites with a vitreous luster of a bluish-gray, or a fine-grained flesh color.

A Section on Moreau, one mile below the forks, represents some of the upper beds, as follows :

No. 1.   90 feet cherty Slope, with fragments of Sandstone.

No. 2.   110 feet of Magnesian Limestone ; the upper 25 feet of Cotton Rock below, is of a dark-ash, with the lower 40 feet a thick bed of light-drab, silicious Magnesian Limestone; the upper part is cellular, with some minute quartz crystals arranged botryoidally, occurring in drusy cavities. A bed of compact quartz, of a few inches thickness, is interstratified.

The junction of Second Sandstone and Third Magnesian Limestone is well exposed at the Ferry on Vienna road. We have here

No. 1.   30 feet Second Sandstone, coarse, white and banded—ripple-marked— the lower beds intercalated with Magnesian Limestone, and some Chert.

No. 2.   105 feet of Third Magnesian Limestone, both fine and coarse, the beds often forming a breccia with Chert; the Chert often oolitic; the layers very irregular.

Thick Chert beds sometimes occur. Near mouth of Little Tavern, we find a Chert bed having a peculiar structure. It may be fucoidal or remotely belong to the PROTOZOA. There seem to be occasional axes from which flag-like bands of Chert shoot out both ways, and anastomose with Chert bands from other axes.

A similarly formed Chert bed has been observed in the Magnesian Limestone beds of the southern part of Madison county.

Of the Third Magnesian Limestone there probably is about 170 feet in this county.

ECONOMICAL GEOLOGY.

The metallic ores found in Cole county, include Iron, Lead and Zinc, with traces of Copper.

IRON ORES.

Brown hematites and sulphurets were observed; the latter at the

"Circle Diggings," 3 miles south of Hickory Hill; and at the Coal mines near Elston. The brown Hematite, or Limonite, is often found on the hills between the Osage and the Moreau, and at a few other localities, but at no place did I observe large quantities. Its origin seems to be in the Chert beds immediately at the top of the Second Sandstone, as the following description will show :

On B. Lothin's land, one-half mile west of St. Thomas, the ore is found attached to the Chert just over the Sandstone, and lies in loose masses for over 100 feet down the hill, becoming fewer as we descend. Near the upper part it is strewn along for 100 feet east and west. It is of good quality, occurring in a columnar form, with probably a ton in sight.

Similar ore is found at several other places in the neighborhood.

On E. W. Gaty's land, one-half mile above the mouth of Bois Brule, several pits have been dug, revealing a good quality of ore. The country here is very much broken, the hills about 200 feet high, and covered with a fine growth of young White Oak. Third Magnesian Limestone extends nearly to the hill-top, along which is strewn large masses of the Second Sandstone Chert. The hill is broken by several deep ravines extending north, along the sides of which, and about 80 feet below the hill top, are the ore beds. The ore was found in some of the pits, but not in others. A soft yellowish, and a harder porous brown Limonite is found. A ton or more of ore was dug and piled up. The ore has evidently been drifted from just above, being the residue of the destruction of the overlying and inclosing rocks. Large masses of ore are often found on the surface, between the Osage and South Moreau, and occasionally north of the Moreau.

In N. W. Sec. 34, T. 44, R. 14, many fragments of Iron ore and silico—ferruginous Conglomerate—are found.

At the county line, 5 miles north of Centretown, are seen small quantities of brown Hematite, associated with Heavy Spar, the Iron ore often penetrating the Spar in the form of small hollow cylinders.

At the Old Circle Diggings, 3 miles south of Hickory Hill, we find some rather nice crystals of brown Hematite, reposing on Heavy Spar, undoubtedly formed since the Heavy Spar was, and assuming in general outline the form of the mass of Spar.

COPPER.

At Smith's "Old Circular Diggings," in Sec. 35, T. 42, R. 13, small quantities of Sulphuret of Copper are found, either disseminated in the Limestone, adhering to the Galena, or else adhering to Heavy Spar. We find the Heavy Spar attached to Limestone with a thin cupriferous band between, of which the central part is Sulphuret, and that next to the Limestone is the green Carbonate, or Malachite, which gradually blends into the Baryta.

ZINC.

Small quantities of Silicate and of Blende, occur at Fowler's Mines, in Sec. 35, T. 43, R. 13. Future mining may yet disclose a greater amount of the Silicate. A very little Silicate was also observed at Streit's Mines, 2 miles of south of Centretown.

The Coal Mines near Centretown also contain Zinc Blende, mingled with the Coal.

At Thos. Caspary's, near Elston, the Zinc traverses the Coal both horizontally and vertically. The horizontal arrangement appears thus, numbering from top down:

    No. 1. Coal.
    No. 2. 1 inch Zinc Blende.
    No. 3. 2 feet Coal.
    No. 4. ¾ inch Zinc Blende.
    No. 5. 8 inches Coal.
    No. 6. 1 inch Zinc Blende.
    No. 7. Coal.

LEAD.

Galena is abundant at many places in this county—the west and south-west including valuable mines. It was found in this county in 1820, and the first mining done by Chouteau in 1827, who had a furnace near where Pratt's Mill now is.

The geological position of the ores in the southern part is the Third Magnesian Limestone; of those in the west, the lower beds of the Second Magnesian Limestone. I observed Galena in openings or crevices in Second Magnesian Limestone and in broken strata in the Third. Small amounts of Lead have been picked up on the surface or associated with surface Clays in almost every neighborhood. It has been picked up at Jefferson City.

ELSTON MINE.

This is in a low hill on the south side of Gray's Creek, a quarter of a mile from the Station. The formation is Second Magnesian Limestone. The Lead occurs in what miners would call an "opening," which was filled with soft Magnesian Limestone containing Galena. The opening is a little over 2 feet square, starting southwardly 15 feet into the hill, then turning south-east 125 feet, thence east 25 feet. The

Lead was found throughout, occurring in a sheet 1 foot wide and $2\frac{1}{2}$ to 3 inches thick—sometimes much thicker, and also almost thinning out. At end of drift, the "opening" is reduced in size, and the Lead is 1 foot wide by $2\frac{1}{2}$ inches thick.

In mining, I was informed that occasional "chimneys" would occur, in which the Lead was found for several feet above.

About 12,000 pounds of mineral have been taken from this mine.

DODSON'S MINES.

Three miles north of Elston, on Missouri bluffs, a little mining has been done in a Magnesian Limestone and Cotton rock, probably of age of First Magnesian Limestone, as I found Saccharoidal Sandstone at foot of hill. The solid rock does not apparently bear the mineral. About 600 pounds is said to have been found in overlying loose Clays.

LEMLEIN & STAEHLIN'S MINE.

This, a very recent discovery, is on land leased of Stokes, 3 miles south of Elston.

The underlying rock is Second Magnesian Limestone, Cotton rock beds, and the mineral chiefly obtained in overlying "Local Drift." The diggings are on a hillside sloping to a small branch of Gray's Creek.

Excavations show as follows:

No. 1. 1 foot Soil, with many pebbles and Chert fragments strewn on the surface.

No. 2. 3 feet red Clay, loose Chert and disseminated chunks of Galena.

No. 3. 3 feet soft, decomposing, drab Magnesian Limestone not generally containing Galena, but in one opening observed two thin $\frac{1}{2}$ inch parallel and vertical veins, 10 inches apart.

In one pit, a small opening of 6 inches square contained some Galena, but the quantity was too small to work and was abandoned.

Mining began here in August, 1874, and since then 2,000 pounds of Galena have been taken out.

Five miles north of Centertown, near the Moniteau county line, and probably in Moniteau county, some mining has been done in Second Magnesian Limestone, and small quantities of Lead obtained. The succession of rocks appears to be—

No. 1. Chert.

No. 2. Red Clay containing Galena.

No. 3. Drab colored Cotton Rock.

No. 4. Sandstone.

I picked up pieces of broken Chert to which the Galena adhered, some forming a brecciated mass with the Chert. The surface of the Chert sometimes contains minute Quartz crystals arranged botryoidally and inclosing Galena.

STREIT'S MINE.

This is in N. E. qr. Sec. 2, T. 44, R. 14, two miles south of Center-town. The formation here is Second Magnesian Limestone. A shaft revealed—

> No. 1. 8 feet red Clay.
> No. 2. 1½ feet drab and buff Shales.
> No. 3. 2 to 3 feet of red Clay with pockets of drab Shale.
> No. 4. 3 feet Cotton rock.

Lead was obtained in crevices with Baryta, in which it was inclosed. A little Zinc Blende and Calamine was obtained.

FOWLER'S MINES.

These mines are in Sec. 35, T. 43, R. 13, about 30 feet below the top of a hill, of which a Section shows:

> No. 1. 10 feet loose Chert, with fragments of fossils and a little tumbling Sand-stone (Second).
> No. 2. 18 feet mottled, fucoidal, ash drab and buff Magnesian Limestone.
> No. 3. 5 feet flesh colored and drab Magnesian Limestone, containing occasional flattened cells. Cracks and rotten openings occur containing Galena; the cracks mostly perpendicular with an occasional oblique or, for a short distance, a horizontal variation.
> No. 4. 50 feet Slope.
> No. 5. 20 feet brecciated Chert.

I regard these rocks as the upper part of the Third Magnesian Limestone. In the openings there is found Lead, Zinc (Sulphuret and Silicate), with Heavy Spar. The Heavy Spar is compact, white, blue or amber colored crystals. Considerable Silicate of Zinc may be obtained here, but the mine, not having been recently worked, was in a poor condition for examination. It was worked in 1869 and shafts sunk 30 feet, and about 30,000 pounds of mineral taken out.

"SMITH'S" OR "OLD CIRCLE DIGGINGS," S. E. SEC. 28, T. 42, R. 13.

The hills have Chert and fragments of Second Sandstone on top, and are about 170 feet high. The Third Magnesian Limestone appears 75 feet from the top and at intervals below. The surface of the ground at the " Circle Mines " is 20 feet above the valley. Twenty feet higher and one-eighth of a mile north, are the " Sand Diggings." They extend 30 feet higher in the hill.

A great deal of mining was formerly done at the " Sand Diggings," but little during the past few years. The ore has been chiefly obtained from the Clay, Sand and debris overlying and filling fissures in the Magnesian Limestone, and mostly associated with white Heavy Spar.

At the " Old Circle Diggings " the mining has extended into the solid rock, but the ore mostly obtained in seams and crevices, associated with a gangue of Heavy Spar, although sometimes adhering to the Magnesian Limestone. The present operator of the mines, Mr. E. W. Gaty, has done a great deal of work here—he has sunk a wide shaft to the depth of 70 feet. Being filled with water, I could not see the lower structure of the rocks. Near the upper part are thick sheets of Heavy Spar, containing Galena.

In these mines are found besides Galena, Sulphuret and green and blue Carbonate of Copper, Oxide and Sulphuret of Iron. Heavy Spar (Baryta) both crystalized and compact, and Calcite. The total yield of these mines I could not obtain, so I can only give partial statistics. The first work was done here by the original owner, Mr. — Smith, in 1840. He sold to Henly, and he to Clark & Eaton, 'and then to E. W. Gaty. I was informed that Smith took out over 800,000 pounds of mineral; Clark & Eaton, over 500,000; Unseeker & Carter, 60,000. Gaty began to work in 1874, and continued regularly for several months. At the " Sand Diggings," ¼ of a mile north, Mr. Carter showed me several shafts from which a stated amount of mineral was obtained, as follows : In one from 10 to 25 feet in depth, 4,000 pounds obtained in 1869 ; another, 35 feet depth, 5,000 tô 6,000 pounds obtained ; another, 30 feet in depth, 8,000 pounds, chiefly in red Clay in crevices. In one of 22 feet depth, 13,000 pounds, in light Sand and red Clay.

Two miles east, on north side of Little Tavern, a little surface mining has been done in crevices of Third Magnesian Limestone, and small quantities of Lead obtained, The Limestone here is either a soft, coarse, bluish-gray Dolomite or very fine-grained flesh-colored. The crevices in the Limestone are often filled with white, heavy Spar apparently maintaining the same horizon at several places. In bluffs of Bois Brulé, in S. E. qr. Sec. 21, T. 42, R, 13, some surface mining has also been done, and the underlying rock quarried out for a few feet depth. The crevices contain red Clay, decomposed Magnesian Limestone, Heavy Spar, and Lead associated with the latter.

Lead in small quantities has also been found at several other places in this vicinity.

One mile south-west of St. Thomas, on land of Leven's heirs, a little " float " mineral has been obtained in shallow pits, in crevices of the Third Magnesian Limestone.

OTHER MINERALS—NOT ORES.

Handsome Crystals, semi-transparent Crystals of Heavy Spar, (Barytes) are found at the old " Circle Mines," also large masses of white Heavy Spar, both here and near by at the " Sand Diggings." Heavy Spar is also found at many other places in the neighborhood. The mines on the South Moreau also afford large quantities of it. At Fowler's mines are Crystals of azure blue, Heavy Spar and of transparent and amber-colored, some beautifully modified.

On the Osage River, a half mile above the mouth of Bois Brulé, Mr. Turner has a mill erected for the purpose of grinding the Heavy Spar. It has been in operation 5 years, and grinds up a large quantity of the mineral, which he ships to St. Louis, where it is used for mixing with white Lead. His supply is chiefly derived from up the Osage River, from whence it is brought in boats to his mill. He had about 150 tons of raw material on the ground and 5 or 6 tons of prepared material ready to ship.

CALCITE.

Beside Sulphate of Baryta, the old " Circle Diggings" afford large crystals of Calcite—generally of a brownish or amber color—it is here often found assuming the common Dog-tooth Spar shape.

QUARTZ.

Associated with the Third Sandstone, are often found minute Quartz crystals, generally closely arranged on a flat surface. Quartz in small crystals, botryoidally arranged, is often found in drusy cavities of Magnesian Limestone.

COAL.

Coal mines have been worked at several places in the county, but all investigations have proved these deposits to be pockets of limited extent. Two miles north of Centretown the Pacific Mining Company have worked out two extensive deposits. They had railways connecting the mines with the railroad at Centretown, but most of their track is taken up, the mines abandoned, and ashes, banks of Clay and Shale and old logs are all that is left. This Company also worked out several similar deposits south of Elston.

A half mile south of Centretown, on a gently sloping point near the foot of a hill, a pit, 18 feet deep, has been dug, passing through chiefly Fire Clay, with small streaks of Coal, irregularly dispersed. The Coal is of a very impure quality; dull looking and crumbly. The Clay also contains a little Selenite. This may be a drifted deposit, as chunks of Chert, with small pieces of attached Galena were thrown out of the pit.

A quarter of a mile south, and on Sec. 2, T. 44, R. 14, is a pit 21 feet deep. Some Cannel Coal has been taken out here, but driftings at bottom show that the Coal extends only 12 feet east, and thins out at 8 feet south. Going 15 feet west, it almost thinned out, but again thickened. The Coal contains Iron Pyrites and small seams of Zinc Blende.

STAEHLIN'S MINE.

This is 3 miles south of Elston, and 180 feet deep. The Coal is said to be 30 feet thick, and mostly bituminous. Not being able to descend into the shaft, I can not give any particular interesting or useful information about the mine. The mouth of the shaft is about 25 feet below the hill-top. The Coal occupies the area of an acre or a little more, and a good deal of Coal has been obtained.

THOS. CASPARY'S COAL BANK.

The pit here is 60 feet deep, entering from a gently sloping hill-side about 30 or 40 feet below the hill-top. The Coal is 6 feet thick, and of an impure, slaty, bituminous variety. Sixty feet southwest, in a shaft sunk 50 feet in depth, the Coal found was only 4 feet thick, which in a short distance pitched down and gave out. Entering the Drift at the bottom of the main shaft, the Coal at first seemed rather irregular, and dipping 10° north-west. Fifty feet back it rises. Horizontal seams of Zinc Blende are met with, and occasionally a vertical vein. Iron Pyrites, in masses and modified crystal forms, is abundant.

A little over a quarter of a mile north-east, Mr. Caspary has a deposit of Cannel Coal, but has not worked it recently.

A half mile south of Caspary's, Mr. Elston penetrated 20 feet in black Slate. He used it in burning Lime, and found it answered the purpose very well; it blazed free but did not burn to ash. It was very near this that Mr. Elston found the singular pocket of Coal named in preceding pages. A little south of this is a pocket of blue

Shale, but no Coal. A quarter of a mile still further south the Pacific
Coal Mining Company have exhausted another Coal deposit. A quarter of a mile further South there is another pocket of probably not
much over a 100 feet square, Staehlin's bank, previously noticed, is
about a half mile further south.

On a small tributary of Bois Brule, in Sec. 21, T. 41, R. 14, some
Coal of an impure slaty character has been obtained, but the deposit
is too limited and quality too poor to work.

A half mile north-east of Hickory Hill an impure Cannel Coal
has been obtained. The bank is situated in a deep valley between
two hills, whose summits and sides are composed of beds of Second
Magnesian Limestone. This deposit is also quite limited in extent.

On Lantrum's land, a few miles north-west of Elston, are several
abandoned Coal pits. They are all pockets of Coal, not connected
with each other, but none of them appear to be extensive. Tumbled
masses of Lower Carboniferous Limestone appear on the hills above,
and a little lower down are some beds of Second Magnesian Limestone. One pit is located in a ravine, 25 feet above the foot of the hill ;
another probably a hundred feet higher up, and still another a short
distance above. At one of these I observed Coal Measure Sandstone,
including plant remains.

C L A Y S .

Beds of good Fire Clay occur at most of the above named Coal
banks, and at some of them are beds of good Potters' Clay.

A silicious Clay stone of a white color is found in hills of Little
Tavern, a short distance from its mouth. This is not a Kaolin as some
supposes, but a silicious Clay stone. It would probably do well to
make it into some kind of stone ware. This rock is interstratified
with the Third Magnesian Limestone.

BUILDING STONE.

Some of the Cotton Rock beds at Jefferson City afford a beautiful
and useful building stone, but great care should be observed in the
selection of quarries. No quarry of this rock should be used until it
is found to withstand the winter frosts, for many of the layers will
not. These rocks should be quarried during the spring and summer,
so as to give them time to dry and season before winter. By following this plan we often have, what would not under other circumstances be a good building rock.

The Limestone in the western wall of the Capitol inclosure, has been proven to stand the frosts well; for many years it lay exposed on the ground, but showed no frost cracks.

The thick beds of Magnesian Limestone near Osage City, afford a useful building material. The piers of the Osage bridge, were constructed of it, and over 20 years exposure show that they are as good as ever.

Similar good rock, with Sandstone layers, occurs at the Moreau bridge.

Near Hickory Hill there is occasionally seen, a short distance below the hill-top, a superior buff Magnesian Limestone. This works free, and is durable; is also ordinarily called Cotton Rock. It belongs near the upper part of the Third Magnesian Limestone. This rock is found at many places near the hill-top, from Locust Mound to Brazito.

The thick beds of the Third Magnesian Limestone, undoubtedly are superior for works requiring strong stone-work. Fine exposures may be seen in the south-west part of the county, on Osage River, and on Bois Brule and Little Tavern Creeks.

The Second Sandstone also affords a strong and useful building stone. It may be found along the Moreau from the Pacific Railroad to the forks. Good quarries could be opened on Vienna road near the Moreau and near the Osage. Some of the beds of this Sandstone seem pure enough for making glass. But the best material for glass-making, is the Saccharoidal or First Sandstone. This is found at several places near Elston, and near Marion. It is well exposed near the mouth of Rock Creek. It is a pure, white Sandstone, and generally more loosely cohering than the other Sandstones. By this it may be easily recognized.

SOILS.

The best lands are the bottom lands, which are generally sufficiently elevated to be above ordinary high water.

The Missouri bottom extends from the mouth of Gray's Creek to Rock Creek.

The Osage River bottoms are from a quarter to a half mile wide; those of the Moreau about a quarter of a mile wide; and even sometimes wider. The Moreau being an exceedingly crooked stream, gives more bottom land to Cole county than it otherwise would.

Rich, pretty valleys occur along the other streams.

The uplands are not desirable farming lands, with this exception : Near Hickory Hill, and most of the country drained by Clark's Fork

G.S—22.

of the Moreau, is a rich body of farming land. This land originally supported a heavy growth of Black Oak, Hickory, White Oak, Ash, Redbud, Red and American Elm, vines, etc. The hills near Jefferson City yield good corn and wheat crops. Occasional good tracts of farming land also occur on the Missouri hills ; for instance, between Elston and the Missouri River, and between Jefferson City and the Osage. But most of the uplands will raise fine wheat crops, and are superior for vineyards. It is generally well adapted to all the fruits of this climate.

SPRINGS.

Good springs are found in most of the valleys. Where the Third Magnesian Limestone occurs, we find the clearest water and most constant supply. We may instance Little Tavern, a very clear running stream, which is supplied by clear, cold running springs.

At Elston there is an Epsom Salt well. It issues from the Second Magnesian Limestone, and seems to contain a large supply of water.

POCKETS AND OUTLIERS OF COAL.

These deposits are found in Lincoln, Warren, Montgomery, Callaway, Cole, Moniteau, Morgan, Benton, Pettis, Saline and Jasper.

They belong, in age, to the true Coal Measures, or Carboniferous formations, and were probably the earliest beds deposited. In some of them I have even recognized a close resemblance to well known beds of the true Coal formation. They generally have their associated Slates, Shales and Fire Clay beds. Their variable thickness, and often great inclination to the horizon, would indicate their deposition in an unquiet sea. They have generally been deposited in valleys, or at a lower horizon than the general surface of the country ; and although sometimes in vertical thickness as much as 20 to 50 and 80 feet, rarely extend horizontally over 300 feet. They are limited by walls of rock of older geological age. The Mammoth and Mastodon banks in Callaway county, are such deposits. The Mastodon—Sec. 4, T. 44, R. 10— is reported to be over 80 feet in thickness, without reaching the bottom. It is located where two hills of gentle slope come together.

From my observations, I do not suppose it to extend much over 100 feet in width and length. The Second Magnesian Limestone appears in a ravine near by.

A half mile S. W. of the Mastodon bank is the Einstein shaft. A Section of this is—

No. 1. 20 feet local Drift.

No. 2. 8 to 10 feet of coarse, rough, sandy Shales.

No. 3. 3 feet bituminous Coal.

No. 4. Cannel Coal—thickness not known. The shaft was sunk in edge of a sharp valley.

A ferruginous Sandstone appears on the hill above. The arrangement of strata appearing so regular here, one is very apt to be deceived. This is undoubtedly a more extensive deposit than the Mastodon, and may extend horizontally several hundred feet. It would seem to have been quietly deposited in an eroded valley and older rocks subsequently drifted over it.

DICKSON BANK—S. W. SEC. 20, T. 45, R. 10.

This would appear to have been a drifted deposit—drifted a short distance from where originally deposited, for the rocks do not lie horizontal, and on the hill-top we find Devonian Limestone, and lower down the Coal dipping from the hill. The dip is S. 80° W., at an angle of 30°. The extent of Coal can not be over 200 feet in width. The Coal occurs with its own rocks thus:

No. 1 7 feet drab Shales, with decomposing Limestone bearing Coal Measure fossils, *Spirifer* ———, *Productus*, etc.

No. 2. 6 inches blue Clay Shales.

No. 3. 1 foot black Shale.

No. 4. 5 inches blue Clay.

No. 5. 22 inches rotten Coal.

No. 6. 9 inches alternate layers of rotten Coal and Clay.

No. 7. 9 inches good bituminous Coal.

No. 8. 2 inches yellow and drab Clay.

No. 9. 2 inches good Coal.

No. 10. ½ to 3 inches gray Clay with Stigmaria.

No. 11. 5 + feet Coal.

The Coal is also exposed 100 feet west, showing over 2 feet of good Coal under 5 feet of rotten Coal.

On the hill-top is ferruginous Sandstone and below it is Devonian Limestone.

JOHN Y. BASINGER'S—S. E. SEC. 30, T. 45, R. 10 W.

This deposit appears in bed of a small branch entering on the west side of Revoir Creek. The valley is not over 100 feet wide with Mag nesian Limestone in regular undisturbed layers cropping out in the hill, and drifted Devonian Limestone in the branch just above. The Coal rocks occur thus:

No. 1. 2½ feet Cannel Coal.
No. 2. 2½ feet bituminous Coal.
No. 3. Slate.

One hundred feet north, borings passed through, 1st, 11 feet Slate; 2d, 11 feet Coal.

LOHMAN & PRICE—N. W. SEC. 30, T. 45, R. 10 W.

A good deal of mining has been done here and the Coal seems to have occupied a rather more extensive area than those places above named. Mining has been prosecuted up and down the branch for probably 200 yards, and side drifts extended into the hill at numerous points. Coarse Sandstone, evidently of the age of the Coal Measure, appears on the hill for over a hundred yards back. Further back on the hill we find Lower Carboniferous Chert. A Section is this:

No. 1. 2 + feet brown Sandstone.
No. 2. 11 inches rotten Coal.
No. 3. 8 inches good bituminous Coal.
No. 4. 2 inches rotten Coal.
No. 5. 6 inches black Slate.
No. 6. 4 inches chocolate colored Clay.
No. 7. 7 inches jointed slaty Coal.
No. 8. 10 inches dark snuff or olive colored Clay.
No. 9. 2 + feet bituminous Coal.

This closely resembles Prof. Swallow's description of Coal below the mouth of Lamine River. Some of the other banks resemble H. L. Brown's, near Boonsboro, Howard county.

[For a description of the Coal pockets of Cole county see report on that county.]

MONITEAU BANK.

This is one mile south of Moniteau Station, Moniteau county. The surface of the ground slopes very gently. No rocks of any kind appear in position near by. A mile east are detached masses of ferruginous Sandstone and Encrinital Limestone, the latter apparently in place. A little lower down the hill is Second Magnesian Limestone. The Coal shaft is being worked by Gen. Shelby and others. The Coal appears very near the surface; dipping, as far as tested, quite regularly at an angle of about 50° at a course of N. 20° W. The Coal is worked on a Slope along its plane of dip on which a track is laid for 200 feet (June, 1874). At the end of the Slope the Coal is 104 feet from the surface in a vertical direction. It is 30 feet in thickness. From the bottom an entry has been extended 80 feet to the right, and half way down there is another reaching 20 feet to the left. The Coal has been made into pretty fair Coke. This deposit at present baffles any attempt to calculate its extent and quantity. This can only be determined by practical experiments in extending drifts or shafts.

For description of other similar deposits we would refer to the various reports in this volume and to the volume of 1873.

GENERAL REMARKS.

The Coals are generally of two kinds, Cannel and Bituminous, and the quality not often so good as the other Coals. Zinc blende is often found traversing the Coal. The Coal beds generally lie at an inclination to the horizon and are never found near a hill-top, and more often in a valley—generally in a smaller valley tributary to a larger one. These valleys seem to have been eroded previously to the deposits of the Coal. The Coal then was deposited in them, but probably soon after the larger or unprotected mass was washed away, leaving issolated pockets in the narrow valleys where they have been protected by adjacent walls of Limestone from being drifted away.

The Cannel Coal deposits also, seem to have been sometimes deposited in small basins or crevices.

These deposits may thus be divided into two classes:

1. Outliers from the true Coal Measures, preserving their regular order of arrangement of Slates, Clays, Coals, etc.
2. Drifted deposits, including—
   a. Drifted in an unbroken mass, and retaining after being drifted a regular succession of beds, as in the first class.
   b. Drifted in broken or comminuted masses, as are some of the Cannel Coal deposits.

CHAPTER XXI.

MADISON COUNTY.

BY G. C. BROADHEAD.

SURFACE, CONFIGURATION, Etc.

The area of this county is about 506 square miles; it is bounded on the north by St. Francois, on the east by Bollinger, on the south by Wayne, and on the west by Iron. It presents every variety of surface, from that of high mountains and high Chert hills, to lower hills, valleys and plains.

No positive anticlinal or synclinal axis was observed, nor any regular system of elevation. The following elevations west of the St. Francois River were noted, the heights being estimated from the neighboring valleys: Daguerre Mountain, 492 feet; Blue Mountain, 551 feet; Smith's Mountain, (porphyritic) 432 feet; Rock Creek Mountain, (porphyritic and Syenitic) 575 feet; Black Mountain, (porphyritic) 467 feet. Another elevation just south of Black Mountain, is probably higher. Near the mouth of Leatherwood Creek the Limestone and Chert hills are about 150 feet high.

Where the Syenite or porphyry approaches the streams from opposite sides, a " Shut-in," as it is called, is formed; that is, the stream is confined to a narrow, rocky, rugged channel, which generally continues until a bench of sedimentary rock sets in. We have such an example where the west end of Daguerre Mountain approaches close to St. Francois River, with a steep, rocky front, and just across on the west side of the River, another high Granitic hill appears to stretch forward to meet it, each hill rising to a height of not less than 250 feet near the stream, becoming higher as it recedes.

Lower down St. Francois River, in N. E. of S. W. qr., Sec. 2, T. 33, R. 50 E., are the "rapids;" here the Syenitic cliffs approach close to the stream on both sides, along which and in the stream on both sides, are many very large tumbling masses of rock, which, especially in time of high water, seriously impede the current, which was the case at the time of my visit to the locality, and the noise of rushing waters was very great. In traveling southward, east of St. Francois River, after leaving Daguerre Mountain, we pass over Conglomerate and Cherty hills, elevated about 200 feet above the River, thence across the wide, pretty valley of Cedar Creek, skirting along the slopes of Reeves' Mountain, rising on our left to an elevation of 660 feet, thence along lower hills to neighborhood of Twelve Mile Creek, where the hills are about 150 feet high, with Limestone at the base and Chert on the top, thence to the south county line, near which, as measured, we find the hill, to be 187 feet high. Occasionally we find wide, rich bottoms of alluvium on the St. Francois. The Limestone and Chert hills 'between St. Francois River and Castor, rise to a hight of 280 to 300 feet. At Berry's, on West Trace Creek, it is 280 feet from the Creek to top of the Chert hills. On Big Creek, near Hoffman's, a Porphyry hill is 269 feet high. At Rickman's, on Shutley's Creek, it is 207 feet to top of the Chert hills.

On Castor, in Sec. 31, T. 31, R. 8, E., the bluff is 163 feet high. At Geo. Whitener's, west of Castor, the bluffs are 251 feet high; near Henry Hildebrand's, 115 feet; on East Trace Creek, 143 feet.

The bottoms on Castor are often a half mile wide, those on most streams are narrow.

The Slopes adjacent to Callaway's Mill Creek, Village Creek, and near Fredericktown, Cedar Creek, Slater's Creek, and part of Mat. thew's Creek, are long and gentle, and their valleys are beautiful.

LIST OF TREES AND SHRUBS.

Alder,	Waahoo Elm, (*Ulmus alata*)	Mulberry,
Amorpha fruticosa,	Summer Grape,	White, Burr, Post, Swamp White, Rock-Chesnut, Pin,
A. caneseens,	Frost Grape,	Laurel and Gray Oaks,
Aralia Spinosa, or "tear-blanket," as it is called by the country people.	Muscadine,	Pawpaw,
	Greenbrier,	Persimmon,
Crab Apple,	Black Gum,	Yellow Pine, (*Pinus mitis*)
White Ash,	Sweet Gum,	Plum, (2 species)
Prickly Ash,	Hackberry,	Rose, (4 species)

Linden,	Witch Hazel,	Raspberry,
Sycamore,	Red Birch.	Red Elm,
Blackberry, (several species)	Common Hazel,	
		Sumach, (3 species)
Bladdernut,	Black Haw,	
		Sassafras,
Red Cedar,	Common Hickory,	
		Serviceberry,
Bumelia lanuginosa,	Shelbark, and thick Shell-	
	bark Hickory,	Thorn, (*cratœgus*)
Black Cherry,		
	Pignut and Bullnut Hickory,	Trumpet Creeper,
Coffee Tree,		
	Hornbeam,	White Walnut,
Coral Berry,		
	Ironwood,	Black Walnut,
Flowering Dogwood, (*cornus florida*)	Honeysuckle,	Spicebush,
Common Elder,	Redbud,	Waaho,
White Elm,	Honey Locust,	Huckleberry, (several spec's)
Red, White and Sugar Maple,		

There is some difference in the relative distribution of certain trees and shrubs, in different parts of the county. The Poplar, or Tulip Tree occurs at a few localities in the southern part of the county, and I was informed that there were a few Beech trees on hills east of Castor, in the south part of the county. Catalpa is found on St. Francois River, in T. 31. Sweet Gum is quite common in T. 31, and portions of T. 32, and the farthest locality north where I observed it, was on Cedar Creek. Leatherwood (*Dirca pulustris*) is abundant on Leatherwood Creek, and on Castor, near Marquand.

The Pine is not very abundant in T. 34. Occasional thick groves are found further south, but in T. 31 and part of T. 32, there are many very dense pine groves of excellent timber. Large forests, of a superior quality of large White Oak trees, are found throughout the county. The White Oak timber in this county, as yet, seems scarcely to have been touched. Five or six miles south and south-west of Fredericktown are quantities of excellent White Oak timber.

On Cedar Creek and vicinity, are some of the finest Cedar groves in the State. On Leatherwood Creek and Gray's Mountains, great quantities of Cedar have been cut off and hauled away, mostly for fence posts. At the old John Francis' place, I noticed a fence a few hundred yards long, composed mainly of Cedar rails. A field on the old Cooper place, on Cedar Creek is also inclosed with Cedar rails. Good Walnut and Cherry timber abound along the various streams. The Sweet Gum often grows very large, and is said to polish quite beautifully.

WATER.

Madison county is generally well supplied with a superior quality of water. Castor River is a very pretty, clear running stream. Its bed can be plainly seen anywhere, so pure is the water. Along its banks are many lasting springs of cool water, which assist in keeping the river water cool throughout the hottest weather. There are several water mills on Castor, which keep at work the whole year round. Cold Water Spring, at the head of Twelve Mile Creek, affords plenty of water for several families the year round.

On Shutley's Creek are many large, clear and cool springs.

SOILS.

Of course, there is not much soil on the mountains, nor do their disintegrating rocks afford a rich soil. But even on the mountain tops are sometimes found spots of arable land. On Daguerre Mountain, I saw a pretty good field of corn. The Chert ridges afford a rather thin soil, especially where the pines predominate.

Around Fredericktown, as far north as Mine LaMotte, and eastward a few miles, extending to the head of the various streams that centre here, we have an elevated valley, rising gently from the streams, probably as much sometimes as 75 feet. The base of this soil is Magnesian Limestone. On this reposes a very red soil, containing a good deal of oxide of Iron, and it is very productive. As a proof, I would cite the fact of a large portion of it having been in cultivation as much as 70 years, and still continuing to yield bountiful crops.

The valleys of Slater's and Matthew's Creek are based on similar formations, and overlaid in part by similar red soils. Southwardly, this soil is sparingly diffused, not seen near Trace Creek and Twelve Mile, but was observed near the mouth of Twelve Mile, and also, in part, on the west side of Saint Francois River, near the southern part of the county. This soil supports a natural vigorous growth of White Oak, Elm, Linden, Hickory, Iron-wood, Hornbeam, Black Walnut, Black Gum, Sassafras and Dogwood.

In the western part of the county, south of the Gravel road, and to south line of the county, are found but few patches of good soil; only occasionally are interposed small valleys of a third class quality, on which the inhabitants manage to eke out a support.

In the northern portion of the county, west of Iron Mountain Railroad, and reaching to the St. Francis River, is an elevated plateau of third class soil based on Syenitic rocks. On this tract tolerably good crops of corn and wheat are raised, and fine crops of all kinds of fruit, peculiar to the county, are annually produced. Good crops of cotton can be raised. The thin lands produce 35 to 40 bushels of corn per acre; the valleys, 60 bushels. The soil on the ridges is generally of a whitish color.

In the streams we find a great deal of Gravel; this mingling with the Soils of the bottoms, and loosely cohering, is easily washed away; hence we often see changes and widening of channel. The soil of all the bottoms contains a great deal of gravel, especially may this be said of Twelve Mile Creek. Near its head we find quantities of Chert and porphyritic boulders and Gravel. Lower down stream the soil is enriched by decomposing debris from Magnesian Limestone. The gravel in this soil performs the function of digestion, and where the comminuted matter possesses richness, the result is a superior soil.

GEOLOGY.

SURFACE GEOLOGY.

Under this head we include the Soils, Local Drift and other loose Drift, if any, and

ALLUVIUM.

This is constantly forming along the streams by deposition from the waters. Local Drift may include deposits of fragments of rock strewn over the surface everywhere—some of it now being deposited, but a large portion in former ages.

Loose masses of rock sometimes occur a little at a place, in other places in large quantities; sometimes comminuted, in other localities are found large and small boulders lying along the surface—these fragments mostly resulting from mechanical agency acting upon the older rocks. At some places large and small boulders are found lying on the surface, but upon their removal and digging a few feet below the surface, a comminuted mass is exposed.

At Apos. Tucker's, in E. half Lot No. 3 of N. W. qr. Sec. 1, T. 33, R. 5 E., a well was dug 75 feet deep, and, as Mr. Tucker informed me, after removing a few feet of boulders and Clay near the top, he dug into a coarse Sand which extended to the bottom, when a fine stream of water was reached. The Sand thrown out seemed to be granitic.

On the east side of Sec. 32, T. 31, R. 8 E., the ground is covered over with Porphyry boulders to a depth of 1½ feet, under which was observed a fine-grained, variegated Potters' Clay. A quarter of a mile east there is a similar bed of coarser Clay covered with Cherty boulders—the Clay at each of the two last named places being entirely free from boulders.

In the Railroad cut, one mile north-west of Fredericktown, near the old Gholson place, we have:

No. 1. 8 feet red Soil and Clay.
No. 2. Beds of dark brown or black sandy Shale, with bands of buff sandy Shale resting on Magnesian Limestone.

A quarter of a mile south of the 103d mile post is seen:

No. 1. 4 feet Soil and red Clay.
No. 2. 4 feet red and dark sandy Shales.
No. 3. Bed of yellow Sandstone (Primordial).

At the 102d mile post are similar beds, but the Shales are dark reddish-brown. At each of the above Sections a considerable quantity of black Sand enters into the various beds of No. 2. This dark sandy bed, I regard as equivalent to that at Gholson's, and probably also at Hick's. It has a dull black appearance, and, under a magnifying glass, seems to be formed of minute, silicious grains, united by a black cement of Manganese and Iron.

Mr. North, in Sec. 19, T. 34, R. 6 E., dug 30 feet through Clays to black Sand, in which he found a fine stream of water.

At Hick's place there appears several feet of this bog ore in the soil, and at the old Gholson place, near Fredericktown, are found tumbled boulders of similar material.

An analysis of a specimen from Hick's, made by Mr. Chauvenet, gave:

Insoluble silicious matter ... . 56.82 per cent.
Peroxide of Iron .... 18.67 per cent.
Sesqui-oxide of Manganese... 14.24 per cent.
Water.. 3.19 per cent.
Traces of Lime and Magnesia.
Metallic Iron in above.. 13.07 per cent.
Metallic Manganese... 9.86 per cent.

ARCHÆAN ROCKS.

Previous to the deposition of the sedimentary rocks, the contour of this county presented alternations of high hills and mountain peaks with low depressions between, and the rocks presented to view were either varieties of Porphyry or of Granite and Syenite, with their various intrusive veins or dykes of Quartz, Greenstone, Dolerite or Specular Iron Ore; the Syenitic rocks being mostly in the northern part of the county and Porphyry towards the Southern. The mountain peaks, many of them, were elevated as much as 700 feet above the valleys, and it is even probable that, previous to the deposition of the unaltered sedimentary rocks, some may have towered to a height of 1,000 feet.

LIST OF ROCKS.

The following is a descriptive list of specimens of metamorphic rocks collected in 1871, the number preceding the description corresponding with that on label attached:

124, 125, 126—Railroad cut at 98th mile post. Very pretty, uniformly colored, fine-grained, dark gray Syenite. Under a magnifying glass are exhibited green spots, with flesh-colored Feldspar and black Hornblende.

127, 130, 131, 132—Near north county line, between Rock Creek and Musco. Dark, reddish gray Syenite, coarser than 124; contains red Feldspar, flesh-colored Quartz and black Hornblende.

129—Same locality as last. Very dark gray Porphyry, with crystals of red, flesh-colored and green Feldspar and dark colored Quartz; contains a little green mineral which is probably Epidote.

128—Same locality as last. Fine-grained, compact, dark red, jaspery Porphyry; resembles 160 and 174.

133, 134—At John Miller's, Sec. 29, T. 34, R. 6 E. Light red granitic rock, composed of coarse grains of Quartz and Feldspar.

135, 136, 137, 138—From N. side of Stout's Creek, Sec. 5, T. 33, R. 5 E. Coarse reddish gray Syenite similar to 134. Contains black Hornblende, red and flesh colored Feldspar and flesh colored Quartz.

139, 140, 141—N. E. qr. Sec. 6, T. 33, R. 6 E. Brownish gray coarse Granite. Contains red Feldspar, rose colored Quartz and silvery Mica. From a N. E. and S. W. vein, at this locality, can be obtained numerous Quartz crystals, of a variety of beautiful colors, viz.: rock crystal, yellow and amethystine.

142, 143—N. W. corner of S. W. qr. Sec. 1, T. 33, R. 5 E. Ferruginous Porphyry; contains a good deal of red Hematite and many fine grains of Quartz. Resembles 215.

144—S. W. qr. Sec. 2, T. 33, R. 5 E. Dark gray Syenite; contains black Hornblende, flesh colored Feldspar and limpid Quartz and Copper pyrites. This specimen is traversed by a blackish green band about 2 inches wide, blending into the surrounding rock. Similar Granite extends from this across the St. Francois River at the "Rapids," when it is traversed by a Dyke of Dolerite 44 inches wide, and bearing S. 60° W.

145, 146, 147, 148, are found in the same locality as the last; are Syenitic, with green mineral resembling Epidote.

149, 150, 151, 152, 153—N. W. of N. E. qr. Sec. 33, T. 34, R. 5 E. A very pretty red Granite or Granulite formed of pink colored Feldspar and limpid Quartz; has diffused through it innumerable shiny flakes of micaceous Iron ore.

154—From the Polk place. A very fine grained Syenitic Greenstone.

155, 156, 157—Top of Burns' Mountain. Deep red Porphyry with lighter red and flesh colored crystals of Feldspar; contains particles of clear Quartz and a green mineral resembling Epidote.

158—North end of Burns' Mountain. Porphyry resembling the last, but is vertically banded by lighter colored and minute quartzose parallel veins, in some of which found the similar green mineral of No. 157.

159—North end of Burns' Mountain. Porphyry also banded vertically and from long continued exposure presents rough, narrow ridges on the upper surface, bearing N. 30° E. magc. Similarly striated Porphyry was observed a half mile west, having the same bearing.

160—North end of Burns' Mountain. Porphyry somewhat resembling the above, but very compact and close grained. Color, a very dark shade of red, almost black; general appearance dark gray.

161—Tolers, 2 miles south of Fredericktown. Porphyry; color like 155, but darker and more crystalline; when magnified appears fine grained and of a similar color to 160.

162—Sec. 32, T. 31, R. 7 E., at Hoffman's. Porphyry; dark red, almost black, and very fine grained, red spotted with small grains of limpid Quartz and red Feldspar and a green mineral. Resembles 164, 165 and 182.

163—Near King's, on Mill Creek, S. W. corner of county. Porphyry; general appearance dark gray; when magnified looks dark red; contains light colored Feldspar and quartz.

164, 165—North end of Rock Creek Mountain. Porphyry; color very dark red; contains some bright red, pretty crystals of Feldspar and some pyrites.

166—Same locality. Pink Porphyry, with deeper colored crystals of Feldspar and small Quartz grains.

167—Same locality. Compact quartz; has stains of specular Iron. This is from a vein in the Porphyry, but its exact position could not be obtained.

168, 169, 170—Sec. 16, T. 33, R. 5 E., east side Blue Mountain. Porphyry; very fine grained; has beautiful wavy bands of light red and black. This is a beautiful rock.

171—Same locality. Black Porphyry; when magnified shows a faint red tinge; in texture and color resembles 160, but is darker.

172—E. hf. N. E. Sec. 15, T. 33, R. 5 E. Gray Porphyry; has light colored Quartz grains and red Feldspar.

173—Sec. 9, T. 31, R. 5 E. Deep red Porphyry; rich appearance, with white crystals of Feldspar.

174, 175—Sec. 15, T. 31, R. 7 E. Black (jaspery) Porphyry; when magnified shows shades of red; observed a little Quartz and a few minute Feldspar crystals. Resembles 162. This rock works freer than any Porphyry in the county, and could no doubt be quarried in good shape.

176 and 177—Sec. 20, T. 34, R. 6 E. Dark, greenish-gray Porphyry, compact, with large crystals and rounded pieces of Feldspar, and a few small particles of Pyrites.

178 and 179—5 miles east of Fredericktown. Dark-green Porphyry; resembles the last, but in this specimen the crystals are of green Feldspar and very minute. Contains a green mineral resembling Serpentine.

180—Sec. 15, T. 31, R. 8 E. Compact, very dark colored Porphyry. This is from a small peak, 110 feet high, surrounded by Slope, covered with Chert, from which were collected many fossils. The Porphyry, if indeed it can be so called, more resembles a dyke of metamorphosed rock; is 6 feet wide and 3 feet high and 50 feet long, bearing north 75 deg. west magnetic.

181. Dark-red, fine-grained Porphyry, with red and flesh-colored crystals of Quartz, and a green mineral resembling Epidote.

182—Sec. 9, T. 32, R. 6 E. Hard Porphyry; fine and coarse; contains red and flesh-colored crystals of Feldspar, and particles of limpid Quartz. Color deep red.

183 and 184—Sec. 15, T. 32, R. 6 E., adjacent to a dyke on Moudy & Michel's land. Very fine-grained, compact, black (jaspery?) Porphyry; very thin pieces show a faint reddish tinge; contains minute crystals of red Feldspar, and on an exposed joint in the rock are scales of Specular Iron; same locality as 188, 189, 190, 191, 192 and 193.

185—From Tin Mountain. Very coarse, dark-colored Greenstone.

186—Sec. 15, T. 33, R. 5 E. Coarse, dark Greenstone; resembles 185. This seems very abundant, strewn up and down the east side of Blue Mountain.

187—North end of Rock Creek Mountain. Fine-grained Greenstone.

188—Sec. 15, T. 32, R. 5 E, S. W. qr. of N. W. qr. Light Green rock, probably Epidote, having alternations of white spots, with a portion beautifully red tinged; same locality as 183.

189—Sec. 16, T. 32, R. 6 E. Coarse, dark-colored Greenstone; a little finer than 185. From west side of West Dyke.

190—Sec. 16, T. 32, R. 6 E. Dark-green Dolerite; contains a few small specks of Pyrites. West side of East Dyke.

191 and 192—Sec. 16, T. 32, R. 6 E. Coarse Greenstone; contains minute specks of Pyrites. From middle of East Dyke.

193—Sec. 16, T. 32, R. 6 E. Fine-grained Greenstone, resembling 187. From east side of East Dyke. The sketch (Fig. 8) illustrates the position of the various rocks in and adjacent to the dyke first spoken of. The course of the dyke bears S. 45 deg. W. The needle was so much affected that I had to hold my compass high in the air in order to get the course. From the sketch we perceive there are two parallel dykes, separated by a belt of Porphyry. On the west side of the East Dyke is a band of Dolerite, a few inches wide. The wall rock of Porphyry is very fine-grained, with a somewhat splintery fracture. The face of contact is smooth and true to a straight line as far as exposed.

194 and 195—Rapids of St. Francis River, S. E. qr. of S. W. qr. Sec. 2, T. 33, R. 5 E. Vein of hard, very fine-grained Dolerite, one inch wide, traversing Syenite. The Dolerite contains Pyrites. The Syenite contains red Feldspar and black Hornblende.

196, 197 and 198—Same location as last. Dolerite; coarser than the last; from dyke 44 inches wide; contains Pyrites. 198 is obliquely jointed.

199 and 200—Same location as last. Dark-reddish, gray Syenite; has light-red Feldspar, and dark Hornblende; part of a vein of Dolerite is attached.

201—Same location as last. Syenite, similar to that named above, but of a lighter color; resembles 144.

202, 203 and 204—Same location as last. Syenite, similar to 199 and 200. 202 shows dyke of Dolerite 4½ inches wide.

205, 206, 207 and 208—John Miller's, Sec. 29, T. 34, R. 6 E. Veinstones, with Specular Iron.

209—Daguerre Mountain. Dolerite, with Pyrite on Syenitic Slope. West end of Daguerre Mountain.

210—Same location as last. Dark-gray, fine-grained Feldspathic Porphyry; Feldspar is dark-red; contains Iron Pyrites. East end of mountain.

211—Same location as last. Quartzose Porphyry; color dark-reddish gray; contains crystals of Quartz and Feldspar. This is from near mountain top.

212 and 213—Same location as last. Black Porphyry, with lighter colored crystals of Feldspar, and some Quartz. Is hard and heavy; slightly resembles 262 and 182.

214—North-east end of Daguerre Mountain. Light-red Granulite ; very coarse ; is formed of red Feldspar and white Quartz.

215 to 220 inclusive—Raub's shaft, 2½ miles south of Fredericktown. Beautiful deep, rose-red Porphyry ; contains some Quartzose grains and a green mineral.

221, 222 and 223—Sec. 16, T. 33, R. 5 E. Coarse Greenstone ; somewhat resembles 191, but is not so dark a color.

124, 227 and 228—E½ of N. E. qr. Sec. 15, T. 33, R. 5 E, on land of Weightman and Waters. Greenstone ; coarse, dark-brown, very heavy.

229, 230, 231, 232, 235 and 224, 234—Same locality as last. Greenstone ; color dark-gray and brown ; said to contain Wolfram. These specimens are from a drift running into the hill-side about 200 feet, and about 50 feet deep at further end. There is said to be a Greenstone dyke 20 feet wide at this place, but it was covered up with debris from above. 236, 221, 224, 225, 226, 227, 228 are all from this locality.

233—Same locality as last. A dark-green, fibrous Hornblendic mineral attached to part of 186. This is from nearly a quarter of a mile east of last named locality.

237, 242, and 243—From shaft near Lloyd's, S. hf. N. E. qr. Sec. 15, T. 33, R. 5 E. White Quartzose rock, with long, slender, dark-green crystals disseminated.

238, 239, 240, 241, 246—Same locality as last. Similar but darker, color gray with green crystals (Actinolite?).

236 and 245—Same locality as last. Compact, white rock, resembling 237 ; but green crystals are wanting. 245 has small brown octahedral crystals of Iron ore, one-eighth inch in diameter.

244—Same locality as last. Resembles last ; general appearance dark. Contains milk-white, rounded particles of Quartz.

The rocks from 224 to 244 inclusive are all from the east half of N. E. quarter Sec. 15, T. 33, R. 5 E., on land of Weightman and Waters.

Near the south part are several shafts. That furthest south exposes a vertical wall or dyke of rock (No. 237, etc.,) 18 inches wide, and extending as deep as the shaft runs, which is about 15 feet, but it probably extends much deeper. The course of the dyke is about N. E. and S. W., and is surrounded by soft Granite or Greenstone Sand. Two hundred feet north-west another shaft has been dug displaying to view a similar dyke, about 2 feet wide and running about north and south. A quarter of a mile east is the Greenstone dyke (Nos. 186 and 233,) eight feet wide and bearing a little west of north. Several pits have been dug in this vicinity and from each one quantities of decomposed (Greenstone) Sand have been thrown out, and I was informed that black Sand had been panned out from it. In washings in the road, a short distance east, I collected black Sand, which proved on examination to be Magnetic Iron.

On waters of Captain's Creek, in Sec. 20, T. 32, R. 6 E., there appears a dyke of coarse Syenitic Greenstone about 75 feet wide, bearing a north and south course, and occasionally traversed by small Epidote veins. The adjacent rock is flesh colored Porphyry.

Two hundred yards west a shallow digging has exposed a deposit of Asbestos, but of its exact mode of occurrence I was unable to determine as the pit was filled up. Washings in the creek near,by show seams of Asbestos in Greenstone Sand.

A few hundred feet west a pit has been dug into Dolerite and Platinum has been reported to be found there, but specimens I submitted to Mr. Chauvenet for analysis did not prove its existence here.

On the Mine LaMotte tract, near the old Fleming dwelling, Sandrock is traversed by a dyke of Dolerite about 6 feet wide and prismatic, the prisms horizontal. The course of the dyke is N. 15° E. The Sandstone adjacent is altered to a Quartzite. On east side of dyke is a Porphyry which is somewhat altered near the dyke. The Porphyry is exposed up and down the branch for 200 feet. Further up and also opposite the dyke and on higher ground, the Sandstone appears unaltered and in horizontal layers.

Granite, from Einstein's property, in Sec. 13, T. 33, R. 5 E., is coarse reddish gray and contains black Hornblende. Some of the Granite in this vicinity is very much decomposed, but there are also extensive outcrops of superior Granite for building purposes. Good Granite quarries can be opened in many places in T. 34, Rs. 5 and 6 and in the N. E. part of T. 33, R. 5 E.

I would remark that the Porphyries, although they are often of a dark or black shade, will show a red tint under a magnifying glass.

PRIMORDIAL ROCKS.

The sedimentary rocks were deposited across the valleys between the mountains and hills. In the order of deposition, commencing at the oldest, we have 1st. Sandstone, Conglomerates and Shales. 2d. Marble beds. 3d. Gritstone beds with some beds of Magnesian Limestone. 4th. Magnesian Limestone. 5th. Chert beds. 6th. Sandstone—the last found on the hill-tops, and is probably the equivalent of the Second Sandstone of the Missouri Report. The Chert (5th,) and Sandstone (6th,) belong to the age of the Calciferous Sandrock. The Sandstone (1st,) and Marble (2d,) beds and Gritstone (3d,) are of Potsdam age.

THE LOWER SANDSTONE

Is mainly developed across the northern part of the county, in Ts. 33 and 34. It occurs either as a fine-grained white or buff Sandstone, or as a coarse brown or red Conglomerate. Near Gholson's, there appears about 45 feet of fine-grained white Sandstone, almost resting on the Granite, it being separated by 4 feet of a coarse red slaty Sandstone, as shown in the following section : (See Fig. 10.)

No. 1. Slope, red Clay and fragments of Quartz rock.

No. 2. 21 feet Magnesian Limestone.

No. 3. 18 feet Silicious Limestone.

No. 4. 23 feet Gritstone.

No. 5. 40 feet of Sandstone near point of contact with Granite, but where the Magnesian Limestone is seen, only 10 feet of Sandstone appears above the water.

No. 6. 4 feet red slaty Sandstone. (No. 13.)

No. 7. Granite.

Specimen (No. 102) of Sandstone, from 10 feet above the Granite is fine grained white with even texture and a few buff stains and minute brown specks. The lower, slaty red Sandstone specimen, marked 113, is very dark red and contains small Quartz pebbles. It has an irregular, hackly fracture and a somewhat slaty cleavage. The red beds are better developed further west. On Gravel road, at the crossing of Pine Creek, they are upwards of 20 feet thick, with alternations of the following described beds :

No. 1. Outcrop of yellow Sandstone on hill-top.

No. 2. 25 feet Slope, occasional outcrops of coarse Conglomerate.

No. 3. 10 inches fine-grained drab Sandstone.

No. 4. 3 feet brown and yellow soft Sandstone.

No. 5. 3 inches Sandstone, flesh drab with black specks.

No. 6. 2 inches coarse red Sandy bed.

No. 7. 8 inches yellow Sand.

No. 8. 2 inches light colored, coarse, soft Sandstone.

No. 9. 2 feet very dark red, soft Sandstone.

No. 10. 4 inches coarse yellow Sandstone.

No. 11. 2 feet coarse red Sandstone.

No. 12. 10 inches hard, coarse gray Sandstone.

No. 13. 8 inches dark red Shales.

No, 14. 6 inches firm bed of coarse Sandstone.

No. 15. 1 foot red Shale bed.

No. 16. 3 inches yellow soft Sandstone.

No. 17. 3 feet red Shales.

No. 18. 10 inches very coarse hard Sandstone.

No. 19. 3 feet red sandy Shales.

No. 20. 3 feet beds of red and drab Conglomerate.

No. 21. 3 feet red sandy Shales.

No. 22. 2 feet yellow Sandstone at foot of hill.

Total thickness of Section here is 50 feet 7 inches. Some of the

G.S—23.

red Sandstone˙contains scales of Mica. Specimens marked 115, 116 and 117 are from this locality.

North of David Rhodes, in Sec. 18, T. 33, R. 6 E., is a quarry of white and buff Sandstone. A part is a tolerably coarse buff with occasional imbedded small pebbles of igneous rocks and a few scattering scales of Mica. Other beds from the same quarry, are fine-grained white and drab, with scales of Mica sparingly diffused. Specimens marked 99, 100 and 101 are from this locality.

At Rhodes house, which is on lower ground, is a red Granite which rises into a high hill to the west. West of this, near St. Francois River, the conglomerate beds occupy the surface on hill-top, and northward, for two miles, are both Sandstone and conglomerate.

On west side of St. Francois River, in N. W. of N. E. quarter Sec. 33, T. 34, R. 5 E., there is exposed 65 feet of Sandstone and Conglomerate, resting directly on the Granite. The upper strata are deep red Porphyritic Conglomerates and Sandstones; the middle beds are fine-grained and the lower gray beds rest on the Granite and are almost cemented thereto. Specimens 114 and 118 are from this place. The underlying granulite is very coarse and just to the south rises high into the hills, cutting off the Conglomerate beds. The Sandstone and Conglomerate strip here is not over a quarter of a mile wide, east and west, and also extends but a short distance to the north.

West of Wachita is a strip, of probably a half mile in width, extending nearly to the north county line, of coarse, red and gray Conglomerate, composed of coarse pebbles of Porphyry and Granite, cemented together by a ferruginous material. This rests directly on the red Granite, which rises into elevated hills on the west. Specimens marked 111 and 112, are from this Conglomerate.

In S. E. of S. E. qr. Sec. 31, T. 34, R. 5 E., near the township line, there is a good quarry of Sandstone in thick even beds.

On Iron Mountain Railroad, at 101 mile post, the railroad cuts through 25 feet of soft, yellow Sandstone, jointed obliquely; the joints presenting as much as 12 feet of even surface. I collected some specimens from this (marked 107, 108, 109 and 110,) presenting beautiful bands of yellow and red. Some specimens from the " chimney stack," near by, appear to consist of a very pure, soft Sandstone of a beautiful pink color, spotted white and pink, with the sides presenting similarly colored bands. Specimens of this are marked 103, 104, 105, 106.

North-west of Mine LaMotte, the white Sandstone is about 90 feet in thickness. West of Rock Creek, near the county line, and just in St. Francois county, there is a remarkable lone Sandstone hill, called Castle Rock, about 200 feet across and about 50 feet high on the upper side, and 80 feet on the lower.

In the southern part of the county the lower Sandstone and Conglomerate beds are wanting, but their place is supplied by the

MARBLE BEDS.

These beds are entirely unknown in the northern tier of townships, and first appear in the southern part of T. 33. Fig. 11, on Twelve Mile Creek, on east side of Sec. 8, T. 31, R. 6 E., shows their relation to the beds above and below. The beds dip east with the lower resting on Porphyry.

The specimens collected here were :

No. 49. From the upper or silicious beds ; is a tolerably fine-grained, dull looking drab, having a small vein lined with crystals of Dolomite.

No. 50. From same place.

No. 51. Ferruginous, gray Marble, with splotch-like veins of coarser green and buff Magnesian Limestone.

No. 52. Decomposing Porphyry, forming a part of a shaly, Conglomerate beneath the Marble ; color variegated red, brown, green and buff.

No. 53. From same bed.

No. 54. Red, gray and dark-colored Porphyritic Syenite, contains some Horn blende, and is perpendicularly jointed.

This nucleus of Porphyry is not exposed over a few hundred feet across.

On the west side of St. Francois River, in Sec. 11, T. 31, R. 5 E., we have the following :

Section 5.

No. 1. Slope, with some oolitic Chert.

No. 2. 4 feet very fine-grained, close textured, dark-ash colored Magnesian Limestone. (No. 37.)

No. 3. 4 feet Magnesian Limestone, very ferruginous, slightly flesh-colored, inclining to drab, contains a green mineral. (Nos. 38, 39 and 40.)

No. 4. 5 feet very coarsely crystalline Magnesian Limestone, cellular; cells with brown lining. (No. 41.)

No. 5. 3 feet exceedingly fine-grained, silicious rock, color drab, faintly buff-banded. (No. 42.)

No. 6. 5 feet very coarse, heavy, buff-stained gray Magnesian Limestone. (No. 43.)

No. 7. 2 feet very fine-grained, somewhat white Magnesian Limestone, has minute cells of wavy form, which are buff-lined. (No. 44.)

No. 8. 4 feet very coarse Magnesian Limestone, with a dip of 22 deg. and course S., 65 deg. W.

No. 9. 20 feet MARBLE beds. (Nos. 45 and 46.)

The Marble here is a fine-grained, light-gray, with occasional disseminated specks of Calcite; is buff-stained on the coarser part; is
also faintly tinged with pink.

On west side of S. W. qr. Sec. 10, T. 32, R. 6 E. :

Section 2.

No. 1. Cherty Slope.

No. 2. 10 feet light-gray, fine-grained Magnesian Limestone, green and buff-
        stained, some beds are whitish.

No. 3. 10 feet outcrops of Marble.

This is a very fine-grained, light-gray Marble with buff stains
(Specimens No. 36.)

No. 35. This is a light-gray, fine-grained Marble, with coarse, buff
stains, very closely resembles No. 36. Locality, Sec. 9, T. 31, R. 5 E.

The best exposure of Marble is on land of Cooper heirs, Cedar
Creek; about 8 feet in thickness as seen; and as it does not perceptibly dip, it probably underlies most of the tract. It occurs in even
layers of a prevailing red color, but always variegated with buff or
white, with occasional spots of Carbonate of Lime, with clear specks,
and spots of the same. Some layers contain minute particles of limpid
Quartz; other beds are coarse, sub-crystalline, colored red and white,
the colors arranged in obscure, broken bands, parallel to the surface
of deposit. The white colors are coarser, but purer Calcite than the
red. Some other layers are finely compact, traversed by reticulated
veins of gray Calcite; others blend beautifully from a drab and flesh-
colored to peach blossom tint. Other variegated Marble beds are found
in Sec. 13, T. 32, R. 5 E.; also in Sec. 35, at Shut-in, on Morris Creek,
and variegated beds in Sec. 34, T. 32, R. 5 E.

GRITSTONE BEDS.

In the above Sections, including the Marble beds, Gritstone is but
thinly represented, and only by a few feet of very fine-grained, silicious rock. Near Fredricktown the silicious beds are much thicker.
The lower beds are represented by strata composed of numerous minute, round silicious grains cemented together.

Fig. 10 shows the lower Magnesian Limestone, Gritstone, Sandstone and Granite, and is more particularly described as follows:

No. 1. 21 feet hard, dark, ash-blue Magnesian Limestone.

No. 2. 18 feet hard, coarse-grained, silicious Limestone.

No. 3. 23 feet Gritstone beds, mostly in thick even strata.

No. 4. Coarse, white Sandstone in creek.

One mile north of Fredericktown, near the railroad, the Gritstone beds were observed 18 feet thick in even strata ranging from 2 inches to 2 feet in thickness—the lower beds the thinnest. In the upper strata are drusy cavities with small and pretty white crystals of Dolomite. I also observed small veins of Calcite and Dolomite, and on one specimen minute crystals of Quartz and particles of Sulphuret of Copper. The rock is generally fine-grained, close-textured, formed of minute round grains of Quartz disseminated in a very compact, hard paste of Magnesian Limestone; color is a light gray or whitish. Nos 75 to 92 are from this quarry. This rock affords a good building material, is mostly very hard, firm and strong, and but little acted upon by exposure.

LINGULA GRITS.

Nos. 61 to 75 inclusive, except 62, are from the bluffs on the north side of Brewer's Creek, and represented by a thin-bedded, brown calciferous Sandrock, abounding in a small species of Lingula (*Lingulella lamborni*—Meek), and also containing small Quartzose pebbles and crystals.

No. 66. Under the last there rests a dark ash-blue Magnesian Limestone containing small crystals of Galena. A Section I made close by, in 1858, is thus:

No. 1.   15 feet Slope from hill-top; outcrop of white Sandstone.
No. 2.   9 feet coarse gray Sandstone.
No. 3.   5 feet coarse drab Sandstone.
No. 4.   11 feet buff silicious Limestone, in thick beds.
No. 5.   5 feet thin-bedded drab Limestone; resembles the last.
No. 6.   9 feet Sandstone, alternating with coarse conglomerate beds; some porphyritic pebbles.
No. 7.   42 feet Slope to bottom.

No. 5 of this Section may be the Lingula bed.

No. 56. At railroad bridge, one mile north of Fredericktown, we have 9 feet of very dark blue, hard, heavy, close and fine-grained Magnesian Limestone. A few small Quartzose pebbles were observed adhering to the outer surface; also, a little green Carbonate of Copper. These beds repose on the Gritstone. Some remains of fossils were observed, among which were *Lingulella lamborni, Orthoceras*, a turbinated *Gasteropod*, a coral resembling in cross section a *Zaphrentis*, and small reniform bodies winding irregularly through the rock, in some places leaving an empty reniform passage less than a quarter of an inch in diameter. Specimens 56 to 62 are from this locality.

MAGNESIAN LIMESTONES.

The various beds of rock previously described may be of an older age than the Third Magnesian Limestone formation. The fossils and low position in the geological series indicate that they are of the age of the Potsdam Sandstone.

We come now to speak more particularly of that group which includes all the other Magnesian Limestones seen in the county. This, together with the overlying Chert beds, may be referred to one and the same group.

The lower beds near Fredericktown, lying above the Gritstone and *Lingula* beds, are mostly of a coarse gray or whitish color, sometimes with stains of buff or green, and contain a good deal of Calcite.

On the Bloomfield road, two miles from Fredericktown, there is a very good quarry of even-bedded, flesh-colored, faintly banded, fine-grained Magnesian Limestone. Specimens marked 20, 21 and 22 are of this.

On the Greenfield road, one mile south of Fredericktown, we pass over thick beds of dark, coarse Magnesian Limestone, good for building purposes. This rock resembles the fossil beds described on page 357. Three-quarters of a mile south, the road passes over a broad exposure of a brownish drab, porous Magnesian Limestone, worn very rough on top and intersected by numerous north and south parallel fissures, and dipping about south at an angle of 5°. Specimens are marked 17, 18 and 19.

A half mile south, in Mr. Toler's field, we find a coarse, gray Magnesian Limestone, intersected by veins of Calcite and closely resembling the rocks at Fredericktown. A small Porphyry hill is exposed 100 feet south, and about 200 yards down a creek to the west is a ledge of very pretty white, inclining to flesh-color, Magnesian Limestone. Still further west a few hundred feet, and just beyond a ravine, we approach another hill of Porphyry. Porphyry also occurs on west side of creek.

We, therefore, conclude that these Magnesian Limestones must be very near the base of the series.

After passing over mostly high Chert ridges to Geo. Birch's, in W. half of N. W. qr. Sec. 34, T. 33, R. 6 E., we find Magnesian Limestones resembling those at Fredericktown—coarse, light gray with buff spots, and veins and particles of Calc Spar.

On the head of Matthews' Creek, at John Boswell's, in N. E. qr. Sec. 34, T. 33, R. 6 E., there is an outcrop of a dark, close-grained Magnesian Limestone.

Passing south, over high Chert ridges, to corner of Secs. 3, 4, 9 and 10, Magnesian Limestone is seen in horizontal strata.   Just west is a hill of dark red Porphyry.

On west side of Sec. 10, the Magnesian Limestone beds appear above the Marble.   Passing across a low divide to waters of Trace Creek, thence along its valley to Barton Berry's, we find a coarse, white Magnesian Limestone (No. 33) near the water, and is the highest Limestone seen on Trace Creek.   The hills above seem to be mostly formed of Chert.

In Sec. 17, T. 31, R. 6, E., on Twelve-mile Creek, the low, whitish beds are very thick.   This place was noticed in 1858, and also in 1871, and the following Section taken :

No. 1.   16 feet Slope—Chert and Magnesian Limestone.

No. 2.   Magnesian Limestone ; coarse, open texture, buff and gray ; below is close-grained and finer ; some is green-tinged, and has small cells containing minute dolomitic crystals ; weathers in rough points sticking upward.

No. 3.   22 feet bed of close-textured, fine-grained, gray Magnesian Limestone ; part has a flesh-colored tinge ; forms a perpendicular escarpment.

Specimens from here, numbered 29, 30 and 31, seem to be nearly pure Dolomites.

No. 28 is from a similar bed on Twelve-mile Creek, below White's.

On the west side of St. Francois River, near the county line, we find a coarse, light gray Magnesian Limestone.

Similar Limestone was found at the foot of a porphyry hill at Hoffman's, on Big Creek.

The lowest rock observed on Mill Creek, above the porphyry, in the south-west part of T. 31, R. 5, E., is a fine-grained, silicious Magnesian Limestone, resembling No. 42, and is of a drab color, inclining to buff.   It may be equivalent to a part of the Grit-stone series. Similar specimens were collected from Sec. 9, T. 31, R. 5, E., from beds occurring a little ways above the Marble.

At Richardson's, on Mowser's Creek, on the west slope of Meyer's Mountain, Magnesian Limestone resembling that described on page 357, dips 15° from the hill.

The Limestones we have been speaking of, may all be referred to the Potsdam Group.

THIRD MAGNESIAN LIMESTONE.

We now come to speak of rocks still higher in the series.

On N. E. S. E. Sec. 18, T. 31, R. 6, E, several pits have been dug
for Lead, and a few fragments found.   The section here made in
1858, is :

  No. 1.   84 feet Chert Slope.
  No. 2.   11 feet coarse Magnesian Limestone, with small, drusy cavities, lined
            with Quartz.
  No. 3.   21 feet, including :
                        1—5 feet, many Quartz crystals.
                        2—5 feet hard Silicious rocks.
                        3—Sandy Limestone.
                        4—Compact Magnesian Limestone.
  No. 4.   Compact drab Magnesian Limestone, in a valley.

On the bluffs of St. Francois River, west of Sec. 3, and across a
ravine half a mile west, we find about 100 feet of mostly thick-
bedded, fine-grained, dark, ash-colored Magnesian Limestone ; the
upper beds coarse, with buff spots; and the slope above is covered
with Chert and agatized Quartz.

On Gimlet Creek, near the centre of Sec. 23, T. 31, R. 7, E., there
is a coarse, drab Magnesian Limestone, with drusy cavities of milky
Quartz.

On Shutley's Creek, at Rickman's, we have :

  No. 1.   127 feet Slope, with Chert on top.
  No. 2.   4 feet light-colored, coarse Magnesian Limestone.
  No. 3.   5 feet coarse-grained, gray, heavy Magnesian Limestone, nearly a
            pure Dolomite. (Specimen marked No. 9.)
  No. 4.   11 feet light gray, coarse Magnesian Limestone ; contains a good
            deal of Chert.
  No. 5.   10 feet, mostly Chert, with some Magnesian Limestone.
  No. 6.   6 feet coarse, gray Magnesian Limestone.
  No. 7.   38 feet Chert and Magnesian Limestone.
  No. 8.   6 feet mostly dark-colored Magnesian Limestone.

Specimens 1 to 9 are from this section; 6, 7 and 8 are from the
lower portion.

No. 6 is compact, buff Magnesian Limestone, traversed by veins
of Chert and Dolomite ; joints show beautiful, aborescent, dendritic
impresssions.

No. 7 is very fine-grained, light, drab, silicious Magnesian Limestone.   One side is covered with minute crystals of white Quartz.   It
is also traversed by very minute veins lined with exceedingly minute
crystals of Quartz.

No. 8 is tolerably fine-grained Magnesian Limestone, slightly crystalline, and contains numerous small wavy cells, which are generally lined with minute white Quartz crystals.

Similar beds occur on Castor River, in Ts. 31 and 32. The following, east of Rhodes', in S. E. qr. Sec 36, T. 31, R. 7 E.

No. 1. 46 feet Chert Slope, contains *Straparollus*, *Orthis*, etc.

No. 2. 45 feet Magnesian Limestone ; fine-grained, somewhat flesh-colored, with small drusy Quartz cavities, and interstratified with Chert in lower part.

On west side of Castor River, in S. W. qr. Sec. 15, T. 31, R. 5 E., Magnesian Limestone, occurring near base of hill, has foliated Quartz crystalizations. On west side of Castor, opposite Geo. Whitener's, our Section shows :

No. 1. 111 feet Slope; some Sandstone near the top, with Chert below ; some of it oolitic and some containing holes of irregular waved outlines.

No. 2. 10 feet dark, coarse Magnesian Limestone.

No. 3. Chert and Quartz crystals on Slope.

No. 4. 2½ feet bed of wavy cellular Chert.

No. 5. 36 feet sandy textured, ashy-gray, coarse Magnesian Limestone.

Specimen marked 10 is from No. 5, and is Magnesian Limestone, to which is attached a mammillary-shaped nucleus of Agate, covered with an aggregation of small, bright Quartz crystals. The Agate bands are of different colors ; the inner white, then a green shade with outer white. A cross section shows beautiful interlocking of crystals at the sinus.

Another Section, taken near this in 1858, is as follows :

Section 15.

No. 1. 111 feet Slope, with Chert, Quartz crystals and oolitic Chert and porous Chert.

No. 2. 16 feet Cherty Slope, with beautiful crystals of rose Quartz.

No. 3. 48 feet Chert Slope.

No. 4. 1 foot bed of Chert.

No. 5. 7 feet close-grained, sandy-textured, gray and drab Magnesian Limestone, with Quartz.

No. 6. 5 feet close-grained Magnesian Limestone ; upper part bluish drab, below buff.

No. 7. 10½ feet somewhat flesh-colored Magnesian Limestone; upper part close and hard, below soft.

No. 8. 7 feet Chert beds, with a few thin beds of gray Magnesian Limestone.

No. 9. 6 feet very coarse, gray Magnesian Limestone.
No. 10. 3 feet drab colored, ashy looking Limestone.
No. 11. 11 feet light-gray Magnesian Limestone.
No. 12. 5 feet brownish gray, coarse Magnesian Limestone.
No. 13. 9½ feet—resembles the last, but somewhat porous.
No. 14. 11 feet Slope to Castor.
No. 15. Magnesian Limestone, with Quartz like No. 5.

At Section, corner of Secs. 16 and 9, T. 32, R. 8 E., the Porphyry approaches close to stream, from each side, forming a "shut-in."

A short distance up river, from the "shut-in," at John Robbin's, the rock is a flesh-colored Magnesian Limestone. The railroad cut just west of Castor exposes a fine-grained, even-bedded and sometimes banded Magnesian Limestone.

On Castor, a half mile below the mouth of Berry's Creek, is a dark, bluish-gray Magnesian Limestone; contains a pulverulent powder. The following Section was taken in N. E. qr. Sec. 20, T. 32, R. 8 E:

No. 1. Slope, Chert and drusy Quartz.
No. 2. 33 feet close-grained, flesh-colored Magnesian Limestone; weathers in very rough small peaks on upper surface.
No. 3. 6 feet slightly flesh-colored Magnesian Limestone, a little coarser than the last.
No. 4. 7 feet—resembles the last.
No. 5. 22 feet very close-grained, grayish, cavernous Magnesian Limestone.
No. 6. 5 feet coarse-grained Magnesian Limestone.
No. 7. 27 feet coarse, gray Magnesian Limestone; upper part darker, middle whitish.

On east side of Castor, in Sec. 21, T. 33, R. 8 E., we have.

No. 1. 56 feet heavy, hard, vitreous looking Magnesian Limestone; color ash gray, shaded with brown.
No. 2, 5 feet Magnesian Limestone.
No. 3. 5½ feet—resembles No. 1; has green and brown shades and contains Dolomite crystals.

At water's edge, near crossing of Jackson road, we find an outcrop of dark colored Magnesian Limestone.

The following Section shows the rocks on East Trace Creek, near county line:

No. 12.

No. 1. 72 feet Slope; some Sandstone and a good deal of Chert, some is cellular with fossils.
No. 2. 3 feet drab Magnesian Limestone.

No. 3. 16 feet bed of cherty Magnesian Limestone; some outer beds of Chert; some of it with beautiful green striæ.

No. 4. 14 feet Slope.

No. 5. 4 feet coarse, buff Magnesian Limestone.

No. 6. 2 feet Slope.

No. 7. 11 feet drab, inclining to buff, coarse Magnesian Limestone.

No. 8. 6 feet thinly-bedded, brittle, silicious Magnesian Limestone.

No. 9. 3 feet Slope to water in creek.

Specimens from Chert bed east of Castor, in T. 31; the bed is equivalent to No. 4 of Section described on page 361, has a wavy outline and open texture as if formed of numerous thin laminæ appressed and united into one bed, sometimes leaving open spaces between the laminæ, which are often incrusted with Quartz crystals.

In the above descriptive Sections we have no record of the Magnesian Limestone reaching higher than 100 feet above the streams. On St. Francois, near Leatherwood, we find it about 100 feet thick; on Twelve mile Creek, about 70 feet; Shutley Creek, 80 feet; East Trace Creek, 59 feet; Castor, in several places, 50 to 75 feet, and at one place 100 feet. Scattered over the hills above is found

CHERT.

Owing to such immense quantities scattered loose over the surface, it is impossible to say what its exact thickness may be, but probably between 100 and 200 feet. On ridge on Bloomfield road, 6 miles S. E. Fredericktown, we find occasional outcrops of hard white Silicious rock sticking up in amorphous masses for several feet. Similar cherty masses and ledges lie along the hills near Trace Creek, near Barton Berry's. From the top down for 153 feet are occasional Chert outcrops; oolitic Chert near the top, with heavy outcrops of Quartz rock and Mammillary and agatized Crystals below. From this down to where the Magnesian Limestone crops out there is 130 feet Slope, covered with Chert and Quartz. The hills and hill sides are covered with large masses of Chert and Silicious rocks, and there seems to be no doubt that the silicious and Chert beds are at least 100 feet thick, and may be 150 feet. On Shutley Creek we have 127 feet of Cherty Slope to top of Limestone beds. On Castor, near Geo. Whitener's, 176 feet Slope, with oolitic Chert near top, and numerous crystalized forms of drusy Quartz and loose masses of Chert strewn along the surface. In Sec. 23, T. 34, R. 7 E., and for 2 miles west and east, towards Castor, the hills are covered with compact and oolitic Chert.

The tops of all the ridges in the county, where there is no porphyry or Granite, are covered with Chert.

Fossils were collected from the following localities from the Chert:

Sec. 19, T. 34, R. 8 E. *Straparollus* and *Murchisonia.*

Sec. 16, T. 33, R. 8, E., *Maclurea*, etc.

Sec. 17, T. 31, R. 5 E., *Straparollus, Orthis, Orthoceras* on hill top.

Sec. 33, T. 31, R. 8 E., a few fossils from Chert.

Sec. 15, T. 31, R. 8. The Chert contains numerous fossils, *Ortho-ceras* (fine spec.) *Maclurea, Straparollus——, Euomphalus Capulus* (fine spec.)

Sec. 33, T. 32, R. 8, E., *Straparollus* in oolitic Chert.

Sec. 26, T. 33, R. 6 E.

Sec. 36, T. 31, R. 7, *Straparollus, Orthis ;* etc.

Sec. 29, T. 32, R. 6, *Straparollus.* These fossils are evidently typ-ical of the Calciferous Sandrock.

Specimens marked 93, 94 and 95, are oolitic Chert from top of these beds. No. 93 is very pretty when magnified. The oolites are white, regularly rounded with small pit in the center. One side is worn, cutting the oolites in two, but not displacing them· In No. 94 some oolites have a solid center, with space separating it from the periphery. In Nos. 95 and 96, we find many oolites cemented into a flattened mass, in which the oolites are scarcely distinguishable.

SECOND SANDSTONE.

Occasional masses of white or gray sandstone, sometimes soft, but more often hard, are found near the tops of the cherty ridges. It was only recognized in south and east part of the county, was rarely found in T. 31, R. 5. E., many masses are found on ridges between Big Creek and Castor ; also east of Castor, near south-east corner of the county, it occurs at a good many places. I there found it containing a species of *Enomphalus.* Specimens marked 230 and 121 were collec-ted from Chert ridge, north-west of Burns' Mountain, and about 150 feet below the mountain top. Specimen No. 119 was collected from hills east of Castor, in T. 33, and is a fine-grained indurated Sandstone, on one side studded with minute crystals of Quartz. This also shows a beautiful example of mudcracks.

Upon recapitulating, we find the various rocks to foot up thick-nesses as follows :

Calciferous	Third Mag. Limestone.	Chert beds............................... 125 feet.
Sandrock.		Magnesian Limestone, Chert and Quartz 100 feet.
		Lower Magnesian Limestone, probably 125 feet.
	Lead bearing.	Gritstone and *Lingula* beds............. 50 feet.
Potsdam.		Marble beds......................5 to 20 feet.
		Sandstone and Conglomerate beds, 5 to 90 feet.

The above does not include the second Sandstone overlaying all, but whose thickness I could not exactly find, probably 20 feet.

MINERAL DEPOSITS.

The following is a brief notice of certain mineral deposits :

IRON ORE.

In W. half N. W. qr. Sec. 34, T. 33, R. 6 E., quantities of brown Hematite lie strewn over the surface. At Geo. Birch's, near by, there is a small Chalybeate spring.

On land of Chas. W. Creasy, in S. E. of S. E. Sec. 36, T. 31, R. 5 E., near county line, red and brown Hematite ores are both found. The red seems more silicious, occurs in a Sandstone and in brecciated Chert ; the brown is massive and sometimes stalactitic in form. The hill here is 187 feet high—Magnesian Limestone cropping out at 75 feet above the base. A thick growth of pines covers the hill.

On Jacob Hoffman's land, on west side of Big Creek, one mile north of south county line, large masses of brown Hematite are found lying in a ravine at the foot of a porphyry hill.

On land of Eli Hovis, in Sec. 29, T. 31, R. 7 E., was observed a good deal of brown Hematite ; some fibrous but mostly massive, some ochrey, some associated with angular fragments of Chert, and some with Sandstone. Same Sandstone shows mud cracks on the surface.

At the old Shutley place, east of Castor, we have :

No. 1. 68 feet cherty Slope ; some fragments of brown Hematite.

No. 2. 53 feet masses of Sandstone, Chert and fragments of Iron ore.

No. 3. 42 feet Slope ; large masses of brown Hematite ; a good deal of Chert, some porous and wavy.

Many masses of Iron ore lie strewn along the ravine. The Sandstone is undoubtedly the Second, and the upper Chert beds may be

beds of passage from Second Sandstone to Third Magnesian Limestone.

There are other places in the Castor Hills where Iron ore seems
quite abundantly diffused.

Brown Hematite is rather abundant at several localities near south
line of county, in T. 31, 7 E.

On Jackson road, six miles east of Fredericktown, was observed
a pit, 4 feet deep, passing through Chert, white and reddish Quartz,
and red Clay. Iron ore was the object of the digging, but none seems
to have been found.

On the same road, three miles from Fredericktown, I observed
many quite large masses of brown Hematite.

At Toler's, two and a half miles south of Fredericktown, washings
in a ravine disclose many masses of a cellular Iron ore mingled with
a soft, ferruginous Clay, and resting on Magnesian Limestone. A little
over a quarter of a mile south are found masses of brown Hematite.
Iron ore is only occasionally found on Powell Callaway's land, one
mile south-east of Toler's.

On a ridge in S. W. qr. Sec. 1, T. 33, R. 5 E., a pit has been dug
into a very ferruginous porphyritic rock.

In Lot No. 3 of N. E. qr. Sec. 6, T. 33, R. 6 E., there seems to be a
good deal of Specular Iron ore on the surface.

On John Miller's land, in Sec. 29 (?), T. 34, R. 6 E., there is a Vein-
stone with Specular Iron. The thickness of the vein could not be
ascertained, but it seemed rather irregular, judging from the appearance of specimens, and is probably less than 2 feet. The vein could
be traced in another ravine bearing N. 15° W., about 200 yards off.
The wall rock is red Syenite.

The old Koch shaft is located on E. half of S. W. qr. Sec. 13, T. 33,
R. 5 E., on land now belonging to Einstein. It is probably 20 years
since it was dug. It was sunk in a Quartz vein and some mineral removed, but at present there are few specimens to be seen on the
ground excepting fragments of Quartz with a little Iron Pyrites attached. In no specimens that I obtained could any valuable mineral
be detected, but Gold and Tungsten are both reported to have been
obtained. The adjacent rock is a reddish gray Syenitic Granite.

At Mrs. King's, in S. W. S. E. Sec. 11, T. 35, R. 5 E., a shaft, 10 feet
in depth, revealed a rich vein of Specular Iron bearing N. E. The surrounding rock is a decomposed granitic Sand. The ore analyzed by
Mr. Chauvenet gave:

Insoluble silicious matter... .... 4.84 per cent.
Peroxide of Iron... 94.18   " "
Metallic Iron.. 65.93   " "

Washings in a gulley near by bring to the surface a good deal of black Sand.

"Black Sand" is found in considerable quantities at several places, among which are the north and east side of Daguerre Mountain, north side of Blue Mountain, in Sec. 19, T. 34, R. 5 E , the eastern part of Sec. 15, T. 33, R. 5 E., and in Sec. 1, T. 33, R. 5 E., also four miles west of Fredericktown and on head of Captain's Creek. At Mr. North's, black Sand was found in a well at 30 feet below the surface.

Specimens examined prove it to be magnetic Specular Iron.

An imaginary line being drawn, commencing at north end of Rock Creek Mountain (where we find Rock Crystal), thence crossing at rapids of St. Francois River at Dolerite Dyke, in Sec. 2, T. 33, R. 5 E., (where Quartz is also found), passing north-east by Quartz vein, in N. E. Sec. 6, T. 33, R. 6 E., thence to Mine LaMotte. Another imaginary line, beginning near Lloyd's, in N. E. Sec. 15, T. 33, R. 5 E., passes direct by Bucholz Mine, in Sec. 11, crossing at St. Francois Rapids, thence near Quartz vein, in Sec. 6, T. 33, R. 6 E., to vein at John Miller's, in Sec. 29, T. 34, R. 6 E.

LEAD.

The Lead mines are more fully described by Dr. Norwood, p. 371, et seq., and Mr. Gage, in his report.

The Lead bearing rock at the Fox Mines, at the O'Bannon place, is a clearly crystalline bluish gray Magnesian Limestone, with many drusy cavities. These cavities are generally lined with Dolomite crystals. The Galena, when present, generally reposes on the Dolomite, Iron pyrites on the Galena, and also on Dolomite. Calcite is also common.

The working shaft is 50 feet deep. Some mineral was found at 14 feet, but mainly below 44 feet depth. Borings were made at numerous places on the tract, some as deep as 90 feet, and Lead mineral found in all. The boring all pass through bluish Magnesian Limestone and Gritstone, thence through a coarse, gritty Sandstone to Porphyry. (See Gage's report and Dr. Norwood's report on p. —-.)

A half mile north, the Sandstone crops out, and is of a coarse, Quartzitic appearance.

Just south of the mines Porphyry appears. The loose, siliceous Limestone beds of these mines occasionally inclose small particles of reddish Porphyry.

MINE LA MOTTE.

Borings one mile north of the chief mines revealed—

No. 1. 80 feet Magnesian Limestone.
No. 2. 63 feet Sandstone.
No. 3. Granite.

The formations at Mine La Motte appear thus:

No. 1. 5 feet red surface Clays.
No. 2. 6 feet deep brown Ochre; probably decomposed Limestone.
No. 3. 22 feet hard, close-grained bluish gray Magnesian Limestone—cap
      rock; contains many small Quartz particles. After long exposure
      they appear studded over the surface of the Limestone, and the
      latter becomes a deep brown.
No. 4. 7 feet coarse or finely crystalline light gray or whitish vitreous
      Lead bearing rock.

At the old Copper mines, the Lead bearing rocks rest against a Porphyry hill on the west, and in the branch, a short distance below the washing rooms, a coarse Sandstone appears.

A sample of Galena from these mines gave, on examination by Mr. Chauvenet,

Copper.. none.
Nickel.. 1.68 per cent.
Cobalt.. .63 " "

Galena with "Gangue," from Neidner's shaft, Mine La Motte, gave,

Lead (metallic).. 63.53 per cent.
Copper.. trace.
Nickel.. 4.26 per cent.
Cobalt.. 1.42 "
Iron present.. (Fe. S_2.)

A sample of Galena from the Jack Diggings gave no trace of either Copper, Nickel or Cobalt.

A Nickel ore from same mines, gave,

Copper.. 2.04 per cent.
Nickel.. 2.27 "
Cobalt.. 1.66 "

Iron present, with traces of Lead: the metals present a Sulphides —no Arsenic revealed. Specimens of ore from Fox's Mines, submitted to Mr. Chauvenet, did not reveal any Nickel.

Near John Revel's, north of Burns' Mountain, some attempts at mining have been recently prosecuted in a hard, crypto-crystalline, dark red Porphyry, in search of Silver. There are 3 obscure veins, with a course of N. 10° E., passing parallel in the Porphyry, and about 8 feet apart. They are 2 inches more or less in thickness. The easternmost one is a dark bluish gray Veinstone, containing many small cubes of Iron pyrites disseminated.

Other minerals observed in the veins were Galena and Zinc blende. The Galena are mostly in the western vein. Its analysis by Mr. Chauvenet gave,

Silver... 4 oz. to the ton (2000 lbs.
Lead... 12.84 per cent.

Mr. Chauvenet says: "If the ore could be concentrated it would contain about 30 oz., or even more, of silver to the ton." The vein is too minute at present to work with profit, and I could see no probability of its increasing to paying dimensions.

GRAY'S MOUNTAIN

Lies partly in Madison and partly in Wayne county. It curves around from Sec. 33, T. 31, R. 5, southward, into Secs. 4, 9, 16 and 17, of T. 30, R. 5. Crane Pond Creek and Big Creek wash it on the west, Big Creek separating it from Logan Mountain which seems to rear itself very high opposite and across the stream. Several varieties of Porphyry, Greenstone and other Archæan rocks are found. High Chert hills appear just east of its eastern extremity.

In Sec. 4, T. 30, R. 5 E., from a shaft, or rather pit, 8 or 10 feet deep, we procured a red Porphyritic conglomerate and grayish rock with pyrites. Some red Shales are also found here. This pit was dug in search of Nickel.

In the valley south, in Sec. 9, T. 30, R. 5 E., we found dark Porphyry, weathers gray; when fractured appears black, but magnified, shows dark red, with flesh colored crystals of Feldspar and feldspathic bands or striae; weathers in gray bands and is very fine grained. Two other specimens of coarse rock from the same locality have a variegated gray appearance, and contain Quartz and a deep purple colored mineral. On Crane Pond Creek, just north of Gray's Mountain, in Sec. 7, T. 30, R. 5 E., we find a hard, very fine grained, pretty, dark but bright red Porphyry, containing small particles of Quartz and a green mineral. At this locality a dyke of coarse, very hard, tough, heavy Greenstone crosses the creek. This rock contains black Hornblende and greenish shaded white Feldspar, and granules of Iron pyrites, and a greenish hornblendic mineral.

On the west end of Gray's Mountain, in Sec. 17, T. 30, R. 5 E., Porphyry—fine grained, splits free, containing compact Feldspar and small granules of Quartz, and a little greenish mineral; color is variegated, black and dark red. A specimen shows small parallel wavy bands, and contains minute yellow specks. One specimen, very compact shows beautiful green crystals of Feldspar, and the rock in variegated shades of light and dark red, with irregular green bands.

From the same locality we have a green, slaty rock (Talcose slate?) It was strewn along up and down the mountain for a width of 20 or 30 feet, but did not see it in place for that width.

Careful examinations of this mountain may result in much interest.

ABSTRACT OF NOTES ON MADISON COUNTY.

BY DR. J. G. NORWOOD.

FRANK O'BANNON'S QUARRY.

The rock here is fine-grained, drab and bluish drab Sandstone ; shaly for an inch or more in the bed planes; rather soft; easily worked. Beds exposed, from 3 to 8 inches thick. Entirely free from joints. Flag stones of bluish tinge, and of any size from 2½ to 3 and 4 inches thick (the thin beds having many fucoidal markings on their surface,) may be obtained. Rock dips S. 25° E., at an angle of 5°. This quarry affords beds of excellent Grit, suitable for grindstones and whetstones.

On O'Bannon's farm a shaft was sunk through Soil, Sandstone, and hard blue Grit-stone, for 47 feet, down to Granite, in search of a Lead vein. The blue Grit-stone has Pyrites scattered through it; and at the bottom of the shaft, brecciated conglomerate, with Fe. S., and apparently Cu. S. and Ni. S.

East and west seams of Galena occur in Sandrock in the bed of the creek below O'Bannon's house.

Frank O'Bannon says he took 300 pounds of Galena from a hole dug a few feet deep in the Sandstone, near where I saw that mineral in fissures.

A section of rocks on the old O'Bannon place shows:

Soil.
Magnesian Limestone (mineral bearing).
Yellow and drab Sandstone.
Blue Grit.
Granite.

NOTE.—The present Fox mines are on O'Bannon's land.

After leaving the village of Symmestown, north of Mine La Motte, Sandstone shows itself all the way to Rock Creek. It is dark drab and yellow, and many of the beds coarse-grained.

At the cave near the old slag furnace, is a granite "dyke" about 40 feet in width, bearing N. E. and S. W., and traversed by a Trap dyke 7 feet wide, bearing N. 15° E.

The overlying Sandstone is not disturbed; the lower 15 feet is shaly; above that it occurs in rather thick beds, and coarse-grained. It extends into St. Francois county, and forms the strata upon which Castle Rock rests.

From the St. Francois county line to Mine LaMotte, the surface shows no rock but Sandstone, with a Granite knoll at one point. The white Sandstone at Mine LaMotte, is probably the equivalent of Frank O'Bannon's quarry beds.

PHILADELPHIA MINE, OR OLD COPPER MINES.

About 100 yards below the opening of the old adit, the Sandstone dips east at an angle of 12° to 13°. (No. 1). About 50 yards higher up, a bed of Magnesian Limestone crops out—a few feet only exposed. (No. 2). In a ravine west of the opening of the mine, is Magnesian Limestone in heavy beds, (No. 3,) dipping S. E. at an angle of 20°.

Lead occurs in the joints and seams; Lead in No. 3 of the ravine. No perceptible dip of the beds is seen at the adit. A fault is exposed north of the mine which has caused the ravine. Nine feet of rock is here exposed. Sandstone below dips east, and the Sandstone over a large district north of the Philadelphia mine, dips east. It is underlaid on the west by a Granite ridge, and is overlaid by mineral bearing Magnesian Limestone, at and in the neighborhood of the mines.

LOCALITIES NEAR FREDERICKTOWN.

On the farm of James Hill, deceased, about half a mile northwest of the dwelling-house, some digging has been done in Magnesian Limestone, and some Galena was found in the Clay overlying the rock. A shaft was sunk to the depth of 16 or 17 feet, (J. Hill, Jr.,) and about 3,000 pounds of mineral taken out. The rock is drab-colored and rather soft, with Galena disseminated through it. This Limestone is underlaid by the same Sandstone which is found on the opposite slope, and over the country between this place and Hick's place.

On Dr. Gosney's land, and on that of Wm. Deguerre, Magnesian Limestone with Galena, shows itself at several points.

On the land of Chris. Buford, Magnesian Limestone crops out in thick beds, and dips W. at an angle of 5°. Lower beds dark colored, very compact and crystalline. Upper beds crystalline, and resemble the Lead bearing beds north-west of this locality.

The country here rises to over 50 feet above the level of the streams, and is as fine agricultural land as any in the State. Nowhere too rolling for tillage, nor too flat for drainage. With the exception of a few granitic and porphyry hills, the whole region is underlaid with the Lead-bearing Magnesian Limestone. I have never seen finer corn in any State, than I saw in August growing over this whole region. With its rich soil to be seen everywhere, and its mineral wealth which will certainly reward the judicious miner, there are few localities in Missouri to be compared with this in real value.

JAMES MARSHALL'S PLACE, T. 33, R. 7, SEC. 15—PART OF OLD ST. MICHAEL GRANT.

No. 1.   Soil and Red Clay with loose Copper ore; one specimen was found weighing 80 pounds.

No. 2.   Magnesian Limestone.

The rock occurs in beds from 1 to 3 feet thick. Mr. M. has opened a vein of Sulphuret and green Carbonate of Copper in an east and west lode. He says he took out about 4,000 pounds of ore from the top of the rock. Mr. Collier sunk a shaft about 8 feet on east end of the diggings, and Mr. M. says the prospect was more favorable the deeper Mr. C. went. The rock at this place has been quarried for piers and culverts by the railroad company. A good deal of brown Hematite is scattered over the surface of the land south of Marshall's place, and some of it has been collected into piles for shipment. The rock forming the creek bed above Marshall's house is traversed by veins of Calcite—"White Tiff"—and 200 yards south of Marshall's mine there is a cavern in the Magnesian Limestone.

In No. 13 Malachite occurs in small druseys cavities in the Hematite, through which the Copper is disseminated. This locality is worth further exploration.

The Buckeye Copper Mines are located on the N. W. qr. of the S. W. qr. Sec. 16, T. 33, R. 7 E. A shaft was sunk 125 feet deep by Pomeroy in 1844, 1845 and 1846, but suspended work in 1847. The ore was obtained in the form of a Sulphuret and Carbonate, with some black Oxide, distributed in a ferruginous cement uniting a brecciated Magnesian Limestone.

On James B. Campbell's farm an opening has been made at the base of a high ridge of Magnesian Limestone and a good deal of Iron ore (Limonite,) thrown out. The surfaces of the lumps are covered by minute crystals of Iron Sulphate and efflorescence from arsenical pyrites, which is abundantly disseminated through the Hematite. The width of the opening is about 40 feet. The Iron ore extends about 6 feet deep to the bedrock of Magnesian Limestone. Mr. Campbell and Col. Foster both say that there are evidences of a vein which dips into the hill at an angle of about 45°.

On Jackson's farm, near Fredericktown, about 300 pounds of Copper are said to have been taken out of a hole 7 feet deep.

MINE LA MOTTE.

Examined the "Jack Diggings," the "Golden Vein" and the "Bluff Diggings."

First, of "JACK DIGGINGS." Depth of shafts 25 to 36 feet. Lead occurs disseminated through Magnesian Limestone, in what is termed a "flat." Thickness of the flat varies from 3 to 4 feet. The average thickness of the Lead bearing strata is about 7 feet 6 inches. The cap-rock is a tolerably close-grained Limestone (No. 52) and forms an entirely safe roof. As a general rule the whole of the Lead bearing rock is taken out, the roof being supported by strong timbers at proper distances. Occasionally pillars are left, but they may be removed with safety whenever it is desired, and those portions of the mine timbered. The roof is quite undulating, and there are generally corresponding undulations in the floor, but not always. This want of correspondence in the roof and floor causes the flat to be pinched down to the thickness of less than three feet at some points. Where this is the case the ore is correspondingly concentrated, so that a square yard of the pinched strata will yield as much Galena as a square yard of the flat of the average thickness—or even where it is 14 feet thick. As the flat increases in thickness the mineral becomes more sparse. There are two systems of faults found throughout the works: One having a direction north and south, the other running east and west. The dislocations of the strata vary in depth from 1 to 3 feet—seldom more than that. In all cases the floor and roof correspond in the dislocation. Between the mineral bearing beds seams of blue Clay Shale are met with, varying from 1 foot to $\frac{1}{4}$ of an inch in thickness. In many places this Shale is full of fossils (No. 53.) Occasional rounded projections are found in the cap rock, with corresponding depressions in the floor beneath them. At one point the flat is traversed by a vein (so to call it,) of Copper Sulphuret, with some Sulphuret of Nickle (No. 54). This vein is 70 feet wide.

There is no dislocation at the junction of the Lead and Copper nor is there a definite line of separation between the ores. They are mingled in the rock for the distance of a few feet, and then the Galena disappears entirely, not a particle of Lead being found for the width of about 60 feet. The Copper-flat has not been worked further than has been found necessary in cutting levels from the main shafts to different parts of the Lead-flat beyond the Copper vein. A considerable quantity of the ore has been taken out for the purpose stated, and is now lying on the ground. This Mine is in the best order in all respects, and is so thoroughly managed, that not a pound of ore is lost. The breast is kept square and clean as the work progresses; the floor free from waste, the tramways (which all center at the main shaft) in complete repair and free from water, and the roof well supported. The cars filled with mineral in the remotest parts of the Mine, are brought to the main shaft, run on to the elevator, hoisted to the surface, moved on to the tramway and started to the dressing works. The grade being a descending one, the cars are carried forward by their own gravity—needing only the attendance of a conductor to regulate their momentum. On reaching the dressing works the cars are elevated to an upper floor and the ore dumped into the crushers. It will be seen from this notice that the ore is not handled from the moment of leaving the breast, where the miners are at work, until it is in the process of separation from its matrix, and nearly ready for the smelter.

The "BLUFF DIGGINGS" are not far distant from those just described, and differ from them in some material respects. The Galena, at this Mine, does not occur in a "flat," but is desseminated through the Magnesian Limestone beds from the surface to the depth of fifty feet. It is, however, more sparsely disseminated than in the Mine just described. The yield is about ten per cent. A bed of Sandstone is found intecalated with the Limestones at this Mine; contrary to the usual consequence at other Mines, it does not "cut off" the mineral, nor is it barren. The Galena is disseminated through the Sandstone in about the same proportion that it is through the Limestone.

The work at the "GOLDEN VEIN" has been done recently. It is situated near the new furnace. The work was begun on a fissure, and sunk through Clays to the depth of about 20 feet; when it opened into a cavern or widening of the fissure. At the distance of a few feet from the cavern, a shaft has been sunk to the depth of 100 feet But at the time of my visit, it could not be entered on account of water which had been allowed to accumulate, because the cribbing was not considered safe—it having been moved out of plumb by the pressure and yielding of the material, filling the fissure on the north and south sides of the shaft. A considerable quantity of Galena was taken out in sinking, and also from the wall rock of the fissure. The wall on the east side is Sandstone, (No. 55,) and on the west side it is Limestone, (No. 56.) Both the Limestone and Sandstone contain Ga-

lena. A rod was thrust into the soft material at the bottom of the
cave to the depth of 40 feet, without finding any obstruction at that
depth. A vein of very fine, tenaceous red Clay crosses the fissure
at right angles, (No. 57,) with yellow and black Clay on either side.
No. 58 was taken from a " pocket" in the wall rock—east side.

OTHER LOCALITES.

Porphyritic Syenite occurs on the north side of Little St. Francois
River, and forms the "Narrows." Just east of the south end of this
mountain, Sandstone, (No. 6,) shows itself in a small rise, dipping
north-east by north, and soon disappears beneath the Magnesian Limestone, (No. 7,) which is liberally exposed on the river banks and in
the slopes, and dipping in the same direction at an angle of 5° to 6°.

The mountain north of the "Narrows" has long been of peculiar
interest to persons in this vicinity. A small vein of Specular Oxide
of Iron has been discovered in it. This mountain is also traversed by
a number of dykes of Dolerite, (No. 9,) which show themselves at its
base, and in the bed of the river, from 2 inches to 2 feet wide. They
run north and south, as does also the vein of Iron ore, (No. 8,) and
probably extend into the mountain on the opposite side of the river
also. The mountain is composed of Porphyritic Syenite, of which
No. 10 is a specimen. It is about 3 miles in extent from north to south,
and 1¼ wide at the widest portion. It includes parts of Secs. 1, 2, 11,
12, 13 and 14.

East and south-east of the South Mountain of the "Narrows,"
which is composed of the same kind of rock as No. 10, the surface
rock is Magnesian Limestone, like Nos. 4 and 5. At one locality, Sec.
—, T. 33, R. 6 E., the surface beds are a very fine-grained, white, with
reddish spots, compact Limestone. This will, I believe, receive a fine
polish, and form a beautiful Marble. Could not ascertain the extent
or thickness of the beds. At the shaft, sunk by Dr. Robb, in Porphyry,
in T. 33, R. 6 E., Sec. 30, N. W. of S. E. qr., could find no evidences of
metallic ore in the debris thrown out. The first few feet of the shaft
passes through Magnesian Limestone.

On Sec. 32, T. 33, R. 6, is a very fine reddish colored Granite.

On headwaters of Captain's Creek, a soft Magnesian Limestone is
exposed, the lower beds of which are quite shaly and silicious ; dips E.,
at an angle of 6° to 8°, on Sec. 8, W. hf. This rock overlies the base of a
Porphyry hill. Magnesian Limestone is of great thickness at many
places, rising into hills over 150 feet high. All the valleys have it exposed, and it also covers the Slopes of the Granite and Porphyry
ridges.

Asbestos occurs in N. E. S. E. qr. Sec. 19, T. 32, R. 6 E., traversed by a small dyke of Dolerite. Other narrow dykes, of decomposed trap, traverse the rotten Granite, with seams and veins of a black material, (Spec. No. 20,) running in irregular directions. The Asbestos is found in a thin bed between thin layers of trap rock, 1 to 2 inches thick. No. 21.

On the Slope of the Porphyry hill, in Sec 20, S. W. of S. W. qr., a shaft was sunk, 8 or 9 feet, to a very black Porphyry or Petro-silex. Over the rock (for 1 foot) a good deal of white Asbestos, in long silky fibres, was taken out.

On Sec. 20, S. W. of S. W. qr., is a dyke of Greenstone, about 30 feet wide, running E. N. E. A shaft has been sunk on this dyke 7 or 8 feet deep. A vein of No. 23 traverses this Greenstone, with veins of Actinolite (?), and some other mineral. Specimens Nos. 24 and 26 are from this dyke.

East of Slater's Creek, in Secs. 14, 23 and 24, T. 33, R. 6 E., is an extensive exposure of Granite, containing reddish Feldspar.

Cedar Creek Mountain commences in Sec. 5, T. 32, R. 6, and extends into Sec. 8 and N. E. part of 7. The north and south ends of the mountain are composed of Porphyry; the central part of Granitic rock (Syenite). About half way up the Slope fragments of Quartz are met with; and still higher, large Quartz veins show themselves in the Syenite; some of them eight feet wide, and running nearly east and west. Immense Quartz crystals have weathered out of this vein; some of them more than a foot in diameter. Saw two veins about 1 and 2 feet wide parallel to the large one.

Marble beds, on Cedar Creek, are in Secs. 31 and 36, and the south part of 25, T. 33, R. 6 E., and show outcrops of reddish colored Marble, in beds from 2 inches to 1 foot in thickness.

In Sec. 31, west half, are heavy beds of Conglomerate on the north bank of Cedar Creek, for the distance of several hundred yards.

Along the headwaters of Cedar Creek, on the south side, Third Magnesian Limestone form perpendicular bluffs, from 20 to 50 feet high. The Slope from them to the general level being as much more, and in some places double that height. Small pieces of Galena are reported to have been picked up in the small branches and gulleys at many places in the lowlands. In fact almost everybody has small pieces of Lead ore picked up in such places or in their plowed fields. Copper is also found in the Soil and the underlying Clay at many points, but I could hear of no lode discovered in the rock.

The bottoms of Cedar Creek are covered with fine timber. The soil is very rich, with numerous Grapevines, some of very large size. Among the trees observed are various Oaks, Maple, Hackberry, Black and White Walnut, Coffee Bean, Pawpaw, Mulberry, Honey Locust, White and Shell Bark Hickory.

Between the Porphyry and Granite ridges, Magnesian Limestone underlies the soil. In some places the Magnesian Limestone forms high ridges, with occasional mural precipices on the sides. In Secs. 17 and 20, T. 33, R. 6, is a high Porphyry ridge, commencing at the river and running southerly to the south line of Sec. 20. The base is surrounded with Magnesian Limestone. East and south-east of this, Granite extends to Matthew's Creek. Between Mathew's Creek and Slater's Creek, in parts of Secs. 15, 16, 21, 22, 23, 26 and 27, Magnesian Limestone was the only rock observed.

In T. 33, R. 6, Sec. 25, S. W. S. E., is a high ridge showing the following Section—ascending :

> No. 1. Level of valley.
> No. 2. Sandstone. No. 36.
> No. 3. Coarse transition beds. No. 37.
> No. 4. Fine, silicious Grit, in thin beds from ⅓ to 2 inches in thickness. (May have come from a higher level, and *seems* to pitch into the ridge.)
> No. 5. Magnesian Limestone in heavy beds. No. 39. These ridges are covered with agatized Chert and drusy Quartz. No. 40.

On Curtis Bolton's land, T. 33, R. 6, Secs. 36, N. E. N. W., a sillicious Iron ore occurs in large masses on the surface of the hill-sides, and extending across the summit.

Very high Limestone ridges occurs in Secs. 25, 26, 27 and 22 of T. 33, R. 6 E., and are covered with Chert, drusy and agatized Quartz.

At Jasper Belken's, or old Newberry place, a number of holes have been sunk by Robt. Slater, to short depths, through the soil and Clay down to the Magnesian Limestone beds, and Copper obtained in small quantities in all of them. In one hole Copper occurs in a fissure in the rock.

The country in Secs. 3, 10, 11, 12 and 13 of T. 32, R. 6, and Secs. 18 and 7 of T. 32, R. 7, comprises that portion between the headwaters of Cedar Creek and Pete's Fork, and other tributaries of Twelve Mile Creek, and lying between the Patterson and Greenville roads. The " State road " runs in a south-east direction through this region. The bottoms are narrow and not cultivated. The district named is made up of high Limestone ridges, covered in many places with Chert and fragments of drusy Quartz. The uplands are broad, gently rolling, and pretty well timbered. Many fine Pines are to be seen, but they are rapidly disappearing under the axe of the lumberman. The Mine LaMotte Lead Company have a saw mill in Sec. 7, T. 33, R. 7. The portions of the trees not fit for the mill are generally used by char-coal burners.

In T. 32, R. 6, Sec. 14, N. E. qr., Conglomerate shows itself on the slope of a cherty ridge, near its base, and many fragments were seen in the beds of a dry run which skirts the ridge. It was also seen on the slope of the opposite ridge, which is of the same character. It is reported that Gold has been found here.

In T. 32, R. 7, Sec. 6, S. E. qr., is a large deposit of similar Conglom-erate or Breccia, very ferruginous, and occurring immediately under the soil. Many very large fragments are strewn over the top of the ground, and holes have been sunk to the depth of six or seven feet into this Breccia. Some of the specimens taken from this locality, (No. 60,) were selected by Col. Foster, and esteemed by him to be "quite rich." I could discover nothing like Gold with the aid of a good lens, but the rock may contain a trace of the precious metal. I doubt of its being worth any attention.

On T. 33, R. 6, Sec. 4, S. E. S. W., on the south-west side of a Por-phyry ridge, an opening has been made to procure indurated red Clay for making pipes. It is like the Powhatan material, and occurs in seams of reddish Clay, and hardens upon exposure.

THE LEAD AND ZINC REGIONS OF SOUTH-WEST MISSOURI.

BY ADOLF SCHMIDT AND ALEXANDER LEONHARD.

A. GENERAL CHARACTERISTICS.

B. DESCRIPTION OF ORES AND ASSOCIATED MINERALS.

C. DESCRIPTION OF ROCKS AND OF MODES OF OCCURRENCE OF THE ORES.

D. SPECIAL DESCRIPTION OF ORE DEPOSITS.

E. MINING AND SMELTING.

GEOLOGICAL ROOMS, WASHINGTON UNIVERSITY,

ST. LOUIS, *August 16, 1874.*

G. C. BROADHEAD, *State Geologist:*

DEAR SIR:—I have the honor of presenting to you, herewith, four reports on the following subjects :

1. THE SOUTH-WESTERN LEAD REGION OF MISSOURI.

2. THE CENTRAL LEAD REGIONS OF MISSOURI.

3. PRACTICAL RULES FOR JUDGING OF, AND FOR DEVELOPING DEPOSITS OF IRON ORE IN MISSOURI.

4. METALLURGICAL PROPERTIES OF THE MISSOURI IRON ORES.

The greater portion of the report on the South-western Lead Region was written by Mr. Alexander Leonhard, late Assistant in the Geological Survey. That report represents the combined results of Mr. Leonhard's investigations at Granby and vicinity, and of my own in the other parts of the South-west region. The Topographical Survey of the Granby District was made by Mr. Carl Henrich. All the maps and sketches were drawn by Mr. T. J. Caldwell.

Wherever I have been at work in the State I have met with great kindness and attention on the part of the citizens, and have received, in several instances, very material aid; for all of which I take this opportunity of expressing my sincere gratitude.

Yours, very respectfully,

ADOLF SCHMIDT, *Assistant.*

CHAPTER XXII.

THE LEAD AND ZINC REGIONS OF SOUTH-WEST MISSOURI.

BY ADOLF SCHMIDT AND ALEXANDER LEONHARD.

A. GENERAL CHARACTERISTICS.

The Lead and Zinc region of South-west Missouri, as far as it is known at present, comprises the counties of Newton, Jasper, Lawrence, Greene and Dade, and the western parts of McDonald, Barry, Stone and Christian counties. The higher portions of this area are occupied by rolling prairies, while the slopes and bottoms along the water courses are mostly covered with timber.

The northern part is watered by tributaries of Sac River, which runs north into the Osage; the southern and western parts by a number of small streams, which flow in a western direction into Spring River. Along three of these latter streams the principal Lead and Zinc ore deposits, known at present, are situated.

It is remarkable that the best ore deposits have never been found immediately on these streams, but always along smaller branches and valleys.

The first and most southern among the three streams referred to, is Shoal Creek, which drains the northern half of Newton county. On a southern branch of this stream are the Granby Mines.

North of Shoal Creek and in the southern part of Jasper county, is Turkey Creek, a much smaller tributary of Spring River, with an extensive mining district situated along some of its southern branches, the most important of which is Joplin Creek.

The third and most northern of these tributaries of Spring River is Centre Creek, with the mines of Oronogo (late Minersville,) situated on a small branch coming from the north.

We may accordingly group the ore deposits in three districts:

1. THE SHOAL CREEK DISTRICT.
2. THE TURKEY CREEK DISTRICT.
3. THE CENTRE CREEK DISTRICT.

The whole region belongs geologically to the Subcarboniferous System. The formation consists of a series of Limestone and Chert beds belonging to the upper part of the so called Archimedes or Keokuk Limestone.

In some places they are overlaid by disturbed layers of Sandstone, perhaps in part the "Ferruginous Sandstone" of Swallow, and in part a Coal Measure Sandstone; in other places by pockets of Slate and Coal belonging to the Lower Coal Measures. The ore deposits in this region lie more often horizontally than vertically. They are connected with certain more or less altered strata of the Archimedes Limestone, and are covered by broken masses of Chert and Limestone.

At Granby the Galena either occurs in loose pieces in Clay or Sand, or in horizontal openings or beds of limited extent, varying in thickness from 1 to 8 feet. The Galena is generally associated with Dolomite, Calcite and Chert. Calamine is mostly found associated with the Galena, and occurs in beds from $\frac{1}{2}$ to 6 feet thick. At Joplin and Oronogo, the Galena forms more or less horizontal veins : i. e., deposits of considerable length but comparatively small section. It also occurs there as irregular local impregnations in Limestone, or it fills cracks in the Chert. Besides, it is frequently found broken up and mixed with large, irregular masses of broken and altered Limestone, Dolomite and Chert, as well as in various conglomeratic rocks, very often associated with Zinc Blende and Iron Pyrites, while Calamine is but rarely met with in these districts. The Limestone and the Conglomerates are often bituminous, and contain small accumulations of fluid or viscid Bitumen.

CHAPTER XXIII.

B. DESCRIPTION OF ORES AND ASSOCIATED MINERALS

The Lead and Zinc ore deposits of South-west Missouri contain the following minerals:

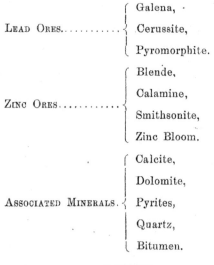

LEAD ORES.............
- Galena,
- Cerussite,
- Pyromorphite.

ZINC ORES...........
- Blende,
- Calamine,
- Smithsonite,
- Zinc Bloom.

ASSOCIATED MINERALS.
- Calcite,
- Dolomite,
- Pyrites,
- Quartz,
- Bitumen.

GALENA,

Sulphuret of Lead, Blue Lead, called "Mineral" by the miners, is the principal ore from which over nine-tenths of all the Lead in South-west Missouri is obtained.

It crystalizes in the monometric system, the cube being the most common form. It has a perfect cleavage in cubes, a metallic luster, a lead-gray color and streak, a hardness of 2.5 to 2.7 and a specific gravity of 7.2 to 7.7. In a pure state it consists of 86.6 p. c. of Lead and 13.4 p. c. of Sulphur.

In South-west Missouri, it occurs in crystals or in compact, crystalline masses. The crystals generally have the form of a cube whose eight corners are taken off by a small development of the planes of the octahedron. In a few localities—for instance, in Brock Hollow (Granby) and in Middle Joplin Valley—crystals are found in which the octahedron is more fully developed and sometimes predominates.

Wherever the crystals are imbedded in Dolomite, or are adhering to solid Chert, they show mostly a smooth, shiny surface; but where they are in connection with Clays or Sand, or decomposed rocks, they are water-worn, changed or coated. Specimens are found in which the original cubes are no longer recognizable.

Cubic crystals of Galena are frequently coated, either by a soft, ashy, dark gray and porous, or by a hard, solid shell of cerussite (carbonate of Lead,) or else by a layer of Calamine (silicate of Zinc). Such cubes in some instances have been partly or wholly dissolved and removed out of their shell, and are in part replaced by crystalline drusy Cerussite, or by Pyromorphite or by Calamine. Sometimes cubes of Galena thickly coated with Cerussite, occur enclosed in Calcite.

At Joplin and Oronogo, the Galena is less frequently altered and pseudomorphosed than at Granby. The most common associate of Galena in the Turkey Creek and Centre Creek districts, is Zinc blende both minerals occurring intimately mixed in numerous localities. Blende is often found deposited on, or enclosing crystals of Galena.

At Oronogo we found small crystals of Blende seated on the somewhat corroded surface of the cubes of Galena.

· At Joplin and Oronogo the Galena is frequently associated with Bitumen, which sometimes surrounds the crystals or entirely impregnates crystalline masses. This bituminous Galena has a darker appearance than the common Galena, being often deep black in color, and emitting, when broken, a bituminous odor.

The following analyses, made by Mr. Regis Chauvenet, of St. Louis, show the Galena of South-west Missouri to be of a very pure variety, containing no Antimony, and only small quantities of Zinc and Iron. All samples contain some Silver, but none of them in sufficient quantity to pay for its separation. All are average samples of clean Galena, in that condition in which it is delivered to the smelting works.

Analyses.

	1	2	3	4	5	6	7	8	9
Insoluble matter......	0.05	0.61	0.12	......	0.44	0.71	0.53	0.33	1.72
Lead......................		84.06	85.84	......	......	......	......	......	......
Zinc.......................	1.32	0.94	0.12	......	0.91	0.73	0.52	trace	0.94
Iron......................	0.09	0.16	0.05	......	0.45	0.196	0.196	trace	0.24
Antimony...............	none	none	none	......	none	none	none	none	none
Silver, ounces per ton......	1	1¼	1¼	1¾	1¼	¾	¾	¾	1
Sulphide of Lead........		97.05							
Sulphide of Zinc........		1.41		......	......	1.36	1.08	0.77	......	1.41
Bisulphide of Iron,......		0.34		......	......	0.96	0.42	0.42	......	0.53

No. 1. Village Diggings, Granby.
No. 2. Holman Diggings, Granby.
No. 3. Trent Diggings, Granby. Galena found imbedded in red Clay.
No. 4. Eastpoint, Granby. Fine-grained structure, and light steel-gray
color. Supposed to be rich in Silver. It contains indeed a little
more Silver than the other samples.
No. 5. Temple Diggings, Joplin.
No. 6. Swindle Diggings, Joplin.
No. 7. Lower Joplin Valley Diggings.
No. 8. Stevens' Diggings, (Turkey Creek District.)
No. 9. Oronogo.

CERUSSITE.

Carbonate of Lead, White Lead ore, called "Dry Bone" by the
miners, is, next to Galena, the most important Lead ore in Missouri.
It mostly occurs in amorphous, compact masses of earthy appearance,
and of white, yellow or reddish color. On account of its non-metallic
appearance it often fails to be recognized by the miners, and is, therefore, sometimes overlooked. It can easily be distinguished from Limestone by its weight, the specific gravity being 6.5, and from hardened
Clays and Barytes by its being readily dissolved in dilute nitric acid
with effervescence. Cerussite occasionally occurs crystalized in brittle
transparent or translucent crystals of the trimetric system. The crystals have an adamantine lustre, and are generally white or gray,
often with a bluish or greenish tint.

The "Dry Bone" of Granby is mostly porous, and only occasionally compact. It often incloses masses of a gray, ashy variety of the same mineral, evidently a product of the decomposition of Galena. This ashy Cerussite generally fills cubical cavities, or surrounds unaltered Galena. When this gray, ashy variety, called "Ash Mineral" by the miners, predominates, the ore is called " Wool Mineral." This is frequently found in Brockhollow, Granby, in the Moseley, Cornwall and other diggings of that district. White, dense but crystalline Cerussite sometimes coats the walls of cubic cavities which were formerly occupied by crystals of Galena, and gray to black translucent crystals of Cerussite project toward the center.

Cerussite is comparatively rarely met with near Joplin, but it is quite frequent again farther north in the Centre Creek district.

At the Oronogo mines specimens were obtained, which show very plainly the gradual change from Galena into Cerussite. Crystals or crystalline masses of Galena, imbedded in altered and softened Limestone, seem to have been coated at first by a compact layer of Cerussite. Through this layer solutions, containing carbonic acid, penetrated and gradually dissolved the Galena, and precipitated a part of the Lead as carbonate on the inside of the coating, but carrying most of it out of the shell, either to deposit it immediately or to carry it away. When this process has been continued for some time, we find a round or oval shell of compact and generally crystalline Cerussite of the size of a walnut, or sometimes much larger, containing a dark transparent, watery fluid, in which a piece of Galena *smooth and rounded, but irregular in shape* is lying loose. The smoothness of these pieces is, under these circumstances, very remarkable and curious. If this process further continues, it is evident that the Galena will dissolve entirely, and that a drusy cavity, lined with Cerussite crystals, must be the final result.

In such cavities, which do actually occur, we find occasionally small yellowish-green, transparent crystals, with an adamantine lustre apparently of trimetric crystallization. They are probably Anglesite, (Sulphate of Lead,) but are too small to be exactly determined.

Cerussite also occur at Oronogo, in porous agglomerations, accompanied by fine, drusy aggregates of large and well developed crystals of grayish-white color. These crystals have mostly the shape of a flattened prism, sometimes over $\frac{1}{4}$ inch in length and $\frac{1}{8}$ inch wide. They occur either in confused aggregations or in stellated compounds of densely packed crystals, so that it is difficult to determine their exact form. It can, however, be seen that the most developed faces are those of two or three different domes; probably brachy-domes, which are always striated horizontally (lengthwise.) The trimetric pyramid and the prism are less distinctly developed at both ends of each crystal.

Pure Cerussite consists of 83.5 per cent of Oxide of Lead (or 77.5 per cent. of metallic Lead,) and 16.5 per cent. of Carbonic Acid.

As generally found, however, it contains some Iron Pyrites.

The analysis of different samples made by Mr. Chauvenet, gave the following results :

	1.	2.	3.	4.
Insoluble matter (mostly Silica)	9.95	6.12	0 36	10.35
Peroxide of Iron	1.51	Some.	0.55	3.11
Oxide of Zinc	0.75			0.73
Lime	Trace.	Some.	0.40	0.75
Magnesia	Trace.			0.36
Sulphur			Trace.	
Metallic Lead	66.35	66.51	72.86	63.64

1. Granby. Flesh red, massive Drybone.
2. Frazier dgs., Granby. Reddish-brown, earthy Drybone.
3. Frazier dgs., Granby. Ashy, Wool-mineral.
4. Circular dgs., Average. Reddish-brown, earthy Drybone.

PYROMORPHITE,

Phosphate of Lead, occurs so rarely in this region that it is of no practical importance as a Lead ore. It is found in small, amorphous masses of light, yellowish-green color, and earthy appearance, or in minute and indeterminable crystals, translucent to opaque, and of dark green color.

It consists of Phosphate of Lead, combined with Chloride of Lead, and contains in a pure state, about 58 per cent. of metallic Lead.

In the Granby district, massive amorphous Pyromorphite is occasionally found in loose rounded pieces, from pea to nut size, associated with loose pieces of Cerussite. The surface of these pieces looks yellowish-green and earthy, while the interior is compact, and of a lighter color, sometimes white.

Mostly, however, the Pyromorphite occurs as a shaly coating; seldom directly on unaltered crystals of Galena, but generally on Cerussite; especially on the gray, ashy variety which, as mentioned before, is directly derived from Galena.

Crystals, also, are sometimes observed in cavities of Amorphous Cerussite.

We have not found any Pyromorphite either at Joplin or at Oronogo. At the Grove Creek diggings, it occurs rarely, coating pieces of Cerussite.

BLENDE.

Zinc Blende, Sulphuret of Zinc. Miners generally call it " Black Jack," but at Granby, where Calamine is called " Black Jack," Blende has obtained the name of " Resin Jack."

Blende crystallizes in octohedral forms of the monometric system, and shows a distinct cleavage parallel to the planes of a dodecahedron.

In South-west Missouri it mostly occurs in compact, crystalline masses, varying in structure from very coarse to fine-grained, and micro-crystalline. Its lustre is resinous to adamantine, and its specific gravity about 4. It is a little harder than Calcite, (3.5—4,) and generally of dark brown color, but often bright red, green and yellow. All these colors can sometimes be observed in different parts of the same specimen.

Blende contains, when pure, 67 per cent. of Zinc, and 38 per cent. of Sulphur.

Two varieties of Blende may be distinguished in South-west Missouri:

A granular variety. The single, small crystalline grains are translucent to transparent, and of bright color, either red or brown or light yellow, and often show an adamantine lustre. This variety occurs either in compact granular masses, or more frequently as small, single crystals disseminated in Sand or Quartzite.

A coarsely crystalline variety, showing broad faces of cleavage, and occurring massive with large and well developed crystals in cavities. This variety is of a yellowish, brown color, sometimes dark and nearly black.

A peculiar kind of Blende occurring only rarely at Joplin and Oronogo, in general appearance and lustre on the faces of cleavage, closely resembles Galena. Mr. Chauvenet analyized pieces of it, and found it to be common Zinc blende, with traces of Lead and Iron.

In many places the Blende seems to pass gradually into Calamine, there being between the two minerals a layer of dark colored, fine-grained Blende, intimately mixed with portions of columnar structure and resembling Calamine. This mixture passes into the regular columnar or fibrous Calamine, which itself is dark colored near the Blende, and is lighter and more transparent the more remote it is from the unaltered Blende. Single crystals or large crystalline ag'gregations of Blende are often surrounded by a thick layer of Calamine of botryoidal form and radiating columnar structure. The surface of the inclosed piece of Blende is then generally corroded and tarnished. Blende, especially the coarsely crystalline variety, is often intimately mixed with Galena. Mr. Broadhead observed at Leadville round globules of one-sixteenth to one-eighth inches in diameter, grayish-brown color, and radiating fibrous structure, on crystals of Galena. Mr. Chauvenet analyized them and found them to be pure sulphuret of Zinc without any Iron or Lead.

Three samples of pure Blende from South-west Missouri, were analyzed by Mr. Regis Chauvenet, who obtained the following per centages :

	1.	2.	3.
Insoluble..	....	0.25	1.41
Silica........,..	2.05	....	....
Metallic Zinc..	64.67	65.92	64.87
Iron...	0.53	0.32	0.37
Cadmium	....	0.509	0.723

No. 1. From Bellew shafts, Granby.
No. 2. From Porter diggings, Joplin.
No. 3. From Leadville.

All three samples were of the coarsely crystalline, dark-colored variety, which alone occurs in larger masses, and which alone is at present sold and used as an ore.

CALAMINE.

Hydrous Silicate of Zinc, is called " Black Jack," by the miners of Granby. It crystallizes in the hemi-hedral forms of the trimetric system, but mostly occurs compact and massive, or else in botryoidal or stalactitic forms with fibrous structure. It is generally transparent and yellow, green or brown, with bright, vitrous lustre. Its hardness is 4.5; its specific gravity 3.4.

When pulverized, it dissolves in heated sulphuric or muriatic acid, and the solution gelatinizes on cooling. It consists, when pure of 67.4 per cent. of oxide of Zinc, (equal to about 54 per cent. of met. Zinc,) 25 per cent. of Silica, 7.5 per cent. of water. It occurs abundantly at Granby, while at Joplin and Oronogo it.is but rarely found. The ,thin lamellar crystals observed at Granby, are either colorless and transparent or gray-green, or yellow and then translucent.

The following combination was observed : Two different prisms— the macro-diagonal faces, one macro-dome and one steep brachy dome. The crystals have a lamellar form and are generally combined in radiated globular or botryoidal groups seated on massive crystalline Calamine, on Galena, on Dolomite or rarely on Chert.

The Calamine of South-west Missouri is also found massive of crystalline, either columnar or fibrous structure, of green, yellow or brown color, translucent to opaque. This variety forms streaks in sub-crystalline Calamine, or in Dolomite, or in hardened Clays, and occurs as a coating over sub-crystalline Calamine, over crystals of Galena or of Calcite, and sometimes over Blende. The largest masses of Calamine are found in a compact, fine-grained or micro-crystalline state, opaque and of yellow or reddish-brown color. Cavities in it are frequently coated with crystals of Calamine or of Dolomite.

The following analyses, made by Mr. Regis Chauvenet, show the composition of the Granby Calamine :

	1.	2.	3.
Silica	27.51	26.83	23.32
Oxide of Zinc	63.05	66.37	67.15
Peroxide of Iron	1.22	0.65	0.61
Water	7.10	6.46	8.59
Lime	1.21	Trace.	....
Metallic Zinc	50.37	52.97	53.95

No. 1. From Village Diggings, Granby.
No. 2. From Frazier Diggings, Granby.
No. 3. From Bellew shaft, Granby.

The specimens analyzed were of the fine-grained and sub-crystalline, mixed with streaks of the crystalline varieties.

SMITHSONITE,

Carbonate of Zinc, crystallizes in the rhombohedral system but mostly occurs in granular or fine-grained masses of light yellow, gray or brown color. Its hardness is 5 and the specific gravity 4—4.4. It dissolves in nitric acid with effervescence.

When in a pure state it contains 6 4.8 per cent. of Oxide of Zinc(= about 51 per cent. of Zinc)—and 35.2 per cent. of carbonic acid.

In South-west Missouri Smithsonite nearly always occurs in con-nection with Calamine, from which it may in most instances be dis-tinguished by its granular structure and its less bright and rather pearly lustre. At Granby, in the Hard-shaft and Crab-tree diggings, it is often found well crystallized. The crystals are either colorless or milky white, translucent, and are of indistinct rhombohedral forms with covered faces and rounded edges. They are either seated on mas-sive granular Smithsonite, or on Calamine.

The massive Smithsonite in the Hardshaft diggings (Granby,) is white or light yellow, and called " White Jack " by the miners. It is densely granular but passes into spongy, porous, and finally into earthy and friable masses near cavities. At the Burch Diggings and some other places the massive Smithsonite is of gray or grayish brown color.

Mr. R. Chauvenet analyzed a sample of the light yellow, massive Smithsonite from the Hardshaft diggings (Granby). It contained—

	Per cent.
Silicious matter	1.22
Peroxide of Iron	1.21
Oxide of Zinc	63.02
Carbonic acid	34.58
	100.03
Metallic Zinc	50.37

ZINC BLOOM,

Hydrated Carbonate of Zinc, forms snow-white, amorphous masses of a specific gravity of 3.5, and a hardness of 2.5. It readily dissolves in Hydrochloric Acid with strong effervescence. In a pure state it con-sists of 71.3 per cent. of Oxide of Zinc, 12.9 per cent. of Carbonic Acid and 15.8 per cent. of water.

We observed it in the Crabtree Diggings (Granby), closely sur-rounding and coating fibrous Calamine, into which mineral it gradu-ally passes and from which it is evidently derived.

PYRITES,

Iron Pyrites, Bisulphuret of Iron, called "Mundic" by the lead miners, crystallizes in cubes, often combined with the octahedron, or into other forms of the monometric system.

It has a light yellow color and splendent metallic luster, a specific gravity of 5 and a hardness of 6 to 6.5.

It can, by its hardness, be easily distinguished from Copper Pyrites, which it resembles in general appearance but which is softer and may be scratched by a knife, while Iron Pyrites will not do so and will strike fire with steel. It consists of 46.7 per cent. of Iron and 53.3 per cent. of Sulphur.

It is found abundantly in certain mines in the Joplin district and less frequently at Granby and Oronogo. It occurs either in compact, crystalline masses cementing broken Chert and Galena, or in specks and crystals disseminated through rocks or in drusy agglomerations of crystals. Pyrites is, at Joplin, generally associated with Bitumen. Crystals of Pyrites are often formed on and over crystals of Galena.

Sometimes the Pyrites is externally altered into Limonite.

Limonite (Hydrated Oxide of Iron) occurs, besides, as yellow or brown Ochre, often mixed with various Clays and Sands, or as a thin coating on Calamine.

DOLOMITE,

Brown Spar, Bitter Spar, commonly called "Soft Tiff" by the miners of Southwest Missouri, crystallizes in the rhombohedral system and has a white color which is often changed to yellow or brown by oxides of Iron. It has a hardness of 3.5 to 4 and a specific gravity of 2.8 to 2.9. It dissolves in acids slowly and with less effervescence than Calcite. It is composed of Carbonate of Lime and Carbonate of Magnesia.

In many mines of South-west Missouri, especially at Granby, it forms the principal gangue of the ore deposits. Missouri miners often mistake it for Barytes, which also they call "Soft Tiff" or "Bald Tiff," and which somewhat resembles it in general appearance. Dolomite can, however, be readily distinguished by its lighter weight and its solubility in acids. We have not found any Barytes in the South-west Lead regions.

In the ore deposits of Granby, the Dolomite generally occurs in single or loosely aggregated crystals, or in dense crystalline masses. The crystals are opaque and have the form of rhombohedrons with curved and distorted faces. They are yellow or reddish brown on the surface and white in the interior. They project from a crystalline, coarse-grained, massive Dolomite, which forms pockets, bands and streaks in Dolomitic Limestone.

Dolomite is frequently associated with Galena, Blende, Calamine and Calcite in a paragenetic order, of which we will give a few examples.

Alternate layers of dark gray, coarsely crystalline Dolomitic Limestone and of light colored, crystalline Dolomite form a banded rock of several feet thickness. The limits between Limestone and Dolomite are not very sharp. Long and narrow drusy cavities, horizontal and parallel to the banded structure of the rock, are frequent in the Dolomite. Large cubes of Galena are found partly or wholly inclosed in the Dolomite. The surface of such Galena crystals is sometimes corroded and partly changed into Carbonate of Lead. The crystals of Dolomite, as well as the projecting parts of the Galena, are frequently covered with small crystals of Calamine in botryoidal agglomerations.

Streaks and seams of Calamine occur in Dolomite, often crossing each other, thus giving the whole a reticulated appearance. In other places, layers of coarsely crystalline, reddish brown Blende, inclosing small crystals of Galena, are in close contact on both the upper and under side, with layers of dark brown Dolomite which gradually passes into white or light yellow aggregates of Dolomite crystals.

Crystalline masses of Calcite often occur in streaks through massive Dolomite.

Mr. Regis Chauvenet analyzed two samples of Dolomite, in which he found:

	1.	2.
Insoluble	1.24	0.26
Carbonate of Lime	54.72	54.52
Carbonate of Magnesia........................	41.98	44.83
Carbonate of Iron..	2.94	1.14
	100.88	100.75

No. 1. From Moon Diggings, Joplin. Loose aggregate of crystals of yellow
        or yellowish gray color, partly of a dull and rotten appearance—
        the crystals being cracked and split into small fragments.
No. 2. From Murphysburg Diggings, Joplin. Reddish white, coarsely crys-
        talline, massive Dolomite.

CALCITE,

Calcareous Spar, Carbonate of Lime, is known to the miners of Missouri by the name of " Glass-tiff," or " Hard-tiff." It crystallizes in the rhombohedral system, and shows a highly perfect cleavage in rhombo- hedrons. The pure crystals are colorless and tranparent. It dissolves very readily in acids, with strong effervescence, and contains 56 per cent. of lime and 44 per cent. of carbonic acid, often with some Carbonate of Magnesia or Iron.

Calcite is frequently found in the mines of South-west Missouri, in crystals or in crystalline masses. The crystals mostly show the form of scalenohedrons, which often combine to form twin-crystals, and are found as large as 6 inches in length and 3 inches in thickness.

Light, spongy or froth-like agglomerations of long, thin, imperfectly developed crystals, of snow-white color, occur occasionally at Granby, for instance, in Holman Diggings.

The crystalline masses of Calcite, as found associated with the Galena, are translucent and white, often with a greenish tint. They sometimes inclose specks or crystals of Galena. Calcite also forms white opaque incrustations in cavities and crevices in the Limestone as well as stalactites and stalagmites.

QUARTZ,

Crystalizes in the rhombohedral system, generally in prismatic or in pyramidal forms. Its hardness is 7, its specific gravity 2.7.

It consists principally of Silica, and is not attacked by acids. In the ore deposits of South-west Missouri, small transparent and splendent crystals of Quartz occur occasionally in small cavities of Chert or of Quartzite.

They show the hexagonal prism and two rhombohedrons. Accumulations of small, often microscopic Quartz crystals, are quite frequent in the ore deposits. They occur either loose as a crystalline Quartz-sand, or aggregated and cemented together as Quartz Sandstone, or as Quartzite, which rocks will be described in the next chapter.

BITUMEN,

Asphaltum, Mineral Picth, termed "Tar" by the Joplin miners, occurs either in a fluid or in a plastic state. It has a black color, and a bituminous odor; melts when heated, and burns with light flame and much smoke. It consists of Carbon, (generally over 80 per cent.,)

Hydrogen and Oxygen in various proportions. It is of quite common occurrence in the Joplin mines, in crevices and cavities of the Limestone, mostly connected with Dolomite, Galena or Blende.

It is found as a brownish-black fluid, but more frequently as black, soft amorphous masses of great tenacity and plasticity, which harden on exposure, and become brittle, and then break with conchoidal fracture.

All the mineral described occur in various paragentic relation to each other, as the following examples of succession will show. We begin in each case with the oldest mineral, over which the others seem to be formed successively:

1. Galena, Blende, perhaps in places found simultaneously.
2. Galena, Dolomite, Calamine.
3. Galena, Cerussite, Pyromorphite.
4. Galena, Calcite.
5. Galena, Pyrites.
6. Blende, Dolomite.
7. Blende, Calamine.
8. Blende, Bitumen.
9. Dolomite, Calamine, Smithsonite, Zinc Bloom.
10. Dolomite, Calcite, Calamine.
11. Dolomite, Bitumen.
12. Pyrites, Limonite.

By combining these examples of succession of minerals, we obtain the following 4 series:

1. Galena, Blende, Dolomite, Bitumen.
2. Galena, Blende, Dolomite, Calcite, Calamine, Smithsonite, Zinc Bloom.
3. Galena, Cerussite, Pyromorphite.
4. Galena, Pyrites, Limonite.

All these minerals may be divided in those of older and those of later formations; most of the latter being produced by alterations of the former, in regard to composition as well as in regard to form and place:

OLDER FORMATION:

      Galena.
      Blende.
      Dolomite.
      Bitumen.
      Calcite.
      Pyrites.

LATER FORMATION:

    Cerussite.
    Pyromorphite.
    Calamine.
    Smithsonite.
    Zinc Bloom.
    Limonite.

CHAPTER XXIV.

C.—A DESCRIPTION OF ROCKS AND OF MODES OF OCCURRENCE OF THE ORES.

The General Geological Section of the Lead and Zinc-bearing for mation of South-west Missouri, is about as follows :

$a...$
- 1 foot to 3 feet Soil.
- 0 to 5 feet Gravel.

$b...$
- 0 to 15 feet Sandstone.
- 0 to 5 feet black Slate, with Coal.

$c...$
- 20 to 75 feet Chert, more or less broken up, sometimes in fissured layers, and in some localities, especially at Granby, altered to soft, porous Chert. The Chert is invariably accompanied by large masses of Clay and Sand.
- 0 to 20 feet Silico-Calcite.
- 0 to 30 feet alternate layers of Limestone and Chert.

$d...$
- 140 feet or more Limestone; in some places gray and coarse-grained ; in others bluish and fine-grained.

(*a*) Alluvium. Frequently contains some ore in loose pieces.

(*b*) Probably Lower Coal Measures, with occasional occurrences of ore.

(*c* and *d*) Upper layers of Keokuk Group. Also called Archimedes Limestone. (Sub-Carboniferous System.)

(*c*) Represents the principal ore-bearing strata; (*d*) the bed rock in which no ore has as yet been discovered.

SOIL.

The Soil in this mining region is generally of a sandy character, and in places somewhat clayish and calcareous. Fragments of hard or of rotten Chert, partly with sharp edges, are lying loose on or in the soil, in places so numerous as to cover one-third of the surface of the ground. They vary in size from the smallest to 4 inches in diameter, and are often larger. Pieces of Cerussite, or of Galena coated with Cerussite, are frequently found in the lower portion of the soil, especially where sandy and cherty.

GRAVEL.

The Gravel consists of loose, more or less water-worn pieces of either hard or rotten Chert, which are often mixed with brown Ferruginous Sand or Clay. It generally occurs, in the bottoms, below the Soil. In the vicinity of Joplin and Lone Elm, it is also found in slight depressions and runs on the prairie plateau.

SANDSTONE.

Sandstone is found in fragments or isolated patches of variable size and extent, in the vicinity of Granby, at Cornwall diggings, near the Joplin Mines, and at the Cooney, Burch, Grove Creek, and Oronogo Diggings.

In the vicinity of Granby, these patches, apparently of considerable extent, overlie the Keokuk Limestone in layers as much as 15 feet thick.

The best exposure was observed in a quarry one mile west of Granby, where it crops out on the top of a high prairie ridge, presenting the following section:

3 feet to 5 feet Soil, with loose pieces of Red Sandstone.

1 foot shaly, broken Red Sandstone, with layers of brown Clay.

4 feet to 5 feet (as far as uncovered) of thickly-bedded Sandstone, red in the upper, yellow in the middle, and white in the lower parts.

The Sandstone consists of small, translucent and colorless Quartz grains, loosely aggregated, with but little, more or less, ferruginous cement, and mixed with some single, but pretty equally distributed lamellæ of white Mica.

One mile south-west of Lone Elm, in the Joplin district, a similar Sandstone, 4 to 6 feet thick, overlies black Slate and Coal. It is red and fine-grained, and broken, the crevices being filled with red Clay.

G. S—26

The occurrence of the Sandstone at the other localities above mentioned, will be described in the special description of mines.

The position and appearance of these Sandstones, as well as the character of the rather indistinct fossils found in the same, make it probable, according to Mr. Broadhead, that it belongs to the Lower Coal Measures.

SLATE AND COAL.

Slate and Coal, in this region, occur as small local deposits, or pockets, which are always greatly disturbed and disrupted when found with the ore.   The Slate is gray or black, either in compact layers or in thin Shales, mixed with some Sand or Clay.   It sometimes passes gradually into an impure, heavy Coal, of a bituminous and slaty character.   Both Slate and Coal often contain thin sheets or crystals of Pyrites.

These pockets of Slate and Coal are not found at Granby, but frequently at Joplin and Minersville.   The following Section was observed in Mitchell and Pierce's shaft, one mile south-west of Lone Elm in the Joplin district: (See Fig. 12.)

    No. 7.   1 to 2 feet of Soil.
    No. 6.   4 to 6 Sandstone.   (Described above.)
    No. 5.   4 feet red and yellow, sandy Clay, with Chert.
    No. 4.   1 to 5 feet black Slate, with pockets of Fire Clay.
    No. 3.   1 to 5 feet Coal.
    No. 2.   1 foot Slate.
    No. 1.   (?) Limestone.

The Coal is heavy and impure, and seems to form a somewhat disturbed basin, five feet thick in the center, and extending about 40 to 50 feet in one direction, and 20 to 25 feet in the other, as far as could be judged from its appearance in summer 1873.   No ores have been found in this locality; the shaft had not yet reached the ore-bearing formation.   Slate patches are spread all along Joplin valley, on or near the surface of the ground.   Some Coal has been found in loose pieces between the broken Chert, at the Four Corner Diggings, and in Beamer's shaft, near Joplin.   Black Clay and Coal also occur at Minersville in different places, especially in the Centre shaft of the Circular Diggings, and generally mixed with much pyrites.

CHERT,

Flint, Hornstone, and Jasper, is amorphous Quartz, often inclosing microscopic, crystalline particles disseminated.   It consists essentially of Silica, sometimes containing small quantities of alumina and Lime.

It strikes fire with steel, (hardness 7,) and is opaque with white, yellow or reddish color. It is brittle like glass, and shows a conchoidal fracture. It sometimes contains drusy cavities with crystals of Quartz.

In South-west Missouri Chert occurs abundantly. Swallow observed 105 feet of Chert above Grand Falls, on Shoal Creek, which he describes as " white, bluish, white and buff, compact, thick-bedded, in regular layers interstratified with irregular beds of brown, impure, ferruginous, porous varieties, of the same rock." This is the greatest observed thickness. In Granby some shafts are sunk through 40 to 60 feet of Chert, but the solid layers from 1 to 6 feet thick, are separated by Sand or Clay.

The Chert is mostly white, gray or yellow, occasionally rose or flesh-colored. The Chert is one of the principal ore-bearing rocks in the Mines of South-west Missouri. It contains Galena in numerous sheets or seams, either deposited between layers of Chert, or filling small cracks in the Chert. It is evident, in all places, that the Galena was formed after the Chert had been formed and hardened, as crystals of Galena or Blende are never found entirely inclosed in the body of the Chert, but always in cracks or cavities. In the lower Joplin valley, crystals or Galena, are found formed on all sides of angular Chert; fragments, showing that this Galena was formed after the Chert had been broken up. Chert is also found in intimate connection with Blende, both forming a conglomerate, in which sharp-edged pieces of Chert are surmounted by crystalline Blende.

In many places the solid Chert undergoes a change and passes into a soft, porous variety. Minute particles of the Chert seem to be dissolved and carried away by solutions, while other particles remain and form a fine-grained and sometimes porous, spongy mass. The pores are then often lined or filled by red oxide of Iron, deposited in them. Gradually with the further progress of the alteration, the porous Chert becomes soft and friable, and is finely crushed and changed into a very fine either white or red Sand, often earthy or Clayish to the touch, on account of its extreme fineness, and of the presence of oxide of Iron. This change was most distinctly observed in the Tripoli quarry, near Seneca, in Sec. 26, T. 25, R. 34 W. Large beds of Chert are there changed into so-called "Tripoli," (altered Chert,) which is white in the lower layers, but colored reddish near the surface by infiltration of Iron solutions from above. It is porous, soft and friable, sandy to the touch, and consists of 99.8 per cent. of Silica, according to an analysis made by Messrs. Chauvenet and Blair. Pieces can often be seen with the interior still containing unaltered compact, white Chert, which gradually becomes porous towards the outside, and is surrounded by entirely porous Chert, and colored red near the surface. The change always begins from the outside of the piece, or from small crevices or cavities. At Granby a thick formation of this soft, porous, altered Chert, (called Cotton Rock by the miners,) overlies the alternate layers of Limestone and Chert, or the solid Chert layers. It is of reddish, white color, and contains sometimes irregular masses of unaltered Chert. The whole mass has the appearance of being first broken and then altered. A regular stratification, if it ever existed in this rock, has been obliterated by the change. Its thickness varies from 10 to 60 feet. It is covered by 10 feet of irregularly broken Chert masses, contains much red Sand, perhaps the product of further disintegration of its own mass. No ore has been found in it. The so-called first ore-opening, consisting of red Clay with little Galena, directly underlies it. The absence of ore in the altered Chert goes far towards proving that the alteration of the Chert must have taken place after the deposition of the ores.

SILICO-CALCAREOUS ROCKS.

Below the bottom of altered Chert beds above described, we find in the South-west districts alternate layers of Limestone and Chert; sometimes the former, sometimes the latter, predominating in quantity. Both are often plainly characterized by their fossils, which are especially numerous in the Chert. The layers are firmly adhering to each other. They are generally horizontal, often wavy. Their thickness varies from 3 inches to 6 feet. The limit between the layers of Chert and those of Limestone in many places assumes an irregular form, and the Limestone encloses smaller or larger concretions of Chert, increasing in number until in places the whole rock presents a confused mixture of the most varied and irregular mixture of concretionary forms of both Chert and Limestone. This mixed rock does not show any stratification. It plays a conspicuous part in the ore formations of South-west Missouri, and we will call it SILICO-CALCITE in the following descriptions. The Limestone of this formation is of grayish-white color, very compact, of a fine-grained to oolitic structure, the latter only occurring in Granby. The Chert is light-colored, mostly yellowish or white, sometimes bluish. The greatest total thickness observed of both the alternate and mixed rocks, is 40 to 50 feet. They contain most of the ore deposits in South-west Missouri. The ores, however, occur only in certain altered or metamorphic portions of these rocks.

The changes to which this formation was exposed before and during the deposition of the ores are of a different character at different points.

The Limestone has undergone in many places a process of dolomization. Solutions penetrating it have dissolved the Carbonate of Lime and partly replaced it by Carbonate of Magnesia. With this change a contraction is connected ; cracks are opened in the mass and filled with crystallized Dolomite. The change always begins either in fissures or on the surface of layers, or of broken off blocks, and gradually proceeds toward the interior of the rock. It seems to have preceded the formation of the ore and to have continued during the whole process. Many blocks and broken masses are nearly entirely changed into Dolomite Limestone and containing bands and irregular streaks of crystalline Dolomite. Such altered blocks are generally softened and sandy on the outside and rounded off (Boulders). The deposition of Zinc ores, especially Calamine, is evidently in intimate connection with the dolomization. At Granby the layers of Calamine are deposited directly on the altered sandy Limestone, and mostly mixed with sheets of Dolomite rocks or crystalline Dolomite in various proportions. The Galena occurs in Limestone only as far as the dolomization or alteration has proceeded in the rock, either in soft or sandy or in regenerated portions, or sometimes in thin fissures in the original rock. The dolomization connected with the formation of the ore beds extends, at Granby, through horizontal zones of irregular outline, called openings, generally 2 to 6 feet high, above which solid beds of Chert and Limestone or of Chert slabs alone, are deposited.

In the Joplin districts the ore deposits are mostly in the form of "runs," extending principally in one horizontal direction rarely more than 5 feet wide, and limited in height by the layers of Chert above and below the Limestone layer, in a crevice of which the run originated. Another mode of alteration of these rocks consists in a gradual dissolution and removal of the Limestone, either unaltered or more or less dolomized. This was undoubtedly effected by water containing carbonic acid, which dissolved the Limestone as Bicarbonate of Lime, leaving the sandy and clayish, and sometimes dolomitic masses and layers as residue of a more or less rotten appearance between the Chert. Large caves are produced by this dissolving process whenever the layers of Chert above did not happen to break down. These caves ($\frac{1}{2}$ to 6 feet high,) extend in one horizontal direction, sometimes for several hundred yards. One of these caves was observed in the Holman diggings in Granby, where several shafts are sunk through it to the ore beds, which lie 3 to 10 feet below the cave. The latter can be traced over several acres of ground, varying in height from ½ to 5 feet. It is cut off in several places by slabs of Chert broken down from the roof, in others it gradually thins out. The bottom in the cave is covered with yellow Sand or red Clay, which lies on the remaining part of the Limestone, whose surface is changed to a soft sandy mass. The walls are in places lined with a sheet of white crystalline Limestone, from which stalactitic forms are projecting. In other places small crystalline masses of Galena are pendant from the Chert roof of the cave. In places where the cave thins out, Calcite with some Galena, is occasionally deposited between the Chert and the Limestone.

Fig. 13 shows a portion of this cave in section.

a=Stalactites.

b=Stalagmites.

c=Galena.

d=Calcite.

e=Red Clay.

Many similar caves occur at Granby, often partly filled with red Clay. They are undoubtedly produced by the removal of Limestone layers. If the Limestone is removed from very large areas, the remaining alternate layers of Chert will either break down irregularly or gradually settle down without extensive disintegration. A formation, over 20 feet thick, was observed at Granby, consisting of layers of Chert separated from each other by horizontal seams, either empty or filled with Clay and Sand.

Likewise Silico-calcite, from which the Limestone has been removed, gradually breaks down and gives rise to large accumulations of irregularly shaped and broken up Chert concretions, sometimes very coarse, at other times of the size of small Gravel or even of Sand. In some places the leached-out and broken-up Silico-calcite is re-cemented, either by newly formed Limestone inclosing Galena, or by Calamine, or by Quartzite inclosing Blende. Thus, the various Conglomerates were formed, which we shall mention in our special description of ore deposits.

Whenever Limestone, after being in part dolomized, was afterwards subjected to the process of leaching, the dolomitic particles seem to have often remained undissolved, and now form the beds of "rotten Dolomite" which are so common in the ore deposits. This "rotten Dolomite" is either a soft and friable, but coherent mass, or else an entirely disintegrated Sand, composed of single loose Dolomite crystals, with corroded and cracked surfaces.

The alterations of Limestone, as above described, the breaking down of the Chert concretions and layers, and the deposition of the ores, although spread apparently over the whole Keokuk formation, in South-west Missouri, yet show a very variable degree of local development. In such localities where these changes have taken place in a higher degree than in others, all the overlying strata broke and settled down to a greater extent, thus producing gently sloping depressions on the surface. Such depressions of the ground are therefore good indications for the miner. As many of these depressions have, from early times, served as water channels, they are often washed out considerably and changed into small branches and sometimes into deep-cut valleys, whose bottoms are filled with enormous masses of broken Chert. These Chert masses occur to a very large extent all over the ore formations, especially in the middle and lower portions of Joplin Valley.

The above remarks explain the fact that so many good deposits are situated along and in the valleys.

CLAYS.

Besides the ores themselves, a number of residuary and of secondary products occur in and above the ore beds, especially Clays of different description, often mixed with Sand or with rotten Dolomite. All these Clays mainly consist of Silicate of Alumina—many, however containing more or less Iron, which gives them a dark red or brownish color. The miners distinguish two principal kinds of Clay— the Tallow Clay and the Red Tough Clay.

The "Tallow Clay" is generally light red, sometimes yellow or white, and very uniform in color and structure. The latter is extremely fine, almost impalpable. This Clay is somewhat greasy to the touch. In the condition in which it is found in the mines, it is not plastic but rather dry and breaks with a smooth conchoidal fracture. When exposed to the air it cracks and falls apart, and finally turns into a greasy powder. When finely triturated by the addition of water, it it becomes plastic.

It is generally associated with Calamine, in which it forms small pockets or streaks. It sometimes forms beds of some extent and as much as 2 feet thick. It frequently incloses crystals of Galena.

The "Red Tough Clay" of the miners is a plastic, ferruginous Clay, often so fine and uniform in color that it might be used as a paint. Its color is either deep red or yellow or brown. It is found in the mines in a perfectly plastic state, and when exposed to the air shrinks from one-half to one-third of its volume, forming a dry, hard mass of even fracture. It mostly occurs between layers of Chert in places where the Limestone has been dissolved and removed, forming beds of limited extent up to 4 feet thick. It frequently contains loose pieces or sheets of Galena. With Sand, it forms a mixture that is common in all masses of broken Chert occurring in the ore-bearing formations.

There is perhaps no essential difference between these two Clays, except in structure and purity. The tallow Clay is very pure, and extremely fine, while the red, tough Clay is coarser and mixed more often with Sand or with Oxides of Iron in larger quantity.

Mr. Regis Chauvenet found, in a sample of red, Tallow Clay, from the Hard-shaft, (Granby,) besides Iron, a large amount of combined water and 34.53 per cent. of Silica.

SANDS.

According to their origin, we may divide the different Sands of the ore-formation into three categories:

1. Sand produced by the disintegration of porous Chert. It generally incloses loose, irregular masses of the latter and passes into it. It contains no ore, except occasional impregnations of Carbonate of Lead.

2. Residuary Sand, which formed a part of the Limestone, and was left when the latter was dissolved. It is calcareous in some places; argillaceous in others. The latter variety was observed at McGee's shaft, in the Dutch diggings (Granby,) where it forms layers ½ to 1 inch thick, in red Clay, and incloses angular, well developed crystals of Galena.

3. Crystalline Sand, often mixed with crystalline Blende, passes into Quartzite, which will be described in the following:

"Yellow Sand," or "Brown Sand," or "Black Sand," are terms applied by the miners to a loose, sandy, or sometimes clayish mass, which in some districts occurs with the ore layers, especially of the layers of Calamine. Their origin can be generally traced to one of the above three. They are often intimately mixed with Zinc ore. The composition of these Clays and Sands is very variable, as may be seen from the following analysis made by Mr. Chauvenet. A soft and somewhat fat Clay, yellow and white streaks mixed, from Shaft 4, Lone Elm, showed:

Silica... 46.15 per cent.
Alumina (including some Peroxide of Iron)........................... 38.55   "
Water... 8.83   "
Lime... some.
Magnesia .... some.

A fine, reddish yellow Clay, associated with tallow Clay, from the Frazier diggings, (Granby,) contained 33.94 per cent. of Oxide of Zinc, or 27.23 per cent. of metallic Zinc; probably an intimate mixture of Clay and Calamine.

A brown, porous and friable clayish substance, accompanying the ores in the Hard-shaft diggings, (Granby,) called "Black Sand" by the miners, proved to be no Sand at all, but principally a Clay strongly mixed with Oxides of Iron and Zinc. Mr. Chauvenet found in it:

Clayish insoluble substance... 43.68
Peroxide of Iron... 27.96
Oxide of Zinc... 14.98
Water (including a little carbonic acid).. 13.33
                                                                               _____
                                                                               99.95

Three analyses were made of different Sands, with the following result:

	1.	2.	3.
Silica	87.82	79.54	93.63
Iron	4.13	some.	trace.
Zinc	4.48		
Lime	1.15	trace.	
Alumina		some.	5.71

No. 1 is a brownish-gray, coarse, crystalline Quartz Sand, from Minersville.

No. 2 is a pale-yellow, porous, fine micro-crystalline Sand, from Village diggings (Granby.)

No. 3 is a white, pretty hard rock; probably finely crystalline Quartz Sand, cemented by some Clay, accompanying and inclosing Galena. From Dutch diggings (Granby.)

QUARTZITE, OR QUARTZ ROCK.

We find in connection with the Zinc and Lead ores of South-west Missouri a very hard rock consisting almost entirely of crystalline Silica; partly fine, partly coarse-grained, and frequently porous. It is occasionally light-gray, but more frequently dark-brown to black, colored by Sulphuret of Zinc, and perhaps by Bitumen. The Quartzite is mostly micro or sub-crystalline. Sometimes, however, the small crystals, of which it is composed, can be seen with the naked eye, and under a common magnifying glass show the pyramidal form. It occurs but rarely at Granby, oftener at Joplin, (Lone Elm,) and is quite abundant at Oronogo. It forms the principal part of a certain Conglomerate, in which angular fragments of Chert or broken concretions from leached Silico-calcite are cemented by this Quartzite, the latter containing much Blende—as disseminated crystals and sometimes Galena in various forms.

The lines of contact between the Chert and the Quartzite are mostly sharp, though sometimes the Chert is somewhat altered and of darker color near its contact with the Quartzite. The ores are never in the mass of the Chert, but always in the mass of the Quartzite. The latter may be in places simultaneous, but is probably in most instances of later origin than the Galena and Blende. The inclosed crystals of these ores are well formed, angular and closely surrounded by the rock.

In some old shafts at Lone Elm single crystals and small crystalline masses of Dolomite are found inclosed in Quartzite. In most places, however, the Dolomite crystals formerly inclosed in the rock were leached out, leaving the rock as a porous, irregularly, spongy, silicious mass, whose cavities show plainly the form of Dolomite crystals of one-eighth to one-tenth of an inch in diameter. Wherever Quartzite occurs it is rarely found without these cavities, or at least without impressions of Dolomite crystals on its surface. Sometimes, however, the cavities seem to be produced by Blende, and occasionally also by Galena. Calamine and Cerussite sometimes line or fill these cavities.

In one instance, at Lone Elm, impressions of pretty distinct bivalves were found in very coarse and distinctly crystalline Quartzite of dark brown color. This seems to indicate that in this locality the quartzite may be, at least in part, metamorphic, being either an altered Sandstone or Chert, or else having replaced the Limestone in Silico-calcite. Mr. G. C. Broadhead thinks that these bivalves are sub-carboniferous fossils. Some further details regarding the Quartzite will be given in our special description of deposits, especially in that of Oronogo Diggings.

BED ROCK.

The alternate layers of Limestone and Chert above described, are finally underlaid by a Limestone whose thickness has not yet been determined. Wherever it underlies the metalliferous layers, the miners call it " bed rock," No ore has ever been observed in it.

At Granby, this Limestone occurs in thick layers, and is hard, gray and fine grained. The grain becomes generally coarser and more irregular with the depth. The coarse grained variety contains numerous fossils. Single concretions of Chert of irregular shape occur in it. In a bore-hole, near the furnace at Granby, this Limestone was struck at a depth of 12 feet, and followed to a depth of 136 feet without a change, and without reaching the end. The Day shaft, a little farther north, was sunk through the same Limestone 130 feet deep. In both places, like in many others where the miners tried to penetrate this Limestone, no ore whatever was found in it.

The surface of this rock below the deposits, is very uneven and strongly undulating, and lies at Granby from 12 to 80 feet below the surface of the ground.

A coarse grained, bluish gray, uniform, somewhat bituminous Limestone, containing many fossils, and occasionally irregular concretions of Chert, has been struck in the Nelson shaft, by the Jasper Lead and Mining Company, on the southern part of Swindle Hill, near Joplin. This solid and unstratified rock was struck immediately below 6 feet of Soil and of loose Chert, and the shaft was sunk to a depth of nearly 50 feet without encountering a change of the rock, and without finding any ore.

This Limestone has also been struck in the Porter shafts, on the north slope of Swindle Hill, and seems to compose the main body of this hill, and to correspond to the " bed rock " of Granby.

Mr. R. Chauvenet analyzed three samples of Limestones and found them to contain:

	1	2	3
Unsoluble matter	1.57	0.23	2.98
Carbonate of Lime	96.43	99.67	91.84
Carbonate of Magnesia	0.81	0.67	2.83
Carbonate of Iron	0.75	0.26	2.04
	99.56	100.83	99.69

No. 1. From Jasper, No. 3 Diggings, Joplin. Light gray, finely crystalline Limestone, from this ore-bearing Strata,

No. 2. From Holman Diggings, Granby. White oolitic Limestone, underlying the ore beds, which contain much Dolomite.

No. 3. From Joplin. Occurred in connection with the ore. Partly Dolomized Limestone, mainly composed of light gray crystalline grains about one-sixteenth inch thick. It is mixed with specks of bitumen.

These results show that the original Limestone contains but very little Magnesia, even in the vicinity of dolomitic layers. Some analyses of Dolomite have been given in the preceding Division, B of the present Report.

When Dolomites of highly dolomized Limestones are dissolved in acids, the residues are in different cases of a very different nature. By examining these residues under the magnifying glass, we found that:

No. 1. Black or dark gray dolomitic rock leaves many small particles of bitumen.

No. 2. Brown dolomitic rock leaves yellowish brown fine Sand.

No. 3. White, or light-gray dolomitic rock leaves small, scaly or botryoidal particles of white opaque Quartz or Chert.

No. 4. Rose-colored dolomitic rock, is pure Dolomite, and leaves no residue whatever.

GEOLOGICAL HISTORY OF THE SOUTHWEST MISSOURI ORE REGION.

PERIOD OF DEPOSITION. *First Period*—Original deposition of the various stratified rocks, namely: The "Bed Rock," the alternate layers of Limestone and Chert, the Silico-calcite, the Slates and Coal, and of the Sandstone.

These several strata, after their depositions, probably remained unaltered for a very long time and became dry, hard and dense before the second period began.

PERIOD OF DOLOMIZATION. *Second Period*—Local dolomization of certain strata of Limestone. Disturbances and ruptures in the Chert in consequence of the contraction of the Limestone during the metamorphic action. Principal deposition of the ores from watery solutions.

This metamorphic action was confined to a part of the alternate layers of Limestone and Chert, and very limited in its vertical extent —rarely exceeding 20 feet.

The dolomization of the Limestone, and the simultaneous deposition of the ores, began either from horizontal crevices and then extended through the whole mass of one stratum of Limestone and was limited by the layers of Chert above and below, or it began from vertical crevices in the Limestone and formed a mass of Dolomized Limestone, with ore extending along the crevice between the Chert layers, and generally from 3 to 10 feet wide. In the first case the "openings" of Granby were formed, in the second the "runs" of Joplin.

PERIOD OF DISSOLUTION. *Third Period*—Dissolution and removal of a part of the Limestone from the Silico-calcite and from the alternate layers of Limestone and Chert. Gradual breaking down of the remaining concretions and of the layers of Chert, and of the strata above. Continued deposition of ores in diminished measure.

In this period the immense accumulations of broken Chert were formed, which in so many places overlie or accompany the ore deposits. The ore (nearly always Galena) was deposited, in many places, in the fissures and little cracks of the broken Chert beds, in sheets between these layers and in crystals adhering to pieces of broken Chert, sometimes on all sides of the fragments, showing plainly that the Galena was formed after the Chert had been broken.

PERIOD OF REGENERATION. *Fourth Period*—Local regeneration of the partially dissolved and softened Limestone by renewed deposition of Carbonate of Lime. Local infiltrations of Quartzite. Continued deposition of ores.

All the conglomerates which consist of Chert-fragments, cemented either by a silicious or by a calcareous mass, the cementing mass inclosing crystals of Blende or Galena, were formed in this period.

PERIOD OF OXIDATION. *Fifth Period*—Oxidation of the metallic Sulphurets, and alteration of these Sulphurets into Silicates and into Carbonates.

During this period the Galena, in many deposits, was more or less completely altered into Cerussite and Pyromorphite, the Blende into Calamine and Smithsonite, and the Pyrites into Limonite. Some of these minerals also, while in solution, were carried over larger or smaller distances and re-deposited as seams or impregnations in Sands, in Clays or in Chert Breccia.

The local corrosion and partial dissolution of the Chert, and its alteration into a porous and more or less friable mass, must have taken place after the deposition of the ores. This is proved by the entire absence of ores in the porous Chert. This corrosion, therefore, belongs to the Fourth and Fifth Periods, and probably continues to the present day. Also, the oxidation of the ores undoubtedly yet continues.

All these mechanical and chemical actions which, according to present appearances, are confined to the upper layers of the Keokuk Limestone, have taken place over a very large area in South-west Missouri, but with different intensities and effects in different districts and localities.

CHAPTER XXV.

D.—SPECIAL DESCRIPTION OF ORE DEPOSITS.

I.—THE DEPOSITS OF SHOAL CREEK DISTRICT.

GRANBY MINES.

The Granby Mines are situated in Newton county, and occupy Sec. 6, T. 25, R. 30 W.

The elevation of this section is from 60 to 160 feet above the railway at Granby City, (1½ miles north of Granby Mines,) or from 670 to 770 feet above the city directrix of St. Louis; or from 1,075 to 1,175 feet above the level of the sea.

The central part of the section forms a basin extending two-thirds of a mile in an east and west, and one-half of a mile in a south and north course. It is surrounded by gently sloping hills, which rise from 60 to 80 feet above the valley.

This basin has only one outlet—through a valley leading north, and through which a small creek, originating in a number of small channels in the surrounding hills, flows northward into Shoal Creek. All the slopes are gentle.

The Limestone crops out in a few places, while generally it is covered by thick beds of Clay and Soil.

A part of the land was formerly covered with timber. This timbered land extends into the bottoms of Shoal Creek, which winds its course 1 to 1½ miles north of Granby, from east to west.

South of Granby, in Sec. 7, a gently rolling prairie begins, which is a part of Oliver's prairie.

The town of Granby is situated near the centre of the northern boundary of Sec. 6, and extends somewhat into the adjoining section. Single houses and cabins are scattered over the whole of Sec. 6, especially in the centre of the basin.

The distribution of the diggings is represented on our topographical map of the Granby Mines, which comprises the whole of Sec. 6, and was drawn after a survey made by Mr. C. Henrich, who was engaged for this work by the Geological Survey.

The diggings lie on the upper part of the slopes surrounding the central basin, and in many places extend over the top of the hill and on the outside slopes. Many shafts are also sunk in the bottom, and on both sides of the valley which forms the northern outlet from the basin.

We will now proceed to describe the relative positions of the various diggings, as they are marked on the topographical map :

Beginning with the north-west quarter of the section, we first observe, west of the town, the Village Diggings, on the slope along the east side of the creek. The creek separates them from the Brockhollow Diggings, which extend west from the creek into a small valley. South of the Village shafts are the Crabtree Diggings—on the north slope of the basin. West of them, the hill rises 60 feet above the valley, and near its summit the Holman Diggings are situated. West of these, on the west slope of the same hill, are the Dutch Diggings—at the upper end of a little valley running north. A number of shafts are sunk on the northern slope of Ashcraft's Hollow, west of the great basin.

In the north-east quarter of the section the hill rises 80 feet above the valley, sloping gently west towards the creek and south towards the center of the basin. The Hardshaft Diggings extend from the top of this hill down the western and southern slopes. Between all these diggings many single shafts were sunk, so that no definite lines can be drawn limiting the various diggings; all forming one complex, which we may comprise under the general name of the Northern Mines. A zone containing but a very few shafts, and running across the central basin, separates them from the Southern Mines, which are spread over the hills on the south side of the basin. Beginning in the south-west quarter of the section, we observe hills rising 70 to 80 feet high, (above the center of the basin,) sloping towards a small water-course, which enters the central basin from the south. A number of diggings are situated on both sides of this stream and on the hill-sides. These we will comprise under the general name of Frazier Diggings. Some shafts north-west of these and rather isolated are called the Chester Shafts. Several diggings extend from the Frazier Diggings through the northern part of south-east quarter of the section, namely : the Hopkins, Bellew, Eastpoint, Poorman's Point, and Mineral Diggings. The Hopkins shafts lie adjoining the Frazier Diggings on the northern slope of the hill. They connect the latter Diggings, with the others just mentioned, which are situated on the different slopes of a knob to the north-east quarter of the south-east quarter of the section, 50 to 60 feet above the bottom of the basin. The Bellew shafts and the Eastpoint Diggings are on the northern and north-eastern slopes, and the diggings at Poorman's Point and Mineral Point on the southern and south-eastern parts of this knob.

The General Geological Section of the strata occurring in the Granby Mines, is as follows, giving the maximum thickness of the strata in feet :

No. 1. 8 feet Soil and Gravel, sometimes mixed with plastic, ferruginous Clay, and in places containing pieces of Cerussite.

No. 2. 15 feet Chert, broken to small angular pieces without regular stratification, and always mixed with more or less brown Sand and red Clay.

No. 3. 20 feet soft, porous Chert, (called "Cotton Rock" by the miners.)

In some places we find an ore-opening from 2 to 20 inches thick immediately below the porous Chert. It consists of red Clay or Sand in which loose, rounded pieces of Galena are imbedded. It is, however, of exceptional occurrence.

Below the above strata we observed two different successions of rocks in different places :

FIRST :

No. 1. 35 feet alternate layers of white or gray, fine-grained, often oolitic Limestone, and of hard, white Chert, the layers being $\frac{1}{2}$ to 3 feet thick.

No. 2. 3 feet first regular ore-opening, containing broken Chert, rotten and disintegrated Dolomite, Clay and Sand, with Galena in thin sheets or in loose pieces.

No. 3. 9 feet alternate layers of Limestone and Chert, same as above.

No. 4. 10 feet second or principal ore-opening, containing the best ore deposits. This will be specially described hereafter.

SECOND :

No. 1. 25 feet hard, solid Chert, in more or less broken layers, from $\frac{1}{4}$ to 3 feet thick, never adhering to each other, but always separated by more or less Clay and Sand.

G.S—27.

No. 2. 2 feet first opening, containing Clay, disintegrated Dolomite, with
       Galena and Cerussite in loose pieces or in thin sheets.
No. 3. 7 feet of Chert; layers as above.
No. 4. 10 feet second or principal ore-opening.

Both Sections are finally underlaid by over 130 feet of Limestone,
called the "bed-rock." In comparing the above two Sections, which
replace each other in different localities, it is evident that the Second
is only an alteration of the First, the Limestone being gradually dissolved and removed, leaving thin residuary beds of Sand or Clay between the Chert layers. The latter in settling down became more or
less broken.

The second or principal ore-opening contains all the Zinc ores and
most of the Lead ores. It is mostly from 2 to 6 feet high and extends
nearly horizontally, generally between a layer of solid Chert and the
"bed-rock," whose surface is mostly altered and softened. It is occasionally empty (forming caves,) but generally contains various materials, as broken Chert, Dolomitic Limestone, Dolomite, Calcspar,
Sands and Clays. These materials contain the ore generally in more
or less horizontal sheets or streaks of variable thickness and limited
extent.

Most of the Zinc ore (almost exclusively Calamine,) is deposited
directly on the altered Limestone, generally mixed with streaks of
Dolomite and occupying the lowest part of the opening in layers
from 1-10 to 6 feet thick. The Galena is found in horizontal sheets,
which are in some places six inches thick in all parts of the opening;
also as loose chunks in the Clay or Sand.

The contents of the openings vary very much and often change
completely within a distance of 10 to 20 feet. The ore that may exist in one part several feet thick gives out entirely within less than 10
feet, and frequently the opening itself thins out or is suddenly terminated by a curved elevation of the underlying Limestone, called
"bar" by the miners.

The very numerous openings at Granby are not all on the same
level, but their absolute elevation depends on that of the underlying
Limestone (the bed-rock). It varies from 45 to nearly 100 feet above
the railway at Granby station, and mostly lies between 60 to 80 feet
above that level. These openings are 15 to 70 feet below the surface
of the ground.

We will now proceed to describe the several mines of Granby
in the following order:

I. NORTHERN MINES.

a. *Central part:*
1. Village Diggings.
2. Brockhollow Diggings.
3. Crabtree Diggings.

b. *Western part:*
4. Holman Diggings, with the diggings in Dutch and Ashcraft's hollows.

c. *Eastern part:*
5. Hardshaft Diggings.

II. SOUTHERN MINES.

a. *Western part:*
6. Frazier Diggings with the Chester shafts.

b. *Eastern part:*
7. Eastpoint Diggings with Bellew's and Hopkins' shafts.
8. Diggings at Mineral Point and at Poorman's Point.

1. THE VILLAGE DIGGINGS

Extend over a piece of ground along the east side of the creek, about 1,100 feet long, in a direction of north 20° west, and from 100 to 200 feet wide. On this ground, about 110 to 120 shafts have been sunk; most of them, however, were worked before the war (1851–1860,) and have caved in since. Only 7 shafts were in operation during the time of our examination. The ground rises toward the east so that the tops of the eastern shafts are 25 to 30 feet higher than those of the shafts along the bottom of the creek.

In these diggings the following General Section was observed:

No. 1. 7 feet Soil and Gravel.

No. 2. 15 feet Chert, broken irregularly with much fine Sandy Limestone and Clay.

No. 3. 18 feet Chert layers, from $\frac{1}{3}$ to 3 feet thick, with little Sand and Clay between the layers.

No. 4. 2 feet first opening, as described in the General Section of Granby.

No. 5. 7 feet Chert layers or in places alternate layers of Limestone and Chert.

No. 6. 5 feet second and principal opening. (?) Limestone, decomposed and sandy near the surface, and gradually passing into a dense, hard gray Limestone. The surface of this Limestone is irregular and wavy as usual, and the highest portions of it are oolitic.

The second or principal opening varies in its composition often and rapidly. To elucidate this we will give a few sections of the openings in this district as we measured and sketched them in the drifts. Thirty feet north-west of shaft 7 the opening consisted of $2\frac{1}{2}$ feet of Chert layers, with 3 seams of Galena between the layers, $\frac{3}{4}$, 2 and 2 inches thick respectively, as represented in the sketch (Fig. 14). Both the Limestone and the opening dip 20° west. About 60 feet west from the shaft and 8 feet deeper than the above Section we saw in the same opening—

No. 1. 2 feet Chert layers without any Galena.

No. 2. 1 foot Dolomite partly disintegrated and sandy, with streaks and pockets of tallow Clay.

No. 3. 2 feet Calamine in wavy sheets, with tallow Clay in pockets.

About 50 feet north-west of shaft 7, near shaft 6, the section of the opening presented itself as follows:

No. 1. Chert on top.

No. 2. 3 feet solid Calamine, with streaks of Galena often 2 inches thick and with pockets of tallow Clay ; softened, sandy Limestone below.

South-west of shaft 7, near shaft 8, we observed the section as represented in sketch (Fig. 15).

Limestone Top.

No. 1. 3 feet alternate layers of Limestone and Dolomite ; in the latter crystals of Galena.

No. 2. 8 inches solid Calamine.

No. 3. 10 inches tallow Clay, with streaks of Calamine. Soft, decomposed Limestone.

All the faces mentioned here belong to one large opening, on which the shafts No. 6 to 11 were sunk. It dips 15° W., like the surface of the ground, so that the western part (at shaft 11) is 13 feet deeper than the eastern points near shaft 7. The patches of Galena above the Calamine, had been mostly worked out before the war, and the Calamine, whose value was not known then, was left. This, like many of the old diggings, was reopened in 1872, and worked especially for the Calamine.

Another portion of the second ore-opening, can be traced from here southward, through the shafts 15 to 28, over to the Crabtree Diggings. It dips like the former to the west, but not as strongly as the surface of the ground. It forms in its western part, the lowest ore-beds found in Granby, being there only 42 to 45 feet above the railway. The composition of this opening also changes very materially.

Near shaft 15 we found :

8 feet decomposed Dolomite and red Clay.

1 to 2 inches Galena.

2 feet Calamine with pockets of tallow Clay.

About 200 feet further south, near shaft 19, the face appeared thus, as represented in Fig. 16 :

No. 1.   6 inches Dolomite and red Clay.

No. 2.   12 to 18 inches Calamine and tallow Clay.

No. 3.   6 to 18 inches pockets of Calcite with Galena.

In the southern part, near the Crabtree Diggings, the face of the rock presented the following Section which is represented by Fig. 17 :

No. 1.   2 feet Limestone, with wavy streaks of Dolomite and Calamine, 1 to 2 inches thick.

No. 2.   28 inches Calamine, with pockets of Blende and Galena, and with streaks of rotten Dolomite and a little tallow Clay.

No. 3.   1 foot tallow Clay.

No. 4.   Limestone, the upper part of which is rotten and sandy to the touch.

To show the relation of the opening to the General Section, we represent a Section through a part of the Northern Village Diggings, of which the following is a description :

No. 8.   Limestone.

No. 7.   Rotten, sandy Limestone.

No. 6.   Oolitic Limestone.

No. 5.   Calamine, with sheets of Dolomite, and some Blende and Galena.

No. 4.   Clay and Sand, with chunks of Galena, and some Chert fragments.

No. 3.   Chert layers.

No. 2.   Broken up Chert.

No. 1.   Soil.

At the north end of these diggings, east of the furnace building, about 25 pits from 4 to 7 feet deep, had been sunk through Soil and Gravel, in which loose pieces of silicious Cerussite (Drybone) were imbedded.

In all these diggings, the frequent occurrence of Cerussite and Pyromorphite in amorphous masses and crystals, is remarkable. They are mostly connected with a brown, hardened and very silicious Clay.

2. THE BROCKHOLLOW DIGGINGS

Are situated on the west side of the creek, opposite the Village Diggings, on both sides of a little hollow, and on the lower part of a slope south of it, and extend about 800 feet from south to north, and 600 feet from west to east. The western part of this ground is about 50 feet higher than the eastern part, near the creek.

120 to 130 shafts have been sunk on this piece of land, but nearly all of them are abandoned at present, and most of them are caved in.

Only 3 shafts were occasionally worked during the progress of our examination.

The shafts were from 15 to 40 feet deep, and showed the following General Section:

3 feet Soil.

10 feet broken Chert

15 feet Chert layers, separated by a little Sand and Clay.

10 feet ore-opening, consisting of Chert Detritus, with occasional horizontal
streaks of Sand, Dolomite, tallow Clay, Galena and Cerussite.

(?) Limestone.

Some Galena, but more Cerussite, (in the form of Drybone and Wool mineral,) was obtained.

3. CRABTREE DIGGINGS.

The Crabtree Diggings, (see topographical map,) extend from the east side of the creek, up the lower part of a hill slope rising toward the east.

They adjoin the Village Diggings on the South, the Holman Diggings on the west, and the Hardshaft Diggings on the east. They cover a space about 700 feet in each direction, the eastern part of which is about 50 feet higher than the Creek.

About 90 shafts are sunk, 11 of which we saw in operation.

The General Section at these digging is as follows:

No. 1. 3 feet Soil and some Gravel.

No. 2. 8 feet loose, broken Chert, with some Sand and Clay.

No. 3. 20 feet soft, porous Chert, (Cotton rock).

No. 4. 25 feet Chert-layers, partly broken, with Sand and Clay between the
layers.

No. 5. 2 feet first opening, mostly red Clay, with occasional small pieces of
Galena.

No. 6. 10 feet alternate layers of Limestone and Chert, 4 to 8 inches each.

No. 7. 9 feet second ore-opening to be described hereafter.

No. 8. 1 foot Limestone.

The second opening presents the following examples of sections

In Shaft 50.   See Fig. 19.

No.   1.   2 feet broken Chert.
No.   2.   ½ inch Galena.
No.   3.   2 feet Calamine, with much Dolomite and Red Clay, and some streaks of Galena.

Near Shaft 55.   See Fig. 20.

No.   1.   3 feet Limestone, with wavy layers of Dolomite, the latter containing streaks and crystals of Galena.
No.   2.   2 feet Calamine, with little tallow Clay.

Near Shaft 51.   Section Fig. 21.

No.   1.   3 feet white tallow Clay, Dolomite, and some Calamine in alternate sheets.   Some patches of Galena 1 inch thick.
No.   2.   1 foot Calamine, with small pockets of tallow Clay.

In Shaft 71.   Section Fig. 22.

No.   1.   16 Inches tallow Clay and Sand.
No.   2.   8 inches sandy, rotten Limestone.
No.   3.   12 inches red Clay.
No.   4.   8 inches Dolomite, with numerous streaks of Galena.

In Shaft 73.

No.   1.   3 feet red plastic Clay.
No.   2.   4 inches Calamine, with tallow Clay.
No.   3.   8 inches black Sand and rotten Dolomite.
No.   4.   18 inches Calamine, with much Dolomite.
No.   5.   5 inches solid Calamine.
No.   6.   6 inches red Clay.
           (?) Limestone.

The opening throughout these Diggings lies deepest in the western and northern parts, and rises towards the south and east. It is 49 feet in shaft 50; 53 feet in shaft 51 ; from 60 to 73 feet in shafts 52 to 74—above the railway level at Granby station.

4. HOLMAN DIGGINGS'

Are situated on the south side of a hill which occupies nearly all of the north-west quarter of the section. They extend from the creek bottom south of Brockhollow Diggings to the top of the ridge, and connect westwards with the diggings in Ashcraft's and Dutch Hollows. They occupy a space 2,000 feet long from east to west, and 400 to 600 feet wide, on which 150 to 160 shafts are sunk—9 of these were

in operation in the summer of 1873. The Diggings at the head of
Dutch Hollow and in the Creek bottom were worked before the war,
while the principal ore-beds near the top of the ridge (shafts 121 to
132) were not discovered until 1866, and have been mined since then
without interruption, and with very great success.

The General Section in this part of the Central Diggings shows the
following strata :

> No. 1. 5 feet Soil and Gravel.
> No. 2. 10 feet broken Chert.
> No. 3. 20 feet soft, porous Chert.
> No. 4. 30 feet alternate layers of Limestone and Chert, which are sometimes
> replaced by :
>> 15 feet Chert layers.
>> 10 feet alternate layers of Limestone and Chert.
>
> No. 3. 3 feet first opening consisting of Limestone, Dolomite, red Clay and
> some Galena in the Dolomite and in the Clay.
> No. 6. 10 feet alternate layers of Limestone and Chert.
> No. 7. 6 feet second opening, described hereafter.
>> (?) Limestone, rotten and sandy in the upper 2 to 10 inches, then
>> oolitic, which structure gradually passes into one dense and fine-
>> grained.

The surface of the ground at these Diggings is 110—130 feet, the
principal ore opening 56—66 feet above the railway level.

The following sections of the ore beds were observed in the Drift :

In Shaft 123.

1st Opening..... { 2 inches Tallow Clay, with crystals of Galena.
{ 3 inches rotten, sandy Dolomite.

> 5 feet Chert, in one solid layer.

2nd Opening.... { 12 inches gray, Dolomitic Limestone and yellowish Dolomite in alternate sheets ; the Dolomite containing Galena, Limestone and
Dolomite form banded masses.
{ 14 inches Calamine, with tallow Clay, Dolomite and some little Galena.

> (?) Limestone.

In Shaft 125.

The principal ore opening consists of (Fig. 23 :)

> No. 1. 12 inches soft, rotten Dolomitic Limestone.
> No. 2. 4 inches Dolomite, with many crystals of Galena $\frac{1}{4}$ to 1 inch in dia-
> meter, well developed.
> No. 3. 1 inch tallow Clay.
> No. 4 14 inches Calamine, with some Dolomite and tallow Clay.

In Shaft 122.

No. 1. 8 inches Chert.

No. 2. 2 inches Galena.

No. 3. 24 inches Chert, with thin sheets of Galena.

Beginning at this place, both the Limestone and the opening dip east 30°, and the opening changes its character entirely, so that in it and only 23 feet north-east of the last mentioned face, and consequently at a level about 5 feet deeper, we found:

> 3 feet of soft, rotten Dolomitic Limestone, with 4 small seams of Galena, each about ½ inch thick, and connected with each other by very thin vertical seams.

In Shaft 129, (Fig. 24.)

No. 1. 8 inches Limestone, partly altered into Dolomite.

No. 2. 4 inches Chert.

No. 3. 6 inches crystalline Calcite, inclosing Galena.

No. 4. 6 inches Calamine, in patches.

No. 5. (?) Limestone.

Shaft 148

Was sunk in March, 1873, by Mr. McGee on the top of the ridge between Ashcraft's and Dutch Hollows. The mouth of this is 148 feet and the principal ore bed 83 feet above the railway level. The shaft shows the following Section:

No. 1. 3 feet soil.

No. 2. 12 feet broken Chert.

No. 3. 20 feet soft, porous Chert.

No. 4. 17 feet Chert layers.

No. 5. 1 foot, first opening, filled with red Clay and a little Galena.

No. 6. 12 feet Chert layers.

No. 7. 6 feet, second opening.

No. 8. 2 feet Chert.

No. 9. (?) Limestone.

In the different drifts of this shaft we noticed the following faces:

North-west of Shaft.

No. 1. Chert layer on top.

No. 2. 1 to 2 inches Galena.

No. 3. 8 inches fissured Chert, with thin seams of Galena in all directions.

No. 4. ½ inch Galena.

No. 5. Limestone.

South-east of shaft is Fig. 15. The Section is Fig. 25.

No. 1. Chert on top.
No. 2. 1 inch Galena.
No. 3. 8 inches soft, rotten Dolomitic Limestone, with some Clay and streaks of rotten Dolomite.
No. 4. 2 inches hardened, white silicious Clay rock, with many crystals of Galena, $\frac{1}{4}$ to 1 inch in diameter.
No. 5. 12 inches tallow Clay and red Clay.
No. 6. 6 inches Chert, with small seams of Galena.
No. 7. 1 inch hard Clay rock, with large crystals of Galena.
No. 8. 8 inches red Clay.
No. 9. 12 inches Chert.
No. 10. 4 feet 2 inches Limestone.

The silicious Clay rock bears on its under side numerous impressions of Dolomitic crystals, and was undoubtedly originally deposited on crystalized Dolomites. At present, however, this Dolomite is replaced partly by Tallow Clay and partly by a very ferruginous tough Clay.

5. The Hardshaft Diggings

Extend east of the Crabtree diggings to the top of a hill which lies near the center of the north-east quarter of the Section. They cover an area of ground about 700 feet wide in every direction, on which 70 to 80 shafts have been sunk. The surface of the ground at these diggings is from 125 to 155 feet, and the principal ore beds 76 to 83 feet above the railway level at Granby station.

The General Section is as follows: the number of feet indicating the greatest observed thickness of the strata:

No. 1. 6 feet Soil and some Gravel.
No. 2. 8 feet broken Chert.
No. 3. 12 feet soft, porous Chert.
No. 4. 24 feet alternate layers of Limestone and Chert.
No. 5. 2 feet first opening, filled with Chert and with red Clay, inclosing some little Galena.
No. 6. 8 feet alternate layers of Limestone and Chert.
No. 7. 8 feet second ore opening.
No. 8. (?) Limestone.

In the second opening we observed the following characteristic faces:

Near Shaft 101.

No. 1. 3 feet Limestone, with streaks of Dolomite and pockets of tallow Clay.

No. 2. 1½ feet white or light yellow, massive Smithsonite.

No. 3. 3 feet Calamine, with small pockets of Galena in the upper part.

No. 4. ——? Limestone.

This is the only place in South-west Missouri where this variety of Smithsonite (called "White Jack" by the miners) was found in large quantity.

Near Shaft 95.

No. 1. Chert top.

No. 2. 2 inches red Clay with pieces of Galena.

No. 3. 14 inches Silico-calcite.

No. 4. 1 inch white Sand, with a seam of Galena ¼ of an inch thick.

No. 5. 7 inches Chert.

No. 6. 1 inch Sand with Galena.

No. 7. 6 inches Chert.

No. 8. 1 inch Sand with Galena.

No. 9. 15 inches Tallow Clay with small streaks of Dolomite.

No. 10. 1 inch Dolomite with Galena.

No. 11. 3 inches Chert.

No. 12. ——? Limestone.

Near Shaft 93.

Chert layer.

1ST OPENING.....{ 14 inches limestone and Chert, with Calcite and crystals of Galena.

2 inches Chert.

1 inch Galena.

8 inches rotten Dolomitic Limestone and rotten Dolomite.

3 feet Limestone.

2 feet Chert.

2ND OPENING....{ 4 feet Chert, with five seams rotten Limestone 1 to 2 inches thick, containing much Galena.

Near Shaft 103.

No. 1. Chert layer.

No. 2. 4 inches tallow Clay.

No. 4. 18 inches Calamine, with pockets of Galena 2 to 3 inches thick.

No. 5. 36 inches rotten Dolomite, white Sand and red Clay, with Galena disseminated through the whole mass.

This Section is one of the few where much Galena was found below the solid sheets of Calamine.

6. THE FRAZIER DIGGINGS AND THE CHESTER SHAFTS.

The Frazier Diggings are situated on both sides of a small valley, through which the creek enters the Granby basin from the south. They occupy, with the Chester Shafts, which are further west, a space of about 1600 feet from east to west and 400 to 600 feet from north to south. From 170 to 180 shafts have been sunk here, seven of which we saw in process of operation. The surface at these Diggings is 105 to 145 feet—the principal ore beds 67 to 84 feet—above the railway level.

These Diggings were partly worked before the war and many have been re-opened a year or two ago for the purpose of getting the Calamine which had been left in the mines.

The General Geological Section of these Diggings is as follows:

No. 1. 5 feet Soil with some Gravel.
No. 2. 20 feet soft, porous Chert.
No. 3. 1 foot first opening, filled with red Clay containing little Galena.
No. 4. 24 feet Chert layers.
No. 5. 10 feet second opening, described hereafter.
No. 6. 2 feet solid Chert.
No. 7. ——? Limestone.

The second opening shows the following various Sections:

In Mine of Shaft 218, South-east from Shaft.

No. 1. Chert layer.
No. 2. 12 inches Limestone.
No. 3. 3 inches Calamine in thin, broken slabs, with pockets of red Clay and tallow Clay.
No. 4. 1 inch Sand.
No. 5. 18 inches Calamine, with small pockets of tallow Clay.
No. 6. 8 inches Calamine, with much red Clay and Sand.
No. 7. Chert layer.

In the Same Mine, North-east from Shaft. (Fig. 26.)

No. 1. 4 feet rounded boulders of Limestone, decomposed on the outside and surrounded by red Clay and tallow Clay.
No. 2. 1½ feet Calamine, with small pockets of tallow Clay.

In the Same Mine, South-west of Shaft. (Fig. 27.)

No. 1. Chert layer.
No. 2. 4 inches tallow Clay and Sand mixed.

No. 3.   13 inches Smithsonite, solid, of grayish brown color, and fine-grained
        or oolitic.
No. 4.   18 inches solid Calamine.
No. 5.   Chert layer.

Near Shaft 220. (*Fig. 28.*)

No. 1.   Chert layer.
No. 2.   4 inches white tallow Clay, with crystals of Galena.
No. 3.   10 inches Chert.
No. 4.   8 inches Clay and Sand, with chunks of Cerussite and a little Galena.
No. 5.   Chert layer.

At Shaft 195.

No. 1.   Chert layer on top.
No. 2.   8 inches tallow Clay, with Galena.
No. 3.   24 inches Sand, rotten Dolomite and tallow Clay in alternate bands.
No. 4.   12 inches Dolomite, with streaks of crystalline Dolomitic Limestone.
No. 5.   21 inches Calamine, with pockets of Blende and Galena.
No. 6.   ——? Limestone.

In the Same Mine, only 10 feet West of the preceding Section.

No. 1.   Chert layer.
No. 2.   1½ inches tallow Clay and red Clay, with a little Galena.
No. 3.   6 inches gray Clay and brown Sand, in alternate streaks.
No. 4.   12 inches red Clay and Sand.

No. 5.   1 inch gray, sillicious Clay.

No. 6.   8 inches tallow Clay, with some Sand.

No. 7.   3 inches Calamine, with some tallow Clay.

    With pockets of Ga-
    lena from 1 to 8
    inches thick.

In the Same Mine, 15 feet West of the last mentioned Section. we saw :

No. 1.   Chert layer.
No. 2.   4 inches rotten Dolomite.
No. 3.   2 inches gray Clay, with streaks of Galena and Calamine.
No. 4.   2 inches Galena in patches.
No. 5.   4 inches rotten Dolomite.
No. 6.   12 inches Dolomite and Sand mixed.
No. 7.   2 inches Chert.
No. 8.   ? feet Limestone.

The above three Sections, taken in shaft 195, at one and the same
mining face, which was about 25 feet wide and 4 to 8 feet high, show
very plainly the rapid changes in the materials filling the opening.
The solid Dolomite and Calamine in the first Section at one end of the
face for about 20 feet is almost entirely replaced by various Clays

and Sands, in which Galena abounds in chunks and pockets. About
15 feet farther again, in the Third Section mentioned, Dolomite appears again, but Calamine and Galena only occur in small streaks.

We will add here two more Sections from openings in the Frazier
Diggings, which are remarkable for a large development of solid Calamine:

Near Shaft 209.

No. 1. 3 feet Limestone with bands of Dolomite and pockets of tallow Clay.
No. 2. 2 feet Limestone and Dolomite in alternate bands, the Dolomite containing crystals of Galena.
No. 3. 8 feet solid Calamine with some Galena. The Dolomite which occurs only in small quantities in the 3 feet layer of Limestone, gradually increases and predominates in the lower portions adjoining
the Calamine.

Near Shaft 236.

No. 1. 8 inches Chert.
No. 2. 4 inches Sand.
No. 3. 24 inches red Clay, with chunks of Galena.
No. 4. 12 inches Chert.
No. 5. 36 inches Calamine, which, in some other places near this shaft,
occurs 6 feet thick.
No. 6. (?) Limestone.

7. THE EASTPOINT DIGGINGS,

Which we will here describe, together with the Bellew and Hopkins'
Shafts, form a belt which extends from the Frazier Diggings about
2,500 feet in the direction of N. 50° E., in a width of 200 to 500 feet.
Over 200 shafts are sunk here, some of which we have been able to
examine. The surface of the ground at these Diggings is from 105 to
155 feet above the railway level at Granby Station.

The diggings at Eastpoint are on the north-east end of this belt,
on the northern and eastern slope of a ridge which gradually rises towards the south-west.

The General Section at these diggings, is as follows :

No. 1. 2 feet Soil.
No. 2. 14 feet soft, porous Chert.
No. 3. 18 feet Chert layers.
No. 4. 1 foot first opening, consisting of yellow Clay and Sand, with loose
chunks of Galena.
No. 5. 7 feet Silico-calcite, in some places replaced by alternate layers of
Limestone and Chert.

No. 6. 7 feet second ore-opening.
No. 7. 3 feet Chert layer.
No. 8. (?) Limestone.

The second principal ore-opening shows a great variety of composition.

We give the following Sections of it as being the most characteristic :

Near Shaft 292, North-west of Shaft.

No. 1. Chert layer above.
No. 2. 6 inches Galena, in patches.
No. 3. 24 inches Chert.
No. 4. 6 inches red Clay.
No. 5. 36 inches Calamine.

In the same Mine, South of Shaft.

No. 1. Chert layer.
No. 2. 1 inch Galena.
No. 3. 8 inches Silico-calcite, the Limestone partly Dolomized and rotten ;
both Limestone and Chert contain Galena in small streaks.
No. 4. Limestone.

Near Shaft 271. (Fig. 29.)

No. 1. 8 inches Chert.
No. 2. 1 inch Galena, connected with the Chert above, and filling all the
indent small crevices in the same.
No. 3. 18 inches Calamine, with tallow Clay and Sand.
No. 4. 6 inches Chert.
No. 5. $\left\{\begin{array}{l}\frac{1}{2}\text{ inch Galena.}\\ \frac{1}{4}\text{ inch Calamine.}\\ \frac{1}{2}\text{ inch Sand.}\end{array}\right\}$ Forming one-banded layer.
No. 6. 2 inches Chert.
No. 7. Limestone below.

THE BELLEW SHAFTS,

South-west of Eastpoint, were not worked at the time of our visit.
They were filled with water. They had been worked before the war
and were re-opened by Mr. Bellew in 1872, to mine the Calamine
which was left at the bottom of old Drifts 3 to 5 feet thick. This Calamine was of the very best quality, of nearly black color, and contained many patches of Blende and Galena.

HOPKINS' SHAFT,

Is situated between the Frazier and the Bellew Diggings. We saw one shaft (No. 236,) at work, which had been sunk through

No. 1. 13 feet broken Chert.
No. 2. 15 feet soft, porous Chert.
No. 3. 30 feet Chert layers.
No. 4. 5 feet principal ore-opening.
No. 5. 3 feet Chert.
No. 6. (?) Limestone.

It had been sunk before the war, and was re-opened in fall 1872, to work out the Calamine.

The principal ore-opening, in various drifts of the shaft, showed the following strata :

38 feet North-west from Shaft.

No. 1. Chert layer above.
No. 2. 2 feet red Clay.
No. 3. 2 feet Chert, with some seams of Galena.
No. 4. 3 feet Calamine, with small pockets of Blende and Galena.
No. 5. Chert layer below.

70 feet North from Shaft.

No. 1. 8 inches Chert.
No. 2. 4 inches yellow Sand.
No. 3. 20 inches solid Calamine.
No. 4. 12 inches Sand and tallow Clay.
No. 5. Limestone below.

The Calamine forms a nearly horizontal layer, $1\frac{1}{2}$ to 4 feet thick, extending 40 to 50 feet in each direction.

8. MINERAL POINT AND POOR MAN'S POINT DIGGINGS.

The diggings at Mineral Point and at Poor Man's Point, situated on a strip of land about 1,400 feet long and 400 feet broad, south of Bellews' shafts and of East Point Diggings, running parallel with the latter. About 60 shafts have been sunk on this ground, 2 of which we had an opportunity to examine. The surface is 120 to 145 feet and the ore beds 60 to 78 feet above the railway bed at Granby station.

The General Section shows the following strata:

3 feet Soil.
10 feet broken Chert.
18 feet soft porous Chert.
25 feet Chert layers.
6 feet principal ore-opening.
3 feet Chert.
(?) Limestone.

In the drifts worked in the principal ore-opening, we noticed the following compositions of faces:
In the mine of shaft 341, north of shaft:

6 inches red Clay and Sand, with loose pieces of Galena.
6 inches yellow tallow Clay.
1 inch white Sand.
1 inch tallow Clay, with Galena.
1 inch Sand and red Clay.
6 inches Calamine, in thin sheets.
24 inches red Clay.
Chert layer.

In the same mine, south of shaft, all the Calamine, Sand, and tallow Clay had given out, and the whole face consisted of:

4 feet red Clay, with loose chunks of Galena, ¼ to 60 pounds in weight, coated with Cerussite.
Chert layer.

The ore formation is generally parallel to the surface of the ground, dipping with the slopes.

Outside of the Diggings above described, about 200 shafts are sunk on the Granby section, making a total of nearly 1,200 shafts.

Most of the outside shafts struck the solid bed rock in a depth of from 15 to 70 feet below the surface, without finding any ore. All attempts made to penetrate through this solid Limestone, with the purpose of finding "lower openings," have failed.

As far as known at present, the ore formation of Granby is confined to a zone rarely thicker than 10 feet, and lying immediately above the solid Limestone, in an altered and more or less broken formation. The disadvantage of this limited vertical extent of the ores, is, however, balanced by their large horizontal extent, which is undoubtedly much larger than has been brought to light by the mining operations to the present day. Especially the southern part of the section, and some parts of Sec. 7, present very favorable prospects. Around the Odd Fellows' Hall, for instance, some shafts were sunk

G.S—28.

which went through a formation very similar to that of the other Diggings, mainly consisting of broken Chert, and of soft porous Chert. In some of these shafts, small quantities of Lead had been found. But all of them were abandoned on account of the water rushing in very heavily before they had reached the solid Limestone. When worked with proper pumping machinery, they may yet strike well-paying ore beds.

Similar favorable prospects exist in other places, in and outside of Sec. 6.

We will now proceed to describe various Diggings in the vicinity of Granby which, though not yielding largely at present, prove the vast extent of the ore-bearing formation in this district.

We begin with the

PRAIRIE DIGGINGS,

Sec. 18, T. 35, R. 30 W.—about 2 miles south of Granby, near the northern end of Oliver's prairie.

The General Section in this part of the prairie, is as follows :

5 feet Soil and Gravel.
15 feet red and yellow Sandstone, which frequently crops out in the prairie.
Limestone, white or gray, of oolitic structure in upper layers, passing into a fine-grained bluish or drab variety below.

Deep depressions in this Limestone are filled with broken Chert, *Chert-breccia*, red Clay and loose boulders of Sandy Limestone. Galena occurs in small, loose sheets between the boulders and in single pieces, adhering to the Chert or lying loose in the red Clay. Also a silicious Cerussite, (Dry-bone,) often partly changed to Pyromorphite, and some Calamine are found in loose pieces in the Clay.

These Diggings are among the oldest in the region, being discovered in 1850. They yielded about 300,000 pounds of Galena, in the first 10 years, but are not worked regularly at present.

The location of the shafts of these Diggings, may be seen in Fig. 30.

Most of the shafts are on a circular space of ground about 300 feet in diameter, east of Mr. Davis' house. They are from 30 to 40 feet deep, in broken Chert and in boulders of sandy Limestone, the latter sometimes 3 feet in diameter. The boulders are deposited in a depression of the Limestone. The latter was struck as a solid mass in the surrounding shafts, at D, E and F, at a depth of only 10 to 15 feet.

South-east of this circle, at G and H, red Sandstone crops out in the prairie.

About 800 feet further north, (at B,) a shaft was sunk which passed through 42 feet of broken Chert and red Clay, with some Galena in sheets and in thin seams in the Chert.

At shaft A the masses of broken Chert and of large Chert slabs, were 70 feet thick, mixed with some red Clay, but containing no ore. Solid Limestone was struck below.

CULPEPPER DIGGINGS.

The Culpepper Diggings, Secs. 1 and 2, T. 25, R. 30 W., are 4 to 5 miles east of Granby, on hills 20 to 30 feet high, covered with small timber, and extending south as far as Oliver's prairie. The higher portions of this ground are covered with pieces of red Sandstone, which also crop out in several places. The Sandstone is underlaid by Limestone, oolitic in the upper, gray and coarse-grained in[the lower layers.

Galena occurs in small quantities, either in small crevices of the Limestone, associated with Dolomite, or loose in red Clay, or between broken Chert, which overlies the Limestone in some places.

A considerable number of shafts have been sunk in this vicinity, but the whole production did not exceed a few thousand pounds of Galena.

In a shaft in Sec. 1, sunk by Mr. Houser, we observed :

10 feet red Clay.
15 feet soft, porous Chert.
(?) Silico-calcite, with small pieces of Galena.

Another shaft called the Hard Shaft, was sunk through :

12 feet red Clay.
35 feet Limestone and Chert, with a vertical seam of Dolomite about 1 inch thick, containing crystals of Galena, and some pieces of Blende. The seam closed, however, at that depth. Similar small seams of Galena in Limestone, were observed near the house of Mr. Skipworth.

HEM DIGGINGS.

The Hem Diggings are 2 miles west of Granby, in the south-half of Sec. 2, T. 25, R. 31 W., on the south-west slope of a hill rising about 40 feet above the bottom of a small creek which runs north-west into Shoal Creek.

The slopes are thickly covered with broken, dense, white, brittle Chert, and some pieces of red or yellow Sandstone.

The shafts, 30 to 40 in number, struck Limestone after penetrating 15 to 25 feet of broken Chert and Chert-breccia. This latter consists of Chert split by numerous cracks and recemented by Quartzite, or by hardened Clay. Red or brown sandy Clay, is mixed with the broken Chert.

Galena, in small pieces, was found loose in the Clay.

The production of these Diggings was small. They were worked in 1859, then abandoned, and will soon be reopened by some parties from Granby.

NEOSHO.

At Neosho and vicinity, Galena has been found in some places, but nowhere as yet in paying quantities.

The formation consists of Archimides (Keokuk) Limestone, which appears at the surface in many places. It is exposed 60 to 70 feet high, at the southern limit of Neosho, on Harold's farm. There it consists of dark gray, coarse-grained Limestone, with many fossils, and with continuous layers as well as irregular concretions of white, dense Chert. The upper layers of the Limestone are of finer grain than the lower ones, and the boulders which lie above the solid rock, are also fine-grained. The same Limestone forms a bluff in the western part of Neosho, near the "Big Spring."

In some places this Limestone is overlaid by strata of hard Chert, of soft, porous Chert, and of red Clay, in the same succession, though of less thickness, than in the ore-bearing formation of Granby.

A railroad cut in the N. E. qr. of Sec. 27, T. 25, R. 32 W., on the land of Mr. Hopkins, shows the following Section:

4 feet Soil, with pieces of broken Chert.

4 to 8 feet hard, solid Chert, in layers separated by layers of red Clay.

2 to 3 feet soft, porous Chert.

3 to 7 feet white, entirely disintegrated Chert, of sandy, and in places, clayish structure.

(?) Silico-Calcite, the Limestone of which is fine-grained and light-colored.

The Chert layers immediately below the Soil, are solid and continuous, rarely broken, and 2 to 8 inches thick. They are not in close contact with each other, but leave in places horizontal clefts, which are in part empty, in part filled with a white, fine, silicious powder, or with dry, red Clay.

The soft, porous Chert below them, is identical with the formation in Granby, called "Cotton rock" by the miners. It occurs in coherent layers 2 to 5 inches thick, and passes gradually into the disintegrated sandy Chert. The latter encloses irregular lumps of soft, porous Chert, not fully disintegrated.

This locality is on higher ground than the bluffs near Neosho, previously described. All the strata have no distinct dip, but seem to be horizontal.

In Neosho, a well was sunk by Mr. McKane, passing through broken layers of Chert and red, sandy Clay between the layers. In several places small crystals of Galena were found either loose in the Sand, or sticking to small pieces of Sandy, fine-grained Limestone. At 20 feet depth a boulder of Limestone was struck lying on red Clay, with some loose pieces of Galena. Several old diggings may be seen on Hickory Creek, south-east of Neosho, where Galena has been found in red Clay, under broken layers of Chert.

THE MOSELY DIGGINGS, T. 26, R. 32 W., SECS. 26 AND 27,

Eight miles west of Granby and 4 miles north of Neosho. They are situated on both sides of a small valley which runs north-east to the bottom of Shoal Creek, about ½ mile distant. The ¡Slopes are steep and 50 to 60 feet high.

The Shafts passed through Soil, masses of broken Chert, broken, soft, porous Chert and accumulations of broken masses rounded and partly altered, of coarse-grained, dark-gray Limestone, which passes locally into a fine-grained, bluish variety. Between these masses and boulders, at a depth of 45 to 60 feet, irregular seams or elongated pockets of Lead and Zinc ores were struck, lying about parallel to the Slope.

Galena is found as seams in soft and rotten Dolomite, as crystals adhering to Chert, or in loose pieces in the Clay between the boulders of Limestone.

Calamine, frequently enclosing pieces of Galena or Blende, occurs in botryoidal forms, as slabs, with the Dolomite, or loose in red Clay.

These Diggings, formerly yielding very largely, (See Swallow's Geological Report, 1855), are but little worked at present.

Near the south-east corner of Sec. 27, in this district, Abbot & Co. sunk a deep shaft on the summit of a hill. It passed through :

No. 1. 20 feet broken Chert.

No. 2. 50 feet boulders and slabs of fine grained Limestone and broken Chert layers. Some of the latter contain vertical seams of Galena, reaching ½ an inch in thickness. These seams do not pass into the underlying layers.

No. 3. 30 feet of coarse-grained and dark-colored Limestone, containing layers and concretions of Chert, but no ore.

THE SAWYER DIGGINGS, T. 26, R. 32, SEC. 27, N. W. QR.

At this locality Culpepper & Sawyer lately began work, and are sinking two shafts about 30 feet apart, on top of a hill, on land belonging to the Granby Mining and Smelting Company.

They dug through 30 feet of broken Chert, and then struck more solid layers of Chert, with coarse red Clay, in which some loose pieces of Galena and Cerussite were found. A few hundred pounds of ore had been raised at the time of our visit.

THE CONLEY DIGGINGS, T. 26, R. 32 W., SECS. 31 AND 32, NEWTON COUNTY,

Form a part of the old Cedar Creek Diggings—belong to Messrs. Thompson & Graves, of Joplin.

They are situated on Spurgeon's prairie, and extend along the west slope of a small water-run the deepest point of which is not over 15 feet below the surrounding prairie. Most of the shafts are less than 20 feet deep.

A narrow run of loose pieces of Cerussite lying in red Clay comes to the surface at the northern end of the Diggings, and dips slightly towards the south, so that it is about 20 feet below the ground at the southern end.

The whole length of the present Diggings is about 500 feet.

Galena has in various places been found in loose pieces at a greater depth. In the centre of the Diggings a shaft has been sunk 110 feet deep. It passed through

No. 1. 15 feet red Clay, with a " run " of loose pieces of Cerussite partly pure, partly sandy, consisting in the latter case of disintegrated porous Chert, strongly impregnated with Carbonate of Lead.

No. 2. 95 feet broken Chert, with some red Clay and Sand.

The shaft did not reach the solid Limestone.

Another shaft was sunk at the south end of the Diggings 95 feet deep.

At a depth of 35 feet some Galena was found adhering to pieces of broken Chert. At 90 feet, the red Clay began to predominate over the Chert, and large pieces and slabs of impure, fine-grained Zinc Blende and masses of dark-gray, fine-grained and spongy Quartzite, enclosing crystalline Zinc Blende were reached.

A quarter of a mile west of these Diggings, in Sec. 31, a "run" of pieces of heavy, massive Cerussite, imbedded in red Clay, with broken Chert lies near the surface. The ore-bearing layer is about 2 feet thick, and lies only 4 feet above the Limestone. The latter has the appearance of being a part of a large, solid body of rock.

T. 26, R. 33, Sec. 36 S. W. qr., are one mile south-west from the Conley Diggings, and are owned by S. B. Corn, of Joplin. They consist of about 20 shafts, situated on a broad and gentle slope extending from a plateau of the prairie in a south-western direction down to a hollow in which Lost Creek originates.

Figure 31 is a topographical sketch of the diggings and a Geological Section.

The layers dip toward the east. The Sandstone crops out about 200 feet west of the shafts, in a belt 50 feet broad, and running south-west to north-east.

West of this, layers and boulders of Chert appear on the surface. Through these latter the sheet shaft was sunk about 500 feet west of the other shafts. The Section is given in the sketch.

About 500 feet south of this shaft the Chert layers, cropping out at the surface, contain some small seams of Galena.

The various rocks of the Section of the Cornwall shafts show the following characteristic features:

The Sandstone is micaceous, mostly gray, occasionally yellow or reddish in the upper portions. It is partly very hard, not very friable and of medium-sized grain. Its lower layers contain some Galena in specks or in seams, between the layers. All the strata are more or less broken. A layer of greenish Clay, varying in thickness from 1 to 14 feet, lies in places between the strata of Sandstone; 3 to 6 feet Sandstone being above and 2 to 4 feet below the Clay.

Loose, rounded pieces and often large chunks of Galena are imbedded in this Clay, one of which measured 1 by 1 by 2 feet.

The tallow Clay below the Limestone is strongly mixed with Sand; the latter being evidently the product of contrition of the Sandstone. The broken Limestone below the Clay is hard, gray and coarse-grained. The single blocks are separated from each other by red Clay, which contains loose pieces of Galena, Cerussite and, in some places, of Calamine. The Limestone contains Bitumen, in cracks and cavities, as well as crystals and crystalline masses of Galena and specks of Blende. The upper part is less broken, and thinly stratified or shaly, and of sandy, fine-grained structure. This part contains Galena in streaks between the slightly waving layers.

T. 26, R. 33, Sec. 1, ¼ mile south of the Cornwall Diggings, are also represented on Figure 31. They are situated at the head of Lost Creek, which flows south-west to Spring River. The shafts have been sunk through masses of broken Chert, with red Clay and Sand and broken Limestone. Galena was found in seams and specks between the layers of Chert and in the Limestone. The shafts A (see sketch) in the northern part of the Diggings, were sunk through masses of broken Chert, with some broken Limestone. Some shafts are 50 feet deep without reaching the solid rock.

Galena was found also in loose pieces a few feet below the surface, and again at 45 feet depth in seams in the Chert.

B B are shallow diggings. The angular broken masses of coarse-grained and somewhat bituminous Limestone are there 3 to 7 feet below the surface, and contain thin seams of Galena.

The shaft C is 20 feet deep, and passed through 6 feet Sandstone before reaching the broken Chert.

The shaft D struck solid layers of Chert, partly mixed with Limestone (Silico-Calcite.)

CARPENTER'S SHAFT,

T. 25, R. 33 W., Sec. 2, about two miles south-west of the Cornwall Diggings, penetrated the following strata:

No. 1. 4 feet Soil and loose pieces of Chert.
No. 2. 6 feet grayish-white Sandstone.
No. 3. 8 feet brown and green Clay.
No. 4. 3 feet boulders of sandy, fine-grained Limestone.
No. 5. 15 feet alternate layers of Limestone and Chert.
No. 6. (?) Chert layers.

The Limestone between the Chert layers is dark and coarse-grained, containing Bitumen in cavities, and some crystals and specks of Galena and Blende.

WILLIAM'S DIGGINGS,

T. 26, R. 33 W., Sec. 14, on Beef Creek, consists of a number of shafts which were sunk through broken Chert and Clay, with streaks of Galena.

SIBLEY DIGGINGS,

T. 24, R. 34 W., Sec. 8, are 1½ miles south of the town of Seneca, close to the line of the Indian Territory. They are situated near the top of a flat, rolling slope, which descends northward into the plain of Seneca.

Mr. Sibley sunk a well near his house, and 3 shafts about 600 feet east of it, and 20 feet higher up the hill. The well is 20 feet deep, and stands in broken Chert with layers of brown Clay, and large quantities of tallow Clay near the bottom. The 3 shafts passed through :

No. 1. 6 feet cherty soil.

No. 2. 20 feet red and yellow sandy Clay, with pieces and occasional layers of hard, gray Chert.

No. 3. 40 feet yellow, sandy Clay, with Chert fragments and boulders, and slabs of fine-grained, yellow, sandy Limestone. The latter inclosing some Chert-breccia and occasional crystals or crystalline masses of Galena. Below this, soft, rotten, white Chert was struck.

In one shaft, at a depth of 35 feet, 2 very thin sheets of Galena were met with in the sandy Clay ; one being 2 feet below the other. They were followed 15 feet to the west, in which direction they dipped at an angle of about 30°.

Paying quantities of ore have not yet been discovered in this locality.

THE THURMAN DIGGINGS,

T. 27, R. 32 W., Secs. 29 and 30, Newton county, are owned by the Thurman M. and S. Co., and leased to Mr. Richards of St. Louis. The situation of the Diggings is represented on the sketch (Fig. 32.)

Several hills, 30 to 40 feet high, separated by small valleys or hollows, rise east of a small creek which flows south-west into Shoal Creek.

The shafts are situated principally along these hollows. The southern hollow is called Roarke's and the shafts in it extend about one-fourth of a mile east to west, and 800 feet north to south. At shafts 1 and 2, (see sketch,) the dark, coarse-grained Archimedes Limestone was struck at a depth of less than 40 feet without finding any ore. Only small quantities of Iron Pyrites occurred occasionally in the Limestone. Shaft 3 passed through Chert and fine-grained Limestone in slabs and boulders, mixed with Chert detritus and Clay, inclosing some Galena in loose pieces. The solid Limestone was struck at 75 feet depth.

Shafts 4 and 5 had 40 feet of broken Chert, with sandy Clay of red or yellow color, in which some loose, rounded pieces of Galena were imbedded.

A number of shafts have been sunk near the mouth of the northern hollow, which lies one-fourth to one-half mile north of Roarke's Hollow. They are sunk in the bottom land, and are the Thurman shafts proper.

Four of these shafts, sunk at distances of 40 to 50 feet from each other, and 35 to 40 feet deep, passed through:

No. 1. 5 feet Soil, with pieces of Chert.
No. 2. 30 to 35 feet irregular mixture of boulders, slabs and irregular fragments of various materials, mixed with Clay.

These broken materials are of very unequal size, becoming larger with the depth. They consist of:

1—Grayish white, hard, angular Chert in large slabs or fragments of 1 to 3 feet diameter, sometimes cemented by sandy, regenerated Limestone.

2—Chert-breccia, the angular pieces of Chert, from pea to head size, cemented by a yellow or brown, fine-grained, sandy Limestone, which in its mass contains specks and pockets of crystalline Galena and Blende.

3—Rounded boulders, 1 to 3 feet in diameter, of soft, coarsely crystalline, reddish gray, Dolomitic Limestone, rotten on the outside, and containing seams and aggregates of Galena.

4—Pieces of Chert of fist to head size, with adhering crystals of Galena; also, masses of Calamine in botryoidal forms, inclosing crystals of Galena. The latter are sometimes mixed with pure, crystalized Calcite, and with yellow or red, porous and Dolomitic Limestone, also inclosing small crystals of Galena.

The Clay is either plastic, ferruginous and gritty or impalpable and fat (tallow Clay), and contains loose pieces of Galena, rounded and coated with Cerussite.

Most of the above materials contain Galena only at a depth of about 30 feet.

From 300 to 400 feet north of these shafts, in the open valley, some old shafts had struck broken layers of bluish black, micaceous Slate thinly stratified—probably belonging to the Coal Measures.

The Locke Shaft (see sketch) is sunk a few hundred feet north-east of the Thurman Shafts, on the summit of a hill, being about 30 feet above the valley. It passed through:

No. 1. 6 feet cherty and sandy Soil.

No. 2. 30 feet broken Chert, with a little sandy Clay.

No. 3. 29 feet very large, angular, broken masses of Silico-calcite, consisting
of about two-thirds of Chert and one-third of fine-grained, gray
Limestone. The Chert sometimes contains small seams of Galena.

These large, broken masses are often cemented together by a
coarse-grained, yellowish gray Limestone, inclosing small pieces of
angular Chert.

Below these rocks is a coarse, solid Conglomerate of broken, white
Chert and of boulders of bluish gray Limestone cemented by yellow,
sandy Limestone—the latter containing crystals of Galena one-fourth
to one-half inch in diameter, distributed through its whole mass. This
latter Limestone is evidently of a more recent formation, simultaneous with the deposition of the ores.

The McCoy Shafts (see sketch) are sunk east of the Locke Shaft,
on the ridge and in the hollow. They were worked in 1872, but had
been abandoned at the time of our visit. The shafts on the southern
slope of the hollow struck yellow, calcareous Sandstones and solid
Archimedes Limestone without finding any ore. But those on the
same hill with the Locke Shaft had considerable quantities of Galena,
principally connected with a yellow, fine-grained or clayish, calcareous Sandstone, probably formed from residuary Sand from dissolved
Limestone. The Galena is also found adhering to Chert or loose in
red Clay ; also, in reddish gray regenerated Limestone, which incloses
Chert fragments. The yellow Sandstone also contains seams of Cerussite.

One quarter of a mile south-east from Thurman Village, on the
southern slope of a hill, Mr. Summers sunk a shaft which struck the
solid Limestone below solid Chert, at a depth of 20 feet. He went 36
feet into it without finding any ore.

THE JOHNSON DIGGINGS,

T. 27, R. 32, Sec. 20, west half, near centre, (Newton county,) two
miles north of Thurman Diggings, are controlled by Mr. S. B. Corn, of
Joplin.

As may be seen from sketch, (Fig. 32,) six shafts are sunk near the
head of a little hollow, which runs south-west towards the Thurman
Diggings.

Shaft 1 seems to have struck large boulders of coarse, gray Limestone, inclosing some fluid Bitumen, crystals of Galena and angular
pieces of Chert.

The shafts 3 to 6 are about 30 to 40 feet deep. They passed through masses of broken Chert, with boulders of coarsely crystalline, light gray Limestone and through boulders of sandy, rotten Dolomite, sometimes in banded sheets. Loose pieces of Galena are found with these materials, forming thin and narrow runs a few feet below the surface, and occurring again 20 to 30 feet deep in larger quantity. The Galena is often adhering to pieces of Chert. Brown Clay and tallow Clay are found in large streaks and masses. Occasionally loose chunks of Calamine occur, inclosing crystals of Galena.

THE CARNEY DIGGINGS,

Situated in T. 27, R. 33, Sec. 15, near center of Section, Jasper county, 3 miles south-west of Joplin, close to the dividing line between the water-sheds of Shoal Creek and Turkey Creek. They are controlled by Messrs. Chapman & Riggin, of Joplin. In the lower part of a small valley descending south-west towards the Shoal Creek valley, a number of shafts had been sunk several years ago. They passed through 58 feet of Chert in fragments and layers, and then struck rotten Dolomite with small pieces of Chert and streaks of Galena or Blende 1 inch to 2½ inches thick. The shafts were then abandoned, owing to the inability of raising the water which was met with in considerable quantity. At present a new shaft is being sunk close by. Other shafts were commenced a few hundred feet up the hollow, for the purpose of testing the locality. They passed through similar materials to those in the lower shafts, but did not reach any ore. In one of these shafts a boulder of grayish-red Sandstone, 2 feet thick, was struck 20 feet below the surface in broken Chert. One shaft passed through 20 feet of broken Chert, and then through 20 feet of bluish-gray Limestone with segregations of bitumen. The whole surface at these diggings, especially the upper part of the valley, is covered with pieces and angular slabs of gray or red Sandstone.

THE BUDLONG DIGGINGS,

About ¼ of a mile north of the Carney Diggings, and on high ground on the summit of the ridge. Three shafts were sunk near together by Moffet & Sergeant, of Joplin, on Mr. Budlong's land. All had a run of loose pieces of Cerussite, ("wool-mineral,") 3 to 5 feet below the soil, in red Clay, mixed with loose pieces of hard Chert, and some Sand. This formation of broken Chert continued for 30 feet down without any farther ore.

South-west of these, another shaft was sunk 30 to 40 feet deep in broken Chert mixed with red Clay and some loose pieces of Galena. The whole surface at these diggings is covered with pieces of hard, white Chert.

CHAPTER XXVI·

II. THE DEPOSITS OF TURKEY CREEK DISTRICT.

The Lead and Zinc Mines of Turkey Creek District are situated in the south-western part of Jasper county, extending principally along the courses of several small creeks which run in a north-western or northern direction into Turkey Creek, the latter flowing nearly due west. The greatest number of Mines are on both sides of the most eastern of these creeks, namely : Joplin Creek.

About 1 mile farther west is a small run of water along the hol. low of Lone Elm, in which the Lone Elm Diggings are situated.

Three miles west of Joplin Creek, or about 2 miles west of Lone Elm, the Leadville Diggings extend along the third of these branches.

Still farther west, 2 miles, are the Stevens' Diggings, ½ mile south of Turkey Creek, on Stevens' Branch ; and finally 1 mile west of the last named Diggings and about 5 miles west of Joplin, we find the Bentley Diggings, on another similar branch.

THE JOPLIN MINES.

Along Joplin Creek, will be described in the following order :

a. Upper Joplin Creek Diggings.

No. 1. Cox & Pierce's and Thomas' Diggings.
No. 2. Schott Diggings.
No. 3. Jasper No. 1 Diggings on Power's Hill.
No. 4. Short & Temple's Diggings.
No. 5. Jasper No. 2 Diggings.
No. 6. Diggings on Swindle Hill.

We have added to this Report a Topographical sketch, representing the whole mining district along the valley of Joplin Creek.

The strata throughout this mining district is generally very irregular in their character and relative position, often varying considerably within short distances.

Near the summits of the hills or ridges, we find sometimes places with pretty regular formation, but rarely entirely undisturbed. The ores are, however, generally less concentrated at such points. The succession of rocks on the slopes remains the same sometimes for long distances, but the layers are always of very variable thickness. The position of the layers is generally strongly disturbed, especially in the lower part of the slopes. The layers almost invariably dip with the slopes. In the bottoms all materials are frequently broken up : the Chert into angular fragments, the Limestone into large blocks or slabs, which are rounded into " boulders" when softened by alteration. A certain regularity of succession is nevertheless perceptible for many miles along the upper part of Joplin Creek. But the diggings in the bottoms of the lower or northern part of the creek show but rarely anything else except immense accumulations of more or less finely broken Chert, and only occasionally masses of altered Limestone or of Dolomite crushed and irregularly mixed with the broken Chert.

A.—THE UPPER JOPLIN CREEK DIGGINGS.

1. The Cox & Pierce and the Thomas Diggings,

Sec. 12, T. 33, R. 27, S. W. qr., on Pitcher's land, leased by Moffet & Sergeant.

A number of shafts have been sunk on the west slope of a slight depression, indicated on our topographical sketch. They cover a belt of ground about 800 feet long from north to south, and 10 to 20 feet broad.

Shaft A is the deepest, and has the following section :

2 feet Soil.

20 feet yellow Clay, with pieces of Chert.

3 feet black slaty Clay.

16 feet rounded boulders of sandy Limestone, containing seams and crystalline masses of Galena, with tallow Clay and yellow Chert Sand between the boulders.

> This sandy Limestone is fine.grained, and contains some Bitumen in cracks and cavities.

30 feet Conglomerate, formed by pieces of broken Chert and loose crystalline masses of Galena, cemented by calcareous Clay, or by argillaceous, regenerated Limestone. Also, specks of Blende occur in it.

12 feet ore-opening, consisting of an irregular mass of boulders of fine-grained yellow, sandy Limestone, with chunks of crystalline Blende, in fine gray, calcareous Sand.

10 feet broken Chert, partly cemented by dark blue Clay.

At B (see sketch) 2 shafts have been sunk 30 feet deep, and are connected by a drift. They passed through :

3 feet Soil.

20 feet yellow, gray and white Clay, in streaks, with pieces of Chert.

4 feet ore-bearing " run," yellow or brown sandy Clay, with loose pieces of Galena in paying quantities.

The run of Galena extends for about 100 feet from north to south, being 6 to 8 feet wide. Below it are Chert with Clay, and some little Galena.

The shaft at C was sunk 65 feet deep through Soil, 20 feet yellow sandy Clay, 20 feet broken Chert with sandy Clay and some Galena. Then a layer, 2 to 3 feet thick, of black Slate, was struck, dipping nearly vertically between boulders of altered sandy Limestone. The shaft followed this Slate downward for 22 feet, without reaching the end of it. At 60 feet depth, some loose pieces of Galena were found in the red Clay between the boulders.

The Thomas Diggings are about 200 yards north-east of the Cox Diggings (see sketch).

The shafts are 25 to 30 feet deep, sunk through Soil and broken Chert, mixed with Sand and rotten Dolomite. Loose pieces of Galena were found in the Sand, but hardly enough, so far, to pay working.

2. SCHOTT DIGGINGS.

The Schott Diggings, E. hf. Sec. 11, T. 27, R. 33, on Pitcher's land, leased by Mr. Schott.

Four shafts have been sunk on a low slope dipping north-east, toward Joplin Creek.

One shaft is 15 feet deep, and struck, immediately below the Soil, layers of black Slate belonging to the Coal Measures.

The other shaft passed through :

   5 feet Soil.
   10 feet boulders of coarse-grained, somewhat bituminous Limestone, with layers of Chert in it.

No ore has been reached as yet.

3. JASPER DIGGINGS, No. 1.

The Jasper Diggings No. 1, S. E. qr. of N. E..qr. of Sec. 11, T. 27, R. 35, on Power's Hill, worked by the Jasper Lead and Mining Company.

This hill rises about 20 feet above the bottom of the creek, on the west side, and presents about the following General Section, the maximum thickness of every stratum being given :

   5 feet sandy Soil.
   20 feet yellow, fine sandy Clay.
   20 feet broken Chert, with streaks and patches of Galena, partly loose, partly in seams in the Chert.
   5 feet Dolomite and Dolomitic Limestone, banded horizontally, containing layers of Galena and of Calamine.
   15 feet small boulders (about head size) of gray, fine-grained Limestone. Loose masses of Galena and Blende occur between the boulders. Seams of these ores are also found occasionally in the boulders themselves, especially when the rock is softened and sandy.
   20 (?) feet alternate layers of gray, fine-grained Limestone and Chert, with large openings filled with red Clay. The layers are broken and disturbed. Galena and Blende occur in loose pieces in the red Clay, and in seams in the Limestone, and in the Chert.

The runs of Dolomite below the broken Chert, are in places rotten and crushed, and are then mixed with fragments of Chert, and with a considerable quantity of loose, mostly rounded pieces of Galena.

The Dolomite, when fresh and solid, forms alternate bands with dark, gray dolomitic Limestone, passing into Dolomite.

Toward the north, these runs thin out, and then the Chert lies directly on boulders of softened sandy Limestone.

The Blende occurs in very irregular streaks and pockets, in the dolomitic rocks.

The Galena occurs in horizontal seams, 2 to 5 inches thick, separated by 1 to 2 feet of rotten Dolomite, extending 3 to 5 feet in width, and 40 to 60 feet in length.

4. THE SHORT DIGGINGS AND THE TEMPLE DIGGINGS, T. 27, R. 33, SEC. 11, N. E. Qr

Are situated on the left side of Joplin Creek, north-west from Powers' Hill, on a level slope, rising 10 to 20 feet above the level of the creek.

The General Section of these Diggings shows the following strata, which however, are very irregular in character and thickness:

No. 1. 3 feet Soil.

No. 2. 5 to 15 feet Clay, yellow or gray, and often mixed with broken Chert.

In the Felton shaft, near the summit of the Slope.
- ½ foot black Slate.
- 3 feet gray Clay, with some pyrites.
- 1-2 foot pyrites.

No. 4. 3 to 30 feet boulders of Sandy Limestone, which often contain in their altered portions small crystalline masses of Galena and Blende, also segregations of fresh semi-fluid Bitumen.

No. 4. 0 to 12 feet solid Chert-layers, with only occasional specks of Galena.

No. 5. 4 to 7 feet Chert-breccia, the angular pieces of Chert cemented by a gray, silicious mass, or by pyrites frequently enclosing crystals and specks of Galena.

No. 5. 2 to 6 feet Dolomite, partly fresh and rose-colored, partly loose, soft and sandy, and black from Bitumen. It is the principal ore-bearing rock containing Galena in streaks and loose chunks and Blende in crystalline masses.

No. 6. (?) Limestone, (perhaps boulders) below.

These Diggings, especially the upper shafts, are remarkable for the occurrence of pyrites in considerable quantity, often connected with black Slate and dark gray Clay. Some of the ore-deposits here to a considerable extent, somewhat resemble the openings of Granby.

Fig. 33 represents a cave discovered in a shaft of the Temple Diggings. This cave, although in close proximity to the ore-deposits, as seen in the figure, contains no ore, but only Clay.

No. 1. Boulders of sandy Limestone.

No. 2. Dolomite Sand, with Galena.

No. 3. Chert-layer.

No. 4. Red Clay.

No. 5. Chert-layers (cap-rock) of the cave.

No. 6. Limestone boulders.

G.S.—29.

5. JASPER No. 2 DIGGINGS, T. 27, R. 33, SEC. 11, N. E. QR,

On Pitcher's land, leased by the Jasper Lead and Mining Company. These Diggings are situated close to Joplin Creek, on the east side, opposite the Temple and the Short Diggings, and extend as far as Swindle Hill.

The Shafts which form the most southern portion of these Diggings, show the following formation:

No. 1. 3 feet Soil.
No. 2. 15 feet broken Chert.
No. 3. 15 feet boulders of dark-gray, coarse-grained bituminous Limestone.
No. 4. 2 feet Breccia, consisting of Chert pieces, cemented by hard, gray silicious rock, containing much pyrites, Galena and Bitumen.

One Shaft disclosed somewhat different strata, as follows:

No. 1. 3 feet Soil.
No. 2. 10 feet broken Chert.
No. 3. 5 feet shaly, white Limestone, with pyrites in cracks and between the layers.
No. 4. 2 feet dark-colored, somewhat hardened clayish Sand, containing some Bitumen and crystals of Galena.

In the bed of the Creek Mr. Jackson sunk two Shafts in loose detritus, mostly Chert, and struck larger masses of Limestone at a depth of 15 to 20 feet, with irregular cavities formed by erosion, in which loose pieces of Galena were found in Clay and Sand.

About 1,000 feet further down the Creek, opposite Swindle Hill, the Jasper Company sunk their pump Shaft, No. 2., (marked P. S. on our map,) which struck a thick layer of black Slate and Clay belonging to the Coal Measures.

This Shaft passed through:

No. 1. 4 feet Soil.
No. 2. 6 feet rounded Chert and Gravel.
No. 3. 40 feet black Slate and Clay, with pieces of Chert.
No. 4. 8 feet Limestone, broken in parts.
No. 5. 25 feet broken Chert, Limestone and Dolomite mixed. Galena in small quantities occurs with the Dolomite also in altered Limestone, or adhering to Chert fragments.
No. 6. 7 feet boulders of fine-grained Limestone, with some Bitumen and Galena in the altered portions.
No. 7. 5 feet alternate layers of Limestone and Chert.
No. 8. 95 feet.

Black Slate was struck in several other shallow Diggings in this vicinity. The opinion prevailing among the miners that no ore is found below this Slate, prevented the continuation of these Shafts.

These Slates are residuary deposits, probably remnants of destroyed Coal Measure Strata, and can neither prove nor disprove the presence of ore-beds in the underlying rocks.

6. DIGGINGS ON SWINDLE HILL.

As shown on our Topographical sketch of the Joplin Lead district, the Swindle Hill rises about 40 feet above Joplin Creek, north-west of the Short Diggings.

East of the hill a number of Shafts form a belt from south to north, containing the Holston Diggings, on the west side, and the Chambers Diggings and Powers Diggings on the east side of the Creek.

The Holston, Chambers and Southern Powers' Diggings are pretty shallow, (not over 30 feet deep), and passed through Soil and broken Chert, then striking boulders of fine-grained Limestone and Galena in loose pieces, in calcareous Sand between the boulders.

The northern Shafts of the Powers' Diggings went 50 to 55 feet deep, and were very similar to the Jasper No. 2 Diggings. The principal ore-bearing rock is Dolomite 3 to 10 feet thick, lying about 30 feet below the surface.

It is white, rose, brown or black. The latter variety is colored by Bitumen, which frequently occurs, and is always accompanied by considerable quantities of Blende and of Galena.

The solid underlying Limestone, perhaps the bed-rock of the ore formation, nearly reaches the surface on the summit of Swindle Hill. The Nelson shaft (see Fig. 34) struck this Limestone solid and coarse-grained, at a depth of 6 feet, and went 40 feet into it, without reaching a different stratum, and without finding a trace of ore. North and west of this point, the Limestone must have a sudden dip, as all the shafts sunk in these directions struck thick masses of Chert, and of boulders of Limestone.

The Hurlbut shaft, the Jasper No. 3 shaft and the Swindle shaft, all situated on the western and northern Slope of the hill. show pretty nearly the same geological character. They were sunk through—

No. 1. 1 to 10 feet Soil and Gravel.

No. 2. 20 feet broken Chert.

No. 3. 2 to 10 feet shaly, white Limestone, with some Bitumen.

No. 4. 5 to 15 feet Chert-breccia, with specks and seams of Galena and Blende.

No. 5. 6 to 8 feet soft Dolomitic Limestone, with streaks of Dolomite, and with large quantities of Galena and Blende, deposited in "runs."

No. 6. (?) boulders of Limestone, with Bitumen and some Galena.

Some shafts met with black Slate below the soil, as much as 20 feet thick in places.

Among the Diggings situated on Swindle Hill, the Swindle Diggings are the most important, having produced an immense amount of ore (several millions of pounds) within the last two years.

Figure 34

Represents the Section through the Swindle shafts, and shows also a longitudinal Section of the main run of ore:

No. 1. Solid Limestone of the Nelson shaft.
No. 2. Rotten Limestone.
No. 3. Rotten, sandy Limestone boulders.
No. 4. Run of ore, both Galena and Blende in the boulders.
No. 5. Broken Chert layers, capping the run.
No. 6. Loose, broken Chert.
No. 7. Clay.

A number of shafts (partly marked in Fig. 34) are sunk on the main run of ore in nearly one straight line down the northern hill slope.

The three highest are 60 to 70 feet deep. One of them reached two horizons of ore; the first at about 30 feet, the second at 70 feet of depth. The ore lies in "runs," parallel to each other, dipping with the Slope, generally 5 to 10 feet wide and 6 to 8 feet high, but very irregular in shape and extent. They consist of accumulations of Galena and Blende, intimately mixed with pieces of Chert and cemented by a gray, bituminous, sandy mass, probably the residue of dissolved Limestone.

Fig. 34 represents a longitudinal Section, and Fig. 35 a cross-section of a run. The single runs are separated by broken and rounded masses of gray, fine-grained Limestone, which contains large quantities of fluid Bitumen, and sometimes strata of black bituminous Clay. Crystalline Dolomite frequently accompanies the runs which widen toward the north and perhaps continue into the Porter Diggings. It can be very plainly seen in this locality that the runs were former vertical clefts in the Limestone layers. Along rich clefts the dolomization of the Limestone and the deposition of the ore were started.

A strange Section is presented in Fig. 36, which was sketched in one of the lower Swindle shafts, 25 feet below the surface. There the main run of ore is separated in two halves by a fresh, unaltered, large block of Limestone, which itself is horizontally divided by a third layer of black Clay.

Figure 36.

No. 1. Limestone.
No. 2. Sandy Dolomite.
No. 3. Dolomite and Chert, with Galena and Blende.
No. 4. Broken-up Chert.

The most southern of the Porter shafts or the north-east Slope of Swindle Hill, struck gray, coarse grained Limestone at a depth of 30 feet, which continued solid for 20 feet down, then began to split into smaller or larger masses by numerous cracks in various directions. The cracks, sometimes one or two feet wide, are filled with red Clay, or less frequently with finely broken Chert and loose pieces of Galena and Calcite. This shaft seems to be just at the edge of a large body of Limestone, perhaps the same which was struck in the Nelson shaft, and which may be supposed to compose the main central body of Swindle Hill, as indicated in Fig. 34.

Shafts C, on map, are very shallow diggings, only a few feet deep, which struck Coal-slate and Clay below the Gravel.

B. MIDDLE JOPLIN CREEK DIGGINGS.

7. THE PORTER DIGGINGS,

Are situated north-west of Swindle Hill, along the eastern Slope of the Murphysburg ridge, on Mr. Porter's land.

The General Section of these Diggings in the southern shafts (No. 1 to 6) is as follows :

No. 1. 1 to 5 feet Soil.
No. 2. 6 to 30 feet broken Chert, sometimes with some boulders of Limestone.
No. 3. 6 to 8 feet light colored, shaly Limestone.
No. 4. 4 to 5 feet Dolomitic Limestone, often mixed with Chert and generally softened, containing some Bitumen. It is the principal ore-bearing rock, inclosing Galena and Blende in pockets.
No. 5. (?) Hard, gray, coarsely crystalline Limestone in boulders, mostly dolomized and softened on the outside.

Some of these shafts have yielded considerable quantities of ore, especially the shafts 5 and 6, which are 40 feet deep, and connected by drifts. Eight men obtained here about 8 to 9000 pounds of Galena a week.

The Galena occurs in these shafts in a run of about the following Section (see Fig. 37) :

No. 1. Chert slabs and Limestone boulders.
No. 2. Fissured Chert layers.
No. 3. Loose, broken Chert, with some sandy Dolomite.
No. 4. Run, streak of finely broken Chert, with much Galena.
No. 5. Broken Chert, with some Sand.
No. 6. Boulders of altered Limestone, occasionally with loose pieces of Galena in pockets.

The shafts further north, (No. 7 to 10,) are more shallow (10 to 25 feet deep,) and generally have a layer of black Slate or black Clay from a few inches to 3 feet thick, directly below the soil. The ore is found between loose masses or boulders of Limestone.

Much Blende occurs in the northern shafts, sometimes in chunks of head size.

In shaft 20, a layer of 15 feet soft, porous Chert, lies beneath the soil, and above alternate layers of Limestone and Chert.

The formation evidently changes here, and passes into that of the Murphysburg Hill Diggings, to be described hereafter.

8. ORCHARD DIGGINGS.

The Orchard Diggings, S. hf. of Sec. 2, T. 27, R. 33, are situated along the east side of Joplin Creek, opposite the Porter Diggings, on lands owned by the East Joplin Mining and Smelting Company.

Between Powers' Diggings and Orchard Diggings, a number of shallow shafts, marked F and G on our map, are sunk 10 to 20 feet deep through Soil, broken Chert and shaly Limestone, in which some little Galena was found in loose pieces.

The shafts K K are shallow. Some black Slate, shaly Limestone, and gray, solid Limestone, were found.

M M are old shafts, sunk along the lower part of the slope. They penetrated much black Slate, broken Chert, (with some Galena at a depth of 25 feet,) shaly Limestone and hard Limestone.

N N are shallow shafts which passed through soil, gray, fine-grained, soft Sandstone and broken Chert, with loose pieces of Cerussite (Drybone).

P P are old shafts, apparently pretty deep.

The old shafts R R, seem to bear some resemblance to those of the Moon Diggings, which adjoin them on the north side.

The masses of broken Chert are frequently soft and porous, and contain Bitumen, Galena in small crystals, and some Calcite. The boulders of hard, gray Limestone, contain streaks of Dolomite, and are generally soft and decomposed at the outside. As far as the decomposition reaches, they contain Galena and Blende in crystalline masses.

The Orchard Diggings were not worked in 1871 and 1872. In the summer of 1873, a few shafts in the northern part of the Diggings, were again opened and sunk deeper, and reached paying Galena deposits at 30 to 40 feet of depth. The formation is very irregular.

9. MOON DIGGINGS.

The Moon Diggings, N. W. qr. Sec. 2, T. 27, R. 33, adjoin the town of East Joplin on the west, and have their largest extent from north to south, for one-fourth of a mile along the western slope of the East Joplin plateau. The slope falls steeply, in places abruptly, toward the bottom of Joplin Creek, below the city. The mouths of the shafts are 40 to 65 feet above the creek. Some shafts have also been sunk along the foot of the ridge, and are called "Lower Moon Range."

The Diggings are named after a miner who first discovered the ore. They are at present leased by Messrs. Moffet & Sergeant from the Joplin Mining and Smelting Company.

About five million pounds of Galena have been taken out from these Diggings.

The formation is greatly disturbed, and the Galena irregularly deposited, in the most northern shafts; while in the southern and central shafts, the ore occurs in regular "runs," in two different horizons.

The Blende does not occur in large masses, and is always intimately connected with the Galena.

Dolomite, mostly soft and rotten, is frequently found accompanying the ores.

The Parr & Rosenberger shafts, at the south end of the Diggings, are sunk through:

2 to 6 feet cherty Soil.
20 to 40 feet broken Chert and red Sand, with Galena and Blende.
30 feet large, broken masses of coarsely crystalline Limestone.
3 feet broken Chert, with some solid Chert-slabs.
2 feet gray, decomposed Dolomite.

The Galena occurs here loose, between the broken masses of Limestone, and also in disturbed streaks or "runs," from $\frac{1}{2}$ to 3 feet thick and 10 to 15 feet wide, in the broken Chert and in gray, silicious Clay; rock about 58 feet below ground, and striking north-west south-east.

No Bitumen is found here, but much Pyrites, which frequently cements pieces of Chert and Galena, and also occurs as loose concretions.

The Barner shaft lies west of the Parr's shafts, at the foot of the hill, about 35 feet deeper, and belongs to the lower Moon Range. It is 20 feet deep, and struck a "run" between large, loose masses of Limestone. The run strikes parallel to the ridge, and is 10 to 15 feet wide and 2 to 3 feet high, filled with broken Chert, in which three streaks of Galena, ½ to 3 inches thick, are imbedded nearly horizon· tally.

Fig. 38 shows the formation in the Barner and in the Parr & Rosenberger shafts.

The shafts between Parr's and the deep pump shaft at the northern end of the Diggings, constitute the principal part of the Moon Range.

The ore-bearing rocks form a belt 30 to 40 feet wide, along the edge of the plateau.

The General Section in the shafts sunk on this belt, is about as follows:

> 30 to 40 feet loose broken Chert.
> 20 to 30 feet Chert, in more regular, yet broken layers.
>   Chert-breccia, cemented by finely triturated Chert, Sand, and hard, silicious Clay.

The ore-bearing layers are from 50 to 80 feet below the surface, and consist of loose, broken Chert, red Clay, and soft, rotten Dolomite. All these materials contain Galena or Blende, either in loose chunks or in streaks. In some places the ores lie in two distinct horizons, one about 20 feet, the other about 80 feet below the surface. The latter, however, was only struck in a few places.

The Coyle shafts, which seem to be the richest in this part of the Moon Diggings, have Galena in regular layers between Chert-slabs, or between streaks of Dolomite. The latter is rotten, and mixed with tallow Clay.

Fig. 39 represents a peculiar face, which was observed in this locality.

> No. 1. Broken Chert layers, with adhering Galena.
> No. 2. Loose Chert fragments, with Clay and rotten Dolomite.
> No. 3. Chert layers, with Galena seams.

The deep pump shaft at the northern end of the diggings is 95 feet deep and struck the first workable ore at a depth of 75 feet, where several loose chunks of Galena, of very large size, were found imbedded in the loose, broken Chert, also, many small pieces irregularly distributed. Boulders of Limestone underlying this Chert contained specks of Galena, Blende and Pyrites.

The East Joplin Diggings

Are situated at the north end of the Moon Diggings, along the foot of the northern slope of the East Joplin Hill (see map), reaching across the valley to Joplin Creek.

All these shafts passed through masses of broken Chert, with some yellow or brown Clay. At depths varying from 9 to 30 feet below the surface, they struck boulders of fine-grained, bituminous Limestone, softened and more or less dolomized on the outside, the dolomization penetrating 1 to 3 inches into the boulders. The Galena occurs in loose chunks or streaks, generally in the Chert, together with sandy Dolomite and red Clay. Blende and Pyrites are occasionally found.

Most of the shafts are shallow, only a few of them going deeper than 30 feet. One of shafts (No. 30) is 70 feet deep, and passed through :

No. 1. 30 feet soft, porous Chert.
No. 2. 25 feet alternate layers of Limestone and Chert.
No. 3. Over 10 feet broken, irregular masses of Chert and Limestone, in which, at a depth of 60 feet, a layer of Galena was found in broken Chert, being ½ to 3 inches thick, and extending almost horizontally for 70 feet towards north-east.

The shafts (36) are 20 to 30 feet deep, sunk through loose Chert fragments and boulders of Limestone. Galena occurred in loose chunks with red Clay. One shaft yielded 10,000 pounds of ore per week in the summer of 1873.

10. The Four Corner Diggings

Received their name from their location at a point in which the lands of four mining companies touch each other, namely, those of Davis & Murphy, of Moffett & Sergeant, of the Joplin Mining and Smelting Company, and of the Granby Company. They are at the north-west end of the East Joplin Diggings, close to the Joplin Creek, on the east side. They consist of the Wilson Shaft, owned by Wilson, Taylor & Co., and four other shafts. These shafts are from 20 to 32 feet deep, and show a very irregular and disturbed formation.

The Wilson Shaft (Fig. 40) struck a thick layer of gray, striated Sandstone standing nearly vertically on its edge. It is overlaid on the south side by black, micaceous Slate about 6 feet thick. Both

combined are evidently a large, detached mass of later, perhaps Coal
Measure rocks, surrounded by loose, broken Chert. A few feet south
of this mass, Galena was found with Dolomite at a depth of 24 feet,
and also on the north side of the Sandstone a streak of Galena and
Blende, in Chert and in rotten Dolomite, at 32 feet. (See Fig. 40.)

The other shafts also struck streaks of Galena in broken Chert at
a depth of about 20 feet.

We found in these Diggings loose fragments of white, hard Chert,
the surfaces of fracture being covered with fresh crystals of Galena—
the latter evidently having formed after the Chert had been broken.
We also found broken Chert cemented together by crystals and crystalline seams of Galena.

11. THE MURPHYSBURG HILL DIGGINGS

Are situated on the north-eastern slope of the Murphysburg Hill (see
map), and extend from the north end of the Porter Diggings (described
above) in a north-western direction. They are owned by the Joplin
Mining and Smelting Company.

The Jackson Shafts (marked 20 on the Joplin map) are 70 to 80
feet deep. They passed through Soil, masses of broken Chert, and
through Chert and Limestone, either irregularly connected as Silico-
calcite or in alternate layers, all of which are much broken. Below
this, a Conglomerate of Chert cemented by gray Quartz rock was
struck, and at a depth of 80 feet boulders of soft Limestone, which
contained horizontal layers of white, yellow or black Dolomite with
crystals of Galena. The Galena was also found in considerable quantities in streaks between Chert slabs and in red Clay.

The Witge Shaft, (No. 21 on map,) a little east of the former, is
about 70 feet deep and presents the following Section :

Figure 41.

No. 1.   60 feet broken Chert, with two sheets of Galena ½ to 4 inches thick, at
depths of 35 feet and of 60 feet. The lower sheet is separated from
a layer of 1 to 10 feet of Blende by 3 to 10 inches broken Chert.

No. 2.   5 feet Dolomitic Limestone, with streaks of rotten Dolomite.

No. 3.   ——? solid, hard, fine-grained Limestone, cracked in some portions, the
clefts being filled by broken Chert with Galena, and by gray Clay.

The Chert and Dolomite contains Bitumen in small quantity.

The Sherman Shafts (22 on the Joplin sketch) show the same conditions. They contain much Dolomite, forming streaks between boulders of Limestone.

12. The McCrum Diggings, (No. 23 on the Joplin map,)

Are situated north-west of the Jackson Shafts, on the eastern slope of the ridge between the Joplin and Lone Elm Hollows.

A number of shafts are sunk in a straight line on a fissure which strikes south-east to north-west through the hill, about in the direction towards the Harrington Diggings, situated on the summit of the ridge. These shafts are sunk through an enormous accumulation of broken Chert, in which, occasionally, boulders of altered Limestone are imbedded. The Chert is mostly coarse, often in very large blocks or slabs. The above-mentioned fissure runs through the whole mass, and is filled with finely broken, loose Chert, containing much Galena in places. The fissure is very irregular, with ill-defined walls, often split up and branching off in various directions.

The pump shaft, (P. S.), near the summit of the slope, is 120 feet deep. The Chert seems to become coarser and less broken in the depth. Most of the shafts are connected by drifts, which followed the streaks of Galena in the fissure and its branches.

Shafts 24, situated north of the McCrum Diggings, near the foot of the same slope, struck, in some places, boulders of coarse-grained Limestone, in others, black Slate with much Pyrites, in strongly disturbed positions in the loose, broken Chert.

C. LOWER JOPLIN CREEK DIGGINGS.

13. Joplin Valley Diggings,

T. 27, R. 33, Sec. 2, W. hf of N. W. qr., and Sec. 3, N. E. qr. of N. E. qr. We designated by the name of Lower Joplin Valley Diggings, all the diggings which lie north of the East Joplin Hill and the Four Corner Diggings, on both sides of the Joplin Creek along the bottom and on both slopes down to Turkey Creek.

The western Slope is very steep in the southern part of this district, forming in one place, opposite Riggins & Chapman's furnaces, a bluff 30 to 50 feet high, called the Chapman bluff. On the opposite, or east side of the creek, there is a wide and gently rising half-circular basin, in which the principal diggings are situated. About half a mile further down the creek, the eastern ridge becomes steeper, and approaches the creek forming the Suess Bluff. A considerable number of shafts have been sunk on various points on the western Slope with more or less success. The main diggings are in the bottom and along the eastern Slope.

At the Chapman Bluff the rock is exposed about 30 feet in height.

It consists of alternate layers of 1 to 3 feet Limestone, and 2 to 10 inches Chert, without any perceptible dip. The Limestone is light-gray, its structure varying from coarse to fine-grained, often within a few feet in the same layer. The Chert is brittle and cracked wherever exposed. The layers are partly broken and disturbed, especially towards the northern end, where the Limestone becomes sandy and decomposed, and the Chert never broken. Yet, it seems, as if both belong to a body of rock which forms the main mass of the hill. No ore is seen in the rocks. Opposite this bluff, north of the East Joplin Diggings, the bottom of this valley is covered by numerous shafts, especially along the east side of the creek. The bottom is there 600 to 800 feet wide. (See Topographical sketch of Joplin Lead District.)

Proceeding from south to north, we have here, in the bottom, the shafts Nos. 45, 46, 51, 54, 56, 59, 63 and 64, the West Diggings and the Suess shafts. Along the eastern ridge, proceeding in the same order, we observe the Ball shafts, shafts 40 to 44; the Beamer shafts, shafts 55; the Lustre shafts, shafts 57; 60 to 62, the Mill's and Cavanaugh shafts. On the west side of the creek are the shafts 65 to 74, and the Maguire shaft.

All these diggings present, in general, very similar features. Yet, the diggings in the bottom are, as a rule, more shallow, have larger masses of red Clay over and in the Chert, and shows the latter broken to smaller pieces than the diggings on the Slopes. The principal rock is Chert broken up and mixed with yellow Sand, red Clay, or gray calcareous Clay; its thickness varies from 30 to 70 feet. It is often changed into soft, porous Chert, 10 to 20 feet in thickness. It is sometimes mixed with boulders of Chert-breccia, in which the Chert pieces are cemented by a mixture of finely crushed Chert, Sand and clayish regenerated Limestone, or by hardened silicious Clay. In these beds of broken Chert, boulders of Limestone are imbedded either single or in larger number, separated by loose Chert and red or black Clay. These boulders are softened and partly dolomized, and contain streaks of Dolomite, and sometimes unbroken thin layers of Chert. Bitumen is frequently found in cavities in the boulders, or adhering to pieces of loose Chert. The boulders are from 6 to 60 feet below the surface, and according to their depth, vary the depth of the ore-beds, the latter being generally found immediately above the boulders in the Chert, or else between the boulders themselves. In the diggings situated on the Slopes, the Galena with its gangue, forms in some places regular " runs," 5 to 12 feet broad, 5 to 8 feet thick, and 20 to 80 feet long. The Galena occurs either in loose pieces or in continuous sheets, 1 to 6 inches thick, sometimes mixed with Blende. The gangue is red Clay, gray calcareous Clay or soft, rotten Dolomite or Dolomitic Limestone. Above the beds of broken Chert is generally a layer of 4 to 15 feet of red or yellow sandy Clay, containing more or less Galena in loose, rounded pieces. Patches of black, micaceous Slate are frequently met with in these diggings between the Soil and the broken Chert, especially in the valley bottom.

In the Ball* shaft a big "run" of Galena was struck at a depth of about 50 feet. It consists of finely broken Chert, with loose chunks of Galena and Blende and with streaks of Galena 2 to 10 inches thick, and extends with a width of 4 to 20 feet, and a thickness of 2 to 10 feet for about 80 feet from north to south, dipping about 70° into the hill. Six men obtained about 10 to 15 thousand pounds Galena per week in summer of 1873.

In the eastern Beamer shaft, chunks of a good quality of Coal were found between the broken Chert, also masses of black bituminous Clay.

In the Western Beamer shafts, streaks of Galena adhering to a sheet of about 6 inches of Calamine, extend from south to north, over a considerable length, at a depth of about 40 feet below the surface.

In shafts 46, broken masses of Silico-calcite accompany the boulders of Limestone.

In shafts 53 and 54, layers of black, micaceous Slate lie below the Clay and above the boulders. Blende, Galena and black Clay are deposited between the boulders.

In Lustre shaft, the ore-bearing formation was reached at a depth of 54 feet and presented the following Section : (Fig. 42.)

No. 1. Broken, loose Chert.
No. 2. Same, with chunks of Galena, also Galena adhering to the Chert.
No. 3. Same, with boulders of Dolomized Limestone ; sandy and bituminous.
No. 4. Fissured Chert-layers.

In the Mill's Shaft a bed 10 to 15 feet of "wash-dirt" was found, 54 feet deep. This wash-dirt consists of very finely broken Chert, with numerous small pieces of Galena and gray, calcareous mud. The West Diggings consist of a large number of Shafts 10 to 25 feet deep, sunk through Soil and red and black Clay, in which considerable quantities of Galena and loose pieces were found. Some deeper Shafts reached broken Chert below. The West diggings formerly counted amongst the richest mines of Joplin.

A short distance farther west are the two Suess Shafts. The south-

* Spelled "Bawl" on map by mistake.

ern of these struck a rich deposit of ore, 50 feet below the surface. This deposit presents an appearance, as shown in Fig. 43.

The Chert pieces, represented in the sketch, are of fist to head-size, surrounded by gray, calcareous Clay, mixed with loose pieces of Galena and some Blende.

Single crystals are often deposited on all sizes of loose Chert-fragments, showing that the deposition of the ore has continued long after the breaking of this Chert. As these crystals are entirely intact, they can not have been subjected to contrition or frictions, but must have been formed, after their surroundings were in their present state, or nearly so.

The northern Suess Shaft, close to the foot of the bluff, was sunk 40 feet deep. through :

No. 1. 1 foot Soil.
No. 2. 4 feet Gravel and Sand, (red, rounded Chert).
No. 3. 10 feet yellow, or white rotten, porous Chert (fossiliferous).
No. 4, 10 feet hard, white, broken Chert.
No. 4. 15 feet alternate layers of Limestone and Chert, fractured but not considerably disturbed.

No ore was thus far found in this Shaft. The Shaft seems to be too near the solid and unaltered rock. The Suess Bluff itself consists of alternate layers of Chert and Limestone.

Shaft 64 struck Limestone at 20 feet depth without finding any ore. In the whole northern part of this valley-bottom, the Chert is generally broken smaller than in the upper valley, and the boulders of altered Limestone become less frequent towards the north, and finally disappear almost entirely, being replaced by soft, gray mud, filling the interstices between the broken Chert.

THE LONE ELM DIGGINGS.

North half of Sec. 3, T. 27, R. 33, and S. hf. of Sec. 35, T. 28, R. 33, Fig. 44, is a map of them.

The Lone Elm Hollow is formed by the confluence of two small branches, or rather of two low depressions in the prairie, which join in the north-west qr. of Sec. 3. At the head of the western branch (in the south-west corner of Sec. 3, and the south-east corner Sec. 4) the Byers and Snead Shafts are situated, having a rather isolated position. At the head of the eastern branch we find the Harrington, the Sutton and the Morse Shaft, which form the beginning of a large number of Shafts sunk along the valley of Lone Elm Creek, on both slopes, nearly to the mouth of the Creek, which lies about one mile north-west of the Harrington Shaft. The slopes on both sides are rather flat, especially on the west side, but gradually become steeper toward the mouth of the hollow, and pass into the bluffs of Turkey Creek.

We will, in the following, give a short account of the more prominent Shafts of this region. The Byers and Snead Shafts are on Norton's land.

The Byers Shaft shows the following section:

No. 1. 2 feet Soil.
No. 2. 2 feet Cherty Gravel.
No. 3. 6 feet broken Chert, with yellow Sand.
No. 4. 10 feet Conglomerate, consisting of Chert fragments, cemented by altered and regenerated Limestone.
No. 5. 1 to 3 feet shaly Limestone.
No. 6. 6 feet Chert-breccia, cemented by Blende and by altered Limestone.
No. 7. 5 feet solid Dolomitic Limestone, with streaks of Dolomite and some Galena.
No. 8. 8 feet alternate layers of Chert and Limestone, the latter softened and partly dolomized. Small streaks of Galena up to $\frac{1}{2}$ inch thick occur in both, but not in paying quantities.

The strata dip correspondingly to the surface. The occurrence of Gravel at this high point is remarkable.

The Snead Shafts are less regular. They passed through the following strata, all dipping about 40° S. S. E.:

No. 1. 4 feet soil and Gravel.
No. 2. 8 feet broken Chert, with yellow Sand and loose pieces of Galena and Blende.
No. 3. 5 feet Chert-conglomerate.
No. 4. 5 feet Silico-calcite, containing little Galena.
No. 5. 10 feet alternate layers of Chert and Limestone, with Galena, as in Byers' Shaft. Both rocks are so mixed in places as to resemble Silico-calcite.

A nearly vertical crack runs through all the strata. It is filled with black or gray Sand, and loose pieces of Galena. The Limestone contains Galena only as far as it is softened and dolomized. At the head of the eastern smaller branch of Lone Elm Creek, may be observed the Morse Shaft, the Sutton Shafts and the Harrington Shaft, all sunk nearly on top of the ridge which divides Joplin Valley from Lone Elm.

The Morse Shaft went through:

No. 1. 3 feet Soil.
No. 2. 5 feet Gravel, with white and yellow Chert.
No. 3. 20 feet yellow Clay, with some Chert and some loose pieces of Galena.
No. 4. 10 feet soft, bituminous Limestone, with some Galena.
No. 5. 10 feet Chert-layers broken, and 3 to 4 inches thick, with little Lime-
stone.

All strata dipping 20° to the east.

The Sutton Shaft

Was sunk through:

No. 1. 3 feet Soil.
No. 2. 10 feet broken Chert, with specks of Galena.
No. 3. 12 feet yellow Clay, with pieces of rotten Chert.
No. 4. 2 feet Silico-calcite.
No. 5. 8 feet alternate layers, ½ to 1 foot thick, of Chert and Limestone.
Some layers of black, bituminous Clay, 1 inch thick, occur occa-
sionally between the rock layers.
The strata dip with the hill about 25°.

The Harrington Shaft,

The highest of these shafts, showed the following succession of
strata:

No. 1. 2 feet Soil.
No. 2. 3 feet red Clay, with some loose pieces of Galena and Cerussite.
No. 3. 15 feet yellow Clay, with some Chert.
No. 4. 10 feet broken Chert.
No. 5. 3 feet soft, coarse-grained Limestone in boulders, and Shales with
seams of Galena and some Blende.
No. 6. 7 feet Limestone and Chert in solid, alternate layers. The Limestone
is predominant; it is fine grained and, in places, strongly bitum-
inous.

The two sketches (Figs. 45 and 46) show the peculiar position of
the rocks as seen in these shafts.

Fig. 45 shows, in place, two runs of Galena crossing near a strongly
dipping layer of Slate and Coal which cuts them off. These runs are
3 to 5 feet wide and 2 to 6 feet high, and consist of finely broken Chert
in which Galena, often connected with Blende, is deposited in streaks
1 to 4 inches thick. Layers of red and brown Clay often accompany
these ores. Some Galena is occasionally mixed with the black
Slate.

Figure 46. (Harrington Shaft.)

Fig. 46 shows a vertical section along a line AB on Fig. 45.   We see here the two runs as well as the Slate layer in Section.

1. Slate.
2. Broken Chert.
3. Two runs of broken Chert, with Galena.
4. Boulders of softened and bituminous Limestone.

The Shafts 2 to 7, (see topographical sketch,)

Are sunk along the eastern branch of Lone Elm Creek down to its junction with the western branch.   They are rather shallow, most of them not being over 20 feet deep.

Below the Soil, we find here:

No. 1.   1 to 3 feet Gravel.

No. 2.   3 to 12 feet yellow Clay, sometimes pure and fat, sometimes mixed with yellow Sand and pieces of rotten Chert.   Boulders of Limestone, altered and softened on the outside, are occasionally found in it.

No. 3.   ½ to 1 foot clayish and sandy, shaly Limestone, which, when dissolved in acid, leaves a residue of fine, white, silicious Clay.

No. 4.   5 feet broken Chert, with loose pieces of Galena.

No. 5.   ? feet hard, blue, often bituminous Limestone in broken masses, which, in places where it is softened and altered, contains Galena in quantities which pay working.

Lone Elm Hollow proper begins at the junction of the two small branches.   It contains the following Diggings:

A.   SHAFTS ON THE EAST SLOPE OF LONE ELM HOLLOW.

THE SHAFTS 12 TO 15, (see General Sketch,)

Include the Hayes, Acton and Slatton Shafts.   Those sunk on the lower part of the Slope are characterized by the section of Shafts 12:

No. 1.   5 feet Soil.

No. 2.   10 feet finely broken Chert.

No. 3.   15 feet coarse, broken Chert.

No. 4.   5 feet slabs of Chert, with Clay and streaks of loose pieces of Galena.

No. 5.   ? feet layers of Chert and boulders of bituminous Limestone.

Fig. 47 shows the form of the ore deposits in Chr. Hayes' Shaft:

1. Soil.
2. Broken Chert.
3. Coarsely broken Chert in distinct layers.
4. Ore-bed ; Chert in more or less broken, irregular layers, with thin layers of
       black, bituminous Sand, and thick seams of pure Galena in the seams of
       the Chert and in the Sand.
5. Stratified Chert.
6. Bituminous Limestone.

John Hayes' Shaft,

A short distance farther north, passed through :

No. 1. 10 feet Soil, Clay and broken Chert.
No. 2. 15 feet layers and slabs of Chert.
No. 3. 5 feet layers of Chert 1 to 2 feet thick each, with 1 to 5 inches layers of
       brown Sand between them, containing much Galena and Blende.
       The Galena forms here basins of 20 to 30 feet diameter. It some-
       times replaces the brown Sand entirely.

This shaft yielded 5,000 to 12,000 pounds per week in the summer
of 1873.

The shafts higher up the slope are mostly shallow, and show a
section similar to that of shafts 12. Some have masses of Limestone,
with openings of brown Sand and Galena. The Limestone in all these
shafts is, in places, very bituminous.

The Acton Shaft,

About in the centre of a depression in the slope, has a pretty regular
ore formation at a depth of 30 feet. It consists of 15 feet of Chert
layers, separated by layers of Dolomitic Limestone, with streaks consisting of brown Sand in the upper and of rotten Limestone in the
lower layers. This Limestone contains streaks of Galena, sometimes
connected with Blende or with streaks of tallow Clay.

The Slatton Shaft

Passed through irregularly broken and mixed masses of Chert. At a
depth of about 45 feet, irregular runs of Galena occur in the broken
Chert. Large cracks and cavities in the midst of the broken Chert
masses are found filled with red or black Clay and loose chunks of
Galena.

THE SHAFTS 24 TO 26,

With Pierce's and Smith's Shafts, in the lower part of the hollow, did
not prove as rich in ore as those sunk in the upper part. The shafts

on the slope are from 30 to 50 feet deep, and passed through Soil, Chert, Sand, rotten Chert and boulders or broken masses of partly dolomized and often bituminous Limestone, containing Blende and Galena. The shafts 25, which lie at the mouth of a small ravine, did not strike any Limestone, but the ore lay here in masses of broken Chert.

The Smith Shaft,

Near the top of the ridge, had the following Section different from the others:

No. 1. 2 feet Soil.

No. 2. 20 feet red, porous Chert, partly disintegrated into a loose, sandy mass and inclosing large chunks of Galena in the lower part of the stratum.

No. 3. 10 feet white, partly rotten Chert, in slabs, dipping nearly vertically.

No. 4. 6 feet black, bituminous Clay, with small crystals of Galena.

No. 5. 2 feet brown or black Clay, with fragments of Chert and some Galena adhering to the Chert.

B. DIGGINGS IN THE BOTTOM AND ON THE WESTERN SLOPE OF THE LONE ELM HOLLOW.

Shafts 6 to 11 (see topographical sketch) in the upper part of the hollow, on the west side of the creek, contain the following strata:

No. 1. 2 to 4 feet Soil.

No. 2. 2 to 4 feet Gravel.

No. 3. 3 to 15 feet yellow, sandy Clay, with Chert pieces.

No. 4. 5 to 10 feet shaly Limestone.

No. 5. 6 to 40 feet broken Chert, with boulders of softened and altered Limestone in layers, or in irregular accummulations. Single runs of Galena occur in both Limestone and Chert.

In shaft 8 the following section presents itself (see Fig. 48):

No. 1. Soil.

No. 2. Gravel.

No. 3. Yellow Clay.

No. 4. Shaly Limestone.

No. 5. Brown Dolomitic Sand, with some Galena.

No. 6. Broken Chert.

The shafts 9 are sunk to a depth of 45 and 70 feet respectively. Runs of ore were found at two different levels; the first at 45 feet, the second at 70 feet depth.

The runs are 3 to 4 feet high, 3 to 10 feet wide, and extend con-

siderably in length. They are connected with the boulders of softened Limestone, and contain Galena, with broken Chert and Clay.

This group of shafts yielded about 100,000 pounds of Galena a
month in summer of 1872.

The layers always dip and strike in the same direction as the
Slope. They also follow all the depressions of the Slope.

The shafts 16 to 19, on land of the Granby Mining and Smelting
Co., are a continuation of the preceding group, with which they form
a zone following the strike of the Slope from south-east to north-west.
The layers of yellow Clay of the former group is partly replaced by
rotten, porous Chert, partly by red and brown Clays, with some Sand.
The boulders of Limestone are represented in some places, and in
others we find masses of altered Silico-calcite in their stead.

Shaft 20 is an old shaft, sunk through broken Chert and Chert-
conglomerate, consisting of a hard mass of fine-grained to sub-crystalline Quartzite of gray or drab color, inclosing angular pieces of
Chert, partly soft and porous. Numerous specks of Blende and crystals of Dolomite are disseminated in the Quartzite. Small Quartz
crystals are often found lining the walls of cavities. The dissolution
and removal of the inclosed pieces of Dolomite and Blende makes
the rock often porous and honey-combed. This Quartz rock has been
evidently formed in many places over layers of Dolomite, from which
crystals of Dolomite project. The Dolomite being dissolved and removed afterward, left the surface of the Quartz rock very rough and
full of impressions of Dolomite crystals.

Shafts 22 are shallow shafts along the bottom 15 to 20 feet deep.
They disclosed Soil, Gravel, black Slate and black Clay, with large
slabs of bituminous, dark, gray Limestone.

Shafts 21, 31, 30, 29 and 27 form a zone of a very disturbed and
irregular character.

Near the steam-pump shaft ("St. P." on the topographical sketch)
the ore is found between the Chert, in runs consisting of layers of
Clay or of Sand as much as 3 feet thick, with Galena irregularly distributed and dipping strongly toward the creek.

Those of the above mentioned shafts that are situated in the valley bottom, show only broken Chert below the Soil, and the ore irregularly distributed in it.

Shafts 30, which lie between a low bluff and the creek, struck
angular broken masses of unaltered Limestone mixed with the Chert.

Galena occurs sometimes in crystals formed on all sides of fragments of Chert.

Shafts 29 and 27 are mostly shallow and sunk through red and white, soft, porous Chert. The deeper shafts struck hard, fine-grained Limestone.

BLUFFS IN LONE ELM HOLLOW.

Three bluffs, marked A and B on topographical sketch, are exposed on the south side of Turkey Creek on both sides of the mouth of Lone Elm Creek. The bluff A lies west of Lone Elm Creek, and consists of immense masses of Chert-Conglomerate in a greatly disturbed position, the layers standing on edge. The Conglomerate is composed of broken white Chert, cemented by some hardened clayish Chert-sand of a reddish color. The whole mass is full of irregular holes, as there is not enough of cementing material to fill all the interstices between the broken Chert concretions. This rock was evidently formed from Silico-calcite by removal of the Limestone and by the breaking down of the Chert, the latter being afterward in part recemented. It is similar to those found in many shafts in the Southwestern Lead Region. It is also found in Pierce's shaft, on the opposite side of the Lone Elm Hollow, where it contains seams and crystals of Galena. In the bluff A, however, it does not contain any ore.

The bluffs marked B are situated near Turkey Creek, and rise about 20 feet above it. They consist of layers of Limestone in an undisturbed position, with irregular concretions and thin layers of Chert. The Limestone layers are 1 to 4 feet thick, and often separated by thin layers (1 to 3 inches thick) of shaly, coarse-grained Limestone.

THE LEADVILLE DIGGINGS,

Sec. 33, T. 28, R. 33, situated along the Leadville Hollow to its junction with Turkey Creek valley. (See Fig. 49.)

The upper portions of the hollow, near Pound's shaft, is very flat, a mere depression of the prairie. The middle and lower portions are deeply cut, and form, in places, quite steep bluffs.

The Pound's shaft at the upper end of the hollow, in Sec. 4, T. 27, R. 33, near the prairie plateau, shows the following section:

No. 1. 3 feet soil.

No. 2. 10 feet finely broken Chert, with yellow Sand.

No. 3. 8 feet finely broken, rotten, gray Limestone, with some Chert and a little Galena.

No. 4. 30 feet alternate layers of fine-grained, gray Limestone (2 to 3 feet thick) and of white dense Chert, (2 to 4 inches thick,) with some Galena.

No. 5. 6 feet solid Limestone.
No. 6. 3 feet solid Chert.
No. 7. 2 feet soft, porous Chert with streaks of gray Limestone.

The northern wall of the shaft consists of finely broken Chert, extending all the distance from the top down, and at 62 feet depth the whole shaft stood in this loose material, and the solid rock entirely disappeared.

It seems from this that a nearly vertical crevice widening below and filled with detritus was struck by this shaft. No workable ore had been found in August, 1873. Shafts 1 and 2, some distance lower down the branch, on the east side of the creek, struck 10 feet of broken Chert and then 15 feet of alternate layers of Limestone and Chert. Both often contain segregations of Bitumen. The layers are nearly horizontal, and the Limestone is partly unaltered and partly softened. In the latter case it frequently contains Blende and some Galena. The ores also occur in seams and chunks between the layers and broken pieces of Chert.

The shafts marked on the map 3 are about 30 feet deep and passed through much broken Chert and Conglomerate, consisting of pieces of Chert cemented by gray calcareous Sand and Blende. Below these Conglomerates are layers of softened and bituminous boulders of Limestone 2 to 6 feet thick, containing Chert layers 1 to 4 inches thick.

The Limestone is more altered than in the former group and partly replaced by calcareous Sand. The Chert is more broken.

The shaft 4 is a pump-shaft, in the bottom, close to the creek.

The section is here as follows:

No. 1. 4 feet Soil and Gravel.
No. 2. 5 feet loose, broken Chert.
No. 3. 4 feet broken masses of hard Limestone.
No. 4. 15 feet broken Chert cemented by gray Sand with some boulders of Limestone and a little Galena.
No. 5. 20 feet broken Chert layers, with Galena and Blende irregularly distributed in fissures and seams.

The ore apparently increased with the depth. No regular strata or solid rocks were struck in this shaft. The Galena was found in paying quantities. Shafts 5 and 6 lie on the lower part of the flat western slope. The formation is more regular, although nearly all the materials are more or less broken.

The Rhonimus shaft shows a characteristic section of an accumulation of broken and partly softened and rounded masses of Limestone. (See Fig. 50.)

No. 1. Soil.
No. 2. Loose Chert and Sand with some Galena and Blende.
No. 3. Boulders.
No. 4. Broken Chert cemented by hardened Sand and some pyrites.
No. 5. Brown Sand with a little Galena.
No. 6. Chert and Sand.

The ores were not found in paying quantity.
The Powell shaft passed through :

No. 1. 2 feet soil.
No. 2. 10 feet broken Chert with yellow Sand.
No. 3. 20 feet Silico-calcite and alternate layers of Limestone and Chert.
No. 4. 3 feet brown Sand and some Chert and Galena and Blende in paying
       quantities.
No. 5. ? Hard Chert layers.

The McCloud shaft penetrated through :

No. 1. 15 to 20 feet loose, broken Chert in yellow Clay.
No. 2. 15 to 20 feet solid Chert layers or Chert slabs.
No. 3. 1 to 6 feet ore-bearing stratum, consisting of broken Chert with Dolo-
       mite and Clay, and horizontal seams 1 to 10 inches thick of Galena
       mixed with some Blende.
No. 4. 7 to 10 teet alternate layers of Limestone and Chert, or else Chert lay-
       ers alone.
No. 5. 3 feet Chert with two seams of Blende.
No. 6. ? Chert.

The sketch Fig. 51 shows the composition of the ore-bearing
strata.

The shafts marked 6, have some resemblance to the McCloud
shaft. The materials are, however, more altered and more disturbed,
and the ore-seams are in broken Chert, at a somewhat higher level.

The Horse-shoe Diggings, on Davis & Murphy's land, have the
form of a half circle or horse-shoe. They are situated on the eastern
slope of the valley, about 30 feet above the creek.

The Horine shaft, which is over 90 feet deep, passed through :

3 feet Soil.
20 feet red, soft, porous Chert.
20 feet white, porous Chert.
30 feet broken Chert, with broken masses of Limestone.
20 feet Conglomerates of Chert and Dolomite, cemented by gray, regenerated
        Limestone, with some Galena, Blende, and Bitumen, and with large
        infiltrations of coarsely crystalline Calcite.

The other shafts were not sunk near so deep as this one, but so far
as they went they showed about the same succession of strata.

Some of the shafts in the middle part of the Diggings, passed through thin beds of black, micaceous Slate, which lay immediately below the Soil. All the shafts at the Horse-shoe Diggings, except the Horine shaft, are at present abandoned.

The shafts marked 7, including Philip's and Webb's Diggings, at the terminus of the Leadville Hollow, near Turkey Creek, are from 15 to 30 feet deep, and were sunk through Soil, broken Chert, and broken Limestone, with hard brown Sand between the fragments. Galena often adheres to the surface of the pieces of Limestone, and beside is irregularly distributed in the hard sandy mass.

The bluffs in the lower part of the hollow, are formed of alternate layers of white Chert and fine-grained Limestone.

GRAVES SHAFT.

The Graves Shaft, N. hf. Sec. 31, T. 28, R. 33, is situated at the head of a small southern branch of Turkey Creek. The Shaft was yet being sunk at the time of our visit, and was 35 feet deep. The location of the Shaft is shown on the topographical sketch, Fig. 52.

The Section is:

> 2 feet Soil.
> 3 feet slabs of white Sandstone.
> 16 feet broken Chert, with yellow Sand.
> 6 feet Silico-calcite, and boulders of Limestone, with segregations of Bitumen.
> 6 feet coarsely broken Chert, in pieces of fist-size and larger, with gray sandy Clay.
> 1 foot gray Clay.

No ores had been found then.
All layers dip north with the hill.

STEVENS' DIGGINGS,

The Stevens' Diggings, W. hf. Sec. 31, T. 28, R. 33, are situated in the upper part of a small hollow called Stevens',Hollow, about one-half mile south of Turkey Creek, as represented on the topographical sketch, Fig. 52.

The shafts marked A, especially the two most northern ones, count among the richest Lead shafts in the south-western region. They were sunk through Soil, broken Chert with yellow Sand, and struck at 25 feet depth a bed of softened dolomitic Limestone boulders 5 to 10 feet thick, and below these, broken Chert.

The ore was principally found in a nearly horizontal run of an oval cross-section, 150 feet long from south-east to north-west, 20 feet broad in the centre, and thinning out toward both ends. Its height varied from 5 to 15 feet. This space is filled with broken Chert and Limestone boulders, and contains numerous large and small irregular seams and chunks of Galena and Blende. The Galena occurs mostly between the Chert; the Blende more in the altered Limestone.

The sketch Fig. 53, represents the vertical-longitudinal section of a portion of this run.

The shaft B, on the eastern slope, went about 30 feet deep, through broken Chert, with boulders of Limestone occurring at a depth of 5 to 15 feet. Galena was found in small quantities in the loose Chert.

The shafts C and D, on the slope west side of the creek, passed through a very disturbed and irregular formation, consisting of:

No. 1. 20 feet broken Chert, with some Galena.
No. 2. 10 to 15 feet slabs and boulders of Limestone, partly dolomized.
No. 3. 10 feet broken Chert.
No. 4. 10 to 15 feet dark gray Clay.
No. 5. ? feet broken Chert, with dark gray Clay.

All strata dip very strongly from 45° to 70°, with the slope toward the east.

BENTLEY DIGGINGS,

The Bentley Diggings, S. E. qr. Sec. 25, and N. E. qr. Sec. 36, T. 28, R. 34 W., (see topographical sketch Fig. 52,) on Lienallen's land, leased by Bentley & Co., extend along a small branch of Turkey Creek, one-half mile west of Stevens' Diggings.

The upper Bentley Diggings consist of a small group of shafts, all sunk through loose Clay, Soil and broken Chert, with loose pieces of Galena and Blende. In some shafts, streaks of Galena were struck at a depth of 30 feet, but proved to be of rather small extent. The Galena is mostly in loose pieces, but is also found adhering to broken Chert.

The Blende occurs as single crystals, or in crystalline masses inclosed in either compact or porous mico-crystalline Quartz rock of gray color.

Boulders of Limestone occur occasionally.

The lower Bentley Diggings lie further down the hollow, one-fourth of a mile from Turkey Creek. There are 12 or 15 shafts, some of which reach a depth of 35 to 40 feet. Here, as in the upper Diggings, no Gravel was found, but the formation below the Soil consisted of large fragments of Chert, (1 to 6 feet in diameter,) with some Chert slabs and some Sand. These materials occur loose and irregularly mixed—or, as the miners call it, " tumbling."

Some Galena is found a few feet below the surface, in loose pieces in the Sand, and then again at a depth of 25 to 35 feet, between the Chert masses. The Chert is in a few places finely broken, and sometimes contains Galena in streaks.

Boulders of Limestone are rare.

Blende is occasionally met with, cementing broken pieces of Chert.

Beside the Diggings above mentioned and described, there are in the Turkey Creek district a number of places where Lead had been formerly found, but which are abandoned at present. Prominent among these were the Duff Diggings on Turkey Creek, 8 miles east of Joplin, which formerly yielded large quantities of ore.

In other localities, parties of miners were prospecting, but had not found any ore at the time of our visit—for instance, on J. H. Taylor's land, Secs. 4 and 5, T. 29, R. 32; and on some points along Short Creek, near the western boundary of the State.

CHAPTER XXVII.

D.—SPECIAL DESCRIPTION OF ORE DEPOSITS—Continued.

III.—DEPOSITS OF CENTRE CREEK DISTRICT.

Centre Creek winds its way from east to west through the southern portions of Jasper county, and joins Spring River a short distance west of the State line.

The land is mostly rolling and forms bluffs and abrupt slopes only in close vicinity to the water-courses.

Lead and Zinc ores have been found principally at the following three localities :

1. Near Sarcoxie (Perry Diggings.)
2. Near Scotland (Birch and Grove Creek Diggings.)
3. Near Oronogo, formerly called Minersville.

1.—THE PERRY DIGGINGS,

T. 27, R, 30, Sec. 12, are 2½ miles west of Sarcoxie (see general map of South-west Missouri,) on land belonging to William Carnahan and H. W. Perry.*

Several shafts have been sunk through :

No. 1. 3 feet Soil.
No. 2. 12 to 15 feet broken Chert and yellow Sand.

---

*See Perry Mines on p. 84 of this volume.

No. 3. 20 to 70 feet alternate layers of Limestone and Chert broken, and con-
        taining small seams and specks of Galena, in both Limestone and
        Chert. One layer of Limestone is 15 feet thick, solid, bluish-gray,
        coarser-grained, inclosing crystalline masses of Galena. The other
        Limestone is mostly light-gray, and contains but little ore. It
        sometimes contains streaks of Dolomite, some little Bitumen and
        always many sub-carboniferous fossils.

In one shaft loose chunks of Calamine, in head-sized boulders,
were found in Chert and Sand, on the surface of the solid rock. The
ore, however, was never found in sufficient quantities to pay working,
and consequently the mines are abandoned at present.

2.—THE MINES NEAR SCOTLAND.

GROVE CREEK DIGGINGS, (see pp. 86 and 87 of this Vol.),

(See topographical sketch, Fig. 54,) T. 27, R. 32, Sec. 12 N. W. qr., are
situated less than a mile south-west of the town of Scotland, on a
south-east Slope, near the head of Grove Creek.

Figure 54 represents a topographical sketch of this locality.

At the northern end of the present Diggings a knob rises about
40 feet above the creek bottom. On the eastern Slope of this knob is
an outcrop of light-gray, sandy Limestone, extending horizontally for
150 to 200 feet. This outcrop is about 15 feet below the mouth of the
highest shafts on the knob, which shafts are less than 100 feet distant
from the outcrop. They were sunk through 15 feet of broken Chert,
and then struck large boulders and slabs of thin alternate layers of
Limestone and Chert. This seems to show that the outcropping strata
do not reach far into the hill, but are perhaps only large portions of
the broken and disturbed strata in the shafts.

The Diggings show the following General Section:

No. 1. 3 to 5 feet Soil.
No. 2. 15 to 20 feet broken Chert, with yellow Sand.
No. 3. 20 to 30 feet boulders of Limestone, softened and altered on the out-
        side, or broken masses of alternate layers of Limestone and Chert.

The ore generally occurs between the boulders, lying in loose
pieces in yellow, sandy, broken Chert.

Carwin & Clow's shafts, in the southern part of the Diggings, have
at a depth of about 30 feet, a regular bed of ore in yellow Sand and
Clay, between the boulders of sandy Limestone, extending over an
area about 100 feet in diameter. The Galena forms a continuous wavy

layer, 1 to 2 inches in thickness, mixed occasionally with crystals and crystalline masses of Blende.

The Tussinger shaft (see topographical sketch) is sunk 40 feet in the lowest part of the Diggings.

Figure 55 represents the 8 feet at bottom of this shaft:

No. 1. Large boulder of hard, coarsely crystalline Limestone.

No. 2. Bluish-black, slaty Clay.

No. 3. Layers of light-colored, sandy Limestone and Chert.

No. 4. Calcareous, yellow Sand, (soft Sandstone,) with loose chunks of Galena and some Blende; sometimes rounded and coated with gray Carbonate.

No. 5. Head-sized boulders of sandy Limestone, with yellow, calcareous Sand, with thick sheets, and streaks of Galena, partly coated and between the boulders.

The mines are worked at present (summer 1873) by about 30 to 40 men, who obtain 25 to 30,000 pounds of Galena per week.

BURCH DIGGINGS, (see p. 88 of this Vol.),

T. 27, R. 32, Sec. 11 S. W. qr. of N. W. qr., are about 1 mile south-west of the Grove Creek Diggings. They are owned by Burch & Co. They lie on high ground, in a slight depression of the prairie, the surface of which is covered with pieces of broken Chert. Boulders up to 6 feet thick, of red or yellow Sandstone, are found on the surface between the Burch and the Grove Creek Diggings. The Burch shafts are generally 30 to 40 feet deep, only one of them being 60 feet. All are sunk through loose materials, without reaching a solid stratum of rock. The upper layers mostly consist of red, clayish Sand, 25 feet thick, with some Chert, and in places with large masses of white Clay. At greater depth, streaks of red tallow Clay and of brown, sandy Clay are met with. The Clay incloses considerable quantities of Galena and of Smithsonite. The latter occurs in the eastern shafts in chunks and slabs, and in the western in solid layers, 1 to 3 feet thick. In the western shafts sharp-cornered slabs of red Sandstone, similar to that seen in the prairie, as above mentioned, are found in the Sand a few feet below ground.

There were about 15 to 20 men at work at these Diggings. Three miners at one time obtained 10,000 pounds of Galena in 6 days from 2 of the eastern shafts.

3.—THE MINES OF ORONOGO (MINERSVILLE.)

These mines are situated in T. 29, R. 32 W., Sec. 31 N. hf. of S. W. qr., and in T. 29, R. 33 W., Sec. 36 N. E. qr. of S. E. qr. The present Diggings at this place are owned by the Granby Mining and Smelting Co., conjointly with other parties. They are situated at the head of a small branch, running south into Centre Creek.

We add to this report a topographical map of these Diggings, from sketches taken in summer of 1873. See Fig. 56.

The Geological formation is the Keokuk Limestone, which is exposed in a small quarry east of the Diggings. This Limestone is in places overlaid by small pockets of Lower Coal-Measure rocks, namely, Slate and Coal.

In regard to the rocks associated with the ore, the Oronogo district is very remarkable for the frequency and considerable development of the Quartzite. This rock occurs to some extent in a few other places, (as in Shaft 20, at Lone Elm and in the Bentley Diggings), but at Oronogo it forms the principal ore-bearing rock in several of the richest runs of ore, especially in Shafts y, v, s. r, m, k, i, also in Shafts 2, 8, 14 and 15, and in the Circular Diggings. This Quartzite must be of much later origin than either the Chert or the Limestone, because it cements together Chert fragments, thus forming the Conglomerates described in our preceding chapter, and because it also encloses broken masses of Limestone occasionally. The Quartzite contains ores in single crystals as well as in seams and streaks. It is, in places, coarsely crystalline, the crystals being of either prismatic or pyramidal type. When thus plainly crystalline, it passes into porous aggregations of crystals, and sometimes into loose crystalline Quartz-Sand. It seems that single loose crystals were at first deposited, which by increasing gradually in number, formed a porous, and finally a dense Quartzite. This rock is of a gray or drab color, which, by the admixture of Blende or of Bitumen, is frequently changed into dark brown or black. The Bitumen has undoubtedly assisted in the precipitation of the ores in this rock. It betrays its presence by its peculiar odor when the rock is rubbed or broken. The Blende, which is nearly always associated with the Quartzite, occurs in large and well developed crystals disseminated through the whole mass. Galena, on the other hand, occurs in this rock, mostly in large vein-like aggregations of various shapes.

In the above mentioned Conglomerates, the limits between the pieces of white or light-gray Chert and dark-colored Quartzite, are generally well defined. In a few instances, however, it was observed that the Chert became gradually dark-colored and somewhat porous, and more crystalline near the lines of contact, and that it has evidently been attacked and altered by the solutions which have deposited the Quartzite. The ores are always in the mass of the Quartzite. never in the Chert-fragments.

The Diggings near Oronogo may be divided into two groups :

a. The Branch Diggings.

b. The Circular Diggings.

a. THE BRANCH DIGGINGS. (See topographical sketch of Oronogo.)

Are situated in the west half Sec. 31, T. 29, R. 32 W., along a small branch of Centre Creek. The Shafts form more or less parallel rows, which correspond to subterranean runs of ore on which they were sunk. There are three such runs on the eastern Slope, one opened by the Shafts 9, another by the Shafts *w* and *t*, and the third by the Shafts *g*. All three seem to join into one in the vicinity of the furnace building, and to continue as one wide but less regular run, along and close to the branch, for some distance south. Another run extends on the west side of the branch, through shafts 3 and 10, and another through Shafts 2 and 8, up the western slope at an angle to the Creek. This latter run may perhaps continue south to Shafts 14 and 15, which are of a similar character.

The Shafts *g, d, c, b,* form the upper run on the eastern slope, and are 15 to 25 feet above the branch. They were mostly abandoned at the time of our visit, because their ore-deposits were not as rich as others in the district. The shafts passed through Soil, yellow Clay, (often tallow-Clay and broken Chert). Boulders of Limestone, either decomposed and sandy, or hard and bituminous, were found 12 to 25 feet below the surface. In shaft *c*, 20 feet of alternate, irregular layers of black bituminous Clay and yellow sandy Clay were struck below the Soil, all dipping with the slope.

The shafts *w, t* and *p*, are sunk on a run of ore nearly parallel to the former, on the same slope. The shafts are mostly 20 to 40 feet deep. They passed through :

No. 1. 2 to 5 feet Soil.

No. 2. 0 to 15 feet yellow, sandy Clay.

No. 3. 10 to 15 feet broken Chert.

No. 4. ½ to 6 feet solid Chert, in slabs or layers.

No. 5. 3 to 10 feet ore-bed, consisting of broken Chert and gray or red Clay, in which Galena, with little Blende, occurs in streaks ¼ to 6 inches thick. The seams of Galena are nearly horizontal, dipping but slightly with the hill.

In shaft *t*, boulders of soft, bituminous Limestone were found, surrounded by gray or green Clay, the latter containing some Galena.

The deepest shaft on this run is the " Pump Shaft," close to the furnace building, sunk for the purpose of draining the whole district. It is 82 feet deep. At a depth of 20 feet a seam of Galena in the Chert was struck, but not followed. At 50 feet of depth the shaft reached a Conglomerate, consisting of angular pieces of Chert, cemented by gray, sandy Limestone, and enclosing single crystals and specks of Blende, and some Galena.

The shafts *y*, *v*, *s*, *r*, *m*, *k*, and *i*, are sunk on the main run of ore. Their mouths are but a few feet above the level of the creek. The following sections were obtained in the several shafts :

	y	*v*	*r*	*m*	*k*	*i*
Soil and Gravel............	5 feet.	....	2 feet.	5 feet.	3 feet.	3 feet.
Slate and Coal............	0	15 feet.	0	0	0	3 to 5 feet.
Yellow Clay··············	0	....	6 feet.	0	0	0
Broken Chert...............	0	0	0	5 feet.	0	0
Boulders and slabs of Limestone..............	4 to 5 feet.	0	0	0	....	0
Quartzite....................	5 to 8 ft.	20 feet.	6 feet.	12 feet.	7 to 9 feet.	7 to 9 feet.
Chert Conglomerate....	....	0	....	....	....	....
Broken Chert.............	0	15 feet.	0	0	0	0
Solid Chert-layers.......	0	0	0	0	3½ feet.	0

This table shows how much the strata vary in thickness and in character in this row of shafts. The level of the layer of Quartzite however, is pretty near the same all through, as the surface of the ground is lower at the shafts *k* and *i*, than at *y* and *r*. The upper layer of broken Chert is occasionally replaced by sand and yellow Clay. The Limestone which occurs in boulders and slabs in the shafts *y*, is entirely missing in the shafts lower down the creek. The Quartzite occurs either massive and without admixture, or else it cements Chert-fragments into a Conglomerate. In some shafts it occurs in both ways, and then the Quartzite overlies the Conglomerate, while loose, broken Chert, or else fissured Chert-layers are found below.

Galena and Blende occur in the Quartzite in the manner above described. In shaft *y* the Quartzite varies much in shade and color. The dark variety contains much more ore than the light colored one, and the ore in the former looks darker itself, than the ore in the lat-ter. The Blende is nearly black, and the Galena has a perceptibly darker hue, and a bituminous odor when broken. This shows that the dark color is to a great extent, due to the presence of Bitumen.

In the most southern of shaft y, are observed the following Sections. See Fig. 57:

Fig. 57. Branch Diggings, Oronogo.

No. 1. 4 feet Soil.
No. 2. 4 feet yellow, sandy Clay.
No. 3. 10 feet broken Quartz rock, with some Galena and Blende, and boulders of softened Limestone.
No. 4. 10 feet solid Quartzite, with much Galena and Blende.

The shaft s, west of the furnace building, nearly in line with the former shafts, was only 10 feet deep when visited by us. At this shallow depth it had disclosed one of the largest chunks of Galena ever found in this region, being 6 to 8 feet long, 3 to 4 feet high, and $1\frac{1}{2}$ to $2\frac{1}{2}$ feet thick, and weighing over 10,000 pounds. It was found loose, imbedded in a mixture of Clay, broken Chert and broken Quartzite, in the manner shown on sketch, Fig. 58.

Fig. 58. Loose Chunks, Oronogo.

No. 1. Soil.
No. 2. Gravel and small Chert fragments.
No. 3. Coarse, broken Chert.
No. 4. Gray Fire Clay.
No. 5. Black Clay.
No. 6. Sand, with broken Chert and Quartzite, and rounded chunks of pure Galena. The large chunk is seen in Section.

In shaft m we observed the Section represented by the sketch, Fig. 59.

Fig. 59. Oronogo.

No. 1. Soil and Gravel.
No. 2. Broken Chert and brown Sand.
No. 3. Broken Chert cemented by gray Quartz rock, with Blende, Galena and Calcite.
No. 4. Alternate layers of Chert and Limestone, bituminous, with some seams and specks of Galena and Blende.

In shaft i, sandy, gray Coal-slate and impure Coal were struck between large, broken masses of black, bituminous Conglomerate—

G.S—31

i. e., Chert cemented by Quartzite—with Galena and Blende, and Calcite. Below this lay a large mass of black, bituminous Quartzite without any ore.

The shafts a are shallow, 5 to 10 feet deep, and struck alternate layers of Limestone and Chert below the Soil, which, in fissures, contained Calcite with some Galena in large crystals.

The shafts f, x, y, u, 3, 9, 10, compose a range along the branch, having about the following Section:

> No. 1. 2 to 5 feet Soil and Gravel.
> No. 2. 2 to 10 feet yellow Clay and Sand.
> No. 3. 4 to 10 feet broken Chert.
> No. 4. 4 to 12 feet broken Limestone, sometimes altered.
> No. 5. ? feet broken Chert.

In addition to this General Section, the shafts f and x, which are the most northern of this range, have, below the Soil:

> 3 to 6 feet of black Clay and clay Slate.

In shafts x, 9 and 10, a stratum of gray, sandy Limestone, 5 to 8 feet thick, and containing streaks of micaceous, black Slate, lies under the Soil. This stratum is, in places, over 15 feet thick, divided into layers of $\frac{1}{4}$ to 4 inches. Its position is strongly disturbed—the strata dipping 25° to 40° east, as shown in the sketch (Fig. 60), which is taken from the shallow shaft 10.

Fig. 60. Oronogo.

> No. 1. 1 foot Soil and Gravel.
> No. 2. 4 feet light gray, slaty Clay.
> No. 3. 5 feet sandy Limestone, with specks, seams and small veins of Galena and Blende.

This range is not near so rich as the former. The ores occur in seams and specks in the Sandstone, and also at greater depth between broken Chert and Limestone.

The shafts g and h, north of the railroad, are sunk 25 to 35 feet deep, through Soil, broken Chert and large masses (15 to 20 feet thick) of soft, rotten Chert, with some single, angular boulders of bituminous Limestone containing segregations of fluid Bitumen. Galena occurs in the Chert, and in the softened, outer portion of the Limestone, but has not, so far, been found there in paying quantities. The shafts h are 15 to 30 feet deep, and had 10 feet of gray Fire Clay below the Soil, and then 10 feet of black Clay and broken Chert.

The shafts 2 and 3 are sunk from 20 to 32 feet deep, on a run of

Galena-bearing Quartzite, striking nearly south-west to north-east The run is overlaid and surrounded by broken Chert, and in places on the west side, by boulders of altered Limestone. The Galena occurs principally in seams in the fissured Quartzite, and is associated with much Blende. Also, the boulders of Limestone are sometimes impregnated with Galena to a depth of 5 or 6 inches.

The shafts 14 are 16 to 20 feet deep. They penetrated:

No. 1. 3 to 4 feet Soil, with loose pieces of Cerussite and Chert.
No. 2. 3 to 4 feet broken Chert and yellow Sand, locally impregnated with Cerussite.
No. 3. Over 10 feet bituminous Quartzite, in places, cementing dark gray Chert fragments.

This conglomeratic mass is itself, in places, fissured and broken. Galena occurs in irregular aggregations or pockets, sometimes 5 to 7 inches thick, and 1 to 4 feet long. Many small seams extend in all directions from these pockets into the adjoining Quartz rock. The shafts 15 are very similar to the former. They are, however, 35 to 40 feet deep, and below the Chert and the Quartzite reached Limestone boulders with some Galena, and masses of broken Chert conglomerated by regenerated Limestone, containing single crystals and bunches of Galena and Blende. Broken masses of half-decomposed Silico-calcite are also met with. Smithsonite is found in pockets and streaks in the broken rocks. The Quartzite in this locality sometimes incloses Limestone boulders, which are rotten, soft and sandy on the outside. This case is represented in the sketch. (Fig. 61.)

No. 1. Solid interior of Limestone boulder.
No. 2. Soft, sandy exterior,
No. 3. Chert-breccia cemented by bituminous Quartzite with Galena.
No. 4. Solid Chert-layer 5 inches thick.

Shafts 1. One of these shafts is sunk 25 feet deep, and showed the following formation: (See Fig. 62.)

No. 1. Soil and Gravel.
No. 2. Clay and Gravel.
No. 3. Limestone boulders, softened on the outside, and rounded, forming a cave about 15 feet high, 15 feet wide, and 15 to 20 feet long.

The cave was filled with a soft mud, consisting, in its various parts, of yellow Clay, gray calcareous Clay, Gravel, pieces of wood, and some fine Galena and Blende, all of which had evidently been washed into it. The existence of this cave proves that the boulders can not have been brought into their present position and rounded shape by drifting, but only by a gradual settlement and thorough chemical action.

Shafts 13, 12, 7, 6, 5, and 4, are sunk on the Slope ascending gradually from the branch west towards the Circular Diggings, which lie on somewhat higher ground. These shafts are mostly shallow, and passed through a formation of Clay and broken Chert, deposited in thick layers. In some places they struck Limestone boulders.

In shafts 5 and 6, broken masses of Silico-calcite were reached at a depth of 20 feet, containing Calcite with Galena in fissures.

In shafts 13, loose pieces of Cerussite were found in the broken Chert below the Soil. But no well-paying deposit has as yet been discovered in these shafts.

B. THE CIRCULAR DIGGINGS,

T. 29, R. 33 W., Sec. 36 N. E. qr., of S. E. qr., (see Topographical sketch of Oronogo, Fig. 56,) consist of a number of shafts, sunk on a natural dyke of circular form. The surface of the ground dips from all sides towards the center of the circle, forming a flat basin. This circle has a diameter of 400 to 500 feet. The west side lies about 10 feet higher than the east side. The dyke is interrupted, in three places, by gaps 20 to 30 feet wide. Two of these are on the west side, and one in the lower or eastern part, where the water runs out to join the Oronogo Branch.

We will describe a few shafts in various parts of the circle to show the Geological features, beginning at the lower gap on the east side:

Shafts 17, near this gap, are sunk 15 to 20 feet through broken Chert, with seams of Galena all through the mass.

The shafts a little farther north, went through 15 feet Chert-layers, with Clay between them, 15 feet massive Quartzite, then boulders of Limestone with some Bitumen, and some Galena as represented in sketch. (Fig. 63.)

No. 1. Soil.
No. 2. Yellow Clay and Chert.
No. 3. Chert-layers.
No. 4. Quartz rock with fissures and gash-veins with Galena.
No. 5. Limestone boulders.

Shafts 18, on the west side of the circle, passed through broken Chert, with Galena seams 1 to 3 inches thick, in fissures, and then struck Quartzite at a depth of 25 feet, with large, irregular gash-veins filled with Galena, as in the sketch shown: (Fig. 64.)

The irregularly stratified formation of Gravel and of broken Chert dips both ways towards the center of the circle, and in the opposite direction.

Shafts 19, south of the preceding, near the gap, are about 30 feet deep, in broken Chert, with loose pieces of Cerussite and Galena. Farther towards the inside of the circle, large masses of gray Clay were found containing considerable quantities of Cerussite, and in places entirely impregnated with it.

Shafts 20 are sunk through a solid mass of dark-colored Quartzite with seams of Galena.

Shafts 21 are 20 to 30 feet deep, and passed through Soil, and then struck

No. 1.   8 feet black Slate and black Clay.
No. 2.   10 to 15 feet yellow Clay, with some broken Chert.
No. 3.   ? feet Limestone boulders, some hard and light-gray, others soft and a little bituminous.

Shafts 22, on south side of circle, passed through 4 inches to 15 feet broken Chert, mixed with yellow Sand and Clay, and also with pieces of Cerussite, and of half decomposed crystals of Galena. Below this, is again broken Chert, and then massive Quartzite, with veins of Galena and with red Clay in fissures.

Shafts 23, situated a short distance outside of the regular circle, are 12 to 15 feet deep in yellow Clay and broken Chert, and then reached a hard, light-gray Limestone, broken and partly bituminous. They did not strike any ore up to the time of investigation.

Shafts 24 had 6 to 10 feet of broken Chert and Chert-conglomerate; 10 feet solid, dark gray Quartzite with specks of Galena and of Blende. This Quartzite sometimes incloses broken Chert of light gray color. Pieces of Cerussite and Calamine occur in the soil and in the loose Chert above the Quartzite.

Shafts 25 are shallow and situated near the steep slope of the eastern gap of the circle. They disclosed a large quantity of very coarse Gravel, and below this, rounded slabs of Sandstone. They did not reach the regular ore formation.

CENTRE SHAFT.

A deep shaft was sunk by the Company in the very centre of the circle, for the purpose of testing the locality, and in the hope to be able to drain all the diggings by it. According to the records which the Superintendent, Col. Young, kindly submitted to our inspection, this shaft passed through the following strata:

Section of Centre Shaft.

NUMBER.	DESCRIPTION OF STRATA.	FEET.
1	Soil	1
2	Clay and broken Chert	3
3	Irregular layers of various Clays, dark blue, gray and yellow	14
4	Gray Fire Clay, becoming sandy lower down.....................................	25
5	Sandy, gray and black Clay, with a chunk of Coal 4 inches thick..........	12
6	Black, slaty Clay, with some Pyrites...	2
7	Slaty Clay full of Pyrites................................	3
8	Same, with Coal chunks	6
9	Hard, slaty Clay, inclosing large and small boulders of sandy Limestone	16
10	Hard, gray Sandstone, with Pyrites..	8
11	Hard, dark blue, slaty Clay, with numerous seams of Galena	4
12	Boulders of sandy Limestone	5
13	Hard Sandstone (?)	2
14	Conglomerate, consisting of angular pieces of Chert cemented by a very sandy regenerated Limestone, inclosing specks of Blende, and also some Galena and Calcite. This is the same rock as found in the pump shaft near the furnaces at a depth of 50 feet.....................................	3
	Total depth	104

The last blast opened a fissure striking north to south, when, for the first time, some water ran into the shaft, rising slowly—about 5 feet in the first 12 hours, and 13½ feet in the first 36 hours. The work was then abandoned. The above Section evidently indicates the presence of a confused mixture of broken Coal Measure rocks in the centre of the circle, and therefore a disturbance on a pretty large scale. The last 10 feet of the Section seem to belong to the Subcarboniferous Ore Formation.

According to the above descriptions, the Circular Diggings would appear in section about as follows: (see Fig. 65.)

Fig. 65. Circular Diggings, Oronogo.

The lowest rock struck by the Centre Shaft is Chert-conglomerate. Above this, we have:

No. 1. Limestone boulders.
No. 2. Quartzite with Galena and Blende.
No. 3. Chert layers.
No. 4. Broken Chert.
No. 5. Clay and Sand with Cerussite.
No. 6. Broken Coal Measure rocks. Slates, Clay, Sandstone and Coal.

The present circular form, which is peculiar to these Diggings, may have been caused by the erosion of a large cavity in the underlying Limestone, and by the breaking down of the upper strata. The condition and relative position of the various rocks, especially the fact that all the layers, irregular as they are, yet invariably dipping towards the centre of the circle, decidedly support this view. The boulders lie about 70 feet deeper in the centre than at the circumference of the circle.

The existence of numerous large and small sink holes all over the Limestone region of Southern Missouri, shows that such local subterraneous erosions, causing circular, funnel-shaped depressions on the surface, are nothing unusual.

The lead-bearing Quartz rock, according to present appearances, is not found inside the circle, but has itself a nearly circular form. The developments made so far do not permit us to decide whether it has been at once deposited in this form, or whether it originated in two separate runs, curved afterwards by the particular manner in which the settling of the ground may have been effected.

CHAPTER XXVIII.

E. MINING AND SMELTING.

HISTORY.

Mining operations began comparatively late in the lead region of South-west Missouri.

In 1850, the Prairie Diggings, one mile south of Granby, were opened, and in 1851, mining began in the Brock Hollow on the Granby section. Soon after, a great number of mostly shallow shafts were sunk in other parts of South-west Missouri, and in many instances met with good success. So the Nobleton, the Moseley and the Cedar Creek mines in Newton county; the Centre Creek, the Duff, the Mineral Point (Leadville), and the Orchard mines (Joplin), in Jasper county, and several others.

The Galena obtained was smelted in simple log furnaces or on small Scotch hearths with one eye. The blast was produced by bellows driven by water power. The Lead was taken by wagons to Fort Smith, and then boated down the Arkansas and Mississippi Rivers, and was shipped to New Orleans, New York and Boston.

The total amount of Galena raised from 1850 to 1854 was estimated by Prof. Swallow, in his Report of 1855, p. 161, at 1,721,679 pounds.

The Granby Mines were the first which actually began to flourish. In 1856, Blow & Kennett obtained a lease on the Granby section from the Atlantic and Pacific Railroad Company, which owns the land. They erected six Scotch hearths with blast produced by fans and steam power. Six other hearths were built and worked by other parties. Miners from all parts of the world flocked to Granby, and the town grew rapidly. The production rose to over 8,000,000 pounds per year. The principal work was done at the Brock Hollow, the Dutch, the Frazier, and at some parts of the Crabtree and Hardshaft Diggings.

We will here mention a few remarkable examples of well-paying shafts worked at that time.

Holman, Hersey, Gatzel and others obtained from two shafts 3,500,000 pounds of Galena in 18 months, which, estimated at $21 per 1,000 pounds, had a value of $73,500.

Frazier's Shaft, at the present Frazier Diggings, yielded, in 1859, an average of 100,000 pounds per month.

The beginning of the war in 1861 stopped the mining operations of the whole region until 1865. Henry T. Blow then obtained a lease of the Granby section and vigorously started and pushed the work. Several valuable disclosures, especially in the Holman, Hardshaft and East Point Diggings, gave a new impulse to it from time to time, and finally the discovery of the Zinc ore, and its value, secured the success of these mines for a lengthy future.

More sudden yet than the rise of Granby was that of Joplin. In 1870 not a single house was in the place where two years afterward a flourishing town stood, which has now grown into a city of 5000 inhabitants.

In 1871 one furnace, owned by Moffett and Sergeant, was more than sufficient to smelt all the ore there raised from the Cox and Orchard Diggings, and some shafts at Leadville, until a miner, named Moon, struck a very rich deposit, now called after him—the Moon Range, or Moon Digging—on East Joplin Hill.

For nearly 20 years (more or less) ore had been found along Turkey Creek, and mined with but moderate success, when suddenly Moon's lucky hit increased the confidence, causing more extensive prospecting, and thus leading to the great development of mining operations in Joplin Creek Valley. Discovery followed discovery in rapid succession, and after hardly two years over 1000 miners were at work, producing near 400,000 pounds of Galena per week. At present 7 Scotch hearths and 16 air furnaces are in operation.

Joplin miners also discovered and worked the Grove Creek and Burch, the Stevens and Bentley, the Thurman, Carney and Cornwall Diggings, and are now prospecting extensively in numerous other localities.

In the Centre Creek District mining had likewise been carried on for about 20 years. The old Centre Creek mines yielded a total amount of about 370,000 pounds of Galena up to the year 1854. The ore was smelted on a Scotch hearth (Harklerode's furnace.) Since the discovery of the rich deposits of Oronogo, (late Minersville,) the operations have been concentrated at this place. Three Scotch hearths were built, and the erection of Zinc works is under consideration.

LEASES AND CLAIMS.

According to the system adopted in nearly all the lead districts of Missouri, the miner obtains from the land owner, or general lessee, a " claim;" that is, a square piece of ground of 100 to 200 feet side-length, on which he has the exclusive right of mining. On this claim the miner works at his own risk and expense. All the ore he gets he has to deliver to the persons who own or control the land at a certain prearranged price per 1000 pounds of Galena, and per ton of Zinc ore; or else, if he prefers to sell his ore to other parties than those who control the land, he pays to the latter a royalty, which varies from one-fourth to one-eighth of all the Galena mined, and about 50 cents for every ton of Zinc ore.

Such claims are operated in two different ways; either two or three miners work the claim conjointly, at their entire risk, or else they unite with business men for the purpose. In the latter case the business men support the miners as long as they are working and fail to find any ore. After they have struck a deposit of ore, the proceeds are equally divided.

In a few instances only have companies worked the land they control at their own risk by hired labor.

A claim is forfeited and falls back to the owner or general lessee of the land as soon as no work is done on it for more than 15 days.

These and other points are stipulated for each case by a special agreement between the interested parties.

MINING.

When a new claim is laid out, the miners begin sinking a shaft. The place in which to do this is often determined by the direction of the ore runs or opening already found on the adjoining lands. If no such indications exist, a depression of the ground on a hill slope is chosen if possible. The working implements used are a double-pointed pick, shovel, windlass with rope and bucket. For boring and blasting, steel drills, about one inch wide, are used, and a hammer about 3 pounds in weight. One man holds and sets the drill, the other strikes. The holes are made 20 to 30 inches deep. Common blasting-powder, as well as Giant-powder are used. The latter is more effective, but its gases are considered to be injurious, and to produce head-ache. Yet in fissured rock it is almost indispensable. The Giant-powder generally used in South-west Missouri consists of Nitro-glycerine mixed with various materials to lessen its explosibility, especially with sawdust and sand. It has the appearance and the consistency of brown wax. It is inclosed in a cartridge, and is lit by a rubber-coated fuse, so as to burn below water or in wet places. A large cap is put over one end of the fuse, and both are pressed into the powder.

The time required for sinking a shaft is, of course, very variable, according to the condition of the ground. While in Clay sometimes 6 feet and more are sunk in one day, it often takes 3 days to sink 1 foot in hard, cherty Limestone or solid Chert.

Ten feet per week is considered a fair average, 2 men being at work.

When the shaft passes through loose material, it is always made square, and fully timbered.

When a run or opening is struck, the miner generally begins " drifting" at once, giving the drift the full height of the opening.

The bucket in which the ores and rock are hoisted to the surface, is taken from the bottom of the shaft to the working place, and when filled, it is slid by hand along the drift to the shaft. This is very hard work, and cannot be done for long distances. The miners therefore sink a second shaft as soon as the drift acquires a considerable length.

The water is also hoisted in a bucket by hand, or in a tub by horses or oxen, and only in case a good deposit is found and much water, does the miner go to the expense of putting up a horse or steam pump. When much water is met with in a new place, where the existence of a good deposit is not confidently expected, or previously proven, the miners often abandon the shaft entirely. Old, abandoned shafts are therefore not proof that there is no ore in that particular place, nor that the ore has all been taken out.

For the purpose of supplying the shafts and drifts with fresh air, a wide tube made of cloth is frequently used, the upper end of which reaches to the mouth of the shaft, and is turned against the wind. If this is not sufficient, a small, plain, wooden fan is placed near the shaft and driven by hand.

DRESSING.

From the materials hoisted, the clean Galena or Zinc ore, is separated by hand, with hammer and chisel, as far as possible. Impure pieces are ;crushed and washed in an inclined wooden trough with a square box at the lower end. A strong stream of water flows over the crushed ore, which at the same time is worked against the stream with the help of a shovel. The best material remains in the trough; the sludge or "smiltum," (impure fine ore,) is deposited in the box; and the greater part of the drift is carried off. The contents of the trough and of the box, are jigged by hand jigs, and the clean ore is thus ready for smelting.

When the Galena is intimately mixed with Chert or with Dolomite, the miners lay it on a small wood pile and burn it. The heat must then be kept low enough not to roast or to smelt the Galena, but just enough to make the rock crack, or at least to make it so brittle as to be easily broken by hand. The burnt and broken ore is picked and washed in troughs.

If the Galena is finely disseminated through the rock, especially if mixed with Blende or Pyrites, it has to be crushed between rollers to less than pea size, and then jigged. However, as rollers exist only in a few places as yet, in South-west Missouri, such materials are often thrown among the refuse.

The troughs are about 10 feet long, 2 feet wide, and 6 inches deep. Two men or three boys, can wash, per day, from 5 to 10 wagon loads of "wash dirt" (impure ore). Each load weighs from 1,800 to 3,000 pounds, according to quality, and yields from 200 to 600 pounds of clean Galena.

SMELTING.

Smelting of Lead ore is done, either in the Scotch hearth or in the air furnace.

The old Scotch hearth, built of stone, and supplied with blast through one single tuyere-hole, has been displaced everywhere in South-west Missouri, by the so-called "Scotch-American hearth," which is made of cast iron, and has a water-cooled tuyere plate surrounding the hearth on 3 sides, and containing in its central portions, 3 tuyere-holes. This hearth is shown in Fig. 66 *a*, in a vertical section. Fig. 66 *b* represents the tuyere and plate.

    a. Entrance of blast.
    b. Wind box.
    cc. Water-cooled tuyere plate, which is represented in a horizontal projection by Fig. 66 *b*.
    d. Nozzle of wrought iron. (Three of these pass through the tuyere plate.)
    e. Basin filled with molten Lead.
    f. Charge of ore and charcoal.
    g. Iron plate over which the Lead runs from the working basin into the kettle in front of the hearth.

h. Small kettle from which the Lead is taken with ladles, to be cast into pigs.
    A small fire is kept below this kettle to keep the Lead hot.
i. Entrance of water.
k. Exit of water.
l. Water circulation.
m. Tuyere-holes.

Fig. 66 *b*, gives a plan of the tuyere plate, which is a very compli-
cated and costly casting.

The nozzles are about 1 inch wide.

The thickness of iron walls of the tuyere plate, is 1½ inches.

All the other dimensions are given in the drawing.

The air passes through the wind box and 3 tuyeres, into the
hearth. The basin *e* is always kept full of molten Lead. It holds
about 2,500 pounds.

The operation is conducted as follows :

The smelter makes a wood-fire on the surface of the Lead in the
hearth, throws charcoal over it, and starts the blast, which enters the
hearth from 1 to 3 inches above the surface of the Lead. He then adds
the remains from the last smelting, which consist of a mixture of
Lead, slag and charcoal. After the Lead in the basin is heated up
well and completely fluid, the regular smelting operation begins.
New charges of charcoal and of Galena, crushed to about pea-size,
are added continually with the shovel, the Galena in portions of 20 to
30 pounds at a time. Some burnt Lime is added as a flux. The ore is
always kept protected by a layer of fresh charcoal. After adding the
latter, the fire remains undisturbed for 4 or 5 minutes. The charge is
then broken up with a long poker and mixed so as to bring new particles of ore in contact with the coal, and raised slowly with a long,
flat spattle to prepare a proper passage for the blast. All these manipulations are repeated with every new charge of 20 to 30 pounds. The
Lead runs almost uninterruptedly over the inclined iron plate into
the kettle, in which it gathers to be cast into moulds from time to
time. The pigs weigh 70 to 80 pounds each. Two smelters melt about
3000 pounds of good ore in less than 8 hours, so that one hearth has a
capacity of working 9000 pounds of Galena in 24 hours. The Galena
yields about 68 per cent.; a little less than in the air furnace, because
the slag of the Scotch hearth is less fluid, and retains more Lead.
This slag is crushed and washed, and the best part of it is smelted
again on the Scotch hearth, in charges of 2400 pounds, yielding 7C0
pounds of Lead.

The poorer slag thereby produced, yet holds 30 to 40 per cent. of
Lead, and is smelted with coke in a small, square blast-furnace, 8 feet
high, 2 to 3 feet square.

The cost of running a Scotch hearth for 24 hours, in 3 shifts of 8 hours, is as follows :

Six smelters, (for each shift) at $2.50 per day...	$15 00
Two engineers (one for day, one for night) $2.50 per day..............................	5 00
Three laborers, at $1.50 per day..	4 50
Forty bushels of charcoal, at 10 cents...	4 00
One cord of wood for the boiler, etc..	2 00
Tools..	25
Total..	$30 75

The 9000 pounds smelted at this expense yield about 6100 pounds of Galena. The cost of smelting for every 1000 pounds of Lead thus amounts to about $5.00.

By running a number of hearths side by side, the above cost may be reduced to less than $4.00 per 1000 pounds.

THE AIR FURNACE

Is in most cases preferable to the Scotch hearth, although the capacity is only about one-third of that of the latter. But it is cheaper to build, because it requires no steam-engine, nor blower. It can work poorer or less clean Galena without great disadvantage; it needs a less skilled and experienced smelter, and, finally, yields 2 to 3 per cent. more Lead.

The sketch (Fig. 67) represents the usual form of these furnaces in plan and vertical section :

   a. Fire-place, heated with 4 feet logs.
   b. Fire-bridge, 6 feet above the hearth *c.*
   c. Smelting hearth, consisting of a cast-iron plate, with 6 inches of slag
        smelted over it.
   d. Sheet-iron stack, 20 feet high.
   e. Door for charging and working.
   f. Door for discharging and cleaning.
   g. Casting-kettle.

The cost of an air furnace is estimated at $500 to $600, including the shed in which the furnace stands.

The charge consists of 1400 to 1600 pounds of Galena, from pea to hazelnut-size, and is thrown into the furnace all at once, through the charging door e. The ore is spread over the bottom of the hearth, and kept there without applying much flame, but under constant stirring, for 60 to 90 minutes; during that time a partial roasting of the Galena is effected. After this a strong fire is given, throwing a long flame on the ore in the hearth. The reducing action begins, and the reduced and molten Lead runs into the lower part of the hearth and through the door f, into the kettle g. This operation is continued until the Lead ceases to flow. The reaction is from time to time assisted by stirring. When the charge gets too hot and threatens to smelt without being reduced, the smelter throws ashes over it to cool and to thicken it. The lead is cast into pigs of 70 to 80 pounds. A charge is smelted in 9 to 11 hours. The yield from pure Galena reaches 70 and sometimes 72 per cent.

The cost of running the furnace for 24 hours, in double shifts, is as follows:

Two smelters at $3.00	$6 00
One laborer in day-time	1 50
One and a half cords of wood, at $2.00	3 00
Tools and repairs	50
Total	$11 00

During that time the furnace produces 2200 to 2300 pounds of Lead, so that the cost of smelting 1000 pounds of Lead would be about $4.90. The cost of smelting is therefore nearly equal to that in a single Scotch hearth. Several Scotch hearths are worked together for a large production; they smelt considerably cheaper than the air furnace, and are, therefore, generally adopted in the larger smelting works.

SPECIAL NOTES ON GRANBY.

The section on which the Granby mines are situated, is owned by the Atlantic and Pacific Railroad Company, and leased by the Granby Mining and Smelting Company. The latter Company is under the administration of the following officers: Henry T. Blow, President, James B. Eads, Vice-President; Barton Bates, Harry Blow and —— Hensey, Directors; Charles Bingston, Superintendent.

The Granby Lead-ores are smelted in place. The Zinc-ores are shipped to the various Zinc-works in St. Louis, at a very high cost of freight. The erection of Zinc-works at Oronogo is therefore contemplated.

The Granby Company has never mined itself, but always let out claims on its leased section of ground. But it has frequently assisted the miners in sinking shafts through hard rock, with the intention of having a new part of the field investigated. In such cases the Company agreed to pay the miners a gratuity of $100, under the condition that they would sink the shafts either to an ore-opening, or at least to a depth of 75 feet.

The Company also put up a large steam-pump in the Valley, south of the furnace-building, in a shaft 94 feet deep. This pump drains a large portion of the Brockhollow and Village Diggings. As all the single-ore deposits, the "openings," are limited in their extent, the continuance of mining in the several Granby districts depends always upon the discovery of new deposits, and this discovery depends upon the degree of activity in prospecting. This is the cause of the fluctuations that have taken place regarding the production of these mines. In 1870 and 1871, when the excitement began at Joplin, many miners left for that place, prospecting diminished, and the production and the reputation of Granby decreased. Happily, about the same time this Zinc-ore began to attract attention, which had before been considered worthless. In November, 1871, Mr. Bellew, agent for the Missouri Zinc Company, in St. Louis, began to work for Lead and Zinc on several old claims, which before that time, had been worked for Lead only. In August, 1872, Mr. Hopkins began doing the same for Messrs. Martindale & Eddy, of St. Louis, and towards the end of 1872, the Granby Company itself began to buy up the Zinc-ore. The whole appearance of the mines was changed by this getting of Zinc-ores. While the sheets and pockets of Galena are comparatively small and scattered, the Calamine occurs in thick layers, often extending over considerable areas. Consequently the risk of the miners is much less in mining the Calamine than in mining the Galena. Hundreds of old shafts which had been left because the Galena was too scattered to pay the miner, were now re-opened. In following the layers of Calamine, the miners were sure to earn pretty good wages. With one foot thickness of the Calamine they earned about $5 per day. All the Galena was an extra profit. In this way many good Galena deposits were discovered and mined, and the productions of Lead-ore increased with that of Zinc-ore. Thus, the knowledge of the value of this Zinc-ore, became of immense interest and advantage to the Granby mines.

Before we close our special remarks on these mines, we will mention the following very interesting fact: As the miners have an interest to hoist as little useless material as possible, they often fill up old drifts with such material, which is here mostly Clay, Chert and Limestone. In the course of years these masses, as the miners say, " grow together," and we were astonished in visiting an old mine in Brock Hollow, which had not been worked for 15 years, to find some old posts of timber buried in a hard Conglomerate of Chert and hardened Clay, the whole having the appearance of an original rock.

The smelting-works of Granby are situated near the creek, in the north-west quarter of the Section, west of the town. The sketch, Fig. 68, represents a plan of the works.

Fig. 68, Granby Smelting-Works.

1 to 4, Scotch-American hearths.

5 to 8, old Scotch hearths.

9, Blake-crusher.

10, Washing trough.

11, Sludge-box.

The heavy line represents wooden blast-pipe, 18 inches square.

The principal building contains 8 hearths, one of which is used for smelting slag. Each hearth has a separate stack. The fan is a large Sturtevant No. 7. The steam is produced by two boilers, 40 feet long and 45 inches diameter. They use 2 cords of wood in 24 hours. The engine runs the fan, a turning-lathe, a pump, 3 jigs, a Blake-crusher and a small saw-mill.

Fifty-two feet east of this main building is a smaller shed, with 2 air-furnaces. These works smelt all the Galena from Granby, Oronogo and from the Company's lands near Joplin.

In 1873 nearly 7 millions of pounds of Galena were smelted, about one-half of which quantity was from the Granby mines. In summer of 1873, about 200 miners were occupied at Granby, producing an average of 70,000 pounds of Galena per week.

NEOSHO FURNACE.

The Neosho Manufacturing Company, —— Stein, President, at Neosho, Newton county, runs one American Lead-hearth, besides its Iron foundry, machine shop and saw-mill. The Scotch hearth gets a sufficient supply of Lead ore from several south-western mines to run about three days in a week. This company smelts not only Galena in the American hearths, but also Dry-bone, which at Granby is invariably taken into the air furnaces. The Galena yields 70 per cent., the Dry-bone 35 per cent. of Lead. In smelting Galena some finely sawed wood is used as fuel, mixed with the charcoal. The slag encloses me-

G. S—32

chanically about 12 per cent. of Lead. This slag is crushed between two rollers to pea-size and smaller, washed in running water, and jigged. The slag thus concentrated is smelted in the Scotch hearth with some burnt and powdered Lime, and yields 15 to 20 per cent. of Lead. One jigger makes about 800 pounds of smeltable material per day. The crusher crushes enough in one day to supply the jig for three days. The Company pays $32.00 per 1,000 pounds for Galena, and $12.00 for Dry-bone.

THURMAN FURNACE.

The Thurman Mining and Smelting Company: President, Colonel Graves of Joplin; Vice-President, Colonel Riggin; Superintendent, Colonel Chapman. It has erected one American hearth, of newest construction, at Thurman, near the Thurman Diggings, T. 27, R. 32 W., Sec 31. Ore, mixed with mush rock is burnt and then smashed by a flat hammer over a cast-iron screen, $3\frac{1}{2}$ feet by $2\frac{1}{4}$ feet, the slits being $\frac{3}{8}$-inch. All the mineral has to pass through these slits which give it the proper size for smelting. The crushed material is jigged. The pure ore is then smelted, while the impure ore is crushed finer by hand on a plain iron plate and washed in a trough. The hearth is run with charges of 2,000 pounds of Galena, which is smelted in four to six hours, and yields 15 pigs of Lead, weighing 80 to 83 pounds each. Twelve charges are made per week, producing 14,500 pounds of Galena. The blast is produced by a Sturtevant No. 5 blower. The Company pays $31.00 for 1,000 pounds of Galena, deducting a royalty of $4.00 when the ore has been taken from their own lands.

SPECIAL NOTES ON JOPLIN.

The general mode of mining in the Joplin District has been described previously.

The water is in many places plentiful and a great impediment to mining in this district. We therefore find here very frequently pumps in use. The most common kind is the Cornish horse-pump. A horse walking in a circle turns a vertical wooden shaft, the upper end of which is connected with a crank to transfer the movement to a walk-.ng-beam. The latter carries the rod and piston of the pump on one end and a counterpoise on the other, and moves up and down, supported by two horizontal pivots. The stroke of the pump is generally 7 feet, the diameter of the piston 8 inches. The rods are either of wood or wrought Iron. In some places steam pumps are in operation, the pumps being worked by movable steam engines. The Cameron pump is often used and does good service for depths of 30 to 40 feet. At greater depths this pump does not work as well on account of the condensation of the steam in the long narrow pipes which carry the steam from the boiler to the pump in the shaft, as well as in the exhaust pipe.

The Galena is generally separated from the Zinc ore and Chert by breaking the ore with hand-hammers, and by picking out the pieces of Galena. The finer materials obtained in this process are washed in troughs and jigged in wooden jigs of rough construction moved by hand. Messrs. Riggins & Chapman have lately begun to dress and separate the ores in a more perfect manner by machinery which they put up at their smelting works at Joplin. The ore is crushed by roll·ers, hoisted by an elevator, separated by screens and cleaned by two large jigs with horizontal piston. All this apparatus, as well as the fan which supplies the blast to three American hearths are moved by steam power. The dressing machinery has a capacity of 24,000 tons of ore in 10 hours. How much Lead and especially Zinc is lost by the ordinary imperfect dressing and washing manipulations may be seen from the following analysis of refuse taken from recent heaps below Swindle Hill. Mr. R. Chauvenet found in it:

Metallic Lead.. 4.23 per cent.
Metallic Zinc ....35.51 per cent.

There is no doubt that as soon as Zinc works will be built in the South-west, or as soon as the present enormous freight on Zinc ore to St. Louis will be reduced to a proper measure, it will pay well to work over such refuse as the above and to separate both the Zinc and the Lead ores, when good and efficient dressing machines are used. The cost of washing Lead ore by hand, as it is now done, varies from two to six dollars per 1,000 pounds of clean Galena. Five smelting works are now in operation at various points along Joplin Creek. They are as follows :

Owners.	Air Furnaces.	American Hearths.
Jasper Lead and Mining Company............................	2	2
Davis & Murphy...	6	0
Moffett & Sergeant...	4	0
Riggins & Chapman..	0	3
S. B. Corn..	4	2
Total..	16	7

While American hearths are usually built in rows side by side,
each hearth having its own chimney, the Jasper Lead and Mining
Company has built its hearths on a new system, according to which
each couple of hearths is placed back to back and has but one common stack. This is represented by Fig. 69.

Messrs. Riggins & Chapman use a No. 5 Sturtevant blower for
three American hearths.

The Joplin smelters pay to the miners, for 1,000 pounds of Galena,
$35, less the royalty, which is paid to the land owners, and which
amounts to from $4 to $8.

One air furnace, the property of Messrs. Davis & Murphy, is
located near the Bentley Diggings, four and a half miles west of Joplin. Another works, which runs exclusively on Joplin ore, is that of
Messrs. Sarver & Co., at Baxter Springs, in Kansas.

One air furnace is in operation near Scotland, seven miles east of
Joplin, one-fourth of a mile from the Grove Creek Diggings and one
and a half miles from the Birch Diggings. They smelt a charge of
1,500 pounds of Galena in nine hours, and obtain over 1,000 pounds
of Lead from it. The furnace is owned by Messrs. Davis & Murphy, and
pays $25 per 1,000 pounds for Galena. The erection of a second fur-
nace in this locality is under consideration.

The smelting works at Oronogo, containing three American
hearths, are not in operation because the Granby Company, which
owns them, prefers to smelt all the Oronogo ores at Granby.

The following analyses of Joplin Lead slag were made by Mr.
Andrew A. Blair, of St. Louis :

	1.	2.	3.
Silica	23.98	14.15	12.32
Oxide of Lead	41.03	59.72	57.72
Peroxide of Iron	4.42	2.98	2.58
Alumina			
Oxide of Zinc	10.14	6.77	11.51
Lime	15.72	11.25	10.37
Metallic Lead	38.00	55.45	53.58
Metallic Zinc	9.15	5.43	9.23
All specimens contain some Magnesia and Sulphur.			

No. 1.　Average sample of slag produced in smelting Galena in the American
　　　　hearth, at the works of Messrs. Riggins & Chapman, Joplin.
No. 2.　Average sample of ordinary, good slag, produced in smelting Galena
　　　　in a reverberatory or wind furnace, at the works of the Jasper Lead
　　　　and Mining Company, Joplin.
No. 3.　Average sample of a slag, of a bluish color and rotten appearance, ob-
　　　　tained near the fire-bridge of the same furnace as No. 2.

All the above slags are so rich in Lead that they will yield a large
and paying percentage of it when smelted over in a shaft furnace.
As they contain a considerable amount of Zinc, the Lead thus produced must be, however, less pure and less valuable than that obtained in smelting the ore. The air furnace seems to produce a much
richer slag than the American hearth.

STATISTICS.

We may estimate the total production of Granby, from the beginning of mining to the end of the year 1873, at about 80,000,000 pounds
of Galena—equal to about 27,100 tons of Lead, worth, at 7 cents per
pound, $3,920,000.

The total production of Joplin district, from 1871 to 1873 inclusive,
was about 50,000,000 pounds of Galena, from which about 17,500 tons
of Lead were smelted, having a value of $2,450,000.

The total production of the whole South-western region until
1873 inclusive, was about 140,000,000 pounds of Galena, corresponding
to 49,000 tons of Lead, and a value of $6,860,000.

The above values are only approximates, but they are sufficiently
accurate to give a general idea of the importance of this mining
region.

We will add here some statistics regarding the production in 1873,
taken from a pamphlet entitled "The Mineral Wealth of South-west
Missouri," by Messrs. Baumann and Lloyd, who gathered the figures
directly from the books of the different mining and smelting companies.

The mining companies produced, in 1873, the following quantities
of Galena:

Quantity of Galena Mined.

NAME OF COMPANY.	POUNDS.
The Granby Mining and Smelting Company :	
From Granby and Oronogo..	4,803,410
From Joplin, Lone Elm and Leadville	2,075,590
Davis & Murphy :	
From Joplin, Stevens and Grove Creek Diggings........................	6,360,000
The Joplin Mining and Smelting Company :	
From Joplin and Thurman Diggings...	5,500,000
Moffett & Sergeant :	
From Joplin and Bentley Diggings..	3,731,000
Lone Elm Company :	
From Lone Elm...	1,120,021
The Jasper Lead and Mining Company, and S. B. Corn and others :	
From Joplin, Cornwall and other Diggings...............................	789,000
Total	24,379,021

Of this total quantity, there was produced at :

MINES.	POUNDS.
Joplin	19,250,000
Granby and Oronogo...	4,803,410
Other mines..	325,611
The above total	24,379,021

The total production of pig Lead in Jasper and Newton counties for 1873, was, according to the same publication, (p. 49,) 16,950,000 pounds, or 8,475 tons. This corresponds to a value of about $1,186,500.

At present, the Joplin district produces, on the average, about 400,000 pounds, and the Granby district 70,000 pounds of Galena weekly.

CHAPTER XXIX.

THE LEAD REGION OF CENTRAL MISSOURI.

BY ADOLF SCHMIDT, PH. D.

A.—GENERAL CHARACTERISTICS OF THE REGION.

GEOGRAPHY.

The Lead region of Central Missouri, comprises the counties of Saline, Cooper, Pettis, Benton, St. Clair, Hickory, Camden, Morgan, Moniteau, Cole, Miller, Osage and Maries.

Lead and Zinc ores have been found also further south, in Laclede, Dallas, Greene, Webster, Wright, Texas, Douglas, Christian, Taney, Stone and Barry counties, forming what we will call the Southern Lead Region of Missouri, a description of which will be published at some future time.

The principal and best-paying deposits so far discovered in the Central region, are situated within a district covering the central and southern portions of Morgan, the northern half of Miller, the south-western portion of Cole, and the southern portion of Moniteau counties. It will be seen from this, that the centre of the Central Lead Region lies about 70 miles north-west from the centre of the Central Iron Region, as described in my published report of 1872.

In a general way it may be said that the Osage River, in its course from Linn Creek, Camden county, to its mouth, near Osage City, forms the limit between the Iron and the Lead regions. This limit is

most abrupt in Miller, Osage and Cole counties, although even
there, Lead ore is occasionally found east of the Osage, while single
deposits of Iron ore are scattered over the whole Central Lead
Region.

Westward from the sudden turn of the Osage River, near Linn
Creek, this river ceases to be the limit, and the Lead region in Camden, Hickory and Benton counties, has a decidedly southern extension.
However, the greater and principal portion of the region lies between
the Osage and Missouri Rivers. No workable deposit of Lead ore is
known north of the Missouri.

TOPOGRAPHY.

The general topographical character of this region is rather broken and rough, the country being cut deeply by numerous tributaries
of both the Missouri and the Osage, as well as by innumerable
smaller water runs and ravines, with steep slopes which are mostly
covered by a silicious soil, mixed with Chert fragments. The region,
however, contains also much excellent bottom land, and large tracts
of good rolling prairie.

GEOLOGY.

The Central Lead Region contains much Lead ore, and some Zinc
ore and Iron ore. These ores are principally connected with the
Lower Silurian Limestones, especially with the Second and Third
Magnesian Limestone, although in some places in northern Moniteau,
and in Cooper and Saline counties, it is found in the Archimedes or
Keokuk Limestone of the Carboniferous Formation: that is, in the
same rock in which the Lead and Zinc ores of South-west Missouri
occur.

The Galena, accompanied by more or less Barytes, is found either
filling fissures in the Limestone and Chert, or cementing breccia of
both, or loose in cherty Clay. In most places, where the Galena occurs in large quantities, the Limestone is softened and altered.

The fissures containing Galena, are in some places very numerous inside of a circular space of ground, and thus form a peculiar
kind of "stockwerk" deposit, with circular outlines called " circles" by the miners.

None of the Lead ore deposits as yet worked, have proved to be-
paying to a greater depth than about 80 feet below the surface. This
fact is independent of the geological position of the single deposit.

It is also a remarkable fact that while Barytes is entirely missing
in the South-western region, the same mineral is in this Central region

a nearly constant associate of the Galena, in the Carboniferous as well as in the Silurian rocks. These facts suggest the idea that the occurrence of Lead ore with its associates, is not exclusively dependent on the geological formation, but that its deposition may have taken place simultaneously, in similar rocks belonging to different geological periods, which rocks happened to be under similar conditions at the time of deposition. If this suggestion is correct, it would throw the origin of all the Galena of the Central and the South-western Lead regions, into a later period than the Sub-Carboniferous.

As Galena is also found in the seams and partings of the Coal strata in Simpson's Coal mine, situated in the Lead district of southern Moniteau county, which Coal strata, although belonging to a separate basin, must be supposed to be formed simultaneously, or nearly so, with the North Missouri Coal field, we may conclude that the Galena is of much later origin even, than the Coal Measures.

CHAPTER XXX.

B.—DESCRIPTION OF ORES AND OF ASSOCIATED MINERALS.

The following minerals are represented in the Lead deposits of Central Missouri :

GALENA,
CERUSSITE,
BLENDE,
SMITHSONITE,
BARYTES,
CALCITE,
QUARTZ,
PYRITES, (in part cupriferous,)
LIMONITE,
MALACHITE,
AZURITE.

GALENA.

Galena, Sulphuret of Lead, is the principal ore found in this region. It occurs as crystals, or crystalline masses. The crystals are sometimes one, two, and more inches in diameter, and have generally a cubic form, the eight corners of the cube being however, taken off by the faces of the octahedron. These faces are mostly very unequally developed on different corners of one and the same crystal, and sometimes produce crystals flattened parallel to two opposite octahedral faces.

Fresh-broken faces of cleavage of the Central Missouri Galena have, like most Galena, a Lead-gray color and a bright metallic lustre. After a longer exposure they generally lose their brightnesss without altering their color. The Galena from the Streit Diggings, (Cole county,) however, assumes a blue, and sometimes reddish tarnish, on exposure.

Galena is often found coated, more or less thickly, with gray Carbonate of Lead, either earthy or crystallized. Galena is also very commonly seen covered and surrounded by Barytes, and in some instances also coated by either massive or crystalline Carbonate of Zinc.

At the Hoff Diggings, (Miller county,) pieces of Galena were found rounded off, and coated thinly with Carbonate of Lead, and associated with stalactites of Limonite, adhering to and partly surrounding the rounded forms of Galena. The Galena is undoubtedly the oldest of all these minerals.

The following analyses of Central Missouri Galenas were made by Mr. Regis Chauvenet, from average samples of clean Galena, in such a condition as it is usually delivered at the smelting works:

Sample 1 is from Walker Diggings, Miller county.

Sample 2 is from Madole Diggings, Morgan county.

Sample 3 is from New Granby Diggings, Morgan county.

Sample 4 is from Streit Diggings, Cole county.

	1.	2.	3.	4.
Insoluble Silicious..	0.15	0.11	0.21	0.13
[Iron	0.24	trace.	0.48	trace.]
Bisulphide of Iron..	0.51	trace.	1.02	trace.
Zinc	trace.	none.	trace.	none.
Silver	none.	trace.	trace.	none.

The Silver is in every case less than $\frac{1}{3}$ oz. to the ton.

Copper and Antimony were sought for in all samples, but with negative results.

Cobalt and Nickel are included in the " Iron," and are not present in a determinable quantity.

The above are all the impurities contained in these various Galenas, which are, consequently, almost pure Sulphides of Lead, and contain in the average about 86 per cent. metallic lead. They are the purest Galenas known.

CERUSSITE,

Carbonate of Lead, occurs as a coating over Galena, as well as in well developed, yellowish or greenish-white translucent crystals of a columnar form, the prisms being prevalent and cut off on both ends by faces of pyramids and of domes. Such crystals are almost invariably deposited on the surface of either coated or fresh Galena-crystals ; they are occasionally of dark-gray to black color.

Massive Cerussite, called " Dry-bone," sometimes with a subcrystalline structure, occurs white and yellow at the Boaz Digging, (Cole county,) and in numerous places, though rarely in large quantities.

BLENDE,

Sulphuret of Zinc, has nowhere in the Central Lead Region been found in sufficiently large quantity to be used as an ore. It occurs as dark-green, yellow or red crystalline specks, or as agglomerations of crystals between broken Chert, for instance at the Eureka Diggings, (Cole county,) or surrounded by Barytes, for instance on Coffin Spring Creek, (Morgan county,) also as horizontal and vertical seams in some of the Coal deposits of Moniteau and Cole counties, where it is evidently a product of reduction from Sulphate of Zinc, through the chemical action of the Coal on solutions, containing the Sulphate.

Blende is also found as amber-yellow, translucent, well developed twin-crystals of the common form, loose in black Clay, at the Stocker Diggings (Morgan county.)

Blende is found in contact with Galena, in Barytes, at the Collins Diggings (Cooper county.) But from the specimens I have seen, I was unable to determine which of the two minerals is the oldest.

SMITHSONITE,

Carbonate of Zinc, occurs in mostly small quantity, in such localities where also Blende is found, from which Smithsonite undoubtedly originates. I found it as a thin crystalline coating, of brown color, over broken Chert, at the Eureka Diggings (Cole county.)

At the Collins Diggings (Cooper county) it occurs massive, intimately mixed with Peroxide of Iron, which gives it a reddish-brown color, but containing no Lead according to Mr. Chauvenet. This massive Smithsonite shows in places incrustations of light-gray crystalline Smithsonite.

BARYTES,

Sulphate of Baryta, called " Bald Tiff," or simply " Tiff," by the miners in Missouri, occurs in large quantities, with or without Galena, in the Central Lead Region. It is often sub-crystalline, with a very fine grain, and white or yellow and opaque, or it is plainly crystalline, translucent, colorless, to bluish-white. At the Doph Diggings, on Indian Creek, (Morgan county,) both these varieties occur together; the crystalline variety being deposited over the sub-crystalline and therefore of later origin.

Another pretty, common variety is white to yellow, opaque, and very coarsely crystalline, with distinctly lamellar structure and cleavage.

A colorless, transparent, and very coarsely crystalline Barytes, with an imperfectly lamellar structure, but with very marked basal and prismatic cleavage, is found in considerable quantity in T. 42, R. 18 W., Sec. 21, near the Clark Diggings, on Coffin Spring Creek (Morgan county.) In the same locality tabular crystals are met with, 1 inch thick, 2 inches wide and 3 to 4 inches long. Very fine transparent crystals of Barytes of the common forms, $\frac{1}{4}$ to 1 inch long, were also found at the Caldwell and the Price Mill Diggings, in Morgan county. Galena is nearly always accompanied by Barytes, though sometimes in very small quantity. But Barytes is frequently seen without Galena; less frequently without at least specks of Blende.

Whenever large quantities of Barytes occur together with Galena, well-formed crystals of the latter are generally surrounded by the former on all sides except one, where it is mostly in contact with altered or unaltered Limestones.

Barytes forms usually veins or vein-like deposits. It is of later formation than other Galena or Blende, and always incloses both, or fills places left between crystals of these minerals. It sometimes incloses fragments of Limestone and of Chert, with crystals of Galena or Blende adhering to these fragments. Some specimens often have the appearance of a Galena crystal, entirely surrounded by Barytes; but these present only a Section through a string of crystals, the last of which will generally be found to be seated on Limestone or Chert. I have not seen a single specimen that proves conclusively that clean Galena can be surrounded by Barytes on all six sides.

CALCITE,

Carbonate of Lime, the "Glass Tiff" of the miners, is often met with as crystals or coarsely crystalline masses, in seams and cavities of the various Limestones in the Central Lead Region. It is, however, rarely found in close association with either Galena or Blende or Barytes, and does not seem to have any particular relation to the ore deposits, as it has been often supposed.

QUARTZ,

Mineral Silica, is not infrequent in the form of columnar or pyramidal crystals lining drusy cavities of Chert. This occurrence is, however, independent of the vicinity of the Lead deposits. Drusy cavities, lined with Quartz crystals, are quite common in the Limestones of the *Eastern* Lead region, and are there known under the name of "Mineral Blossom." In the Central region they are but rarely found in Limestone.

PYRITES,

Bisulphide of Iron, is frequently found in small quantities in and near the Lead deposits as well as in many other places. It is rarely seen in direct contact with either Galena or Blende. In one specimen I have from the Collins Diggings, Cooper county, it seems to inclose crystals of Galena. It is often accompanied and covered by crystallized Calcite.

Much of the Pyrites of this region is cupriferous, and therefore, whenever in part decomposed, it is associated not only with Limonite, but also with Malachite and Azurite (Carbonate of Copper.) I observed Pyrites deposited on broken Chert at the Cordray Diggings, Morgan county; disseminated in crystalline Limestone at the Gabrielle Diggings, Morgan county; deposited on laminated Barytes at the Marmaduke Diggings, Saline county; as specks and seams, also containing some Galena, in Barytes and in clayish Ochre at the Collins Diggings, Cooper county; filling irregular cavities in Barytes, and deposited over Barytes and covered by crystallized Calcite at the Walker Diggings, Miller county. These associations show that the Pyrites is of comparatively late origin.

In a specimen from the Collins Diggings, Cooper county, Mr. Chauvenet found 20.96 per cent. of metallic Copper, showing that some of these cupriferous Pyrites are very rich Copper ores. The cupriferous Pyrites may be distinguished from the pure Iron Pyrites by their inferior hardness and only rarely by their color, because they are all generally bronze-yellow. True Chalcopyrite (Copper Pyrites), with its greenish, brass-yellow color, has not been discovered in such quantity as to determine its existence with surety.

LIMONITE,

Hydrated Peroxide of Iron, occurs both as an original mineral and as a product of pseudomorphism from Pyrites. In the latter case, it is often accompanied by Carbonates of Copper—the latter being always inferior in quantity to the Limonite.

I observed Limonite as an apparently original mineral, lining cavities in Barytes at the Thomas Diggings, Camden county; and as Stalactites, cementing rounded and coated Galena, at the Hoff Diggings, Miller county. In the vicinity of the Hoff Diggings, it also occurs in stalactitic forms in considerable quantity, forming an Iron ore bank, as will be seen from the description in division D of this report. Limonite occurs in smaller or larger quantity as concretions and segregations in innumerable localities, without any distinct relation to the Lead deposits.

MALACHITE,

Green, Hydrated Carbonate of Copper, with about 56 per cent. of metallic Copper, is generally, in this region, a product of decomposition of cupriferous Pyrites, and is nearly always associated with decomposing Pyrites and with Limonite—this latter being also produced by the decomposition (pseudomorphism) of the former. From the fact that the Limonite is found in such instances intimately mixed with the undecomposed Pyrites and passes into the latter gradually, while the Malachite is always deposited in cavities or in seams of the Limonite, and often in the adjacent rocks, it appears that, while the transformation of the Sulphide of Iron into Limonite is effected without change of place, the Sulphide of Copper on the contrary is not only decomposed and changed into a Carbonate, but also dissolved, extracted and redeposited. The Malachite is bright green, vitreous, crystalline, and has generally a fibrous and radiated structure. .

The pieces of half-decomposed Pyrites, with Limonite and Malachite, sometimes contain a sufficient amount of metallic Copper to constitute a good Copper ore. But the ore has not been found as yet in paying quantities. The largest accumulations of it which are known to me in this region, are at the Collins Lead Diggings, Cooper county, and at Abbott & Gantt's Copper bank, T. 39, R. 15 W., Sec. 13, Miller county.

AZURITE,

Blue Hydrated Carbonate of Copper, mostly accompanies the Malachite, and is then deposited over the latter and fills the inmost portion

of cavities which were but partially filled by the Malachite. It is
azure blue, in part crystalline. It is found in very small quantities
only.

PARAGENESIS.

From the description of specimens above given, we may establish
the following paragenetic series, beginning with the oldest minerals:

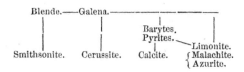

CHAPTER XXXI.

C.—DESCRIPTION OF ROCKS AND MODE OF OCCURRENCE OF THE ORE.

The following rocks occur in or near the Lead deposits in the Central Missouri Lead region:

1. SOIL.
2. SANDSTONE.
3. CLAY.
4. CHERT.
5. LIMESTONE.

I will now describe these rocks, and the mode of occurrence of Lead ores in them, and will finally add some more general remarks on the various

6. FORMS OF DEPOSITS

Of Lead ore in this region.

1. SOIL AND SURFACE INDICATIONS.

The Soil in the Central Lead region is either sandy or silico-argillaceous, and almost invariably mixed with more or less Chert fragments. These latter are, in places, very abundant. They are sometimes fresh and hard, sometimes more or less altered or disintegrated, so as to be, in places, converted into a soft, silicious rock, and finally into a powder of clayish appearance.

The impression prevails in some districts that the accumulation of Chert fragments in and above the Soil indicates the existence of Lead ore deposits below. This is, however, incorrect. We find in many places good deposits underneath a Soil with but little Chert, and very cherty hills have often been searched for Lead ore in vain. As the Galena is frequently found in the vicinity of oolitic Chert layers, the presence of oolitic Chert fragments, whether in large or small quantity, may be considered as improving somewhat the chances for finding Lead ore.

The best indication, however, is a clayish soil of dark red or brown color, especially when observed in or near a depression of the surface of the ground. I consider this even a better indication than the existence of loose pieces of Galena in a soil of light color. The reason will be apparent from the contents of the following Article 3 on " Clays," as well as from the special descriptions of deposits. In the best districts of the central region, *some* Lead ore is nearly always found in localities bearing the above characteristics. This fact is well known to all practical miners of some experience. No external sign however, is known from which this presence of ore in paying quantities could be safely predicted. Loose, small Galena, often rounded and coated, occurs occasionally in the soil, also massive Cerussite and porous or softened Chert, impregnated with carbonate of Lead. These are not unfavorable indications. But the deposit from which such ores are derived lies very often not right beneath these indications but at some higher point of the same slope, which point is sometimes difficult to discover.

2. SANDSTONE.

Fragments, slabs or broken layers of a rather loose, not very coarse-grained and frequently red colored Sandstone, are found with or below the soil, especially in the northern half of the central Lead region. This Sandstone consists of colorless, clear, irregular Quartz grains, with very little cement. The latter seems to be a clayish Oxide of Iron, and produces the red or brown color of the rock. This Sandstone often contains layers or concretionary masses of oolitic Chert, the limits between the two rocks being sometimes sharp, sometimes indistinct. It also contains lenticular concretions of common gray Chert, in the vicinity of which the Sandstone is sometimes transformed into oolitic Chert and passes into it gradually. A specimen we have from the Otter Diggings, (Morgan county,) shows this gradual transition of Sandstone into oolitic Chert and finally into common gray Chert very plainly. There can be no doubt that the oolitic Chert was, in many cases, at least produced by the same cause which produced the Chert concretions in this Sandstone, namely by the infiltrations of Silica into pre-existing cavities. The oolitic Chert frequently contains drusy cavities, lined with Quartz crystals.

No fossils have been found in the Sandstone just described; but if we compare the above description with that which Prof. G. C. Swallow has given of the "Saccharoidal Sandstone," on pp. 117 and 118 of the Missouri Geological Report of 1855, we feel inclined to believe in the identity of both rocks. Mr. G. C. Broadhead has observed similar Chert beds in the lower layers of the Second Magnesian Limestone and in the Second Sandstone. The Sandstone above described, therefore, probably belongs to the Lower Silurian System.

This rock generally contains no Lead ores. At the "Eureka-Scott" Diggings, however, in Cole county, I observed fragments of it on which Galena was directly deposited. The appearance and position of these fragments shows that the deposition of the Galena must have taken place after the breaking and consequently long after the formation of the Sandstone.

3. CLAYS.

The Clays play an important part in the Lead deposits of this Central Region. In the best deposits so far discovered the Galena is associated with red Clay.

The origin of these Clays is not very plain. In some places they either seem to be purely residuary matter from dissolved Limestones or else it appears as if the solutions that dissolved the Limestone simultaneously deposited white or greenish-gray Clay, or peroxide of Iron mixed with Clay. In other places they seem to originate from a gradual disintegration of the Chert through chemical action, in which case they are no true Clays, but fine, soft Silica, mixed with some Clay and with hydrated peroxide of Iron. This subject could not however, be cleared up satisfactorily, except by a series of careful chemical analyses of judiciously selected samples.

We may distinguish four kinds of Clays bearing some relation to the Lead formations of Central Missouri:

1. The shaly or stratified Clay, grayish-white or greenish-gray, with alternate yellow layers. It is always silicious, often also calcareous. It passes into shaly Limestone, and is undoubtedly of residuary origin, though perhaps mixed with newly deposited silicate of alumina. It frequently contains gray Chert concretions similar to those found in the Limestones. Good Galena seams, mostly parallel to the stratification, are found in it. When it occurs in a very fine, soft and uniform state with almost or entirely obliterated stratification, the miners call it "Soapstone," on account of its being slightly

soapy and very smooth to the touch. Its thickness is generally from 3 to 10 feet.

2. The white or slightly yellow Pipe-Clay which occurs in numerous places in flakes or in irregular layers, between other Clays and between broken rocks, mostly not many feet below the surface. It has been found in considerable quantity in a shaft near the Buffalo Diggings (Morgan county). It is very fine, pure and uniform and would be an excellent material for the manufactory of pottery. Mr. Regis Chauvenet found in it—

	Per cent.
Silica	73.81
Alumina	18.46
Iron	Trace.

Lime and Magnesia are both present in small quantity, less than one per cent. According to his analyses the " Pipe-Clay " is a mixture of Clay with extremely fine, free Silica, the latter perhaps a production of the disintegration of Chert.

3. Red ("tallow") Clay, a pretty constant companion of the Lead ores. It is fine-grained and plastic. It contains much Iron and much water. It is generally mixed with more or less altered and softened Chert concretions, also with fragments or fine detritus of porous and ferruginous Chert. Its relative position is not definite. It occurs in alternate streaks with Pipe-Clay. It occurs both below and above the shaly Clay and shaly Limestone. It is found in many places immediately below the soil or even touching the surface. It mostly reaches down to the surface of the Limestone, its total thickness being sometimes 40 or 50 feet. It encloses nearly always at least some loose Galena, especially within a few feet from the Limestone. The presence of this Clay is the best indication a miner can have.

4. Black Clay (" Fire-Clay,") together with dark gray Slate, and sometimes with some Blende and Galena, occurs in patches in the northern half of the region mixed with pieces of Limestone and of Chert with numerous impressions of crinoids. It is always found above the Lead formation and is undoubtedly derived from destroyed carboniferous strata.

4. CHERT.

Chert is much less extensively represented in the Central than in the South-western Lead region. Yet thick and extended Chert beds are met with, especially in the galeniferous Keokuk Limestone of Cooper and Saline counties. Most of the Chert found in this region is concretionary, or else it occurs as comparatively thin and non-continuous beds. It varies in its character according to the geological formation to which it belongs.

A bluish-gray, microcrystalline Chert, with dark gray to black streaks, and sub-carboniferous fossils is found in the Lead diggings in the northern part of Morgan county, near Otterville, and in those situate on the line between Cooper and Saline counties.

The oolitic Chert which has been spoken of in (No. 2) this chapter, (Sandstone,) is the most common in the vicinity of Lead Diggings in the greater portion of the region, especially in Morgan, in southern Moniteau, in Cole, and in northern Miller counties.

Nearly everywhere, though not frequently in very large quantity, we find a white Chert with gray streaks, in the main amorphous, with smooth, sub-conchoidal fracture, probably belonging to the Second, or sometimes to the Third Magnesian Limestones. This latter Chert is often found in thin, streaky or banded layers, or else as round or lenticular, jasper-like concretions, with rather smooth outer surfaces. These jasper concretions when broken, are seen to consist of concentric bands, colored gray in various shades, and contain sometimes, a drusy cavity in the centre.

All the different kinds of Chert above mentioned, occur partly loose in the Clay as fragments or concretions, partly as layers or concretions in the Limestone.

Galena is sometimes found adhering to broken Chert, or filling seams and spaces between the fragments. This is very extensively the case at the Anderson Diggings, (Camden county,) where most of the Galena occurs in this form.

The Cherts of the Central Lead Region, undergo similar changes to those described in our report on the South-western Region. They turn gradually into a light, soft, and very hygroscopic mass, having the exterior appearance of a Clay, yet consisting mainly of Silica. I found lenticular Chert concretions changed in this wise, and yet showing their original concentric structure, loose in the red Clay, at the Blockberger Diggings (Cole county).

The oolitic Chert undergoes similar alterations, during which the grains are attacked first. They become opaque and gradually changed into a white clayish mass, and are finally removed, leaving the cement behind in the form of spongy Chert.

In some cases, on the contrary, we find the cement removed and the grains left. This happens particularly, when the oolitic Chert is exposed to weathering on the surface of the ground.

We find sometimes altered, porous, or disintegrated Chert, im-

pregnated with Cerussite. But we never find it impregnated with Galena. This shows that the alteration of the Chert has taken place in
a later period than the deposition of the Galena.

5. LIMESTONE.

The Archimedes, or Keokuk Limestone, met with in the several
Lead Diggings of Cooper and Eastern Saline counties, is a dark gray,
dense, crystalline Limestone. At the Old Scott Diggings, (Cooper
county,) some layers are very coarsely crystalline, and full of Crinoid stems resembling the Encrinital Limestone. These Limestones
alternate with thick fossiliferous Chert layers. The Galena occurs
with Barytes as sheets and seams in the Limestone; also loose between Limestone boulders, broken Chert and Clay. The rock is
somewhat softened and in part disintegrated, in the vicinity of the
Galena.

The so-called Second and Third Magnesian Limestones of the
Lower Silurian formation, are the principal galeniferous rocks in the
Central Lead Region. They are spread over the whole region, and gen-
erally compose the interior bodies of the Lead-bearing hills. The Sec-
ond is more largely represented in the northern and western, and the
Third more in the southern and eastern half of this region.

These Magnesian Limestones, when found fresh and unaltered,
are light gray, crystalline, hard, and contain numerous small cracks
and cavities, one-sixteenth to one-fourth inch wide, lined with Dolomitic crystals. In this form this Limestone is generally found in the
bluffs along the creeks and rivers, and sometimes contains specks or
thin seams of Galena.

Larger deposits have not so far been found in this unaltered rock.
This rock invariably underlies the ore deposits, in the vicinity of
which its upper layers are broken into larger and smaller blocks, and
mostly softened, and sometimes entirely disintegrated and changed
into loosely-aggregated masses of rhombohedric crystals, sandy in
appearance and to the touch. These soft, sandy, broken masses of
Magnesian Limestone, are always more or less rounded through the
disintegrating action itself, and through the slower movements which
must have been the consequence of that action, and are therefore
called "Sand Boulders," by the miners.

The interior of many of these boulders is yet unaltered and hard.

A specimen of the outer and entirely disintegrated portion of
such a boulder, from the New Granby Diggings, (Morgan county,)
was analyzed by Mr. Regis Chauvenet, with the following result:

Insoluble silicious (of clayish appearance)........................ 14.71 per cent.
Peroxide of Iron... 1.68   "
Lime.. 26.11   "
Magnesia.. 17.17   "
Carbonic Acid... 40.21   "
                                                            —
    Total.. 99.88   "

This result shows that there is actually no Sand in these masses of sandy appearance.

The boulders, as well as the larger, slightly softened masses of fissured Limestone, which are often found adjacent to the ore deposits, show frequently dendritic specks, probably hydrated peroxide of Iron, in their interiors. These dendritic specks evidently follow extremely fine cracks, entirely imperceptible before the rock is broken. The specks are one-sixteenth to one-eighth of an inch in diameter, and pretty evenly distributed over the surface of fracture. The miners call this rock "Calico Rock," and justly consider it a good indication.

In some districts—for instance, along Buffalo Creek, (Morgan county,)—the Galena is found immediately in the Sand boulders; more frequently, however, it is found in the form of slabs or broken sheets, between and above the boulders, associated with broken "Cotton Rock," of which I will speak hereafter.

The thickness of the Sand-boulder formation varies from 2 to 30 feet, within comparatively short distances of 60 or 100 feet. The boulders do not constitute a geological horizon, but are only of local occurrence. They are often missing entirely, and the various Clays and detrital rocks rest immediately on the somewhat sandy surface of the solid surface of the Limestone, which surface is washed off irregularly, forming large pockets, hollow runs, deep chimneys, and occasionally extensive caves. Good deposits of float Galena, are often found in the red Clay in these various excavations, on or near the surface of the solid Limestone. Galena seams sometimes run downward into the latter.

In some places veins of Galena and Barytes, traceable over several hundred feet, set down through solid Limestone, and have been followed to a depth of over 70 feet. They were, however, not paying, nor were they found to improve with the depth. Overlying the crystalline Limestone above described, and above the "Sand boulders," and undoubtedly derived from the latter, we meet in most of the richest Lead mines with a more or less silicious Magnesian Limestone of an entirely different character, and eminently Lead-bearing. This rock has a yellowish-gray or drab color, a very fine grain, and is either

sub-crystalline or earthy, and perceptibly softer than the above described unaltered crystalline rock. Like this latter Limestone, it contains often dendritic specks in fine seams.   Locally, and especially in
the vicinity of the Lead ores, it gradually becomes softer and more
earthy, and is then called "Cotton Rock" by the Central Missouri
miners. (It will be noticed that this rock is entirely different from the
porous Chert, which the miners of South-west Missouri call "Cotton
Rock.")

Through further disintegration, this rock passes into a soft, clayish,
friable mass, and finally into a silicious and often also calcareous, shaly
Clay, which has been described in No. 3 of chapter 31. It contains in
places concretions and concretionary beds of Chert, with brown dendritic specks in fissures occasionally of the same description as the
dendrites in the Limestones.

This drab colored, fine-grained Magnesian Limestone is the principal Lead-bearing rock in the Central Missouri Lead Region. It contains the Galena in the form of sheets and seams, which, when locally
accumulated, constitute the various forms of workable deposits, to be
characterized in No. 6 of chapter 31. The Galena, although itself
nearly always adhering to the Limestone, or to fragments of it, is
mostly accompanied and enveloped by more or less Barytes, which
mineral must, as a rule, be considered of later origin than Galena.

The form of the Lead ore, as found in the mines, is invariably
seam-like, and often conglomeratic, the Galena cementing together
fragments of Limestone, or of Chert, or of both. In most places the
Galena-seams are themselves again broken, and the empty spaces
filled with Barytes. In many localities, finally, the whole conglomeratic mass thus formed is again broken up, and lies in loose chunks in
the Clay. In this case, however, the Limestone fragments inclosed in
the Conglomerate are either changed into a soft calcareous Clay, or
else, have disappeared entirely, leaving only the Galena and the Barytes, with perhaps some little Clay or Sand. The cavities formerly
occupied by the Limestone are generally perfectly angular, showing
that the Limestone was hard at the time when Galena began to be deposited in its fissures. In these cavities we now find frequently crystals of Carbonates of Lead or Zinc, as drusy aggregates.

It is evident from these descriptions:

1. That the deposition of the Galena must have taken place
originally in the hard or but slightly altered Limestone after the latter
had been cracked and fissured in various ways.

2. That the deposition of the Barytes must have followed that of
the Galena.

3. That the softening and partial deposition of the Limestones
and their alteration into "Sand Boulders," and into "Cotton Rock,"
and residuary Clay, which caused a gradual diminution of volume of
the layers operated upon, and a gradual breaking down of the layers
above, has been effected *mainly* after the deposition of the Galena,
and also after that of the Barytes, and undoubtedly continues in some
measure to the present day.

In regard to the above point, 3, I will remark, that the occurrence
of Galena cementing broken Chert concretions, further, the occurrence of Galena as well developed crystals in residuary Clays and
Sands, and, finally, the occurrence of Galena as disseminated crystals
in the softened and sometimes regenerated outer portion of solid
masses of barren Limestone, have been observed occasionally. Although these occurrences are but exceptional, yet they show that in
some localities at least the dissolution of the Limestones may have
begun before, and continued during the deposition of the Galena.

6. FORMS OF DEPOSITE.

The various forms of Lead ore deposits in the Central Region are
as follows :

1. SEAMS AND SHEETS,

Either in hard or in altered and softened Limestone, the Galena and
Barytes filling horizontal partings between the strata, penetrating into
fissured Chert layers, also filling vertical cracks and irregular cavities
in the Limestone. The extent of such deposits is generally more horizontal than vertical; the net work of seams sometimes extending
horizontally over several acres of ground, but not often reaching to a
greater depth than 50 or 60 feet. Single and very thin seams sometimes not thicker than a knife blade, often reach deeper, to a depth as
yet unknown.

Most of the main seams strike from north-west to south-east.

Deposits as just described rarely pay working when in this crystalline Limestone, but they are often quite rich when in the earthy,
drab colored Limestone, or in " Cotton Rock."

2. VEINS.

The vertical seams show in places a vein-like character, continuing over considerable distances, and to a considerable depth, without
being connected with many horizontal or vertical cross-seams, and
without deflection or interruption. Such deposits are at the Mineral

Point Diggings, in Moniteau, and at the Doph Diggings, in Morgan county. The former deposit contains very little, the latter much Barytes. The former strikes north to south, the latter north-west to southeast. The Doph vein has been followed to a depth of over 70 feet, without either widening or narrowing, without getting richer or poorer in Galena.

3. CIRCLE,

Is a name given by the miners to a kind of *stock-werk* of circular outline and of the shape of a truncated cone, being somewhat wider below than above. It consists of a more or less conglomeratic accumulation of softened Limestone fragments, with Galena-seams, and of broken masses of both Galena and Barytes. The wall consists of a somewhat harder, yet altered Limestone, and is sometimes quite distinct and even smooth, while in other instances, or on another side of the same deposit, the Galena-seams reach into the wall rock.

In most "Circles" the best portion of the deposit lies along the wall, which is itself in places covered by a thick sheet of Galena. The broken mass becomes less rich toward the centre, so that the principal and richest shafts will lie in a circular line on the surface.

Some of these "Circles" are over 100 feet in diameter, and have been dug into to a depth of 70 to 90 feet. At that depth the rock begins to lose its conglomeratic character and to become simply fissured and less rich, although single seams of Galena yet continue deeper.

The origin of these deposits must be explained by a gradual disintegration and breaking down of a circular mass of Limestone underwashed by a vertical water course or spring in the underlying Limestone. The mode and time of deposition of the ore and of the Barytes do not appear to be different in the "Circles" than in all the other deposits, and has been treated of in No. 5 of chapter 31.

4. FLOAT DEPOSITS,

In which the Galena and Barytes occur broken and loose, imbedded either in completely disintegrated, silicious and clayish Limestone, or in red and brown, silicious Clays. The mines worked in the latter are known by the name of "Clay Diggings." The float deposits have been, up to this time, the best yielding and the most paying of the region, because the ore is more concentrated and more abundant in them than in those previously described, and because the work can be exclusively done with the pick and is therefore cheaper than where blasting is required.

The deposits have undoubtedly originated from a partial destruction and abstraction of the rocks from sheet, vein and circle deposits, and in many cases show their origin plainly by their shape and by their passing into the original deposit in the depth. Sheets and seams of Galena, starting in float deposits and running into the solid, nearly unaltered rock, are frequent. At the Bond Diggings, Morgan county, and at the Mineral Point Diggings, Moniteau county, the main vertical seam continues into the rock, and the broken slabs of Galena found above the rock in the red Clay, stand upright, exactly or nearly in the vertical plane of the seam; yet the heaviest part of each slab or piece generally turned downward. This shows not only that the float Galena is derived from the seam in the solid rock, but also that the alteration and diminution of the rock, and the consequent breaking and settling down of the Galena, has been a very slow and gradual process—so slow, indeed, as neither to disturb nor to throw over the loose Galena slabs. In none of such diggings could I find a proof of any kind of sudden or violent disturbance on a larger scale.

The Boaz Diggings, Cole county, furnish an example of circular Clay diggings. The circular float deposit in Clay near the surface, turns into a circle deposit in the fissured "Cotton Rock" below.

CONCLUSION.

It will be seen from the above general, as well as from the following special description of the Lead deposits in the Central Missouri Lead Region, that, from the present appearance of the diggings, the Lead ore seems to extend more horizontally through the rocks than into the depth, and to be more extensively developed in certain strata than in others; also, that the local development is exceedingly variable, there being besides the numerous favored spots where large quantities of Galena are accumulated, numerous others where the Galena, although present, is not found in paying quantities.

The prospect of finding Lead ore in greater depths than that into which the deepest of the present mines have penetrated, are not just now very encouraging. However, as it sometimes happens in stratified rocks that ore bearing and barren or richer and poorer strata alternate, and as the seams of Galena lead downwards in numerous places in this region, it is by no means impossible that, at a greater depth, other lead-bearing strata may be found, or that the veins may grow richer. So long as this has not been practically ascertained, we must say that, according to our present experiences, Lead ore deposits in Central Missouri have been found paying to a moderate depth only, but that many deposits are quite extensive and that they are very numerous in certain districts, although undoubtedly many existing are yet undiscovered. An important practical consequence of this is that large stock enterprises should never be made dependent on one single district or locality, however rich it may appear; but that they must be based on the possession of extensive tracts of land, situated in promising districts, to have a chance for becoming financially successful.

CHAPTER XXXII.

D.—SPECIAL DESCRIPTION OF DEPOSITS.

The special description of Lead deposits in the Central Missouri Lead Region will be given after counties in the following order:

1. DEPOSITS IN SALINE AND COOPER COUNTIES.
2. DEPOSITS IN PETTIS, BENTON, ST. CLAIR AND HICKORY COUNTIES.
3. DEPOSITS IN CAMDEN COUNTY.
4. DEPOSITS IN MORGAN COUNTY.
5. DEPOSITS IN MONITEAU AND COLE COUNTIES.
6. DEPOSITS IN MILLER, OSAGE AND MARIES COUNTIES.

Detailed descriptions will, as a rule, be given of such deposits only as I have visited personally. Others will be simply mentioned by name and location with the addition of a few short remarks based on reliable information. I have thus endeavored to make the list as complete as possible. New discoveries are, however, constantly being made in this Region, which is, comparatively, but little developed. Most of the following observations were made in May and June, 1874, and present the state of things at that time. The notes on Camden county make an exception, they being taken in May, 1873.

1. LEAD ORE DEPOSITS IN COOPER AND SALINE COUNTIES.

An old Lead mining district, already mentioned by Prof. G. C. Swallow in his report on Cooper county, of 1855, p. 199, situated on both sides of the line between Saline and Cooper counties, is at present being re-opened at the old as well as some new localities. The Lead-bearing rock in this district is the Archimedes or Keokuk Limestone of the Sub-carboniferous formation, consequently different from that met with in nearly all the other Lead Diggings in the Central Region, but similar to that with which the Lead ores are connected in the South-west. The localities so far known are the following :

MARMADUKE DIGGINGS,

Sec. 19, T. 49, R. 19 W., Saline county, on Salt Fork of Lamine River ; owned by Vincent Marmaduke and Company.

The location of these Diggings is on the east side of the Salt Fork, on the great bend near the centre of the Section. A thinly stratified, crystalline, somewhat cherty Limestone crops out along the Creek, dipping towards the latter.

A shaft was sunk between this Creek and the bluff, following a crevice in the Limestone filled with loose masses of Barytes with Galena. The shaft struck an opening in the Limestone at 15 feet depth, containing a considerable quantity of loose Barytes and Galena. The great affluence of water caused by the proximity of the Creek, stopped the work temporarily.

Another shaft is now being sunk through the Limestone a short distance south of the former, and if the prospect proves favorable there, it is intended to turn off the Creek into a new channel across the bend, so as to leave the Diggings dry.

Work was begun in March, 1874, and 20,000 pounds of Galena had been obtained in June.

A reverberatory furnace for Lead smelting, usually called "air-furnace" in Missouri, is in course of erection in the vicinity of the Diggings.

OLD SCOTT DIGGINGS,

T. 49, R. 19 W., Sec. 26, N. E. qr., Cooper county, on a branch of the Lamine River ; owned by J. A. Shedd and others.

This locality was described by Prof. Swallow. It was first worked about 30 years ago ; was worked a second time in 1871, by Dills & Co., who also built an air-furnace and smelted about 400 pigs of Lead. It is now being worked again by Mr. Shedd. Mr. Reynolds and others have also commenced work close by. As the old and the new Diggings are situated along a small branch, this strike of the deposit seems to be N. W. S. E.

The rocks consist of crystalline, fossiliferous Limestone, alternating with thick, fossiliferous Chert layers, in places altered and softened. The position is nearly horizontal. Seams of Barytes are frequent between and through this Limestone strata.

The new shafts, 25 to 40 feet deep, made in the bottoms, passed through various Clays mixed with unaltered, broken Chert. They struck at first a small accumulation of float Galena, somewhat altered and mixed, some Carbonate with Barytes, at a depth of 20 feet, another at 30 feet, and the solid Limestone at 35 feet. The shafts are being worked through the Limestone in search of a deeper galeniferous stratum. The quantity of ore raised from the new shafts is as yet inconsiderable.

COLLINS DIGGINGS,

T. 49, R. 18 W., Sec. 19, S. E. qr., S. W. qr., Cooper county; owned by S. R. Collins, J. W. Alexander and A. Hamilton.

Two shafts are sunk on a flat hill slope through white, yellow and red Clays 15 feet thick, then reaching a layer of Clay mixed with broken Chert, much Galena in broken seams, and some Barytes; also masses of disintegrated, crystalline Limestone, ("Sand boulders,") with adhering Galena crystals surrounded by Barytes. Masses of brown-colored, massive Smithsonite, containing no Lead, but much Iron, according to Mr. Chauvenet, are seen in places above the Galena. Single crystals of Zinc Blende are occasionally found with the Galena, and a $\frac{1}{2}$ to 3 inches streak of the same mineral, mixed with cupriferous Iron pyrites, (20 per cent. Copper,) lies below the Galena. The galeniferous streak is $\frac{1}{2}$ to $1\frac{1}{4}$ feet thick, and dips into the hill South-east 20 to 30°, following the surface of the solid, coarsely crystalline Limestone, which was struck a few feet below.

The mine was opened in the summer of 1873. Since that time, four men worked about one-half of their time, sinking shafts and building an air-furnace for smelting, which is about a quarter of a mile distant from the mine.

25,000 pounds of Galena were taken out, and 240 pigs of Lead, 60 pounds each, were produced and shipped down the Missouri and Mississippi Rivers to St. Louis. The pigs are branded thus: C. & CO. MO.

There are several other places in the north-western part of Cooper county where traces of Lead and Zinc ore have been found. In T. 48, R. 18 W., Sec. 5, W. hf., N. W. qr., on J. W. Willis' land, I saw a seam of Barytes several inches wide, with specks of Blende, in a hard, gray, crystalline Limestone, containing some stems of Encrinites.

2. LEAD ORE DEPOSITS IN PETTIS, BENTON, ST. CLAIR AND HICKORY COUNTIES.

Occurrences of Galena and of Copper and Zinc ores have been discovered years ago in numerous localities in the south-eastern part of Pettis, in the western half of Benton, in the south-eastern part of St. Clair and in the northern part of Hickory counties, and some mining has been carried on in several points. Very little, however, was done since the beginning of the civil war. But the interest of the mining public in this district is now beginning to revive, and the explorations have again been taken in hand in some places.

The late Dr. B. F. Shumard, of the Missouri Geological Survey, wrote, in 1867, a private report on this district for R. H. Melton, of Warsaw, who controlled the better portion of the Lead lands then known in the district. This report has been published in a pamphlet from which I will here communicate the following extracts. Dr. Shumard frequently uses the miners' expression "mineral" for Galena:

"WHITE DIGGINGS,

T. 39, R. 21, W. Sec. 28, N. W. qr. of S. W. qr., Benton county. They were opened about fifteen years ago on the east side of a low range of hills. The diggings extend a distance of about 100 yards in a direction a few degrees east of north. The shafts are numerous and from 3 to 25 feet deep. The ore, a pure variety of Galena, is found in a perpendicular fissure, cutting through soft gray, sandy-textured Magnesian Limestone. The fissure contains, besides the mineral, Sulphate of Baryta in abundance and of very good quality. From careful inquiries I learn that from 6,000 to 10,000 pounds of ore have been raised from these mines and smelted upon a temporary log furnace, the remnants of which are still to be seen near the diggings. The fissure exhibited no evidences of exhaustion at the time the work was suspended. The indications appear to me to be favorable that the mines may be made to yield largely by a judicious system of mining."

"GUSTKA DIGGINGS

Lie a short distance east of the preceding, near the base of the hills. An experimental shaft has been sunk here to the depth of 20 feet through sandy, sub-crystalline Magnesian Limestone. In sinking this shaft small quantities of Galena were found all the way down, mingled with Barytes, which occurs in massive and in transparent crystals. The prospect is flattering that both Lead and Barytes will be found in paying quantities."

"HOOPER DIGGINGS,

T. 39, R. 22 W., Sec. 2, N. E. qr. of S. W. qr., Benton county. At this place a shaft has been excavated to the depth of 54 feet in the Second Magnesian Limestone upon a Spar vein (" glass-tiff,") containing carbonate of Copper (azurite) and Sulphuret of Lead. The vein continued downward as far as the excavation was carried. At the time of my visit the shaft was partially filled with rubbish so that I could not ascertain the true character of the vein, but the surface indications and the material thrown out show that the 'prospect' is a promising one and worthy of further exploration."

"DEER CREEK MINES,

T. 39, R. 20 W., Sec. 6, E. hf. S. E. qr., Benton county. The principal mining for Lead has been done in a ravine at the base of a ridge 200 feet high. At this place 3 shafts have been sunk, the deepest of which is 25 feet. From these shafts Mr. Robert Nicholson raised about 9,000 pounds of mineral. The ore occurs with Barytes in masses embedded in sandy Clay, and in fissures in the Magnesian Limestone. Small quantities of mineral have also been found at several other localities upon this tract. It is a rich Sulphuret of Lead and probably contains a small per centage of Silver. Very little labor has been expended in developing these mines. For the small amount of work done the results have been highly satisfactory."

"COLE CAMP MINES,

T. 42, R. 21 W., Sec. 32, N. E. qr. N. E. qr., Benton county. The principal workings are on the northern declivity of a hill, a few feet above its base, and about 100 feet below its summit. The first discovery of Lead was made here about 30 years ago, but no mining was carried on until about the year 1848, when Mr. Glenn purchased the property and began a rude system of mining operations upon a very limited scale. From a few shallow pits sunk in the Clay he obtained considerable ore, but he was compelled to abandon the work in consequence of too great an influx of water, no precautions having been taken to secure the necessary drainage. During the year 1859 James Atkinson, becoming possessor of the mines, resumed operations after a somewhat more systematic method. The work of reopening the mines was entrusted to Edward Stemmer, who has had considerable experience as a miner in the Lead regions of South-east Missouri and the Hartz mines of Germany. Mr. Stemmer, assisted by his son, commenced operations by cutting a channel along the course of the min-

G.S.—34.

eral lode, beginning at the foot of the hill and extending it in a direction nearly south a distance of 70 feet. The depth of this channel at
its southern extremity is 18 feet; its width is from 3 to 4 feet. In excavating it Mr. Stemmer encountered several mineral caves or openings, one of which, near the end of the cut, was found to be quite
extensive, and gave prospect of being very productive. A shaft was
sunk to the depth of 35 feet, with a view of reaching this opening,
but from some miscalculation it was excavated too far south and
failed to strike it. Considerable mineral, however, was taken out in
sinking this shaft. Mr. Stemmer also states that near the end of the
channel he encountered an east and west lode of mineral nearly a
foot thick. He took its bearings and sunk a shaft upon it, reaching
the lode upon striking the Magnesian Limestone strata. It was followed only a few feet in the rock, as water set in too strongly to permit him to proceed further without employing pumps. Previous to
the war Mr. Stemmer, assisted by one and occasionally two hands,
worked two seasons in these mines, during the fall and winter, and
raised about 50,000 pounds of ore, which was stored in a mineral-house
near the mines. Most of this mineral was obtained in cutting the
channel, and chiefly from the eastern wall."

"Carter Diggings,

T. 38, R. 21 W. Sec. 18, S. W. qr. of N. E. qr., Hickory county, near the
base of a ridge about 100 feet high. The formation here is soft earthy,
Magnesian Limestone (Cotton rock,) underlaid by thick-bedded, light,
earthy, buff Magnesian Limestone. A shaft has been sunk to the
depth of 15 feet upon a small vertical vein of Galena, about half of
an inch thick, and bearing nearly east and west. The mineral is associated with Barytes. Between 400 and 500 pounds of ore have been
obtained from this place."

"Barytes Diggings,

T. 38, R. 21 W., Sec 18, N. E. qr. of S. E. qr., Hickory county, upon the
eastern declivity of a low ridge. A few pounds of ore have been
raised from a Clay fissure, running east and west through the same
strata as at Carter's. The fissure contains, besides the mineral, pure
white Barytes in considerable quantity. The prospect is good and
worthy of more thorough exploration. On the same ridge, south of
this place, a good deal of Barytes occurs with mineral disseminated."

" Stearns' Diggings,

T. 38, R. 21 W., Sec. 18, S. E. qr. of S. E. qr., Hickory county. At this
place a shaft, 20 feet in depth, has been sunk upon a vein of Barytes,

cutting through a mottled, gray Magnesian Limestone, and bearing east and west. The opening of the shaft is about twenty feet above the level of Galena branch. The vein contains, besides Galena, Carbonate and Sulphuret of Copper, and Sulphuret of Zinc. This appears to be a regular vein. According to Mr. Stearns, who made the discovery, and sunk the shaft, the thickness of the vein was found to increase the deeper he went. The prospect here is certainly very promising and I believe that systematic mining will develop a rich deposit of ore at this point. About 500 pounds of mineral were raised in excavating the shaft."

Dr. Shumard mentions some other localities in this district: among these the "Irish Diggings," in the S. E. qr. of the S. W. qr. of the same section, in which locality he expresses great confidence ; also the "Post Oak Diggings," one mile north-west of the Irish Diggings.

"DANIEL'S DIGGINGS,

T. 38, R. 22, W., Sec. 13, N. E. qr., Hickory county. These Diggings occupy the north-west corner of the tract, near the summit of a high ridge of Second Magnesian Limestone. Two shafts have been sunk here, each 10 feet deep, from which some mineral has been raised. The ore occurs in a fissure, with Barytes as a gangue. The latter is abundant, and the embedded mineral is sometimes found in large pieces. The prospect here is a good one. Mineral has been picked up also at several other places upon this tract, and Tiff is abundant in masses, scattered over the surface and in veins traversing the Magnesian Limestone."

"BROWN DIGGINGS,

T. 38, R. 22, Sec. 12, S. W. qr. of S. E. qr., Hickory county. They are located on the eastern Slope of a low ridge. They are the oldest Lead mines in the county. They were opened about 20 years ago, and have afforded several thousand pounds of mineral. A series of shafts, varying from 5 to 25 feet in depth, extend a distance of about 100 yards along the spur of the ridge, and from all of them more or less mineral was obtained. The mineral is a pure variety of Galena, occurring in cubical masses, some of them of large size."

Dr. Shumard also mentions briefly the "Southard's Diggings" in N. hf. of S. W. qr. of Sec. 11, in the same township.

3. LEAD ORE DEPOSITS IN CAMDEN COUNTY.

The Lead district of Camden county lies south and east of Linn Creek, the county seat, and several Diggings are within a few miles from that town, where an air-furnace for smelting the Lead ores, owned by Draper, McClurg & Co., is in operation 3 to 4 months in every year.

The furnace is of the same construction as those used in other places in the State, and as described in our report on the South-western Lead Region. It is charged with 1500 pounds of clean Galena, which is smelted in about 10 hours, yielding 1050 pounds of good pig Lead in the average. This is 70 per cent.; weight of pigs about 85 pounds. Nearly one cord of Oak-wood, also Hackberry, Ash or Maple, is used for each charge. One smelter and one helper are employed in the work. The furnace was started in the middle of October, 1871, and produced, until May, 1873, in all 1895 pigs. The Lead is shipped by boat to the mouth of the Osage, and thence to St. Louis by boat or by rail.

The hills near the upper part of the town of Linn Creek show the following successions of rocks, beginning from above:

No. 1. 10 to 20 feet conglomeratic Chert bed, with porous, cherty Cement, reddish, passing into massive Chert, or in places into reddish-brown Sandstone.

No. 2. 30 to 40 feet yellowish, rather soft Limestone, thinly bedded, sometimes shaly, sandy in the upper layers.

No. 3. 3 to 4 feet layer of solid, glassy Chert.

No. 4. 80 to 90 feet, to the foot of the hill, bluish, crystalline, thick-bedded Magnesian Limestone.

About one mile east of this locality are the Ferry Diggings.

FERRY DIGGINGS,

T. 38, R. 16 W., Sec. 5, N. W. qr., and Sec. 6, N. E. qr., owned by Mr. Patterson. The hills at these Diggings show about the following Geological Section :

No. 1. 1 to 2 feet Soil.

No. 2. 10 to 30 feet loose, red Clay and broken Chert, with loose Galena and sometimes Limonite.

No. 3. 50 feet alternate layers of Second Sandstone, gray and porous, with beds, several feet thick, of solid Chert.

No. 4. 20 feet white, calcareous Sandstone, with broken Chert and Chert-conglomerate.

No. 5. 150 feet Third Magnesian Limestone, gray, crystalline, inclosing some
Chert concretions.

The Galena is found loose in the red Clay, sometimes irregularly
disseminated, sometimes in more or less extensive accumulations.

MURPHY DIGGINGS,

T. 39, R. 17 W., Sec. 36, owned by McClurg, Murphy & Co. The Galena
occurs here in the same manner as in the Ferry Diggings. The layers
of red Clay and broken Chert is in places over 50 feet thick, and
seems to directly overlie the Limestone. Slabs of pure Galena, $\frac{1}{2}$ to
1 inch thick, are often found between the Clay and the Limestone. In
some places these slabs or fragments of Galena seams are accumulated and piled up in considerable quantity. Very thin seams of Galena are occasionally seen to penetrate into the solid Limestone.

THOMAS DIGGINGS,

T. 39, R. 16 W., Sec. 21, leased from Mr. Thomas by McClurg & Co.
Large quantities of loose Galena, with some Barytes, are found in the
red Clay, mixed with broken Chert, in a depression, near a small ravine. The Galena has the form of broken seams, yet occurs sometimes in pieces $\frac{1}{2}$ to 1 foot in diameter. The pieces lie mostly in rows
or " runs " on the sandy surface or along the sandy walls of the Limestone. Ledges or slabs of Heavy Spar with Galena are sometimes
found in an upright position, between a Limestone wall and the red
Clay. Specks of Galena are often seen in the Limestone, as well as
seams, $\frac{1}{8}$ to $\frac{1}{4}$ inch thick.

Calcite has rarely been found; Cerussite and Zinc ores never.

The total production of these Diggings had reached 40,000 pounds
at the time of my visit.

ANDERSON DIGGINGS,

S. E. qr. of S. W. qr. Sec. 35, T. 39, R. 16 W. Owned by Mr. Bender and leased by Mr. Anderson. Situated 6 miles east of Linn
Creek.

The Galena is there deposited at a depth of a few feet only below
the surface, in a layer in part of spongy, in part finely broken, white,
fossiliferous Chert, cemented by seams of Galena into a conglomeratic mass. This layer is from 6 inches to 2 feet thick, and lies about
horizontally above the irregular surface of the Limestone, the upper
part of which is softened and disintegrated into a sandy-like grit.

The Lead-bearing Chert layers are, however, in most places, separated from the Limestone by a red or brown Clay or loam, which fills the cavities on the surface of the Limestone, and varies from nothing to several feet in thickness.

The Galena is so intimately mixed with the Chert, that the ore has to be crushed and washed, which is done near the smelting furnace at Linn Creek.

BRUIN DIGGINGS,

S. E. qr. Sec. 27, T. 39, R. 16 W. Owned by the heirs of John Anderson; leased by McClurg & Co.

These Diggings are situated on a very steep western slope, in which the Limestone crops out in places, containing fine seams of Galena.

The digging is done in red and brown Clay, which is spread over the whole slope, and which contains float Galena in broken chunks and slabs, principally along the Limestone wall and in cavities in the Limestone. It is associated with a grainy Barytes.

The Limestone is altered, and sandy externally.

DAYTON WILLIAMS' DIGGINGS,

N. ¼W, qr. Sec. 34, T. 39, R. 16 W. Owned by Dayton Williams and leased by McClurg & Co.

These Diggings are of the same character as the former. They are situated at the foot of the eastern slope of a hill, opposite to and a short distance from the Bruin Diggings.

Both these Diggings are worked, and are said to yield handsomely.

FIELDING CLARK DIGGINGS,

Sec. 33, T. 37, R. 16 W., one mile west of Decaturville, near the southern line of the county.

Some fine-grained Galena had been dug from a shaft, some years ago. This Galena is intimately mixed with a dark gray, calcareous Clay, and has a different appearance and darker color than the Galena from the other Diggings.

This locality has not yet been tested sufficiently, and is not worked at present.

4. LEAD ORE DEPOSITS IN MORGAN COUNTY.

Morgan county comprises the most developed Lead district in the Central region. The mining operations are rapidly increasing in number, and have been carried on within the last two years, with rising success.

The production of Morgan county from July 1 to December, 1873, exceeded one million pounds of Galena, 80 to 100 miners, on an average, being employed during this period.

The miners generally pay 10 per cent. of the ore as a royalty, to the land owner, and sell the ore to the highest bidder.

The Galena is all smelted in the county, and is sufficient in quantity to occupy seven smelting furnaces during a considerable portion of the year. These seven furnaces are the following:

1. CLARK'S AIR FURNACE,

N. E. qr. S. W. qr. Sec. 21, T. 42, R. 18 W. On Coffin Spring Creek. Built in 1867. Owned by J. P. Clark, of Versailles. Galena smelted during the year 1873, 500,000 pounds.

2. BOND'S AIR FURNACE,

S. E. qr. N. E. qr. of Sec. 16, T. 40, R. 17 W. Built in 1867. Owned by T. S. Bond and his two sons. Leased by Wangelin, Bradbury & Co., of Jefferson City. Brand of pigs: "Gravois."

This furnace has the following dimensions:

Length of fire chamber	6 feet.
Width and height of fire chamber	2 feet.
Fire bridge above grate	1¼ to 1½ feet.
Interior length of hearth	8 feet.
Greatest width of hearth	3 feet 8 inches.

The hearth tapers in both directions, and is only 1½ feet wide near the doors. The fall of the hearth from the chimney to the discharge door is 18 inches.

This furnace smelts 3 charges, or 3,600 pounds of Galena in 24 hours.

Three-fourths of a cord of wood is used on 1,000 pounds of Galena.

Daily smelting expenses, about $4, the yield varying from 70 to 75 per cent. of metallic lead, from well-cleaned Galena—72 per cent. being the average.

The furnace has been running, so far, about three months in every year.

3. WYANT SPRING AIR FURNACE,

S. E. qr. N. W. qr. Sec. 32, T. 42, R. 17 W. Built in 1873. Owned by the Wyant Spring Lead Company (T. M. Avery & Co. of Chicago).

Runs during about two weeks in every month, smelting all the Galena from the company's own Diggings, as well as some that is bought from other parties.

4. HANDLIN AIR FURNACE,

West hf. Sec. 9, T. 42, R. 17 W., near the New Granby Diggings. Built in 1873. Owned by the Jackson County Mining Company.

5. BUFFALO AIR FURNACE,

Sec. 1, T. 41, R. 19 W., near the Buffalo Diggings. Built during the winter of 1873-74. Owned by the Buffalo Mining Company, of Versailles. Brand of pigs: the image of a buffalo. Weight of pigs about 83 pounds. Smelts the Galena from the Buffalo, and from the adjacent Johnson Diggings.

6. OTTERVILLE AIR FURNACE,

Sec. 21, T. 45, R. 19 W., near the Corday Diggings. Owned by the Otterville Smelting Company. Built during the winter of 1873-74. Brand of pigs: "Otterville Co." Total amount of ore smelted up to June, 1874, about 35,000 pounds of Galena, obtained from the various Diggings on Flat Creek.

7. O'BRIEN'S SCOTCH HEARTH,

Sec. 17, T. 41, R. 17 W. Very old and old-fashioned Scotch hearth, with bellows moved by water-power. Smelts the Galena from the O'Brien and other adjacent Diggings.

GALENA.

All the Galena so far found in Morgan county, occurs in the Lower Silurian Limestone, especially in the lower part of the so-called Second, and in the Third Magnesian Limestones.

The former rock prevails in the mining districts of the northern and central, the latter in those of the southern portions of the county.

Mr. F. B. Meek furnished, several years ago, a careful report on the Lead district of Morgan county, which may be read in the "Reports on the Geological Survey of Missouri, 1855-71," published in 1873, on pages 152 to 155. Since that report was written, many new and valuable deposits have been discovered in the county, as will be seen from the following descriptions:

T. 40, R. 17 W., Sec. 26, W. half of N. E. qr. and E. half of N. W. qr.
Owned and worked by Johnson & Davidson. These Diggings are at
present carried on on a south-east flat slope, the surface of which is
covered with clayish Soil and much broken Chert. The Galena is
mostly found at a depth of from 6 to 10 feet, lying loose in the Clay.
It extends several hundred feet along the slope. One shaft was carried down to a depth of 40 feet, and passed through Soil, 6 to 8 feet of
Clay with broken Chert and loose Galena, 30 feet Limestone, somewhat cherty, partly fissured, partly solid. They finally drilled 18 feet
deeper from the bottom of the shaft without reaching a change of
rock. The upper part of the Limestone was altered and softened, with
cavities and horizontal fissures lined with small crystals of Dolomite
or of dolomitic Calcite. It was also broken in all directions by larger
fissures containing in places streaks of Galena. The last 7 feet of
rock in the shaft were solid and hard, granular to sub-oolitic, unstratified, and contained no Galena. The Diggings have been worked inter-
ruptedly by two to four men for nearly three years. Mr. Johnson gives
the total production at about 15,000 pounds, but I heard from other
reliable sources that it has been considerably larger. The Galena is
smelted at Bond's furnace.

BOND DIGGINGS,

T. 40, R. 17 W., Sec. 9, S. W. qr. of S. W. qr., and Sec. 16, S. E. qr. of N.
E. qr. Owned by T. J. Bond and his two sons, H. P. and W. I. Bond.;
at present leased by Wangelin, Bradbury & Co., of Jefferson City. The
Diggings are situated on two separate hills, on both sides of a branch
of Milk Creek. In both places, the principal portion of the Galena
is found loose in the red Clay, occasionally associated with Barytes.
It is frequently found in loose sheets in part standing upright, the
heaviest part downward, and extends in several parallel, nearly
straight lines over distances of 100 to 300 feet. The direction of the
deposit is about N. W. to S. E. The galeniferous Clay is 6 to 8 feet
thick, and in several places vertical seams and horizontal sheets are
found running into the solid Limestone, yet hardly ever thick enough
to be worked with profit. In the the western Diggings, a shaft was
being sunk at the time of my visit, near the summit of a spur of the
hill. It had then penetrated through:

No. 1.   8 feet Soil and red Clay.
No. 2.   15 feet porous, altered and fissured Magnesian Limestone.
No. 3.   15 feet solid, cherty Magnesian Limestone.
No. 4.   15 feet soft, altered and fissured Magnesian Limestone with irregular
         cavities.

Zinc Blende occurs but rarely in the Bond Diggings. Calcite is in some places in Sec. 16 quite common. Barytes is found sometimes with the Galena, sometimes without it.

There are now 20 miners at work. The total production of the Diggings during five years amounted to 800,000 pounds of Galena. About 10,000 pounds were raised per month during the year 1873. All the Galena is smelted in Bond's air furnace, which is situated in Sec. 16, close to the Diggings, and which has been described above.

JANUARY DIGGINGS,

T. 40, R. 17 W., Sec. 11, E. half N. E. qr. Owned by the January heirs and Spurlock. Not worked at present. The amount of Galena taken out by miners since 1868 is estimated at 60,000 pounds.

GRANBY COMPANY'S DIGGINGS,

T. 41, R. 16 W., Sec. 30, W. half. Owned by the Granby Mining and Smelting Company. This locality was worked 15 years ago, and is marked as Lead land on Mr. F. B. Meek's Geological Map of Morgan county. It is now being opened again by Hon. G. Stover of Versailles.

LOWER INDIAN CREEK DIGGINGS,

T. 41, R. 17 W., Sec. 26, N. E. qr. Owned by H. P. Bond of Bond's Mines. These Diggings extend about 600 feet along a small ravine on Indian Creek, in an east and west direction. They are right in the water run and the water causes much trouble to the miners. Loose Galena is found in red Clay, either above the sandy, soft Limestone, or in irregular openings and under a "cap" or roof consisting of bluish Chert between soft, yellow, thinly stratified to shaly Limestone. The Limestones are full of Dendrites near the deposit. The work was carried on with long interruptions for three years, and has been taken up again lately. Several shafts had to be abandoned on account of the inability of the miners to remove the water. The production was never very large, yet amounted to several thousand pounds of Galena during the year 1873.

T. 41, R. 16 W., Sec. 18, W. half of E. half, near Sidebottom's farm on Indian Creek. Owned by Th. V. Jones, of St. Louis; leased by Doph. A very good description of this locality is given in Mr. F. B. Meek's Geological Report on Morgan county, published by the Missouri Geological Survey in 1873, on page 154 of the small volume. In the present stage of development, this deposit. represents a vein, striking north-west to south-east, of galeniferous Barytes, in the Magnesian Limestone. The Barytes is frequently banded, and incloses fragments of softened Limestone with crystals of Galena adhering to them. The vein, which can be traced across depressions and ridges for about a quarter of a mile, was followed to a depth of nearly 70 feet without altering either its character or its thickness of 3 to 12 inches. But the wall-rock grew harder with the depth, and the amount of Galena raised was not sufficient to pay for the work. The work is at present suspended, but will, I am informed, be resumed soon. This would be undoubtedly a proper place to attempt a practical solution of the question whether the Central Missouri Lead deposits belong exclusively to these geological strata which lie at present near the surface of the ground, or whether they are in places connected with lead-bearing strata which lie deeper.

T. 41, R. 16 W., Sec. 8, S. W. qr. of N. W. qr., close to Indian Creek. Owned by Hiram Madole, Jr.; leased by George H. Stover & Co. The General Section of these Diggings is represented by Fig. *a*. It consists of:

No. 1. 2 to 4 feet cherty Soil.
No. 2. 8 to 40 feet Clay with loose Chert.
No. 3. 0 to 6 feet Chert slabs or loose fissured Chert layers.
No. 4. 3 to 30 feet "Sand boulders"—loose, broken masses of soft, sandy Limestone.
No. 5. ? feet solid Magnesian Limestone, containing near the south end of the Diggings a horizontal cave about 5 feet high and 6 feet wide.

The bottom of this cave is not Limestone but Clay, and has never been investigated. The cave has been struck 40 feet below the surface in a shaft, and extends from this shaft eastward over a distance of about 150 feet, when it touches the surface of the hill-slope near the creek. It is connected, near the shaft mentioned, with an opening in the rock filled with Clay and Galena, and running nearly at a right angles to the cave and parallel to the ridge. This cave is evidently an old water outlet from the Galena deposit.

It will be noticed in the above sketch that there are two depressions in the profile of the slope. These extend nearly 800 feet along the slope from S. E. to N. W. On these depressions, sometimes called " breaks," two parallel rows of shafts have been sunk, most of which struck loose Galena in considerable quantities, partly in irregular streaks in the upper Clay, partly below the Chert slabs and between the softened Limestone masses down to the irregular and mashed surface of the Limestone. The Galena varies from pea to fist-size, is frequently rounded off and coated and associated with red Clay. It also occurs in large loose sheets. No Barytes has been found except some loose rounded pieces in the cave. The softened Limestone masses, " Sand Boulders," are more or less rounded off and vary generally from fist to head-size, but reach sometimes a diameter of 4 feet. These diggings were worked four years ago, and after a long interruption the work was resumed in January, 1874, at first with two men until May 1st, when the number was increased to 4. From January to the middle of May most of the work was expended in opening and sinking shafts. About 14,000 pounds of Galena were taken out during this period. The total production of these diggings is estimated at 300,000 pounds, most of which was found at a shallow depth in the red Clay.

KELSEY DIGGINGS,

T. 41, R. 16 W., Sec. 5, S. E. qr. of S. E. qr., one mile north of the Madole Diggings—owned by Kelsey's heirs and leased by Estell. The deposit is not worked now. The Galena is said to exist in seams and sheets in the Limestone and without Barytes. Total production about 8,000 pounds.

STRONG DIGGINGS,

T. 42, R. 16 W., Sec. 27, N. W. qr. N. W. qr., on a branch of Upper Indian Creek, near the edge of the prairie ; partly on Strong's and partly on Burch's land. The latter portion is leased to Jones, of Independence, who raised, I am told, 4,000 to 5,000 pounds of Galena in January, 1874, from the red Clay.

O'BRIEN DIGGINGS,

T. 41, R. 17 W., Sec. 17, N. hf. of S. W. qr., and T. 41, R. 18 W., Sec. 24, E. hf. N. E. qr. Shallow Clay diggings—yielded largely in summer of 1873. The Galena is smelted at the place in O'Brien's Scotch hearth.

BRUSHY DIGGINGS,

T. 41, R. 18 W., Sec. 12, S. E. qr., near center. The land is owned partly by Allen and partly by Fair and leased by the Morgan County Mining Company.

The diggings are on an eastern slope, and the main streak of ore seems to run N. E. S. W. The Galena is found loose in the red Clay. At a depth of from 20 to 40 feet broken masses of pretty hard Limestone were struck, with some Chert, mixed with rounded pieces of Barytes and some Galena. The slope is 70 to 80 feet high, and shows a distinct " break " near the middle of its height.

The total production of these and the following Gray Horse Diggings together, is estimated at over 200,000 pounds of Galena. The diggings are being worked with interruptions and were so for several years past.

GRAY HORSE DIGGINGS,

T. 41, R. 18 W., Sec 13, N. E. qr., N. W. qr., on widow Allen's land, on the west slope of the same ridge, on whose east slope the Brushy Diggings are situated. The Galena is found loose in red Clay on the surface of the Limestone, in many places only 10 feet below the surface of the ground. Loose pieces of Barytes are met with occasionally. The diggings extend along the slope in a north-east direction and also along a steep ravine, striking eastward. Worked irregularly for the past 3 years with 4 to 6 men. Total production of these and the Brushy Diggings together, about 200,000 pounds of Galena.

NEW JOPLIN DIGGINGS,

T. 41, R. 18 W., Sec. 13, S. E. qr. of N. W. qr.; owned in part by Taylor of Joplin, in part by the Granby Mining and Smelting Company and J. H. Stover. Worked in 1872 and much Galena is said to have been taken out by the miners. It is expected that work will be resumed this year.

CALDWELL DIGGINGS,

T. 41, R. 18 W., Sec. 14, N. E. qr. of N. E. qr., a half mile from the Brushy Diggings, near Caldwell's farm. Owned by the Central Missouri Lead Company (T. M. Avery & Co. of Chicago). A shaft was sunk nearly 100 feet in depth, on a south-east spur of a high ridge, about 80 feet above the Brushy Creek. There being no work done at present I could not get into this shaft. The mining superintendent of the mining company says the shaft passed through 40 feet red and yellow Clay with loose pieces of Barytes and with much float Galena. Fifty-five feet large sandy boulders with white dense Barytes, broken, and some Galena. Below this, yellow, sandy Clay, with loose Barytes and some Galena and some water.

Clark, Libby and others mined about 80,000 pounds of Galena out of the upper 40 feet of Clay three years ago.

BLOW DIGGINGS.

T. 41, R. 18 W., Sec. 23, S. W. qr.; owned by the Granby Mining and Smelting Company. A few shallow trial shafts were sunk here and some Galena obtained.

WILD CAT DIGGINGS,

T. 41, R. 18 W., Sec. 12, N. W. qr. S. W. qr.; owned by Judge Rice. Production of 1873 estimated at 30,000 pounds of Galena.

PROCTOR DIGGINGS,

T. 41, R. 18 W., Sec. 29, N. W. qr. and Sec. 30. Indications of Galena in the Limestone on the land of J. N. Hit, on the Upper Proctor Creek. No regular mining has been done there as yet.

WILSON DIGGINGS,

T. 41, R. 19 W., Sec. 12, W. hf. S. E. qr.; owned by William P. Wilson, of St. Louis. Old diggings reopened in the fall of 1873. Seams of Galena in Chert and in Limestone.

BUFFALO DIGGINGS,

T. 41, R. 19 W., Sec. 1, S. E. qr. of N. W. qr., near the head of Buffalo Creek; owned by the Buffalo Mining Company (Stover, Walker & Clark, of Versailles). On a north-west slope of a ridge, a few hundred feet from the creek, two shafts were sunk in September, 1873, about 30 feet apart, both of which struck a deposit of Galena which must be considered one of the richest so far discovered in the county. One of these shafts struck the Galena immediately below the soil, the other passed through a few feet of Clay and of disintegrated sandy Limestone. The latter rock is here the Lead-bearing rock, and undoubtedly before its disintegration reached a very high degree, contained a rich net-work of thick Galena seams without any Barytes. At present we find the Limestone broken and soft, the seams and irregular masses of Galena broken and piled up above each other, the interstices being filled with a sandy mass consisting of loose crystalline grains of Magnesian Limestone.

The main portion of this deposit seems to be circular or elliptic in its outline, as far as can be judged from the present development, with a diameter of about 30 feet. Within these limits the Galena forms from 10 to 20 per cent. of the whole mass. But branches of the deposit reach much further out; one such having been struck by a shaft about 80 feet distant, and farther up on the Slope. The main deposit has been excavated by a large shaft, 16 feet wide in both directions, to a depth of 50 feet, at which depth the deposit becomes rather less rich in Galena. An open mining cut is now being made into the hill-slope. Streaks of red " tallow " Clay, and occasionally Chert concretions are met with in the deposit.

The shaft above mentioned, which was sunk further up the hill-slope, at about 80 feet distance, shows the following Section :

No. 1. 3 feet Soil, with some slabs of red Sandstone, and with much coarsely broken Chert.

No. 2. 30 feet red " tallow Clay," with Chert fragments and some float Galena.

No. 3. 10 feet disintegrated and sandy but not much broken Limestone.

No. 4. 10 feet large, broken masses, 3 to 5 feet in diameter, of the same rock, (" Sand-boulders,") with thick, broken seams of Galena, running in a north-western direction toward the main deposit.

Some trial-shafts, sunk 100 to 150 feet north-east of the main shaft, and from 10 to 20 feet deep, struck a little Clay and then " Sand-boulders," without so far reaching any Lead ore. The Johnson Diggings, to be described hereafter, have struck a good deposit on the same slope, about 700 feet south-east of the Buffalo mine, which fact gives an indication that the Buffalo deposit might extend in that direction. The Buffalo Diggings have been worked with an average of 6 men since September 1, 1873, and had produced 190,000 pounds of Galena on May 1, 1874. The Buffalo air-furnace, erected near the Diggings, smelts the ore.

JOHNSON DIGGINGS,

T. 41, R. 19 W., Sec. 1, on the same tract of land as the Buffalo Diggings, about 700 feet south-east of the latter, on the same slope of the hill, are worked by Laridy & Johnson.

The shafts passed through Soil, 10 to 15 feet red Clay, 5 to 10 feet disintegrated and fissured Limestone, 10 feet " Sand-boulders," with much Galena, of similar appearance and occurrence as that of the Buffalo mine. The work began in October, 1873, and was carried on rather irregularly with 3 men. The production, on May 1, 1874, had exceeded 30,000 pounds of Galena.

POTTER NO. 2 DIGGINGS,

T. 42, R. 18 W., Sec. 31 N. W. qr., owned by Prof. W. B. Potter, of St. Louis, and Alexander Leonhard. Four shafts were sunk near a ravine, in Clay, with loose Galena and Chert fragments; also Barytes and Calcite. In places finely broken Chert is found cemented by hardened Clay and by Galena, forming a Conglomerate, which also occurs in the Clay.

Work began here in December, 1873. Production, until April, 1874, 5000 pounds of Galena.

WOLF-DEN DIGGINGS,

T. 42, R. 18 W., Sec. 30, S. W. qr. of N. W. qr., owned by widow Mc-Ghea. Float Galena in red Clay. Also seams in the Limestone. Has not been, as yet, very productive.

FERGUSON DIGGINGS,

T. 42, R. 18 W., Sec. 28, S. W. qr., on Crow branch of Gravois Creek, owned by Prof. W. B. Potter, of St. Louis, and others. I owe the sketch Fig. B, and the following notes on these Diggings to the kindness of Mr. Alexander Leonhard, late Assistant in the Geological Survey.

Fig. B, a, a, is a crevice in Limestone, 6 to 12 feet wide, dipping from 45 to 60°. A Chert layer of nearly 1 foot thickness forms the roof of the crevice. The lower wall rock is Limestone. The crevice is filled with broken masses of half disintegrated Limestone, containing a net-work of seams of Barytes, some as much as 3 inches thick. The Barytes incloses cubic crystals of Galena, $\frac{1}{4}$ to 2 inches thick, forming in places one-fourth of the mass.

Red Clay fills the interstices between the loose "boulders" of Limestone, and contains large chunks and some fine crystals of Barytes and loose pieces of Galena.

The contents of the deposit are more altered and disintegrated than in the depth, and near the surface of the ground the crevice is filled with sandy, yellow Clay, loose Galena and well developed crystals of Barytes.

Several shallow shafts, bb, were sunk on the outcrop of the deposit and have traced it on the surface over a length of 30 feet so far.

The main shaft, c, passed through the Soil, through 20 feet of hard Limestone, 1 foot of Chert, and then struck the deposit, and excavated it in the shape indicated by the zig-zag line in the above sketch.

Water rushing in from below in considerable quantity has for the present interrupted the work, which will, however, be resumed shortly in a more regular and systematic manner.

SIMMONS' DIGGINGS,

T. 42, R. 18 W., Sec. 20, S. E. qr. of S. E. qr., on Coffin Spring Creek, owned by Simmons. Caves and cavities in the Limestone, filled with red Clay and loose Galena. Total production about 25,000 pounds. Not worked since summer of 1873.

CLARK DIGGINGS,

T. 42, R. 18 W., Sec. 21, S. E. qr., S. W. qr., on Coffin Spring Creek, owned by J. P. Clark, of Versailles. Galena has been and is yet mined in several places in this vicinity, along Coffin Spring Creek. Opposite Clark's smelting furnace, close to and on the west side of the creek, the outcrops of numerous seams of Galena and of Blende and of Barytes, $\frac{1}{4}$ to 3 inches thick, are seen in the Limestone. The main seams strike east to west, and are connected by cross-seams. Some of the Galena and Barytes seams cross the creek at an angle of about 45°, and seem to extend into the opposite hill. The Limestone dips toward the creek about 20°.

Blende and Galena is not generally found together. On the west side of the creek, one east and west Barytes seam separates the deposit in two parts, the northern of which contains the seams of Galena and Barytes, the southern those of Blende and Barytes.

Several shafts were sunk in this place from 6 to 15 feet deep, and about 20,000 pounds of loose Galena was obtained from the Clay covering a part of the net-work of seams. The seams themselves were not followed to any depth. The net-work of seams covers an area about 50 feet long and 30 feet wide, but thin seams of Galena and of Barytes are seen crossing the rock in the creek for some distance to the south. All along the creek, on the east side, are old, shallow Clay diggings 2 to 6 feet deep, which used to be quite productive; but in all the Limestone was struck at a depth of only 2 to 6 feet. They extend over the line into Sec. 28, where less float ore is found, but where a large district of perhaps 200 feet diameter exists in which the Limestone contains Galena disseminated in its mass in numerous small specks. This has been observed in the Diggings as well as in the bed of a small branch running south-west into Coffin Spring Creek.

On the west side of the creek, numerous shafts have been sunk along a pretty steep ravine, up to the top of the ridge. Here we find

G.S—35

a cherty Soil and 5 to 15 feet Clay below with considerable quantities of loose and often rounded and coated Galena on the irregular, sandy surface of the Limestone. Some Barytes occurs occasionally. In places, large slabs of Chert or of Limestone lie above the galeniferous Clay, and have to be pierced to reach the "opening."

The total production of these Diggings has been about 500,000 pounds of Galena during three years.

A shaft sunk on the summit of the ridge, 60 feet deep, passed through Soil, 15 feet Clay, 15 feet Chert rock and Limestone, 5 feet Clay with loose Galena and some disintegrated Limestone, then struck the surface of the solid Limestone and went 25 feet deep into it without meeting with any traces of Galena. One hundred and sixty thousand pounds of ore were taken out of this shaft.

About a quarter of a mile south of this, in Sec. 28, a cave 6 feet wide enters the Limestone bluff at the southern end of the same ridge, but no indications of Galena have as yet been found in it.

A few hundred feet further down the Creek, between the Creek and the Limestone bluff, a deposit of beautiful, clear and translucent Barytes is observed covering an area of ground 15 feet long and 8 feet wide. A connection with the rock cannot be plainly seen, nor are there any traces of Barytes in the adjacent bluff. The character of this Barytes deposit cannot, therefore, be ascertained without digging. As Barytes is a valuable mineral, selling raw at $8 per ton in St. Louis, this place would be worthy of a closer investigation by the owner of the land. No Galena has been observed at this last-described locality. The Barytes is unusually clear and pure.

POTTER NO. 1 DIGGINGS,

T. 42, R. 18 W., Sec. 21, N. W. qr., on Coffin Spring Creek. Owned by Prof. W. B. Potter, of St. Louis, and Al. Leonhard. A crevice 1 to 4 feet wide, in solid, somewhat softened Limestone, traceable over about 300 feet in a south-west to north-east direction, was followed to a depth of 80 feet. The crevice is filled with red Clay, broken Chert, large masses of crystallized Calcite and loose pieces of Galena, some of which are as heavy as 40 pounds. Worked irregularly during the past two years. Total production about 25,000 pounds of Galena.

STOVER DIGGINGS,

On Coffin Spring Creek, T. 42, R. 18 W., Sec. 21, S. W. qr. of N. W. qr. J. H. Stover, agent. Two crevices of a similar character and running in the same direction as that just described. Worked since 1866 with long interruptions. Total production about 30,000 pounds.

ARGENBRIGHT DIGGINGS,

T. 42, R. 18 W., Sec. 18, S. E. qr. of S. E. qr.   Owned by Argenbright
& Co. Sixteen thousand pounds of Galena were taken out during
summer of 1873.

FAIR DIGGINGS,

T. 42, R. 18 W., Sec. 18, S. E. qr. of N. E. qr. Owned by William Fair.
Worked in winter of 1873 and a few thousand pounds of Galena produced.

MERRITT DIGGINGS,

T. 42, R. 18 W., Sec. 23, S. W. qr. of N. W. qr. Owned by the Granby
Mining and Smelting Company. Irregular crevices and cavities in
Limestone with Clay and loose Galena. Worked intermittently for
several years past. Total production estimated at 50,000 pounds.

NEILSON DIGGINGS,

T. 41, R. 17 W., Sec. 6, N. W. qr. of N. E. qr. Owned by Mayor Brown
of St. Louis. A number of shallow shafts have disclosed some float
Galena imbedded in red Clay. A more thorough investigation of this
locality is now in progress.

WYANT SPRING DIGGINGS,

T. 42, R. 17 W., Sec. 32, S. E. qr. of N. W. qr. Owned by the Wyant
Spring Lead Company (T. M. Avery & Co., of Chicago.) A long row
of shallow shafts were sunk along an eastern hill-slope on a line striking N. N. W. to S. S. E., over a distance of about 1,000 feet. These
shafts sunk 10 to 20 feet deep into either yellow or red Clay with more
or less loose Galena. Some places were found to be very rich.

One shaft, situated in about the middle of the row, was sunk
deeper and struck a fissure, $\frac{1}{2}$ to $2\frac{1}{2}$ feet wide, in the solid Limestone.
The fissure has the same strike as the Diggings, and is filled with
black Clay, triturated black Slate and some Chert, also boulders of
disintegrated Limestone. Galena in considerable quantity was found
adhering to the wall-rock, as well as to the boulders. The fissure is
slightly inclined towards the west. The shaft reached a depth of 55
feet.

Another shaft was sunk 35 feet further up the slope and outside
of the line of the main diggings, and was likewise carried down to a
depth of 55 feet. This shaft struck considerable float Galena in the
red Clay and then another fissure, 1 to 3 feet wide, in the Limestone,

parallel to the former and filled with red Clay, softened Limestone and some Galena. This fissure dips slightly east.

In several shallow shafts sunk on this second fissure along the slope, much Galena was found in yellow Clay.

Shallow test shafts, sunk yet higher on the slope, disclosed but little ore in the Clay. Eight or ten such shafts were also made on the summit of the ridge to depths of 10 to 20 feet, and below 10 feet of Clay, struck a softened, stratified Limestone with more or less Galena in thin seams and sheets.

About 30,000 pounds of Galena were taken out of some shallow diggings in the Clay, situated on a southern hill-slope in the northern prolongation of the main Diggings, separated from the latter by a small valley. This gives hope for a continuation of this deposit in a northern direction, while the attempts to find a continuation in a southern direction have been, so far, without any favorable result. The fact that the shafts forming the southern portion of the main Diggings show a decrease in the quantity of Galena, and the appearance of Barytes in its stead, is interesting in this connection. In all other parts of these Diggings, Barytes is but rarely found.

The Wyant Spring Diggings have been worked the past eighteen months, during eight or ten of which the work was steadily carried on with an average force of ten men. The total production was, up to May, 1874, about 300,000 pounds of Galena. One-half of this amount was taken out by the Wyant Spring Lead Company in about four months work, with ten miners.

The Galena is smelted in the Wyant Spring Air Furnace, which has been erected in the immediate vicinity of the Diggings.

SCHULTZE DIGGINGS,

N. E. qr. of N. E. qr. Sec. 33, T. 42, R. 17 W. Owned by Schultze & Cooper, of St. Louis. Specks and pockets of Galena in Limestone. Also, loose pieces in Clay. This locality is now being opened.

SPURLOCK DIGGINGS,

N. W. qr. of S. E. qr. Sec. 24, T. 42, R. 17 W. Owned and worked by Spurlock. Shallow shafts in Clay. Worked at intervals during the last three years. Total production, 8.000 pounds.

TOWNLEY DIGGINGS,

N. W. qr. of N. W. qr. Sec. 23, T. 42, R. 17 W.; and the Gunn Diggings, in the N. E. qr. of N. W. qr. of same Section, are owned by George S. Wright, of St. Louis, and Alexander Leonhard. Surface Diggings near the head of a branch of Gravois Creek. Shafts 10 to 20 feet deep in Clay and disintegrated Limestone. The Galena occurs loose in Clay, and also in seams in Limestone. Much broken Chert and Chert Conglomerate are found in the Soil and Clay of this District. Total production during two years, 30,000 to 40,000 pounds. The work has been taken in hand more vigorously of late, and 2 to 4 farmers now dig out about 1,500 pounds of Galena per week.

MORELAND DIGGINGS,

N. hf. Sec. 22, T. 42, R. 17 W. Owned by Moreland, worked by Jliff. Worked intermittingly for two years. Production until end of 1873, about 30,000 pounds of Galena.

NEW GRANBY DIGGINGS,

S. hf. of S. W. qr. Sec. 9, T. 42, R. 17 W.

The southern portion of these Diggings is owned by the Granby Mining and Smelting Company, the northern portion by the Jackson County Company.

We include under the name of New Granby Diggings, all which are more specially known by the names of Woods, Jliff, Crossroad, and Wilkinson Diggings, which are all situated on the summit and on the south-western slope of a long meandering ridge, whose general direction is about N. W. S. E.

The Wilkinson Diggings are situated on the most northern spur of this ridge, about 1,000 feet N. W. of the Crossroad Diggings. There are several shafts which struck the Limestone at a short depth, and some of which have been sunk 20 feet through the Limestone, containing specks of Galena. They are being continued in the hope of striking an opening below.

The formerly so-called Crossroad Diggings, lie about 1,000 feet further south, and nearer the summit of the ridge. The shafts were 15 to 20 feet deep, and worked on float Galena in the red Clay, on the surface of the altered Limestone. One district, about 30 feet wide and 70 to 80 feet long, was especially rich in ore.

Lower down the slope, are shallow old Clay Diggings, formerly called the Grass-root Diggings.

On the summit of the ridge are the Jliff Diggings, which have yielded large quantities of ore. Some trial shafts are now being sunk further north on the summit of the ridge, in the hope of striking similar deposits. McCoy's shaft has pretty well succeeded in this. It passed at first through 20 feet of red Clay, with broken Chert, but *without ore*, then through 20 feet of immense boulders of soft, sandy

Limestone, with *much Galena* in broken sheets and seams. These Galena fragments are all in rather irregular positions, but the heaviest parts always turned downward.

James Wilkinson sunk a shaft a short distance to the north-east, to a depth of 75 feet, passing through 10 feet of Soil and Clay, 65 feet through solid, hard Limestone, with specks and thin sheets of Galena.

All these Diggings are on the north and west side of the road from Versailles to Tuscumbia. The Crossroad Diggings are situated very near the road. Eight or nine hundred feet south-east of this road, near the summit of the same ridge, we find the New Granby Diggings proper, also called the Wood's Diggings. Ten to 15 feet of red and yellow Clay, here covers a large part of the western slope, being only overlaid by a dry, Cherty Soil. Much float Galena has been dug out of this Clay.

There is, however, a district of elliptic outline, say 100 feet long and 70 feet wide, which has been opened by several shafts, 20 to 30 feet deep, and by drifts. Here are immense broken and more or less rounded masses of very soft, yellow or white Magnesian Limestone, with numerous broken veins of 1 to 6 inches pure Galena between, and with numerous thinner seams of Galena through them. This rich district has in some places a pretty sharp limit. It seems to get wider with the depth, yet the richest portion lies at about 25 feet below the surface. This deposit seems to be a rather indistinctly developed "circle." A shaft sunk 10 or 15 feet east of the apparent limit of this rich place, and another sunk about 60 feet north of it, struck the solid, barren Limestone, and the eastern shaft passed 40 feet into this rock without reaching a change.

The Jackson County Company produced from their portion of the New Granby Diggings, in the year 1873, 150,000 pounds of Galena, which was smelted in the Handlin air furnace, located at the foot of the slope.

The Granby Mining and Smelting Company, worked in the average 4 shafts, with an aggregate number of men of 12 to 16, and produced in the year 1873, 500,000 pounds; and from January to April, 1874, 150,000 pounds of Galena.

GUM SPRING DIGGINGS,

S. E. qr. Sec. 8, T. 42, R. 17 W., near the Handlin furnace, at the foot of the same slope on which the New Granby Diggings are situated. Owned by the Jackson County Company. Shallow shafts in Clay worked in 1873, when they yielded Galena in large quantity. Not worked at present.

AFRICAN DIGGINGS,

N. E. qr. of S. W. qr. Sec. 5, T. 42, R. 17 W.   Title under litigation.

These Diggings occupy several acres of ground on the summit and western slope of a ridge, on a small branch of the Upper Gravois River, 1½ miles east of Versailles. The summit is 80 to 100 feet above the water course. The Diggings are shallow. Their main direction is about N.—S.

On the lower part of the slope, the shafts present the following section:

No. 1. 3 feet Soil, with slabs of red Sandstone.

No. 2. 2 to 10 feet red Clay, with some float Galena.

No. 3. 6 feet softened, fine-grained Magnesian Limestone, in 1 to 3 feet layers.

No. 4. 5 feet loose mixture of Shales, Clay, Sand, and very soft Limestone, with specks and aggregated masses of Galena lying in streaks between the various detrital materials mentioned.

(?) Harder, sub-crystalline Limestone.

Higher up the slope, much loose Galena is found in numerous shallow shafts in red Clay, immediately above the Limestone, at a depth of 3 to 10 feet. Banded oval Chert concretions (Jasper,) are frequently found loose in the Soil and Clay.

These diggings were worked from January to October, 1873, and are again worked at present.

The total production, so far, is about 50,000 pounds of Galena.

VERSAILLES DIGGINGS,

T. 42, R. 17 W., Sec. 5, N. E. qr, of S. W. qr., east of Versailles, close to the town. Worked 10 years ago, when Galena was found in paying quantities.

GABRIELLE DIGGINGS,

T. 33, R. 18 W., Sec. 17, N. W. qr. of N. E. qr. Owned by the Gabrielle Mining Company, Dr. L. Pim, of St. Louis, President. On a flat, northwestern spur of a plateau, a short distance from the Upper Richland Creek.

The formation in this flat slope is variable, yet mostly as follows:

No. 1. Soil.

No. 2. 6 to 12 feet red Clay with loose broken Chert and float Galena. The latter occurs occasionally in slabs and chunks of very large size.

No. 3. 20 to 30 feet altered Magnesian Limestones and residuary Clays (Soapstone,) dipping very irregularly, mostly however, with the Slope.

The Limestone is found in places in very large, detached, softened layers, containing Chert seams and forming sometimes the "caprock" of Galena deposits. The latter are generally associated with more broken and disintegrated Limestone, with finely broken Chert and with Clay. The Galena is mostly deposited irregularly, but in some places it is found accumulated in more or less straight lines, extending over some distance. This is especially the case on the north side, where such a "run" of Galena has been followed over a distance of near 100 feet. One shaft in the southern portion of the diggings was sunk a depth of 65 feet, having on one side large broken and in part altered masses of both fine and coarse-grained Limestone, on the other side black (Coal Measure?) Slate with much Pyrites, dipping straight down between the broken Limestone.

The Gabrielle Mining Company does not lease claims to miners but works at its own expense and risk.

The diggings have been worked since June, 1873, with an average of 6 or 7 men. The total production in May, 1874, amounted to 250,-000 pounds of Galena.

PERRY ROSS DIGGINGS,

T. 43, R. 18 W., Sec. 10, S. W. qr. Property in litigation. Locality mentioned in F. B. Meek's report on Morgan county, p. 152. The Galena is said to occur disseminated in pretty hard Limestone. About 6,000 pounds of it was raised during the summer of 1873.

PRICE MILL DIGGINGS,

T. 44, R. 19 W., Sec. 35, E. hf. of S. E, qr. Owned by Henry Kuhlman. Leased by W. M. Coventry and others. The mining is done in the hard and fresh Limestone forming the bluffs on the east side of Little Richland Creek. A large and several small veins in the Limestone, filled with Galena, and Barytes crop out in the bluff. The large vein strikes N. W. S. E., and is very variable in width, 6 inches being the maximum. The Galena adheres to the walls of the vein and sometimes fills the whole of it, but mostly leaves a space which is filled by Barytes. The smaller veins or seams strike about at a right angle to the large vein. A shaft has been sunk 25 feet deep on the principal vein. The proximity of the creek caused a considerable influx of water, disturbing the work considerably. It is, however, being continued. The Galena so far raised does not exceed 1,500 pounds.

OTTEN DIGGINGS,

T. 44, R. 19 W., Sec. 36, in center. Owned by Otten. Leased by Stover, Walker and Leonhard. Several shallow shafts struck some loose
Galena between the sandy Limestone boulders below the red Clay.
Sheets and specks of Galena are seen in a small Limestone bluff in
the ravine. Work began but lately.

STOCKER DIGGINGS,

T. 44, R. 19 W., Sec. 25, N. W. qr. of S. W. qr. Owned by Stocker.
Leased by Stover, Walker & Leonhard. A hole was dug near a spring
and disclosed black Clay and black Slate, with loose crystals of Galena and of Blende. Another hole, dug close by the above, struck red
and yellow Clay. The place will be better opened and investigated
in the course of the present summer.

TWIN SPRING DIGGINGS,

T. 45, R. 18 W., Sec. 19, S. E. qr. of N. E. qr., on Richland Creek.
Owned by John Lewis. Leased by J. H. Robeson of Otterville. Crevices and washed out cavities in the Magnesian Limestone, extending
N. E. to S. W. along the slope. The surface of the Limestone is from
5 to 15 feet below the surface of the ground. The Galena is found
loose and mostly rounded, imbedded in red Clay on the Limestone.
It is occasionally associated with some Barytes. The external indications are all very favorable, but the Galena has not yet been found in
well paying quantity. A small vein of Barytes, $\frac{1}{2}$ to 4 inches thick, is
visible in softened sandy Limestone in the bluff of Richland Creek,
near the diggings. The latter have been worked intermittingly since
the beginning of the present year, with two men. The production
has not yet exceeded 500 pounds.

WEAR DIGGINGS,

T. 45, R. 19 W., Sec. 34, S. E. qr., on Hawk Creek. Owned by Wear
& Thomas of Otterville. Situated on a pretty steep north-western
slope. A shaft has been sunk 50 feet deep, and struck below the cherty
soil, an irregular mixture of more or less softened Limestone fragments, partly rounded, partly sharp, with red Clay and many loose
pieces of Barytes, white and opaque, many of which inclose Galena
in considerable quantity. The broken Limestone masses seem to get
larger and harder with the depth. The galeniferous Barytes reaches
to the bottom of the shaft and probably continues deeper. This place
was worked one month with two men, who made the shaft and produced about 500 pounds of Galena.

ZOLLINGER DIGGINGS,

T. 45, R. 19 W., Sec. 34, S. W. qr. and N. E. qr., a few hundred yards south of the Wear Diggings. Owned by A. L. Zollinger of Otterville, Jennie Sanders and W. Williams. Explorations were made at three points on this ground. A shaft was sunk on the south-eastern slope of a ridge 18 feet deep in loose Clay and Chert, and struck two streaks of small loose Galena, one at 3, another at 10 feet depth. The shaft finally struck hard, shaly Limestone. Worked one month. About 2,000 pounds of Galena taken out.

Two more places were opened nearer the foot of the hill on both sides of the same ridge, and loose, rounded pieces of Galena were found in the Soil and Clay, but struck the solid Limestone a few feet below the surface. The Limestone is shaly in its upper layers. It contains $\frac{1}{8}$ to $\frac{1}{2}$ inches of Galena. Some small holes dug on the summit of the ridge disclosed a red Clay of very favorable appearance.

CORDRAY DIGGINGS,

T. 45, R. 19 W., Sec. 22, N. W. qr. of S. W. qr. Near the Otterville air-furnace. owned by Cordray, Myers & Co. Three shafts are sunk on a steep northern slope near a ravine, the depths of 15, 20 and 35 feet. They met with broken masses of softened and rather shaly Magnesian Limestone, mixed with chert-fragments, Clay and loose Galena. The latter is frequently found adhering to the Chert, and occurs in part in rounded masses, in part in regular cubes reaching 2 inches in diameter. Some large crevices were found to be filled with black Clay inclosing crystals of Zinc Blende. Much of the Chert found in this locality is highly fossiliferous, and has the appearance of being of Carboniferous origin. These diggings have been worked since the middle of August, 1873, with two men, and have produced 6,000 pounds of Galena.

EDWARDS' DIGGINGS,

T. 45, R. 19 W., Sec. 15, S. E. qr. of S. E. qr. Owned by Andrew Atkison, leased by George Edwards. A shaft was sunk in a depression on a south-western slope, 34 feet deep, through yellow Clay and Chert, and struck some streaks of Barytes boulders, but no Galena. Large masses of broken Sandstone are seen a short distance below the shaft near the foot of the hill.

T. 43, R. 16 W., Sec. 19, N. E. qr. of N. E. qr.   Near Excelsior Mills.
Owned by Ratcliffe.   Loose Galena in Clay.   Production in summer
of 1873, is estimated at about 20,000 pounds of Galena.

5 LEAD-ORE DEPOSITS IN MONITEAU AND COLE COUNTIES.

Moniteau county has been carefully examined, and was fully reported on by F. B. Meek, in the Missouri Geological Report of 1855,
pp. 95—120.   Mr. Meek there either described, or directed the attention to the following localities, in which Lead ores were found:

T. 47, R. 15, Sec. 24.   Near a small branch of Howard's Creek.

T. 46, R. 15, Sec. 25.   (Perhaps what is now known as Klinger
Diggings.   See the following :)

T. 45, R. 14, Sec. 5.   On English and Powell's land.

T. 45, R. 14, Sec. 17.   Worked by English, Saxton and Wells.

T. 45, R. 15, Sec. 10.   (Now known as the Mineral Point Diggings.
See the following :)

T. 44, R. 15, Sec. 33.   Near Burrows' Fork.

T. 44, R. 17, Sec. 12.   In the bed of Straight Fork.

T. 44, R. 17, Secs. 24 and 25.   On Smith's Fork.

T. 43, R. 16, Sec. 3.   On a branch of Burrows' Fork.

T. 43, R. 15, Sec. 17.   Near High Point village, and known as the
High Point Lead Mine.

Descriptions of these various localities will be found on pp. 115
to 119, of Meek's Report on Moniteau county.

I will add a few remarks in regard to some of these, and describe
a few more localities which have since been discovered:

Since the publication of Meek's Report, the deposits of Cole county, which will follow those of Moniteau in the present description,
have mostly been found and opened within the last few years.   Most
of them probably belong to the Second Magnesian Limestone.

T. 43, R. 15 W., Sec. 17, N. E. qr., Moniteau county.   Owned by D. C.
Sterling, of High Point.   For Meek's description and illustration, see
pp. 117 to 119, of his Report of Moniteau county.   The Mine was opened in 1854 by Harrison, Berthoud & Co., of St. Louis, and worked until
1857.   It is said, that when left off, their Circular Mine was 90 feet
deep, and 120 feet wide, and that a considerable quantity of Galena
was yet in sight, although this deposit was less rich at that depth than
at a higher level.   At present the Mine is filled with water to the rim,

and used as a pond. It is situated near the lowest point of a high
rolling plateau, on a small branch of Burrow's Fork. The debris,
large heaps of which are seen near the Mine, consist of altered Limestone, Chert, fresh and hard Limestone, Galena, Blende and very little Barytes, the latter associated with and surrounding the Galena
crystals. It is assumed that a common horse-whim has always been
sufficient to keep the Mine clear of water while it was worked.

REED DIGGINGS,

T. 45, R. 15 W., Sec. 12, N. E. qr. of S. W. qr., Moniteau county. Leased
by the "Moniteau Mining Company," of California. A shaft was
sunk 120 feet deep on a flat, eastern Slope, through

No. 1. 15 feet Clay, in which one chunk of Galena was found loose.
No. 2. 15 feet broken masses of soft, yellow Magnesian Limestone.
No. 3. 30 feet, the same, with large pockets of Galena, also with pockets filled
with Barytes and with Clay.
No. 4. 30 feet, the same, with smaller pockets of Galena.
No. 5. 30 feet, the same, with only occasional traces of Galena.

Two other shafts, sunk on the same Slope, were sunk to a depth
of 18 and 28 feet, respectively, and did not strike paying deposits.

All this work was done early in 1874, and 7,000 pounds of Galena
were obtained. The explorations will probably be continued.

MINERAL POINT DIGGINGS,

T. 45, R. 15 W., Sec. 10, N. qr. of N. E. qr., Moniteau county. On a
branch of Brush Creek. Meek has described this locality on p. 116,
of his Report of Moniteau county. Since then, new developments
were made by the Mineral Point Company, of California. One vein
of Galena in Limestone, ¼ to 2½ inches thick, and striking N. and S.,
has been traced by a number of shafts over a distance of 750 feet,
from the foot to nearly the highest point of the Slope. The Galena is
pure and but rarely associated with Barytes. Another vein of the
same character, parallel to the former, and about 75 feet east of it,
has also been traced over several hundred feet. The shafts struck 6 to
12 feet of Soil and ochrey Clay, with some Sandstone slabs and loose
plates of Galena standing upright in the Clay, above and parallel to
the veins, the heaviest part turned downward. Below this is 15 to 20
feet yellow or drab-colored, soft Magnesian Limestone, with numerous
dendrites, alternating with Chert-layers and with some shaly, clayish
Limestone, and containing the Galena veins above described. One
shaft was sunk deeper and struck at 30 feet depth, a layer of very hard
"glazed" Sandstone. (?) (A gray Quartz rock of light-gray color.)
These diggings have been worked since the beginning of the year 1873,
with 1 to 3 men. Total production, 15,000 pounds.

BATY DIGGINGS,

T. 45, R. 15 W., Sec. 4, N. W. qr. of S. E. qr., Moniteau county, on Brush Creek. Owned by the California Mining Company of California, Missouri. Shallow Clay diggings, 5 to 10 feet deep. Worked during two months in 1873, producing 10,000 pounds of Galena.

TIFF DIGGINGS,

T. 46, R. 15 W., Sec. 35, N. E. qr. of N. E. qr., Moniteau county. Owned by J. K. Hodge; leased by the California Mining Company. Open quarry on a north-western slope, showing a face about 50 feet wide and 24 feet high, consisting of immense blocks and broken veins of white Barytes between softened, fine-grained Limestone. Galena is found occasionally in small quantity. The veins seem to continue into the depth. One hundred car loads of Barytes have already been taken out.

KLINGER DIGGINGS,

T. 47, R. 15 W., Sec. 25, S. W. qr. of S. W. qr., Moniteau county, three miles north-west of Jamestown. Owned by Klinger of California, Mo. Several drifts have been made into the foot of a low ridge, and passed through yellow sandy Clay with some Chert concretions, and with numerous large and small, mostly rounded, masses of Barytes, and in places with some float Galena. The mine has produced nearly fifty car loads of Barytes, and also some Galena has been shipped to Eanes & Berry's Lead furnace.

EANES' DIGGINGS,

T. 44, R. 14 W., Sec. 32, N. half, Moniteau county. Owned by Judge W. H. Eanes, of Russellville, and Clark Berry, who have also erected an *air furnace* close to the Diggings. The latter are situated on the northern slope of a high and pretty steep hill. The older Diggings, near the summit, had much float Galena in 10 to 15 feet of red Clay, then struck the Limestone with Galena in seams and pockets. Occasionally, some little Barytes is met with in the seams.

At present, digging is carried on lower down on the slope, where the red Clay is 15 to 20 feet deep, and also contains considerable quantities of Galena. None, however, has as yet been found in the seams in the rock in these lower diggings.

The deposit was discovered eighteen months ago. Total production, nearly 200,000 pounds. At present, it is worked by two to four men, producing 10,000 to 12,000 pounds of Galena per month.

Eanes & Berry's *air furnace* is situated at the foot of the slope, near the Creek. It is of the usual construction, and works almost without interruption, being supplied with Galena from various places in Moniteau and Cole counties. It makes three charges of 1,200 pounds of Galena in 24 hours. Charges of 1,500 and of 2,000 pounds have been tried, but were found disadvantageous in regard to the yield of the ore. The pigs weigh 72 to 80 pounds, and are branded thus : "Moniteau Co. Furnace."

DUNLAP DIGGINGS,

T. 45, R. 13 W., Sec. 5, Cole county, six miles from Centretown. Owned by Dr. M. A. Dunlap, of Centretown. Worked four years ago with two men during twelve months. Production, 20,000 pounds of Galena, found in cavities in the Limestone along a steep slope.

WEAVER DIGGINGS,

T. 45, R. 14 W., Sec. 25, Cole county, one-half mile from Centretown. Owned by Weaver, of Centretown. Steep eastern slope. A vertical crevice, 2 to 3 feet wide, in the Limestone is filled with Clay and fine Chert with some Galena. All these materials have the appearance of being washed down from above, and red Clay is met with in several places on the hill. A few hundred feet north of this crevice, specks and seams of Barytes are seen in the Limestone. Some work was done in 1873 near the above-mentioned crevice.

ELSTON DIGGINGS,

T. 45, R. 13 W., Sec. 35, Cole county. A short distance from the railroad station at Elston, seams of Galena occur in the Limestone. The locality is now being investigated by mining operations.

STREIT DIGGINGS,

T. 44, R. 14 W., Sec. 2, E. half, Cole county. Owned by Streit and others. Several shafts have been sunk 15 to 25 feet deep. The Section is as follows :

No. 1.   3 feet Soil.
No. 2.   6 to 10 feet red Clay with Chert and some Galena.
No. 3.   1 to 4 feet white or greenish gray, tough Clay, passing into shaly Clay, shaly Limestone and not shaly but soft Limestone.
No. 4.   10 feet broken masses of softened Limestone with broken seams and lumps of Galena, generally with more or less Barytes—the Galena adhering to the Limestone or to oolitic Chert fragments.

The Galena is found in lumps, some of which weigh 200 to 300 pounds, with 1 to 1½ inch crystals. The Galena found here obtains a fine blue or reddish tint after being exposed some time to atmospheric influence.

Worked intermittingly for the past two years by Streit Brothers. Production, about 15,000 pounds of Galena.

BOAZ DIGGINGS,

T. 43, R. 14 W., Sec. 2, S. W. qr. of S. W. qr., Cole county. Owned in part by Henderson, in part by Winston; leased by E. D. Boaz. This rich deposit has a nearly circular form and is about 150 feet in diameter, situated near the summit of a flat ridge. Inside the circular outline, loose Galena in red Clay was struck in nearly every place, and in some places very large accumulations of pieces from fist to head size were found, so rich that two men could raise 8,000 to 10,000 pounds per day from some of the shafts. All the richest portions lie in an annular space near the outer line of the deposit, while the central portions yield less. This annular space is from 25 to 50 feet wide and contained the main part of the float Galena in the red Clay with broken Chert. Several shafts, however, have been sunk deeper and, after passing through 6 to 15 feet of the above-mentioned Clay, etc., struck a circular deposit of Galena in the underlying softened Magnesian Limestone, into which they penetrated 25 to 30 feet, at which depth the Limestone gets less altered and harder, and the Galena seams diminish in number and size.

The outer limit of the deposit in the Limestone is formed on the upper or east side at least, by a thick but variable circular seam filled with Galena, and numerous smaller seams run from it towards the centre of the circle, extending from 3 to 10 feet in that direction, but then become very thin or close entirely. As this whole circular deposit gets wider with the depth, it has actually the form of a truncated cone.

Some of the seams contain some Barytes besides the Galena, but most of them are free from it. Various kinds of massive and crystallized Cerussite ("Drybone") are found occasionally in the Clay, sometimes over 20 feet below the surface.

Work commenced at these Diggings on September 1st, 1872, and was carried on very irregularly with a force varying from one to thirty men. The total production amounted to about 600,000 pounds of Galena up to May, 1874.

STEENBERGEN DIGGINGS,

W. hf. Sec. 11, T. 43, R. 14 W., Cole county.   Owned by Peter Steen-bergen.

Some 20 shafts, 12 to 20 feet deep, are sunk in one N. and S. line, down a very flat southern slope.   The Galena is found float in the red Clay, associated with much oolitic Chert, as well as between broken masses of softened and altered Limestone.   Worked at intervals since spring of 1873, by two men.   Production, 25,000 pounds of Galena.

HENDERSON DIGGINGS,

S. hf. Sec. 14, T. 43, R. 14 W., Cole county.   Own ed by widow Hender-son.   On the edge of a plateau.

The Galena, so far as known at present, seems to be confined to an elliptic area of ground, about 80 feet long and 40 feet wide, the main axis lying N. W. and S. E.   All the paying shafts are within this limit.

They passed through :

No. 1. 1 foot cherty Soil, with many long and thin fragments of Sand-stone.
No. 2. 8 to 12 feet red and brown sandy Clay, with Chert and with much loose Galena.   The latter is in some places more accumulated than in others.   No Barytes accompanies the ore.
No. 3. 15 feet softened Limestone, (Calico and Cotton Rock,) with seams of Galena and glazy Chert.

The shaly Limestone occurs in places, and is generally very rich and full of Galena seams.   Calcite is sometimes found.   Worked ir-regularly since 1871.   Total production about 60,000 pounds.

ENLOE DIGGINGS,

N. E. qr. of S. W. qr. Sec. 15, T. 43, R. 14 W., Cole county.   Owned by Ben. S. Enloe.   Situated on a western slope.   The main strike of the deposits is N. E. and S. W.   The shafts are 25 to 30 feet deep, and reach the ore at about this depth.

The General Section is :

No. 1. 15 to 25 feet Soil and Clay, with Chert.
No. 2. 2 to 3 feet "Cap Rock," shaly Limestone.
No. 3. 3 feet "Clay opening."
        (?) feet "Bed Rock," fine-grained, massive Limestone.

No boulders nor broken masses are generally met with.

One deep shaft was sunk on the top of the hill, and passed through:

No. 1. 3 feet Soil.
No. 2. 4 feet Clay, with Chert.
No. 3. 6 feet yellow and red Clay.
No. 4. 4 feet "Cap Rock."
No. 5. 4 feet opening, filled with Clay, Galena and Barytes.
No. 6. 22 feet Limestone, fine.grained, with specks of Galena.
No. 7. 3 feet "second opening," yellow, gray, partly bituminous Clay, without ore.
(?) feet hard Limestone.

These Diggings have been worked at intervals since January, 1872. Total production estimated at over 300,000 pounds. At present they are worked very steadily with 3 to 8 men, the production being between 5,000 to 10,000 pounds of Galena per month.

DOOGAN DIGGINGS,

S. E. qr. of S. W. qr. Sec. 15, T. 43, R. 14 W., Cole county. On old Chouteau lands. Some residents, however, have tax titles on various portions.

The Diggings are on a S. E. slope. A run of loose Galena in red and yellow Clay, with both hard and rotten Chert fragments. Strikes about E. to W.

Galeniferous cavities in the soft Limestone are connected with it. Worked the last 2 to 3 months with two men. Production 25,000 pounds of Galena.

EUREKA SCOTT DIGGINGS,

S. E. qr. of N. E. qr. Sec. 23, T. 43, R. 14 W., owned by the Eureka Mining Company; and S. W. qr. of N. E. qr., owned by the Pioneer Mining and Smelting Company.

Both companies are mining different portions of one and the same deposit, situated in the south-west corner of Cole county, one mile north of Pratt's Mill, on Brush Creek.

The deposit is circular, and each company owns about one-half of it. It lies near the southern edge of a broad ridge. Fig. C gives a vertical section through the centre of the "circle," and is principally intended to show the distribution of the ore in the circle, and the relative position of the whole deposit to the surrounding strata of softened Limestone.

G S—36

The circle has a diameter of 110 feet at the upper edge of the deposit, and widens out conically so as to reach a diameter of about 130 feet at a depth of 65 feet. The surrounding, somewhat altered Limestone, is plainly stratified with a dip toward the north. The same stratification and dip can be observed in the least altered central portions of the deposit. The conical wall is in some places very marked, and has then a seam of Galena adhering to it. In other places, it is less distinct. Seams of Galena extend sometimes from the wall into the surrounding strata outside. Inside of the wall the whole mass of rock is strongly altered and broken, and mixed, especially near the wall, where also by far the largest masses of Galena are found in broken veins and irregular pockets associated with Barytes. This rich district along the wall, is the richest on the south side, and is there 15 feet wide in the average, although very variable, as is to be seen from the sketch. In some places, the fifth part, or 20 per cent. of the whole mass is Galena. On the north side this rich district is only about 5 feet wide, and contains 5 to 10 per cent. of Galena. The whole central portion of the deposit is broken up into large blocks, with thin and thick broken Galena seams, but is much less rich than the district along the wall.

The mining operations have been carried to a depth of 65 feet. Explorations made into a greater depth have shown that the rock becomes harder, less altered, and less broken, and contains much less Galena, either in single seams or locally in a disseminated form; also as sheets between the strata.

Barytes occurs in large quantity with the Galena, in this deposit, in thick, broken veins, sometimes 5 to 8 inches wide. The Galena seams also reach a thickness of 4 and 5 inches, and crystals are found of 3 inches diameter. Some little Zinc Blende occurs occasionally with the Galena and surrounded with Barytes. It seems to increase somewhat in quantity with the depth.

The Eureka Mining Company has all the cleaning and washing of the ore done by hand, and smelts its ore in its own Eureka air-furnace, located at a short distance from the mine. The Company also buys ore from the Boaz and other Diggings, and has smelted near 500,000 pounds of Galena within six months.

The Pioneer Mining and Smelting Company has the cleaning of the coarser lumps of Galena ("block mineral") done by hand, while all the ore much mixed with Barytes or Limestone is crushed, jigged and washed in a small but elaborate ore-dressing establishment, erected near Pratt's Mill, close to the Pratt's Mill Air-furnace, owned by the same Company. This establishment, which seems to do good service, contain two cast-iron rollers for crushing, a chain-pump for hoisting,

two large double jigs, and a rotary hearth for washing, all driven by a
moveable steam engine. This establishment produces from 1000 to
2700 pounds of Galena in 10 hours. The furnace smelts the cleaned
Galena.

As regards the production of the Eureka Scott Diggings, I owe
the following statements to Mr. C. Norfleet, of the Eureka Company
and to Mr. Hacker, local superintendent of the Pioneer Company :

The Eureka Company produced, from January 27, until September
12, 1873, about 267,000 pounds of clean Galena, 8 to 10 men being at
work pretty steadily.

The Pioneer Company produced from this mine, in the year 1872,
which was the best year :

> Large, hand-cleaned Galena ("block mineral").................... 337,000 pounds.
> Adding to this the amount of Galena washed out of the
>   "wash-dirt," at the dressing establishment, estimated
>   at about.. 150,000 pounds.
>
>   The total production in 1872 was......................... 487,000 pounds.

At present the Pioneer Company employ 7 men, producing 1125
pounds of Galena per day, the " wash-dirt " not included, which may
contain 200 to 250 pounds more daily.

The Eureka Scott Diggings were first opened in August, 1871, and
their total production during the last $2\frac{1}{2}$ years, from both companies
together, may amount to about 2,000,000 pounds of Galena.

WHITE'S DIGGINGS,

T. 43, R. 14 W., Sec. 25, Cole county, owned by J. D. White, of Jefferson City. Worked since March, 1873, with the purpose of investigating the ground. Worked at present with 3 men. Total production
estimated at 5,000 pounds of Galena.

WINNUP DIGGINGS,

T. 43, R. 14 W., Sec. 25, Cole county, $\frac{1}{4}$ mile south-east of Pratt's Mill,
owned by D. Winnup. It has been worked during the past 3 years.
Production estimated at 75,000 pounds of Galena. Not worked at
present.

JUNGMEYER DIGGINGS,

T. 44, R. 13 W., Sec. 29, N. W. qr., Cole county, a few hundred yards
from Fluegel's house, north-west of Stringtown. Some holes, 6 to 8

feet deep, were dug in a small water-run, in fine broken Chert, Sand and Clay, and 2 to 3000 pounds of loose Galena, small and large, were raised. Not worked now. There are indications of Galena on several other points in that neighborhood.

RAPP DIGGINGS,

T. 43, R. 13 W., Sec. 3, N. W. qr., Cole county, close to G. Rapp's house, near Stringtown. Small, loose Galena was at first found in a small ravine, at the foot of a flat south-western Slope. Several Shafts, 12 feet deep, were sunk on the Slope, penetrating through Soil, with broken Sandstone, red Clay, with some Chert-fragments and float Galena, without any Barytes. This Clay was 3 to 5 feet thick. The Galena is generally from pea to fist-size, and frequently coated. Below the Clay broken masses of altered, soft Limestone, with brown specks and dendrites, and in places thick seams of Galena was struck. One shaft is being sunk deeper. This locality has been worked at intervals for 2 years. Total production about 40,000 pounds of Galena.

BLOCKBERGER DIGGINGS,

T. 43, R. 13 W., Sec. 3, Cole county, ¼ mile east of Rapp's, owned by Adam Blockberger. Many shallow holes are dug on a flat, western Slope. They met with yellow Clay below the Soil, and pieces of Sandstone, and of softened, colored Chert, the latter apparently passing into the yellow and red Clay. Loose Galena in the Clay, and numerous fragments of oolitic Chert in Soil and Clay. Worked irregularly during the past year. Production estimated at 10,000 pounds.

Several other places in the vicinity and south of Stringtown have a very favorable appearance.

FOWLER DIGGINGS,

Near Brazito, Cole county.

BELCH DIGGINGS,

T. 42, R. 13 W., 3 miles east of Smith's Circle, (see fol.,) Cole county.

GOETZ DIGGINGS,

T. 42, R. 12 W., on Bois Brule Creek, Cole county.

SMITH'S CIRCLE,

T. 42, R. 13 W., Sec. 28, N. E. qr. of S. E. qr., Cole county, formerly worked by Clark & Eaton, and afterward by E. W. Gaty, of St. Louis.

The shafts are now filled with water. A reliable informant describes these Diggings as constituting a true " circle," or circular deposit, 120 feet in diameter. The only portion rich enough to pay for mining was along the outline, on an annular space of ground of the above exterior diameter, and 15 feet wide. The diameter grew somewhat larger with the depth. But at 20 feet depth the galeniferous portions ran out into an annular edge, pointing downward, and a shaft sunk by Mr. Gaty, 75 feet deep, into the solid Limestone, did not reach another galeniferous stratum. Smith's Circle is said to have produced very heavily, some say about 1,000,000 pounds of Galena.

CENTRAL DIGGINGS,

T. 42, R. 13 W., Sec. 21, S. E. qr., Cole county, close ¡to the southern county line, owned by Squire M. H. Belcher, of Locust Mound. At the north-western foot of a hill a crack in the Limestone, containing Clay and loose Galena, was followed horizontally about 30 feet, by a ditch on the surface. Finally a small cave was reached filled with red Clay, yellow Ochre, Chert-concretions, concretions of Pyrites, partly converted into Limonite, and much float Galena. Near the summit of the same hill a shaft was sunk through yellow Clay and Chert, struck the Limestone at 20 feet, and followed a " chimney " or vertical cavity full of red Clay, with much loose Galena. These Diggings have only been worked since 1873. The lower place furnished about 4000, the upper 3000 pounds of Galena.

6. LEAD ORE DEPOSITS IN MILLER, OSAGE AND MARIES COUNTIES.

The Osage River divides Miller county into nearly equal halves, the northern of which contains valuable Lead districts, the southern a rich Iron district. In a few exceptional places only is Lead ore found south, and in a few others Iron ore is met with north of the Osage River.

Most of the Galena deposits of Miller county seem to belong to the Second Magnesian Limestone.

Osage county is, as far as known at present, more an Iron than a Lead county. Lead ore having been discovered exclusively in a small portion of the south-western corner of the county. Lead ore is also found in the western half of Maries county, and some deposits have been opened lately with good success. Miller county has two Lead-smelting furnaces, namely : the Pioneer and the Grassroot furnace.

T. 41, R. 13 W., Sec. 6, N. E. qr. of N. E. qr,, Miller county. Owned by R. B. Hoff. These diggings are situated close to the northern boundary of the county, ¼ mile south-east of the Central Diggings above described, on a broad and flat north-western hill-spur, between two small ravines. Galena was first discovered in the year 1872, as loose pieces in the western ravine. By digging on the slope north-east of this place, a crevice was discovered striking S. W. N. E., connected with numerous chimneys and caves in the Limestone, which contained loose Galena in red and yellow Clay. The shafts sunk on this crevice passed through 20 to 30 feet of Clay with Chert concretions, then struck the Limestone and followed the cavities on the surface of the latter to an additional depth of 10 to 20 feet. The Limestone is fine-grained, more or less altered and soft, and often speckled with dendritic oxides of Iron. Some crystalline Calcite was found with the ore, but no Barytes.

A crevice, striking at a right angle to the one above mentioned was afterward discovered, and by being followed led to the discovery of another crevice parallel to the first, and 120 to 130 feet distant from it, running across the summit of the spur, S. W. N. E., and not unlikely in some relation to a cave existing near the eastern ravine and situated in the prolongation of this second crevice. The latter also is connected with galeniferous cavities in the Limestone. A few hundred yards south of these Lead diggings, on the upper part of the western ravine, a Limonite deposit is observed on the surface, consisting of fragments of good, stalactitic, partly hard, partly ochrey Limonite, one to two feet in diameter, extending about 50 feet along the ravine on both sides.

The Lead diggings have been worked by two men since 1872, with interruptions, and produced from that time until May, 1874, 21,000 pounds of Galena.

T. 42, R. 14 W., Sec. 15, N. W. qr., Miller county. These diggings, which were known for some time past, have taken a great start of late, as I am informed, and are now worked steadily with 10 to 12 men, with excellent success.

T. 42, R. 14 W., Sec. 35, Miller county. Owned by McMillan & Hill. They are situated on high, nearly level ground, and extend about 150 feet from north to south, and 80 feet east to west. The Galena was found 12 to 15 feet deep, loose in the Clay, and again in cavities in the Limestone. The latter lies from 10 to 25 feet below the surface, is altered and soft and in places contains thin seams of Galena. Some Barytes occurs near the northern end of the deposit. The diggings were worked with interruptions by a few men from 1870 until 1873, and have produced about 200,000 pounds of Galena.

WALKER DIGGINGS,

T. 41, R. 14 W., Sec. 5, N. W. qr., Miller county. Owned by the Pioneer Mining and Smelting Company. J. W. Conlogue of St. Louis, President. These diggings, which are the richest so far discovered in Miller county, occupy a pretty extensive district on both sides of a branch of Saline Creek, which branch flows from north to south. On the west side of this branch a hill slope, called Anderson Hill, is covered with holes and shafts which are said to have produced 400,000 pounds of Galena. On the eastern slope we find the old diggings on the so-called Jew's-harp Hill, extending south across a ravine to the north-west slope of the adjacent hill. Their total production is estimated at 200,000 to 300,000 pounds. They join toward the north those diggings which are worked at the present time and whose total production so far may be estimated at a minimum of 200,000 pounds. These latter diggings are spread to some extent over the slope of a hill-spur. Their best and principal part, however, consists in a row of shafts sunk on the slope in an east to west direction. These shafts followed a crevice in the altered rocks and were very productive. The uppermost shafts, sunk on the summit of the spur, struck finally a very large circular deposit which is being worked at present.

The shafts passed through about:

No. 1. 3 feet of Soil.
No. 2. 6 feet of fractured Chert layers, with Chert Sand.
No. 3. 10 feet Clay, with Chert fragments.
No. 4. 15 feet hard, bluish crystalline, Magnesian Limestone, porous, owing to numerous denticulated cavities throughout the whole mass.

This rock exists here in fissured layers. Below it a very large circular "opening" was struck, 30 to 40 feet wide above and getting rapidly wider with the depth and filled with loose, soft and wet red Clay ("tallow Clay,") in its upper part, while the lower part was filled with broken down masses of Limestone more or less altered and softened, mostly angular, with broken veins and seams of Barytes and Galena through and between them. Large cavities between the broken masses are filled with red Clay. The whole mixture contained in its main portion 5 to 10 per cent. of Galena, mostly in thick slabs and chunks. The excavation has now reached a depth of 85 feet, at which depth the deposit has a diameter of nearly 80 feet. The walls are in some places very marked and cut off the Galena; in other places, however, thick seams of Galena run into the pretty hard wall rock. Some of these have been followed to a distance of over 30 feet. Seams of Galena also extend into a greater depth, but the rock seems then to get harder and more solid. Copper Pyrites or cupriferous Iron Pyrites, and some Malachite are often found associated with the Barytes. The Galena is always deposited directly on the Limestone, and the Barytes fills the spaces left and thus surrounds the Galena. Fine, transparent, colorless crystals of Barytes, $\frac{3}{4}$ of an inch long and $\frac{3}{8}$ inch thick are occasionally met with in drusy cavities.

The Walker Diggings have been worked for about three years. Miller is said to have discovered the Galena on Walker's land. Walker sold the land in 1872 to Fox, and the latter shortly after sold it to the Pioneer Company, about 100 acres. The figures stated above may give an approximate idea of the total production, which can not be far from 1,000,000 pounds. The present production from the circular deposit which is the only portion now being worked and in which 7 men are steadily occupied, is somewhat over 4,000 pounds weekly.

The Galena is smelted in the Pioneer air furnace, situated in T. 41, R. 14 W., Sec. 25, N. W. qr., Miller county, on Saline Creek, 6 miles south-east of the Walker mines. This furnace is also owned by the Pioneer Mining and Smelting Company.

BLACKBURN DIGGINGS,

T. 41, R. 14 W., Sec. 10, N. E. qr., Miller county. Owned by Bill Blackburn. They extend over several acres of ground on a rather flat, easttern Slope. The Galena exists loose in red Clay at shallow depths, and also in long subteranean water channels (caves.) The production has been quite large for some time.

TEMPLE E. BELL DIGGINGS,

T. 41, R. 14 W., Sec. 2, S. W. qr., Miller county. Owned by K. G. Martin, of Tuscumbia. Old Diggings, not worked at present.

CURTEY DIGGINGS,

T. 41, R. 14 W., Sec. 11, N. E. qr. of N. W. qr., Miller county. In litigation between D. M. Curtey and the Pioneer Company. They are considered as good diggings.

FLETCHER RYAN DIGGINGS,

T. 41, R. 14 W., Sec. 10, S. E. qr., Miller county. Much Galena is said to have been raised here in 1873.

HACKNEY DIGGINGS,

T. 41, R. 14 W., Sec. 14, S. W. qr. of N. E. qr., Miller county, 5 miles from Tuscumbia. Owned by Wesley A. Hackney. The diggings are on both slopes of an E. W. ridge. The greatest number of shafts are at present on the southern Slope, the surface of which is strongly wavy. The shafts generally pass through

No. 1.   3 feet Soil, with fragments of Sandstone.

No. 2.   3 to 15 feet yellow Clay and broken Chert.

No. 3.   6 feet "cap-rock," altered Magnesian Limestone, in places shaly.

No. 4.   2 to 10 feet red, tallow-clay, with loose Galena and often much fine Chert.

No. 5.   10 to 25 feet "Sand boulders," broken masses of half disintegrated Magnesian Limestone, with broken seams of Galena, with more or less Barytes.

The solid Limestone has not been reached as yet. The depth of the shafts varies from 10 to 50 feet. The diggings occupy an area of about 800 feet long and 400 feet wide. They have been worked since March, 1872, but more actively since February, 1873. The production is very irregular and very different in different places. In one of the richest places 3 men obtained 100,000 pounds of Galena in 14 months. The total production until May, 1874, may be estimated at 300,000 lbs. About 270,000 pounds were raised since February, 1873. From January till May, 1874, 15 men were at work in the average, and produced about 120,000 pounds of Galena, or 30,000 pounds per month. The Galena is smelted partly in the Grassroot, partly in the Pioneer, and partly in Eanes & Berry's furnaces.

GRASSROOT DIGGINGS.

T. 41, R. 14 W., Secs. 23 and 26, Miller county. Owned by James J. Blackburn. The principal diggings are situated on all sides of a pretty steep and high hill. The shafts are, however, the most numerous on the north-eastern Slope. Nearly all of them struck loose Galena in red Clay, at depths from 10 to 20 feet. On the upper part of the north-eastern Slope, a shaft was sunk to a depth of 80 feet, and passed through 25 feet of Clay, so rich in Galena, that 100,000 pounds were raised. The shaft then struck solid Limestone with occasional seams

and specks of Galena, and penetrated 55 feet into it, until it struck a
Chert-layer. As the Galena was very scarce, and the work not paying, the exploration was stopped for the present. Slabs of Sandstone
occurs on the surface of the south-western Slope of the hill. These
diggings have been worked since 2 years ago, and have produced
about 500,000 pounds of Galena. The latter is smelted in the *Grass-
root-air Furnace*, erected in the vicinity of the diggings, and owned
by Blackburn and Johnson. The pig-lead is shipped per boat down
the Osage River, and from Osage City by rail to St. Louis.

WILLIAMSON DIGGINGS,

T. 41, R. 13 W., Secs. 7 and 8, Miller county.

CAPP'S DIGGINGS,

T. 40, R. 13 W., Sec. 12, N. W. qr., Miller county. Near Humphey's
Creek, south of the Osage River. Owned by King & Kirby, of Jefferson City. Leased by Capp's and others. The Diggings lie along a
south-western Slope, near the summit of a high, steep ridge. Large
outcrops of Magnesian Limestone may be observed below the diggings on the same Slope. The Slope round the diggings is covered by
a cherty Soil, below which red Clay with float Galena is found. This
galeniferous Clay extends also into both horizontal and vertical cavities in the Limestone. Sheets and seams of Galena, in hard Limestone, are also met with, but too thin to pay. The Galena is often
found adhering to broken oolitic Chert. I noticed some Calcite, but no
Barytes, associated with the Galena. These diggings are said to have
been worked, from time to time, during the last 20 years. They are
worked at present with 2 to 3 men, irregularly. The total production
is estimated at 30,000 to 40,000 pounds, of which 10,000 to 12,000 pounds
were taken out in 1873. A few hundred yards north of the Capp's
Diggings, in T. 40, R. 12 W., Sec. 7, near the summit of the same
ridge, on the opposite Slope, specular ore is seen in loose pieces on
the surface, together with Chert-conglomerates, and with ferruginous
Sandstone and some Limonite.

JONES' DIGGINGS,

T. 41, R. 13 W., Sec. 36, S. hf. of S. E. qr., Miller county, south of Osage
River. Owned by Lewis Jones. Leased by Charles Himrod. I am
informed that these diggings were worked with good success in spring
and summer of 1873.

SUGAR CREEK DIGGINGS,

T. 41, R. 11 W., Sec. 17, near centre, Osage county, on Sugar Creek, south of the Osage River. This locality is mentioned in G. C. Broadhead's Report on Osage county. (See Reports of Mo. Geo'l Sur. 1855 and 1871, p. 34.) Some work has been done there since by the Pioneer Mining and Smelting Company, which also built an air-furnace called the Sugar Creek Furnace in that vicinity, near Scheiler's ferry. Neither the diggings nor the furnace are at present in operation.

WILLIAMS' DIGGINGS,

T. 39, R. 10 W. On upper Maries Creek, Maries county. This locality was opened in the spring of 1874, and is said to be now worked successfully.

CHRISMAN DIGGINGS,

T. 40, R. 11 W., Sec. 34, N. W. qr., Maries county. This place is mentioned and described in G. C. Broadhead's Report on Maries county. (See Mo. Geo'l Reports 1855 and 1871, p. 22.) Another occurrence of Galena in Maries county is there mentioned in T. 41, R. 11 W., Sec. 20, S. E. qr.

E. LIST OF LEAD ORE DEPOSITS AND OF LEAD SMELTING FURNACES.

A. DEPOSITS.

DIGGINGS.	SECTION.	TOWNSHIP.	RANGE.
Saline County.			
Marmaduke	19	49	19 W.
Cooper County.			
Old Scott	ne qr 26	49	19 W.
Collins	se qr sw qr 19	49	18 W.

Deposits—Continued.

DIGGINGS.	SECTION.	TOWNSHIP.	RANGE......
Benton County.			
White..	nw qr sw qr 28	39	21 W.
Gustka..	nw qr sw qr 28	39	"
Hooper	ne qr sw qr 2	39	22 W.
Deer Creek...................................	e hf sc qr 6	39	20 W.
Cole Camp...................................	ne qr ne qr 32	42	21 W.
Hickory County.			
Carter..	sw qr ne qr 18	38	21 W.
Barytes	ne qr se qr 18	38	"
Stearn's.....................................	se qr se qr 18	38	"
Daniels'.....................................	ne qr 13	38	22 W.
Brown	sw qr se qr 12	38	"
Camden County.			
Ferry	nw qr 5 and ne qr 6	38	16 W.
Murphy	36	39	17 W.
Thomas......................................	21	39	16 W.
Anderson	se qr sw qr 35	39	"
Bruin	se qr 27	39	"
Dayton Williams........................	nw qr 34	39	"
Fielding Clark............................	33	37	"
Morgan County.			
Johnson-Davidson......................	{ w hf ne qr 26 } { e hf nw qr 26 }	40	17 W.
Bond..	{ sw qr sw qr 9 } { se qr ne qr 16 }	40	17 W.
January......................................	e hf ne qr 11	40	"
Granby Company's......................	w hf 30	41	16 W.
Indian Creek.............................	ne qr 26	41	17 W.

Deposits—Continued.

DIGGINGS.	SECTION.	TOWNSHIP.	RANGE......
Morgan County—Continued.			
Doph..	w hf e hf 18	41	16 W.
Madole ..	sw qr nw qr 8	41	" "
Kelsey ..	se qr se qr 5	41	" "
Strong	nw qr nw qr 27	42	" "
O'Brien	17	41	17 W.
O'Brien	24	41	18 W.
Brushy ..	se qr 12	41	" "
Gray Horse	ne qr nw qr 13	41	" "
New Joplin	se qr nw qr 13	41	" "
Caldwell	ne qr ne qr 14	41	" "
Blow..	sw qr 23	41	" "
Wild Cat....	nw qr sw qr 12	41	" "
Proctor ..	nw qr 29	41	" "
Proctor	30	41	" "
Wilson	w hf se qr 12	41	19 W.
Buffalo	se qr nw qr 1	41	" "
Potter No. 2	nw qr 31	42	18 W.
Wolf Den	sw qr 30	42	" "
Ferguson	sw qr 28	42	" "
Simmons	se qr se qr 20	42	" "
Clark	se qr sw qr 21	42	" "
Potter No. 1	nw qr sw qr 21	42	" "
Stover	sw qr nw qr 21	42	" "
Argenbright	se qr nw qr 18	42	" "
Fair	se qr ne qr 18	42	" "
Merritt	sw qr sw qr 23	42	" "
Neilson	nw qr ne qr 6	41	17 W.
Wyant Spring	se qr nw qr 32	42	" "

Deposits—Continued.

Diggings.	Section.	Township.	Range.
Morgan County—Continued.			
Schultze	ne qr ne qr 33	42	17 W.
Spurlock	nw qr se qr 24	42	"
Townley ..	nw qr nw qr 23	42	"
Gunn ..	ne qr nw qr 23	42	"
Morland	n hf 22	42	"
New Granby	se qr sw qr 9	42	"
Gum Spring	se qr 8	42	"
African..	nw qr ne qr 8	42	"
African..	se qr sw qr 5	42	"
African..	sw qr se qr 5	42	"
Versailles..	ne qr sw qr 5	42	"
Gabrielle	nw qr ne qr 17	43	18 W.
Perry Ross	sw qr 10	43	"
Price Mill	e hf se qr 35	44	19 W.
Otten..	centre 36	44	"
Stocku	nw qr sw qr 25	44	"
Trim Springs	se qr ne qr 19	45	18 W.
Wear	se qr 34	45	19 W.
Zollinger	sw qr 34	45	"
Zollinger	ne qr 34	45	"
Cordray	nw qr sw qr 22	45	"
Edwards .	se qr se qr 15	45	"
Excelsior	ne qr ne qr 19	43	16 W.
Moniteau County.			
High Point	ne qr 17	43	15 W.
Reed ..	ne qr sw qr 12	45	"
Mineral Point	near centre 10	45	"

Deposits—Continued.

DIGGINGS.	SECTION.	TOWNSHIP.	RANGE.
Moniteau County—Continued.			
Baty	nw qr se qr 4	45	15 W.
Klinger..............	sw qr sw qr 25	47	" "
Eanes................	w hf 32	44	14 W.
Cole County.			
Dunlap................	5	44	13 W.
Weaver...............	25	45	14 W.
Elston	35	45	13 W.
Streit...............	e hf 2	44	14 W.
Boaz.................	sw qr sw qr 2	43	" "
Steinbergen	w hf 11	43	" "
Henderson...........	s hf 14	43	" "
Enloe	ne qr sw qr 15	43	" "
Doogan..............	se qr sw qr 15	43	" "
Eureka-Scott........	se qr nw qr 23	43	" "
White...............	25	43	" "
Winnup..............	25	43	" "
Jungmeier	nw qr 29	44	13 W.
Rapp	nw qr 3	43	" "
Blockberger.........	nw qr 3	43	" "
Fowler..............	near Brazito	...	....
Belch...............	3 miles east of Smith's circle	42	13 W.
Goetz...............	on Bois Brule Creek	42	12 W.
Smith's Circle......	ne qr se qr 28	42	13 W.
Central	se qr 21	42	" "

Deposits—Continued.

DIGGINGS.	SECTION.	TOWNSHIP.	RANGE.
Miller County.			
Hoff	ne qr ne qr 6	41	13 W.
Clay	nw qr 15	42	14 W.
McMillan	35	42	" "
Walker	e hf nw qr 5	41	" "
Blackburn	ne qr 10	41	" "
Temple E. Bell	sw qr 2	41	" "
Curtey	w hf 11	41	" "
Fletcher Ryan	se qr 10	41	" "
Hackney	sw qr ne qr 14	41	" "
Grassroot	23 and 26	41	" "
Williamson	7 and 8	41	13 W.
Capps	nw qr 12	40	" "
Jones	se qr 36	41	" "
Osage County.			
Sugar Creek	near centre 17	41	11 W.
Maries County.			
Williams	on upper Maries Creek	39	10 W.
Chrisman	nw qr 34	40	11 W.

B. FURNACES.

FURNACES.	SECTION.	TOWNSHIP.	RANGE......
Saline County.			
Marmaduke Air Furnace......................	19	49	19 W.
Cooper County.			
Old Scott Air Furnace..................................	26	49	19 W.
Collins Air Furnace. (Brand: "C. & Co., Mo.")	19	49	18 W.
Camden County.			
Linn Creek Air Furnace...............................	25	39	17 W.
Morgan County.			
Clark's Air Furnace..................................	21	42	18 W.
Bond's Air Furnace	16	40	17 W.
Wyant Spring Air Furnace............................	32	42	"
Handlin Air Furnace..........	9	42	"
Buffalo Air Furnace................................	1	41	19 W.
Otterville Air Furnace...............................	21	45	"
O'Brien's Scotch Hearth............................	17	41	17 W.
Moniteau County.			
* Eanes & Berry Air Furnace	w hf 32	44	14 W.
Cole County.			
Eureka Air Furnace.................................	se qr nw qr 23	43	14 W.
Pratt's Mill Air Furnace............................	ne qr 26	43	"
Miller County.			
Pioneer Air Furnace	nw qr 25	41	14 W.
Grassroot Air Furnace	se qr sw qr 23	41	"

CHAPTER XXXIII.

PRACTICAL RULES FOR JUDGING OF AND FOR DEVELOPING DEPOSITS OF IRON ORE IN MISSOURI.

BY ADOLF SCHMIDT, PH. D.

In the perusal of my treatise on the Iron ores of Missouri, con - tained in the Geological Reports for 1872 of this State, it has been noticed undoubtedly that, generally speaking, no practical conclu- sions for the miner or smelter were drawn in that treatise from the observed geological facts, and from the results of the numerous che- mical analyses, and that it was avoided even to draw such conclusions in places where they would have come in naturally. The reason of this is that I had intended to spare all the practical results, as much as possible, for two separate chapters; one for the miner or land owner, and another for the smelter, which chapter were to be appended to, and to conclude the treatise. As the time allowed to me last year for preparing my report was too limited to enable me to add these chap- ters, I will now present them to the public. The one will give practi- cal rules for judging of, and for developing deposits of iron ore in the State, the other will treat of the metallurgical properties of the Missouri Iron ores. The former will be principally based on the observations contained in Division C, the latter on results contained in Division B of my report of 1872. As that report gives all the data required for the following considerations, many readers, having already drawn the proper conclusions from these data, will not find anything new in these two chapters. However, considering the exaggerated views often held by practical miners, regarding subterranean treasures, considering the great excitement, well excusable in itself, and the consequent confusion of judgment of many land owners, when they discover some useful mineral on their property, considering, finally, how much capital may be, and how much really has been spent uselessly by injudicious " prospecting," these lines certainly will not appear superfluous.

The observations by which the character and extent of unopened deposits of Iron ore in Missouri may be ascertained or estimated with a greater or less degree of safety, from their exterior appearance, must refer principally to the following points:

1. Character of the ore.
2. Size, shape and extent of the surface ore, or of the outcrops.
3. Character, shape and extent of the associate rocks.
4. General geological position.
5. Geographical and topographical position of the deposit.

1. CHARACTER OF THE ORE.

A careful determination of the character of the ore is of great importance, not only because it is one of the elements necessary to judge of the character and extent of the deposit, but also, in a more immediately economical point of view, because it gives an approximate idea of the value of the ore itself. The chemical analyses published in last year's report show that the specular ores of Missouri are uniformly very pure, regarding Sulphur, Phosphorus and other injurious ingredients; the red Hematites less so, and the Limonites less than the latter. In the same way as the impurities increase the per centage of metallic Iron decreases in these ores. In the great average it may be said that:

Specular ores contain............................ .... 65 ⎤
Red Hematites contain... 60 ⎬ Per cent. of metallic Iron.
Limonites contain.. 55 ⎦

We see that there is a descending scale of value from the Specular, through the Red, down to the Brown or Limonite ores. The difference in value of these ores is, from certain metallurgical reasons, considerably greater than it would appear from the above figures.

I have explained on pp. 50 to 52 of my former report how these three kinds of Iron ores may be generally recognized and practically distinguished from each other by their color, streak and hardness, in brief thus:

Table.

	COLOR.	STREAK.	HARDNESS.
Specular ore..............................	Dark bluish-gray.	Dark-red............	Scarcely to be scratched with a knife.
Red Hematite......................	Red to reddish-gray..................	Light-red............	More or less easily scratched with a knife.
Limonite...............................	Yellowish-brown.	Yellowish-brown	Scarcely to be scratched with a knife.

With the help of this simple table, it will be possible, in most cases, to determine and distinguish Missouri Iron ores. In comparing several specimens of the same kind of ore with each other, darker color, darker streak, greater hardness and weight are indications of greater richness in metallic Iron.

For obtaining a correct view on the character of an ore bank, it is often important to determine the origin of the various ores which origin may be a different one for the same kind of ore in different localities. Such determinations are, however, sometimes very difficult and have to be made with great care. The following rules may guide in them :

SPECULAR ORE

May have originated either in Porphyry or in Silurian Sandstone. The ore from the Porphyry is mostly very hard and compact; that from the Sandstone can generally, with some effort, be scratched with a knife, and is full of small, irregular cavities and cracks, so small sometimes as to be hardly perceptible with the naked eye.

As the Specular ore from Porphyry has not, so far, been found in stalactitic forms, the presence of such forms is an indication that a certain specular surface ore has originated in the Sandstone. As the Sandstone ore undergoes transformations into soft, red Hematite and into Limonite, neither of which transformations has been observed taking place with the Porphyry ore, the occurrence of red ore, or of Limonite, together with the Specular, shows that the latter originated from and perhaps rests on the Sandstone.

We shall see in the following portions of this chapter how important it is, in valuing an ore bank, to ascertain facts as those just mentioned.

RED HEMATITE

Occurs in Missouri either as a product of alteration from specular ore or as an apparently original mineral in the carboniferous formation. These two kinds, although very similar in color and streak, can in most cases be readily distinguished from each other.

The Red Hematite produced by alteration has always a partly earthy, the carboniferous ore a more stony fracture. While the latter can be scratched with a knife without great difficulty, the former is so soft as to be easily scratched with the finger nail or crushed between the fingers. The red ore formed by alteration frequently incloses bright crystalline particles, disseminated through the red, earthy mass. Whenever this is not the case, this ore is either greasy or clayish to the touch, and often mixed with small flakes of white Clay. None of all these characteristics are ever observed in the carboniferous red ore, which is never crystalline or clayish. Thus their distinction is easy.

When fresh or half decomposed specular ore is found with the red ore, the latter must always be considered as produced by alteration.

Although this red ore from alteration is never seen to pass into brown Limonite, and although the carboniferous red ore does this very frequently, the mere presence of Limonite is no proof of the carboniferous origin of the red ore, because the same specular ore which is transformed into red Hematite under certain circumstances, is under other circumstances changed into Limonite; and, therefore, the red ore and the Limonite may occur together in the same bank without the latter being necessarily produced by an alteration of the former.

LIMONITE

May be derived from three different sources :

1. From a transformation of specular ore.
2. From a transformation of carboniferous red Hematite.
3. From original deposits in the Silurian Limestone.

These three Limonites can not always be well distinguished from each other. Yet it may be said that nearly all Limonites having a stalactitic or botryoidal structure, and all those associated with pyrites, or existing as pseudomorphs in the crystalline form of pyrites, are original Limonites. When the pores seen in the fracture of dense pieces have the shape of thin cracks with denticulated or slightly ragged outlines, the ore is mostly an altered specular ore. When the structure is spherulitic, amygdaloidal, or else when it is sponge-like, the ore is mostly an altered red Hematite.

2. SIZE, SHAPE AND EXTENT OF THE ORE.

An untouched ore bank may show the ore either as surface-ore, or as outcrops, or as both surface-ore and outcrops.

The larger in size and the more angular in shape the surface-ore is, the greater is the probability of finding a deposit in that vicinity. This probability increases with the greater concentration and accumulation of surface-ore on certain spots. On the other hand, small, rounded surface-ore spread sparingly over a large area is no sure indication of the presence of a good deposit.

Outcrops of solid ore are a more valuable sign than the surface-ore. The thicker, the more extensive, the less rounded and boulder-like they are the better. Outcrops may have the appearance of veins or of beds, or of rounded pockets or of other irregular deposits. The specular ore alone has so far been found in veins, and then exclusively in Porphyry. But the same ore occurs also in small irregular deposits in Porphyry. The specular ore occurring in Sandstone is found in regular, often very large lenticular pockets of well-defined, irregular basins (?) or elliptical outlines. The carboniferous red Hematite is found in continuous beds with Sand and Sandstones. Original Limonite is always found in very irregular deposits on or in Limestone.

Thus, if specular ore is in some locality found in Sandstone, it must be considered as a pocket, according to our present experiences, however closely it may resemble a vein in its surface.

If Limonite is found outcropping along the slope of a Limestone hill, it should not be judged as a bed running through the whole hill, but as an irregular, though possibly large deposit.

The mania of seeing veins and beds everywhere has led to great errors and loss of capital within the last few years.

3. CHARACTER, SHAPE AND EXTENT OF THE ASSOCIATE ROCKS.

In investigating ore-banks, the character of the associate rocks must be considered of the greatest importance.

I have shown in my report, the relations existing between the different iron ores and rocks. The following facts seem to be well established:

Specular ore occurs either with Porphyry or with Sandstone.

Red Hematite with Sand or Sandstone.

Limonite with Limestone.

Thus, if you find Specular ore on a Limestone hill, without Sandstone, or else original Limonite on a Porphyry hill, without any Limestone in the immediate vicinity of the ore, the deposit is to be considered as residuary or drifted. If you find a circular accumulation of specular surface ore, surrounded by an annular outcrop of Ferruginous Chert-breccia and of brown Sandstone, the latter getting lighter in color as you move away from the ore, you may expect to find a good pocket of massive specular ore, extending over the whole interior of the circle, and from one-sixth to one-third as thick as it is wide.

If you find no regular outcrop of Chert-breccia or brown Sandstone, but these same materials as loose fragments on the surface, round a circular or elliptic accumulation of specular surface ore, you may yet have considerable confidence in the value of the deposit.

If boulders of Specular ore, partially altered into red ore, and showing in other respects the characteristics of that kind of Specular ore which occurs in the Sandstone, are found over the surface of a Porphyry hill, do not expect to find veins of ore in the Porphyry, but consider the deposit as residuary, if not drifted.

It will be noticed that in some of the instances just mentioned, the study and determination of the origin of the ore, is of the utmost and even decisive importance for judging of and for mining an ore bank correctly.

4. GEOLOGICAL POSITION.

The Sandstone in which Specular ores occur in Missouri, has been found to be the Second (Silurian) Sandstone, which has its place above the Third and below the Second Magnesian Limestone. This fact has been established in all those instances in which the geological position of the ore could be at all determined. The chances for discovering good Specular ore deposits in the strata, are therefore more favorable in this particular Sandstone than in others. This Sandstone is extensively represented in the central part of Southern Missouri.

Specular surface ores found on some other Sandstone, or on Limestone, is not so likely to lead to a coherent deposit.

That kind of Specular ore which occurs in Porphyry, is mostly found in the vicinity of the flesh-red Porphyry. This color of the rock would therefore somewhat improve the chances.

The strata of red Hematite occur in the sub-Carboniferous formation, or in the lower strata of the Coal Measures, and their out-croppings will therefore have to be looked for along the border of the

North Missouri Coal fields, from Vernon and St. Clair, in a range across the whole State to Lincoln and St. Charles counties.

The original Limonite does not seem to be connected with any particular formation, but to occur indiscriminately in almost any Limestone, from the Coal Measures down to the Lower Silurian. The study of the geological formation is, therefore, of less value for judging of Limonite deposits.

5. TOPOGRAPHICAL POSITION.

A comparatively elevated position of an ore bank is always a favorable indication. Nearly all the best ore banks occupy such positions. The chances for finding solid and undisturbed deposits are then much greater. A fine show of surface ore in a bottom or in a ravine, or even on the lower portion of a slope, proves sometimes very deceptive, while on high ground it is almost invariably connected, if not with some large deposit, yet with a deposit of some value.

6. GEOGRAPHICAL POSITION.

What I have said (under 4) will show the importance of considering the geographical position of an ore bank in connection with its geological position in certain cases.

It is, beside, important under the following point of view: A look on the ore-bank map which accompanies my report of 1872, will show that all the various kinds of ore banks form richer, as well as less rich districts, the former presenting evidently greater advantages to the explorer than the latter. Of the Specular ore deposits in Sandstone, it may, moreover, be said that they occur in more or less distinct small groups, generally composed of one or two larger and little disturbed banks, and of some smaller and less regular ones; also, that the largest deposits so far discovered, are centrally located within the central ore region. I mention this however merely as a fact. For there is at present no intelligent reason for supposing that such large deposits could not be found in other parts of the region.

As regards the eastern Porphyry district, where the Specular ore partly occurs in veins and beds, it is evident that a deposit situated in the prolongation of the Iron Mountain or Shepherd Mountain veins, or in that of the ore bed on Pilot Knob, would inspire more confidence than one not thus located.

All the various points treated of are to be considered not only in estimating the extent and value of untouched deposits of Iron ore in Missouri, but also in opening and developing them. Much money has been and is yet being wasted by inconsiderate or improper mining operations, partly through miners who arrive from other States where the natural conditions of the deposits may be entirely different from those in Missouri, partly by geologists and engineers who work on the basis of obsolete or of false geological theories. Any person who thinks that every stone he finds on the surface of the ground has been thrown out by a volcano; that every hill owes its existence to an upheaval through subterraneous action, and that all metalliferous minerals have been squeezed into a molten condition from the interior of the earth, must needs conclude that indications of ore on the surface prove the presence of more ore below, and that the deeper one goes the more he must find, because he approaches the source. Such, however, is not the general experience in other States and countries. On the contrary, in by far the most mining districts the ore deposits are limited below or decrease in volume with the depth.

Here in Missouri, quite especially, we shall have to accustom ourselves to the idea that the majority of our ore deposits, both Iron and Lead, were brought into that position in which we now find them, by a gradual downward movement, being originally deposited in strata of rocks which have been long since destroyed or dissolved and carried into the rivers and the seas, leaving the less alterable matters, such as flint and ores, behind. We must accustom ourselves to the idea that the ores, in many instances, have come into their present position from above and not from below.

If, therefore, we find surface-ore in a valley or over a slope, we have to look for the deposit from which it may be derived, not by a deep shaft at the lowest points, but by examining the ground on the upper part of the slope, and to commence digging at such a spot where either the larger size of the surface-ore or the deeper color of the surface-rocks point towards the existence of a deposit of Iron ore. The nearer the summit of the hill we can find such a place the better are our chances for success. Again, if we have found a deposit and sunk a shaft through it, and strike a rock below which is either not ferruginous or is getting less so with the depth, and contains no seams of ore leading downward, we may safely stop operations in that direction, instead of going deeper as has been done on the strength of the theory above mentioned, and in the hope of reaching a larger body of ore below.

We see from the above the great practical importance of geological theories. It is certainly not one of the least duties of a State Survey to correct erroneous and practically injurious views on geological subjects. This must be done by the substitution of better and more natural ones, a process which is neither quick nor easy. For many will rather believe in the most wonderful and supernatural actions and occurrences, than to think one moment that the mechanism of nature might be simple, its ways plain, and its workings, as we may daily observe, smooth and slow, but wondrously steady.

METALLURGICAL PROPERTIES OF MISSOURI IRON ORES.

BY ADOLF SCHMIDT, PH. D.

Iron ores are used at the present time, principally, for two purposes namely, for fettling in the puddling process and for the manufacture of pig iron, the latter of which is by far the most important.

A good fettling ore must be able to stand a high temperature without cracking and falling to pieces and without smelting. It should therefore not contain much water, nor much Quartz, nor any admixture which would be liable to lower its smelting point, as Alumina, Lime, Magnesia, Alkalies. Neither should it contain much Sulphur or Phosphorus. It should be compact so as not to smelt and to dissolve too rapidly when in contact with the iron-bath in the puddling-furnace. It should finally be neither too brittle nor too tough, so as to be conveniently broken into that shape in which it just happens to be needed for fixing up the puddling-walls.

Missouri contains excellent ores for this purpose, especially the Specular ores from Iron Mountain, Shepherd Mountain, and from the Central ore-regions. The last named ores, however, have to be picked, so as to separate the softest ore and to obtain the hard, unaltered ore as pure as possible.

The second and most extensive use made of iron-ores is in the manufacture of pig-iron in blast-furnaces.

In taking under consideration the value of iron-ores for this manufacture, we can not say *in a general way*, which is a better and which a less good ore. But we have to inquire into the special use intended to be made of the pig-iron which we wish to produce.

No sufficient attention has been paid as yet, to this subject, by the majority of our western pig-iron manufacturers, and the opinion yet prevails that a good ore will make good iron, and that good iron can be used for any purpose. This is, however, correct only within certain limits, while on the other hand, irons which may be generally considered as inferior, may be of superior value for certain purposes. The reason for this is that certain impurities which are injurious for one purpose, may be beneficial, or even necessary for another purpose. Sulphur, for instance, is required in an Iron good for the manufacture of cut nails and spikes, because it makes the wrought Iron tough when cold, and because the red shortness it produces, is no great impediment to the manufacture of this speciality. Silicon is required in Bessemer-pig, Phosphorus in foundry-Iron. Scotch-foundry-Iron, for which the highest prices are paid in St. Louis, is one of the most impure Irons made, containing from one to two per cent. of Phosphorus. It is superior for foundry purposes, although entirely unfit for any other use. Another remarkable fact to be mentioned in this connection is this, that the St. Louis Rolling Mills, though having the pure Missouri pig-Irons at their disposition, so to say, in unlimited quantities, have to buy and mix in, impure Eastern brands to make a good Iron-rail.

These examples may suffice to show the necessity or usefulness existing for the pig-Iron manufacturer to distinguish between different ores, and to select and to mix his ores carefully with reference to their composition and properties, as well as to the properties which they are expected to impart to the pig-Iron.

The principal uses of pig-Iron are :

a. In foundries for making castings.

b. In forges and rolling-mills for making wrought-Iron bars, rails, plates, etc.

c. In Bessemer works for making rail-Steel, etc.

d. In crucible Steel works for making tool-Steel, etc.

a. Good *foundry-iron* for remelting has to be in the first place gray and graphitic, and to be fully charged with carbon. It shall contain some Phosphorus, and may contain as much as 2 per cent. of it without serious injury for common castings. It should be as free as possible from sulphur and silicon. The latter can not be avoided in this Iron, because a very gray Iron can only be made at a high temperature, which never fails to reduce silicon in some degree. A very gray coke or Coal-Iron generally contains about 3 per cent. of Silicon. Too much Silicon makes the pig-Iron weak and the castings brittle.

The presence of Sulphur in the blast-furnace prevents the complete saturation of the Iron with Carbon, and makes the Iron inclined to become white, hard and brittle.

The ores fit for making a good foundry-iron should be therefore :

1. Not too compact so as to be easily reduced and carburized.
2. Non-silicious.
3. Non-sulphuric.
4. Phosphoric.

They should be smelted in capacious furnaces, with pure Coke or sulphurless Coal, with a highly heated blast. Very compact or hydrated ores should be calcined.

b. Mill-Iron, or pig-Iron used for the manufacture of wrought-Iron in hearths or puddling furnaces, does not need to be gray. It may be the more mottled or white the purer it is in regard to Silicon, Phosphorus, Sulphur, etc. It is evident that whenever the blast-furnace-materials are so pure and good, that a white pig-Iron produced from them, will make a good puddle-bar, it would be an absolute waste of material, labor and time, in the smelting as well as in the puddling-operation to make a gray forge-iron instead of the white. On the other hand, when the ores and other materials used contain much silica, especially when combined or intimately mixed with the oxides of Iron, or else much phosphorus or sulphur, the pig-Iron will have to be made gray to give a satisfactory product in puddling.

Silicon is injurious in bar-iron under all circumstances, making it brittle when cold and inclined to rot in the fire and to crumble under the hammer.

Sulphur makes the Iron red-short, that is cracking at the edges when worked at red-heat, but it makes it very tough when cold.

Phosphorus makes it cold-short and somewhat brittle, but imparts to it a certain hardness and resistance to wear by friction. Phosphorus also seems to make the wrought Iron hammer and roll smoothly, and, therefore, in a certain measure, and within certain limits, to counteract the bad effects of red-shortness. An Iron may, however, be both red-short and cold-short, when both Phosphorous and Sulphur are present in considerable quantities.

Some Sulphur is desirable in Iron to be used for making cut nails, mentioned above. Some Phosphorus is desirable in Iron to be used for heads of nails, because it makes them hard and durable. Nevertheless, with a few exceptions of this kind, these substances must be considered as injurious. A good wrought Iron for ordinary purposes, should not contain over

0.15 per cent. Silicon,
0.15 per cent. Sulphur,
0.20 per cent. Phosphorus.

The amounts admissable in the pig-Iron will depend greatly as its degree of carburization, and on the mode of conducting the refining processes. Generally a mill Iron may contain about

> 0.2 per cent. Silicon,
> 0.3 per cent. Sulphur,
> 0.5 per cent. Phosphorus,

Without necessarily producing a puddled Iron of inferior quality. Whether an Iron entirely free from Silicon, Sulphur and Phosphorus, would be the best, is very doubtful, not only because Silicon improves the welding capacity, and because Sulphur increases the toughness of bar-Iron, but also from the following more mysterious reason: Very pure Irons, with but traces of Phosphorus and Sulphur, are frequently red-short, perhaps owing to an imperfect reduction in the blast-furnace, and a consequent retention of some combined Oxygen during the refining processes, or from some other cause as yet unknown. However this may be, it seems probable that small quantities of Phosphorus, Silicon and Sulphur, are beneficial to bar-Iron. As Silica is always contained in the smelting materials, not its absence, but only its excess is to be feared, especially when it is intimately mixed with the ore.

Thus the ores adapted to the production of the best mill-Iron should be

> 1. Non-silicious,
> 2. Slightly Sulphuric,
> 3. Slightly Phosphoric.

They should be carburized as little as their general quality will allow, and smelted at a comparatively low heat. The more Sulphur and Phosphorus the fuel and flux contain, the less of these impurities is admissable in the ores. Nearly all the Phosphorus, and on the average about two-thirds of the Sulphur contained in all the smelting materials, enter into the composition of the pig-Iron in the blast-furnace process. The more Limestone is used as flux, and the more basic the slag is, the less Sulphur combines with the Iron.

c. Bessemer pig, or pig-Iron to be used in the Bessemer process, must, as a first and indispensable requirement, contain a certain amount of Silicon. About 2½ per cent. of it are needed for continued success, unless the Iron contains a considerable per centage of Manganese, in which case, the the Silicon may be less. Phosphorus and Sulphur have to be avoided, and neither of these should, as a rule, exceed 0.11 per cent., although pig-Iron with 0.14 per cent., and even somewhat more Phosphorus, may be worked into a good rail-steel under favorable circumstances. Copper above 0.2 per cent.: Aluminum or Calcium above 0.1 per cent., are considered injurious.

An important requirement in Bessemer pig is, uniformity of composition, and as the gray Irons are generally more uniform than the half-gray or mottled, the former are preferred even then, when the latter may be obtained with a sufficient quantity of Silicon, which is not often the case.

An excess of Silicon, say over $3\frac{1}{2}$ per cent., is injurious, and over-silicious Irons have, therefore, in the the Bessemer process, to be mixed with Charcoal Irons, with only 1 to $1\frac{1}{2}$ per cent. of Silicon.

Ores adapted to the production of Bessemer pig have, therefore, to be

1. Silicious,
2. Non-Phosphoric,
3. Non-Sulphuric,
4. Uniform in their chemical compositions.

Ores which are either hydrated, or very compact in their structure, should be calcined.

In making Bessemer pig, all the ores should be smelted with particular care, with pure fuel and pure flux. If the ores are highly silicious, and liable to produce an over-silicious pig-Iron, large furnaces, rather cool blasts, wide tuyeres and a large quantity of blast are to be recommended, so as to reduce and carburize the ore gradually and thoroughly at the lowest possible temperature, while at the same time accelerating the smelting operation, thus to prevent the reduction of too much Silica. If either the ores or the fuel contain Sulphur in objectionable quantity, the highest possible amount of a pure Limestone should be used as flux. If this is not sufficient to keep the Sulphur low in the pig-Iron, it will be advantageous, in some localities, to add a moderate quantity of Manganese ore, or of Manganesic Iron ore to the charges.

I know of no means to prevent any part of the Phosphorus from entering into composition with the Pig Iron, whenever it is present in the smelting materials. The latter must, therefore, be carefully watched in this respect, and frequently analyzed.

d. For the manufacture of *crucible steel*, especially for tool steel, the very purest Pig Irons only can be used, and the ores of which, to make such a Pig Iron, should contain Silica, Sulphur and Phosphoric Acid, in as small quantities as possible, and should be smelted with great care, with a non-phosphoric flux, with charcoal as fuel, and as an effective means for keeping the Silicon low, with cold blast.

We have seen above, what kinds of ores are required for the manufacture of the different kinds of Pig Iron. Let us now examine how far the qualities of the various Iron ores of Missouri correspond to those respective requirements.

1. IRON MOUNTAIN ORES.

The Specular ores from Iron Mountain, of which ores a description and analyses will be found on pp. 52 to 56 of my report on Iron ores of Missouri, contained in the Vol. of 1872 of the published parts of the Geological Survey, are very rich, (66 per cent. of Iron,) very compact, moderately silicious and phosphoric, nearly free from Sulphur, very uniform in their physical character, somewhat less so in their chemical composition. The free Silica varies from $1\frac{1}{2}$ to $4\frac{1}{2}$ per cent., and is mostly very intimately mixed with the Oxides of Iron. Phosphorus varies from 0.03 to 0.11 per cent. This substance is principally contained in the crystals of Apatite, (Phosphate of Lime, etc.,) which are found in the ore along the walls of the veins, in some places in great abundance.

For making a good, strong, highly carburized *foundry Iron*, these ores, being very compact and, therefore, rather difficult to reduce, should be calcined and smelted in very capacious furnaces, with Coke or Coal, and with highly heated blast. They may be mixed with softer ores to advantage, as, for instance, with calcined Limonites, or with red and specular ores from the Central Ore Region ; provided that the ores selected are not too silicious nor too sulphuric. When smelted in small furnaces, or with charcoal, such an addition is very desirable to insure a continuous good operation of the furnaces.

The Iron Mountain ores make also a good *Mill Iron*, although wrought Iron made from it is often found to be somewhat inclined to red-shortness, which may be due to the insufficient capacity of the blast furnaces in which it is at present smelted, and to the use of raw Coal in these furnaces, as well as to the use of very sulphuric Coal in puddling mills.

All the ore taken from central part of the different veins in the Iron Mountain, and, therefore, free from Apatite, makes a Pig Iron of sufficient purity to be used in the BESSEMER process. When smelted with Coke or Coal, the Pig Iron takes up a sufficient amount of Silicon to be used in this process without admixture of other irons.

When the Iron Mountain ore is smelted with charcoal, the Pig Iron produced contains less than $1\frac{1}{2}$ per cent. of Silicon, which is not sufficient. Under all circumstances, in making Bessemer Pig, constant attention must be paid to the purity of both the fuel and the flux in regard to Phosphorus, also to the uniformity in size of the smelting materials, and to the regularity in charging, so as to obtain not only a pure but also a very uniform product. Calcination of the ore is recommendable.

To produce Pig Iron for the manufacture of *crucible steel,* the Iron Mountain ore should be smelted with charcoal and under all possible precautions, regarding impurities in admixtures and fluxes.

2. PILOT KNOB ORES.

The description and analyses of the Pilot Knob Specular ores are given on pp. 56 to 60 of my report on the Iron Ores of Missouri, contained in the Vol. of 1872 of the published reports of the Geological Survey. These ores are very compact, variable in richness, highly silicious, very pure in regard to Phosphorus and Sulphur. The latter ingredient is somewhat variable, depending on the greater or less quantity of Barytes, (Sulphate of Baryta,) which is found in the fissures and on the faces of cleavage of the ore. It varies from 0.006 to 0 08 per cent. The free Silica varies from 5 to 12 per cent. in the western and central portions of the main ore bed, but rises as high as 30 per cent. near the eastern outcrop, and is exceedingly variable in the ores above the seam filled with Clay, which forms the roof of the main deposit. If we, therefore, divide the Pilot Knob ores in No. 1 ores from the western and central portions of the main ore bed below the seam, with about 60 per cent. of iron, and in No. 2 ores from the eastern portion of the main ore bed, and from above Clay seam, with 36 to 55 per cent. of Iron, a division which can be carried out in practice, we find that the No. 1 Pilot Knob ores are very good and useful for most purposes, while the No. 2 can be used only for certain purposes in a limited measure. *The No.* 1 *ores,* although too silicious to produce a good *Foundry Iron,* when smelted alone with Coke or Coal, would, however, with charcoal and with proper fluxing, make a Pig Iron to be used extensively in foundries when mixed there with more phosphoric coke Irons.

When this ore is mixed with other less silicious and more phosphoric ores, a very fair foundry iron may be obtained, even with coke and coal as fuel. The Big Muddy Iron Company at Grand Tower, Ill., smelted in 1872 and 1873, a mixture of one-half unselected Pilot Knob ore (which may perhaps be considered as consisting of ¾ No. 1 and ¼ No. 2,) and of one-half Central Missouri mixed hematites (in part soft red, in part specular,) with pretty good results.

The remarks just made may also apply to the manufacture of *mill Iron.*

The Pilot Knob No. 1, being silicious and very low in phosphorus,. is specially adapted for making *Bessemer Pig.* For this purpose it may either be mixed with at least one-half its weight of other less silicious, non-phosphoric ores, and smelted with Coke or Coal, or else it may be smelted with little or no admixture in a Charcoal furnace. The ore should be calcined and broken to pieces of pretty uniform size. Although sufficiently free from phosphorus the Pilot Knob ores are less adapted for making Pig Iron to be used in the *crucible steel* process. The No. 1 may, however, be used as an admixture in the production of such Iron.

No. 2. PILOT KNOB ORE.

See analyses 5 to 8 on p. 58 of my report on Iron Ore of Missouri contained in the volume of 1872 of the published Reports of the Geological Survey.

This ore is exceedingly silicious, so much so as to be utterly unfit to be smelted alone. But when mixed with a large proportion of softer and less silicious ores it will produce a good *Bessemer Pig* and also a fair *foundry* and *mill iron.* The ore should be calcined and broken and well mixed with crushed Limestone and smelted with Charcoal in comparatively large furnaces, with wide tuyeres and with a large quantity of not very hot blast, so as to obtain a quick yet cool run of the furnace. Calcined Missouri Limonites will prove an excellent admixture in smelting this ore on Foundry Pig.

A pig Iron made at the Pilot Knob furnace in 1872 from a charge, consisting of one-third of Shepherd Mountain ore and of two-thirds of a mixture of No. 1 and No. 2 Pilot Knob ore, contained, according to Mr. A. A. Blair's analysis: Sulphur, 0.017; Phosphorus, 0.062; Silicious, 2.624. This is a most excellent Bessemer pig, besides being very valuable as foundry Iron.

The Pilot Knob ores will prove an exceedingly valuable admix· ture in any (especially Charcoal,) blast furnace where there is a difficulty in obtaining a sufficient amount of silicious in the pig Iron, for Bessemer purposes.

No. 3. SHEPHERD MOUNTAIN ORE.

The analyses communicated on p. 62 of my report of 1872, show that the Shepherd Mountain ore is very uniform in its chemical composition, very rich in Iron (66 per cent.), almost free from Sulphur and Phosphorus. It contains 5 to 6 per cent. of free Silica. It is less hard and dense than the Iron Mountain ore and therefore easier to reduce and to smelt, and liable to make a softer and tougher pig Iron. It.

counts among the best and purest Iron ores known. It is actually too
pure and contains too little Phosphorus to be smelted alone on *foundry
pig*, except with a highly phosphoric flux and fuel. It will make an
excellent *mill Iron*, but is especially valuable for all *Steel* purposes
where purity is always the main requirement. Whenever the flux
and fuel used are not very impure, this ore will, under all circumstances, furnish a superior pig Iron for the use of crucible Steel works
as well as for that of Bessemer works. For the latter purpose, especially when smelted with Charcoal, an admixture of a more silicious
but otherwise pure ore, as for instance, that from Pilot Knob will be
advantageous, calcination will be found useful, although less important with this ore than with those from Iron Mountain and Pilot Knob.

4. CENTRAL MISSOURI SPECULAR ORES.

The specular ores occurring in the SILURIAN SANDSTONE of Central Missouri, including the ores from Scotia, Steelville, Meramec,
Salem, Iron Ridge, St. James, Rolla and other districts, are described
on pp. 66 to 85 of my report on Iron Ores, in the published volume of
Geological Reports for 1872. They contain in the average about 60
per cent. of Iron. Nearly all are to a greater or less extent softened
and partly altered into soft red ores. The numerous analyses and considerations given in the published report of 1872, show invariably that
the hard blue, unaltered portion of these ores have about the same
chemical composition as the purest of the Iron Mountain ore, and
may be put to the same uses as the latter. As they are less silicious,
less hard and compact, and therefore easier to reduce, they actually
constitute a better ore. There are, however, but a few localities in
Central Missouri where this unaltered specular ore is found in larger
coherent masses and unmixed with the soft red ore which is less rich
and less pure. Such of the Central Missouri Specular ores as are
mined and shipped at present, consist of hard and soft ores irregularly mixed, and may be said to be rich in Iron, easy to reduce and to
smelt, not very uniform, neither physically nor chemically, moderately phosphoric, as a rule non-sulphuric and non-silicious. The per
centage of Phosphorus is very small in the hard blue ore, but rises to
over 0.2 per cent. in the soft red ore, especially when the latter is
mixed with yellow Ochre. These ores, when properly treated, will
make a good *foundry* as well as *mill Iron*.

The least disintegrated and purest of these ores make a pig Iron
pure enough to be used in the Bessemer process. Those, on the contrary, which are soft, earthy and red in color, must be mixed with
about their double quantity of purer ores to produce an Iron adapted

for that process. The Limestone used in smelting should then be nearly free from Phosphorus.

The sample of pig Iron which I took in 1872 at the Scotia Iron Works, made from Scotia ores with Charcoal, contained 0.116 per cent. of Phosphorus. This figure is pretty high for Bessemer purposes, and yet it is the lowest obtained in any of the Central Missouri specimens. One taken at the Meramec Iron Works and made from Meramec ores with Charcoal, contained 0.165 per cent.; one taken at Moselle, and made from Iron Ridge and St. James ores with 8 per cent. Limonite, contained 0.196 per cent., according to Mr. A. A. Blair's analysis. [See Missouri Geological Report of 1872, p. 43.]

The several Irons above mentioned, like most Charcoal Irons, are low in Silicon, especially the Meramec, which is made with cold blast. In the latter Iron Mr. Blair found 0.942 per cent., in the two others about 1.3 per cent. of Silicon. To make a Bessemer pig for exclusive use these Central Missouri ores have to be selected and smelted with Coke or pure Coal.

5. RED HEMATITES.

The original red Hematites occurring as strata in the Carboniferous Formation, have not yet been mined extensively. From the description and the analyses communicated on pages 85 to 87 of my report of 1872, we see that these ores are very variable in character, composition, richness and purity. All of them will however prove a valuable admixture in the manufacture of foundry pig.

6. LIMONITES.

The Missouri Limonites are described on pages 87 to 92 of my report on Iron ores contained in the volume of 1872, of the published Reports of the Geological Survey. They contain in the great average, 50 to 55 per cent. of Iron. They are moderately silicious and sulphuric. Most of them are rather phosphoric, containing from 0.1 to 0.3 per cent. of Phosphorus. Some ores from the middle and upper Osage River, make an exception, being much lower in Phosphorus.

All Limonites contain from 11 to 14 per cent. of water, and have therefore to be calcined before being smelted. Belonging naturally, not among the very compact ores, they are all made porous and very easy to reduce and to smelt, by being calcined. They are therefore principally adapted to produce a gray, soft, foundry Iron, and will do so with any kind of fuel. When smelted with Coal or Coke, they are likely to produce a foundry Iron similar to the Scotch.

Many Limonites will also make a fair mill Iron, and the Osage ores seem to be mostly pure enough to be used as an admixture in the production of Bessemer pig.

In general, the value of the Limonites as an admixture in smelting the very compact Specular ores from the Iron Mountain district, is not yet sufficiently recognized. If the companies which smelt these compact ores would erect calcining kilns, and mix three-fourths or two-thirds of these hard ores with one-fourth to one-third of good, non-sulphuric Limonites, in a calcined state, they would not only produce a superior quality of foundry pig, but they would undoubtedly also correct in some measure the red shortness of their mill iron.

The following tables will show the respective fitness of each kind of ore for the various purposes. Each series begins with the best ore for the particular purpose mentioned, and ends with that which is least adapted to it. The ores are beside classified in three grades, thus:

GRADE 1.—

Very good. The ore may be used exclusively, or nearly so.

GRADE 2.—

Pretty good. The ore may be used in considerable proportion (to one-half or more) in a mixture with better ores.

GRADE 3.—

Not adapted to the respective special purpose. The ore cannot be used at all for that purpose, or else in a small proportion only.

The Specular ores from Central Missouri, which are all more or less mixed with soft red ores, will be mentioned as " Central Missouri Mixed." In regard to these ores, it must be kept in mind that they are variable, and contain the more Phosphorus the softer they are. In the following classification it is assumed that they consist, in the average, of one-half Specular and one-half soft red ore:

FOR FOUNDRY IRON.

Ores.	Grade.	Remarks.
a. Charcoal as Fuel.		
Limonites...........................	1	
Central Missouri Mixed...................	1	
Iron Mountain..........................	1	Hardly Phosphoric
Shepherd Mountain.....................	1	enough.
Pilot Knob, Nos. 1 and 2...............	2	Too silicious.
b. Coke or Coal as Fuel.		
Limonites.............................	1	
Central Missouri Mixed................	1	
Shepherd Mountain....................	1	Hardly Phosphorus
Iron Mountain	1	enough.
Pilot Knob, No. 1....................	2	Too silicious.
Pilot Knob, No. 2....................	3	Too silicious.

FOR MILL IRON.

Ore.	Grade.	Remarks.
a. Charcoal as Fuel.		
Shepherd Mountain.....................	1	
Iron Mountain.........................	1	
Pilot Knob, No. 1.....................	1	
Central Missouri Mixed................	1	
Pilot Knob, No. 2.....................	2	Too silicious.
Limonites.............................	3	Too phosphoric.
b. Coke or Coal as Fuel.		
Shepherd Mountain....................	1	
Iron Mountain.......................	1	
Central Missouri Mixed...............	2	Too phosphoric.
Pilot Knob, No. 1	2	Too silicious.
Limonites	3	To phosphoric.
Pilot Knob, No. 2....................	3	Too silicious.

FOR BESSEMER IRON.

[Bessemer Iron should contain 2.5 per cent. Silicon, and not over 0.11 per cent. Phosphorus.]

ORES.	GRADE.	REMARKS.
a. Charcoal as Fuel.		
Pilot Knob, No. 1..	1	
Shepherd Mountain......	2 ⎱	Not sufficiently si-
Iron Mountain...	2 ⎰	licious.
Pilot Knob, No. 2	2	Too silicious.
Central Missouri Mixed.................................	2	Too phosphoric.
Limonites.......	3	Too phosphoric.
b. Coke or Coal as Fuel.		
Shepherd Mountain.......................................	1	
Iron Mountain...	1	
Pilot Knob, No. 1	1	Rather silicious.
Pilot Knob, No. 2	2	Too silicious.
Central Missouri Mixed.................................	2	Too phosphoric.
Limonites..	3	Too phosphoric.

FOR STEEL IRON.

ORES.	GRADE.	REMARKS.
a. Charcoal as Fuel.		
Shepherd Mountain.......................................	1	
Pilot Knob, No. 1...	1	Rather silicious.
Iron Mountain...	2	Too phosphoric.
Pilot Knob, No. 2..	2	Too silicious.
Central Missouri Mixed.................................	3	Too phosphoric.
Limonites..	3	Too phosphoric.

FOR STEEL IRON—Continued.

Ores.	Grade.	Remarks.
b. Coke or Coal as Fuel.		
Shepherd Mountain...	1	
Pilot Knob, No. 1...	2	Too silicious.
Iron Mountain...	2	Too phosphoric.
Central Missouri Mixed.......................................	3	Too phosphoric.
Pilot Knob, No. 2...	3	Too silicious.
Limonites..	3	Too phosphoric.

The Limonites should be calcined under all circumstances, but especially when the furnace gases are to be used for heating the blast, or the boilers, and when the furnace-top is closed. Calcination will also prove to be of advantage with the Iron Mountain and Pilot Knob ores, as well as in some measure with the Shepherd Mountain and Central Missouri ores. Wherever raw Coal is used in the furnaces, the calcination may be effected by the waste gases, without additional fuel.

CHAPTER XXXIV.

Prof. G. C. Broadhead, *State Geologist* :

Sir—I have the honor to herewith submit a report of examinations made in the "Lead District of South-East Missouri," during the latter part of spring and summer of 1873.

I would take this opportunity of tendering thanks to Messrs. Scott and Lockwood, of Mine LaMotte, and their Superintendent, Mr. Allen, to Mr. Frank Pratt, of Valle Mines, and to Mr. Fox, of "Fox Mines," at Fredericktown, and to many others, for kind attention and much valuable information.

Very respectfully,

JAS. R. GAGE,
Ass't on State Survey.

LEAD MINES—SOUTH-EAST MISSOURI.

BY J. R. GAGE.

The Lead Districts of Missouri embrace not only the most important deposits of this ore on the western continent, but by the late discoveries of the enormous deposits in Morgan, Newton and Jasper counties, would seem to entitle her to the claim of being ranked as the richest and most important Lead region, as far as yet known, in the world.

Besides the Lead mines of the Mississippi Valley, there are none of much commercial value except those of the European Continent and the British Isles, but neither the mines of Spain, Germany or England, nor any of those in our sister States, have ever yielded within a given area such quantities of Lead-ore as has lately been mined in Morgan, Newton and Jasper counties.

The Lead deposits, besides possessing interest to the land owners, the capitalist and the economist, present in their varied geological distribution, their mode of occurrence as layers, impregnations, *stock werk* and veins, and the paragenesis of associate minerals, a study of especial interest to the Geologist.

The Lead deposits of Missouri are divided into three great districts, Middle, South-west and South-east. I examined a number of mines in the South-east District.

This Lead mining region is principally confined to Franklin, Jefferson, Washington, St. Francois, St. Genevieve and Madison.

I have thought it advisable for a better understanding of the subject, to render my report under the following order of arrangement: Divisions A, B. C.

A. This division contains a general description of the topographical features of the South-eastern District and the geology taken as a whole, then a general idea of the mode of occurrence of the metalliferous ores, the different forms in which they are found, the paragenesis of associate minerals, and as far as advisable the relations which these forms geologically and mineralogically bear to each other and the rocks in which they are found.

B. This division will comprise a detailed description of special deposits, showing the geographical location of the mines, the topographical and geological features of the District, an account of the mining and smelting operations of each mine, with a description of the dressing floors and furnaces, and as far as could be obtained, statistics showing the amount of ore raised, smelted and shipped ; with cost of mining the ore, facilities for transportation, and cost of placing the products of the mines on the market.

C. This division will contain a summary of the Lead mining statistics in tablet form, showing amount of Lead raised and smelted. Then a special mine will be described, showing the manner of the operation and the cost of mining, dressing and smelting the ore ; the various furnaces will be described, and an estimate of the cost of their erection—with some suggestions as to the most economical and judicious method of carrying on mining and smelting operations.

DIVISION A.

This region embraced in the South-eastern District, is very broken and hilly, traversed by ridges not more than two hundred feet in height, but with an occasional knob which rises higher. The region contains a great many fertile valleys, well adapted for agricultural purposes, irrigated by an innumerable number of streams too small for navigation, but invaluable to the miner, as they furnish inexhaustible and unvarying supplies of water for mining operations. If Crawford county is excluded from this district, the Lead deposit would then begin in the southern half of Franklin county, extending west into Jefferson county, with a width of about twenty-five miles, then striking southeast, somewhat increasing in width in the southern part of Washington, but retaining 25 miles as an average width, extending on through St. Francois, taking in the western half of St. Genevieve and the northern half of Madison, making an area of about 25 miles in width by about 100 in length. This whole area is not by any means entirely underlaid by Lead deposits, nor does it necessarily follow that the country lying outside the boundary line of this district is entirely devoid of Lead-ore, for in portions of Iron county, south half of Madison, and in parts of Bollinger, I have seen the occurrence of the mineral, but in such small quantities as not to entitle them to be included in this District.

The geological formation of this district is almost entirely composed of a subdivision of Lower Silurian, known in Missouri as the Third Magnesian Limestone (occasionally capped by the Second Sandstone. This is almost the principal rock of Franklin county, where little, if any, igneous rocks occur. This same Third Magnesian Limestone extends on through Washington, Jefferson, St. Francois and Madison, and fills all the valleys of the Porphyry mountains of Iron county. The formations of the above named counties, (except Iron, which is chiefly igneous,) though principally of sedimentary origin, still contain igneous rocks which are frequently met with, especially as ridges commencing in the southern part of Washington and extending on through the south-western portion of St. Francois into the southern part of Madison. These igneous rocks are more rarely met farther east, but sometimes occur, as in the form of Granite at Knob Lick, St. Francois county, or as Porphyry at several points. There is a Porphyry ridge to be seen cropping out near the Bluff Diggings at Mine LaMotte. The ridge can be traced several hundred yards; it has a strike of N. W. S. E. Porphyry is also to be seen on the railroad at several points above Mine LaMotte Station.

The igneous rocks of this region are older than the overlying stratified rocks; for wherever they come in contact the latter lie against the former in horizontal beds—in most cases with scarcely any perceptible dip, showing no indication of disturbance in position or change from metamorphic action.

Though there have been no changes since the deposition of these rocks from internal action, the changes in denudation produced by the forces of nature, both mechanical and chemical, have been prodigious. The Porphyry ridges have been worn down and ravines formed in their sides, which have afterwards been filled by the washing down of the decomposed mineral forming the mass. Then the Silurian sea came and deposited the Third Magnesian Limestone and afterwards the Second Sandstone was formed. The latter has almost entirely disappeared, but remnants of old beds are frequently found capping the Limestone ridges. Rains and chemical action have worn deep ravines of several hundred feet in the Limestone, thus bringing about a complete change in the aspect of the country since the first deposition of the rocks.

The Porphyries of this region are very silicious and so hard that they cannot be worked to advantage, but the Granites, especially those of Knob Lick district, are of the best quality for building purposes, being of a gray color, very much in appearance like the Vermont

Granite, is easily worked, and as it takes a beautiful polish, is well adapted to ornamental and monumental purposes.

The Limestones of this region sometimes vary much in color, texture and quality. Most of them can be used as rough material for building purposes, while a large per centage is adapted to the manufacture of Lime and Cement. The formation is almost entirely devoid of fossils. I found but a single species, (a *Lingula*,) which occurs in considerable numbers inclosed in a Clay Slate in the Lead-bearing rock at Mine LaMotte.

The Lead-bearing Limestone is, throughout the whole district, very similar in character, more usually of a light-gray, sometimes owing to the presence of a greater quantity of Dolomite passes into different shades of yellowish gray, very uniform in its crystalline texture, though at times so dense as to appear compact, yet the crystalline particles, though very minute, still exists, as can be seen under the glass. Frequently cavities occur both in the dense crystalline and in the more granular portions of the rock, containing crystals of Galena, Copper Pyrites, Iron Pyrites, Calcite and Dolomite.

In its physical character, the Limestone appears to be very uniform throughout the district. Analyses made by Chauvenet and Blair show the rock to contain the Carbonate of Lime and Carbonate of Magnesia nearly in the proper proportion for forming Dolomite.

Limestone from Iron County.

	A.	B.	C.
Insoluble silicious	5.11	3.85	2.06
Peroxide of Iron	4.67	1.07	none.
Carbonate of Lime	47.50	52.50	54.32
Carbonate of Magnesia	42.19	42.56	43.82

This Limestone (especially B) is very similar to the Galena Limestone of Iowa and Wisconsin, as seen from the following analysis taken from Wisconsin Report:

Limestone from Dubuque.

Insoluble	2.46
Carbonate of Iron	1.35
Carbonate of Lime	52.00
Carbonate of Magnesia	43.93

I found it impossible to take different portions of the Limestone series and so connect them as to calculate the entire thickness of the Lead-bearing rocks, and I can only say that we proved the Magnesian Limestones to reach as high as the 300 foot contour line along the ridges; and at a different point, where the country was comparatively level, a shaft was sunk 180 feet before coming to the Lead-bearing Limestone, thus indicating a thickness of four or five hundred feet.

MINERALOGY.

The ores of the Lead district are:

LEAD ORES ....
{
Galena—Sulphuret of Lead.
Cerussite—Carbonate of Lead.
Pyromorphite—Phosphate of Lead.

COPPER ORES......... { A mixture of the Sulphuret and Carbonate.

ZINC ORES..............
{
Calamine—Carbonate and Silicate of Zinc.
Blende—Sulphuret of Zinc.

NICKEL AND COBALT ORES.

There are a great many minerals, as Quartz, Calcareous Spar, Iron Pyrites, etc., which occur associated with the above-mentioned ores, but a description is omitted as they are of no practical importance.

LEAD ORES.

Sulphuret of Lead—universally known to the miners of the West as "mineral." When perfectly pure, Galena contains:

Sulphur... 13.34 per cent.
Lead.. 86.66 per cent.

The Galena of the Mississippi Valley is remarkably pure, and in this State has a specific gravity of 7.3 to 7.6, possesses a very characteristic cubic cleavage, a bright metallic lustre and Lead color. By these qualities it may be readily distinguished from all other minerals.

It is frequently found crystalized in the form of cubes, and occasionally as octahedrons, this is especially the case in the cave deposits, but the most common occurrence is in the dense, massive form, and both in the crystalline form and general occurrence, the Galena of the Mississippi Valley presents a remarkable uniformity. Wherever the crystalline faces have had an opportunity to develop themselves, they have crystallized as cubes without modifications, except occasionally the corners of the cubes are cut off by the planes of the octahedron; it is also the characteristic of the cubes, when found in the caves or Clay diggings, that the surface of the cubes are of a dull, lead lustre, with a rough, corroded appearance. This rule only holds good in the case of the cave and similar formations, for in the cavities of the mineral bearing rock of Mine LaMotte, I have observed beautiful brilliant cubes sometimes plain, and again with the derived forms of the regular system, from the microscopic size to an inch square; besides the cube I saw, but more rarely, the octahedron and dodecahedron. These small crystals are called by the miners "dice mineral," large crystals "cog mineral," and when indistinctly crystallized, "chunk mineral;" where the terms of "sheet mineral" or "block mineral," are applied to large masses of ore inclosed in the rock, or lying loose in the caves.

The ores of Missouri are remarkably free of Silver, as may be seen from a list of analyses made from more than twenty fine specimens taken at different points, and given by Dr. Litton on page 13, Volume 2, of the Missouri Geological Report for 1855, the per centage of Silver usually averaged from 00.1 to 00.2, that is less than one ounce to the ton, being too small to repay for its separation.

On the Continent, where labor is cheaper, ores containing 7 or 8 ounces of Silver to the ton, can be desilverized with profit; and, although the igneous rocks of our State may contain Galena sufficiently argentiferous to justify separation, it can be seen by the analysis made from the Lead-ores of the Limestones, that we have not yet found Galena sufficiently rich for that purpose.

CERUSSITE,

Carbonate of Lead, or more universally known to miners as "Drybone." This mineral is found in considerable quantities in the various mining localities of the world, and is of some commercial importance; when found in quantity, is a very valuable ore. It was at one time mined and smelted at Mine LaMotte, but owing to the large quantities of Galena found, it has lost nearly all its economic importance. When found in Missouri, it is usually in the Lead bearing veins, or in the loose Clay near the surface, and is, no doubt, of secondary formation, being a product from the decomposition of the Galena.

Its chemical composition consists of Carbonic Acid, 16.4, and Oxyde of Lead, 83.6, or 77.7 per cent. Metallic Lead. When pure and crystallized, is generally white, but often gray, brown or black, of a diamond lustre; specific gravity, 6.4. When uncrystallized, it has the appearance of *dry bones*, and breaks with a conchoidal fracture; when found in any quantity, it is usually in the latter form. Very beautiful crystals of this mineral occur coating the Galena in the crevices at Mine LaMotte, but the finest specimens I saw, were found at the Valle Mines. On breaking large cubes of Galena, I frequently found them hollow with the interior walls lined with crystals of Cerussite and Anglesite; these two minerals also frequently occurred in the cavities of the solid masses of Galena taken from the caves at the Valle Mines, but in the latter case the minerals did not posses the bright diamond lustre as seen in the hollow crystals.

ANGLESITE,

Sulphate of Lead. This mineral is in its mode of occurrence very similar to the Carbonate, but more rarely found; like the latter, it is produced from the decomposition of the Sulphuret; when pure, consists of 26.4 of Sulphuric Acid, and 73.6 of Oxyde of Lead, or 68.28 per cent. of Metallic Lead.

ZINC ORES.

The ores of Zinc are quite as numerous as those of Lead, but the former metal like the latter, for commercial purposes, is nearly all obtained from a very few ores, the most important of which are Zinc Blende, (Sulphuret of Zinc,) the Carbonate of Zinc and the Silicate of Zinc.

The ores of Zinc like those of Lead, are distributed throughout nearly all of the geological series, and scattered through nearly every mineral district, but the principal supply of the metal, for commercial purposes, is furnished by a few localities. In reference to their geological position the Zinc ores are divided into two classes: the first includes all of the Zinc ores occurring in the regular veins of the older rocks, and associated with other metalliferous deposits.

The second mode of occurrence, and in fact, the only one of real importance, at least in Missouri, is that occurring in the Third Magnesian Limestone of the Lower Silurian. The Zinc ore deposits of Missouri are seldom found alone, they usually occur associated with Galena in the cave formation. The principal localities furnishing Zinc-ore, are the Granby and Joplin Districts, and the Valle Mines.

ZINC BLENDE,

Or Black-jack, is composed of 33.10 parts of Sulphur, and 66.90 of Zinc.

It is frequently found in beautiful crystals, as in the South-west, and when pure, is transparent and of a white or of a fine honey color, with a resinous lustre; it, however, almost invariably contains more or less Iron, which causes it to become opaque and change to a dark-brown or black color, and it is under this form known to miners as Black-jack.

The Sulphuret of Zinc, next to the Sulphuret of Lead and Iron, is one of the most widely diffused minerals in the West; but as a long and careful roasting is necessary in order to free the ore from its Sulphur, and necessarily the process becoming very expensive, this ore is yet but little used in the West for the production of the metal, nor is it necessary, as the Carbonate and Silicate occur in such profusion, and can be smelted so much more cheaply.

A specimen of Black-jack, analyzed by Dr. Chandler, gave:

Zinc	66.37
Iron	.79
Sulphur	33.41
Insoluble	trace.

100.57

SILICATE OF ZINC,

Known to the Mineralogist as Calamine, (electric,) or Galmei, and to the miner as "Dry Bone," usually occurs crystallized, associated with the Lead ores in the cave formation.

This mineral crystallizes in the Prismatic System, and occurs here in very small, fine crystals, fixed on the inner walls of cavities, whose incrustation are found of the same material, but in a dense uncrystallized mass, has a specific gravity of 3.35, hardness about the same as the brown Hematite, usually colorless, but occasionally passing into different shades of yellow and gray—as at Granby and Valle Mines—generally very transparent, with a glassy lustre. The crystals through heating acquire polarity; the positive pole being at the upper and the negative pole at the lower end of the crystal. When pure, this silicious Oxide of Zinc contains, according to the analyses of Berzelius, 7.5 per centage of water, 25.5 of Silica and 67.0 Oxide of Zinc. This is one of the most important of the Zinc ores, and furnishes a very large per centage of the Zinc of commerce. It is certainly by far the most abundant and valuable ore in Missouri for the extraction of the metal.

G.S—39.

CARBONATE OF ZINC,

Zinc Spar, or Smithsonite, and also called " Dry Bone " by the miners. This Zinc ore is very similar in general appearance to the Silicate. It differs by crystallizing in a different system, (the Hexagonal,) being a half degree softer, less brilliant in its lustre and heavier, possessing a specific gravity of 4.1 to 4.5. It is very readily distinguished from the Silicate, as it contains carbonic acid, and the addition of muriatic acid immediately causes effervescence. When pure, according to Berthier, it contains 35.5 of carbonic acid and 64.5 of Oxide of Zinc. Before the Blow-pipe it soon looses its carbonic acid, and then acts as Oxide of Zinc.

This is probably the most important of all the Zinc ores, and from which most of the metal of commerce is derived. In Missouri it is invariably associated with the Silicate, though not so abundant; is frequently found in crystals, though the largest masses occur in an earthy, friable form, and generally contain impurities, especially the Oxide of Iron.

This Carbonate, like the Silicate, derives its name of " Dry Bone " from its cellular, bone-like texture, which is so characteristic of both when found in the massive form.

The mode of occurrence and general appearance of the Carbonate of Zinc would seem to demonstrate that this mineral is of secondary origin. It is almost invariably found associated with the Sulphuret of Zinc, ("Blende,") occurring as pseudomorphs after this mineral, and frequently gradual transition from the Sulphuret into the Carbonate can be observed in the same mass, without any of the peculiarities of structure being changed. The changes always begin on the outer surfaces, and frequently when the transition has not proceeded through the entire mass. If the piece is broken, a nucleus of Sulphuret is found in the interior.

ZINC-BLOOM

Is another of the Zinc ores. I observed it at the Valle Mines as an incrustation on the Carbonate. It contains 71.28 per cent. of Oxide of Zinc, but as it occurs in such small quantities it possesses no economic value.

SULPHURET OF COPPER

Is found in considerable quantities in the Mine LaMotte property, associated with Lead, Nickel and Cobalt ores. The Lead is separated, and a matt formed of the Copper, Nickel and Cobalt, and in this shape barrelled and shipped to Europe, where these metals are separated and sold at immense profits.

There is no reason why furnaces should not be built here for their separation, thus adding large profits to the owners and wealth to the State.

NICKEL AND COBALT.

Besides the Zinc and Copper ores, the only metalliferous deposits of any importance, associated with the Galena, are the Nickel and Cobalt ores. These ores occur intimately mixed with the Galena, in more or less quantities, throughout the whole formation at Mine LaMotte; very little of the Galena being entirely free from some traces. These two ores occur in two forms, one as a very soft, blue, earthy mass, sometimes mixed with the Galena, in seams, and again cemented in cavities, and again as small crystals in the Clay-slate between the beds of Limestone. The two ores occur as Sulphurets and Arseniurets, and will be more particularly described under a detailed description of the Mine LaMotte Mines.

Nickel is a very useful metal, as it enters into combination with other metals, forming valuable alloys, the most important of which is German Silver, formed by the addition of 8 parts Copper to 3 of Nickel and 3½ of Zinc. As the proportion of Nickel increases the whiter becomes the metal; besides, the proportion being changed, other metals can be added, forming different products.

Cobalt also forms several valuable alloys with the different metals; but its principal value lies in its property of imparting beautiful and various shades of permanent blue to glass-ware.

The Lead ores of the United States are profusely scattered throughout the country, especially in the Mississippi Valley, and have yielded a larger revenue, for the amount of capital and labor invested, than any other metal except Gold and Iron, (possibly the mining of Silver and Coal have been equally as remunerative). Though the Lead ores are widely scattered throughout the country, the paying mines are embraced in a comparatively small district, being principally situated in the two regions known as the Upper Mississippi and Lower Mississippi regions, the former comprising Wisconsin, Iowa and Illinois, the latter chiefly confined to Missouri.

HISTORY OF LEAD MINING IN MISSOURI.

The first excitement on the subject of mining was created by the famous expedition of LeSeur, which passed up the Mississippi in 1700, but active operations did not commence until 1720, when under a patent granted to Law for the exclusive privilege of mining through the Mississippi Valley, Renault and LaMotte commenced their explorations; they were rewarded by numerous discoveries of Lead deposits, the most important of which were the mines of Mine LaMotte and the different localities in the neighborhood of Potosi, but the Company was sorely disappointed in not finding Gold and Silver, which were reported to exist so abundantly, and for which purpose the Company had been chartered and organized.

GEOLOGICAL POSITION OF THE LEAD ORES.

The geological position of these metalliferous deposits, as previously stated, is confined to the Third Magnesian Limestone, (a subdivision of the Lower Silurian) and to the Clay deposits imbedded in the superficial soil, immediately overlying the Limestone; in the latter position the masses of ore are called "float-mineral," and when sufficintly concentrated, pay large returns on the capital invested and the labor expended, but the ore is very irregularly distributed, and this kind of mining, termed "Clay-Digging," is very uncertain. As the "Clay-Digging" of the South-east is such an unimportant feature in the economic Lead mining of that district, a detailed description of this mode of occurrence will be omitted. I have arranged the mode of occurrence of the Lead-ores in this district under the following heads:

DEPOSITS IN LIMESTONE.

I.　"Disseminated ore."
II.　Deposits in "flat-sheets."
III.　Deposits in "vertical-fissures."
IV.　Deposits in "horizontal-fissures."

THE DISSEMINATED LEAD-ORE

Usually occurs in a stratum of Limestone, varying from 2 to 6 feet, occasionally reaching a thickness of 15 or 20. The beds of Limestone are nearly horizontal, usually having a dip of 8 to 10°, but rarely does the inclination become greater.

The Galena in this formation seldom occurs alone, but is usually associated with Iron and Copper pyrites, and at some points in considerable quantities, and in some cases, as at Mine LaMotte, Cobalt and Nickle-ores occur.

Fig. 70, taken at Mine LaMotte, will give an idea of this mode of occurrence.

Figure 70.

a. Represents the roof-rock, which is a dense, almost white, crystalline Lime-
    stone, 10 feet thick.
b. A Limestone 10 inches thick, very similar in character to the roof-rock, but
    containing small blotches of Galena disseminated through the rock.
c. Represents the true "Lead-rock" of this region, here in this cross sec-
    tion given as only 19 inches in thickness, this being the case at the point
    where the sketch was made, but this "Lead-rock" throughout the Dis-
    trict varies very much in thickness, this is especially the case at Mine
    LaMotte, where it changes in a short distance from 2 or 3 feet to 8 and
    10, and at some points has reached a thickness of 20 feet, the whole
    mass of rock containing the mineral in sufficient quantities for mining.
    This stratum besides being very rich in Galena at certain points, con-
    tains Copper pyrites in considerable quantities.
d. Represents a 4 inch Clay Slate, which widens and diminishes in thickness
    more or less throughout the mines of Mine LaMotte; this Slate is very
    interesting, as it contains the only organic remains (a *Lingula*,) I have
    observed in the formation; it is also the depository of the only crystal-
    lized specimens of the Nickel and Cobalt ores. I have observed in this
    Slate, and especially under the microscope, beautiful cubes of Cobalt
    glance, (Cobalt pyrites.) These crystals have a bright metallic lustre
    very much resembling Iron-pyrites, color almost Silver white, with a
    reddish tinge, and when scratched on a rough surface of Porcelain gives
    a grayish-black streak, has a specific gravity of 63, quite as hard as feld-
    spar, not being cut with a knife, is very brittle, and easily crumbling
    under the stroke of a hammer.

This disseminated occurrence of the Lead-ore is probably the
most valuable we have in Missouri, for although not yielding so largely
in a given area as the "Clay Diggings" and "Cave-formations" of
middle and South-west Missouri, the mining is more remunerative and
certain, and the yield more constant.

DEPOSITS IN "FLAT-SHEETS."

There are two ways in which the "Flat-Sheets" occur—one is
a stratum containing the disseminated ore, and is caused by greater
quantities of the ore being concentrated at certain points, presenting
the appearance of "sheet-mineral," but when this is the case the
sheets are of small dimensions, usually a few inches in extent, rarely
extending even a few feet; but more persistent in its extent is the
other form occuring as "sheet-mineral" in a Limestone containing
very little or no disseminated ore, and instead of lying imbedded directly in the rock, the sheets are enclosed in horizontal layers of
"Heavy-Spar" ("Baryta.") The sheets of mineral are usually from 1
to several inches in thickness, and though confined to the bed in which

they occur, are usually constant as far as this particular bed extends.

The layers of "Heavy-Spar" usually contain cavities filled with crystals of Galena, associated with crystals of Quartz and calc-spar, (dog-tooth spar.)

Fig. 71 is a cross section representing a horizontal deposit.

a. Represents the Magnesian Limestone.

b. Eighteen inches of "Heavy-Spar."

c. Sheet of Galena varying from a half inch to 2 inches in thickness.

This sketch was taken at the bottom of a shaft about 30 feet below the surface, near Potosi.

III. Vertical Fissures.

These may be subdivided into "True Veins," "Gash Veins," and " Stock Werk."

a. A true vein is a vertical opening almost invariably filled with a gangue; and if a Lead ore vein the gangue usually consists of Galena, frequently in crystals, associated with Quartz, Calc Spar, Heavy Spar, Iron Pyrites, Copper Pyrites, and not infrequently Fluor Spar, Zinc Blende, Silver ores and other minerals. The Lead ore found in true veins is usually so argentiferous as to pay for the separation of the Silver, and especially is this the case when the vein occurs in the older crystalline or metamorphic rocks.

The "true vein" is the most important mode of occurrence of the metalliferous deposits. Unlike all other deposits, they seldom give out; in fact, I believe, no well defined vein has ever been found entirely terminating in depth, though some of them, as at Freiberg, Saxony, have been worked from the time of the Romans, nearly a thousand years ago, and some of the veins are now worked at a depth of nearly 3,000 feet.

IV. Horizontal Fissures.

The Lead ores of Missouri, when found in a horizontal position, occur in "caves," "pipe veins," and "stock werk."

" Cave Formation."—This mode of occurrence is one of the most interesting to the scientist, and, on account of the quality and quantity of the ore thus found, is one of the most important to the economist.

The "caves" are horizontal fissures in the rock which have neither been produced by internal agencies, as the "true veins," nor by shrinkage, as the " gash veins," but have been slowly produced by the dissolution and removal of the *softer portions* of the rock. The formation in which the caves occur is composed of several beds of Limestone

That bed in which the Lead ores occur is invariably *softer* than either the overlying or underlying strata of Limestone, and consequently water or any solution percolating the rock seeking an outlet would naturally follow the softer and more porous rock as a conductor; the solution acting upon the rock as a solvent would dissolve out portions, until a perfect net-work of horizontal fissures would be formed, passing into each other at every angle, and varying in size from a few inches to many feet in height and width, according to the nature of the rock. After the formation of these caves, which were probably at first open, water passed through, slowly refilling them by depositing the various minerals held in solution. It is possible that the metalliferous deposits were formed synchronously with the formation of the caves, as the same water which dissolved the rock away may have also, at the same time, held the various minerals in solution.

These caves are sometimes completely filled throughout all their ramifications, and again portions will be only partly filled. Both of these occurrences are to be met with at the Valle Mines, while again, as is the case in Wright county, the caves are open and sometimes so large as to admit of a person walking upright. In the latter case there is little mineral, which occurs usually in small bunches or cubes along the roof and sides of the cave. The gangue in the filled caves, as seen at Valle Mines, consists of Galena surrounded by red Clay, intermixed with Calc Spar, Heavy Spar, and detritus from the adjacent rock. Not infrequently, besides the Galena, are alternate layers of other metalliferous deposits, as Silicate and Carbonate of Zinc (called by the miners " Drybone "), and Sulphuret of Zinc, often accompanied by Iron Pyrites and brown Hematite.

This association is frequently met with at the Valle Mines. The accompanying cross section represents this mode of occurrence sketched in the mine.

Figure 72.

a. Limestone.
b. Red Clay.
c. Silicate of Zinc.
d. Galena.
e. Heavy Spar.
f. Clinker Zinc or Drybone.

Fig. 72 is a cross section representing the head of a drift in the Valle Mines. The drift at this point was 4 feet wide and five feet high —some blasting being necessary, as the cave was only 3 feet wide by

2½ feet in height. The ores occurring at these points will be more minutely described in Division B.

At another place, the brown Hematite occupies the place of the Silicate over the Galena.

In these cave openings, mining is carried on with great ease and very little labor, as the contents of the caves are entirely removed without blasting. When the caves are 4 or 5 feet high by several in width, blasting can be dispensed with entirely.

In some of the caves, as at Valle Mines, the Zinc ores occur in such quantities that it pays better to mine for them than for the Galena.

The "pipe vein" and "stock werk" formations were probably originated by the same agencies. They are very similar in character, with the exception that the former is more continuous. In some respects they resemble the cave openings, but differ by being confined to smaller spaces and devoid of all gangue matter, simply containing a deposit of "block mineral."

Mining in these two deposits is very precarious and deceptive, as they are very rich for short distances.

DIVISION B.

DETAILED DESCRIPTIONS OF SPECIAL MINES.

VALLE MINES,

T. 38, R. 5 E., Secs. 7 and 8, Jefferson and St. Francois counties.

The Valle Mines are situated nine miles south-east of DeSoto, a station on the Iron Mountain Railroad. The property, about 4,500 acres, is situated along the county lines—mining operations being carried on in both counties. The principal mining work is confined to about 40 acres on a ridge in Sec. 7. On the north and east side, Galena predominates, and considerable mining is done by miners who sell the ore to the company at a stated price. On the west and south side of the hill the Zinc ores predominate, but are accompanied by large quantities of Galena.

A large number of shafts have been sunk on this and the adjoining hill, but most of them have been abandoned. There are now only three or four in use. The principal one, known as the "new shaft," is 160 feet deep and represented by the following section:

Figure 73, is a Section of shaft at Valle's Mines.

This shaft is 164 feet deep, being 110 feet above the valley; the

floor rock of the lowest cave is consequently 54 feet below the bed of
the valley.

In sinking, the shaft passed through 6 or 7 feet of red Clay mixed
with Chert boulders, then over a hundred and thirty feet of Limestone
of a very hard, dense texture, a light cream shade being the predominating color as far down as the roof of the upper cave; from this point
to the floor of the lower cave, a distance of about twenty-five feet, the
Limestone very perceptibly changes its character, being much softer
and looser in texture, and disintegrates much more rapidly than the
overlying rock, it is also very porous containing a great many cavi-
ities filled with crystals of Calc-spar, Dolomite and Quartz. Besides
crystals in the cavities, the Limestone also shows, especially the portions which have been exposed and partly undergone disintegration,
small but well defined crystals of Dolomite. This Limestone, in
places, is very silicious, which is very perceptible on weathered surfaces, the Limestone in part having disappeared, and the Silica deposited in the forms of grains of Sand. Frequently the Silica is met
in a more concentrated form, and occurs as irregular masses of Chert
or crystallized Quartz, known to the miners as "mineral blossom."
This "mineral blossom" is found in large quantities lying scattered
over the surface of the adjoining hills, having been weathered out of
the Limestone.

As previously stated, there are a series of three caves in which
the mining operations are carried on, but at present the work is chiefly confined to the lowest cave. Formerly a large amount of Lead ore
was taken from the first and second cave, but they have now been
nearly abandoned, not because they were exhausted, but because the
lowest proves to be so rich and the yield is so much greater on the
same amount of labor expended.

The depth at which the caves lie below the surface, depends upon
the point of the hill at which the shaft is sunk.

At the foot of the new shaft, there are five drifts leading off in different directions; these drifts have been openings in the rock produced
by the forces of nature posterior to the deposition of the Limestone,
the openings then afterwards filled by Clay, tumbling rock and the various minerals which they now contain. These caves are one *continuous* opening, observing no general direction, but winding on through
the hill at all angles, continually crossing each other, forming a complete net-work, represented by a sketch of Dr. Litton in his Report
contained in the Geological Survey of Missouri, on Plate No. 9, page
35, Volume 2.

These caves, although at times greatly changing in size, never
completely close; sometimes the chambers are reduced to the size of

a pocket a few inches in height and width, and then spreading out into large rooms 10 or 12 feet high and as many feet wide, but they usually are not less than 2 by 3, nor greater than 3 by 5 feet. These caves not only form a complete net-work of communication in each distinct series, but the three series are connected by *vertical* openings, called by miners "chimneys." These chimneys almost invariably occur where two or more drifts cross each other, though several may cross without necessarily forming a chimney. Another and almost invariable result of the crossings of these openings, is that the caves become much higher and wider, in most instances forming large chambers.

The Limestone in which the caves occur, is entirely free from all traces of mineral, the deposits being confined exclusively to the openings which are filled with red Clay, containing very irregular mixtures of Lead and Zinc ores, the first in the form of Galena (Sulphuret of Lead,) with a few crystals of Cerussite, (Carbonate of Lead,) in the cavities of the Galena, and the Zinc ore principally in the form of the Silicate, with a small occasional quantity of the Carbonate ; also quite frequently small quantities of Iron ores occur as Pyrites and thin sheets of brown Hematite.

Figure 72 represents the occurrence of these minerals; the solid Limestone contains a fissure entirely filled with minerals and gangue ; the minerals are completely enveloped by the red Clay, above are two thin folds of Silicate of Zinc, separated from each other and from the Limestone by the red Clay ; the folds of Zinc ore are sometimes perfectly solid, being from 1 to 6 inches thick, and consisting of alternate layers of the same material in very compact folds ; again the mass of Zinc ore is from 1 to 6 inches in thickness, but instead of being dense, consists of a thin crust, with a cavity, whose interior walls are lined with beautiful, brilliant crystals of the Silicate, and occasionally the Carbonate of Zinc ; more rarely crystals of Galena occur in the cavities, but in this case, are invariably covered with a thin coating of the Silicate, and not unfrequently portions of the cavities are partly filled with red Clay, highly impregnated with Oxide of Iron and has the appearance of a highly decomposed brown Hematite. Occasionally Heavy Spar (Barytes,) lies in a dense mass in close contact with the Zinc ore, but more frequently it is associated with the Galena. Often, but not invariably immediately below the folds of Zinc ore, occur irregular masses of the Zinc ore in the crystallized form, as pseudormorph or Galena.

The characteristic position of the Galena is in dense *uncrystallized* or undeveloped crystals, lying under the Zinc ore; occasionally large cubes, several inches square, will occur, but always of a very dull, lustreless appearance, usually covered by a thin coating of the Carbonate. Frequently crevices occur both in the crystals and dense masses of Galena, and it is in these crevices that the beautiful, brilliant crystals of the Carbonate and Sulphate of Lead are found. The Barytes, (Heavy Spar,) occur in close contact with the Galena, especially is this the case in the western part of the hill. The Heavy Spar, like the other minerals, lie loosely in the fissure, completely surrounded but separated from the Limestone by the red Clay.

Besides this red Clay is another Clay called by the miners "tallow Clay," it is white, very soft, and of a greasy feel. I have made no analysis of either, but presume both are Clays, (the Silicate of Alumina,) the white being more pure, the red owing its color to the presence of Oxide of Iron. On exposure to the atmosphere both these Clays—lose some of their moisture and become very dry and brittle—in a few hours crumbling away to a powder.

Besides the above described minerals, there also occurs quite frequently thin sheets of brown Hematite, (probably a decomposed product of the Sulphuret,) and more rarely, irregular, uncrystallized pieces of Sulphuret of Zinc. I observed no crystal forms of this latter mineral.

MINING.

The ore, on account of its occurring in the fissure, is mined with very little blasting. It is dug out with picks, and loaded into cars, which are run on small trucks to the foot of two different shafts, and then raised to the surface by horse power. Water not being available, steam power is dispensed with, and whims used instead. At the time of my visit, 56 men were on the pay roll, most of them negroes, receiving as wages $1.50 to $1.75 a day. Beside these men, employed by the company, a number of miners were working on the property on their own account, and paying a royalty on the ore mined.

All the ore, except the larger masses of Galena, which is separated by hand, is first calcined in kilns, like Lime kilns, 12 feet high, with grate bars. Two charges of 8 tons each are passed in 24 hours. The charge is made by sprinkling on thin alternate layers of Coal and the ore.

The Zinc ore which is free from Galena, is hauled to De Soto, (the shipping point on the Iron Mountain Railroad,) by wagon, at a cost of 25 cents per hundred, and from that point shipped to Carondelet, where it is treated for metallic Zinc.

The Galena is hauled by wagon from the mines to the dressing works, where the impurities are separated by first crushing, and then washing in jigs and in wash floors. When sufficiently pure, the ore is not washed, but immediately passed through a crusher, and then rollers; is then mixed with the washed ores, weighed, and then placed on the furnaces.

The furnaces, two in number, are "Scotch hearths," and consist of solid cast iron sides and bottom, built on a Limestone rock foundation. The blast is furnished by a No. 6 Sturtevant blower. The engine also runs the dressing works.

There is but one shift a day, consisting of six hours, during which time 3,500 pounds of mineral are smelted on each furnace, yielding in all, 70 pigs at 70 pounds each. Two brands are produced from these ores called the "Vallé" and "Rozier." The former has been picked and dressed, but is not entirely free from Zinc ore. The Rozier brand is very soft, being entirely free from Zinc, and made from the "block mineral."

Beside the two Scotch hearths, there is a blast furnace which is used for treating slags, the refuse of the Scotch hearths.

The Scotch hearths, in producing 70 pigs of Lead, consume each 7 bushels of charcoal, and one-sixteenth of a cord of light wood. The company cuts the wood at a cost of 75 cents per cord, and supplies it to Coal burners, who in turn deliver the charcoal to the company at 8 cents per bushel.

STATISTICS.

It is now impossible to obtain an accurate statement of the total amount of Lead ore produced by these mines, as a perfect record from 1824 to 1854 was not preserved; but from 1854 to 1873, nearly all mined has been recorded, and the following statement, though not giving the total amount, may be taken as a fair estimate of what was mined by the present owners, and furnished me from the books of the company by Mr. Pratt, the Superintendent:

From 1824 to 1830	5,229,146 pounds.
From 1830 to 1834	5,000,000 "
From 1834 to 1839	2,890,959 "
From 1839 to 1845	2,227,495 "
From 1845 to 1850	1,559,040 "
From 1850 to 1854	2,577,137 "
Total	19,483,777 '

During 1854.. 783,407 pounds.
During 1855.. 722,210 "
During 1856.. 534,357 "
During 1857.. 750,000 "
During 1858..1,089,783 "
During 1859.. 644,985 "
During 1860.. 765,600 "
During 1861 }
During 1862 } ....1,145,295 "
During 1863 }
During 1864 } ....1,086,621 "
During 1865 }
During 1866 }
During 1867 } ....1,371,215 "
During 1868 }
During 1869.. 357,425 "
During 1870.. 372.240 "
During 1871 }
During 1872 } .... 842,300 "

                                           13,463,648 "

Total amount—
    From 1824 to 1854... 19,483,777 pounds.
    From 1854 to 1873... 13,463,648 "

                                             32,947,425 "

Up to the year 1869, the Zinc ores were considered of no economic value, and were consequently thrown away; but since that time they have been utilized, and these mines now furnish a large per centage of the ore from which the metal is extracted in this State, and these Zinc ores, at present, yield larger profits to the company than the mining of the Lead ores.

The following statement shows the amount of Zinc ore shipped by the company during the last three years:

From 1869 to 1872—
    Shipped to the Missouri Zinc Company............................... 2,830,640 pounds.
       "   Hesselmeyer.. 1,858,849 "
       "   Beck.. 1,369,031 "
       "   F. F. Rozier... 2,016,468 "
       "   Martindale & Eddy .... 1,298,189 "
       "   Richards.. 872,715 "

    Total amount in three years.......................................10,245,822 "

BISH MINES,

Jefferson county, T. 38, R. 5 E., Sec. 18. These mines are very near the Vallé mines, situated in the adjoining section, on the same range of hills, and is separated from the latter mines by a slight ravine. The general geological formation is very similar to that at the Vallé mines, though the paragenesis and position of the minerals and ores are somewhat different. There are two series of caves on the same level—or three at the Vallé mines. The two series are also connected by chimneys. The Limestone is lighter in color, and more dense and crystalline than at the Vallé mines, and containing many more cavities filled with " mineral blossom."

A great deal of blasting is necessary, as the fissures are very small and contain little or no Clay, but are filled generally with " block mineral " (Galena)—seldom in crystals. The Zinc ore is entirely wanting. Occasionally a small quantity of Baryta and brown Hematite is found. With these differences, the formation very much resembles that at the Vallé mines.

MINING.

The mining is carried on in the usual way, a driller and striker working together. The ore is conveyed from the head of the drifts to the shaft and raised by a whim. When a sufficient quantity of ore is accumulated it is smelted in an air furnace. I visited the mines several times but was unable to procure any statistics in regard to the amount of mineral raised or smelted.

AVON MINES,

Or Saline Valley Mining Company, Ste. Genevieve county, T. 35, R. 7 E., Sec. 12.

The geological formation at this point is very similar to that of Mine LaMotte. A similar Magnesian Limestone occurs, containing disseminated Galena, though the occurrence of the Galena is on a much smaller scale than at Mine LaMotte, the seam of Limestone containing the disseminated mineral not being more than two feet thick.

On extending my examinations into the adjoining Sections, I found wherever the faces of the rocks were exposed, that the valleys and hills were underlaid by the Third Magnesian Limestone, the Limestone on the hills generally being capped by the Second Sandstone. In the beds of streams where the Third Magnesian Limestone has been subjected to the action of water, impregnations of Galena are exposed showing the formation throughout to be the same.

MINING.

At the time of my visit 8 men were employed in an open cut blasting off the Limestone containing the Galena. The superintendent informed me that they averaged in blasting one ton to the man, and each ton of rock yielded 500 pounds of mineral rock, and 25,000 pounds of mineral rock yielded 5,000 pounds of washed mineral. This is 20 per cent., an enormous yield, and I doubt if the yield is so great. In smelting, 5,000 pounds of washed mineral yields 4,000 pounds of the metal. There were 18 boys employed at $1.12½ a day to break the rocks with hammers in order to prepare it for the rollers. I strongly advised the company to procure a Blake crusher at a cost of $1,500, which would accomplish ten times the amount of work as the boys, and as they already had a good engine the rock could be crushed at a nominal cost.

After the rock is blasted it is carried up to the dressing works; here the boys separate the poor rock from the disseminated Galena; the latter they break with hammers into fragments about the size of hen eggs. These fragments are then passed between two rollers and then carried to jigs, where, by a washing process, the rock and lighter materials are separated from the ore. The latter is then crushed very fine under a stamping mill and from these passed to the furnace.

FURNACES.

There are three furnaces, two of them air furnaces and one blast furnace, the latter for smelting the slags of the two former. Only one of the air furnaces was in operation during my visit. Two charges are made in 24 hours. At each charge 1,200 pounds of the ore is put in, from which, on an average, they get one pig to every hundred pounds of ore. The slag from the air furnace is again smelted in a blast furnace, which yields from 8 to 15 per cent of metal.

MISCELLANEOUS.

About two miles distant from these mines, in Sec. 7, T. 35, R. 8 E., is an old abandoned Marble quarry. The rock occurring here is a white, dense, very hard Limestone, containing abundant crystals of magnetite, and traversed by veins filled with a yellow coloring matter caused by the decomposition of the magnetite. I had several pieces polished in Mr. Parks' Marble works of St. Louis, but he informed me on account of the hardness of the stone and the difficulty of polishing it that it was useless for monumental purposes.

In the same section, township and range, on Mr. Brigg's farm, occurs a large deposit of brown Hematite. Boulders, varying in weight from a few ounces to several hundred pounds, thickly strew the ground for several acres. Some of the ore is very much decomposed, forming a soil in places several feet thick. Some of the ore, especially the larger boulders, when broken show a smooth chocolate brown conchoidal fracture and seems to be of a good quality. The analysis of the ore has not yet been made. The property has never been worked, but should the ore prove to be free of Sulphur and Phosphorus, and of a good quality, it could no doubt be worked to advantage, as the quantity is certainly considerable.

I was unable to procure any statistics in regard to the amount of ore raised and shipped by the Saline Valley Mine.

ST. JOE MINES.

St. Francois county, T. 38, R. 4 E., Sec. 33. These mines are situated 5 miles south-east of the Valle mines and six miles from Cadet, its shipping point, a station on the Iron Mountain Railroad. The property embraces 1,800 acres of fine ridge and timber land, supplied by a sufficient amount of water for mining and smelting purposes.

MINING.

The principal mining operations are carried on at a depth of 85 to 90 feet in a bed of ore averaging two feet in thickness. Above this rich bed is an 8 or 10 foot bed of poor rock with some little Galena very thinly disseminated. Overlying this comes a seam ranging from 4 to 10 inches of very rich disseminated ore, making a thickness of 11 to 12 feet of rock to be worked out. Pillars are left at proper intervals to support the roof, which consists of a thick bed of solid Limestone. The rock here is much harder than at the Valle Mines. As so much blasting is necessary the diamond drill is used *in the mines* to great advantage. It is worked by forcing steam down pipes from the engine. Each diamond drill does the work of five miners drilling by hand, being able to drill 25 feet in each shift of 8 hours.

The rock in which the ore occurs is in the Third Magnesian Limestone, of a dark-drab to dark-gray, very much resembling that at Mine LaMotte. The mode of occurrence at this mine and at Mine LaMotte present a remarkable uniformity. The Galena, like that of Mine LaMotte, is slightly argentiferous. Occasionally with the Galena occur as associate minerals, small quantities of Copper pyrites, and, more rarely, Nickel and Cobalt ores. There are 250 to 350 feet worked out.

The ore is moved from the head of the drifts by wheelbarrows to the bottom of the two shafts, one of which is worked by steam and the other by horse power. When it reaches the surface it is removed by cars to the dressing works, and then thrown into a Blake Crusher, from which it drops to a lower floor and is then fed to rollers arranged with levers and comb weights to relieve the strain when large and hard pieces are to be crushed.

From the rollers the fine ore is carried by a Jacobs-ladder to the story above and fed to the end of an inclined, revolving screen cylinder, the fine ore passing through into a trough below, where it is met by a stream of water, and then carried to the jigs in the adjoining building. The coarser particles which cannot pass through, fall out at the end of the cylinder and are delivered again to the rolls. There are six double jigs worked by horizontal plunges.

FURNACES.

The furnaces are those known as air-furnaces, and are managed in the same way as at other mines ; the same amount of mineral put in at one charge, the same quantity of wood and coal used, and about the same wages paid as elsewhere.

I was unable to procure exact statistics, but the mines have been in operation several years, and yield more mineral than the furnaces can smelt. On an average 120 pigs of Lead are smelted each day. From present appearances the mines can not only continue to furnish mineral for the same number of pigs, but the production could be considerably increased, and will certainly continue in its yield for many years.

MINE LAMOTTE.

The Mine LaMotte property consists of an old Spanish reservation situated in Madison county, and covering an area of nearly 24,000 acres.

As this is one of the most important mines in the State, in an economic view, and one of the greatest interest both to the economist and scientist, a more detailed description will be given than has been done for the other mines.

The property is situated 100 miles south-east of St. Louis, on the Iron Mountain Railroad. The principal mining is done at the village of Mine LaMotte, 3 miles east of Mine LaMotte Station.

Extensive mining is now being commenced a mile and a half west of said station. At present all the ore smelted is hauled in wagons from the works to the Station and there shipped. A good dirt road connects the mines with the station. The country being moderately undulating, with no deep ravines or high hills and but one stream to cross, a 3 mile railroad connecting the works and station could be constructed at a small cost.

TOPOGRAPHY.

The mines are situated in a valley surrounded by small hills, the country for 15 miles being of an undulating character. Through the larger ravines several streams find their way, which are utilized by the dressing houses for washing ores, and by the furnaces for running the engines and other purposes. The quantity of water furnished by a single stream is sufficient to meet all the wants of the mines, dressing and smelting works.

The hills, like a great portion of that district, are heavily timbered with a fine growth of oak and pine, in such quantities as to furnish charcoal material for the smelting works and material for timbering the mines for many years to come.

GEOLOGY.

The rock of the country is a hard, dense, highly crystalline Limestone, which forms the beds of the streams, and, in fact, underlies the whole valley, and forms the principal mass of the hills. This Limestone belongs to the Lower Silurian, probably the Third Magnesian or older. It is, so far as I have observed, entirely free from petrifaction. I saw but one fossil in the formation, which was a small *Lingula*. This fossil occurs in large quantities in a seam of Clay-slate inclosed in the Limestone, and usually underlying the disseminated mineral.

The Limestone overlying the mineral possesses many good qualities as a building stone, and is extensively used in the construction of furnaces, foundations for the houses, supports in the mines, etc.

Besides the Limestone there is but one other rock occurring at this point in any quantity, which is a large-grained, dense Sandstone of a reddish-brown color, being highly impregnated with the oxide of Iron.

Besides these rocks, at several points a Porphyry is visible. This rock crops out as a ridge running N. W. S. E. It is sometimes visible for 50 or 60 feet and then disappears, but is again seen some distance on, but always in this same line. The ridge is never more than 30 or 40 feet in width. The rock is a very hard, dense, liver-colored Porphyry, and breaks with a smooth, even fracture. No crystals of Feldspar are seen, but occasionally a crystal of Quartz is visible.

This ridge divides the "Jack Diggings" from the "Bluff Diggings." These two mines are the principal point at which the mining is now carried on.

It is impossible, in a single cross section, to give an idea of all the various modes of occurrence of the metalliferous deposits in these mines, but figure 70 will give an idea of one mode of occurrence, and a very characteristic one. By reference to it will also be seen a description of the geological position of the minerals. The thickness of the mineral bearing rock at these mines varies very much, sometimes not being more than 2 or 3 feet, and again increasing to 25 feet of mineral paying rock.

At the Jack Diggings the shaft passed through 12 or 15 feet of Limestone. Near the foot of the shaft I observed 6 inches of Limestone with no mineral; then 8 inches of Clay-slate; then 10 inches of Limestone with disseminated mineral; then 6 inches of almost solid Galena, mixed with sheets and solid masses of Sulphuret of Copper; then several feet of Limestone reaching down to the floor-rock, but containing very little mineral.

At this point only the 6-inch sheet of Galena and Copper Pyrites paid for mining; but further on the sheet became much thicker, though not so solid. The Clay-slate was filled with small cube crystals of the Sulphuret and Arseniuret of Cobalt and Nickel. This Slate formerly was thrown out as useless, and on exposure has crumbled away to a powder; but the richness of its Cobalt and Nickel ores having been discovered, all these piles of Slate are now being collected and hauled to the furnaces, where the Slate mass is smelted and a matt made of the Nickel and Cobalt.

Going south-west from the Jack Diggings, the formation changes very much; the Copper Pyrites almost disappear, and the Clay-slate seam becomes thinner, until the Porphyry ridge is crossed, when the Clay seam disappears entirely, and scarcely any Copper Pyrites is found. The Galena in quantity and general appearance makes but little changes. The Nickel and Cobalt ores lack in quantity, and in their mineralogical aspects make very great changes. Instead of occurring here at the "Bluff-diggings" as cube crystals in the Clay-slate as they do at the Jack Diggings, these ores occur sometimes intimately associated with the Lead, covering its surface with a soft, blue powder; again they occur in pockets, much more concentrated, occasionally as a soft mass, but generally brittle, and can be easily crumbled by a pressure in the hand. At this point I found the first and only disturbance that I have observed in this district.

The beds of Limestone seem to be almost horizontal, but observations made at different points show them to have a dip varying from 6 to 10°.

A number of analyses made by Mr. Chauvenet, the State Chemist, show the ores to contain a variety of metallic ores. A few characteristic ores I herewith subjoin:

	JACK DIGGINGS.		BLUFF DIGGINGS.	
	No. 1.	No. 2.	No.	No. 2.
Copper metallic...,	13.90	21.00	16.25	1.00
Nickel	3.25	4.50	3.66	18.10
Cobalt	2.00	5.16	4.65	13.90
Lead	37.10	6.40	trace.	17.45

Assay No. 3 (not given here) of Jack Digging, from the 6-inch seam of Galena, yielded pure Sulphuret of Lead, with 4 ounces of Silver to the ton. Assays Nos. 1 and 2, from same Diggings, taken from mixed ores. No. 2, from Bluff Diggings, is from a very characteristic deposit in that formation, the deposit in places being several inches in thickness, and being chiefly composed of Nickel and Cobalt ores, with some Galena. New discoveries have just been made. The assays by Mr. Setz, the chemist of the Company, show some of the deposits to be pure Nickel and Cobalt ores, entirely free of Lead and Copper. One assay gave 38 per cent. of metallic Nickel.

MINING.

The mining at present is not carried on as extensively as it was a year ago, owing to a fire which occurred in the summer of 1872, which destroyed 12 Scotch hearths, being the greater portion of the Smelting works. The 4 furnaces now in operation are not near competent to smelt the ore raised by the 170 miners now at work.

At the Jack Diggings, 5 acres of rock have been excavated; the whole mining being confined to one immense room, the vault being supported by stone columns, either left as a support during the mining or built up from the refuse rock.

Shafts have been sunk, and borings carried on over more than a thousand acres, and at every point, showing the same formation to exist, and proving its great extent. Some shafts lately sunk a mile distant, passed through this same mineral-bearing Magnesian Limestone. From these facts, and other data, I am inclined to think the whole valley of this region is underlaid by this mineral rock, having at different points the ores more concentrated than at others.

Owing to the incapacity of the furnaces to smelt all the ores raised within the last two years, a very large amount has accumulated; there now being no less than a million of pounds of the different ores piled up on the surface near the various shafts.

DRESSING WORKS.

The ores are transported from the mines to the dressing works, in small cars, capable of carrying from 4 to 10,000 pounds of ore; the mines being much higher than the works, the cars are carried down by their own weight. The Nickel and Cobalt ores are not washed, but alternate layers of the ore and charcoal are placed on a log-heap and then roasted. When they have been sufficiently long subjected to heat to free them of the Sulphur, they are smelted in a blast-furnace, which produces a matt of Nickel and Cobalt, some little Copper and usually traces of Lead. This matt is broken up into fragments of several pounds weight, and then barrelled, and in this form shipped East and to Europe, where refining works separate the Nickel and Cobalt. The matt is worth at the railroad about 75 cents a pound.

When the rock chiefly contains Galena, with a small per centage of the other ores, it is taken to the dressing works, where it is crushed in a Blake-crusher, and then reduced to a powder by being passed through rollers and then washed.

A description of the washing apparatus will be omitted as the old works had been removed and new ones were in process of erection during my visit.

FURNACES.

At present there are 4 furnaces in operation—2 Scotch hearths, 1 blast furnace and 1 furnace for smelting the Nickel and Cobalt ores.

On the 1st of January, as an experiment, 53,000 pounds of ore were smelted with washing, and yielded 37 per cent. of metallic Lead, and also a matt of Nickel and Cobalt, which sold at the rate of $68.00 a thousand pounds, making the ore, before smelting, worth 7 cents.

At present the Company is very much interested in experimenting with furnaces for the reduction of the Nickel and Cobalt ores, but they, notwithstanding, smelt from 6 to 800 pigs a week, weighing 80 pounds, and ship, on an average, 30 to 40 barrels of matt a week, weighing from 12 to 1500 pounds per barrel.

Statistics.

From June 1 to December 31.	Dressed mineral	No. Pigs.	Weight of pig.
1868...	3,122,118	23,398	} 70 pounds.
1869...	6,699,800	62,504	
1871...	15,853,100	44,643	} 80 pounds,
1872...	5,511,600	39,912	
Total.................................	32,186,618	170,457	

Was unable to procure any statistics previous to 1868.

COPPER MINES.

These works belong to the Mine LaMotte Company, and are on the same reservation, situated one and a half miles west of the Mine LaMotte Station. The geological formation is similar to that at the Jack Diggings. The ores are hauled in wagons to the Mine LaMotte, where they are smelted with the other ores. Formerly this mine was worked for Copper, and in the washing all the Cobalt and Nickel ores were lost. The mine not proving profitable it was abandoned, and work has only lately been resumed and is now carried on for the Cobalt and Nickel. The ridge in which the mine is worked extends a mile almost due south, at the end of which is situated the

FOX MINE.

T. 33, R. 6 E., Sec. 12. These mines have just been opened. A shaft of 50 feet deep proves the formation to be identical with that of the Copper Mine just described. There is, at the bottom of the shaft, 20 feet of disseminated ore—the last 7 or 8 feet being very rich. I had two tons of the richest ore crushed. From the two tons, I crushed 100 pounds still finer, and then powdered 10 pounds of this, from which I took a gramme for analysis. My first analysis yielded:

Metallic Lead.. 16.4
Metallic Iron 2.00
Metallic Copper... Not determined.
Metallic Nickel... Trace.
Metallic Cobalt .... Trace.

From the strong reaction in the qualitative tests, I thought the presence of Nickel and Cobalt must be considerable, and not being satisfied, concentrated the ores and made two more assays, which yielded :

Metallic Lead.. 29.37
Metallic Copper... Not determined.
Metallic Iron .... Not determined.
Metallic Nickel.. Trace.
Metallic Cobalt.. Trace.

No work has been done except at the bottom of the shaft, as the formation is the same as at the other end of the ridge.

A number of shafts have been sunk within a radius of a mile—all with the same results, showing the formation to be uniform through-out the valley.

BURNETT'S DIGGINGS, (Texas County,)

These Diggings are situated in Sec. 22, T. 28, R. 12 W. The report of mineral being found at this point created considerable excitement, and at the time of my visit active operations were being carried on.

The mineral (Galena) was first discovered in an open cave. This cave is 5 feet high and 4 feet wide at the entrance, but on being pene-trated the size becomes very variable, sometimes decreasing so greatly that we find it necessary to crawl, and occasionally we were compelled to lie flat and pull the body along. The cave sometimes enlarges at points to 8 and 10 feet wide and as many high. The roof, sides and floor are mostly covered by a layer of red Clay, varying in thickness from that of a knife blade to several feet—the Clay being continually deposited by the dripping water.

The cave, on penetrating the hill, follows no definite direction, but continually changes its course. Numerous smaller caves branch off from the main cave at every angle, nearly all of which were too small for examination.

The Limestone varies in color from a dark cream into lighter shades, is free from any fossil remains, and belongs to the Lower Silu-rian Formation, (the Third Magnesian Limestone.)

Several shafts are sunk on the hill, but the Limestone seems to be entirely free of Galena, and I found this mineral only occurring in the crystallized state as large cubes along the roof and sides of the caves.

The cave, about 200 feet from the entrance, is 5 feet high and 8 feet wide. Large crystals of Galena are fastened to the rock, but are easily detached by a hammer. Of these, quite a number are to be seen, but not sufficient in quantity for any commercial value. The roof has also occasional small patches of a soft, dark brown Hematite, together with Stalactites and Stalagmites formed by the dripping and evaporation of water holding Lime in solution. On penetrating the caves for several hundred feet in different directions, I found the same general occurrence of Galena crystals along the roof and sides of the cave, but only in small quantities. Several shafts having been sunk demonstrated the fact that the rock did not contain the mineral in the disseminated form. I now learn (six months later) that active operations have been carried on, but without success.

Several other points were visited in the neighborhood where "Clay diggings" had been worked, and "float" mineral was said to have been found in two or three of the open pits. A few small particles of Galena were to be seen lying loose in the Clay, but this was the only indication of its occurrence.

THE LEAD HILL DIGGINGS,

Sec. 27, T. 28, R. 12 W., Texas county. These Diggings are situated some eight or ten miles east of the Burnett Diggings.

A shaft 12 feet deep is sunk on the top of the hill, passing through 8 feet of red Clay and 4 feet of gray Magnesian Limestone. The rock taken from the bottom of the shaft contains the Galena very sparsely disseminated, and would not yield more than one per cent. of the mineral. Near the shaft is a large outcrop of the rock, being exposed for several hundred feet. At one point a very narrow seam of Galena not more than the thickness of a knife blade, could be traced for 20 feet. Some work had already been done on it, and the owners were inclined to continue, but I advised them to discontinue as it was not a true fissure vein but a gash vein and would lead to no permanent results; but they concluded to continue. After a time, not meeting with any success, the whole work was abandoned.

THE INDIAN DIGGINGS,

At several points on the road from Hartville to Marshfield, in Webster county, are to be seen old diggings in the Clay, said to have been the work of the Indians in search of Lead ore, and though it is currently reported they mined the mineral in considerable quantities, the fact is to be doubted, as there is no indication of its existence.

ENLOE MINES.

The Enloe Mines are situated in T. 40 in the line of Rs. 1 and 2 W. The county lines of Franklin, Washington and Crawford. corner on the hill where the mining operations are conducted. The presence of Galena on this hill has been known for a great many years, but no systematic mining has ever been carried on. The farmers of the neighborhood have been allowed to come here and mine at their pleasure. No record has ever been kept of the amount of mineral mined. A farmer who had also mined on the hill, and a perfectly reliable and competent man, told me he was confident that at least a half million pounds of mineral had been raised.

This ore was principally found in the Clay between 5 and 20 feet from the surface. No successful mining has been carried on in the rock. The principal deposits occur in loose irregular masses, mixed with Chert, at about 18 feet below the surface.

Several attempts were made to mine in the rock but the ore occurring in such irregular deposits made the mining unprofitable. At three different points on the hill the rock has been attacked; the principal ore is in the " tunnel." This is the true pipe-vein formation, and as previously stated, is a very irregular deposit of the ore, and very rarely the mining for these deposits proves unsuccessful.

At the present time this hill and several similar mines in the neighborhood have been abandoned.

FRUMET MINES,

T. 40, R. 3 E., Secs. 28, 33 and 34, Jefferson county. The Frumet mining property is situated in Jefferson county, $8\frac{1}{2}$ miles distant from De-Soto, its shipping point, a station on the Iron Mountain Railroad. The tract embraces upwards of 1,300 acres but the mining at present is chiefly confined to a few acres, and active operations are now going on at four points. There are numerous outcrops at various points, but as yet undeveloped. The results obtained on those veins already worked would warrant the developing of a number of outcrops I examined.

The country is undulating, some of the hills rising several hundred feet in height, the physical features of the land furnishing a fine drainage to the mining district.

The property is bounded on the west by Big River, which furnishes inexhaustible stores of water power and supplies all the water required for mining, the dressing works and the furnaces.

GEOLOGY.

The metalliferous deposits occur in a bed of Limestone belonging to the Lower Silurian formation, and as far as I was able to determine in my short visit, the Limestone is that known as the Third Magnesian Limestone.

MODE OF OCCURRENCE.

The deposits of Lead ore occur in veins and approach nearer to a *true vein* than any occurrence I have observed in Missouri. All over the land outcrops can be seen, varying from a few feet to 50 in width. This outcrop is composed of decomposed Baryta, brown Hematite and fragments of Galena, varying in weight from a few grains to several ounces. Several of these veins have been developed by driving in open cuts from the sides of the hill. The cuts vary in width from 12 to 50 feet, depending on width of vein, all the vein matter being excavated between the wall rock. It is impossible at present to say to what depth these veins extend, and am unable to determine whether the deposits are confined to the sets of beds in which they occur or whether they extend on down through the Limestones into the older underlying rocks. The veins have been worked at several points at a depth of from 40 to 85 feet with no indication of diminution in yield; in fact the deposits seem to grow richer as the depth increases.

The wall rock is a very hard, dense, crystalline Limestone, inclosing veins crossing each other at all angles. The vein matter is at some points chiefly composed of Baryta very much decomposed, sometimes dense and again crystalline, with irregular concretions of Chert, crystallized Baryta and Galena mixed. This deposit is very easily mined. Sometimes the miners, simply with the use of a pick, are able to follow the vein forty feet without putting in a single blast. At other points the vein matter is more dense ; in this case much of it is composed of Limestone. Whenever the Galena occurs in Limestone it is found in the disseminated form, when not in Limestone it occurs mixed with Baryta and Chert in irregular masses, varying in weight from a few ounces to many pounds. Besides Galena, Baryta and Limestone very few other minerals occur in the vein matter. Occasionally Iron Pyrites and decomposed brown Hematite occur, but not in sufficient quantities to affect the mining.

MINING.

The Lead ore, on account of its mode of occurrence, can be mined at very little cost, as open cuts can be driven, thereby avoiding the necessity of timbering, and on account of the softness and decomposed state of the vein matter in many places blasting can almost entirely be dispensed with.

The natural advantages for mining at this point are unequalled by any mining district I have ever seen, and science has united with nature and made the work complete.

The ore is mined in the open cuts, dumped into the cars, and the cars, without any other locomotive power than that of gravitation, immediately pass to the dressing works.

DRESSING HOUSE.

This building is a most complete work. It is built of heavy timber on a rock foundation, low down on the bank of the river; the stream, some 6 to 10 feet in depth and 75 feet in width sweeps by furnishing an inexhaustible supply of water all the year. The engine, crusher, jigs, rollers, etc., are all under one roof.

The works are so complete but very little handling of the ore is necessary. The cars pass down from the mines into the roof of the house where they dump their contents into a No. 9 Blake crusher, which crushes 100 tons of material in 12 hours. The crusher empties the material into a large screen which acts as a separator, separating the ore into four classes. From the large screen the material passes to four smaller screens, and thence to the jigs. There are six jigs for the ore and six for the tailings. The richest ore taken from the jigs is put into barrels and is ready to be transported to the furnace. The poorer quality has to undergo a further separation; a portion goes back to the rollers and from thence again to the jigs, where it undergoes the same washing process. Another portion, called the tailings, is further washed and separated, and after this final process the waste material is almost absolutely free from Galena.

These are the most complete works I have seen in Missouri, as the amount of manual labor is reduced to a minimum, and accomplish the greatest amount of work at the least cost.

I have not seen the St. Joe works, which are said to be very complete; but leaving out of consideration what science has done, these mines possess natural advantages unequaled by any other.

FURNACES.

There are two furnaces, a Flintshire and a round Cupola, and two Scotch Hearths. Since the erection of the former, the latter are very little used.

The manipulations of the ore in this furnace is precisely the same as the common reverberatory furnace. The advantage claimed for this furnace is that more ore can be smelted with a given amount of fuel, and a larger per centage of metal obtained than from any other furnace.

ZINC MINES.

The Zinc Mines situated on the same property, and a short distance from the Lead Mines, are now being worked.

The hill seems to be a mass of Carbonate of Zinc, and wherever excavations have been made, some ore was found. A large face on the western side of the hill is now exposed showing a mass of the ore; as it can be quarried with picks, with little or no blasting, the expense of mining is very small.

I advised the proprietor to prosecute the work, as cost of mining was so trifling, for one man can mine a ton a day, with a cost of $2.75, to be delivered at the railroad where it is worth $15. Should active operations be carried on here, I believe the returns would be as great if they did not exceed those of the Lead Mines. My short stay prevented me from determining the extent of the deposit.

Professor Forest Shepherd, one of the Directors of the Geological Board, examined this deposit, and says: "The Zinc ore can be traced one half of a mile in a southeasterly direction, and over 1,000 feet in width; the quantity of ore in sight is very large indeed, and the amount of production seems altogether to depend upon the number of hands employed."

My brief stay did not admit of my determining the extent of the metalliferous deposits on this property; but in respect to the Lead deposits, Prof. Shepherd says:

"One of the veins, known as the Great Mother bearing vein, is estimated to be not less than 50 feet in width, and of unknown depth. Where it has been opened at different distances along its course, gives the most satisfactory evidence of its ability to supply countless stores of profitable ore for many years to come. By calculating the plainly visible part of the Mother vein where it has been uncovered on the surface, and opened in the centre by a shaft, and by the north and south cut about 1,000 feet in length, an average depth to the present level of the railroad 100 feet, and 50 feet in width, (the vein being much wider on an average,) we have upwards of 185,000 cubic yards of ore, or vein-stone in sight; and at the rate of 100 tons a day, would require over 15 years to work out this small fractional part of the ' Great Mother vein.'"

The value of this small fraction, calculated at the rate of 5 per cent. of mineral, would give over 55,000,000 pounds of mineral, and at the rate of 4 cents per pound, over $2,000,000 worth in sight still leaning to the level of Big River, 120 feet deeper.

There are a number of other veins equally as rich and productive, some of which are partly developed, and there are many outcrops not yet opened, but would certainly warrant being worked.

Taking into consideration all the advantages these mines possess, both naturally, and those which science and capital have added, the extensive deposits of Lead and Zinc ores, the inexhaustible supply of water, fine drainage, abundance of timber and accessibility to market, which will soon be increased, should the contemplated railroad be built connecting the Iron Mountain and Pacific Railroad; all these considerations give these mines advantages possessed by no other. And so far as our geological knowledge is able to determine, the deposits are practically inexhaustible, and the ore is so rich as to yield profitable returns, which is now and will further be increased by adding to the number of laborers employed. The amount of yield seems to be limited only by the number of workmen and capacity of the works.

CHAPTER XXXV.

THE IRON ORES OF SOUTH-EASTERN MISSOURI.

BY P. N. MOORE.

The South-eastern Ore District was named and described, in outline, by Dr. Adolf Schmidt, in the Report of the Geological Survey for
1872, pp. 46 and 88, and special descriptions of some deposits of this
region given on page 176, *et seq.*

Since that report was written, a somewhat more detailed examination of this region was made by the writer of this, which resulted in
finding that the area over which the ores are found, is somewhat
wider, and that their centre of greatest development is situated further south than supposed.

It embraces, so far as we at present know it, the southern portion
of Iron and Madison, the greater part of Wayne and Bollinger, and
the northern part of Butler and Stoddard counties. It is probable
also, that on investigation, it will be found to extend into Reynolds,
Carter and Ripley counties, and even farther west. There are also
deposits known to exist in Cape Girardeau county, but these would
be embraced in the "Ore District along the Mississippi River," of Dr.
Schmidt's classification.

The ores of this district are essentially all Limonites, or so-called
brown Hematites; although in the northern portion one specular ore
deposit has been examined, and it is not unlikely that others may be
found in connection with the Porphyry hills, which here frequently
occur. The Limonite deposits are so vastly in the majority, however,

that it is not improperly called the South-eastern Limonite District.

The Limonites occur in great variety of character, from the soft, porous, Ochrey, light-colored Stalactitic ore, through a number of dark, amorphous and more massive varieties to the porous, dark, red ore, which often gives a red streak and powder, and can hardly be distinguished from red Hematite, save by the fact that it contains chemically combined water in almost the same proportion as the lighter ores.

The Stalactitic ore occurs as often as any other variety, and is commonly known under the name of Pipe ore. In some deposites the Stalactites are larger, and of well-defined concentric structure—each one possessing a distinct individual character, while in others they are so small as to be almost microscopic. Usually the Stalactites, especially when small, are of uniform length, parallel, and cemented together, both at top and bottom, by more solid ore. But occasionally they are found inclined at angles to each other, and at one locality (T. 26, R. 5 E., Sec. 12, Butler county) a specimen was found which consisted of a large number of Stalactites of pure ore, of various sizes, which had been broken and thrown together at all angles, and then loosely cemented again by amorphous, cherty ore.

These changes prove that the deposition of the ore continues after the disturbance from the position where it was begun ; for the Stalactites are only formed in a vertical position, by the gradual infiltration from above into cavities in the Limestone, of water holding Iron in solution.

They are formed in exactly the same way as the Stalactites of Carbonate of Lime, which are so abundant in caves in many portions of the country.

Hollow concretions, or shells of Limonite, commonly called bombshell, or pot ore, are often found, and are especially abundant in Bollinger county. Some of them are of large size, and partially filled with a whitish Clay. In others, small, needle-like Stalactites, tipped with Quartz, occur ; while in others still, *mamelons* of fibrous Limonite, from which depend small, irregularly conical Stalactites. They are usually found lying on the surface or in the Clay, and broken Chert near the surface, but not often at any great depth below.

The stalactitic and concretionary ores, are generally of good quality, and reasonably free from any impurity, unless it be an occasional admixture of Ochre. The more massive and amorphous ores, however, show a much greater variation in quality. The changes from pure to cherty or sandy ore, take place so often and so suddenly, that it is extremely difficult to form in advance any reliable opinion as to the amount of available ore in a deposit.

The prevailing impurity through all this region, is Chert or flint. In Madison and Bollinger counties, Sulphur is present in sufficient quantities to materially injure the value of some deposits, but further south this does not seem to be the case.

In the northern part of the region under consideration, Chert is found mixed with the ore of nearly all the banks, from that degree where it is only an occasional lump, to that where the ore is nothing more than a Chert-breccia, the Limonite serving as a cement or matrix which holds together the mass of broken Chert lumps. To the south, in the southern part of Wayne, and in Butler and Stoddard counties, the relative amount of Chert is less, and the common impurity is a coarse Sand. This, in its turn, is found in all proportions up to where the ore becomes nothing more than a Ferruginous Sandstone. Many specimens of this kind seem to have been originally a silicious Limestone, in which the Carbonate of Lime has been replaced by Oxide of Iron, by the infiltration of Ferruginous waters, probably containing free carbonic acid, which dissolved the Carbonate of Lime, precipitating in its place the Oxide of Iron, and leaving unaffected the silicious matter. The variation in the quality of these ores is great, but not quite so sudden as in those which are cherty.

In some deposits in Wayne and Butler counties, is a light, olive brown amorphous Limonite, which to the eye appears very pure, but on inspection with a glass it is seen to contain much finely intermixed Silica.

It shows stalactitic structure rarely, though very fine *mamelons* of fibrous Limonite occur, filling crevices in the more solid ore.

The silicious nature of this ore will be seen from the following analysis by Mr. Chauvenet:

		2
Water	8.56	8.46
Insoluble silicious matter	37.88	28.18
Peroxide of Iron	53.26	68.05
Metallic Iron	37.28	44.13

No. 1. Specimen from the L. Johnson bank, Wayne county—No. 30 of the ore bank list.

No. 2 Specimen from Speer's Mountain, Wayne county—No. 24 of the ore bank list.

These specimens are not average samples of the whole deposit, but are merely taken to show the composition of the light-colored ore.

The ores of this district, as far as I had the opportunity of examining them, belong to that class of ores which, in the reports of 1872, page 87, have been described as original Limonites, being originally deposited in about their present form and composition.

In some localities, some of the Limonite found, has undoubtedly been formed by the decomposition of Pyrites; but these are exceptional, and as a rule in this region, the Limonite has the appearance of being original mineral. In all cases it has been deposited from aqueous solution, and in nearly all, upon Limestone, in depressions in its surface or in cavities near the surface.

There are some facts which go to prove that occasionally the ore deposition is continued in the Clay and Chert detritus, after disturbance from its original position and destruction of the associate Limestone; but there is not enough known as yet to enable us to fully understand the circumstances of, nor the laws which govern this later deposition.

The Limestone which carries the ore through all this region, is the Third Magnesian.

The chemical reactions which produced the deposition of the ore, were probably two—one a precipitation of Oxide of Iron from an aqueous solution by the carbonates of Lime and Magnesia of the Limestone, which were dissolved and carried away at the same time the Oxide of Iron was deposited; the other partook more of the nature of a deposit from solution by oxidation and evaporation.

The amorphous massive ores seem to be a result of the first method of deposition by precipitation. Waters charged with oxide of Iron, and probably also carbonic acid infiltrated through the Limestone, dissolving and carrying it away, depositing in its place the oxide of iron. The infiltration in most instances seems to have come from above, and the iron may have been obtained wholly or in part from the Second Sandstone which formerly overlaid the Third Magnesian Limestone in many places in this District, for the ore is often found high in the hills, and associated with broken fragments of Sandstone, which are the remnants of a destroyed stratum. This theory of deposition accounts for the prevalence of Chert in so much of this amorphous ore. The siliceous Cherty materials existing in the Magnesian Limestone were unaffected by solutions which readily dissolved the calcareous portions, and the precipitated oxide of Iron at once became intermixed with and surrounded the Chert.

G.S—41

The method of deposition of the stalactitic ores has been briefly alluded to before. They were deposited by the second method from solution by evaporation in pre-existent cavities in the Limestone. Their stalactitic structure itself, their comparative purity and freedom from Chert, and the fact that specimens have been found showing the position of the walls of the cavities where the ore was in contact with the rock, all go to prove this beyond reasonable doubt. The solutions in this case must also have been infiltrated from above.

The chemical constitution of these ores will be seen from the following analyses by Mr. Chauvenet.

They were all made from average samples taken at the ore-banks, in the summer of 1873, and in selecting the samples for analysis, no specimens were taken from those portions of the deposits (if any) where the ore appeared to the eye so sandy or cherty as to be worthless.

ANALYSES OF SOUTHWEST MISSOURI.

LIMONITE ORES.

	Nifong Bank.	Glenn Emma Bank.	Myers Bank.	Bear Mt. Bank.	Spiva Bank.	Black River Bank No. 1.	Black River Bank No. 2.	Shrout Bank.	St. Francis Bank.
	1.	2.	3.	4.	5.	6.	7.	8.	9.
Water....................	11.43	8.92	10.38	8.99	10.97	6.72	8.50	8.57	9.58
Insoluble siliceous matter..	7.46	33.97	14.72	15.29	17.19	42.25	16.46	25.97	25.88
Peroxide of Iron............	79.57	58.37	74.37	74.87	70.43	50.01	74.71	64.18	68.25
Sulphur..................	0.017	trace	....	0.087	none	trace	0.016	0.003	trace
Phosphoric acid..........	0.323	0.143	....	0.154	0.130	0.096	0.164	0.153	0.147
Metallic Iron............	55.70	37.86	52.06	52.41	49.30	35.01	52.30	44.93	44.27
Phosphorus	0.141	0.062	....	0.067	0.057	0.042	0.071	0.066	0.064

It will be seen that these ores, although not equal to the specular ores of this State, are yet rich enough in Iron and poor enough in injurious impurities to be of great value.

Nos. 1, 2, 3, 4, 5 and 9 are samples of the ordinary porous and cherty Limonite.

Nos. 6 and 7 are samples of the dark-colored reddish Limonite which bears so close a resemblance to Hematite. They are mixed with both Chert and Sand. No. 6 especially being very cherty. Notwithstanding their red color and streak, they show in proportion to the Iron present, about the same amount of combined water as the lighter ores.

No. 8 is a sample of Limonite in which the impurity is a coarse Sand instead of Chert. It will be seen that it does not differ greatly in its composition from the others.

The following two analyses of specimens from the Indian Ford region, were made by Messrs. Chauvenet and Blair, for Mr. James E. Mills, and kindly furnished by him for publication:

	1.	2.
Silica	9.100	....
Oxide of Iron	75.140	77.11
Alumina	2.580	....
Lime	0.26	....
Magnesia	0.15	....
Manganese	1.12	....
Sulphur	0.012	0.076
Phosphoric Acid	0.126	0.181
Water	11.44	8.46
	99.928	....
Insoluble silicious matter	10.56	10.98
Metallic Iron	52.60	53.98
Phosphorus	0.055	0.079

No. 1. Average sample, by Mr. James E. Mills, from T. 26, R. 7 E., Sec. 35, N. hf. N. E. qr.

No. 2. Average sample, by Mr. James E. Mills, from T. 26, R. 7 E., Sec. 22, S. W. qr.

The variation in size of the ore deposits is as marked and great as the variation in quality, but the great majority are of limited extent. Any Iron manufacture which may be established in this region and which relies upon these deposits for a supply of ore, must, if it would be permanent, control a large number of them in order to secure a sufficient amount of ore to last for any length of time.

In Madison and Bollinger counties a number of banks have been opened, so that their character can be pretty well ascertained; but in Wayne and Butler counties there are only a few in which any development at all has taken place. The majority of the banks, and those too in the most promising locality of all—the Indian Ford region—are as yet wholly undeveloped.

The ore at the undeveloped banks is usually seen lying upon the surface and partially imbedded in the Clay and broken Chert, which almost invariably covers thickly the surface, and often occurs to a great depth, completely hiding the underlying rock. In most cases no rock is seen in position near the ore, but when it is, it is mentioned in the description of the deposit.

The ore deposits of this region may be classed under two general divisions, in each of which there is admitted a wide range of variation as to character, size, quality and position. They are:

CLASS G. Deposits of Limonite on Limestone.

CLASS H. Disturbed or drifted deposits of Limonite.

This is the system of classification, adopted by Dr. A. Schmidt in the Report of the Geological Survey for 1872, and there explained at some length by him. Observations during the past season have served to confirm the correctness of this system in its general features. As all who read this report may not have access to that volume a general description of these classes of deposits, as displayed in South-eastern Missouri, will be given before proceeding to the detailed description of deposits:

CLASS G. DEPOSITS OF LIMONITE ON LIMESTONE.

The Limonite deposits of this region seem to have been originally deposited on the Third Magnesian Limestone, which is the prevailing rock.

These deposits are not in veins or masses of any regular shape, but occur in a great variety of forms, as may be inferred from the manner of deposition.

The form which is rather more common than any other is the horizontally bedded lenticular mass of irregular outline but this is not universal, nor does it occur often enough to make it the rule.

There is a popular opinion that the ore occurs in true veins of large size and regular course, which run continually through the

hills, and that the masses of ore found are outcroppings af the main
vein. Nothing can be further from the truth and nothing tend more
to incorrect valuation of the deposits or mistakes in mining than this
theory. The facts can not be too prominently kept in view, that these
deposits are not true veins ; that they are not of inexhaustible extent, and that a large outcrop does not indicate of necessity that there
is a correspondingly greater amount beneath the surface.

CLASS H. DISTURBED OR DRIFTED DEPOSITS OF LIMONITE.

Many of these deposits in South-east Missouri, in fact the great
majority of them, seem to have been disturbed from the position
where originally deposited. We find them in all stages of alteration,
some merely slightly tilted or moved and lying near the original position ; others are completely broken up by the dissolving or washing
away of the surrounding and underlying Limestone, and nearly destroyed, so that they should perhaps be more properly called residuary deposits. Of this class are some few deposits of Limonite which
are found resting in the porphyritic detritus near the base of Porphyry
hills. They are probably residual from Limestone, which once extended farther up the hill and has since been worn away by slowly
acting erosive agencies. The proof of this is found in the fact that
these Limonites are never found at any great height on the Porphyry
hills, and that with them is usually found more or less Clay and
Chert, the invariable accompaniments of the erosion of Magnesian
Limestone.

These deposits occur in a great variety of positions, but usually
lying in much broken, irregular masses, buried in the Clay and Chert
or oftentimes merely resting on the surface. From this can readily be
seen their very uncertain and unreliable character.

There is almost no class of mineral deposits which require more
careful and intelligent examination in order to determine their true
value, and none the surface appearance of which is more deceptive,
many banks showing a fine outcrop of ore on the surface, prove on
opening to hold little or none beneath. It is this feature which leads
to the over estimation of many deposits, some of which will be described. They show a large amount of ore lying thickly and almost
solidly over the surface, which a careless observer would naturally
infer to be the outcrop of large solid masses, but when shafts come to
be sunk or other thorough means of exploration used, they prove to
be nothing more than residuary deposits resting on the Clay.

DESCRIPTION OF SPECIAL DEPOSITS.

CLASS G. DEPOSITS-OF LIMONITE ON LIMESTONE.

NIFONG BANK,

T. 31, R. 8 E., Sec. 2, S. E. qr., two miles from Marquand, Bollinger county.

At this bank, two large cuts have been made in the top of a high hill, about a quarter of a mile from the Iron Mountain Railroad west. The larger of these cuts, of irregular shape, is about 30 feet deep, running in a north and south direction. The ore is exposed at its best on the south wall. It is seen here in an irregular mass 8 or 10 feet thick and about 20 feet long, inclined toward the west at a high angle, overlaid by a mass of reddish Clay and Chert, which shows semi-stratification in about the same direction. The ore at the south end of the cut is of good quality, a dense Limonite and comparatively free from Chert. That exposed on the east wall is very cherty, so much so as to be almost worthless. An analysis of the ore, averaged from such of it as is marketable, is given on page 643.

About 125 feet east, just over the top of the hill towards the railroad, another cut has been driven in a westerly direction, about 60 feet long and 20 feet deep at the head, where it has exposed a mass of very cherty ore, 6 to 8 feet thick, and tilted at the same angle as in the first cut.

RHODES' BANK,

T. 31, R. 8 E., Sec. 14, S. W. qr., Bollinger county. As will be seen from the sketch (Fig. 74), the ore here lies upon the south-east slope of a low hill. It has also been exposed by the two cuts. The upper cut reveals nothing but pieces of ore in the Chert and Clay. At the lower, is exposed over an irregular area, perhaps 40 feet in diameter, ore, Chert and a peculiar porous Quartzite with cavities filled with Ochre. The ore is frequently found adhering to this, but is present in very small quantity in comparison with it. The surface of the hill above is covered with large boulders of ore and Chert, but the ore is freer from cherty admixture than would be expected. At the upper cut the ore is better, but the same Quartzose rock is found adhering to it.

T. 30, R. 9 E., Sec. 11, N. E. qr. of N. W. qr., Bollinger county. At this place at the time of my visit, the ore had been disclosed by two cuts on the north slope of a hill, near the top. The main cut is some 30 feet deep and shows an extremely irregular mass of ochreous, cherty ore, which in its general direction dips steeply toward the north. Much Ochre is associated with the ore, and at places the ore is almost replaced by Ochre. Lying above the main body of ore is found, in irregular pieces, a peculiar, silicious red ore, a specimen of which, on analysis by Mr. R. Chauvenet, gave the following results:

Peroxide of Iron	36.81
Insoluble silicious residue	57.92
Combined water	4.96
Metallic Iron	25.76

It is said to occur often in long, stalactitic pieces standing upright in the Clay.

Scattered over the surface of this hill and the next one north, and occurring in the Clay and Chert at the cut, are found large numbers of hollow concretions of good ore—the so-called "Pot" ore—some of them of considerable size.

T. 29, R. 7 E., Sec. 3, W. half lot 2, N. W. qr., Wayne county, is a high hill in the ridge or divide between Turkey Creek and Bear Creek. The ore occurs almost exactly on top or inclining a little towards the eastern slope. It is in almost solid masses lying irregularly over an area about 45 feet wide and 150 feet along the ridge, while the broken pieces extend down the hill about 100 feet. The surface of the hill is covered with soil, and no rock is visible save occasional Chert lumps. The ore is porous and contains Chert in small pieces, usually not over one-half inch in diameter, which occur at pretty regular intervals. The uniformity of the Chert admixture is unusual, and while sufficient to injure the value of the ore, it does not render it worthless.

T. 26, R. 7 E., Sec. 24, S. half N. W. qr., or possibly N. half S. W. qr. Butler county. As will be seen from the topographical sketch (Fig. 75), that the ore here occurs on a steep hill about 80 feet high, which rises almost from the edge of the water, on the west side of the St. Francois River. The ore has been traced for a distance of 550 feet along the hill, and it lies scattered in immense boulders from the 65 foot level down the slope. None is found above the 65 foot level. At this height, for a distance of 200 to 300 feet, the ore shows a persistent outcrop, which seems at a number of places to be solid and in position. The thickness of it could not be well ascertained.

At the southern end of the hill, the ore lies in greatest abundance over a wider surface and lower down on the hill; but though lying thickly, almost completely covering the ground, it is in broken pieces of greater or less size, and evidently not in position.

Some 200 to 300 yards to the south-west, at a point not shown in the sketch, on the banks of a small branch that flows into the St. Francois River, is a large amount of ore lying scattered in large boulders on both sides of the creek. The ore is of only medium quality, being porous and sandy with small Chert admixture at some places. An analysis, by Mr. R. Chauvenet, of a sample from this bank has been given on page 643.

This deposit is the best one seen in the Indian Ford region.

INDIAN FORD BANK, No. 1,

T. 26, R. 7 E., Sec. 24, N. half N. E. qr., Butler county. Here the ore is found upon a low hill, not above 50 feet high, which is quite near to the old Indian Ford of St. Francois River. The ore lies upon the south-east slope of the hill in an oblong mass, (or rather two masses with a vacant space between,) about 300 feet long and 100 feet at its widest, with its longest diameter in a north-east and south-west direction. It reaches about 100 feet down the hill—about half way. The most of the ore outcrop is in large pieces, but in the centre they lie so closely connected as to seem an almost solid mass of unbroken ore. In quality it is porous and cherty rather than sandy, but is pure enough to be valuable.

INDIAN FORD BANK, No. 2,

T. 26, R. 7 E., Sec. 23, N. E. qr., Butler county, is upon a hill, about 110 feet high. The principal mass of ore lies upon the S. E. Slope, and shows at its thickest about 10 feet below the top, although it is thinly scattered over the top and thick again at about the same level on the northwest. It reaches some 30 feet below the top, extending down in a belt about 80 to 100 feet wide. In its most prominent outcrop it shows apparently solid but limited in extent, while the most of the ore is in large pieces. The quality of the ore is so poor, however, being both cherty and sandy, as to materially detract from the value of this otherwise promising deposit.

INDIAN FORD BANK, No. 3,

T. 27, R. 7 E., Sec. 23, N. E. qr. of S. W. qr., Butler county. The ore here occurs upon the south-eastern Slope of a low hill, about 30 feet high. Near the top it shows an almost or entirely coherent mass, about 75 to 100 feet long, and extends with this width down the Slope about 150 feet, in an outcrop of broken pieces, ranging from 6 inches to 3 feet in diameter. The ore is porous and quite free from Chert, but is inclined to be sandy.

INDIAN FORD BANK, No. 4,

T. 27, R. 7 E., Sec 22, S. hf. N. W. qr., Butler county. This is a large deposit of ore, occurring on the north-western Slope of a hill, about 50 feet high. Near the top the ore lies in an apparently coherent mass, and below it scatters, spreading over a large area.

The value of the deposit is, however, greatly injured by the poor quality of the ore, which is lean, soft and sandy, and almost none of it of first quality.

BLUE SPRING BANK,

T. 26, R. 7 E., Sec. 26, S. E. qr. of S. E. qr., Butler county (Fig. 76.) Here the ore is found in large and small pieces, and in one place in solid outcrop, overlying an outcrop of 10 feet of Third Magnesian Limestone, which shows at 30 feet above the bottom of the hill. The ore is not seen in any great amount, the outcrop being only about 75 feet along the Slope, and 30 feet wide; but it is interesting as showing more plainly than usual the relation of the ore to the Limestone. In quality it is not first class, being quite sandy.

SPIVA BANK,

T. 27, R. 8 E., Sec. 26, Stoddard county. This deposit is upon one of the high hills south of Mingo Swamps, on the southern Slope, but quite near the top. The ore first occurs in large lumps, about 20 feet below the crown of the hill, and some 120 feet down the Slope. At about 30 feet down is a solid ledge of ore, which shows an average thickness of 4 or 5 feet, and is continuous for 100 to 120 feet in length. From the sketch (Fig. 77) the relative position of this ledge will be seen. After an interval of about 40 feet the ore is seen again at about the same level, and apparently a continuation of the same ledge. Broken ore, lying in almost solid masses beyond the visible end of the solid outcrop, is seen, and it also covers the surface for 200 feet or more down the hill. In the sketch only the top of the hill is attempted to be shown.

The ore is of fair quality, porous, with pockets or cavities, filled with Sand, and occasionally somewhat cherty. An analysis by Mr. Chauvénet of ore from this bank is given on page 643.

This deposit is the most promising one seen in Stoddard county.

Shrout's Bank,

T. 27, R. 6 E., Sec. 16, N. E. qr. of N. E. qr., Butler county, upon the western Slope of a steep, high ridge, running north and south, overlooking Black River. The ore lies scattered in broken lumps, some of which are of large size, for a distance of 500 feet along the Slope, and perhaps 100 feet wide, while at one place, near the top of the hill, a solid outcrop is seen, showing some 6 or 7 feet thickness of very flinty and silicious ore. This outcrop of solid ore does not show for any great length. There are in it occasional seams of better ore running through the mass, but the best showed Silica in coarse grains. The quality of the whole outcrop is poor, being extremely sandy, some of it so much so as to be little more than a ferruginous Sandstone. The ore of the solid outcrop is both cherty and sandy.

An analysis of a sample from this bank is given on page 643.

Upon the same tract of land, ½ mile south, on the N. E. qr. of the S. E. qr. of same Section, there is a smaller outcrop of ore in large and small pieces, scattered thickly over an area 100 feet east and west, by 175 feet north and south, and at some places the mass seems to be solid. The ore is porous, semi-concretionary, and quite cherty, while many of the cavities of the concretions are filled with Sand; yet, notwithstanding this, it will average better than the larger outcrop just described.

Swattler Bank,

T. 25, R. 6 E., Sec. 28, N. E. qr. of N. W. qr., Butler county. The ore, in a belt about 75 to 100 feet wide, lies along the ridge, and down the point to the bottom, a distance of about 500 feet, on a low hill pointing north. Down the Slope it is in broken pieces, mostly of large size; but higher up it lies in apparently solid mass, which shows at one place about 10 feet thick. This solid outcrop is, however, of limited extent, and the great proportion of ore seen is broken. It is of medium quality, porous and sandy.

At other places on this tract, ore is found outcropping, and at one place, on the N. E. qr. of the same section, a considerable quantity is seen, which seems to be in position; but the quality is so poor that it is not worth a special description.

MORRIS CREEK BANK,

T. 27, R. 4 E., Sec. 35, S. E. qr., Wayne county (Fig. 78.) Upon the east Slope of a low hill, about 75 feet high, and scattered into the bed of the creek, which here runs north into Black River, the ore is found. It lies thickly about 200 feet along the Slope, and extending up to the 40 foot level, but none above. All the ore is lean and cherty, and often little more than a ferruginous Chert. It seems to have come from a ledge of ferruginous Chert, or very cherty ore, which shows a persistent outcrop of the 40 foot level for about 150 feet. That which is broken and lying in pieces over the surface shows a larger proportion of good ore than the solid mass, but even in this there are irregular masses of better ore.

The value of the bank is much injured, however, by the quality of the ore, which, taken as a whole, is poor.

In addition to these already described, the Gregoire, West, Peterburger, Big Lake Creek and other banks are probably deposits of this class in the South-eastern Ore District.

CLASS H. DRIFTED DEPOSITS OF LIMONITE.

FOSTER BANK,

T. 33, R. 7 E, Sec. 16, N. E. qr., Madison county. At the time of examination, three cuts had been made at different places in this quarter section. The upper cut was made near the end of a tramway, constructed to carry the ore down to the Iron Mountain Railroad, about half a mile distant. This cut was about 80 feet long, running into the hill near the summit in an easterly direction. Considerable ore had been obtained, but it was all found as broken pieces or boulders lying in the Clay and Chert, and no solid mass was found. The ore was very cherty.

About 250 to 300 yards north, by the side of the tramway, another small excavation was made without reaching any solid ore, but much ore in pieces, mostly of small size, was found in the Clay. This was a much better quality than in the upper cut, being dense, dark-colored, often Stalactitic and quite free from Chert.

At still another point, west of the last described, an excavation of about 10 feet deep had disclosed a mass of ore of irregular shape, the extent of which could not be seen. It was lying in the Clay mixed with much yellow Ochre and ferruginous Chert. The ore itself was dense, cherty and very silicious. No rock was visible near the ore save the associated Chert, which was found in abundance, both lying with the ore and scattered over the surface of the hill.

GLENN EMMA BANK,

T. 30, R. 9 E., Sec. 16, Bollinger county. This bank was described in the Geological Report for 1872, by Dr. Schmidt, under the name of the Murdock Bank. Since that time considerable development has taken place, which has shown more clearly the character of the deposit, and up to the time of examination some 1,500 tons of ore had been mined and shipped.

The bank was opened low down upon the hill at a point about 20 feet above the level of the valley. Here three irregular excavations had been made along the hill-side, in all some 200 feet along the Slope, and the deepest of them about 80 feet into the hill. Two principal ore masses were disclosed. Of these, the most southerly was a broken mass, seemingly formed of concentric layers of ore in small pieces. Considerable of this was cherty, but in the northern mass a much larger proportion of Chert was seen, so much as to render a large amount of ore valueless.

The ore in the extreme north part of the cut was better quality, but mixed with much Ochre. An analysis of an average sample of such ore as is not too cherty to be marketable from this bank, is given in the table of analysis. Were the whole averaged the per centage of Iron would be much less than is here shown, and the silicious matter correspondingly greater.

TIBBS' BANK,

T. 31, R. 10 E., Sec. 29, S. W. qr. of S. E. qr., Bollinger county. Upon the north Slope of a hill about 60 feet high, the ore is exposed by a cut at the 40 foot level. It is seen at the head of the cut which runs in a southerly direction, lying in a broken, irregular mass, much mixed with Ochre, and imbedded in the Clay. There is not much Chert present, but the ore is full of Ochre, and occasionally sulphurous. A great deal of very good Ochre can be obtained from this bank; in fact, so far as can be seen, there is more Ochre than ore present.

Much ore is scattered over the surface, and several small test pits have been dug, but without revealing the presence of any solid mass of ore.

ROBBIN'S BANK,

T. 31, R. 9 E., Sec. 10, Bollinger county. Here the ore occurs upon the north Slope of a high hill on the divide, between Hurricane and Crooked Creeks. The ore lies in many broken pieces of uniformly large size, in a belt about 200 feet long, N. and S., and 75 feet wide. It is dense, hard ore, silicious rather than cherty, and much of it dark-red in color. There are many Chert pieces scattered with the ore on the surface, and considering this fact, it is rather surprising that there is so little mixed with the ore.

T. W. SHELL BANK,

T. 29, R. 9 E., Sec. 10, N. E., qr. of S. E. qr., Bollinger county. The hill, upon which this deposit is found, is low and flat, and singular, in that almost no Chert is found upon it. It seems to be deeply covered with Soil, and the only rock visible is the ore, which lies in a belt 50 or 60 feet wide and 200 feet long, over the top of the hill. The most of the ore is upon the S. E. Slope, and is in large boulders. It is dense, sometimes Stalactitic, and usually pure and free from Chert.

MYERS' BANK,

T. 30, R. 8 E., Sec. 32, S. E. qr. of N. E. qr., Bollinger county. This deposit occurs upon the S. bank of Davault's Creek, a branch of Castor River. The ore is found low down upon the hill, not rising over 20 feet above the bottom. It lies very closely along the foot of the hill, for about 100 feet, in large boulders that seem almost solid. A little prospecting has been done at two places by means of small cuts, which have revealed the presence of large boulders of ore underneath the surface, which were so large as to be unmanagable by the prospectors. The ore is comparatively free from Chert and other impurity. An analysis, by Mr. Chauvenet, is given on page 643.

REED BANK,

T. 28, R. 8 E., Sec. 17, N. W. qr. of N. W. qr., Bollinger county, Fig. 79. This deposit is a singular one, in that the outcrop of ore which is usually large and heavy, occurs near the foot of a gentle Slope, which can hardly be called a hill, in the high lands between Castor River and Lost Creek. The ore is near the level of a dry branch with a southerly course, and the Slope deeply covered with Soil, and showing no rock in position, with only few Chert lumps, rises gently toward the east at the rate of about 5 feet in 100. The ore covers an area about 300 feet long, N. and S., by 100 feet wide. It lies thickly over the surface, and at about the centre is an irregular mass perhaps 100 feet long, which seems at first sight to be solid and coherent, but on closer examination proves to be formed of large pieces lying closely together. It is quite porous, of only medium quality, and inclined to be coarsely silicious rather than cherty. The bank is wholly unprospected, save at one point near the heavy outcrop, where a small test pit had been dug. What was its original depth could not be ascertained, but that it had revealed no ore was pretty certain, from the character of the material thrown out and lying at the mouth, which was a whitish Clay mixed with Chert.

REESE CREEK BANK,

T. 28, R. 6 E., Sec. 5, Wayne county. The ore of this bank shows itself in a zone about 100 feet wide and 300 feet long, lying across the top of a very high hill or ridge. The largest amount occurs almost at the top of the ridge, where it is in large boulders 3 feet or more in diameter, but there is no solid mass or close outcrop appearing nearly solid ; on the contrary, it is all broken and much of it in fine pieces. The ore is mostly dense, close-grained and of fair quality, although at places it is both silicious and cherty. Some specimens give a reddish streak. Towards the edges of the outcrop it grows more cherty, at some places shading off insensibly into a ferruginous Chert.

PETTIT BANK,

T. 27, R. 7 E., Sec. 19, S. E. qr., Wayne county. The ore here occurs in two principal outcrops upon the east side of a high hill, quite near the top. Neither of them seem to have been much disturbed or far removed from the place of deposition. The southern outcrop shows one mass that appears nearly solid, and a large amount broken and scattered down the hill over an irregular area, perhaps 125 feet diameter. This outcrop, in a limited space, shows a great variety of ore— some of it pure and dense, some stalactitic, some very sandy, and some cherty. The northern outcrop is about 250 feet distant, at about the same height, and is smaller but more solid. The ore, too, is of poor quality, being porous, sandy and cherty.

RAMSAY BANK,

T. 27, R. 6 E., Sec. 23, Wayne county. [Fig. 80]. The ore of this deposit is found lying in the St. Francois River and embedded in the alluvium of its west bank. The bank is formed of Clay and mud and rises 20 to 30 feet above low water. This level extends back 100 to 200 feet on the west side, where it strikes the foot of the hills. The ore is scattered along the bank for about 50 feet, but does not rise to within 10 feet of the top. Large pieces of Chert and cherty Limestone are found embedded with the ore, which is all stalactitic, in large masses, showing stalactites of unusual length, some 3 or 4 feet long. There is no Chert mixed with the ore, but considerable Ochre in the intestices between the fine stalactites. No rock is seen in position anywhere near, but at a point a few yards below the ore there is a ford in the river which is there quite shallow and runs among many boulders of Limestone or Chert. At time of high water the whole deposit would be covered. It is evident that it is a residuary deposit of limited extent.

Mann Bank.

T. 27, R. 6 E., Sec 21, N. E. qr., Wayne county, is upon the top of a high hill, north of Otter Creek, which runs here in a large bend on three sides of the hill, which is the highest in the neighborhood. It is covered with Chert, but no solid rock is visible. The ore lies close, almost covering the top, over an area 250 feet north and south by 175 feet east and west, but it does not extend more than 20 feet below the top down the slope. It occurs in large pieces, that do not seem much disturbed. In quality it is poor—the prevailing impurity being Ochre, but Sand and Chert are also present, and the ore is almost always mixed with one or the other.

Otter Creek Bank.

T. 27, R. 5 E., Sec. 3 S. W. qr., N. hf. S. E. qr., and Sec. 4, lot 1 N. E. qr., Wayne county. Along the top of the range of hills just north of Otter Creek there are a number of small outcrops of ore in scattering boulders, but the largest of them is situated on the N. E. qr., Sec. 4. Here, upon the south slope of the hill, near the summit, the ore covers an area about 200 feet in length along the slope, and 60 to 75 feet in width. Over the crown of the hill, at about the same level, on the north slope, a small amount of ore is seen. The ore is mostly in quite small pieces, and of poor quality, being quite sandy and often cherty.

Upon the S. W. qr., Sec. 3, lying low on the hill near the Creek, there is a small outcrop over an area 40 to 100 feet, of very good statactitic ore, but it is in small pieces, and the total quantity seen is so little that it does not promise to be of any importance.

HANEY BANK,

T. 26, R. 5 E., Sec. 5 S. W. qr., Wayne county, is another one of this class of deposits where the ore is found only on the summit of a high hill. It is one of the largest of three and likely to be thought much more extensive and reliable than it really is. It occurs on a high ridge, which here forms an elbow, turning from a north-east course to north. The ore lies scattered over an irregular area along the summit, from 500 to 600 feet in length and 200 feet wide. It is in patches more or less thick, but at no place is anything like a solid outcrop seen, and it does not extend over 20 feet below the top of the hill. A number of large boulders are seen, but the greater part of the ore is in small pieces, which are not rounded but flat. It is, however, of unusually fine quality, being dense, somewhat inclined to botryoidal forms and almost entirely free from Chert, Sand or other impurities. Occasionally there is some of it porous, but the cavities in it are not filled with Sand but with a fine Clay and not much of that. There is no rock seen in position on this hill, but considerable Chert and cherty Limestone on the slope below the ore outcrop, while on the east side there are a few large pieces of ferruginous Chert lying with the ore. The ore disappears both to the north and south with the slope of the hill but reappears again a few hundred feet to the north at about the same level in much less quantity. The depression between the two outcrops is only a few feet deep, and from this fact it seems probable that the extension in depth of the ore is very limited.

BEAR MOUNTAIN BANK,

T. 29, R. 3 E., Sec. 2, N. W. qr., Wayne county. The appearance of this bank around the ore outcrop can be seen from the accompanying sketch, Fig. 81, but the general geology needs a slight explanation.

Bear Mountain is an oblong Porphyry hill, having its greatest diameter N. and S., and some 400 to 500 feet high. Detritus of sandy Limestone, Chert, Clay and broken Porphyry covers the base of it for from 100 to 125 feet up, and it is in this that the ore has been found. As shown by the sketch, the surface is covered at several places with ore, and several shafts and cuts have been dug in search of a solid body of it. The lower cut was run altogether in a light-colored Clay. The upper one revealed, at the end, a considerable mass of broken Limonite lying in cherty Clay and a disturbed, decomposed sandy Limestone. The shaft above the cut was sunk 30 feet in light colored Clay or decomposed Chert, passing through a few thin seams of ore, and ending in the Clay without reaching any solid body of ore. The upper shaft was only a few feet deep, all in the same Clay.

The ore in the upper cut is much broken and shattered, drawing from the mass in rectangular pieces of 2 to 3 inches to the side. There is considerable Chert mixed¦with it. Upon the surface much ore is of stalactitic structure, and quite pure.

YANCEY MOUNTAIN BANK,

T. 30, R. 4 E., Sec. 35, N. W. qr. of N. E. qr., Wayne county. This deposit and the one following are peculiar in that the Limonite ore is found at the foot of a Porphyry hill, lying scattered in large and small pieces upon the Porphyry and in the porphyritic detritus. Little or no Chert or Clay is present, and the ore is singularly free from Chert. At the lower part of the outcrop the ore is brown in color, free from impurity; a true Limonite of first quality. Higher up it grows more siliceous and darker in color, and finally presents the appearance of a decomposed Porphyry, highly ferruginous.

KISTER BANK,

T. 30, R. 4 E., Sec. 35, N. E. qr. of N. W. qr., Wayne county. This deposit is upon the flank of the same hill as the last described, and similar to it in the absence of Chert detritus. The ore lies some 50 or 60 feet higher on the hill upon a ridge between two ravines, and running down into them both. At the bottom it is Limonite of poor quality, being quite siliceous; but on ascending the hill it grows redder and leaner, and presents the same changes into an apparently decomposed red Porphyry that were seen in the last described deposit.

CEDAR BAY BANK,

T. 28, R. 3 E., Sec. —, Wayne county. The ore of this bank lies upon the western slope of a high hill, about two-thirds distance to the top, and covers a surface perhaps 200 feet square.

An excavation has been made in the hill side about 250 feet in length, but not at any place more than 12 feet deep, and a large amount of ore, mostly in small lumps not over one foot in diameter has been found, but no solid body has been reached. The surface ore is mostly in small pieces, stalactitic and of good quality, while that in the cut is dense and often cherty.

INDIAN CREEK BANK,

T. 26, R. 6 E., Sec. 35, N. W. qr., Butler county. At this place the ore lies upon the top and down the south slope of a low hill not over 50 feet in height. Ore is thinly spread over an area perhaps 150 feet in diameter, perhaps rather more in an east and west direction. It occurs mostly in small pieces, save at one place, where is an almost solid outcrop of perhaps 20 feet diameter. The ore is of poor quality, being either cherty or porous and full of Sand.

Miller Bank,

T. 26, R. 6 E., Sec. 35, N. W. qr. of N. E. qr., Butler county, is another, and quite characteristic instance of the deposits of this class which are found capping the hills, apparently not far removed from the place of original deposition, but still showing no solid ore masses. The features of it can be seen from the accompanying sketch, Fig. 82. The ore lies upon top of a hill on the south side of Indian Creek, in two outcrops. These cap the highest points of the hill, but are separated by a shallow depression in which no ore at all is found, nor does it extend far down the slope. In quality it is very poor, being sandy and ochreish—the southern outcrop so much so as to be almost worthless, as is it is little more than a ferruginous Sandstone.

Black River Bank No. 1,

T. 26, R. 6 E., Sec. 18, Butler county ; Fig. 83. The ore of this deposit was first found upon the top of a hill about 70 feet high.

A large circular excavation has been made here about 10 to 15 feet deep, from which much cherty ore has been taken in pieces usually of small size, and a large mass of the same ore of irregular shape is disclosed in one wall of the cut. Much very ferruginous red Clay and larger masses of Chert are associated with the ore. About 30 feet below the summit a cut has been run, and from the end a tunnel, which has penetrated below the main cut, but no ore of any amount has been reached by it. At the lower cut, near the surface, some ore was found, but it did not extend to any depth. The tunnel runs through red and yellow Clay, tumbling Chert, and occasionally small seams or streaks of siliceous ore, but these disappear towards the centre of the hill. The excavation above had not been opened down to the tunnel at the time of my visit, so that the exact extent of the mass of ore seen in the wall could not be told, but that it does not extend far is proved by the fact no trace of it is seen in the tunnel below.

The ore is usually of a dark red color, but of a very poor quality, being very cherty and sandy. An analysis of an average sample of such of it as is marketable is given in the table of analyses.

T. 26, R. 6 E., Sec. 18, Butler county, (Fig. 84.) This deposit, both in its character and in the way in which it has been opened, is very similar to the last. It is not quite a quarter of a mile distant, upon top of a hill about 40 feet high, and the ore has been exposed by a summit excavation of irregular shape. A tunnel has also been run about 20 feet below the summit, under the ore, and the excavation has been opened down to the tunnel. The materials through which the tunnel penetrated are about the same as in No. 1, save that less Chert was found and the Clay was not quite so ferruginous.

The principal ore mass exposed is on the side of the cut opposite to which the tunnel penetrated and the bottom of it was not well shown, but it seemed of irregular shape, broken and lying in the Clay. Not much Chert was found with the ore. It is of much better quality than at No. 1, and shows the same variations in mineralogical character. Much of it is red and gives a red streak, and in its lustre and fracture appears like Specular ore, but that it is not is proved by the fact of its containing combined water. It is this ore which has given to this bank the name of a Specular ore deposit, and it was recorded as such in the list of ore banks in the Geological Report for 1872. Specimens of this ore, showing Stalactites and botryoidal forms, are often found adhering to and passing insensibly into true brown, ochreous Limonite. These Stalactites show every appearance of Specular ore, but on analysis by Mr. Chauvenet, were found to contain 9.39 per cent. water—thus proving the ore to be very nearly a true Limonite. Much of this ore which appears red will give a brown streak upon porcelain, showing at once and without the trouble of further examination that it is Limonite. An analysis of an average sample of the ore from this bank will be found in the table.

A number of other banks owned by the same company occur in this region, but they are mostly unopened, and present few peculiarities which are not found in other banks.

ALLEN BANK,

T. 24, R. 6 E., Sec. 4, W. half N. W. qr., Butler county. This bank shows the ore upon the western slope of a low hill not above 40 feet high. The ore lies along the slope some 300 feet or more, and is perhaps 50 feet in width. It occurs in pieces of various sizes, but shows no solid mass. In quality it is porous and sandy, but not enough so to render it worthless.

There are a large number of other banks of this class in South-east Missouri, as can be seen from the accompanying list, but the descriptions given are believed to be fairly typical instances of the character and appearance of these deposits.

DEPOSITS OF SPECULAR ORE.

The only deposit of Specular ore seen in this region was in Wayne county and called the "Cheeney Bank," T. 29, R. 4 E., Sec. 21, N. E. qr. of S. E. qr.; (Fig. 85.)

Specular ore of very fine quality was here found scattered over a large surface down the south slope of a high ridge, between and in two ravines, and a considerable distance down the main ravine formed by the union of these two. In the west ravine, Limonite was also found in considerable quantity upon the surface, but it proved, on being tested, to be only a disturbed deposit of limited extent. A number of cuts and test pits had been dug between the ravines in search of Specular ore, but no large mass of it had been found. At the time of examination, one shaft had reached a depth of 30 feet, but no Specular ore was found after passing the first 4 or 5 feet below the surface. The same thing was noticed in the cuts below this shaft. The Specular ore occurred in Clay quite near the surface. The shaft was sunk in a red Clay with much broken, ferruginous Chert intermixed. In the cut and shaft at top of the hill, considerable Limonite was found in scattering pieces. No rock was seen in position anywhere near this bank. The top of the hill was covered with Chert and sandy Limestone, and much ferruginous Chert was found in the cuts.

It is reported on reliable authority that afterwards another shaft was sunk about half way between the 30 foot shaft last described and the top of the hill. A large boulder of ore was found here near the surface, and ore in larger and smaller pieces in the Clay and Chert all the way down, to a depth of 90 feet, where the shaft stopped without reaching solid rock.

It is not improbable that other deposits of Specular ore will be found in the northern part of Wayne county, but time failed for a complete examination of the whole county.

LIST OF ORE BANKS.

The accompanying list of ore banks has been made upon the plan of that by Dr. A. Schmidt, published in the report of the Geological Survey for 1872. It may be regarded as merely a continuation of the list there given of the ore banks of the South-eastern Limonite District. No deposit is here given which has not been visited by Dr.

Schmidt or myself. It is not of course a completed list; but for some portions of the region, it is believed to approach it, as for instance, that portion of Bollinger county around Marble Hill, and the northern and the north-eastern (but not the western) parts of Butler county.

In the south-eastern part of Wayne county, east of the St. Francois River, are reported a number of valuable deposits of ore, but unfortunately they could not be examined at the time with the others.

Many so-called ore banks have been visited in this region, which have not been included in the list, for the reason that they are not deemed of sufficient size and importance to deserve it. Of this class are a few deposits which were reported in the last list, but not visited by any member of the Survey.

These ore deposits, nearly all, must find their exit to market over one or the other branch of the Iron Mountain Railroad, or by the partially completed Illinois, Missouri and Texas Railroad, a line from Poplar Bluff to Cape Girardeau.

The classification of ore deposits remains the same as that adopted by Dr. A. Schmidt, in the last volume of the Missouri Report, and the same symbols are used to indicate the probable nature and extent of the deposits.

As the deposits are so nearly all Limonite, it will be sufficient here to republish only the divisions of these, and the symbols for them. They are:

  g. Deposits of Limonite on Limestone.
  h. Disturbed or drifted deposits of Limonite.

The signs used in the column indicating probable size, are also the same as before:

  1. Estimated at less than 20,000 tons.
  2. Estimated at 20,000 to 100,000, etc.

COLUMN 1—
   Consecutive numbers.
 COLUMN 2—
   Names of deposits or banks. These names are such as are commonly used to designate the deposits in the neighborhood, or they have been given them from the owners, or from some stream, town, county, or other object having some relation to the deposit.

COLUMN 3—

Location of deposits. This was obtained from the most reliable sources attainable, and is generally correct, but there may be a few instances in which the number of the section or the quarter section, is incorrectly given. It is not believed, however, that an error of more than a half mile will be found in the location of any of the banks.

COLUMN 4—

Counties in which deposits are situated.

COLUMN 5—

Names of owner or lessee.

COLUMN 6—

Probable character of deposit, indicated by the signs just described.

COLUMN 7—

Probable size of deposit.

COLUMN 8—

Distance from railroad.

Number one of this list is equivalent to No. 40 of the ore bank list of Dr. A. Schmidt, in the report for 1872:

LIST OF ORE BANKS.

Number	Name	Location	County	Owner or Lessee	Probable character of deposit	Probable size of deposit	Distance from nearest Railroad.
1	Matthew's Bank	T. 32, R. 6 E, Sec. 3	Madison	Dundas and others		1	St. L. I. M. & S. R. W., 9 miles.
2	Ford's Bank	T. 33, R. 7 E	"	Ford & Burll	G	2	" ½ mile.
3	Gregoire Bank	T. 33, R. 7 E	"	H. Gregoire	"	2	" ½ mile.
4	Foster Bank	T. 33, R. 7 E, Sec. 16, N. E, qr.	"	Madison Mining Company	H	1	" 1½ mile.
5	Nifong Bank	T. 31, R. 8 E, Sec. 2, S.E. qr.	Bollinger	Nifong, Belken & Ruth	G	1	" ¼ mile.
6	Rhodes' Bank	T. 31, R. 8 E, Sec. 14, S. W. qr.	"	——— Rhodes	"	1	" 3 miles.
7	Gilman Bank	T. 31, R. 8 E, Sec. 1, N. W. qr.	"	Mr. Gilman of Frederickt'n.	H	1	" ½ mile.
8	Deal's Bank	T. 31, R. 8 E, Sec. 2	"	Col. Deal, Charleston, Mo...	G	1	" ½ mile.
9	Turkey Hill	T. 31, R. 10 E, Sec. 32, N. W. qr.	"	Mr. Brown, St. Louis	H	1	" 2½ miles.
10	Poblick's Bank	T. 32, R. 8 E, Secs. 23 & 24	"	Mr. Gilman, Fredericktown	"	1	" 2 miles.
11	Glenn Emma Bank	T. 30, R. 9 E, Sec. 16	"	Missouri Furnace Company	"	1	" 3 miles.

No.	Bank	Location	County	Owner					Distance
12	Cushman Hill	T. 30, R. 9 E., Sec. 18, N. E. qr. of N. E. qr	"	"	H	1	"	"	6 miles.
13	Jesse Lute's Bank	T. 30, R. 9 E., Sec. 11, N. E. qr. of N. W. qr	"	Antrim & Tyler	G	1	"	"	3 miles.
14	Francis Bank	T. 30, R. 9 E., Sec. 25	"	R. O. Thompson and Co	H	1	"	"	6 miles.
15	Philip Baker Bank	T. 31, R. 10 E., Sec. 2, N. E. qr	"	J. R. Keep	"	1	"	"	1½ mile.
16	Tibbs' Bank	T. 31, R. 10 E., Sec. 29, S. W. qr. of S. E. qr	"	A. J. Tibbs	"	1	"	"	1½ mile.
17	Robbins' Bank	T. 31, R. 9 E., Sec. 10	"	R. O. Thompson and others	"	1	"		1 mile.
18	Peter Baker Bank	T. 30, R. 10 E., Sec. 6, N. E. qr	"	Orth & Severing	"	1	"	"	1 mile.
19	John Lute's Bank	T. 30, R. 10 E., Sec. 7	"	Gilman & Stevens	"	1	"	"	1½ mile.
20	Mouser Bank	T. 30, R. 9 E., Sec. 35, N. W. qr	"	E. Mouser	H	1	"	"	6 miles.
21	T. W. Shell Bank	T. 29, R. 9 E., Sec. 10, N. E. qr. of S. E. qr	"	T. W. Shell	"	1	"	"	8 miles.
22	Chilton Bank	T. 30, R. 9 E., Sec. 13	"	Mr. Jessop, of St. Louis	"	1	"	"	2 miles.
23	Myers' Bank	T. 30, R. 8 E., Sec. 32, S. E. qr. of N. E. qr	"	Mo. Furnace Co	"	1	"	"	13 miles.
24	Speer's Mountain Bank	T. 29, R. 7 E., Sec. 3, W. hf. Lot 2 N. E. qr	Wayne	E. C. Cushman	G	1	"	"	16 miles.
25	Sim's Bank	T. 29, R. 7 E., Sec. 2, W. hf. Lot 2 N. W. qr	"	J. S. Sims	H	1	"	"	15 miles.
26	Reed Bank	T. 28, R. 8 E., Sec. 17, N. W. qr. of N. W. qr	Bollinger	U. Reed, of St. Charles	"	1	"	"	20 miles.

LIST OF ORE BANKS—Continued.

Number.	Name.	Location.	County.	Owner or Lessee.	Probable character of Deposit.	Probable size of Deposit.	Distance from nearest Railroad.
27	Reese Creek Bank.	T. 28, R. 6 E., Sec. 5.	Wayne.	Graff, Bennett & Co.	H	1	St. L. I. M. & S. R. W., 15 miles.
28	Roe Bank.	T. 28, R. 6, E., Sec. 15, S.W. qr. of S. W. qr.	"	" "	G	1	" 15 miles.
28	Atkins' Bank.	T. 28, R. 6 E., Sec. 6, S. W. qr.	"	J. A. Atkins.	H	1	" 14 miles.
30	Lewis Johnson B'k	T. 28, R. 6 E., Sec. 15, N. E. qr. of S. W. qr	"	Mrs. N. T. Dalton.	"	1	" 15 miles.
31	Pettit Bank.	T. 27, R. 7 E., Sec. 19, S. E. qr.	"	L. M. Pettit.	"	1	" 8 miles.
32	Otter Creek Bank.	T. 27, R. 6 E., Sec. 35, S. E. qr.	"	"	"	1	" 5½ miles.
33	Dewine Bank.	T. 27, R. 6 E., Sec. 25, S. E. qr.	"	Estate of J. W. Dewine.	"	1	" 7 miles.
34	Joiner Bank.	T. 27, R. 6 E., Sec. 19, N. E. qr. of N. E. qr.	"	L. Joiner.	"	1	" 5 miles.
35	Ramsay Bank	T. 27, R. 6 E., Sec. 23.	"	Singer, Nimick & Co.	"	1	" 7½ miles.
36	Mann Bank.	T. 27, R. 6 E., Sec. 21.	"	H. Mann.	"	1	" 6 miles.

No.	Name	Location		Owner				Distance
37	Dalton Bank	T. 27, R. 5 E., Sec. 4, lot 3 N. W. qr.	"	J. Dalton	H	1	St. L., I. M. & S. R. W., 6 miles.	
38	Sloan Bank	T. 27, R. 5 E., Sec. 15, N. E. qr. of N. E. qr.	"	A. Sloan	"	1	"	3 miles.
39	Haney Hollow B'k	T. 27, R. 5 E., Sec. 5, S. W. qr.	"	C. McCormack	"	1	"	3½ miles.
40	Bosanban Bank	T. 27, R. 5 E., Sec. 9, S, E. qr.	"	Bosanban, of St. Louis	"	1	"	3 miles.
41	—— Bank	T. 27, R. 5 E., Sec. 8, S. E. qr.	"	Jno. S. Wilson	"	1	"	2½ miles.
42	Otter Creek Bank	T. 27, R. 5 E. Sec. 4, N. E. qr.	"	O. H. P. Williams	"	1	"	5 miles.
43	Morris Creek Bank	T. 27, R. 4 E., Sec. 35, S. E. qr.	"	O. H. P. Williams	G	1	"	2 miles.
44	Haney Bank	T. 26, R. 5 E., Sec. 5, S. W. qr.	"	A. F. Burns	H	1	"	2½ miles.
45	Daniel's Bank	T. 29, R. 3 E., Sec. 26, N. E. qr.	"	Mrs. G. C. Bowen	"	1	"	1½ mile.
46	Bear M't Bank	T. 29, R. 3 E., Sec. 2, N. W. qr.	"	McKenzie Mining Co	"	1	"	1½ mile.
47	*Cheeney Bank	T. 29, R. 4 E., Sec. 21, S. E. qr.	"	Clark & McCabe	D	1	"	6 miles.
48	Maxwell Bank	T. 29, R. 4 E., Sec. 25, S. E. qr.	"	Estate of A. Brown	H	1		

* Specular ore.

LIST OF ORE BANKS—CONTINUED.

Number	Name	Location	County	Owner or Lessee	Probable character of deposit	Probable size of deposit	Distance from nearest railroad
49	†Yancey M't Bank	T. 30, R. 4 E., Sec. 35, N. E. qr	Wayne	T. C. McCormack	H	1	St. L. I. M. & S. R. W., 5 miles.
50	†Kister Bank	T. 30, R. 4 E., Sec. 35, N. W. qr	"	J. C. Kister	"	1	"　　" 5 miles.
51	Cedar Bay Bank	T. 28, R. 8 E., Sec. —	"	Clarkson & Bro	H	1	"　　" 2 miles.
52	Clarkson Bank	T. 28, R. 4 E., Sec. 19	"	"	"	1	"　　" 2 miles.
53	Big Lake Creek B'k	T. 28, R. 4 E., Sec. 1, S. W. qr	"	C. H. Hickman	G	1	"　　" 7 miles.
54	Little Lake Creek Bank	T. 29, R. 5 E., Sec. 31, S. E. qr	"	O. H. P. Williams	H	1	"　　" 8 miles.
55	Mason Bank	T. 28, R. 5 E., Sec. 6, N. E. qr	"		G	1	"　　" 8 miles.
56	Spiva Bank	T. 27, R. 8 E., Sec. 26	Stoddard	James M. Spiva	G	1	I. M. & Texas Railroad, ½ mile.
57	Leach Bank	T. 27, R. 8 E., Sec 24, S. E. qr	"	G. C. Williams	H	1	"　　" 7¼ miles.
58	West Bank	T. 27, R. 10 E., Sec. 5, N. W. qr	"	Mrs. J. West	G	1	"　　" 2 miles.

† Limonite on Porphyry.

No.	Bank	Location		Owner						Distance
59	Spencer Bank	T. 27, R. 9 E., Sec. 1, N. E. qr.	"	R. Spencer	H	1	"	"		1 mile.
60	Loufoy Bank	T. 27, R. 9 E., Sec. 1, S. E. qr.	"	J. Loufoy	"	1	"	"		1½ miles.
61	Scott Bank	T. 26, R. 7 E., Sec. 33	Butler	—— Scott	"	1	"	"		3½ miles.
62	Blue Spring Bank	T. 26, R. 7 E., Sec. 26, S. E. qr. of S. E. qr.	"	W. H. Rigger	G	1	"	"		½ mile.
63	Ferguson Bank	T. 26, R. 7 E., Sec. 28, N. E. qr.	"	J. S. Ferguson	H	1	"	"		2 miles.
64	Rigger Bank	T. 26, R. 7 E., Sec. 26, W. hf S. E. qr.	"	Singer, Nimick & Co.	"	1	"	"		1 mile.
65	Romine Bank	T. 26, R. 7 E., Sec. 35, N. E. qr.	"	"	G	1	"	"		1 mile.
66	St. Francois Bank	T. 26, R. 7 E., Sec. 24, S. half N. W. qr.	"	"	"	2	"	"		1½ miles.
67	Indian Ford Bank No. 1	T. 26, R. 7 E., Sec. 24, N. half N. E. qr.	"	"	"	1	"	"		1 mile.
67	Indian Ford Bank No. 2	T. 26, R. 7 E., Sec. 23, N. E. qr.	"	"	"	1	"	"		1½ miles.
69	Indian Ford Bank No. 3	T. 26, R. 7 E., Sec. 23, N. E. qr. of S. W. qr.	"	"	"	1	"	"		1½ miles.
70	Indian Ford Bank No. 4	T. 26, R. 7 E., Sec. 22, S. half N. W. qr.	"	"	"	1	"	"		2½ miles.
71	Indian Ford Bank No. 5	T. 26, R. 7 E., Sec. 22, S. E. qr.	"	"	H		"	"		2 miles.
72	Gibson Bank	T. 26, R. 7 E., Sec. 27, N. W. qr.	"	"	"	1	"	"		2½ miles.

LIST OF ORE BANKS—CONTINUED.

Number	Name	Location	County	Owner	Probable size of deposit	Probable character of deposit	Distance from nearest railroad.
73	Mud Creek Bank	T. 26, R. 7 E., Sec. 26, S. half N. W. qr	Butler	Singer, Ninick & Co.	H	1	I. M. & Texas Railroad, 1½ mile.
74	Connor Bank	T. 26, R. 7 E., Sec. 16, N. W. qr	"	A. F. Burns	"	1	" 3½ miles.
75	Indian Creek Bank	T. 26, R. 6 E., Sec. 35, N. W. qr	"	G. C. Thillenius	"	1	St. L., I. M. & S. R.W., 4 miles.
76	Indian Creek Bank No. 2	T. 26, R. 6 E., Sec. 33, N. half S. E. qr	"	"	"	1	" 4 miles.
77	—— Bank	T. 26, R. 6 E., Sec. 35, S. half N. E. qr	"	U. S. Government land	G	1	" 4 miles.
78	Miller Bank	T. 26, R. 6 E., Sec. 35, N. W. qr of N. E. qr	"	Jacob Miller	H	1	" 4 miles.
79	Peterberger Bank	T. 26, R. 5 E., Sec. —	"	A. F. Burns	G	1	" 1 mile.
80	Turkey Pen Hollow Bank	T. 26, R. 5 E., Sec. 27	"	J. M. Smith	H	1	" 2½ miles.
81	Watt's Bank	T. 26, R. 6 E., Sec. 18, N. E. qr	"	Elizabeth Watts	"	1	" ½ mile.

No.	Bank	Location		Owner					Distance
82	Black River banks.	T. 26, R. 6, E, Sec. 18	"	Taylor & Williams	H	1	"	"	½ mile.
83		T. 26, R. 6 E., Sec. 18	"	"	H	1	"	"	½ mile.
84		T. 26, R. 6E., Sec. 18, S. E. qr	"	"	H	1	"	"	½ mile.
85		T. 26, R. 6 E., Sec. 18, S._E. qr	"	"	H	1	"	"	½ mile.
86		T. 26, R. 6 E., Sec. 19	"	"	H	1	"	"	½ mile.
87		T. 26, R. 6 E., Sec. 19, N. E. qr	"	"	H	1	"	"	½ mile.
88	Huskey bank	T. 25, R. 4 E., Sec. 24, S.E. S. E.	"	Jno. Huskey	H	1	"	"	8 miles.
89	Post bank	T. 26, R. 4 E., Sec. 12, N. W. qr	"	F. Post	H	1	"	"	4 miles.
90	Sutton bank	T. 26, R. 6 E., Sec. 20, S. W. qr. of S. W. qr	"	A. H. Dunn	H	1	"	"	1 mile.
91	Allen bank	T. 24, R 6 E., Sec. 4 W hf. N. W. qr	"	E. Allen	H	1	"	"	1½ miles.
92	Shrout bank	T. 25, R. 6 E., Sec. 16, N. E. qr. of N. E. qr	"	Orth & Levring	G	1	"	"	1½ miles.
93	Hill bank	T. 25, R. 6 E., Sec. 9, W. hf. S. E. qr	"	Mrs. D. W. Hill	H	1	"	"	¼ mile.
94	Dillard bank	T. 25, R 6 E., Sec. 17, S. E. of N. E	"	Jas. Dillard	H	1	"	"	1½ miles.
95	Hendricison bank	T. 25, R. 6 E., Sec. 16, N. W qr	"	Estate D. Hendrickson	H	1	"	"	1 mile.
96	Swattler bank	T. 25, R. 6 E., Sec. 28, N. E. qr. of N. W. qr. and N. E. qr. of N. E. qr.	"	G. C. Thillenius & A. H. Dunn.	G	1	"	"	2½ miles.
97	Dunn bank	T. 25, R. 6 E., Sec. 17, E. hf. S. W. qr	"	A. H. Dunn	G	1	"	"	2 miles.

APPENDIX A.

NOTES ON THE HISTORY OF LEAD MINING IN MISSOURI.

BY HENRY COBB.

The first step taken by the white man in the Mineral Region of Missouri was during the summer of 1541, when DeSoto, a grandee of Spain, who had distinguished and enriched himself while aiding Pizarro in the conquest of Peru, being appointed Governor of Cuba, determined to explore the central region of North America, in the hope of discovering rich mines of Gold and Silver, and establishing a colony in the El Dorado, which would secure for him fame and fortune more brilliant than Peru afforded to Pizarro, or Mexico to Cortez, and where he would rise above all his rivals in the list of historical immortality.

Only a short sketch will here be given of this adventure, which should be elaborated with more minute details hereafter in the history of the Geological Survey of Missouri, and in the heroic poems to be written of the bold enterprise displayed in those early days; as it is manifest in the past that the motive of the Spaniard in Missouri, in 1541, fired the breast of the French, in 1719, when Renault & LaMotte came with their band of miners and artisans to re-explore this mineral region, and discover the mines of Gold and Silver, whose existence the igneous rocks of Granite and Porphyry suggested, the signs of Gold Quartz and Argentiferous Lead indicated, and the Indian rumor asserted; although the coveted prize had eluded the search of DeSoto; and a kindred motive impelled Schoolcraft, in 1818, to view the mines of Missouri, and trace the track of the Spanish hero from the sources of the St. Francis, along the summit of the Ozark range, to the sources of the White River; and, although in his survey Schoolcraft found no mines of Gold or Silver, he discovered the Lead mines of South-west Missouri, and built the first furnace there in January, 1819. Renault and LaMotte having made discoveries and started the first Lead furnace in South-east Missouri, in 1720; and it is manifest in the present that, though the mines of precious metals are not yet discovered in Missouri, those of useful ones—particularly of Iron, Lead and Zinc—are so abundant and productive, and the impulse given to their development is so strong that several millions dollars, in value, yearly flow from this source; and, by the manufacture of mineral, vegetable and animal materials, mainly of Missouri, its great metropolis in 1874, is producing, in value, yearly, more than $200,000,000; and thus the dream of wealth and fame in which DeSoto indulged, 333 years ago, is now a reality to St. Louis.

DeSoto, according to Bancroft, left Cuba with 600 men, many of them cavaliers and noblemen, with 300 horses, splendidly equipped, and, passing into Florida, fighting several fierce battles, traversed the Southern country, discovered and crossed the Mississippi River, in May 1541, ascended into the mineral region, and remained 40 days, from the 19th of June to the 29th of July, at Pacaha, "a spot which can not be identified;" having passed on his way tribes of Indians cultivating fields of corn, sent an exploring party north, toward the Missouri, into a land of hunters and buffaloes; then, turning westward, during August, followed the range of the Ozark Mountains to the high lands of White River; and, though he found the country was a mineral region, "the mountains offered neither gems nor Gold." Marching to the south in the land of the Tunicas, he wintered in Arkansas, at the town of Autiamque, then returning to the grandest object he discovered, DeSoto died, May 21, 1542, and was buried at midnight in the middle of the Mississippi.

The scientific and researching spirit of Schoolcraft was dissatisfied with the uncertainties in the narrations of the course pursued and places visited by DeSoto in Missouri, and endeavored to locate them with more accuracy, while traveling over the reputed ground from the South-east to South-west Missouri and Northern Arkansas in 1818 and 1819.

Among his various and valuable productions, Schoolcraft wrote a report of these researches, entitled "Scenes and Adventures in the Semi-Alpine Region of the Ozark Mountains of Missouri and Arkansas, which were first traversed by DeSoto in 1541," and from his investigations in Madison county, where he mentions "mineral discoveries —not of Gold, indeed, which was DeSoto's search, but of Tin, Lead, Copper, Iron, Cobalt and Antimony," he states: "I was now in the probable region of DeSoto's Coligoa, the utmost north-westwardly point of his exploration, and it ceased to be a matter of surprise that the Indians had given him such wonderful accounts of the mineral wealth of the sources of the St. Francis." "The Iron Mountains of Belleview, so called, are part of this development."

But in the greatest work of Schoolcraft's life on the "Indian Tribes of the United States," published by authority of Congress, in 1853, he furnishes a "Map of the route of DeSoto," drawn by S. Eastman, U. S. A., from which it appears that the river was discovered at the lower Chickasaw Bluffs, near what is now the north-western corner of the State of Mississippi, in the county of DeSoto, where the route ran north of west to the St. Francis River, in the land of the Casqui Indians; thence east of north to the present Missouri line near what is now the site of New Madrid, when he fought the Capahas; thence west of south and across the St. Francis, to Quiguate, below and near the mouth of the L'Auguille; thence north, along Crowley's ridge, to the Missouri line, and on between the St. Francis and Black Rivers, to Coligoa, the land of mineral wealth, which seems to have been located, according to this map, in what is now known as the valley of Arcadia, described by Schoolcraft as being "at the foot of the high granitical peaks of St. Francis county, Missouri, celebrated in modern days for the Iron Mountains, and the Lead and Cobalt mines of LaMotte;" thence west of south across Black and Current Rivers in Missouri, in search of a rich province called Cayas; and, probably, crossed White River at Tanico, in Arkansas ; thence west through Tula, and over the Pawnee, now Boston Mountains, to Autiamague, now Fort Gibson, where, among the Quipana Nation, he wintered in a fruitful country of meadows ; thence down the Arkansas River to its mouth, where, according to Schoolcraft, DeSoto died.

This bold adventure of DeSoto, in the mineral region of Missouri, within fifty years after the discovery of America, by Columbus, has been viewed with mingled feelings of admiration at the enterprise, and regret at the failure ; the history of the event is involved in clouds of obscurity by reason of the vague reports made of the expedition, upon which Schoolcraft, by his researches, has thrown much light, which may be increased by future investigation in Missouri, as it has been lately in Arkansas. Yet, withal, the influence of DeSoto is still felt by many scientific and practical seekers after mineral wealth, as it was felt in France in 1717, when the first great practical impulse was given to open the mines of Missouri.

Some facts in the history of the Company of the West, chartered in Paris, August 23, 1717, were noted by Dr. Litton in the Geological Report of Missouri 1854, to which a few more may be added in this sketch.

Philip Francis Renault, agent of the "Company of St. Philips," an association of individuals which had been formed under the patronage of the Western Company for prosecuting the business of mining Gold and Silver in the Upper Country of Louisiana and Illinois, as the Missouri region was then called, left France in the year 1719, with 200 artificers and miners, provided with tools and means to execute the objects of the Company. On his way, at the Island of St. Domingo, he purchased 500 slaves to work in the mines. LaMotte, a companion, an agent versed in the knowledge of minerals, in one of the earliest excursions, in 1720, discovered the Lead mines on the St, Francis River, which bear his name ; and soon after those extensive mines north of Potosi—the Old Mines and others—were discovered by Renault, to one of which his name was given. Many other mines of Lead were discovered, among them the Mine a Gerbore, and numerous deep holes were dug throughout the mining region, from the waters of the St. Francis to those of the Meramec, by these searchers for Silver and Gold ; but no Silver, except the small per cent. found in the ore of LaMotte and near Mine a Renault, was discovered, although the LaMotte was called "Gold Mine," on account of the immense size of the vein.

The Lead produced by Renault supplied the hunters who roamed and the settlements located through the French possessions from Canada to New Orleans. The largest portion of it, which is reported a very great quantity, was shipped for France. In 1731, after the Company of the West was united with the Royal Company of the Indies, the whole Territory of the Mississippi Valley—bounded by New Mexico on the west, and by the lands of the English of Carolina on the east—watered by the river of St. Louis, heretofore called the "Mississippi and its tributaries," "with the exclusive privilege of the commerce of Louisiana and the working of the mines," which had been ceded to the Company, was retro-ceded to the crown of France. Renault, however, remained in the country until 1742, when, having sold his slaves, he, with many of his workmen, returned to his native land, and the mining interest languished.

In 1762, France ceded Louisiana to Spain, and although the possession of the country remained unchanged until 1769, in the meantime, the mining spirit seems to have revived, as Francis Burton, born in 1710, and while a youth employed under Renault, having changed the pursuit of mining to that of a hunter, on an excursion for game about the year 1763, made one of the richest discoveries in the mineral region, which was called Mine a Burton, now known as Potosi ; and the Mine a Robina, two miles from the Mine a Burton, was discovered about the same time. Miners were working in the Old Mines at this date, when it was abandoned for many years, and the workmen were gathered from the Old Mines and others to the New Mines, where the mineral was found lying in great abundance on the surface of the ground, and large quantities of ore were raised from these mines on their first discovery.

The historical facts regarding Renault's operations, were first published in 1819, by Schoolcraft, who gained them by his researches among papers, documents and testimony in law suits on land claims, by the heirs of Renault, and data derived from the obscurity of private life, both in France and America; and the progress of mining, during the latter half of the eighteenth century, with the prospect in 1804 was shown, mainly, by the report of Moses Austin to the President of the United States, which most valuable document, on the early history of the "Lead Mines in Upper Louisiana," is preserved among the American State Papers and reproduced in this Appendix.

Under the Spanish Government, the mining business seems to have been moderately conducted with very little change, and with uncertain data of the quality or value of the mineral produced, until near the end of the last century. The process of smelting was rude and imperfect, only common open log furnaces were used and the Lead ashes wasted, so that not more than fifty per cent. of metal was turned out of the ore; and neither shot nor any other manufacture of Lead was produced until the year 1799.

Early in this era and as a pleasant relief to the weary searcher among the obscure events of history, Longfellow has thrown some rays of social light, through the poem "of Evangeline," by introducing his leading characters in this region, and locating the devoted heroine, at that time, here for a year.

> " Into this wonderful land, at the base of the Ozark Mountains,
> Gabriel far had entered, with hunters and trappers behind him."
> " Mounting his Mexican steed, with his Indian guides and companions,
> Homeward Basil returned, and Evangeline stayed at the Mission."

This Mission may have been at the village of St. Michaels, now Fredericktown, near Mine La Motte, or at Mine a Burton, now Potosi; as these must have been the chief villages among the valleys of the Ozark Mountains in the days of the wandering "sad and afflicted" Acadian.

Although the history of mining in Missouri, during the eighteenth century, is so obscure that it is difficult to form an estimate of the quality and value of the metal produced, yet, from the year 1800, so much light has been thrown on this subject by Austin, Schoolcraft, Litton and others, that a close approximate estimate may be formed of the production during the seventy years, and of the production during the four years between 1869 and 1874, the exact facts are known.

It would be interesting to gain at least a reasonable, speculative estimate of the production during the 80 years the mines were worked in the last century, and with the history of the 700 workmen who commenced operations in 1720, together with the historical and statistical facts stated in Austin's Report of 1804, hereto appended, the chief factors are furnished to operate in the demonstration, which each curious critic may test.

The large number of workmen under Renault, might raise the presumption of a greater production than the other facts in the case justify, and, doubtless, the most of them were engaged in other pursuits than mining. Besides the six mines already mentioned by Austin, four more are recorded by him : The Mine a Lanye, discovered in 1795 ; the Mine a Maneto, or American Mines, and the Mine a la Platte, both being discovered in October, 1799 ; also, the Mine a Joe, now called the Bogy Mine, which was discovered in 1801. Although it appears that not more than five of these ten mines were operated in 1804, and that the three of Burton, Old and LaMotte, furnished nearly all the metal made, according to the condensed, specific statement by Austin, of the yearly production in 1801-4, as follows:

Mine a Burton	366,667	pounds.
Old Mines	133,333	"
Mine a LaMotte	200,000	"
All the other Mines	30,000	"
Total	730,000	"

The price of lead was $5.00 per hundred, making the yearly value of metal $36,-500. To which value Mr. Austin added $30.00, for each thousand on 120,000 pounds manufactured into shot and sheet Lead, $3,600, making the total annual value $40,100, which he states was the average annual product for the years 1801, 1802 and 1803.

Austin also states that men were operating Mine LaMotte, Old Mines and Mine a Gerbore in 1763, when Mine a Burton was discovered; that Mine LaMotte "furnished almost all the Lead exported from the Illinois," about the years 1738-40; that the mineral was formed in regular veins from two to four feet solid; that five of the veins have been opened and the Lead found within four or five feet of the surface; and that for the years 1802 and 1803, about 30 men were employed in this mine from four to six months in each year; and that, of all the other mines in the district, there were 91 families, consisting of 728 in total population. From all these and many other facts, which might be adduced, it seems reasonable to conclude that the annual production of all the Lead mines, during those 80 years, was at least equal to the annual production of Mine LaMotte and Old Mines in 1801, if not to one-half the total production of all the mines at the latter date. The difference being small, assuming the lowest estimate, 333,333. The total production during the 80 years from 1720 to 1800, was 26,666,666 lbs., being about equal in quantity to the total production in the single year of 1873; and estimating the price, at the rate stated by Austin, the annual value equalled $16,666, and the aggregate for the 80 years amounted to $1,333,333. By assuming the higher estimate, the total quantity amounts to 29,200,000 pounds, and the value, $1,460,000, which still is less in value than the production of 1873. It is possible, however, that one may be justified in estimating the total quantity, in the last century, at 40,000,000 pounds, and the total value at $2,000,000, though 30,000,000 pounds in quantity, and $1,500,000 in value, may be the estimate sustained by the strongest probabilities.

Accepting the last stated estimate as the most reasonable one attainable, and adding it to that furnished by Austin, which represents an aggregate quantity of 2,190,-000 pounds, the value of which was $109,500, it appears that before the Government of the United States came into possession of this country, at the end of 1803, the mines of Missouri had produced 32,190,000 pounds of Lead, valued at $1,609,500.

In addition to the important historical and statistical facts above noted, from the report of Austin, he estimated the number of workmen employed, including miners, smelters, wood cutters and carters, at 150 men, at all the mines; and that of this number 120 worked four months, and 30 the whole year—each man employed in the business averaging $43.00 per month; from which data accurate and valuable results are gained, showing that the average number of workmen during the whole year was 70, and that their annual wages, which seem to have mainly included the profits of the proprietors, amounted to $36,120.

Austin went to Mine a Burton in 1797. In 1798 he sunk the first regular shaft, and built a reverberatory furnace which did the work of 20 French log furnaces then there; and in 1799 he erected a shot tower and a manufactory of sheet Lead. " The Spanish arsenals at New Orleans and Havana, drew a considerable part of their supplies for their navy from this source." Austin's report on the Lead mines, communicated to Congress by message from the President, doubtless speedily drew a large amount of capital and workmen to this newly acquired and rich region.

The next era in the mining business includes the 15 years of territorial order from 1804 to 1819. In determinining the facts of this period, the chief source of information is found in the very valuable publication by Schoolcraft of his " View of the Lead Mines of Missouri," for which an everlasting debt of gratitude is due him by the State ; and this entire work which now is almost out of print, should be reproduced, both for its intrinsic value and as an honor to the memory of the author for the services he rendered this cause.

Such an immense variety of important facts are furnished in this work, that the task is difficult to epitomize them properly, for the purpose of this sketch ; therefore, only a few of the leading ones, pointing to the most valuable final results, may be here noted. One of the main final results sought, is the annual production. This is furnished, with evidence and skill commanding strong confidence, by first discovering the quantity shipped during three years, from Ste. Genevieve and Herculaneum, where the Lead from the mines was mainly delivered, and adding the quantity manufactured into shot at Herculaneum, which latter item was found to be 1,356,700 pounds for three years, making a total sum of 9,515,512 pounds, and an annual average amount of 3,171,837 pounds ; and afterward securing estimates from each mine of the productions during the three years; by which process it was found that the total sum amounted to 11,180,-000 pounds, and that the average annual product was 3,726,666 pounds.

As a picture in the history of the Missouri mines at the end of the territorial era, a copy from Schoolcraft may be here presented, representing the main result sought for—the production in detail, and total of the area, together with the number and names of all the mines, the number of hands employed at each, and a list of the mines not worked at that time :

Estimate of the Workmen and Production at all the Mines of Missouri, during three years ending June 1, 1819.

No.	Mines.	Pounds of Lead.	No. of Hands.
1	Mine a Burton..	1,500,000	160
27	Mine Shibboleth..	2,700,000	240
43	Mine LaMotte..	2,400,000	210
39	Richwoods...	1,300,000	140
41	Bryan's Mines...	910,100	80
42	Dogget's Mines..		
6	Perry's Diggings...	600,000	60
28	Elliot's Mines..		
26	Old Mines...	45,000	20
29	Bellefontaine...		
17	Mine Astraddle..		
33	Mine Liberty..		
34	Renault Mines...	450,000	40
36	Mine Silvers..		
35	Miller's Mines..		
30	Canon Diggings..		
32	Becquet Diggings..	75,000	30
10	Little Mines..		
11	Rock Diggings...		
5	Citadel Diggings..		
25	Lamber's Mines..	1,160,000	130
9	Austin's Mines..		
10	Jones' Mines..		
19	Scott's Mines,..		
3	Mine a Martin...	50,000	20
2	Mine a Robina...		
	Total...	1,1180,100	1,130

List of Mines not Worked.

No.	Mines.	No.	Mines.
4	New Diggings.	38	Pratt's Mine.
40	Mine a Joe.	44	Gray's Mine.
8	Rosenburg's Mine.	23	Moreau Diggings.
22	Henry's Mine.	7	Hawkin's Mine.
15	Bibb's Mine.	24	Tapley's Diggings.
37	Fourche a Courtois.	21	Micheaux's Diggings.
18	Masson's Diggings.	16	Tebault's Diggings.
13	Brushy Run Diggings.	19	J. Scott's Diggings.
45	McKane's Mine.		

"In this estimate are included all persons concerned in the operations of mining, and who draw their support from it—wood cutters, teamsters and blacksmiths, as well as those engaged in digging and smelting Lead ore, etc. The estimate is supposed to embrace a period of three years, ending 1st June, 1819, and making an average product of 3,726,666 pounds per annum, which is so near the result arrived at in the preceding details, as to induce the conclusion that it is essentially correct, and that the mines of Missouri, taken collectively, yield this amount of Pig Lead annually.

"The United States acquired possession of the mines in the year 1803, 15 years ago last December ; and assuming the fact that they have annually produced this quantity, there has been smelted under the American Government, 55,000,000 pounds of Lead."

The average value of Lead, during these 15 years, was estimated by Schoolcraft at four cents per pound; and he had a good opportunity to reach the closest approximation to the fact, through Austin, who had been actively engaged in the business during that period. Allowing the above estimate of quantity and price, the result follows that the total value of the Lead produced from 1804 to 1819, was $2,200,000.

The estimate of quantity appears very high since the annual production in 1803, as stated by Austin at the time, was only 730,000 pounds. Yet, when one considers the fact that immediately on the transfer of the country to the United States, a new era was started, that the discovery of several immense bodies of ore near the surface of the ground greatly increased the fame of the mines and the number of the miners; that during 1811 the new mine, Shibboleth, yielded 5,000,000 pounds of mineral, equal to 3,125,000 pounds of Lead, and in 1819 only about 1,000,000 pounds ; that Mine a Burton, which in 1818 produced only 500,000 pounds, had previously yielded as high as 3,000,000 per annum, and that the Richwoods and Bellefontaine became amazingly productive on their discovery, confidence in the estimate stated is confirmed ; and by adding this total production to that gained under the French and Spanish Governments, one finds that in 1819 the mines of Missouri had yielded Lead to the amount of 87,190,-000 pounds, and $3,809.500 in value.

From the days of the Report of Schoolcraft and the formation of Missouri into a State, another era was started in the mining business and extended to the date of the first Geological Report of Missouri in 1854.

Dr. Litton, Assistant Geologist, rendered the State great service by giving a minute and scientific account of many of the mines and most of the furnaces in the mining region, and especially for the tables of production he has presented on pages 63 and 64 of his Report, to which the reader is referred. All these statements are declared by Litton to be "incomplete," yet, so far as they extend, are to be highly prized. The shipments from the three points of Selma, Plattin Rock and Rush Tower, from 1824 to 1854, are stated at 86,709,605 pounds, to which is added the production of Valle's mine sent elsewhere, increasing the sum to 106,193,882 pounds; yet no statement is made of the shipments during this period from Herculaneum and Ste. Genevieve, at which points all this business was transacted in 1819, when, as above shown, it amounted to more than 3,700,000 pounds yearly, and was divided nearly equally between those points. This order of business seems to have continued until 1831, when Selma supplanted Herculaneum, and, therefore, the shipments from the previous points during twelve years, which at previous rate amounted to 44,400,000 pounds, together with the Lead shipped at Ste. Genevieve from 1831 to 1854, estimated on same basis at over 40,000,000 pounds, should be added to the sum gained by Litton, and the result would show the total amount of Lead shipped from 1819 to 1854, by the Mississippi River below St. Louis, to be more than 170,000,000 pounds.

To this should be added the shipments from the mines in Franklin, Crawford, Newton, Jasper and other counties up to 1854—the famous Virginia Mines of Franklin having been discovered in 1834, and having yielded 10,000,000 pounds of *ore* up to 1854, and the Mount Hope Mine nearly 2,000,000 pounds of Lead during the five years previous to this date, while the mines of Newton and Jasper, as reported by Prof. Swallow, were discovered in 1850, and, during four years, produced 1,551,022 pounds.

The production of these four counties, previous to 1854, can be estimated at not less—but doubtless much more—than 10,000,000 pounds, and therefore the total production of Missouri Lead, from 1819 to 1854, may be stated at 180,000,000 pounds, which is a little above an average of 5,000,000 pounds yearly.

Upon a careful investigation of the average price in the pages of the "Western Journal and Civilian," and elsewhere, it was fixed at four cents per pound, and thus the value of this quantity was shown to be $7,200,000, which, with the quantity added to the previous production, swelled the total amount to 267,190,000 pounds in quantity and $11,009,500 in value.

In confirmation of the last estimate, a portion of an "incomplete statement," by Dr. Litton, of the annual production, in pounds of Lead, in three counties of Missouri, may here be reproduced :

COUNTIES.	1850.	1851.	1852.	1853.
Franklin..............	496,744	380,606	378,630	658,169
St. Francois	1,350,395	1,270,334	1,281,068	1,311,275
Washington............	2,211,586	2,294,194	2,376,742	2,099,638
Total	4,058,725	3,945,134	4,036,440	4,069,082

It thus appears that these three counties, during four years from 1850 to 1854, produced 16,109,381 pounds, making their average annual production at that time 4,027,345 pounds.

To this should be added the production of several other counties above mentioned, and particularly Jefferson and Madison. In the latter, Mine LaMotte yielded 800,000 pounds per annum from 1816 to 1819.

This mine, which was opened more than 150 years ago and which has been steadily worked, produced, as above shown, 200,000 pounds per annum from 1801 to 1804, and continued increasing in its production until in the single year of 1870 the amount arose to the immense figure of 5,128,000 pounds, as determined that year by the Iron Mountain Railroad Company in transporting it to the St. Louis market. This production of Madison county, let it be remembered, was entirely omitted from the United States Census of that year; as the production of all the mines of Missouri was also entirely omitted by the Census of 1860.

Moreover, the Sandy Mines, of Jefferson county, which were discovered in 1824, soon after Schoolcraft made his report, yielded 886,905 pounds of ore from the southern third of the mine during the year ending September 23, 1826. This fact is derived from high personal authority and an investigation of the record at the time of the transaction, and now in the possession of Charles S. Rankin, of Pevely, Jefferson county, Mo. From other evidence derived from the same source, it appears that the northern third of this lode, in 1832, was yielding ore at the rate of 666,666 pounds yearly; and those who are most familiar with these mines, and especially with the superior yield of the middle one-third partly described by Litton, estimate their production during the thirty years from 1824, at 10,000,000 pounds.

The Mammoth, the Tarpley, Gopher, Plattin and other mines of Jefferson county, which have produced several millions of pounds, according to Litton, must likewise be considered; also, the mines of Crawford and of Newton and Jasper, as above stated, and their production added; and further, it should be observed that the production of the rich mines of Golconda, Valle and Skewes, the Cove and Short Lode, Evans, Mount Hope, Darby, Virginia and others of Franklin county, all discovered after the Report of Schoolcraft was made, was very incompletely reported in 1854, to which year the total production of Franklin county was stated at only 1,914,149 pounds, as above shown; while, during this period, Litton allowed the estimate of the production of 10,000,000 pounds of ore from the Virginia Mine alone. Also, it must be remembered that in the years 1816, 1817 and 1818, the annual production of all the mines was 3,726,-666 pounds. Therefore, since all these things are so, the conclusion arrived at, that the production of these thirty-five years was 180,000,000 pounds of Lead, is strongly sustained by the facts in the case.

The next stage in the progress of the history of mining in Missouri brings us at home, from the distance of twenty years between 1854 and 1874.

The facts of production during this space of time are more easily attainable, from living witnesses at the mines, from merchants engaged in the trade, from the reports of their Exchange, and most particularly from the records of the railroads which bring nearly all the Lead produced in the State directly to the St. Louis market, and latterly have kept a separate account, easy of access, by which the amount in pounds of the different mineral productions for each year can be exactly determined.

By the use of the latter means in 1870, when the "Scientific American" of New York reported the annual production of Missouri Lead at less than 2,000,000 pounds, the problem was proved with mathematical precision that the production of Missouri Lead, during the year ending June 1, 1870, was 13,658,000 pounds.

Here, the process of arriving at the desired estimate may be shorter and even more reasonable than that previously employed.

Take the average annual production determined for 1854, and by adding it to that still more accurately determined for 1870, the sum amounts to 18,000,000 pounds. One-half of this amount, 9,000,000 pounds, represents the theoretical average annual production from 1854 to 1870. Extend the application of this average to the end of 1873, and the result gained is that the total amount of production of Missouri Lead, during the twenty years from 1854 to 1874, reached 180,000,000 pounds, which, by a singular coincidence, is exactly equal to the estimate of total production during the thirty-five years preceding 1854, and which result, theoretically deduced, is firmly corroborated by practical facts too numerous to mention, which may be introduced in evidence hereafter—many of them being presented in the body of this volume, and a few very significant ones added to this Appendix.

Although the supply has vastly increased yet the demand has surpassed the supply, and the price has risen from 4 to 7 cents, where it ranged a long while, and frequently rose far higher during this term, reaching 10 cents in 1864, and ended at 6 cents per pound December 31, 1873.

Taking, therefore, 7 cents as a moderate average figure, it follows that the average annual value of the Lead produced in Missouri, during this term, was $630,000, and that the total value during the 20 years was $12,600,000. But the value of the total production, preceding 1854, was shown to be $11,009,500; therefore, by adding these values and omitting the fraction of a few thousand dollars, a demonstration is presented which is doubtless somewhat within the bounds of the reality, showing the total value of Lead produced in Missouri during the 134 years, from 1720 to 1874, was $23,600,000; and, in the same way, by adding the quantities developed—267,190,000 and 180,000,000— and omitting the final fraction, the amount of Lead produced in Missouri during the century and a third, from 1720 to the present year, is shown to be 447,000,000 pounds.

In conclusion of these notes on the history of mining in Missouri, so far as they relate to the Lead business, a few more items of evidence may be adduced to show the rapidly rising power and honor gained for Missouri in the ranks of the United States, by plying the energies of the people to mining and other congenial industrial interests.

The United States Census of 1870, with all its errors against the credit of our State, acknowledges that, in the production of Lead, Missouri has as many establishments as, and more capital invested than all the rest of the United States—all the United States, by this authority, having 62 and Missouri 31 establishments; and the capital invested in the Missouri Pig Lead works being stated at $1,428,600, although Mine LaMotte, one of the largest Lead works in the United States, was omitted from both the number and the capital invested; and the total capital invested in the Pig Lead works of all the United States was put at only $2,191,600; and further, in the year 1870, when the *Scientific American* of New York, as above mentioned, reported the Lead product of Missouri at less than 2,000,000 pounds, and the United States Census stated it at 8,794,000; the railroads of Missouri, which are the best authority, proved that the amount of Pig Lead freighted by them from the furnaces of Missouri to market, during the year ending June 1, 1870, was 13,658,000, and during the year ending December 31, 1870, was 14,128,725 pounds, and finally the railroads prove that the production of Missouri Lead in 1871 was 13,676,883, and in 1873, was 27,676,320 pounds, being an increase of more than 100 per cent. in the last two years.

MISSOURI LEAD.

Prices During 30 Years at St. Louis.

Table of average price of Lead per 100 pounds for 30 years, from 1874 to 1844, as determined by Henry Cobb, on data derived from various sources, especially from Messrs. Chadbourn & Forster, of the St. Louis Shot Tower Company, the Merchants' Exchange, the "Missouri Republican," and the "Western Journal and Civilian :"

Year.	Price.	Year.	Price.
1873	$ 6 87½	1858	$ 5 20
1872	6 87½	1857	6 00¼
1871..A	7 00	1856	6 22
1870	7 25	1855	5 74½
1869	8 75	1854	6 19
1868	9 00	1853	5 98
1867	9 00	1852	4 35
1866	10 00	1851	4 28½
1865	10 00	1850	4 60
1864	12 80	1849	4 07
1863	8 62½	1848	3 68
1862	6 50	1847	3 71
1861	5 25	1846	3 42½
1860	5 25	1845	3 30½
1859	5 25	1844	3 02½

MISSOURI LEAD.

Quantity and Value Produced During 5 Years.

According to the circular dated January 2, 1874, of Messrs. Ferd. F. Rozier & Co., merchants of St. Louis, and large dealers in Pig Lead, the quantity of Missouri Lead produced, each year, for five years, from 1874 to 1869, is stated; and according to the figures gained in the price table with these, the quantity and value of Missouri Lead, produced each year for five years, is shown on the following table:

Table.

Years.	Pounds.	Value.
1873...	27,676,320	$ 1,902,747
1872...	20,427,120	1,404,364
1871...	13,676,883	957,381
1870...	14,128,725	1,024,322
1869...	12,963,975	1,134,347
Total 5 years...	88,873,023	$ 6,423,171

WHITE LEAD WORKS OF ST. LOUIS.

When Pig Lead is brought to market it is turned into bar, sheet, pipe, shot, plumbing and white lead, and all these industries are driven energetically at St. Louis, the white lead business being the leading branch, with works of a capacity and commanding influence unsurpassed by any others in the United States, although neither the white lead nor the lead paint of St. Louis is mentioned in the census of 1870, while the value of their productions, the same year, amounted to $1,768,777.

The white lead works of St. Louis deserve further notice than can be bestowed on them here, where the object is to present merely a statistical table of their production from data furnished mainly by the Collier, White Lead and Oil Company and the Southern White Lead and Color Works.

WHITE LEAD PRODUCTION OF ST. LOUIS IN 1873.

Number of establishments..	4
Hands employed..	352
Capital invested...	$1,850,000
Wages paid..	237,600
Cost of raw materials...	1,450,000
Annual value of product...	2,228,000

To which table may be added an item of the capacity of these works for yielding white lead, yearly, to the value of $3,250,000.

SHOT, PIPE, SHEET LEAD, ETC.

The St. Louis Shot Tower has turned out about $9,000,000 since 1858, producing on an average $600,000 yearly, although this establishment also was unmentioned and no shot reported for St. Louis in the census of 1860 and none in 1870.

The two establishments of Pipe and Sheet Lead in St. Louis yield products amounting to an annual value of $200,000.

Without including the Plumbing business, in which the article of Lead is extensively used, a reasonably comprehensive and minute view of the

LEAD INDUSTRY OF ST. LOUIS,

Based on the raw materials of the mines of Missouri, is here presented: by which it appears that the yearly increase of permanent wealth from this source amounts to

$4,882,424 ; which rivulet of tribute, together with the annual scores of millions flowing from a hundred kindred streams of

OTHER INDUSTRIES OF ST. LOUIS:

Flour, Pork, Lumber, Iron, etc., amounting, in 1873, to the value of $200,000,000* is kept at home, accumulating domestic wealth, and filling the treasuries of the people with wages of workmen, cost of raw materials, interest on investments and profits on products; thus insuring to St. Louis an independent, easy, London like seat of capital.

Abundant evidence is at hand to prove that this business has increased on an average fully 10 per cent. per annum since 1870 ; a few effective facts, on only one branch of industry, being above presented, touching this point; and, therefore, by simply adding 30 per cent. to the annual value of products manufactured in St. Louis, according to the ninth census of 1870, it appears that the annual value of products manufactured in St. Louis in 1873, was $206,389,319.

---

*The United States Census of 1870, on Industry and Wealth, reported the annual manufactures of St. Louis, as follows :

Number of establishments	4,579
Hands employed	40,856
Capital invested	$60,357,001
Wages of workmen	24,221,717
Cost of raw materials	87,388,252
Annual value of products	158,761,013

APPENDIX B.

8TH CONGRESS.]   No. 103.   [2D SESSION.

DESCRIPTION OF THE LEAD MINES IN UPPER LOUISIANA.

COMMUNICATED TO CONGRESS NOVEMBER 8, 1804.

(Extracted from the " American State Papers, " Public Lands, Vol. 1, p. 188.)

By message from the President of the United States, of which the following is an extract .

"The Lead mines in that territory (Louisiana) offer so rich a supply of that metal as to merit attention. The report now communicated will inform you of their state, and of the necessity of immediate inquiry into their occupation and titles."

ST. LOUIS, *June 16, 1804.*

SIR: In consequence of a request made me by Captain Lewis, before he left this, I now do myself the honor of enclosing you a copy of a dissertation on the Lead mines in Upper Louisiana, furnished by Moses Austin, Esq.

This gentleman owns an extensive mine, situated about thirty-eight miles back of Ste. Genevieve, which he has worked for some years past, and, from his education and experience, I conceive him to be better calculated to give correct information on the subject than any other man in this quarter.

I am, sir, with sentiments of high respect,

Your very humble servant,

AMOS STODDARD,

Captain and first Civil Commandant of Upper Louisiana.

The PRESIDENT *of the United States.*

Sir: Agreeably to your request, I have annexed a memorandum of the number, extent and situation of the lead mines in Upper Louisiana, with an estimate of the average quality of mineral produced, and the number of hands employed at each mine; with the probable quantity which may annually be produced, when the country becomes populated so as to afford workmen sufficient to occupy the mines to advantage.

NAMES OF THE MINES.

1. Mine a Burton,
2. Mine a Robina,
3. Old Mines,
4. Mine Renault,
5. Mine a Maneto,
6. Mine a la Plate,
7. Mine a Joe,
8. Mine a Lanye,
9. Mine a LaMotte,
10. Mine a Gerbore.

1. The Mine a Burton, situated thirty-eight miles west north-west of Ste. Genevieve, was discovered by Francis Burton, about the year 1763, on a fork of Grand River, * ten miles from its junction with the main River, after which it takes the name of Renault's Fork of the Meramec, and unites with that River, about twenty-five miles above its junction with the Mississippi. Fourche Renault is navigable in the spring season, within ten miles of the Mine a Burton. In the year 1798, a concession of one league in superficies, comprehending about one-third part of the mine, (on condition he should erect a smelting-furnace, and establish a lead manufacture,) was granted to Mr. Austin, all of which he has carrried into execution. Francis Burton, also, obtained a grant of four acres, as a compensation for the discovery.

There is a small village at this place, of twenty families, who cultivate a little land near the mines, but have no concessions. Two grist-mills, with a saw-mill, furnish the inhabitants with grinding and plank.

The greatest part of the workings at Mine a Burton are in an open prairie, which rises nearly a hundred feet above the level of the Creek. The mines may be said to extend over two thousand acres of land; but the principal workings are within the limits of one hundred and sixty acres; and perhaps no part of the world furnishes Lead ore in greater quantities and purity. The mineral is found within two feet of the surface of the earth, and it is seldom the miners dig deeper than ten feet; not that the mineral discontinues, but because they find it troublesome to raise it out of the ground; the French miners being unacquainted with the utility of machinery, and generally are able to procure plenty nearer the surface.

The manner in which the mines have been wrought renders it impossible to determine whether the mineral terminates in regular veins or not; for when the miner finds himself ten or twelve feet below the surface, his inexperience obliges him to quit his digging and begin anew, notwithstanding the appearance of mineral may be good. Thus, one-half his time is taken up in sinking new holes or pits.

The mineral is of two qualities, gravel and fossil mineral. The gravel mineral is found immediately under the soil, intermixed with gravel, in pieces from one to fifty pounds weight of solid mineral. After passing through the gravel, which is commonly ·

---

* Now called Big River.

from three to four feet, is found a Sand-rock, which is easily broken up with a pick, and when exposed to the air easily crumbles to a fine sand. This rock also continues five or six feet and contains mineral nearly of the same quality as the gravel; but mineral of the first quality is found in a bed of red Clay, under the Sand-rock, in pieces from ten to five hundred pounds weight, on the outside of which is a white, gold, or silver-colored spar or fossil,* of a bright, glittering appearance, as solid as the mineral itself, and in weight as three to two; this being taken off, the mineral is solid, unconnected with any other substance, of a broad grain, and what mineralogists call potter's-ore. When it is smelted in a common smelting-furnace, it produces sixty per cent.; and when again smelted in a slag-furnace, produces fifteen per cent. more, making cleanly smelted, seventy-five per cent. The gravel mineral is incrusted with a dead-gray substance, the eighth of an inch in thickness; has small veins of Sulphur through it, and will not produce more than sixty per cent. when cleanly smelted.

When I first knew the Mine a Burton, in the year 1797, the French smelted their mineral in stone furnaces, somewhat similar to Lime-kilns. At the bottom they put a floor of the largest logs to be found, setting smaller ones around the sides of the furnace. In a furnace thus arranged, is put from three to five thousand pounds weight of mineral; and a fire being lighted under the bottom of the furnace, is kept up until the mineral is entirely smelted, burnt or lost in the ashes. In this way, each miner smelted his own mineral; extracting about three hundred and fifty pounds of lead from each one thousand pounds weight of mineral; but, since my works have been established, they have found it more advantageous to sell their mineral than to smelt it themselves.

In the year 1798, there were twenty French furnaces, but, in 1802, one only was in use.

The time for working the mines is from August to December. After harvest, the inhabitants of Ste. Genevieve and New Bourbon resort to the mines; the rich send their negroes, and the poor class depend on the mines to furnish them with Lead to purchase all imported articles. From the middle of August to the fifteenth or twentieth of December, there are from forty to fifty men employed in digging mineral; the remainder of the year but little mineral is drawn from the mines, and but few hands employed. From the year 1798 to the year 1803, the average quantity of mineral may be stated at five hundred and fifty, or six hundred thousand pounds, French weight, each year; procured, mostly in four months, by not more than fifty men. The same number of hands employed the year round would produce at least fifteen or sixteen hundred thousand pounds, making proper allowance for spring rains. From the extent of the mines one thousand men might be employed to equal advantage.

2. Mine a Robina, two miles east south-east of the Mine a Burton, was discovered about the same time. This mine has not been wrought for many years, until the last season; a few experiments were made and a small quantity of mineral raised. The old diggings are not extensive, although it is said large quantities of mineral were drawn from the mines on its first discovery. It is public property, and there is every reason to believe will become advantageous when the population of the country shall afford workmen to open and work the mines.

3. Old Mines, so-called from being discovered many years before the Mine a Burton. It is said the Old Mines were opened and wrought by Mr. Renault, about the year 1726, when he explored this country for the famous Law and Company. It is situated five miles north-east of the Mine a Burton, on the discovery of which it was abandoned, mineral being found in great abundance at the new mines. The Old Mines remained in this situation until February, 1802, when fifteen French families made a set-

---

* This mineral (a fossil as he calls it.) is undoubtedly Heavy Spar—sulphate of Baryta.

tlement near the mines, and have formed a village, since which the mines have been opened, and the last year produced three hundred and sixty thousand pounds weight of mineral of an excellent quality, not inferior to the best produced at the Mine a Burton. A Gold-colored fossil,[*] similar to that found at the Mine a Burton, is also connected with the mineral taken from this mine.

The prospect of obtaining immense quantities of mineral from the Old Mines, is at present very flattering, and there is not the least doubt of there being as extensive as the Mine a Burton. The present workings, with the old, include about one hundred acres of land. The mines are elevated, and may be easily drained to the depth of a hundred feet.

In the year 1799, a grant for four hundred acres of land was obtained, and surveyed in 1800, but includes no part of the workings; therefore, the mine, with the adjacent lands, excepting that concession may be considered public property. No smelting furnace has, as yet, been erected at this place, except a French one—most of the mineral being transported to the Mine a Burton to be smelted. The greatest number of hands employed at the Old Mines, at any one time since the late establishment, has not exceeded twenty-five or thirty, and those only for a few months. It is not improbable that the space between the Old Mines and the Mine a Burton may produce mineral in as great abundance as either of the mines. The Foueche Renault is navigable within seven miles of this mine.

4. Mine Renault, situated six miles north of the Mine a Burton, on a creek of the same name. Little can be said relative to this mine, it not having been wrought for more than seventy years, but, from information, and the extent of the diggings, a large quantity of mineral was drawn from it. It was discovered and opened by Mr. Renault about the year 1724-5, with an expectation of finding Silver ore. The country near the mine is hilly and broken. It is supposed that Renault's concession, granted by the King of France, if ever it should be brought forward will comprehend the mine.

The mineral drawn from these mines is of a good quality, generally found in Lime stone rock, in regular veins, and is said to be inexhaustible. I know of no reason why they have been so long neglected, unless I attribute it to the discovery of mines nearer the settlements, and the small number of workmen to carry them on. As they are within ten miles of navigation, by the Fourche Renault, great expectations of their utility to the public may justly be entertained.

5. Mine a Maneto, or American Mines, on Grand River,[†] was discovered and opened in the month of October, 1799, by the Americans settled on Grand River, is situated twelve miles east, south-east of Mine a Burton. The appearance of the mines being very flattering, a plan was executed by Messrs. Valle and Pratt, of Ste. Genevieve, to dispossess the Americans of the privilege allowed in such cases, of four acres in superficies, as a compensation to the discoverers of mines. In 1803, Mr. Pratt brought forward two concessions, one for himself, of one thousand acres, the other in the name of his son, a minor, for eight hundred acres. In consequence of these concessions, the Americans have been excluded from the mines.

The Mine a Maneto, from its flat position, will not admit of deep mining, the water rising at the depth of fifteen feet, and the situation is such it cannot be drained. The mineral is found within two or three feet of the surface of the earth, in a soft, gray Limestone rock, in small particles. The rock lies in a horizontal position, in sheets of five or six inches in thickness. Two or three layers of this rock are found one under the other; between each is a layer, either of Clay or mineral, one or two inches thick,

---

* Heavy Spar or Barytes.

† Big River.

most commonly mineral. In places where the rock will admit of sinking eight or ten feet, the mineral is found in thin flakes, covered with an Iron colored rust. Before the mineral can be smelted, it requires to be pounded and washed; after passing through this operation, out of one thousand pounds, as it is taken from the mines, three or four hundred only is found to be mineral. Notwithstanding this additional labor, the ease and facility with which the mineral is procured would leave a handsome profit in the hands of experienced workmen; but, to the present holders, yields but little. There is not the smallest appearance of the Marcasite to be found in these mines. The land carriage to Ste. Genevieve, from the Mines a Maneto, is about twenty-six miles.

6. Mine a la Plate, situate on a river of that name, about two miles from its junction with Grand River, and eighteen miles south-east from the Mine a Burton, was discovered in October, 1799, by an American; but the injustice done the settlers at Grand River, in the affair of the Mine a Maneto. discouraged those concerned in the discovery from making any great attempts to open and improve it. In 1800, thirty thousand pounds weight of mineral was drawn from this mine by two Americans, obtained near the surface. The mineral assumes the appearance of regular veins, and there is not a doubt but that this mine will be very productive. A Silver-colored fossil is found at this mine, but not in such quantities as at the Mine a Burton. The mine, at present, is unoccupied, for the reasons before mentioned, and will remain so until a more favorable moment. The land carriage from the mine to Ste. Genevieve, is about twenty miles. The mine may be considered as the property of the public.

7. Mine a Joe, on Grand River, about four miles from the Mine a la Plate, and fourteen south-east of the Mine a Burton, was discovered by Messrs. Baker and Ally, American settlers at Grand River, in September, 1801, but was taken from them in 1802, by one of those acts of injustice not uncommon in absolute governments.

While Messrs. Baker and Ally were suffered to work the mine, they obtained mineral in abundance, but since it has been in the hands of the present holders, it has produced but little. This mine is said to be private property, which renders it difficult to ascertain its extent and richness, but, from circumstances, it is supposed not to be very extensive. The mineral is found in pieces of several hundred pounds weight, pure and solid.

8. Mine a Lanye; this mine is situated six miles west of the Mine a Joe, and sixteen miles south, south-east of the Mine a Burton. It was discovered about the year 1795, and bears the name of its discoverer. The mine has not been much wrought, and, from what I can learn, never produced any large quantity of mineral. It is not in much repute, and at present, is unoccupied.

9. Mine a la Motte, is situated on the waters of the River St. Francois, six miles from the main river, and thirty south south-east of Ste. Genevieve, was discovered by Mr. Renault about the year 1723 or 1724, who made an exploration, but finding no Silver ore, he abandoned it. About the year 1723, a man by the name of LaMotte opened and wrought the mine, after whom it is called.

Mine a la Motte differs in every respect from the mines on Grand River and its vicinity. The situation is flat and low; the water bad and unhealthy. The mineral is found in regular veins, from two to four feet solid. Five of the veins have been opened and wrought. They are found within four feet of the surface, with a declination of about forty-five degrees, but cannot be mined deeper (on account of water) than twenty-five feet, and to that depth only in the dry season.

The mineral is of a fine steel grain, said to contain fifty ounces of Silver to a ton of Lead, and is highly charged with Sulphur. Notwithstanding the French inhabitants of this country have followed the mining business upwards of eighty years, yet they have not advanced in the art of smelting a step beyond their ancestors; the methods they pursue bespeak their surprising ignorance.

As the Mine a la Motte differs from those already described, so does their mode of smelting. The first process is, by depositing the mineral in a pile of logs, after the manner sea shells are burned to Lime; the piles being set on fire and consumed, the quantity of Lead produced is five per cent. It is then put into a furnace of stone, such as before described; from this process, if well attended, is produced fifteen per cent. more. After this second burning, they consider the mineral in a proper state for smelting; therefore, collecting it from the ashes they again put it into the furnace, arranged with logs at the bottom and sides, and make an end to smelting. From the last process they commonly obtain about fifteen per cent., making thirty-five per cent. the greatest quantity obtained.

At the Mine a LaMotte is also found in beds what miners call Gravel Mineral, because it is found intermixed with the Soil like fine gravel, in particles from the size of a pin's head to that of a hickory nut. This mineral, after an imperfect washing, is put into a furnace where it is suffered to melt into a slag, no attempt being made to create a fluxility of the metal from the dross. It is then put into a furnace not unlike a miller's hopper, with a grate at the bottom. Underneath a fire is lighted, and continued until the slags are all melted and a partial fluxion effected. This mode of smelting produces about 250 pounds of Lead to 1,000 of mineral. Notwithstanding the immense loss in smelting, the richness of the mines and the small expense of obtaining the mineral, leaves an astonishing profit to the proprietors. I found by experiments, that the mineral in the hands of skilful smelters will produce 60, and some of the veins 70 per cent.

About the year 1738–40, the Mine a LaMotte was considered as public property, and the people in general were allowed to work at it. At that time it furnished almost all the Lead exported from the Illinois; but soon after the discovery and opening of the Mine a Burton, the Mine a LaMotte was in a great measure abandoned, the mineral at the Mine a Burton being much easier melted. The Mine a LaMotte is at this time claimed as private property, in consequence of which the inhabitants in general are denied the privilege of working. Therefore, the annual quantity of Lead is greatly reduced. For the years 1802 and 1803, the quantity of Lead made at the Mine a LaMotte did not exceed 200,000 pounds weight, although about 30 men were employed from four to six months in each year. It is evident that 50 men, under a proper manager, with a good smelting furnace, might produce five or six hundred thousand pounds weight of Lead per annum.

It is difficult to say what part of the mine is private property, but from the best information about 50 or 60 acres have been granted at different times. The mine, although not so extensive as the Mine a Burton, is supposed to comprehend a much larger boundary than what is granted to individuals, and may be of consequence to the public. The river St. Francois will not admit of navigation for a hundred miles below the mines; therefore the produce of the mines must be transported by land to Ste. Genevieve, which is the nearest to water carriage.

10. Mine a Gerbore, on the waters of the river St. Francois, 18 miles north of the Mine a LaMotte, is also a discovery of Renault, who made an explorement in 1745, but not finding Silver ore, the principal object of his researches, he abandoned it; after which it was wrought by a Mr. Aura and others, until the Mine a Burton was discovered when it was again abandoned. The old Diggings are extensive, but the quantity of Lead produced, I have not been able to ascertain. It is said to be equal to any of the

mines in the country. The commandant of New Bourbon has a concession of a league in superficies, comprehending the mines.

GENERAL OBSERVATIONS.

Within 12 months past, several discoveries have been made near the Mine a Burton. Valuable Lead mines have likewise been discovered about 200 miles up the river Meramec. Some of the mineral I have seen, is of good quality. In short, the country, for 12 or 15 miles round the Mine a Burton, exhibits strong appearances of mineral. In all the small creeks mineral is found, washed down from the hills; and it is not uncommon to find in the draughts, leading to creeks and rivers, and in gulleys made by the spring rains, mineral in pieces from 10 to 50 pounds weight, brought down by the torrents. Some hundreds have been collected in this way. No country yet known, furnishes greater indications of an inexhaustible quantity of Lead mineral, and so easily obtained. One motive to render the mining business generally advantageous is, that every farmer may be a miner, and when unemployed on his farm, may by a few weeks' labor, almost at his own door, dig as much mineral as will furnish his family with all important articles. From a view of the Lead mines in Upper Louisiana, it may be seen that nothing is wanting but an increase of population, to augment their produce to a surprising degree. It is also evident there are valuable discoveries yet to be made. It may therefore be matter of consideration with the Government, whether the donation of four acres in superfices to the discoverers of mines, would not be advantageous to be continued. The Spanish Government has also allowed the inhabitants to work on public land, free from any kind of tax. A continuation of this privilege will exhaust both the mines and the timber, without the least advantage to the public. On the other hand, if a heavy imposition is imposed, it may discourage the mining business; yet the man who can, with his pick and shovel, make his $30, $40, and sometimes his $100 per month, may well afford to pay a small tax to Government.

The country about the mines is broken, but not mountainous, and furnishes the best land for cultivation, and streams of water sufficient for all kinds of water works. Grand River rises 10 miles south-west of the Mine a Burton, and in its course forms nearly three parts of a circle round the mines, and loses its name in the Fouche Renault, which is navigable to the Mississippi. They unite ten miles north of the Mine a Burton, and it is remarkable that in forming this circle, its distance from the mines does not exceed 14 miles in any one place. It also furnishes both land and water of a superior quality, sufficient for eight or nine hundred families.

Thus situated, the time cannot be far distant when the country will furnish Lead sufficient not only for the consumption of the United States, but all Europe, if moderate encouragement is given by the Government, and protection against the Osage Indians, who yearly plunder the inhabitants.

The mines on the waters of the St. Francois, are capable of furnishing vast quantities of Lead.

The Mine a LaMotte has been termed the Gold Mine, as descriptive of its wealth, and if under proper management would verify the observation.

From the annexed estimate, it will be found that the gross produce of all the mines now occupied, amounts to $36,500. The whole number of workmen employed, including miners, smelters, wood-cutters and carters, has not exceeded 150 men, of which number 120 may be supposed to work four months, and the remaining 30 the year round. From this calculation, it will be found that each man employed in the business, averages $43 per month.

To this may be added the increased value on 120,000 pounds weight, manufactured at the Mine a Burton into shot and sheets, which makes the export valuation $40,100 per annum, the average produce for three years past. Admitting 1,000 men to be employed the year round, at the different mines now known, and the quantity of Lead produced to be in proportion to what is now obtained by 150 men, a supposition by no means extravagant, the proceeds are found to amount to $500,000 and upward. This calculation, perhaps, by some, may be deemed incredible; but the riches and extent of the mines justify the calculation.

An estimate of the Produce of the several Mines.

Mine a Burton, 550,000 pounds mineral, estimated to produce 66⅔, is 366,666⅔
    pounds Lead, at $5, is.. .... $18,333 33
To which add $30 (on 120,000 pounds manufactured) to each thousand, is.....   3,600 00

                                                           $21,933 33

Old Mines, 200,000 pounds mineral, estimated to produce 66⅓, is 133,333⅓
    pounds Lead at $5 per hundred weight, is...   6,666 67
Mine a LaMotte, 220,000 pounds Lead at $5 per hundred, is....................... 10,000 00
Suppose at all other mines 30,000 pounds Lead, at $5, is..............................   1,500 00

    Total amount is.. .. .. $40,100 00

When the manufacture of White and Red Lead is put into operation, the export valuation will be considerably augmented on the same quality of Lead.

The folowing table will show the present population of the Mine a Burton and its vicinity :

Table.

DIVISION OF SETTLEMENT.	Distance from Mine a Burton	American Families.	French families.	WHOLE NUMBER OF INHABITANTS.
Mine a Burton, including several plantations		14	12	Suppose each family to con-
Bellevue	10	20	....	tain 8 persons, the whole
Old Mines....................................	5	....	15	number will be 728 souls.
Grand River.................................	12	30	....	
Total	....	64	27	

In June, 1799, when I removed my family to the Mine a Burton, the whole number of inhabitants settled on the Grand River and its waters did not exceed 63 or 64 persons, consisting of eight families.

N. B.—Some late transactions, by order of the Governor of St. Louis, if valid, will entirely change the situation of the public property within ten miles of Mine a Burton. Surveys of all the lands worthy of notice have been made with an intention to include every spot of land supposed to contain mineral. These surveys amount to thirty or forty thousand acres, and have been made, except in a few instances, since the first of the present month.

The above observations and estimates are as accurate as the nature of things would permit and the shortness of time I have had to collect information.

All of which are submitted with respect.

MOSES AUSTIN.

February 13, 1804.

APPENDIX C.

METALLIC STATISTICS OF MISSOURI.

[UNION MERCHANTS' EXCHANGE REPORTS FOR 1872.]

Lead—Importations to St. Louis from 1856 to 1872.

YEAR.	Total pounds.	YEAR.	Total pounds.
1856	16,372,480	1865	9,330,880
1857	13,004,400	1866	11,966,720
1858	25,311,760	1867	11,564,400
1859	21,150,400	1868	14,865,840
1860	19,059,280	1869	18,264,240
1861	9,220,720	1870	18,963,120
1862	7,664,000	1871	18,396,880
1863	6,385,840	1872	22,861,520
1864	7,442,800	1873	*30,090,050

* From Circular of F. F. Rozier.

Lead received in St Louis from 1865 to 1872, by the following routes :

Year	Upper Mississippi—pounds	Lower Mississippi—pounds	Missouri River—pounds	Iron Mountain R. R.—pounds	Atlantic and Pacific R. R.—pounds	Missouri Pacific R. R.—pounds	North-Missouri R. R.—pounds	Illinois Railroads—pounds
1865	2,610,000	729,920	....	3,630,560	....	418,560	....	1,596,880
1866	861,600	1,711,200	....	4,282,640	....	1,758,640	....	2,560,400
1867	2,643,200	1,417,440	....	4,467,120	....	2,266,640	....	770,000
1868	2,260,880	2,760,000	....	5,084,560	....	4,194,320	....	1,063,680
1869	3,349,120	2,236,960	....	9,088,000	....	3,756,320	....	561,360
1870	3,352,320	340,400	6,320	11,264,808	2,460,880	692,400	556,800	80,320
1871	2,806,960	124,480	53,440	9,126,160	3,569,680	1,127,600	1,001,920	626,640
1872	1,596,640	....	57,920	8,270,135	4,463,360	6,316,080	1,181,680	16,480

Of the foregoing amount 1,580,640 pounds were shipped from Galena; 869,680 pounds from Omaha, and 20,411,200 pounds produced in Missouri during 1872.

From data furnished by the different railroads we find that the amount of Lead shipped from their stations, within the State of Missouri, during 1872, were as follows :

STATION.	COUNTY.	POUNDS.	TOTAL.
By the Atlantic and Pacific R. R. :			
From Granby	Newton	3,760,000	
From Carthage	Jasper	1,160,000	4,920,000
By the Iron Mountain R. R. :			
From Desoto	Jefferson	746,385	
From Vineland	"	145,090	
From Blackwell	"	190,030	
From Potosi	Washington	1,307,435	
From Hopewell	"	193,740	
From Cadet	"	2,761,870	
From Mineral Point	"	95,870	
From Mine LaMotte	Madison	2,829,775	8,270,135
By the Missouri Pacific R. R. :			
From Centretown	Cole	240,000	
From Tipton	Moniteau	120,000	360,000
Total production of Lead in Missouri			13,550,135
Importation from other States			9,311,385
			22,871,520

Zinc Ore, in form of Carbonate of Zinc, often mixed with the Silicate and Sulphuret, was shipped to St. Louis from the following stations:

STATION.	COUNTY.	POUNDS.
From Granby	Newton	4,838,440
From DeSoto	Jefferson	3,280,000
From Blackwell	"	146,000
From Potosi	Washington	2,918,000
From Hopewell	"	400,000
Total for 1872		11,582,440

Which total equals 5,171 and 1710-2240 tons of 2,240 pounds or 5,792 and 750-2000 of 2,000 pounds. Of these, nearly 5,000 tons were smelted for Zinc, giving 1,727,450 pounds, or an average yield of 34 per cent., while the rest was used in the manufacture of White Oxide of Zinc.

Barytes, used in the manufacture of White Lead, was shipped to St. Louis by the Iron Mountain Railroad as follows:

STATION.	POUNDS.
From Vineland	2,208,250
From Blackwell	62,200
From Cadet	7,961,920
From Potosi	38,000
From Mineral Point	167,050
Total for 1872	10,437,420

Which equals 4,659 and 1265-2240 tons of 2,240 pounds each, or 5,218 and 1420-2000 tons of 2,000 pounds each.

Pig Iron produced and shipped to St. Louis :

WHERE FROM.	COUNTY.	TONS OF 2,240 LBS. EACH.		TONS OF 2,000 LBS. EACH.	
		Tons.	Pounds.	Tons.	Pounds.
Moselle..	Franklin............	2,836	....	3,176	1,456
Leasburg	Crawford	6,742	....	7,550	800
St. James	Phelps	3,109	....	3,481	400
Carondelet............................	St. Louis :				
1. Vulcan Iron Works...	....	22,000	....	24,640	....
2. Missouri Furnace Co....	....	22,000	....	24,640	....
3 Carondelet Iron Works	....	6,400	....	7,168	....
4. South St. Louis Iron Works	....	14,750	....	16,520	....
Total	....	59,930	....	87,176	656
From this amount was exported	....	55,930	....	62,641	....
Used in Missouri	....	21,907	....	24,535	656

Iron Ore brought to St. Louis during the month of December, being an approximate estimate, except Iron Mountain and Pilot Knob :

WHERE FROM.	TONS OF 2,240 LBS. EACH.		TONS OF 2,000 LBS. EACH.	
	Tons.	Pounds.	Tons.	Pounds.
By the Atlantic and Pacific Railroad :				
Ironridge	14,847	....	16,628	1,280
Leasburg	326	1,100	367	1,720
St. James	12,905	900	14,454	320
Taylor's...................................	512	1,400	574	112
Burkland	1,734	1,200	1,942	1,280
Beaver...................................	9,578	400	10,716	1,760
Kelly's...................................	218	400	244	320
Hancock...................................	676	800	757	1,360
By the Iron Mountain Railroad :				
Iron Mountain...........................	264,284	850	295,998	1,010
Pilot Knob................................	12,272	830	13,744	1,610
Cornwall................................	2,626	910	2,941	1,150
Marquand................................	384	290	430	450
Marble Hill.............................	412	420	461	1,300
Fredericktown	45	1,340	51	140
Bessville	80	1,300	90	500
Glenn Allen	17	1,920	20	....
Giving for 1872 a total shipment of.	280,123	640	359,424	312

Two hundred and ninety-one thousand two hundred tons, each 2,000 pounds, of ore were exported and the ore necessary for producing the 87,000 tons of pig Iron made in Missouri was about 122,000 tons (taking 60 per cent. as the average yield); the whole amount of Iron ore mined in Missouri then cannot be less than 509,200 tons, each 2,000 pounds, equal to 454,643 gross tons, each 2,240 pounds.

APPENDIX D.

MINERAL SPRINGS.

BY G. C. BROADHEAD.

This does not pretend to be a full description or to be a full list of Mineral Springs —others are included in county reports, and there are still others which we have not seen.

IRON OR CHALYBEATE SPRINGS.

These may be seen flowing from Drift Sands or else chiefly Sandstones. Several fine springs were observed at BIRD PRICE'S, on Ramsey Creek, PIKE county. One indicated the presence of considerable Iron; others had a pleasant but no particular mineral taste, while others were inaccessible on account of the marshy character of the ground. The water from one is said to act on the kidneys, another to be beneficial to dyspeptic persons. The neighboring ground is low and flat, and no beds of rock are seen near by. From this "flat" the country spreads off into rich, rolling, heavily timbered, beautiful valleys gradually merging into the surrounding knobs, which are capped with Burlington Limestone reposing on the Chouteau beds. Lower down the valley, we find occasional outcrops of the shaly, pyritiferous beds of the Cincinnati Group. The springs being near the horizon of this Group, probably flow from these shaly beds. We certainly do believe that the Sulphur Springs of this vicinity owe their origin to *reservoirs in these beds.*

At W. B. SITTON'S, in Lincoln county, near Louisville, is a mild Chalybeate Spring. A brown deposit is found in the adjacent wells.

On Bryant's Creek, near the Mississippi River bottoms, are also several springs of similar character.

At LEXINGTON, Lafayette county, there is a Chalybeate Spring which has been somewhat resorted to. Its flow is weak, but it has a strong taste and seems to flow probably from Shale beds of the Coal Measures. The overlying surface deposits are ferruginous and sandy, and may probably somewhat affect the character of this water.

On Clear Fork of Blackwater, six miles north of Knob Noster, Johnson county, a weak Chalybeate Spring issues from Coal Measure Shales. Another fine Chalybeate Spring is said to be ten miles south of Warrensburgh.

In the northern counties, where the Sands of the Drift abound, the waters are often colored by Oxide of Iron. Such waters and many such springs may be found in Knox, Adair, Sullivan, Mercer and Harrison.

In KNOX county, in Sec. 12, T. 62, R. 10 W., is a fine Chalybeate Spring, that is much esteemed as a mild cathartic and good tonic.

In ADAIR the waters of some of the streams flowing through beds of Coal Measure Sandstone, partake of a Chalybeate character. The waters of Hog Creek, Hazle Creek, etc., have marked diuretic properties, and on waters of Hog Creek are several Chalybeate Springs.

In SULLIVAN county, in Sec. 24, T. 64, R. 21 W., a Chalybeate Spring issues from Coal Measure Sandstone. It is of pleasant taste and has marked diuretic properties.

A few miles north-west of PRINCETON, MERCER county, in Sec. 16, T. 65, R. 24 W., numerous springs issue from the drift sands, most of them containing much Oxide of Iron in solution and a thick, rusty crust is deposited on the adjacent ground.

Near MT. MORIAH, HARRISON county, a fine Chalybeate Spring flows from drift sands, in which a small Nautilus and other cretaceous fossils were found.

Near SMITHTON, WORTH county, a Chalybeate Spring issues from sands of altered Drift.

Two miles north of NEVADA, VERNON county, there is a very pleasant Chalybeate Spring.

SALT AND SULPHUR SPRINGS.

In RALLS county are many noted Springs. BUFFALO Lick, in Sec. 28, T. 55, R. 7 W., issues from Chouteau Limestone. A Saline taste is perceptible. About the year 1820, or a few years since that time, Salt, in remunerative quantities, was made at this place by the Messrs. Ely. Bones of Buffalo are found imbedded in the marshy ground near the Spring, and on the north side of Salt River a Buffalo trace was observed from two to five feet in depth and from twenty to fifty yards wide. The waters of Buffalo Lick are very healthy, and are said to be good for liver complaint.

TRABUE's Lick, near Spencer Creek, is a mild Sulphur, and probably issues from the Shales of the "Cincinnati Group." Further down Spencer Creek Valley is an extensive "Lick." Around the Spring the ground is marshy, and near by it has the appearance of being a resort of cattle for many years.

FREMON's LICK, in Sec. 33, T. 56, R. 5 W., is a strong Salt Sulphur Spring, and many years ago Salt was made here, but the settlers becoming frightened by the presence of Indians, the kettles were thrown into a well and the works abandoned. The source of the Spring seems to be from the Shales of the Cincinnati Group. The upper Spring does not afford much water, but is decidedly Saline. The lower one is a strong blue Sulphur, much stronger than Elk Lick. A blue coating has been formed on the adjacent gravel as well as on the gum which incloses the Spring. Cattle and horses are very fond of the water.

At BOUVET's or TRABUE's LICK (or as now more often called MULDROW's,) formerly much Salt was made, and the owners realized good profits. This water issues out boldly from the Black River Limestone Group. Borings have been made to the depth of 300 feet, reaching Salt water. This would place its fountain head in the Magnesian Limestone series, about the base of the Saccharoidal Sandstone, which is Saliferous in other places. Its location is in Sec. 25, T. 56, R. 6 W.

The Spring at SAVERTON somewhat resembles Fremon's, but the water is not so strong. A dark indigo blue deposit is formed on the gum composing its wall; without is a black deposit, and in the branch is a whitish deposit. Salt and Sulphur are predominant.

In PIKE county there are many Mineral Springs. Most of them contain Sulphur and Magnesia, etc., in combination, and they generally issue from Shales of the Cincinnati Group. I would include the following, reputed to possess valuable medicinal properties.

ELK LICK, on Spencer's Creek, is very much resorted to by invalids and pleasure seekers during the summer months. The water is a mild white Sulphur and very much valued for its medicinal properties. There are three springs. Their source is in the Cincinnati Group.

The three springs on BUFFALO LICK probably possess as valuable properties as Elk Lick.

Other springs are: EPSOM SALT SPRING at Mrs. MERRIWETHERS, and of less note are MUD LICK Spring (Sulphur,) near Louisiana and Frankfort Road: FRANKFORT Salt Spring; Spring on the J. W. DAVIS' farm; LINDSAY'S LICK; the FORD Spring, on Big Ramsey, near Paynesville Road.

On Mr. THOMAS' land, in N. W. qr. of Sec. 6, T. 53, R. 1 W., at upper part of the Lick, are two acres of marshy ground. The water apparently contains Iron. At the lower part a Sulphur Spring breaks out. Flint pebbles strewn around are covered with a bluish incrustation. Mastodon teeth and other ancient bones have been found near the spring.

MUD LICK occupies a wet area of about three acres, on which are two Sulphur springs. Cattle seem very fond of the water. Shales, probably referable to the Cincinnati Group, crop out in the spring.

At Mr. JOHN W. DAVIS' a spring issues forth from near the junction of the Hudson River Shales (Cincinnati Group,) and Upper Trenton Limestone (Galena Group). It contains Sulphate of Magnesia and Iron. A brown deposit settles on the mud and a scum on the still branch water. The water is clear and occasionally a slight ebullition takes place, and gas arises.

The springs at Mrs. MERRIWETHER'S resemble the springs at Mr. DAVIS'. They are Epsom Salt issuing from the upper bed of Trenton Limestone. When stationary, a dirty scum will collect on the surface; a ferruginous deposit lies on the earth mound, seemingly in a semi state of crystillization. This water is much esteemed as a diuretic.

About three quarters of a mile above the junction of Big and Little Ramsey is LINDSAY'S LICK, a large spring, covering an area of half an acre; Sulphuretted hydrogen rises from it frequently.

FORD SPRING, three-quarters of a mile above Lindsay's, flows out copiously—contains Salt and Sulphuretted Hydrogen.

On BUFFALO Creek, in S. E. qr. Sec. 34, T. 54, R. 1 W., is a Salt Spring with a Lick of several acres seemingly quite barren, and is mostly covered with a white saline incrustation. Many small concretions of Oxide of Iron are found and also bones of large animals. Lower down the creek is another Sulphur Spring.

In LINCOLN county, near waters of Cuivre, sulphur springs are reported to exist.

L'OUTRE LICK, west of Danville, Montgomery county, is a Salt Sulphur, and during the early settlements much Salt was made here. The water issues from the Second Magnesian Limestone.

The Spring at GOREHAM'S LICK, Randolph county, is 12 feet deep, and embraces 10 square feet of surface. The adjacent wet ground covers an area of about 20 square feet. The water seems to be strongly saline, and on stirring it, bubbles of Sulphuretted Hydrogen arise. Much Salt was formerly made here. Some of the ruins of old works, including ashes and fragments of posts, were yet to be seen a few years ago. Cattle are very fond of the water.

SWEET SPRINGS, on Huntsville and Glasgow road, in Sec. 17, T. 53, R. 15 W., contains common Salt, Epsom Salt, and some Salt of Magnesia. The water is very beneficial in some diseases. Its action appears to be chiefly on the bowels, as a regulator and tonic, and is, therefore, good for dyspeptic persons. It has a Sulphurous taste.

Nine miles west of Marshall, Saline county, are several large Salt springs and Salt ponds; they occupy a flat valley, depressed but a little below adjacent hills. Some of these springs are quite Saline, and it would probably pay well to manufacture Salt here.

On Salt Creek, Chariton county, are several Salt springs.

At Linn's Coal Mine, 2 miles north of Brunswick, Chariton county, there is a strong Copperas spring, with quite an abundant flow of water.

An account of the Howard county Salt springs will be found in the Report of that county,

Sulphur Springs, on Iron Mountain Railroad, 20 miles below St. Louis ; Meramec Springs, Cheltenham Springs, in St. Louis county, and Chouteau Springs, in Cooper, have been much resorted to.

SWEET SPRINGS, near Brownsville, Saline county. These springs flow from cavities in the Upper beds of the Burlington Limestone. The hill here is 47 feet high, above water in Blackwater, spreading out back in a flat table land. The spring itself is about 20 feet above the river, and has a sweetish, alkaline taste. It is useful to promote general good health, and is much resorted to in the proper season. It is owned by the Rev. J. L. Yantis, who informed me that he used the water for ordinary cooking and drinking purposes, for which it was very suitable, except for making tea. Dr. Y. has evaporated the water and obtained a Salt resembling Rochelle Salt. Dr. Litton made an analysis of the water and found it to contain the following constituents, arranged in regular order as to quantity, the greatest first :

Sodium,
Potassium,
Magnesium,
Calcium,
Chlorine,
Sulphuric Acid.

Also, traces of Iron, Manganese, Alluminum, Silica, and Phosphoric Acid. Organic matter was also present, whether in water or from the vessel could not be ascertained.

Just below, at edge of water, in River, is a very pleasant tasted Sulphur spring.

On Mr. Carpenter's land, 2 miles north-east of Knob Noster, Johnson county, is a well of very clear and pleasant tasted water, reputed to contain Alum.

MONAGAW SPRINGS, in St. Clair county, are much resorted to in watering season, but I have not seen them. An account of other springs in South-west Missouri will be found in the county Reports.

There are probably many other good mineral springs in the State, which have not come under my notice.

APPENDIX E.

Saint Louis, *Oct. 23, 1874.*

Mr. G. C. Broadhead, *Director of Missouri Geological Survey:*

Dear Sir: Herewith I hand you the results of most of the chemical work done in connection with the State Survey, during the past year.

Many analyses, chiefly qualitative, are not included in these tables.

The results of most of these examinations are given in the various reports, in which are also included the greater part of the present work, here presented in a systematic and tabular form.

Respectfully yours,

REGIS CHAUVENET.

CHEMICAL ANALYSES.

BY R. CHAUVENET.

The following tabular statements of analyses do not include the results of all the chemical examinations made in connection with the field work of the survey. In numerous instances, samples were sent to the laboratory, the nature of which being uncertain, qualitative examination was required to settle the question. In other cases, the per centage of one constituent only was required, or some special test was directed to be made. A statement of the result obtained in any given case, is made in the proper connection in the report of the field work, and no mention made of it in the present report. Analyses made in a regular series, however, and illustrating the nature of important deposits, are here brought together, and the tables may be found convenient to refer to, although most of the analyses are given in their proper connection in the body of the work.

Some of the results, however, are to be found only in the present report. Among these are the analyses of Limestones taken from various depths of the artesian well at the Insane Asylum, St. Louis county, which were originally made for the report of 1872, but not published. A number of Coals are here given, not elsewhere mentioned, and a few examinations of spring and well waters from Howard and other counties. In reference to these last it should be said that they are by no means exhaustive analyses, but are intended merely to indicate the nature of the saline contents of the waters. In the Salt springs, Lime, Magnesia, and Sulphuric Acid were determined so as to give a fair idea of the probable quality and purity of their product.

A few peculiarities in some of the results on Lead and Zinc ores, may be pointed out as of some interest. Among these is the fact that while Zinc was usually found in the Galena from the Granby region, the Blende of the same region is free from Lead. This, of course, applies only to single crystals of the two minerals in question, since in numberless instances, Galena and Blende are found associated, and often intermixed in the same mass of ore. Taking a mass of this kind, however, and separating the crystals of Blende and Galena by hand, the latter would be found to contain a small per centage of Zinc; the former, no Lead.

The presence of Cadmium in the Blende from the South-west, is of some interest. In making the analyses from which the per centages of Cadmium were determined, 20 grammes of the Blende was the quantity used. From the solution, Cadmium was thrown down by Sulphuretted Hydrogen, (accompanied by no small amount of Zinc,) the Sulphides redissolved in Muriatic Acid, and the same separation repeated. A third precipitation from solution in Sulphuric Acid, the slightest excess of the latter being carefully guarded against, gave a perfect separation. The Cadmium being now re-dissolved, precipitated and weighed as Oxide, was always brought again into solution, and carefully tested for Zinc. The "Cyanide" method was used also for separating the two, the results given being a mean of several trials, all agreeing within 0.05 per cent.

The method used for the "proximate" analysis of Coals, was the same as that described in the report of 1872. A brief account of it precedes the present tables.

The locality of each sample is indicated by section, township and range, in most instances, and when these are not known, the name of the owner of the bank is given. For more particular descriptions of localities, mode of occurrence and size of deposits, whether of Coals or ores, reference must be made to the proper reports of the field work.

The analyses of Slag from the Joplin Lead furnaces, were made by Mr. A. A. Blair, to whom I am also indebted for much assistance on other parts of the work, more especially on the Iron ores analyzed in connection with the report of Mr. Ph. N. Moore.

Analyses showing Average Composition and Purity of Galena from the Granby Region.

	No. 1.	No. 2.	No. 3.	No. 4.	No. 5.	No. 6.	No. 7.	No. 8.
Silicious	0.61	0.12	0.05	1.72	0.53	0.71	0.44	0.33
Lead	84.06	85.84						
Iron	0.16	0.05	0.09	0.24	1.96	1.95	0.45	trace.
Zinc	.0.94	0.12	1.32	0.94	0.52	0.73	0.91	trace.
Lime	0.42	trace.	none.	trace.	trace.	0.86	trace.	none.
Silver	1¼ oz. to ton	1¼ oz. to ton	1 oz. to ton	1 oz. to ton	¾ oz. to ton	¾ oz.	1¼ oz.	¾ oz.

Silver in all cases obtained by fire-assay.

Iron and Zinc are here estimated as in the state *of metal*. For example, in No. 1, the Zinc (0.94) estimated as Blende would be 1.41 p. c., and the Iron (0.16) as Pyrites would be 0.34 p. c.

LOCALITIES AS FOLLOWS:

No. 1. From shafts 20 and 22, Holman Diggings, Granby; as delivered to smelting works.

No. 2. Shaft 499, Trent Diggings; cleaned, and in condition as delivered to smelters.

No. 3. Shaft 215, Village Diggings, Granby; pure, as delivered to smelting works.

No. 4. Minersville, Jasper county; cleaned, but not washed.

No. 5. Joplin Mining and Smelting Company; cleaned and washed sample, as delivered at Riggins' and Chapman's Furnaces.

No. 6. Swindle Diggings, Joplin; washed.

No. 7. Temple Diggings, Joplin.

No. 8. Stevens' Mines, near Joplin.

In all of these samples, search was made for Antimony, Arsenic and Copper, but no trace of any of these metals was detected in a single instance. The direct determination of Lead was usually omitted, the objects of the examinations being to ascertain the nature and the amount of the impurities.

Galena from Miller and Morgan Counties.

	No. 1.	No. 2.	No. 3.	No. 4.
Silicious	0.15	0.11	0.21	0.13
Iron (met.)	0.24	trace.	0.48	trace.
Iron Pyrites	(0.51)	....	(1.02)	....
Zinc	trace.	none.	trace.	none.
Silver	none.	trace.	trace.	none.

Neither Copper nor Antimony could be detected in these Galenas.

No. 1. Walker Mine, Miller county.

No. 2. Madole Diggings, Morgan county.

No. 3. New Granby Diggings, Morgan county.

No. 4. Streit Diggings, 2 miles south of Centretown,

A softened Limestone from the "New Granby" Diggings, known as "Limesand," contains:

Silicious matter, (Clay).. 14.71 per cent.
Peroxide of Iron... 1.68   "
Lime... 26.11   "
Magnesia... 17.17   "
Carbonic acid... 40.21   "

Total... 99.88

Carbonates of Lead, (known as "Dry-bone" at the Mines :)

	No. 1.	No. 2.	No. 3.
Silicious..	0.36	9.95	10.35
Lead (metal)..	72.36	66.35	63.64
Peroxide of Iron......................................	0.55	1.51	3.11
Oxide of Zinc...	none.	0.75	0.73
Lime (Carbonate).....................................	0.72	trace.	1.34
Magnesia...	none.	trace.	0.75
Water...	trace.	none.	none.
Sulphur..	trace.		

No. 1.   Frazier Diggings, Granby; altered Galena, bluish-gray in color, (wool-mineral,) shows remains of Sulphur.

No. 2.   Granby; massive; of brownish-red color; the Iron exists in this and next No., as peroxide.

No. 3.   Ennis' shaft, Minersville; this is a loose, Clay-like mass, which is washed, yielding, however, only the small amount of 30 per cent. of Carbonate of Lead by the process.

Analyses of Slag or "Cinder," from Lead Smelting Furnaces.

	No. 1.	No. 2.	No. 3.
Silica...	23.98	14.15	12.32
Oxide of Lead...	41.03	59.72	57.72
Metallic Lead..	(38.09)	(55.45)	(53.58)
Peroxide of Iron...	4.42	2.98	2.58
Oxide of Zinc..	10.14	6.77	11.51
Metallic Zinc..	(8.13)	(5.43)	(9.23)
Lime..	15.72	11.25	10.37

All contain traces of Magnesia and of Sulphur. No. 3, contains Carbonic Acid, from having been exposed to the air for some time after cooling.

No. 1. Cinder from Scotch hearth, Riggins and Chapman, Joplin.

No. 2. Jasper County Smelting Works, Joplin; ordinarily good Lead cinder from reverberatory furnace.

No. 3. Same works as last; bluish and somewhat burned, from near firebridge of the reverberatory furnace.

A sample of "tailings," or refuse from the washing and jigging operations, being well mixed and ground, gave:

Metallic Lead.. 4.23 per cent.
Metallic Zinc... 35.51   "

The Lead being present as Galena, and the Zinc as Blende. This sample was from Joplin, and illustrates the intimate mixture of Galena and Blende, ("Black-jack,") in the neighboring deposits.

The following analysis shows the composition of various Zinc ores from the Granby Region:

1. CARBONATE OF ZINC (White Jack).

This sample was from shaft 23, Hart Shaft District, Granby, taken from a large mass:

	Per cent.
Silicious matter	1.22
Peroxide of Iron	1.21
Oxide of Zinc	63.02
Carbonic acid	34.58
	100.03.

2. SILICATES OF ZINC.

	1.	2.	3.
Silica	23.32	27.51	26.83
Peroxide of Iron	0.61	1.22	0.65
Oxide of Zinc	67.15	63.05	66.37
Water	8.59	7.10	6.46
Lime	None.	1.21	Trace
Totals	99.67	100.09	100.31

No. 1. Bellew's shaft, East Point District, Granby. Represents average of the ore.

No. 2. Village Diggings, Granby, cleaned.

No. 3. Frazier Diggings, Granby. Shaft 408, as delivered to smelting works.

3. BLENDE.

Average sample from Bellew's shaft, East Point, Granby, gave—

	Per cent.
Silicious matter	2.05
Iron (as metal,)	0.53
Zinc "	64.67
Lead	None.

The composition of most of the samples of Blende sent is very nearly the same as this, but the following two are very interesting :

	1.	2.
Silicious	1.41	0.25
Iron (metal)	0.37	0.32
Cadmium (metal)	0.623	0.509
Zinc (metal)	64.87	65.92

No. 1. From Leadville. Dark, greenish yellow in color. Crystalline.

No. 2. Porter's Diggings, shaft 18, Joplin. Same description as No. 1.

Other samples of Blende from the same region failed to give even a trace of Cadmium.

4. "BLACK SAND,"

So called by the miners, is a Clay impregnated with Peroxide of Iron and containing a small per centage of Zinc. It is of very variable composition.

	1.	2.
Silicious (Clay)	43.68	87.82
Peroxide of Iron	27.96	4.13
Oxide of Zinc	14.98	4.48
Water and CO_2	13.33	....
Lime	....	1.15

No. 1. From Hart shaft 27, Granby. Yellowish-brown, soft and Clay-like.

No. 2. Crystalline Sand from Minersville. In this sample the "Silicious matter" was nearly pure Silica.

For various qualitative analyses and examinations of ores and minerals found in Zinc deposits, reference may be made to description of same in Dr. Schmidt's report.

LIMESTONES,

Accompanying Lead ores in the Joplin region.

	1.	2.	3.
Silicious	1.24	2.98	0.26
Peroxide of Iron	2.03	....	....
Carbonate of Iron	....	2.04	1.14
Carbonate of Lime	54.72	91.84	54.52
Carbonate of Magnesia	41.98	2.83	44.46
Totals	99.97	99.69	100.38

No. 2 contains a very trivial amount of Bitumen.

No. 1. Soft, gritty "Spar." Parr shaft, Joplin Hill. A loose aggregation of small crystals of reddish-yellow color.

No. 2. "Altered Limestone," Joplin, showing black specks of Bituminous matter.

No. 3. From Sherman shaft, Joplin. Resembles Spathic Iron ore. Full description of these Limestones will be found in Dr. Schmidt's report.

	4.	5.
Silicious	1.57	0.23
Peroxide of Iron	0.52	0.18
Lime	54.04	55.82
Magnesia	0.39	0.32

No. 4. Light gray crystalline. Watkin's shaft, Jasper, No. 3 District, Joplin.

No. 5. White oolitic Limestone, from Holman Diggings, Granby.

CLAY.

A yellow "Tallow Clay," from shaft 195, Frazier Diggings, Granby, gave 33.94 per cent. Oxide of Zinc. The Zinc was present as Carbonate, as was evident from the effervescence of the Clay with acids.

A yellow Clay, taken from shaft 4, Lone Elm, gave—

Water.. 8.83
Silica.. 46.15
Alumina*. 38.55

Lime, Magnesia and Alkalies not determined.

*Includes Oxide of Iron.

NICKEL AND COBALT ORES.

1. Mine LaMotte, "Old Jack" Diggings. The Galena obtained here was found to contain no Nickel, but an accompanying ore gave—

	Per cent.
Metallic Copper	2.04
" Nickel	2.27
" Cobalt	1.66
" Lead	Trace.

Iron Pyrites being present in much larger amount.

2. Mine LaMotte, Niedner's shaft. Here the Galena is intermixed with Nickel and Cobalt. A sample, containing some Gangue, gave—

	Per cent.
Lead (metal)	63.53
Copper (metal)	Trace.
Nickel (metal)	4.26
Cobalt (metal)	1.42

3. Galena from "Old Copper Mine," same region, gave—

	Per cent.
Copper	None.
Nickel	1,68
Cobalt	0.63

The following analysis of a slag from the furnaces of the "St. Joseph Lead Company," shows the curiously mixed character of the ores found in the S. E. Lead Region. It was made for the Company, and is published by permission of Mr. C. B. Parsons, Superintendent:

Water	1.89
Silica	2.04
Carbonic acid	4.35
Lime	9.98
Magnesia	4.84
Potash and Soda	2.10
Lead (metal)	41.42
Copper (metal)	1.10
Iron (metal)	14.44
Nickel (metal)	1.24
Cobalt (metal)	1.43
Zinc (metal)	1.19
Sulphur	6.46
Oxygen, required by metals less that replaced by Sulphur	7.47

99.95

This slag had been exposed to the air for some time, absorbing water and carbonic acid. Antimony, absent.

S I L V E R , (Argentiferous Galena).

A sample from the so-called "Madison County Silver Mine," Sec. 9, T. 32, R. 6 E., a thin vein in Porphyry, on land of John Revels, gave :

Silver.. 4 ounces to the ton.
Lead............................... .... 12.84 per cent.

Most of the "fine-grained" Galena in Madison county will yield from 2 to 7 ounces of Silver per ton, the latter figure being rarely reached.

C O P P E R .

The only sample examined which contained a noteworthy per centage of Copper was one of mixed Iron and Copper pyrites, with Gangue, from Collins' Diggings, Cooper county. This yielded 20.96 per cent. metallic Copper.

I R O N O R E S

From Coal Measures, Cedar, Vernon and Barton counties. Partial analyses, giving silicious matter, water and Iron. Localities described in report of Mr. Broadhead, Director of the Survey.

Analyses.

	No. 1.	No. 2.	No. 3.	No. 4.	No. 5.	No. 6.	No. 7.	No. 8.
Silicious....................	12.22	43.94	24.22	4.71	8.69	21.10	24.81	31.51
Water....................	11.33	8.91	10.66	13.27	12.59	*.........	11.90	12.02
Peroxide of Iron..............	76.38	47.02	65.04	81.90	78.30	....	63.20	56.29
(Metallic Iron)..............	53.46	32.91	45.53	57.33	54.81	38.12	44.24	39.40

*Organic matter and Protoxide of Iron present.

No. 1. Vernon county. Lower Coal Measures; Sec. 34, T. 34, R. 33.
No. 2. Cedar county. ; Lower Coal Measures; Sec. 15, T. 34, R. 27.
No. 3. Cedar county. Lower Coal Measures; Limonite. Sec. 15, T. 34, R. 27.
No. 4. Cedar county. Coal Measures; bed 3 to 5 feet thick; Limonite. S.
      W. part of county, Sec. 22, T. 34, R. 28.
No. 5. Cedar county. Underlies No. 4; bed 1½ feet.
No. 6. Barton county. S. E. part of S. W., Sec. 10, T. 33, R. 33.
No. 7. Barton county. Coal Measures. Sec. 18, T. 33, R. 33.
No. 8. Barton county, near Lamar. Sec. 25, T. 32, R. 31.

Two "stray" ores are here inserted:

	No. 1.	No. 2.
Silicious	6.81	4.84
Peroxide of Iron	75.32	94.18
(Metallic Iron)	(52.72)	(65.93)
Lime*	10.09	....
Magnesia	trace.	....
Sulphur	trace.	....
Phosphoric acid	0.356	....

No. 1. S. W. corner of Cole county, from vicinity of "Locust Mound."
No. 2. Madison county. S. E. qr. S. W., Sec. 11, T. 33, R. 5 E.; Mrs. King's
      land.

*Contains Carbonic Acid and trace of Protoxide of Iron.

Iron ores analysed in connection with the report of Mr. Moore.

	No. 1.	No. 2.	No. 3.	No. 4.	No. 5.	No. 6.	No. 7.	No. 8.	No. 9.	No. 10.	No. 11.	No. 12.
Water	8.56	4.96	8.46	6.72	8.50	10.97	10.38	8.57	8.99	9.58	8.92	11.43
Silicious	37.88	57.92	28.18	42.25	16.46	17.19	14.72	25.97	15.20	25.88	33.97	7.46
Peroxide of Iron	53.26	36.81	63.05	50.01	74.71	70.43	74.87	64.18	74.87	63.25	53.37	79.57
(Metallic Iron)	37.28	25.76	44.13	35.01	52.30	49.30	52.06	44.93	52.41	44.27	37.36	55.70
Sulphur				trace.	0.016	none.		0.003	0.037	trace.	trace.	0.017
Phosphoric Acid				0.096	0.164	0.130		0.153	0.154	0.147	0.148	0.323
(Phosphorus)				0.042	0.071	0.057		0.066	0.067	0.064	0.062	0.141

No. 1. L. Johnson, T. 28, R. 6 E., Sec. 15, N. E. qr. of S. W. qr., Wayne Co.

No. 2. Jesse Lute, T. 30, R. 9 E., Sec. 11, N. E. qr. of N. W. qr., Bollinger Co.

No. 3. Spear's Mountain, T. 29, R. 7 E., Sec. 3, w½ lot 2 of N. E. qr., Wayne Co.

No. 4. Black River Bank, T. 26, R. 6 E., Sec. 18, Butler Co.

No. 5. Same as No. 4, T. 26, R. 6 E., Sec. 18.

No. 6. Spiva Bank, T. 28, R. 8 E., Sec. 26, Stoddard Co.

No. 7. Myer's Bank, T. 30, R. 8 E., Sec. 32, S. E. qr. of N. E. qr., Bollinger Co.

No. 8. Shrout's Bank, T. 25, R. 6 E., Sec. 16, N. E. qr. of N. E. qr., Butler Co.

No. 9. Bear Mountain Bank, T. 29, R. 3 E., Sec. 2 N. W. qr., Wayne Co.

No. 10. Poblick's Bank, T. 32, R. 8 E., Secs. 23 and 24, Bollinger Co.

No. 11. Glenn Emma Bank, T. 30, R. 9 E., Sec. 16, Bollinger Co.

No. 12. Cushman Hill Bank, T. 30, R. 9 E., Sec. 18, N. E. of N. E., Bollinger Co.

MANGANESE ORES.

No pure Binoxide of Manganese has been found in Missouri. Many of the ores containing Manganese show in places a crystallization resembling that of Pyrolusite, but none of them give as high an Oxygen ratio as is required for a commercial article.

Four miles north-west of Fredericktown, Madison county, (Hick's place,) a mineral occurs giving:

Silicious matter	56.82
Peroxide of Iron	18.67
Sesquioxide of Manganese	14.24
Water	3.19
Metallic Iron	13.07
Metallic Manganese	9.86

With some Lime and Magnesia undetermined.

In Reynolds county, S. W. qr. of S. W. qr. of Sec. 16, T. 3, R. 2 E., (Lindsay's ore bed,) an ore occurs giving the following results, (a partial analysis only was made):

Silicious	28.81
Iron (as Peroxide)	4.81
Manganese (estimated as Protoxide)	50.84
Lime	6.24

The "Silicious" in this ore is Feldspar, containing 71.50 per cent. Silica and 14.85 Alumina. Potash was qualitatively determined only. Similar replacements occur elsewhere.

In the Report for 1872, analyses occur of ores containing both Iron and Manganese in proportions suitable for the manufacture of "Spiegeleisen." No other ores of this kind have since been found in the State, but from the fact that at least one such deposit is known to exist, and in view also of the contiguity in several instances of Manganese and Iron ores, it seems well worth the while of those owning hitherto useless deposits of Manganese to develop their property somewhat, and ascertain whether, as is occasionally the case, they "run into" Iron, or into ores containing both metals.

COALS.

The "proximate" analyses here given show per centage of water, volatile matter (gas), fixed carbon and ash. Per centage of coke may be found by summing the two last per centages. The method of analysis employed* was:

First—For *water*: exposure to temperature of 105° to 115° C., loss of weight indicating moisture.

Second—For *volatile*: strong ignition for three minutes in a closed Platinum crucible.

Third—For *fixed carbon*: heating the coke with free access of air until completely "burned off."

Fourth—For *ash*: simply weighing same, it being the residue from the last operation.

Some of the best coals in these tables are, in Barton county, Flack's, Sec. 29, T. 32 R. 33; Coal from S. W. of Sec. 23, T. 32, R. 33; Neil and Gilbert's, N. W. of Sec. 29,, T. 33, R. 33; Coal from Sec. 18, T. 33, R. 33; and from S. W. of Sec. 17, T. 31, R. 32.

In Vernon county: Cassell's, N. W. of Sec. 7, T. 37, R. 33; the top of the Osage Coal Company's Bank, Clayton; and Webster's.

In Bates county: Hecadon's Coal, except bottom of seam; Goodman's; Wright's; Mrs. Holt's; and Hosey's.

In Howard county: Garvin's, Sec. 28, T. 50, R. 17; Robb's, Sec. 36, T. 52, R. 16; Dr. Scroggin's bank; and Gilmore's, N. W. of Sec. 16, T. 49, R. 17.

It is believed that the samples sent for analysis were fair averages of the beds represented. The Coals above mentioned are chosen on account of their showing less than the amount of ash and more than the average of fixed carbon. Many others nearly approach them in both respects.

---

* More fully described in Report of 1872.

ANALYSES OF COALS.

JASPER COUNTY.

Name of Coal.	Water.	Volatile.	Fixed Carbon.	Ash.	Color of Ash.
T. C. Arnot's, top, N. W. Sec. 35, T. 30, R. 33	0.28	36.05	55.05	8.62	Purple slate
Same, bottom	1.04	32.44	55.54	10.98	Light purple

BARTON COUNTY.

Name of Coal.	Water.	Volatile.	Fixed Carbon.	Ash.	Color of Ash.
Henry Flack's, Sec. 29, T. 32, R. 33, top	2.14	38.56	56.02	8.28	Faint purple
Same, middle	1.89	34.04	58.71	5.36	Purple gray
Same, bottom	1.54	37.51	56.65	4.30	Drab
Sec. 30, T. 33, R. 31, top	2.85	33.81	51.91	11.43	Light reddish brown
Same, middle	2.45	33.53	50.75	13.27	Light brown
Same, bottom	1.63	36.93	51.03	10.41	Pale chocolate
W. hf. of Sec. 25, T. 32, R. 31, top	1.50	40.76	52.35	5.30	Chocolate
Same, middle	0.81	39.49	54.55	5.15	Warm gray

BARTON COUNTY—Continued.

Name of Coal.	Water.	Volatile.	Fixed Carbon.	Ash.	Color of Ash.
Sec. 5, T. 30, R. 31, top	2.14	36.31	56.96	4.59	Pink brown
Same, bottom	1.27	39.62	53.43	5.68	Pinkish gray
Sec. 32, T. 32, R. 30, top	1.67	35.03	50.02	13.28	Pink
Same, middle	1.36	36.79	53.59	8.26	Yellowish pink
Same, bottom	1.38	34.91	51.69	12.02	Same
S. W. Sec. 23, T. 32, R. 33, top	1.87	32.94	59.85	5.84	Very pale brown
Same, middle	1.91	35.41	59.41	3.27	Gray
Same, bottom	2.07	32.65	55.91	9.37	Yellowish gray
Neil & Gilbert's, N. W. Sec. 29, T. 33, R. 33, top	4.18	31.22	58.57	6.03	Drab
Same middle	1.71	37.85	57.22	3.22	Light brown
Same, bottom	0.35	36.55	58.62	4.48	Dark gray
Kelley's, Sec. 30, T. 32, R. 29	1.72	38.61	49.82	9.85	Light purple
G. M. Evans, N, hf. W. Sec. 22, T. 31, R. 31	1.07	34.66	44.30	19.97	Purple gray
Beebe's, S. part of Sec. 7, T. 30, R. 33	1.12	34.98	50.68	13.22	Pinkish gray
McKerrow's, Sec. 30, T. 33, R. 32, top	1.53	35.62	53.45	9.40	Light brown
Same, bottom	6.52	35.71	46.29	11.48	Pink
A. Cline, Sec. 30, T. 31, R. 31	1.54	33.79	50.21	14.46	Gray

	Water.	Volatile.	Fixed Carbon.	Ash.	Color of Ash.
Sec. 18, T. 33, R. 33, middle...............	1.58	32.79	57.51	8.12	Pinkish brown..........
Same, bottom.......................	2.08	35.09	59.51	3.82	Dull brown...........
S. W. of Sec. 17, T. 31, R. 32, bottom........	3.98	35.13	57.37	5.52	Straw color...........
S. E. of S. E. Sec 12, T. 30, R. 33.........	1.05	37.44	52.15	9.36	Gray............

VERNON COUNTY.

Name of Coal.	Water.	Volatile.	Fixed Carbon.	Ash.	Color of Ash.
Cassel's, N. W. Sec. 7, T. 37, R. 33, top........	2.58	38.39	53.91	5.12	Gray........ ....
Same, middle............	2.84	37.01	55.44	4.71	Faint gray...........
Osage Company's Coal (Clayton)............	2.42	45.06	49.11	3.41	Very pale brown........
Same, middle............	3.14	38.99	50.19	7.68	Faint purple............
Same, bottom............	1.22	37.16	46.75	14.87	Brown............
Medlin's, S. W. Sec. 8, T. 35, R. 33............	1.86	44.27	46.98	6.89	Dull purple............
J. D. Cox, near top, S. E. qr. of S. E. qr. Sec. 26, T. 38, R. 31.........	3.83	39.27	50.71	6.19	Light brown...........
Same, middle............	2.98	40.15	52.91	3.96	Light brown...........
Same, bottom............	2.75	40.11	48.26	8.88	Gray........ ....
John McLaughlin, N. E. Sec. 21, T. 34, R. 30........	1.57	40.94	53.33	4.16	Cream............
Same, bottom............	3.01	33.87	45.59	18.03	Rich brown ....

VERNON COUNTY—Continued.

Name of Coal	Water.	Volatile.	Fixed Carbon.	Ash.	Color of Ash.
Moundville, Sec. 5, T. 34, R. 32........	1.72	39.24	52.35	6.69	Light gray........
N. hf. S. E. qr. Sec. 8, T. 36, R. 30, top........	5.97	45.57	30.27	18.19	Iron rust........
Webster's, N. W. Sec. 7, T. 34, R. 32........	2.13	43.48	48.42	5.97	Gray........
English & Karnes, S. W. qr. of N. E. qr. Sec. 7, T. 34, R. 32........	2.27	40.37	45.73	11.63	Pink brown........
Parker's, N. W. of Sec. 5, T. 37, R. 31, top........	8.97	41.62	47.32	7.09	Pale slate........
Same, middle........	3.75	39.60	46.60	10.05	Brown........
Same, bottom........	2.34	43.71	46.97	6.98	Pinkish brown........

BATES COUNTY.

Name of Coal	Water.	Volatile.	Fixed Carbon.	Ash.	Color of Ash.
Cooper's, top, N. E. Sec. 5, T. 40, R. 33........	5.58	36.04	48.29	10.09	Rusty brown........
Same, bottom........	5.07	38.13	47.99	8.18	Pinkish brown........
Heedon's, top, N. E. Sec. 16, T. 40, R. 32........	2.57	44.93	49.72	2.78	Pink........

Same, middle	4.89	42.89	50.18	2.54	Light brown
Same, bottom	5.09	35.36	47.51	12.04	Light brown
W. F. Goodman	4.57	45.30	48.08	2.05	Light brown
Wm. Arnott, lot 44, Sec. 6, T. 39, R. 33	4.55	33.45	48.74	18.26	Reddish brown
B. Yates', top, S. E. Sec. 4, T. 39, R. 29	1.96	36.29	48.19	18.56	Light gray
Same, bottom	1.87	30.95	47.89	19.29	Light brown
Wright's, top, S. E. Sec. 8, T. 40, R. 31	2.87	36.01	57.79	8.83	Light brown
Same, middle	2.62	37.79	55.74	8.85	Light brown
Same, bottom	2.42	35.99	55.77	5.82	Light brown
Carr's, S. W. Sec. 33, T. 39, R. 31, next to top	6.43	33.71	49.66	10.20	Nearly white
Same, top	6.82	33.73	43.94	15.51	Reddish brown
Same, middle	4.56	39.99	48.85	6.60	Pale brown
Conley's, top, Sec. 18, T. 39, R. 33	3.94	34.28	51.97	9.86	Pale brown
Same, bottom	3.45	36.51	49.27	10.77	Light brown
Leonard heirs', middle, S. W. Sec. 19, T. 88, R. 33	3.16	32.99	52.29	11.56	Nearly white
Same, bottom	2.83	34.60	52.84	9.64	Pale brown
Mrs. Holts', top, S. W. Sec. 14, T. 39, R. 20	5.93	37.72	51.48	4.87	Salmon
Same, bottom	6.89	35.55	51.50	6.06	Salmon

CEDAR COUNTY.

NAME OF COAL.	Water.	Volatile.	Fixed Carbon.	Ash.	Color of Ash.
B. Marcus', top, N. W. Sec. 16, T. 36, R. 27	2.99	39.46	44.55	18.10	Dull red
Same, middle	3.15	40.05	51.17	5.63	Dull red
Same, below middle	3.43	40.67	46.41	9.49	Dull brown
Same, bottom	3.13	37.82	50.95	8.10	Light brown
Miller's, bottom, Sec. 20, T. 33, R. 28	2.21	40.94	50.98	5.87	Light purple
Hosey's, top, N. E. S. W. Sec. 16, T. 35, R. 26	2.27	39.15	54.47	4.11	Light brown
Same, middle	2.19	39.28	51.85	6.68	Pale brown
Same, bottom	1.23	47.52	41.28	9.97	Light purple

JOHNSON COUNTY.

NAME OF COAL.	Water.	Volatile.	Fixed Carbon.	Ash.	Color of Ash.
Porter's, top, near Dunksburgh	3.62	46.36	35.53	14.49	Very light brown
Same, middle	4.18	42.69	37.75	15.38	Chocolate
Same, near bottom	5.30	44.23	38.93	11.54	Nearly white
Same, bottom	2.84	28.09	27.72	41.35	Light chocolate

PUTNAM COUNTY.

Name of Coal.	Water.	Volatile.	Fixed Carbon.	Ash.	Color of Ash.
Wage's, N. E. qr. of N. E. qr. Sec. 11, T. 65, R. 17........	5.58	38.11	45.86	10.45	Full brown.............
Mrs. Nancy Parton, S. E. of Sec. 6, T. 64, R. 16.........	4.76	40.77	49.07	5.40	Red brown.............

SULLIVAN COUNTY.

Name of Coal.	Water.	Volatile.	Fixed Carbon.	Ash.	Color of Ash.
David Sodder, S. W. qr. of S. W. qr. of Sec. 27, T. 63, R. 26.......	7.68	37.37	50.03	4.92	Very light brown.....
Same, middle........	4.88	33.45	47.29	14.38	Full brown.............
*S. Beeler's, Sec. 26, T. 64, R. 18........	8.27	32.62	12.88	51.23	Dark red...............
Wm. Kirby, N. E. qr. of S. W. qr. Sec. 21, T. 61, R. 20....	6.34	40.08	47.59	5.99	Pale brown............
Mrs. Downing, Sec. 18, T. 64, R. 18....	5.02	45.05	44.05	5.88	Gray...................

* This is not a Coal, properly speaking—("Mother of Coal.")

ADAIR COUNTY.

NAME OF COAL.	Water.	Volatile.	Fixed Carbon.	Ash.	Color of Ash.
J. M. Williams', S. W. qr. of Sec. 15, T. 63, R. 17	5.48	36.94	43.76	13.82	Dark brown
Same, bottom	5.13	38.99	49.69	6.19	Nearly white
Beeman's, S. E. of Sec. 3, T. 63, R. 16	1.12	35.31	48.75	14.82	Light purple
McPhetridge, Sec. 36, T. 63, R. 18	5.75	41.32	44.69	8.24	Light brown
Jno. Stanley, S. W. of Sec. 15, T. 63, R. 17	6.64	39.52	48.58	5.31	Brown
Jas. Campbell, S. E. qr. of S. W. qr. of Sec. 36, T. 63, R. 17	5.84	40.68	45.89	7.59	Chocolate

LINN COUNTY.

NAME OF COAL.	Water.	Volatile.	Fixed Carbon.	Ash.	Color of Ash.
Edwards'	1.91	45.37	42.56	10.16	Light brown
Same, lower seam	4.78	43.57	48.29	3.36	Drab
St. Catharine	5.44	41.91	48.12	4.53	Brown
Jacob Van Bibber	7.95	40.45	47.54	4.06	Light yellow

CHARITON COUNTY.

Name of Coal.	Water.	Volatile.	Fixed Carbon.	Ash.	Color of Ash.
McAdams', top bed, 2 miles E. of Salisbury	5.80	39.36	44.35	10.43	Light red brown
Same, bottom	8.05	38.13	48.11	5.71	Dirty white

HOWARD COUNTY.

Name of Coal.	Water.	Volatile.	Fixed Carbon.	Ash.	Color of Ash.
Skinner's, Sec. 18, T. 51, R. 15	5.45	31.01	44.63	18.91	Red brown
Garvin's, Sec. 28, T. 50, R. 17	4.88	40.74	48.93	5.45	Red brown
Rob's, Sec. 36, T. 52, R. 16	5.04	42.86	47.47	4.63	Dark red brown
Robt. Digg's, S. E. Sec. 8, T. 50, R. 14	3.40	35.35	45.54	15.71	Gray
H. L. Brown's Bank, Sec. 5, T. 49, R. 17	3.47	35.52	42.73	18.28	Rusty brown
Dr. Scroggin's Bank, Sec. 2, T. 52, R. 17	4.68	41.21	48.52	5.59	Chocolate
Gilmore's, N. W. of Sec. 16, T. 49, R. 17	5.67	38.44	50.91	4.98	Light brown
Powel's, N. W. of Sec. 18, T. 50, R. 14	4.61	38.24	44.20	12.95	Chocolate
Todd's Bank	4.12	35.03	51.50	9.35	Light brown

MONITEAU COUNTY.

NAME OF COAL.	Water.	Volatile.	Fixed Carbon.	Ash.	Color of Ash.
Moniteau Coal and Coke Co........	4.01	46.89	44.61	4.49	Pale gray............
Coke, from same.........	1.59	2.65	79.28	16.98	Reddish brown........

Three of the Bates county Coals will not coke, viz: Carr's, Mrs. Holt's and Conley's. Carr's is the best example met with in the series, of a perfectly non-coking Coal.

COAL—AMOUNT OF SULPHUR.

Sulphur was determined in a few Coals only. The following table shows the average per centage to be high:

BARTON COUNTY.

	Per centage.
H. Flack's, Sec. 29, T. 32, R. 33	2.97
W. hf. of S. 25, T. 32, R. 31	2.55
Neil & Gilbert, N. W. Sec. 29, T. 33, R. 33	1.42
Beebe's, S. W. Sec. 7, T. 31, R. 33	6.48
McKerrow's, S. E. qr. Sec. 31, T. 33, R. 32	1.85
A. Cline's, Sec. 34, T. 31, R. 31	5.59
Sec. 18, T. 33, R. 33	2.54

JOHNSON COUNTY.

Porter's, near Dunksburgh	6.93.

SULLIVAN COUNTY.

Kirby's, N. E. S. W. Sec. 21, T. 61, R. 20	2.29
Mrs. Downing's, Sec. 18, T. 64, R. 18	3.48

MONITEAU COUNTY.

Moniteau Coal and Coke Company, Moniteau Station	5.207
Coke from same	4.612

BATES COUNTY.

Hecadon's, N. E. Sec. 16, T. 40, R. 32	1.86
B. Yates', S. E. Sec. 4, T. 39, R. 29	4.10
Wright's, S. E. Sec. 8, T. 40, R. 31	3.55
Carr's, S. W. Sec. 33, T. 39, R. 31	2.28

CEDAR COUNTY.

B. Marcus', N. W. Sec. 15, T. 36, R. 27	4.95
Hosey's, N. E. S. W. Sec. 16, T. 35, R. 26	3.26

ADAIR COUNTY.

J. M. Williams', N. E. Sec. 16, T. 63, R. 17	4.41
Beeman's, Sec. 3, T. 63, R. 16	7.18

LINN COUNTY.

Edward's, Sec. 13, T. 57, R. 21	4.33
St. Catharine	3.63

HOWARD COUNTY.

Todd's.. 2.369

The Moniteau Coal contains 0.75 per cent. Iron, which would require only 0.857 per cent. Sulphur (as Pyrites.) In a great majority of the above Coals however, Sulphur is present as Sulphide of Iron. (Fe S₂.)

The following analyses of spring and well waters are, as mentioned in the introductory remarks, by no means complete. Much too great a time had in most cases elapsed, between the times of taking the waters and analyzing them, and in several, more Carbonate would appear in solution than appear in these tables. In fact, in more than one of them, a sediment of Lime and Magnesia was found to have settled out.

In the three Salt springs, however, in Howard county, the analyses are probably accurate, at least the water was in good condition and without sediment, as brought to the laboratory :

VERNON COUNTY—Capt. Houtze's Spring, S. E. of Sec. 1, T. 36, R. 29.

This water gives only 34 grains to the gallon of solid residue, chiefly Chloride of Sodium. Sulphates are absent. No quantitave analysis was made.

" ELLIS' " WELL—N. W. of Sec. 28, T. 36, R. 31, 2½ miles N. of Nevada, Vernon county.

	Grains to gallon.
Carbonate of Lime	6.80
Carbonate Magnesia	7.76
Chloride of Sodium	30.19
Chloride of Calcium	9.91
Chloride of Magnesium	8.62
Sulphate of Lime	5.85
	69.13

VERNON COUNTY—Spring Six miles South of Nevada.

This water was not brought in a fit condition for analysis; probably it will not keep at all when exposed to the air. Although full of a muddy sediment when examined, it was made clear by acid (Muriatic), and then yielded by qualitative tests, Iron, Alumina, Sulphuric Acid, Lime, Magnesia and Alkalies. This indicates an Alum of some kind as one of its constituents.

MR. PREWITT'S WELL, near Nevada, Vernon county, gives.

	Grains to gallon.
Carbonate of Lime	13.93
Sulphate of Lime	22.28
Sulphate of Magnesia	20.37
Chloride of Sodium	7.70
	64.28

BARTON COUNTY—Water from Milford gave

Sulphate of Lime..	43.44
Sulphate of Magnesia..	66.66
Sulphate of Soda...	63.81

No Chlorine. The jug contained a sediment; Carbonates of Lime and Magnesia.

HOWARD COUNTY—" Lewis' " Spring, near Glasgow.

	Grains to the gallon.
Sulphate of Lime..	122.91
Carbonate of Lime..	23.71
Carbonate of Magnesia...	73.12
Chloride of Calcium..	37.29
Chloride of Sodium...	951.30
	1,208.33

" BOON'S LICK " (Howard county.)

Sulphate of Lime..	119.27
Chloride of Calcium..	81.47
Chloride of Sodium...	972.29
	1,173.03

" BURKHART'S SPRING. "—(Howard county.)

Sulphate of Lime	135.08
Chloride of Calcium......................	93.74
Chloride of Magnesium...	116.89
Chloride of Sodium...	1,082.48
	1,428.19

Limestones, from various depths of Artesian Well, at Insane Asylum, St. Louis county.

	1,329 feet.	1,620 feet.	1,627 feet.	1,646 feet.	1,800 feet.	1,842 feet.	1,888 feet.	2,188 feet.	2,217 feet.	2,747 feet.	2,997 feet.	3,447 feet.
Carbonate of Lime..........	83.03	27.24	30.69	38.85	43.28	38.17	41.52	50.80	48.37	48.05	55.57	48.94
Carbonate of Magnesia....	6.14	21.35	25.09	31.13	33.32	29.06	26.96	39.92	35.68	37.25	36.54	34.06
Silicious	10.13	49.15	38.65	28.36	22.19	30.13	28.96	7.91	13.14	9.94	1.99	13.96
Peroxide of Iron...........	0.97	2.79	5.07	1.82	1.41	2.02	1.72	1.62	*2.26	2.56	3.71	2.71

* Includes a small amount of Alumina.

INDEX.

INDEX.

ERRATA.

Page 98, 12th line, for "springs" read "wells."

Page 116, near middle, on 2d line of Chemical Analysis, omit "H2 O4."

Page 139, in Norwood's Report, for "Chalybeate" read "Sulphur."

Page 166, in middle of page, for "calcereous" read "calcareous."

Page 181, the words "Coal Measures" should be in the same type as "Ferruginous Sandstone" is, and in line just above the latter words.

Page 185, for "Dithocorinus" read "Dithocrinus."

Page 245, in capital heading, near bottom of page, omit the word "Lower" before "Carboniferous."

Page 318, for "David Smith" read "Daniel Smoot."

Page 357, 4th line from bottom, for "reniform" read "vermiform."

On Madison County Map, in title, for "C. J. Norwood" read "J. G. Norwood;" and

In Sec. 11, T. 33, R. 5 E., the sign for Copper should be erased and insert the sign for Iron; and

In T. 32, R. 7 E., for "Mine L. & Motte Mill" read "Mine LaMotte Mill."

On Cedar County Map, near left side, at top, for "R. 23," read "R. 28."

On Barton County Map, T. 33, R. 32, for "McKennon" read "McKerrow."

Page 643, Moore's Report, in capital heading, for "Southwest Missouri" read "South-east Missouri."

[I would add that I am under many obligations to Mr. S. H. Trowbridge, formerly of Glasgow, Mo., now of Aurora, Ill., who rendered voluntary assistance in the field during the months of July and August, 1873.]

ERRATA AND CORRECTIONS.

Page 385, line 10 from bottom, instead of "horizontal veins" read "horizontal runs."

Page 390, line 18 from bottom, instead of "average" read "Oronogo."

Same page, line 6 from top, the whole line should be stricken out.

Page 394, line 1 from bottom, instead of "into" read "in."

Page 397, line 4 from bottom, instead of "Mineral Picth" read "Mineral Pitch."

Page 398, line 8 from top, instead of "mineral" read "minerals," and instead of "relation" read "relations."

Same page, line 12 from top, instead of "found" read "formed."

Page 401, line 19 from top, instead of "Cooney" read "Conley."

Page 403, line 19 from bottom, instead of "Chert; fragments" read "Chert-fragments."

Same page, line 16 from bottom, instead of "surmounted" read "surrounded."

Page 405, line 13 from top, instead of "Dolomite Limestone" read "Dolomitic Limestone."

Page 411, line 3 from bottom, instead of "this" read "the."

Page 412, line 8 from top, instead of "ot highly" read "or highly."

Page 446, line 12 from top, instead of "is generally" read "are generally."

Page 481, the following lines should be stricken off:

"Fig. 57. Branch Diggings, Oronogo."

"Fig. 58. Loose Chunks, Oronogo."

"Fig. 59. Oronogo."

Page 486, the line "Fig. 65, Circular Diggings, Oronoga," should be stricken off.

Page 492, line 3 from top, instead of "smiltum" read "smittum."

Same page, line 4 from above, instead of "Drift" read "dirt."

Page 493, lines 5 and 7 from bottom, instead of "Scotch hearth" read "American hearth."

Page 494, lines 1 and 16 from top, instead of "Scotch hearth" read "American hearth."

Same page, line 11 from bottom, instead of "6 feet" read "6 inches."

Same page, line 3 from top, instead of "for each shift" read "two for each shift."

Page 495, line 13 from bottom, instead of "single Scotch hearth. Several Scotch hearths," read "single American hearth. When several American hearths."

Same page, line 3 from bottom, instead of "Hensey" read "Hersey," and instead of "Bingston" read "Kingston."

Page 497, line 7 from bottom, instead of "Scotch hearth" read "American hearth."

Page 498, line 3 from top, instead of "Scotch hearth" read "American hearth."

Same page, line 14 from top, instead of "mush" read "much."

Page 499, line 15 from top, instead of "tons" read "pounds."

Page 501, line 4 from top, instead of "wind furnace" read "air furnace."

Page 509, line 9 from bottom, instead of "other" read "either."

Page 514, line 17 from top, instead of "this presence" read "the presence."

Page 516, line 18 from top, instead of "manufactory" read "manufacture."

Same page, line 12 from top, after the words "Iron * * * * trace," add the following sentence: "What lacks to make 100 in this Clay analysis is mainly water."

Same page, line 14 from top, instead of "his analyses" read "this analysis."

Page 517, line 10 from top, instead of "Blockberger" read "Blochberger."

Same page, line 7 from top, instead of "slower" read "slow."

Page 519, line 16 from top, instead of "solid surface of the Limestone" read "solid Limestone."

Same page, line 4 from bottom, instead of "and undoubtedly derived from the latter," read "which are undoubtedly derived from it."

Page 521, line 1 from top, instead of "deposition" read "decomposition."

Same page, line 8 from top, instead of "in this crystalline" read "in the crystalline."

Page 524, line 4 from top, the words "district or" should be stricken off.

Page 535, line 8 from top, instead of "daily smelting expenses about $4, the yield averaging," read "smelting expenses per charge about $4. The yield varies."

Page 556, line 6 from top, instead of "It is assumed" read "it is assured."

Page 563, line 7 from top, instead of "Hacker" read "Harker."

Page 564, lines 17 and 19 from top, instead of "Blockberger" read "Blochberger."

Page 574, line 12 from top, instead of "Stocku" read "Stocker."

Same page, line 11 from bottom, instead of "Trim Springs" read "Twin Springs."

Page 575, line 6 from top, instead of "Blockberger" read "Blochberger."

Page 581, line 6 from top, instead of "existing as" read "with."

Page 582, line 18 from top, instead of "irregular basins (?) or elliptical outlines," read "circular or elliptical outlines."

Same page, line 24 from top, instead of "in its surface" read "in its surface appearance."

Page 585, line 9 from the top, instead of "squeezed into" read "squeezed, in."

Page 589, line 8 from top, instead of "mentioned above," read "as mentioned above."

Same page, line 7 from top, instead of "nails" read "rails."

Page 590, line 4 from top, instead of "0.2 per cent." read "2 per cent."

Same page, line 1 from top and line 11 from bottom, instead of "admissable" read "admissible."

Page 591, line 5 from top, the words "of which" should be stricken off.

Page 592, line 8 from top, instead of "parts" read "reports."

Page 594, line 11 from top, the words "No. 2, Pilot Knob ore," should be printed small and in line with the succeeding text.

Same page, lines 9 and 13 from top, instead of "silicious" read "silicon."

Same page, line 7 from top, instead of "No. 3" read simply "3."

The following Errata occur in Geological Report of Missouri Geological Survey for 1872, R. Pumpelly, Director. Printed in New York, by Julius Bien, 1873.

[Persons having the volume containing this Errata can cut this out and insert in that volume.]

PART I.

CHAPTER IV.

Page 61, line 7, instead of "one-eightieth" read "one-eighth."

Page 67, "uniform," in line 11, and "local" in line 14, from bottom, should be italics.

Page 71, line 15 from bottom, instead of "the uppermost layer of boulders" read "the outer layer of each boulder."

Page 72, line 11 from top, instead of "9.039" read "0.039."

Page 74, lines 7 and 8 from bottom, instead of "this sample consisted only of one-half inch good specular ore," read "one-half of this sample only consisted of good specular ore."

Page 77, line 9 from top, instead of "cropping" read "crossing."

Page 85, line 9 from top, instead of "the third Chapter" read "this fourth Chapter."

Page 87, line 9 trom top, instead of "chapter (III)" read "chapter (IV)."

CHAPTER V.

Page 93, line 5 from top, instead of "Chapter II and III" read "Chapters III and IV."

Page 100, line 7 from top, instead of "eastern portions" read "western portions."

Page 100, line 2 from bottom, instead of "western portion" read "eastern portion."

Page 101, line 8 from top, instead of "north-west" read "north-east."

Page 101, line 3 from bottom, instead of "Fig. 6" read Fig. 16."

Page 114, illustrations Fig. 21, the thickness of the main ore-bed should be "30 feet" instead of "40 feet."

Page 114, line 6 from bottom, instead of "nearly 40 feet" read "about 30 feet."

Page 115, line 4 from top, instead of "Fig. 11" read "Fig. 21."

Page 115, line 5 from top, instead of "Fig. 10" read "Fig. 20."

Page 115, line 11 from bottom, instead of "8 and 9" read 18 and 19."

Page 116, line 13 from bottom, instead of "Fig. 8" read "Fig. 18."

Page 117, line 9 from top, instead of "but C" read "Cut C."

Page 120, line 13 from top, instead of "Fig. 13" read "Fig. 23."

Page 120, line 4 from bottom, instead of "Fig. 13" read "Fig. 23."

Page 122, line 20 from top, instead of "Big Bogg" read "Big Bogy."

Page 124, line 8 from bottom, instead of "Chapter III" read "Chapter IV."

Page 124, line 3 from bottom, instead of "Chapter II" read "Chapter III."

Page 125, line 22 from top, instead of "Chapter V" read "Chapter VI."

Page 151, lines 2 and 3 from top, the words "Gilkerson's Ford, on Grand River, Henry county," should be stricken out.

Page 154, line 13 from top, instead of "Chapter V " read " Chapter VI."

Page 158, line 3 from bottom, instead of "Chapter V " read " Chapter VI."

Page 159, line 11 from top, instead of "layer" read "larger."

Page 160, line 14 from top, instead of "Chapter V " read "Chapter VI."

Page 160, line 17 from top, instead of " Chapter IV " read "Chapter V."

Page 165, line 1 from bottom, instead of "Chapter V " read " Chapter VI."

Page 167, line 3 from top, for "chapter V " read "chapter VI."

Page 167, line 20 from top, instead of "chapter V " read "chapter VI."

Page 169, line 3 from top, instead of " chapter I and described in chapter II," read "chapter III, and described in chapter IV."

Page 176, line 12 from top, instead of " chapter II" read "chapter III."

Page 179, line 14 from bottom, instead of "chapter IV " read "chapter VI."

Page 179, line 22 from top, instead of "Lutz " read " Lutes."

Page 183, line 12 from top, instead of "chapter V " read "chapter VI."

Page 189, line 13 from top, instead of "Mangua " read "Niangua;" instead of " Carl " read " Carroll."

Page 191, line 3 from top, instead of "Murdoch " read "Murdock."

Page 191, line 13 from top, instead of "Lutz " read "Lutes."

CHAPTER VI.

Page 194, line 12 from top, instead of " I. C." read " V. C."

Page 194, line 15 from bottom, instead of " I. A." read "III. A."

Page 197, No. 16, instead of " Big Bogg " read " Big Bogy."

Page 198, No. 32, instead of " Gilvy " read "Silvy."

Page 199, No. 47, instead of " Lutz " read "Lutes."

Page 199, No. 48, the figures "9, 2 " should be stricken out in the 6th and 7th columns.

Page 199, No. 54, instead of "Leetz " read " Lutes."

Page 199, No. 56, instead of " Spion " read "Spiva."

Page 199, No. 57, instead of " Grungstown " read " Youngstown."

Page 203, No. 95, instead of "Revold " read " Ravold."

Page 208, No. 157, instead of " Jones' estate " read " James' estate."

Page 209, No. 173, instead of "—— bank, T. 39, R. 11 W., Sec. 5," read " Chrisman bank, T. 39, R. 11 W., Sec. 6."

Page 212, No. 218, instead of "Carl" read " Carroll."

PART II.

CHAPTER I.

Page 5, for " Chilhomee " read "Chilhowee."

CHAPTER II.

Page 17, for " Gilkenson's frod" read Gilkinson's ford."

Page 18, for "Lepidastrobus " read " Lepidostrobus."

Page 19, in 11th line from bottom, for "dip " read " slip."

CHAPTER III.

Page 46, 15th line from bottom, for "*castatus*" read "*costatus*."
Page 48, 4th line from top, for "vein" read "seam."

Page 51, 6th line from top, for "*Meekelea*" read "*Meekella*," and in 7th line from top, for "*castatus*" read "*costatus*."
Page 62, for "Wörsten" read "Würster."

CHAPTER IV.

Page 88, in No. 218, omit comma between "*Entolium*" and "*aviculatum*." "*Subcumata*" should be "*subcuneata;*" "*Marconianus*" should be "*Marcouanus;*" "*Fistulafora*" should be "*Fistulapora*."
Page 89, in No. 211, for "*Syncladia*" read "*Synocladia*."
Page 89, in No. 210, for "*punctalifera*" read "*punctulifera*."
Page 90, in No. 206, omit comma just after "*Pleurotomaria*."
Page 90, in No. 197, for "*microspivus*" read "*mucrospinus*."
Page 91, in No. 188, for "*Marconianis*" read "*Marcouanus*."
Page 92, in No. 152, "*Monoptira*" should be "*Monoptera*."
Page 92, in No. 150, "Chest" should be "Chert."
Page 92, in No. 150, for "*Syntriolasma*" read "*Syntrilasma*."
Page 94, in No. 21, for "*Spirifuria*" read "*Spiriferina*."
Page 94, in No. 112, omit comma after word "*productus*."
Page 94, in No. 110, for "*Syntriclasma*" read "*Syntrilasma*."
Page 94, in right hand column, opposite No. 110, for "Saul, Missouri," read "Sam'l Morrow."
Page 95, for "*eutolium*" read "*entolium*."
Page 95, in No. 98, for "*Syntuclasma*" read "*Syntrilasma*."
Page 95, in No. 96, after "*Myalina*" omit "?."
Page 96, in first column at bottom of page, for "3 feet 8 inches" read "5 feet 8 inches."
Pages 107 and 112, for "*Eutolium*" read "*Entolium*."
Pages 119 and 120, for "Jatan" read "Iatan."
Page 126, sixth line, omit the words "in *scalenohedra*."

CHAPTER VI.

Page 193, second line from top, for "flue" read "fire."
Page 199, line 3 from bottom, for "Lymington" read "Symington."
Page 205, for "Cocknell" read "Cockrell."

CHAPTER IX.

Page 290, for "Collins" read "Colliers."
Page 291, line 3, for "red chestnut" read "rock chestnut."
Page 293, in No. 20, erase word "limestone."
Page 302, for "Ch. Marster" read "Ch. Würster."

CHAPTER XIII.

Pages 361 and 373, "Tarkie" should read "Tarkio."
Page 364, line 22, for "Took" read "Zook."

CHAPTER XIV.

Page 377, in line 22 from top, for "Suieda" read "lucida."
In several places for "Tarkie" read "Tarkio."
Page 384, for "Vaugundy" read "Vangundy."

CHAPTER XV.

Page 393, line 7 from bottom, omit comma after "*Rhombopora.*"
Page 396, for "*Ælis*" read "*Aclis;*" also for "*Cetenacanthus*" read "*Ctenacan-thus.*"
Page 400, for "Lund county" read "Sand Creek."

APPENDIX C.

Page 417, No. 27, for "*nanes*" read "*nanus.*"

Fig 1.

No. 1		Slope to Hill top
No. 2	28'	Sandstone at top with tumbled masses and occasional outcrops of the same below
No. 3	5'	Porous Brown Hematite
No. 4	16"	Red & Brown Ochre containing many plants
No. 5	7"	Ochre somewhat concretionary
No. 6	6"	Red Sandy Shales
No. 7	1'	Blue Shaly Sandstone
No. 8	6"	Shaly Coal

Bed of Iron Ore in Sec. 22 T. 34. R. 28. Cedar Co.

Fig. 2.

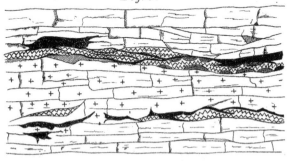

| Galena | Zinc Ore | Chert | Limestone |

Sketch in Old Shaft at Leadville

Scale. 3 Ft. = 1 inch

A. Gast & Co. Lith. St. Louis.

Fig. 3.

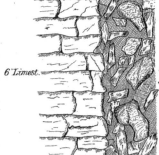

6' Limest.

Chert, Clay and
Soft Dolomite

Sketch in Keiths Shaft, Joplin
40 Ft. below the Surface

Fig. 4 a.

Fig. 4.

Caches in Sandstone
at Hallys Bluff
Osage River

Fig. 5.

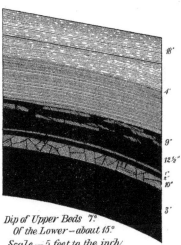

No. 1. Calcs Slate

No. 2. Bit. Sh & St.

No. 3. Slaty Coal
No. 4 Coal
No. 5 Dark Clay
No. 6 Impure Coal
No. 7. Clay

No. 8. Coal

18'

4'

9"

12½"

1"
½"
10"

3'

Dip of Upper Beds 7°.
Of the Lower – about 15°.
Scale – 5 feet to the inch
H. L. Browns Coal Bank, Howard County.

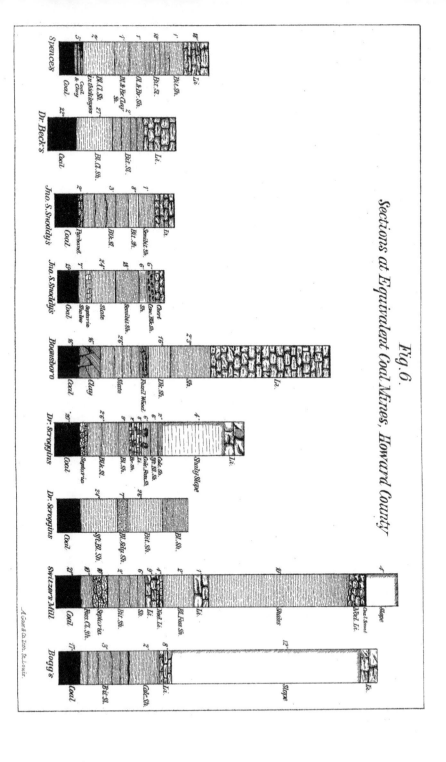

Fig. 6.

Sections at Equivalent Coal Mines, Howard County

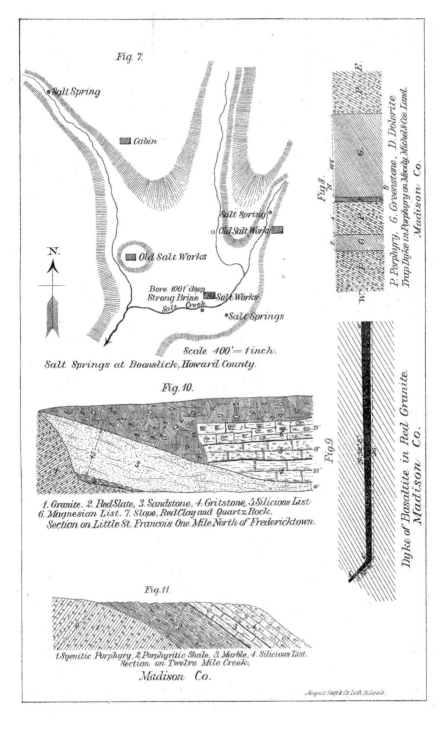

Fig. 7.

Salt Spring

Cabin

N.

Salt Spring

Old Salt Works

Old Salt Works

Bore 1001' deep
Strong Brine
Salt Creek

Salt Works

Salt Springs

Scale 400' = 1 inch.

Salt Springs at Boonslick, Howard County.

Fig. 8.

P. Porphyry. G. Greenstone. D. Dolerite
Trap Dyke in Porphyry on Moody, Michel & Co's Land.
Madison Co.

Fig. 10.

1. Granite, 2. Red Slate, 3. Sandstone, 4. Gritstone, 5 Silicious List
6. Magnesian List, 7. Slope, Red Clay and Quartz Rock.
Section on Little St. Francois One Mile North of Fredericktown.

Fig. 9.

Dyke of Basaltite in Red Granite.
Madison Co.

Fig. 11.

1. Syenitic Porphyry, 2. Porphyritic Shale, 3. Marble, 4. Silicious List.
Section on Twelve Mile Creek.

Madison Co.

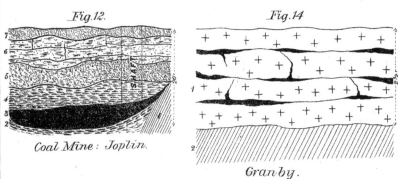

Fig.12.

Coal Mine: Joplin.

Fig.14

Granby.

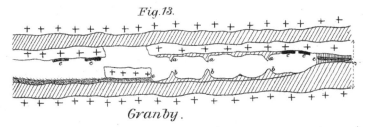

Fig.13.

Granby.

Fig.15.

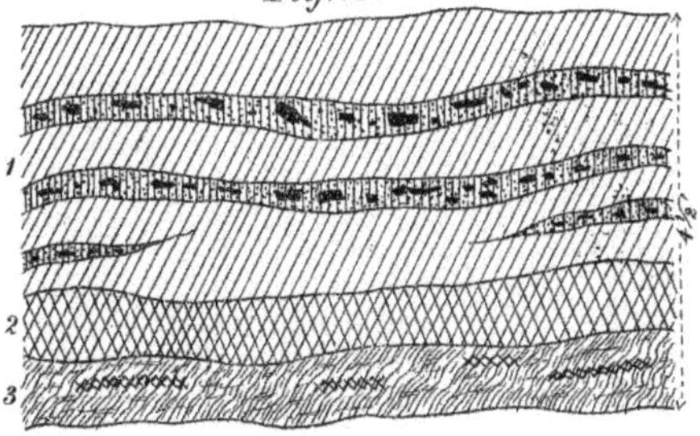

Granby.

Fig.16.

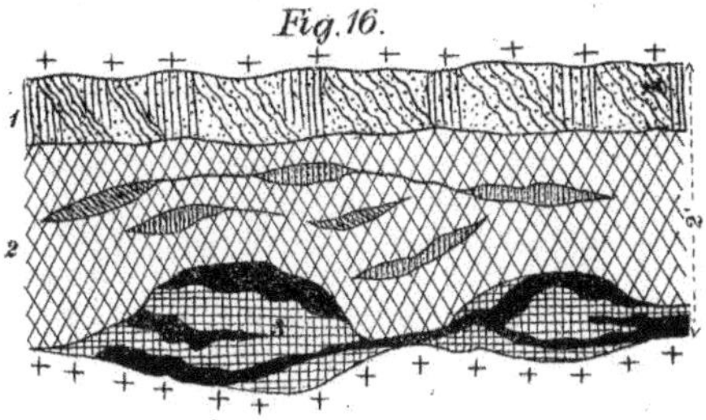

Granby.

A.Gast & Co. Lith. St. Louis.

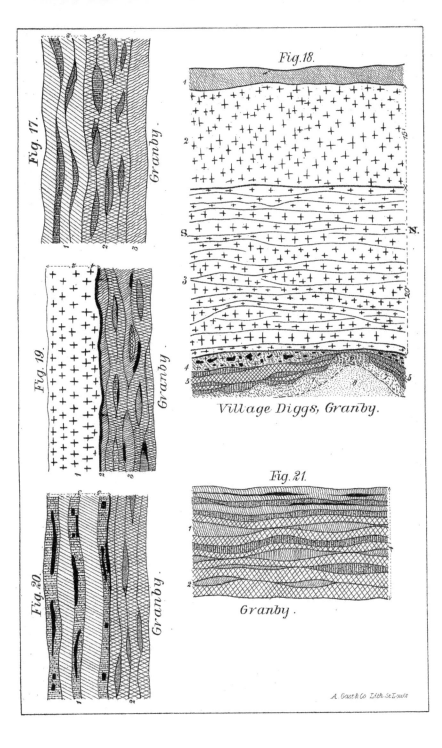

Fig. 17.

Granby.

Fig. 18.

S. N.

Village Diggs, Granby.

Fig. 19.

Granby.

Fig. 20.

Granby.

Fig. 21.

Granby.

A. Gast & Co. Lith. St. Louis

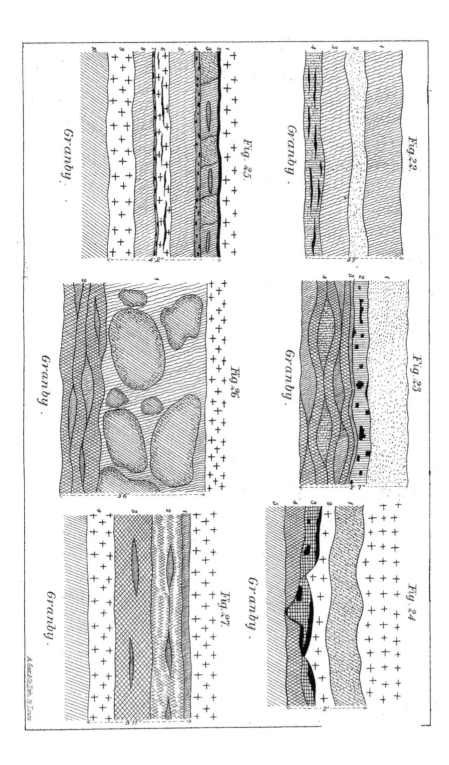

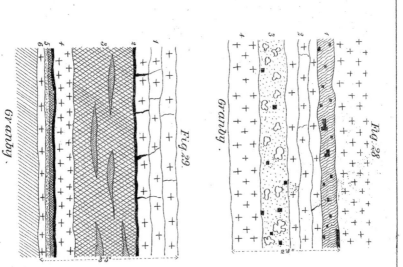

Fig. 28.

Granby.

Fig. 29.

Granby.

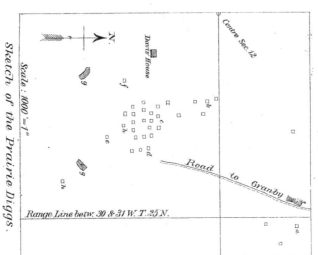

Fig. 30

Centre Sec. 12

Davis House

Road to Granby

N.

Scale: 1000' = 1"

Sketch of the Prairie Diggs.

Range Line betw. 30 & 31 W. T. 25 N.

A. Gast & Co. Lith. S. Louis.

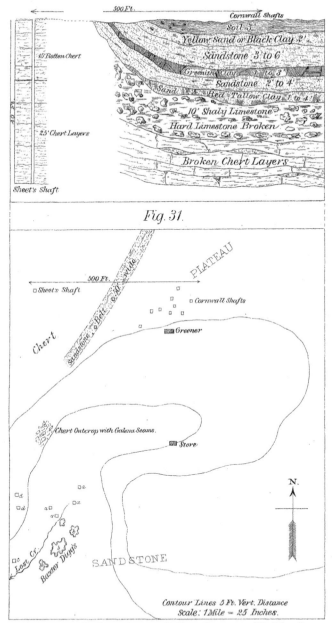

500 Ft.

Cornwall Shafts

Soil 3'

Yellow Sand or Black Clay 2'

Sandstone 3 to 6

Greenish Clay 1 to 3

Sandstone 2' to 4'

Sand & Red Tallow Clay 1 to 4

10' Shaly Limestone

Hard Limestone Broken

Broken Chert Layers

15' Rotten Chert

25' Chert Layers

40 Ft.

Sheet's Shaft

Fig. 31.

PLATEAU

500 Ft.

Sheet's Shaft

Cornwall Shafts

Sandstone's Belt 8 to 10' wide

Chert

Greener

Chert Outcrop with Galena Seams.

Store

d

a

d

a

a

a

c

Lost Cr.

Basler Diggs

SANDSTONE

N.

Contour Lines 5 Ft. Vert. Distance
Scale: 1 Mile = 25 Inches.

Plan and Section of the Cornwall Shafts.

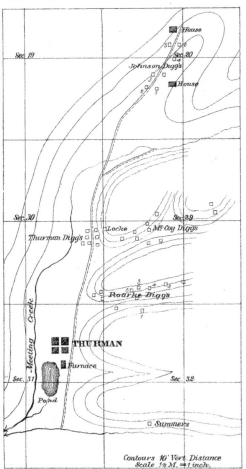

Sketch of Thurman District.
Fig. 32.

Fig. 33.

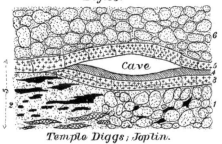

Temple Diggs; Joplin.

Fig. 37.

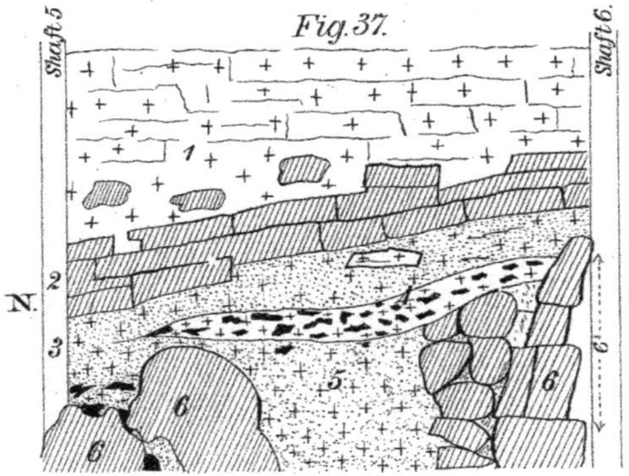
Shaft 5
Shaft 6.
N.
S.
1
2
3
4
5
6
6'

Porter Diggings, Joplin.

Fig. 34

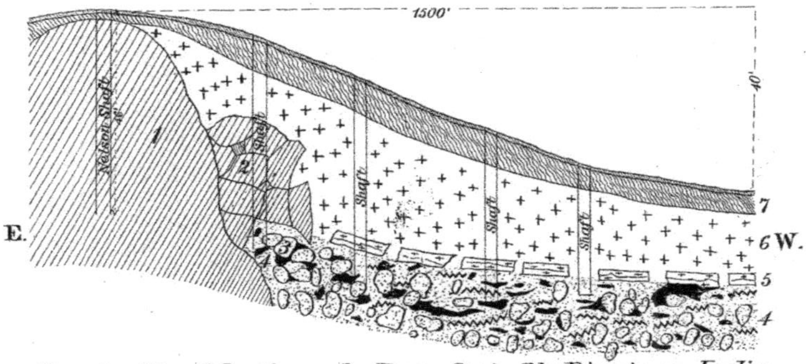
1500'
40'
Nelson Shaft
Shaft
Shaft
Shaft
Shaft
E.
W.
1
2
3
4
5
6
7

Longitudinal Section of a Run, Swindle Diggings, Joplin.

Fig. 36

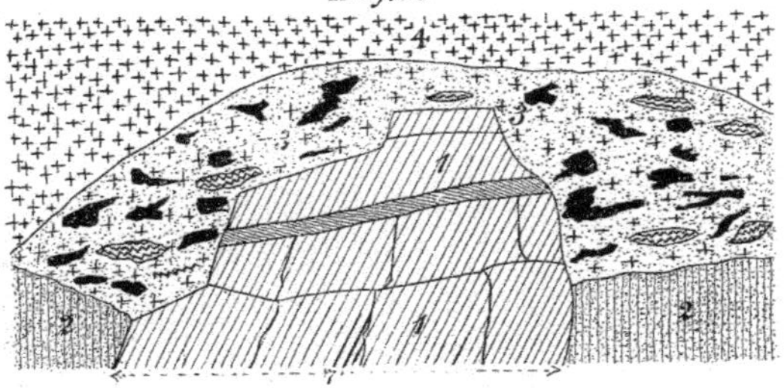
1
2
3
4
7'

Swindle Diggings, Joplin.

Fig. 35.

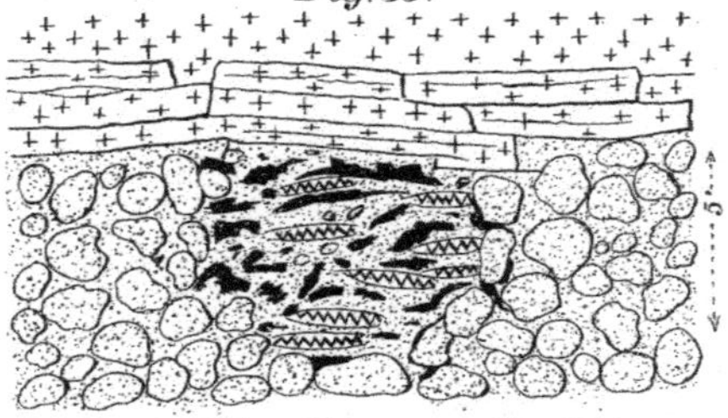
5'

Swindle Diggs, Joplin.
Cross Section of a Run (Compare Fig. 34)

A. Gast & Co. Lith. St. Louis.

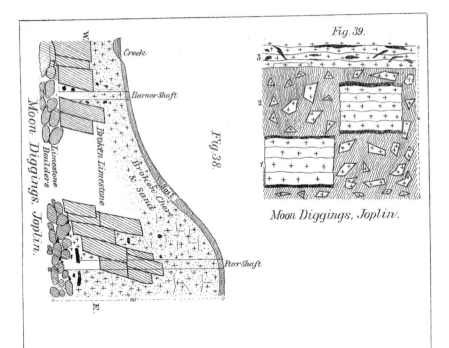

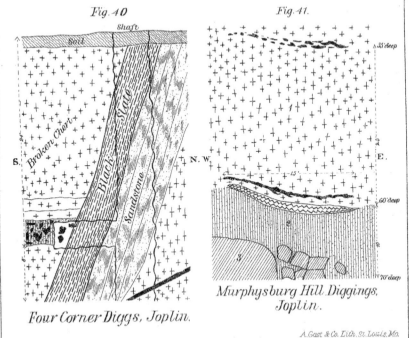

Fig. 39.

Moon Diggings, Joplin.

Fig. 38.

Moon Diggings, Joplin.

Fig. 40

Four Corner Diggs, Joplin.

Fig. 41.

Murphysburg Hill Diggings,
Joplin.

A. Gast & Co. Lith. St. Louis, Mo.

Fig. 42

S.W.   N.E.

1
2
3
4

Lustre Shaft, Joplin Valley.

Fig. 43.

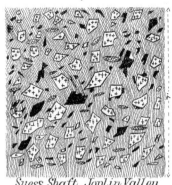

Suess Shaft, Joplin Valley
(50 Ft. below surface)

Fig. 45

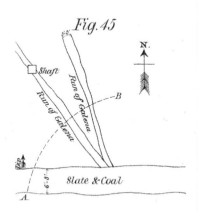

N.

Shaft

Run of Galena

Run of Galena

B

A

Slate & Coal

Harrington Shaft

A. Gast & Co Lith St Louis

Fig. 44

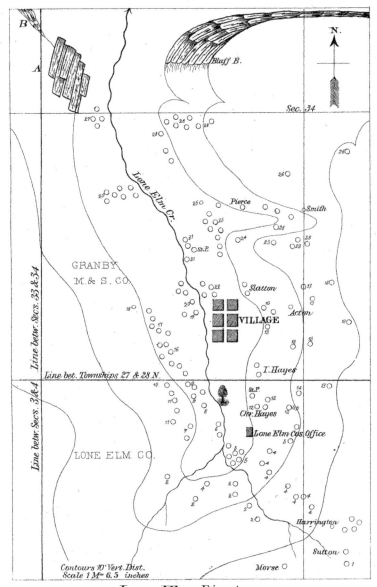

Lone Elm Diggings.

Contours 10' Vert. Dist.
Scale 1 M = 6.5 inches

A. Gast & Co. Lith. St. Louis.

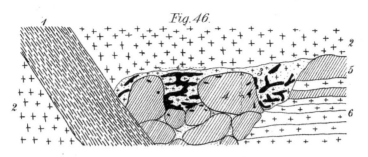

Fig. 46.

Cross Section of Two Runs (A.B.) Fig. 45.
Harrington Shaft, Joplin

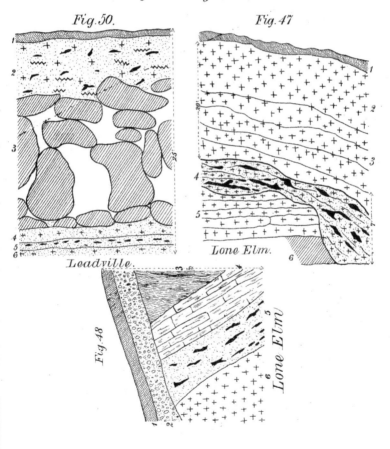

Fig. 50.

Fig. 47

Lone Elm.

Leadville.

Fig. 48

Lone Elm

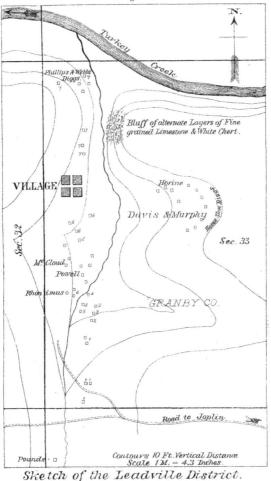

Fig. 49.

N.

Turkey Creek

Phillips & Webbs Diggs

Bluff of alternate Layers of Fine grained Limestone & White Chert.

VILLAGE

Horine

Davis & Murphy

House Shoe Diggs

Sec. 32

Sec. 33

Mc Cloud

Powell

Rhonimus

GRANBY CO.

Road to Joplin

Pounds

Contours 10 Ft. Vertical Distance
Scale 1 M. = 4.3 Inches.

Sketch of the Leadville District.

Fig. 51

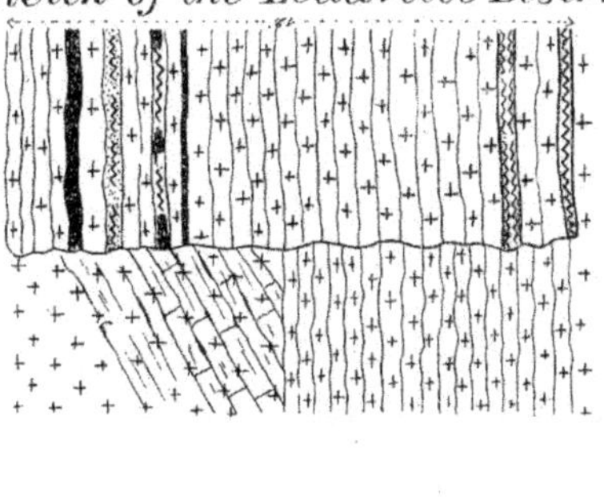

Leadville.
Galena Blende

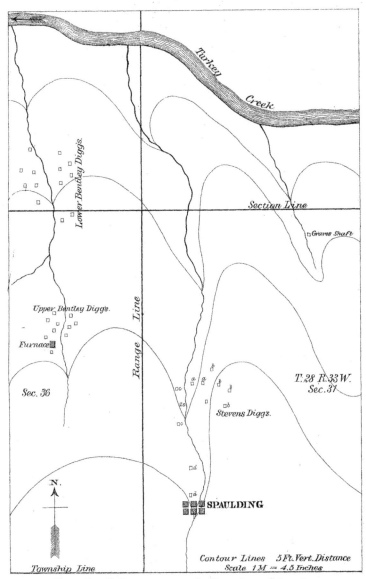

Fig. 52

Sketch of Stevens and Bentley Diggings.

Fig.53.

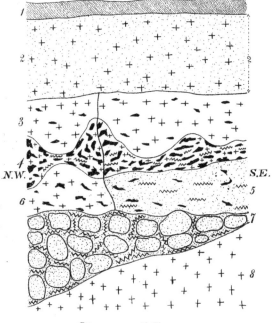

Stevens Mines

Fig.55

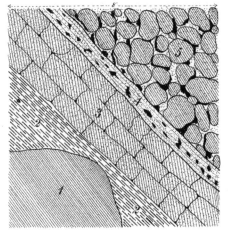

Grove Cr.Diggs.

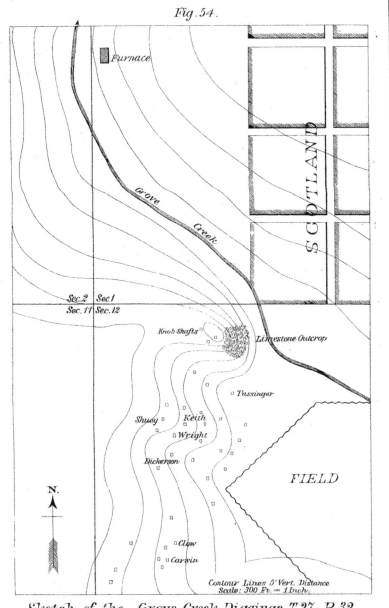

Fig. 54.

Furnace

Grove Creek

SCOTLAND

Sec. 2 | Sec. 1
Sec. 11 | Sec. 12

Knob Shafts

Limestone Outcrop

Tussinger

Shuey   Keith
      Wright

Dickerson

FIELD

N.

Clow

Carwin

Contour Lines 5' Vert. Distance
Scale: 300 Ft. = 1 Inch.

Sketch of the Grove Creek Diggings, T.27. R.32.

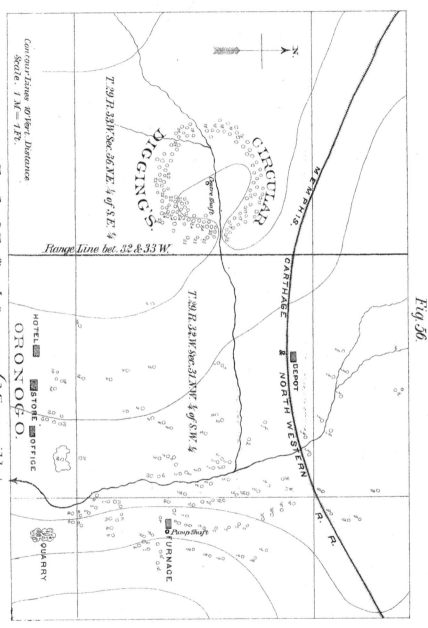

Fig. 56.

Sketch of Shafts at Oronogo (Minersville)

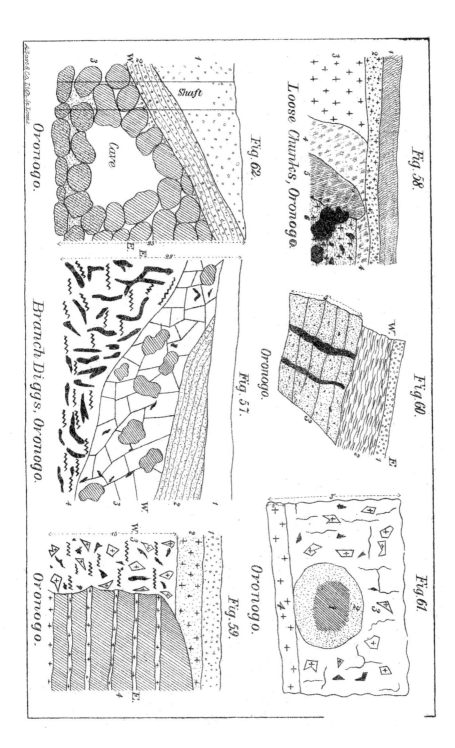

Fig. 58.

Loose Chunks, Oronogo.

Fig. 60.

Fig. 62.

Oronogo.

Fig. 57.

Oronogo.

Shaft

Cave

Oronogo.

Branch Diggs, Oronogo.

Fig. 59.

Oronogo.

Fig. 61.

Oronogo.

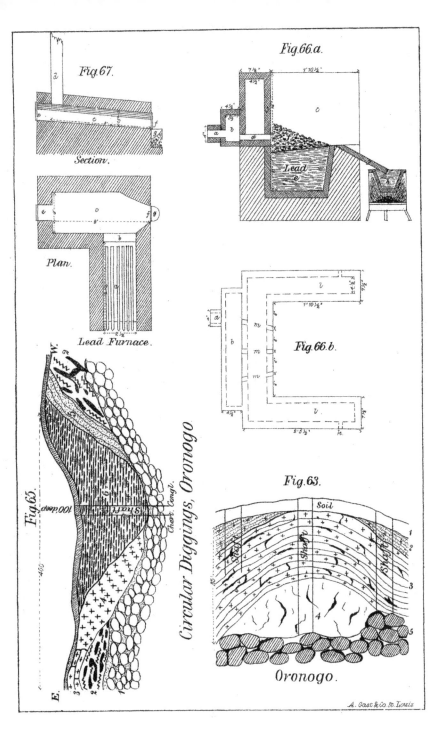

Fig.67.

Section.

Plan.

Lead Furnace.

Fig.66.a.

Lead
e

Fig.66.b.

Fig.65.

100 deep

Shaft

Circular Diggings, Oronogo.

Fig.63.

Soil

Shaft

Shaft

Shaft

1
2
3
4
5

Oronogo.

A. Gast & Co. St. Louis

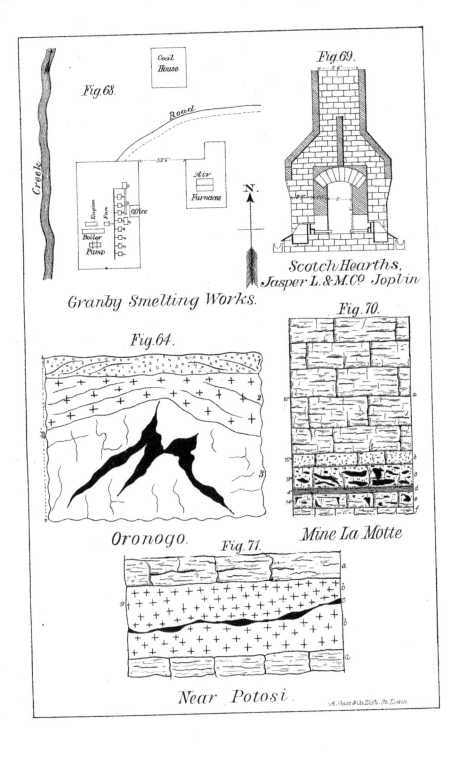

Fig.68.

Coal House

Road

Creek

52'6"

Engine
Fan
Office

Air Furnaces

Boiler
Pump

N.

Granby Smelting Works.

Fig.69.

Scotch Hearths,
Jasper L. & M. Cº Joplin

Fig.64.

Oronogo.

Fig.70.

Mine La Motte

Fig.71.

Near Potosi.

A. Gast & Co. Lith. St. Louis.

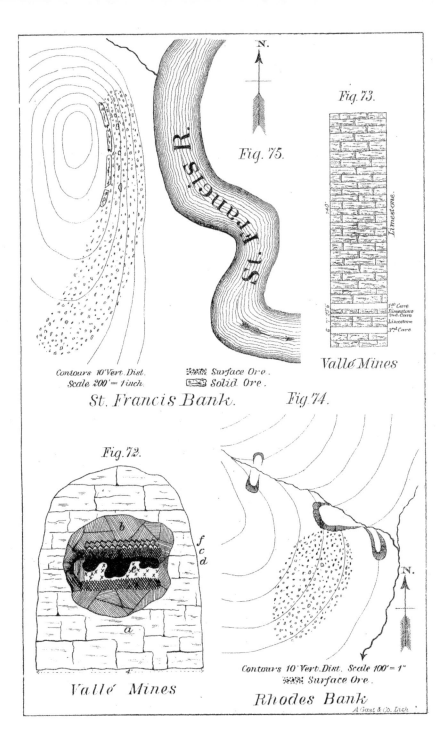

Fig. 75.

N.

St. Francis R.

Contours 10'Vert. Dist.
Scale 200' = 1 inch.

Surface Ore.
Solid Ore.

St. Francis Bank.

Fig. 73.

Limestone.

1⁵ᵗ Cave
Limestone
2ⁿᵈ Cave
or
Limestone
3ʳᵈ Cave

Vallé Mines

Fig. 74.

Fig. 72.

b

f
c
d

a

4'

Vallé Mines

N.

Contours 10'Vert. Dist. Scale 100' = 1"
Surface Ore.

Rhodes Bank

A. Gast & Co. Lith.

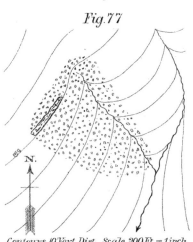

Fig. 77

Contours 10 Vert. Dist. Scale 200 Ft. = 1 inch.
Surface Ore.   Solid Ore.

Spiva Bank.

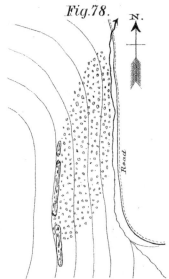

Fig. 78.

Road

Contours 10' Vert. Distance.
Scale.150'=1"   Surface Ore.   Solid Ore
                                &Cherty List.

Morris Cr. Bank.

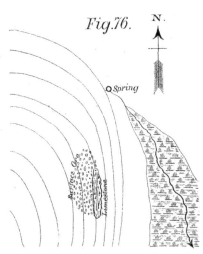

Fig. 76.

Spring

Surface Ore

Limestone

Contours 10' Vert. Dist. Scale 100' = 1 inch.

Blue Spring Bank.

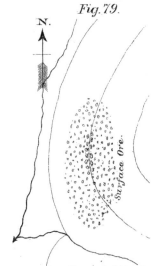

Fig. 79.

N.

Surface Ore.

Contours 5' Vert. Dist. Scale 200'= 1"

Reed's Bank.

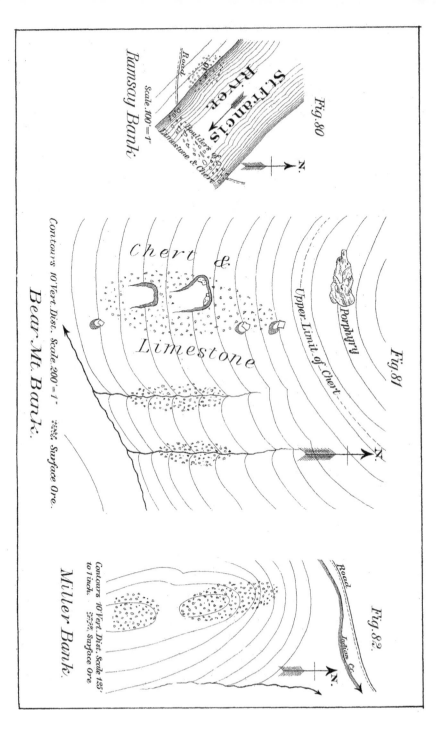

Fig.80

Strangs **River.**

Road

Limestone & Chert

N.

Scale 100 = 1"

Ramscy Bank

Fig.81

Chert &

Limestone

Porphyry

Upper Limit of Chert

N.

Contours 10 Vert. Dist. Scale 200" = 1". Surface Ore.

Bear Mt. Bank.

Fig.82.

Road

Indian Cr.

N.

Contours 10 Vert. Dist. Scale 125'
to 1 inch. Surface Ore

Miller Bank.

Fig. 83.

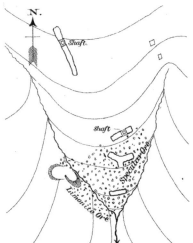

Tunnel

N.

Road

Contours 10' Vert. Distance
Scale 200'=1" Surface Ore.

Black River N⁰ 1.

Fig. 85.

N.

Shaft

Shaft

Specular Ore

Limonite Ore

Contours 10 Vert. Dist. Scale 125'=1"
Surface Ore.

Cheeney Bank.

Fig. 84.

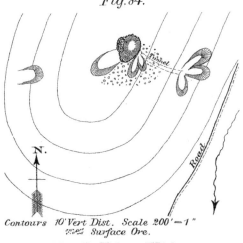

Tunnel

Road

N.

Contours 10'Vert Dist. Scale 200'=1"
Surface Ore.

Black River N⁰ 2.

Milton Keynes UK
Ingram Content Group UK Ltd.
UKHW040631170124
436182UK00004B/132